A Friendly Little War

John Sherman

In loving memory of

John Sherman

(1934-2007)

Ian Sherman

(1972-2009)

REPÚBLICA MEXICANA

SECRETARÍA DE ESTADO

Y DEL

DESPACHO DE HACIENDA Y CRÉDITO PÚBLICO

El Exmo. Sr. Presidente sustituto se ha servido dirigirme el decreto que sigue:

MIGUEL MIRAMON, General de Division y Presidente sustituto de la República Mexicana, á los habitantes de ella, sabed: Que en uso de las facultades de que me hallo investido, he tenido á bien decretar lo siguiente:

ART. 1º El Supremo Gobierno hace una emision de bonos por valor de quince millones de pesos.

ART. 2º Se suspende la emision de igual cantidad de los bonos creados por la ley de 16 de Julio último.

ART. 3º Los bonos á que se refiere el presente decreto serán admitidos en un veinte por ciento, en el pago de todos los derechos y contribuciones que deba percibir el fisco, exceptuando el contingente nacional.

ART. 4º Los mismos bonos ganarán un rédito de seis por ciento anual.

ART. 5º De este rédito el tres por ciento lo garantiza por cinco años la casa de los Sres. J. B. Jecker y Cª, que lo pagará cada seis meses en los dias del 1º al 30 de Junio, y del 1º al 30 de Diciembre, y cuya firma autorizará los bonos.

ART. 6º El tres por ciento de réditos que queda á cargo del Gobierno, representado en cupones, se admitirá en el veinte por ciento de los pagos que tengan que hacerse al erario, lo mismo que los bonos.

ART. 7º Los réditos correrán desde la fecha en que se emita cada bono.

ART. 8º Los actuales tenedores de bonos tienen facultad de convertir los que ahora poseen, por los nuevos, pagando un veinticinco por ciento por los de la última emision que causan réditos, veintisiete por ciento por los que creó la ley de 30 de Noviembre de 1850 y veintiocho por ciento por los de la última emision que no causan rédito.

ART. 9º Estas cuotas se calcularán sobre el importe de los bonos y de sus cupones vencidos hasta el dia de la conversion.

ART. 10. Al efecto, los tenedores presentarán sus bonos á la Tesorería General, que previa la liquidacion de los cupones los amortizará, y espedirá á los interesados una certificacion en que conste la cantidad total y la clase de bonos que convierten.

ART. 11. En vista de esta certificacion, la casa de los Sres. J. B. Jecker y Cª, entregará en bonos de la nueva emision, un valor igual al amortizado en la Tesorería General, previa la exhibicion de la cantidad que corresponda, segun el art. 8º

ART. 12. Por ningun motivo podrá autoridad alguna de la República suspender los efectos de este decreto respecto á la amortizacion de los bonos una vez emitidos, bajo pena de destitucion é inhabilidad perpetua para obtener cargo público.

ART. 13. Esta pena no impide que se haga efectiva la responsabilidad pecuniaria por los daños y perjuicios causados á los interesados, que contrae cualquier funcionario que suspenda ó contribuya á suspender los efectos de este decreto.

Por tanto, mando se imprima, publique, circule y se le dé el debido cumplimiento. Dado en el Palacio del Gobierno Nacional de México, á 29 de Octubre de 1859.—*Miguel Miramon.*—Al ministro de Justicia, Negocios eclesiásticos é Instruccion pública, encargado del Hacienda y Crédito público, Lic. D. Isidro Diaz.

Y lo comunico á V. para su inteligencia y efectos correspondientes.

Dios y libertad. México, Octubre 29 de 1859.—*Diaz.*

Vº Bº
El Ministro de Hacienda.

El Tesorero General.

El Contador General.

Espedido en 13 de Marzo de 1860.

14699

3ª SERIE

LETRA C

VALOR $100.

LETRA C. NÚMERO 12.500

El Gefe de la Seccion de Crédito Público del Ministerio de Hacienda

Teniendo ó jujos del Libro de Bonos del veinte por ciento.

QUINTO DIVIDENDO.

DÉCIMO DIVIDENDO.

NOVENO DIVIDENDO.

DÉCIMOQUINTO DIVIDENDO.

OCTAVO DIVIDENDO.

VIGÉSIMO DIVIDENDO.

SÉTIMO DIVIDENDO.

DÉCIMO DIVIDENDO.

Part 1

"Exactly. A friendly little war, one might say. For us, it's an attractive course of action." Russell held up a hand and ticked off a finger. "First, we can prevent Napoleon from establishing a permanent base in the Americas. Second," another finger, "we put ourselves in a position to help the Confederates - if that suits us - or to keep them out of Mexico if they win their war."

Chapter 1

The war had at last begun. Two generations of fear, distrust and hatred pushed the North and the South to the precipice and then over it, down to the conflict willed by God.

The Union Army promptly lost Fort Sumter and the great naval base at Norfolk. President Lincoln ordered out seventy-five thousand militia to serve for ninety days, then called for half a million more to volunteer for three years. In their thousands, the volunteers crowded the recruiting stations, eager, raw and certain that the war would be won by Christmas.

The days grew longer and hotter, and the cry of "On to Richmond!" grew louder. All believed that a single decisive battle would end the rebellion.

The direct route to Richmond by rail lay through Manassas Junction, about twenty-five miles south of Washington and occupied by the Confederate Army of the Potomac, some twenty two thousand strong. The main Union force was ordered to attack this army, which waited on the far side of a stream called the Bull Run.

*   *   *

One evening in mid-July, Lieutenant Charles Bartlett, U. S. Army, picked his way through the muddy chaos of the First Division's encampment on the Arlington Heights. He was searching for the headquarters of the division's Third Brigade, and he was worried.

Bartlett's orders to report immediately to the brigade had arrived two days before at his tiny study at West Point. He had settled his affairs at the Academy, disentangled himself from one young lady, buttoned himself into his newer uniform and set out for Washington.

All trains headed south were packed with soldiers, but in New York he had managed to bluff his way on to a first class car for the price of the second-class fare. This triumph had allowed him enough for a good lunch, and he was still feeling pleased with himself when he arrived in Washington and settled into one of the coaches hired by the army to carry officers to their postings outside the city.

By now, though, Bartlett had lost his good humor. The location of Third Brigade headquarters remained a mystery, it was dark and his valise was tearing at his shoulder. At length, he circled once more behind a row of tents and saw a wooden sign announcing the presence in that tent of the Third Brigade Adjutant. He ducked his head and went in.

The adjutant was a tubby, moon-faced major named Hoyt. He greeted Bartlett with warmth and said, "We knew that you were assigned to the brigade, Bartlett, but your records haven't arrived. God only knows where they are." He held up his hands helplessly. "Anyway, I'll take you right now to report to the brigade commander, Colonel Sherman, and we can decide where to put you."

Hoyt led the way to a larger tent a few yards away and stopped before a figure seated outside on a campstool. "Sir," he announced, "Lieutenant Bartlett has turned up. You said you wanted to speak to him as soon as he did. I've explained that we haven't yet decided where to assign him."

"Thank you, Major. Stay a few minutes," Colonel Sherman replied as he returned Bartlett's salute." Sit down, gentlemen."

Bartlett gratefully lowered his long frame on to a wooden bench. He was facing a tall, slim, intense man in a rusty uniform and slouch hat. Sherman wore a reddish beard, a cigar and a worried frown.

"Welcome, Lieutenant" he said. "You find us in a state of some disorganization, I fear. The brigade was formed last month and Major Hoyt and I arrived only two weeks ago, so we're still finding our own away around."

"Thank you, sir, I'm glad to be here. I got here as soon as I could but it's a long way from West Point."

"It is, indeed, in more ways than one" Sherman agreed. He drew on the cigar. "Now, all we know about you, Lieutenant, is that you're an artillery officer with a regular army commission. Tell us about yourself - briefly, if you please."

"Yes, sir." Bartlett was ready for this kind of request. "Well, I'm from New Hampshire - Concord - and I was commissioned in the artillery from the Academy in 1851. My first posting was to Fort Leavenworth for three years as a battery officer with the Fourth Artillery." He hesitated, remembering the endless emptiness of the Kansas prairie. "After that, four years at Fort Pickens, in Pensacola - two years as executive officer and two years on the post commander's staff. I was promoted and sent back to the Academy as an instructor for the last three years, teaching gunnery and Greek."

"Greek?"

"Yes, sir. Greek." He kept a straight face. "It's an optional course with, fortunately, few takers. I barely manage to stay ahead of them."

"Concord, eh?" Sherman mused. "You may know a Colonel Stoddard, Miles Stoddard, from Concord. A classmate of mine."

"Yes, sir. My uncle."

"Is that so? A clever man, your uncle." Another pull on the cigar. "Tell me... you're married? Single?"

"Single, sir."

"Just as well." Sherman rubbed his chin and dropped his voice. "Our situation is this, Bartlett. We expect the brigade to move out in the next day or two. So there'll be no time for you to get to know your duties, or the officers and men, if we send you to our artillery battery. Besides, I think Captain Grace is fully staffed already. Am I right, Major Hoyt?"

"Yes, sir. Lieutenant Bartlett's seniority would qualify him as Executive Officer, but Lieutenant Morrison arrived late last week to fill that position, if you remember."

"Ah, yes. The Texas cowboy." Sherman paused again, studying Bartlett. "Well, that settles it, then. The sensible course, Lieutenant, is for you to join my staff at brigade for the present. I have no other artillerist on the staff. There will be openings in the battery before long, I have no doubt, and until then you can make yourself useful to me directly."

"Fine, sir," Bartlett said. This was welcome news. He had tired of battery duty while at Pickens, had grown weary of the daily routine of dealing with the men's petty problems and complaints.

"Well, I think that's all for now, Bartlett. We're glad to have you with us." Sherman stood up. "I'm wanted at General McDowell's headquarters in a few minutes. Major Hoyt, see that Bartlett is settled in, if you will. Good night, gentlemen."

The next day was a busy one for Bartlett. He completed his paperwork, drew his equipment and then met the other officers on Sherman's staff. They were an assortment of elderly majors in the regular army, uneasy politicians from the militia regiments and two recent graduates of West Point. The staff were convinced that combat would be soon and that the army was already in motion. McDowell's broad plan of campaign had been approved and the one question was when the army would strike south.

Before then, Bartlett needed a horse. He found the temporary remount stables in a scrubby square of mud. Sergeant Moulton, a former dragoon, was in charge.

During his time at Leavenworth, Bartlett had of necessity made himself a passable horseman but he had never lost his fear and distrust of the beasts. "Good morning, Sergeant," he blustered. "I understand that you're the man who can supply me with a horse."

Moulton stopped picking his teeth. "Glad to, sir. What do you have in mind?

"Oh, they're all much the same, aren't they? Bite at one end and crap at the other, hah, hah?"

"Hah, hah," agreed Moulton. He surveyed the yard. "Let me see... yes, I think that big grey should suit you. Called Attila, like that Roman general. Bit of a hard mouth, but he'll run all day for you, he will." He pointed to a rangy brute with a rolling eye and the disposition of a rattlesnake. "I'll saddle him up."

A few minutes later: "He's a leetle testy, sir, so you just show him who's the boss and he won't give you no trouble," Moulton said as Bartlett eased himself into the saddle.

Attila needed less than five minutes of bucking, rearing and corkscrewing to show who was the boss, and it was not Bartlett. Thus began a grim, silent struggle of wills between man and horse that the man soon came to believe would not end until the end of the war itself.

First, the war had to begin. It began for Bartlett early the following day, when McDowell's army at last moved out. "Stay close to Colonel Sherman, Lieutenant," Major Hoyt ordered him. "Make yourself available to him and the senior staff officers as a courier. What's wrong with that horse, by the way?"

Bartlett's principal duty as a staff officer was to help maintain some sort of discipline among the troops of the Third Brigade. The march to Manassas became first a stroll, then a picnic and then a carnival. The troops routinely broke ranks to drink from farmyard wells, to pick blackberries, sleep, chase chickens, shoot pigs and even to loot and burn houses beside the road. Their officers screamed and cursed, threatened them with pistols, all to no effect. Bartlett screamed and cursed with the rest.

"This isn't an army, it's a mob, an armed mob." said Sherman at one point, riding up to Bartlett on a hill. He was even more worried than before. "They will hate us in Virginia for all time. I can think of no greater curse, Lieutenant, than to be invaded by a volunteer army."

"No, sir," Bartlett agreed, grinning. "Except perhaps to command one?" he heard himself ask.

Sherman stared at him. "We'll see, we'll see." He shook his head and rode toward the head of the column.

The leading offenders against discipline were the Forty Ninth New York. Their scarlet-legged uniforms may have been copies of the Turks' but every man in the regiment was born in Ireland, every man was a volunteer and every man was ready to swear on his mother's grave that his enlistment was already up. The Forty Ninth's collective sense of outrage was sharpened on the second night when Sherman ordered it to bivouac in a dripping swamp.

Bartlett was a regular visitor to the Forty Ninth. Its staff could always be found by the enormous green banner awarded to the regiment for some civic misdemeanor in its home state. His usual message, "Colonel Sherman says to keep in ranks." or "Colonel Sherman wants you to stay on the road." soon became a joke to the troops. On one of his visits an anonymous rich brogue broke in:

"Sure and who is this mighty Colonel Sherman, then? God himself? If you please, sir, tell him he can kiss my..."

"Shut up, private!" shouted his sergeant.

... sister, then?" Bartlett rode off to hoots of Hibernian laughter.

*   *   *

For three days the huge army shambled south along the dusty road in the heat and brilliance of the green Virginia countryside. Bartlett began to question if the brigade, so badly trained that it could not even march as a unit, would pull itself together to fight. But Major Hoyt had no doubts on this score. The short, round adjutant had turned out to be a tougher character than Bartlett had supposed.

"Don't worry about that, Lieutenant," he drawled. "I saw plenty of movements like this in Mexico. These shit-kickers will fight when the time comes. These boys will do all right."

"The Wisconsin regiment, sure, and maybe the New York Highlanders, but the Forty Ninth?" Bartlett shook his head in disagreement. "Hell, they're all right off the boat from Dublin so this isn't even their fight. Besides, they want to go home and they want to go right now. One of their officers told me he's leaving for New York tomorrow and asked if ther was there anything he could do for me when he gets there."

"Those Irish will fight, you'll see, even if they can't march. They hate the Colonel and they'll fight just to show him they can fight, if nothing else."

Two nights later Sherman summoned his regimental commanders and his staff to a conference at his quarters. The army would attack the next day, he said, pointing his cigar at the map pinned to the wall of the dusty tent. "The army will scatter Beauregard's army, seize the railhead at Manassas and destroy the rail line to Richmond. Beauregard's positions and ours are shown on this map. The rebels are strung out along the south side of Bull Run, with most of their strength on their right. We're formed on the north side near these two fords, here. General McDowell's plan of attack is just like the plan you've been studying all day, so you all know your responsibilities."

He peered hard at the men and went on. "Early tomorrow First Division will move west to take up positions near this stone bridge on the main road across Bull Run. Following behind us, Second and Third Divisions will keep going west and then swing south to positions far around to our right, turning Beauregard's left flank." He jabbed at the map. "They'll attack him here, near these springs. His flank is thinly defended and so, if they show a bit of dash, they'll soon push him back across our front. We'll cross the stream and hit them hard on their flank. That will be about ten o'clock." He turned back to face his men. "Are there any questions?"

No hand rose. "No? Fine. Third Brigade will lead the division column and we leave at four o'clock sharp. The usual line of march except that your artillery, Captain Grace, will move up last. You all know the terrain by now so there will be no excuse for any delay. Make sure your men carry the minimum. It will be a long, hot day. Good night, gentlemen."

Bartlett slept not at all that night. He could not force himself to accept that he had no choice but to go into battle the next day, that there was no way out. He felt trapped, helpless, devoid of will. And he sensed the fear would come later.

Besides, he hurt. He hurt in every bone, every muscle, every follicle. Three days aboard Attila had almost finished him. His shoulders, the insides of his thighs and his back would never be right again, he was certain.

Reveille was at two o'clock and at four the division was formed and moving north by west in the moonlight. All too soon, the day grew bright, still and hot, steaming hot, as the sun raced up the sky.

Sherman's brigade turned left off the dusty road and formed a line on the wooded hillside that sloped down to the Bull Run half a mile in front. The men brewed coffee and rested in the shade as they waited for the order to attack across the high-banked stream. There was little talk.

Noon came and Sherman still waited. The staff knew that the timing of the attack had gone all wrong. They heard intense, sustained fire, musket and cannon, from the direction of the low hills across the river. A rolling bank of smoke poured over those hills and over the plateau in between. The rebels fought ferociously and were being pushed back much more slowly than expected.

Bartlett hitched Attila to a tree, sat on a low branch and swabbed his forehead. Through his field glasses, he saw that the rebels were now falling back from his right to his left under the force of a determined Union infantry assault, well supported by artillery.

"It must be soon," he said to Waller, one of the young West Pointers. "We should be hitting them now, now!"

"I hope to hell it's not soon," was the reply. "The Colonel won't use the bridge because it's defended, we still haven't found a decent crossing and I'm not much of a swimmer."

At this, a young Confederate major in the gaudy uniform of the Louisiana Tigers rode out from the trees bordering Bull Run and galloped up the slope toward Sherman and his staff. He stopped a hundred yards away and shouted:

"What are you waiting for, Yankees? You cowards! Yellow Yankee scum! Damned nigger-loving sons of whores! Come on over and fight, damn you, with the rest of your abolitionist pigs! We've whipped their asses real good, and we'll whip your black asses too, all the way back to Father Abraham, you shit-faced fairies!"

"A saucy turn of phrase," Sherman remarked. He raised his field glasses and then shouted, "Don't shoot him!" as the Southerner turned his horse. "He found a way across the creek... perhaps we can use it, too." He lowered the glasses. "Bartlett, you and Waller follow that noisy fool and see where he crosses, then see if we can get the brigade across there."

Attila was very tired and very thirsty. Bartlett had only to aim him at Bull Run, where the water glinted through the trees, and he was off down the hill at top speed. Bartlett sawed on the reins and kept him in the edge of the woods on the left, where he hoped for cover from the rebels he expected to find waiting on the far slope.

Crashing through the trees, Attila opened up a long gap on Waller and reached the high bank of the stream as the gaudy major scrambled up the other side. Bartlett saw no Southerners on the slope but he dismounted and dived behind a bush, dragging Attila after him.

The major wheeled and snapped off three shots at the bush with an enormous pistol. His aim was so bad that Bartlett did not even hear the bullets hit. The major raked back his spurs and disappeared over the bank as Waller joined Bartlett behind the bush.

"The ford must be right here in front of us," Bartlett hissed. "Let's have a look... stay on my right."

They rode down the steep bank and found the ford, whose gravel bottom was about twenty feet wide. They crossed the stream at either side of the ford and agreed that the maximum depth was two feet. Attila lowered his head and noisily began to drain the stream.

"This looks all right for infantry and horses," Bartlett said, "but tricky for the artillery. I wouldn't cross the battery here unless I was certain the far side was clear of rebels for half a mile or so. What do you reckon?"

"Whatever you say, Lieutenant, whatever you say. Me, I'm getting the hell out of here," and Waller was racing back up through the trees.

Attila had not finished his drink so he bit Bartlett savagely on the knee when asked to withdraw. He was still snapping at that convenient joint when they regained headquarters, where Sherman was giving Waller a "Well done" and Bartlett a long look.

Within the hour, the brigade had splashed across Bull Run in good order and mounted the shallow hill on the far side, where irregular ravines and clumps of young oaks gave good cover. It formed a line of battle whose left rested on a sunken roadway, which gave partial protection from the thunderous cannon fire a few hundred yards ahead. The rebels were in full retreat across the brigade front and Sherman was at last ordered to attack over the crest of the first hill and take the second, steeper hill, marked by a stone farmhouse.

"This is insane," he growled, the worried frown even deeper than before.

"I've been told to advance our regiments one by one. We should be *massing* them!"

First over the hill went the Wisconsin farm boys, to be driven back in a dozen bloody minutes. The retreating Confederates now rallied on the Virginia regiments that had somehow withstood the first Union onslaught and were standing fast on the bare plateau. Their guns were sited behind a slight swell in the ground. Their shot cleared the swell by less than a yard and the recoil ran the six-pounders back to even lower ground, where only the gunners' heads were visible to their enemies. Southern canister methodically cut the Union formations to shreds at point blank range.

Bartlett stuck close to Sherman as he moved up and down the front line and waited for orders. The shattering noise of the guns, the rifle fire and the screaming of men and horses deafened him, the bluish smoke of the field guns almost blinded him. Over all the roar of battle rose the occasional boom of the Parrott thirty-pounder rifle on their right.

Next over the bloody hill went the New York Highlanders, bayonets gleaming, yelling, scrambling up the sunken road. Their commander was cut down by the second volley and their left flank was mangled by shrapnel. After a fierce, frantic fire fight, they too fell back across the hill, panting, screaming, terrified.

At last Sherman called on the Irishmen of the Forty Ninth New York. A quick benediction from their chaplain, a drum roll and a cry of, "Come on, boys! You've got your chance at last!" Their enormous green banner flew and the ancient battle cry "For Ireland and Fontenoy!" rang before them as the regiment leapt forward.

Their first charge carried them up the slope of the farmhouse hill, where they were beaten back by withering canister fire from the Southern battery behind the slope on their left. Again they charged, scarlet pantaloons streaming up the hill. They ran past men cowering behind empty ammunition boxes, past men drinking from muddy puddles, past other men dying. They fired as they ran, closing the gaps in their ranks, Sherman galloping among them. Up and over the hill they surged, to be thrown back by volleys of rifle and cannon fire. They charged again, and then again, only to fall back, their ranks ripped apart, on the bloody hillside.

Bartlett saw their bright green banner abruptly struck down, its color sergeant surrounded by cheering rebels and hustled toward the rear. After a few steps the sergeant pulled out a hidden pistol, shot his two guards and raced back to the field, the banner aloft.

"Did you see that?" Bartlett cried to Waller, who rode on his right. But Waller wasn't there. He was on the ground, flat on his back with his eyes open and only a rush of blood where his throat had been.

Bartlett fought back the bile. He and one of the elderly majors - Edwards? Edison? - pulled the body back to the trees, where he hitched Waller's horse.

'Major Edmonds! Lieutenant Bartlett! Get back here, if you please!" Sherman called to them. He pointed ahead. "Look over there - on our left flank, about half a mile ahead. Do you see it? A Union formation on that road?"

Bartlett squinted through his glasses and saw a column of blue-clad infantry swinging toward them around the base of the farmhouse hill. He could not quite make out the regimental flag hanging lifeless from its staff in the haze.

"That must be part of Schenk's brigade, up from the stone bridge at last," Sherman said. "Now we can safely bring up the artillery."

He pulled out a message pad and, as he wrote, instructed Bartlett. "Lieutenant, take this message to Captain Grace back behind the stone bridge. Tell him to move his guns up over the bridge double quick and direct his fire at that rebel battery. It's holding up the entire attack on this side."

Attila was thirsty, bone tired and sick of the day's work. He spread his forelegs, arched his neck and refused to move. Bartlett hauled frantically on the reins and dug in his spurs, but the horse was having none of it. In despair, Bartlett dismounted.

"Horse is lame, sir. I'll take Waller's," he unlooped the reins and climbed on the dead man's bay.

"Take anything that moves. But get going, damn it."

Bartlett, off again, found a trail through the scrub that led back toward the stone bridge. It was quieter here, the guns were farther away and the vegetation dimmed the screams. He kept the blue column in sight on his right most of the way, so he was astonished when he rode out of the woods and onto a group of three sergeants squatting by the trail. Their blue jackets were unbuttoned and their caps lay on the ground.

"What unit are you?" he demanded as he reined up. He'd had an idea.

The sergeants, taken off guard, stood up. After a moment, one looked sideways at the other two and grunted, "Kentucky militia, sir... Company B, Tenth Kentucky Volunteers."

Bartlett noted the soft, slow vowels and peered again at the regimental colors down the road. They still told him nothing. But any additional manpower, even militia, was welcome. He had a tactical inspiration.

"Take a message to your company commander," he said, "At once, if you please. Tell him that Colonel Sherman, Third Brigade, would like your regiment to advance quickly and support his left. He's over that first ridge there and being pinned down by that battery up ahead."

"Let me see if I got that right, sir," said the spokesman. "Third Brigade wants us to support their left, over that ridge?"

"That's right, sergeant. They'll try to flank that rebel battery as soon as you get in position." He hoped they would, anyway.

"Right, sir. I got that."

"Then hurry, will you? Tell your commander..."

"Tell him yourself, asshole," said the sergeant, reaching for something behind him. Something like a rifle.

Bartlett's innards dissolved. These were Confederates, still wearing the old regulation blue uniform!

Somehow he ducked low and yanked the bay back into the woods before the sergeants could unlimber their antique rifles. One misfired and the other two missed, the bullets snicking the leaves behind him. By then he was hidden by the scrub and moving steadily back toward the Union lines.

Now he was truly petrified, shaking, scared enough to bear left instead of right at a fork in the trail. This took him out onto the fringe of the open battlefield and into the plain view of Southern skirmishers. Another volley of rifle fire and the whisper of bullets over his head, another dive into the woods and he clattered down the hillside.

He was not lost, just disoriented. To find Grace's battery he had to keep going downhill, reach the Bull Run and double back to the stone bridge. Too far right and he would be a target for Confederate rifles again. He had to be careful so he slowed to a trot, still gulping air.

He was at once caught up by dozens of Union soldiers walking away from the battlefield and down towards the stream, singly and in groups of two and three. Many wore the red pantaloons of the Forty Ninth New York. They said nothing and appeared to be in no hurry, as if they were walking home from work when the day is over. Many were stained with blood, many dragged a foot. As he went on, their numbers grew.

Bartlett dismounted and asked a limping corporal of the Forty Ninth where he was going.

"Back to Washington, sir. We're done fighting for today and now we're headed back to camp.

"But Washington's twenty five miles away. You won't make it today. Where are your officers?'

"Don't know, sir. Up ahead somewhere, I expect. Or dead, maybe," was the dull reply.

Bartlett remounted and spurred ahead faster. Forget the battery, he thought, I've got to find Colonel Sherman before these stragglers turn into a rout.

He burst into a small clearing, almost on top of four Union soldiers. One turned at the noise and, wild-eyed, yanked both arms up in surrender and cried, "Don't shoot!" at Bartlett. In his right hand he held his loaded rifle, which fired as it crossed the horse's head.

The bay screamed and plunged into the brush, Bartlett hanging grimly to its neck. His face was bathed in blood from the long bullet crease in that neck and he fought for control as they careered off through the scrub.

Their wild ride ended abruptly. The bay tried to jump a sunken creek bed but landed half way up the far side, throwing Bartlett on to its head. The horse tried to rise, hindquarters first, and Bartlett kept going over its head. He felt himself falling, then a blow to his shoulder and then nothing. Nothing at all.

Chapter 2

Paris

The bedroom was long and light, with a stone fireplace at one end. The walls were covered in pale satin with gilt moldings, and a full-length portrait of Queen Hortense of Holland took pride of place in the center of one long wall. Bright carpets and scattered prayer rugs covered the parquet floor. At the far end stood a vast canopied bed, with doors on either side that led to the dressing room and to a private staircase.

The man sitting on a chair in the center of the room wore an ermine-lined dressing gown and red Turkish slippers. He was about fifty years old and had a large, perfectly round head that was perfectly bald except for the wings of dark hair above his ears. His hooded eyes were blue, the greyish blue that gives nothing away. His short imperial beard and moustache were benefiting from his valet's close attentions with razor, scissors, wax and towel. These attentions often lasted more than an hour. In his youth it was said that he managed his business affairs between dances; now, that he managed France between shaves.

One of the man's grandfathers was the illustrious Talleyrand, who dallied once too often with the wife of the Count de Flahaut and fathered the Count's heir, Charles de Flahaut. His grandmother on his mother's side was Josephine de Beauharnais, the first wife of Napoleon Bonaparte. His mother was Hortense de Beauharnais, Josephine's daughter by her first husband and stepdaughter of the great Napoleon. The Emperor married Hortense off to his youngest brother, Louis and made them King and Queen of Holland.

Louis was a miserable misanthrope who wanted only to be shot of Hortense, so after bearing the obligatory male heir, plus a spare, she looked around for more congenial companionship. Her ravenous eye fell on the formidable young soldier, Charles de Flahaut, and it was but a matter of time before she dragged him, protesting feebly, back from the eastern front and into her bed. In due course she repaired incognito to furnished rooms in Paris, just in time to produce another son.

In the custom of the day, the boy was put out to nurse with a reliable tradesman and his wife from the Auvergne. For a thousand francs, they registered him under their name, Demorny, and undertook to raise him until de Flahaut could arrange for his further care.

Now, after distinguished careers in the army, industry and politics, he was Charles-Auguste, Count de Morny and perhaps the most influential man in France. This eminence he owed equally to his rare combination of talents and to his connection with Hortense's older son, his half brother, the Emperor Napoleon III.

Morny was no longer Minister of the Interior, the post he held ten years earlier when he conceived, planned and executed the December coup that transformed Louis Napoleon from a weak President of the Republic into the all-powerful Emperor of France. Now his only official post was the presidency of the legislative body. The debates in this quarrelsome assembly were controlled by a bell on the president's desk, a small clapper bell like a schoolmaster's, and Morny insisted that the amusement he got from ringing the bell was the only reason he stayed in office.

But everyone knew that his support was the surest path to the official assistance one needed to carry out any significant project in France. It was also, rarely, the path to the door of the Emperor. So the reception room on the ground floor of his presidential palace, the Petit Bourbon, was packed every morning, packed with men who hoped for five minutes of his time. This day was no different.

Morny had just finished with Judge Rost, sent to Paris by the Confederacy to persuade the Emperor that, if France wanted cotton for its spinning mills, breaking the Yankee blockade was its only hope. "These Southern gentlemen importune too crudely, Henri," he complained to the valet. "They are so inspired by the sanctity of their cause that they forget elementary courtesy. Imagine," he snorted," the good judge attempted to bully me. Me! He went off with a flea in his unwashed ear."

"Yes, yes, I was right here at the time," Henri observed, stepping back, razor and towel held high. A short, square man with a round, red face, he had earned that tone of voice by knowing his master from childhood and serving him for forty-five years. "Why don't you send the rest of them away and allow me to finish with the moustache? I have other duties to perform as well, you know."

"Cretin. Let me have the list." Morny scanned a paper. "Ah, Herr Jecker is back. He wrote yesterday, professing important news. Have him sent up, Henri."

"The German banker? The skinny one from Mexico, whose bank went *pouf*? The one with the imaginary bonds? What do you want with him, for Heaven's sake?"

"He was in fact Swiss, but by now he may be French. The bonds are real, curious as that must seem to an Auvergnat peasant like you. I have confirmed it." He turned to see Henri's reddening face. "The last one today, I promise you. Tell them downstairs."

Jean Baptiste Jecker had indeed been Swiss when he first approached Morny two months earlier, on a stifling hot day in June, with an extraordinary proposition. He explained that he was a banker who had done business for many years in Mexico, and that he had completed an 'interesting' loan contract with the government of President Miramon, the ousted predecessor of Benito Juarez.

The impecunious Mexican government had issued to Jecker bonds with a face value of thirty million dollars, against his obligation to pay it one million dollars in cash. "That is correct, sir. One million, no more," he had grinned toothily. In addition, he was granted the exclusive license to explore for silver in Baja California and Sonora. He managed to pay the government less than half a million dollars before Juarez booted out Miramon. The new Radical treasury demanded the balance of the one million, intending to revoke the bonds and the license once it got the cash.

So Jecker went conveniently bankrupt. His exploration license was suspended but the bonds were not. Their terms were still valid. At this point, Jecker learned that the Emperor was considering a military expedition to Mexico to recover the money owed to France and its citizens. His next step was obvious - to become a citizen of France. To accomplish that, he needed Morny's help. To secure that, he pleaded for an interview, granted at last, at which he offered the great man a large slice of the proceeds from the bonds, the details to be agreed later.

"But this conversation is entirely conjectural, Herr Jecker - you do realize that?" Morny had warned the Swiss at their first meeting. "True, Mexico's failure to pay our citizens is intolerable to the Emperor. I also concede that he may occasionally be tempted by such an expedition, but reality always intrudes in the end." He didn't add that it was he who made sure of that intrusion.

"And what reality is that, Excellency?"

"America, my dear sir, America." Morny flicked his wrist to one side. "Specifically, its Monroe Doctrine, so-called. Mr. Seward and Mr. Lincoln know that Jefferson Davis and his friends have long wanted to seize the northern flank of Mexico, along with Cuba and Jamaica." Jecker looked surprised. "Oh, yes, for many years. So you can imagine how the Yankees will react if French troops appear in Veracruz, apparently in league with the South."

"But surely the Americans are too engaged in their own war to try to defend Mexico as well?" Jecker protested.

"Probably. But it is not certain. We shall have to see." Jecker's face sagged. "But until then, Herr Jecker, I know of no reason why you should not apply for French citizenship. France needs more men like you, adventurers, risk-takers."

Morny turned around to his valet. "Henri, a pen, if you will." He scratched a few lines on his card. "Take this with my compliments to Mr. Braco at the Interior Ministry. He will, I think, accommodate you."

Jecker studied the card and bowed himself out with intense expressions of gratitude. "Your Excellency will permit me to inform you of any change in the situation?"

"I will require it. Good day." Morny reached for his hand mirror.

This time Jecker beamed as he presented himself. "You see before you, sir, the newest and proudest citizen of France," he exclaimed, "and my gratitude to you can not be adequately expressed."

"My congratulations. I will endeavor to think of something," Morny drawled from his chair. He isn't skinny, thought Morny, cadaverous is more accurate. Jecker's lean frame and bony, hairless face were topped with an incongruous tangle of curls, so that he looked rather like a well turned out mop. "But, as one Frenchman to another, what is your important news? I have been in the provinces all week, out of touch. Henri, surely you are finished by now?"

Henri muttered something. Jecker stood closer and said, "Great news, Excellency. The American Federal army has been defeated, destroyed, in a battle outside Washington. A place called Bulls Run. Lincoln and his cabinet have panicked and abandoned the city to the Southerns." He stopped to catch his breath. "And Juarez has suspended all payments on the foreign debt of Mexico."

"And just why is all this good... ah, I begin to see," Morny smiled. He sat up, surprising Henri. "Juarez has insulted France and her worthy citizens. He has made it impossible to collect our just debts except by force, and he has put the Emperor publicly in a position where he must take action." He smiled again, shaking his head. "Not so clever, Señor Juarez, I think."

Jecker, almost bouncing on his feet, added, "He has done the same to Spain and England. The Emperor will have the allies he insists upon."

"I agree. But now to Washington. What is your source for this startling news?"

Jecker had realized that the only way to deal with Morny was with complete honesty. "A... friend in the foreign ministry here, in the Latin American section. Quite reliable."

"You derive benefits from your French citizenship already, I see, and in the traditional French manner." Jecker started to correct him but stopped. "Bulls Run, eh? And I suppose 'Yankees Run' as well, *hein*? Ha." Morny waved Henri away, stood up and moved to the gilded looking glass on the wall. He turned to the side, lifted his chin and patted his neck beneath it hopefully. He sighed and turned back to the eager Jecker.

"Which means that the Federals will be incapable of resisting a move on Mexico," Morny went on, as if talking to himself. "Especially if we were to move at once and make the usual protestations about our peaceful purposes... our *limited* and peaceful purposes."

Jecker couldn't believe his luck. Morny's ideas vaulted beyond his own wildest hopes.

"I confess to a certain skepticism about these reports of Lincoln's cabinet fleeing Washington," Morny said, "and will require proof that the situation is so desperate." He walked down the room to the bed. "The mouse colored trousers, I think, Henri, don't you agree? I may tell you, Mr. Jecker, that I've not been idle since we last met. A few friends have formed a syndicate to buy the bonds from you" - his hand went up to forestall Jecker's protest - "on terms that I am sure you will find reasonable, even generous."

"I expect I will, Excellency," the banker stammered.

"You must sell the bonds because, as a bankrupt, you can have no assets if the Mexicans should sue you and win. Also, you can see that if friends of mine own them, my government will treat these bonds with more... regard than bonds owned by one newly hatched French citizen, however esteemed."

Jecker nodded his agreement. Morny swept on.

"As payment for the bonds," he pronounced, "my friends will pay you one franc. Plus two thirds of all moneys recovered from any Mexican government under the terms of the loan. They will retain one third of such moneys. And they will retain the mining exploration licenses."

The licenses were the sting in the tail. Jecker wanted to protest, but reason prevailed. By himself he could do nothing with them, and the friends who could help him had left Mexico. More important, he had a strong sense that Morny's terms were not negotiable. "I accept," he said quietly, "you are indeed most generous, sir."

They shook hands. "Come back in two weeks, Mr. Jecker," Morny commanded, "I expect in that time to have something more precise to discuss with you." He turned toward the Chinese cupboard that half hid Henri. "The mouse colored, I said, not the dove grey. Will you never learn, relic of my youth?"

He poured on his handkerchief precisely two drops of the same English toilet water that his grandfather, Talleyrand, had always used.

Morny had from birth been a dandy, even when he returned to Paris from the Algerian campaign, young, poor and jobless. He believed in making himself a work of art for all to admire. When Henri finished with him, he brushed a speck from his tight-waisted coat and set forth to delight the town.

He was more than usually pleased with himself. The prospect, however hazy, of ten million dollars added more wrist than usual to the swing of his gold-tipped cane. He was already an extremely rich man, but another ten million dollars is always useful. And there might emerge another, much grander reward from this venture. For himself.

Chapter 3

A few hours later, Lieutenant Commander Robert Jones, USN, was leaving a noisome café near Montparnasse. Luncheon had been a success; his new agent had produced a drawing of the breech of a new rifled cannon that the French navy considered promising.

Jones was a short, deep-chested, swarthy man with no neck and thinning black hair who closely resembled a Bulgarian wrestler. Jones wore a shapeless grey suit and a battered hat that could not conceal the military set of his back and shoulders, which distinguished him from the rest of the café's customers. For he was a navy man and had been one for much of his life.

He had been born Alexei Petrovich Ivanov, the oldest son of a Russian fisherman and his Mexican wife, who lived north of San Francisco. When Alexei was eighteen, his father foresaw that their Mexican rulers would soon be sent packing by the Americans arriving in numbers and that until then California was a dangerous place for a young foreigner. He pulled Alexei off the family fishing boat and sent the protesting boy to Mrs. Ivanov's relations in San Antonio.

There, far from the sea, Alexei sullenly learned English and became a citizen of Texas, as planned. Soon afterward, Texas was admitted to the Union and he found himself an American citizen.

This was not planned, but it gave the relations their first chance to rid themselves of the troublesome Alexei and they took it. They sent him off to the Naval Academy at distant Annapolis, which was scraping the newer states for cadets. They explained ambiguously to the Ivanovs that the opportunity was one that might never be repeated.

Alexei flourished at the Academy once he had exchanged his unpronounceable name for plain Robert Jones. He discovered an aptitude for naval architecture which took him to the top of his graduating class and then to a post with a planning section of the Navy Department in Washington. There, in the stifling, seniority-ridden inertia of the peacetime navy, he developed a contempt for military bureaucracy and a friendship with a group of young staff officers struggling to prepare the armed forces for what they saw as the inevitable war with the Southern states. One of the group was Miles Stoddard, Charles Bartlett's uncle.

Jones was a combative type by nature who needed an obstacle to overcome, and this experience of fighting for a cause helped to complete his transformation from Russian to Yankee. He now seldom mentioned his origins and, despite the occasional stilted turn of phrase, he was certain that he spoke like an educated New Yorker.

His masters belatedly awoke to the fact that France and other European countries were moving rapidly in new directions for the design of warships and naval ordnance. They thought it might be useful to have a man in Paris to keep an eye on these developments, so they inspected their files for suitable candidates. Among these, Jones stood out because he spoke two foreign languages, two more than any of the others.

So he was posted to the Paris legation in 1858 as military attaché. That meant that he was a spy, an accredited one. At first he spent his time studying the French navy, which had just built *La Gloire*, the first ironclad ship of the line. Then last year the intentions of the southern states grew obvious. He was ordered by Stoddard and Henry Wise, the chief of naval intelligence, to recruit agents in France and England. With substantial success, it must be said.

He controlled agents in the customs houses, port offices, post offices, insurance firms, and even in the British Admiralty itself. Some were criminals, forgers, safecrackers and the like, but he needed them all, because the rebels hadn't been sitting on their hands. He suspected that some of his people were also working for the South on the side.

It was lonely work, and he couldn't even confide in his wife. Maria Jones was a sturdy country girl from Delaware. She had met Jones at his graduation from Annapolis, where her brother was an instructor, and married him a month later. His accent, his bull-like magnetism and his raw ambition fascinated her. Men like Jones were thin on the ground in Sussex County, so she had thrown her hat in the air and accepted him almost before he finished proposing.

She had spent her days since then regretting it. She disliked the formalities of military life and she didn't care much for Jones, either. Overbearing and selfish were her kindest words for him.

Like any good Slav, Jones thought that a change of scene and a child would be enough to pacify her, so he had taken the posting to Paris and got her pregnant. Sadly, neither Paris nor baby Emily did anything for her disposition.

She disliked France, the French and her small apartment in the Malesherbes district. She longed to take little Emily back to her family farm, without Jones. To this end she nagged him about his failure to be given command of a warship. Once he was at sea, she calculated, she and Emily could escape to the farm, perhaps for good. She was relentless. "With all your fancy friends, like this General Miles Whatsis, Alexio," a nickname he hated, "why won't they give you a ship? Why?"

"Patience, my pigeon, patience," he would urge, to no effect whatever. "I want a ship as much as you do, even more, but I'm waiting for a good ship, not one of these jumped-up trawlers we're using now." And off would go another pleading letter to Stoddard and Wise.

Partly in consequence, he attended more official dinners and receptions than were necessary, where he drank too much wine and generally cut a rather dismal figure. And he began to meet some curious people. Civilians, one of them a certain Mexican gentleman.

Jose Manuel Hidalgo, a Mexican of pure Spanish blood, was related to the grandest families of Andalucía. His own family had foresightedly shifted a large part of their fortune from Mexico to Europe a dozen years earlier and young Jose Manuel, a diplomat, had soon followed it across the Atlantic. A tall, burly man with a round face and a brown beard, he had exquisite manners and unlimited charm. When he heard that Jones was a Mexican with the American ministry, he had a friend introduce them at a reception in the Austrian legation. Jones's Spanish was rusty but he held his own, and he was pleased when, after a few more minutes of polite exchange, Hidalgo invited him to lunch the following day.

Jones was of course familiar with the history of Mexico in that century. Since its independence from Spain in 1821, the country had been ruled by a rotating succession of so-called generals, all of them ruthless, corrupt and brief. The people got poorer, the church got richer and the Americans got Texas and one third of the rest of the country.

Most of the people were poor Indians or *mestizos,* and they had nothing in life but hunger and grief. The white landowners, the generals and the church, who were very Catholic and very conservative, had it all.

But three years before, things had changed. Benito Juarez, a lawyer, a pure-bred Indian, started a revolution against the conservative government led by General Miramon. A year before, he had finally won and taken Mexico City. The country was in chaos, a shambles. He made all religions equal and expropriated the church's property. When he threw many of the bishops out of the country, the rich conservatives followed right behind. Paris was full of them.

But the fundamental problem was money. A great deal of money, in fact. Mexico was so poor that its rulers had always needed to borrow from other countries. Then, when it couldn't borrow any more it began to steal from the foreigners - customs payments that were pledged, a couple of silver shipments, even the cash that was kept in foreign legations. The total of what the country had borrowed and stolen like that was enormous.

And now the foreigners wanted it back. They wanted all of it, and they wanted it right away, before the country fell completely apart. France, England and Spain were the biggest creditors.

Each of these three countries had for at least ten years thought about sending a punitive expedition over to Mexico, to collect the outstanding debts and see which chunks of Mexican territory they could keep as compensation for their trouble. They had all been deterred by the Monroe Doctrine, which proclaimed that the United States would resist any attempt by a foreign power to intervene in the affairs of a Latin American country.

But the Europeans had never been too shy to let their armies negotiate for them elsewhere. What they had done to India, Russia and China in the past ten years was proof enough. So they waited, watched and planned.

Jones had duly gone to lunch at Hidalgo's *hotel* in the Rue d'Angouleme the next day, the middle of August. For a mere ex-secretary of legation, Hidalgo lived in the grand manner - four footmen, six courses, fine wines and all the rest of it. The long dining room was paneled with some sort of light wood, quite plain. A fireplace at each end burned spiced woods and they dined off very heavy and very old silver plates.

"Commander," Hidalgo said over the soup, "a diplomatic initiative is taking shape that, in my opinion, should be made known to your government, but only through an unofficial channel. When you have heard me out, you may choose to serve as that channel. If you choose otherwise, I will deny that this conversation ever took place."

"Of course," Jones replied, trying to sound off-hand. "Please proceed."

"I am a member," Hidalgo continued, "perhaps the leader, of a group of Mexican émigrés, exiles, in Europe who are convinced that our poor country can not possibly save itself from the chaos, the misery inflicted on it by forty years of civil war. Mexico lacks, and will always lack, the people, the institutions and the money to save itself. This Juarez, this *indian,* is the ultimate disaster, in our view."

Jones nodded sympathetically and his glass was refilled. Hidalgo was in full spate now.

"Our group are equally convinced that no so-called democratic regime can save our country. That its only hope of salvation, of its regeneration, lies in the establishment of a proper monarchy." He paused for Jones's reaction to this proposition, but there was none.

"And finally, that a proper monarchy can only be established by a foreign country, or countries, under a prince of a European royal house."

"You mean to import a king?" Jones asked. "Which one?" He drank deeply to conceal his surprise.

"That I can not reveal... yet." He waited as his soup plate was removed.

"But I can reveal that, after many years in which we made no progress at all, years of repeated frustration, I believe we are now close to success. The Emperor himself is actively studying our proposal and I have good reason to hope that his decision will be a positive one." He looked at Jones with an air of authority, almost of triumph.

He's gloating, Jones thought, but he needs something from me. "Well, sir, I wish you good fortune with this, ah, project, but please tell me how I can be of assistance to you."

"Won't you try some more of the duck, Commander? No? Perhaps I will have one more slice." The tray appeared at Hidalgo's elbow as he spoke.

"Your famous Monroe Doctrine is an obstacle, plainly. We thus need to inform your government - to convince them - that France has no territorial designs of any kind in Mexico, none. The monarchy will be established only at the request of the people of Mexico. It will therefore be a strictly internal matter."

Sure it will, Jones thought, and I'm the Queen of the May. "But surely our legation here..."

"Would be an official channel. Please forgive my interrupting, Commander. Any communication to Washington through your minister must, for reasons of protocol, originate with the French foreign ministry. Too many people would be involved, here and in Washington. So many, in fact, that your foreign secretary might be forced to make an official reply, and one can guess how his reply would of necessity read."

"One can, indeed," Jones admitted. He now saw where Hidalgo was leading.

"So, if we can make our position clear, unofficially, to the responsible officers of your government, we are confident that we can satisfy them with respect to our intentions in Mexico, and there will be no need of any official response from them."

"Precisely who are 'we', sir?"

Hidalgo nodded. "The right question to ask. We are only the Mexican émigrés in Europe of whom I spoke. However, as we can accomplish nothing without the help of France, any views and information we communicate to your superiors will have the tacit approval of the proper French officials." He seemed for the first time to be slightly off balance.

"We... I will satisfy you on this score." Hidalgo rang a small glass bell and the table was cleared of food.

Jones was now enjoying himself and decided to press Hidalgo a bit. "I am sure you can, and I look forward to seeing - meeting? - your proof."

Hidalgo relaxed visibly. "Once you have a positive response from Washington, I shall attempt to arrange such a meeting. Do I make myself understood, Commander?"

"Completely, sir." Jones put down his fork and spoon. "I naturally can not comment on your reasons for wanting such an informal channel but, as we in the military say too often - why me?"

Hidalgo chuckled. "Who better? Your Mexican blood, your close relationship with General Miles Stoddard, who we know has the confidence of Mr. Seward and of General Scott, who in turn have the full confidence of Mr. Lincoln. And to that I might add your prowess in the field of, shall we say, intrigue?" He looked closely at Jones, who was struggling with an elaborate dessert.

Jones ignored the last allusion, but he couldn't ignore the logic of Hidalgo's argument, if he assumed that everything the Mexican said was correct. He'd try to confirm his story and would ask Stoddard to do the same. Meanwhile he perceived little risk in playing along. If the story was true, Washington could only gain from having an informal channel to the conspirators. If it wasn't, he'd merely wasted some of his time.

"You're most persuasive, Mr. Hidalgo," he said at length. "I see no reason why I shouldn't report this conversation directly to General Stoddard. You can rely on him to take the appropriate action." Whatever that means, he thought. "I can of course give no assurance how he will respond, or even that he will respond."

"Of course." Hidalgo was plainly delighted by this speech. "We must hope that he will."

Jones had at once reported this lunchtime conversation to Stoddard and asked him to confirm the rest of Hidalgo's story. He also put his own Paris sources to work.

*   *   *

Weeks later, while they were waiting for Stoddard's reply, Hidalgo relaxed over a drink one day and unburdened himself further. He told Jones that many years earlier, when he was posted to the Mexican Legation in Madrid, he came into the company of a vivacious widow named Madame de Montijo. Like all women, she found the young Mexican a charming companion and became fond of him. "We were only friends," he stressed, "nothing more."

The widow Montijo, daughter of an immigrant Caledonian wine salesman and a woman of modest Irish descent, had married well. Her full name was the Duchess of Penaranda, Countess of Teba and Marchioness of Moya. When her duke had the decency to die and leave her his estates, she set forth to carve a prominent place in European society and to settle her two daughters in magnificent marriages. The older girl, Francisca, captured the hand of the Duke of Berwick and Alba, but only after that young grandee was told by the widow that he must choose between the two sisters, and choose soon.

For the younger daughter, Maria Eugenia, her mother had even grander plans. She had in her sights an eminent forty five year old bachelor of eccentric habits. The ladies transferred to Paris and, after a tortuous courtship made notorious by her steadfast refusal to enter her lover's bed before the priest had done his duty, the daughter emerged as Eugenie, Empress of France.

For the Emperor politically, this was a serious mistake. As a foreigner, and a non-royal one at that, Eugenie was no legitimizing help to her parvenu husband. And any ruler who at forty-five married for love was a ruler to worry about.

Eugenie soon discovered that her husband's concept of marital fidelity was remarkably elastic, and for this reason and others she began to take a vigorous interest in politics.

Traveling in her coach to a bullfight in Bayonne five years later, she recognized a man who waved to her from the street as Jose Manuel Hidalgo, a friend of her youth in Madrid. He accompanied her to the *corrida*. "First, I told her all the gossip from Madrid," he said to Jones, "and afterwards I spoke of the agony of Mexico and my vision of a European prince placed on its throne by a European power."

Eugenie was enthralled by Hidalgo's vision. She and the Emperor had arranged to picnic on their yacht the next day and she insisted that Hidalgo join them on board. There, over hard-boiled eggs on the Bay of Biscay, Hidalgo began the task of persuading the imperial couple that destiny called them to the enormous opportunity that awaited them in Mexico.

"His Majesty has been fascinated by Latin America for many years," Hidalgo finished. "And with the help of the Empress, my task has not been as difficult as one might imagine."

*   *   *

A few weeks after his lunch with Hidalgo, Jones got a private note from Miles Stoddard:

> "Robert
>
> Well done meeting Hidalgo. Reviewed your report with Seward, Wise. Seward wants us to open the unofficial channel to his exile group, but Hidalgo must understand that it is open one way only – from them to us. Because of Monroe Doctrine and our commitments to Juarez government, we can not communicate anything to them that might be interpreted as acceptance of their plans.
>
> You should know that we do not accept their plans. The Emperor has had his piggish eye on Latin America for years. So have the Confederates, especially on Cuba and Jamaica. The military risk to us is obvious.

Keep close to H. and report everything to me. Wise
confirms that H. is indeed on intimate terms with Nap.
and Eug., but probably more social than political.
MS"

Jones'ss agents in Paris gave similar reports. Hidalgo was often seen
with Their Majesties at the Tuileries, Compiegne and their other palaces.
He was said to enjoy the personal confidence of Napoleon III and his
Empress in equal measure.

So Jones reported to Hidalgo that his informal channel to Stoddard was
open. Hidalgo absorbed this news with his placid courtesy, with no sign
of the relief or pleasure that he must have felt.

Then two things happened that changed everything: Juarez suspended
all payments on Mexico's foreign debts, and the North was routed at Bull
Run. It was plainly in no position to enforce the Monroe Doctrine, and
the French believed they now had a clear run at Mexico.

Chapter 4

"For Heaven's sake, Lieutenant, do keep still! I enjoy this even less than you do." The nurse stood back and surveyed Bartlett sourly as she wiped her sweaty forehead. "I must change the dressing or that cut will take weeks to heal... months, even."

"All right, Sister, all right." Bartlett submitted with bad grace and held his head still while she fussed with the bandage below his left cheekbone. The cut still hurt. Every day he awoke hoping that the nurses would leave it alone, and every day he was disappointed.

He hated the hospital - the heat, the noise, the smells. But most of all he hated the loss of control over his own actions. He felt as if he had surrendered some part of his being to the nurses, even to the orderlies. And that he had done it willingly.

He had in fact been lucky and he knew it. When he pitched forward over the head of his borrowed horse, he had tried with both hands to break his fall on to the tree stump that jutted from the bank of the dry creek. His left shoulder and head slammed into the stump, fracturing the collarbone and slicing open his cheek.

Much worse than the injuries were the anger and shame that twisted in his gut when he thought of his disgrace. How could he have been such a fool? To give orders to the rebels? To get himself wounded by his own side? He couldn't bear to think about it, but he couldn't think about anything else.

Now, in the stifling heat of the ward, Bartlett gloomily considered his wounds and his immediate future. It was barely possible that the story of his antics at Bull Run would not make all the rounds. But Washington was a small town and the regular officer corps was even smaller; rumors of all sorts were circulating and scapegoats were needed. His prospects were bleak, no doubt of it.

"Good morning, Charles. How do you feel?" asked an unmistakeable voice behind him. He turned the wheelchair and smiled when he saw the patrician features of his uncle, Miles Stoddard.

As always, Bartlett's first reaction was to wonder that his mother and this immaculate apparition could be sister and brother. Mrs. Bartlett was a handsome, if faded, widow with considerable New England dignity but little beauty. Miles, her much younger brother, was almost too handsome and his open, direct charm was famous. The white hair and moustache, the black eyebrows and the sinuous smile were a formidable combination.

It was said of him that he had no need to marry because so many men kept a wife for him.

"Fine, thank you, sir. One cracked shoulder and a scratched face," Bartlett replied. "And my congratulations, General," when he saw the stars on Stoddard's well-tailored shoulders. He noticed that the tailor had made the new stars look as if they had been there for years. Trust Uncle Miles to insist on that.

"That's kind of you, Charles. We're all brigadiers now. Very encouraging what a war can do for one's career."

"What brings you to this hell-hole, Uncle Miles - sorry, General?" Since his father's death, his uncle had often seemed to turn up at critical moments.

"*Sir* will satisfy army regulations, I think." Stoddard smiled and sat on Bartlett's bed. "Well, I've been posted temporarily to help old General Thomas at the Adjutant General's office. My responsibility is to select the best officers and put them where we most need them."

He scanned the ward. "I've come to see for myself when they will be fit for duty. But, what about you? How long will you be in here?"

"The doctor says I need another month in here, then a month's rest before the shoulder is back in one piece and sound enough for active duty. I'll report back to Colonel Sherman's brigade then."

"*Brigadier* Sherman - see what I mean? - is posted to Kentucky, and his brigade is being reorganized. So you appear to be jobless." Stoddard thought for a moment. "I may be able to find another regiment for you, but I must tell you that it will be difficult after your misadventures in Virginia." He smiled slyly.

"I was afraid of that. What have you heard, sir?"

"Nothing much. Only that you jumped on the wrong horse and rode off in the wrong direction. And gave the wrong orders? To the wrong unit? Have I missed out anything?" Stoddard was enjoying himself.

Bartlett tried to joke. "The orders *were* correct. Still, I suppose that does about cover it," he admitted. Then slowly, "Does that mean I've no chance of getting a battery?"

"It no doubt suggests you are not the first choice of many senior commanders. But I'll tell you what. I will do my level best for a week or so to find a line unit for you. If I can not, you will consider favorably any other position I propose. What could be fairer than that?"

Bartlett was relieved. Perhaps his situation wasn't hopeless. "That's very fair, sir. Thank you again."

"Not at all. It's the least I can do for my sister's only son. Come see me as soon as you escape from here." And he was off, with another smile and a half-salute that was more like a wave of the hand.

Again Bartlett saw his own facial resemblance to his uncle. Both had the same angular face, the flat planes of the cheeks, the straight hair, his own still black, and the dark grey eyes. These features had sometimes led him to wonder if there was a Pequot brave or two smirking, half hidden somewhere in the branches of his mother's family tree.

Another month of pain, heat and boredom, and Bartlett was walking shakily down Massachusetts Avenue in the direction of the new office Stoddard had commandeered on 14th Street. Stoddard had written to require his presence at three that afternoon and on the way he was testing the extent of his recovery. He moved with care; each step jarred his shoulder, which was still uncertainly settled in its proper position.

At three o'clock he pushed his way through the soldiers who crowded the entrance to his uncle's building and was directed by a superior clerk to a waiting room on the second floor. It was an enormous, high-ceilinged room with indifferently painted scenes from the Mexican War hanging between the dirty windows. The atmosphere was calm, peaceful, almost academic.

"My apologies, Charles," said General Stoddard when Bartlett at last was ushered in. He stood behind his marble desk in an office that was a smaller replica of the waiting room. "I'm on a joint board that looks at the long term strategy for the war and our meetings tend to drag on. Please sit down. Our board does some interesting work, by the way. Perhaps something for you will come out of it."

"Fine, sir." Bartlett tried to look enthusiastic. "Well, here I am, at your disposal."

"Right," the general said. "Now I have to report that at present there are no openings in our regular artillery units. None. I had them all checked. Perhaps in two or three months; right now none at all."

"I see," Bartlett said. That was not the whole truth, he knew. Regardless, this was bad news. Bad news, indeed. "I was hoping for – I need – a line job, sir, so I can – "

"Of course, there are hundreds of slots open in the volunteer units," Stoddard interjected. He picked up and waved one of the piles of papers on his desk. "In fact, our mutual friend Billy Sherman has asked for you. Yes, here's his letter. He seems to like you. He's still out in Kentucky raising and training new regiments."

"What do you advise, sir?"

"I advise you to stay as far from Kentucky as you can and from any other militia post, for that matter. Training these farmers is hard, frustrating drudgery with no prospect of any real action for at least six months."

Stoddard picked a yellow cigarette from the ivory box on his desk. He lit it, leaned back and blew a perfect smoke ring. "Besides, I have in mind something much more interesting for you: London. England. As our military attaché."

"What?" Bartlett stared at him. "Sorry, sir."

Stoddard laughed. "I thought that would surprise you. Let me explain." He paused to arrange his thoughts. "England is a hostile country, Charles, very hostile. There are many reasons for this but I'll let our Minister in London, Mr. Adams, spell out most of them to you. I'll just mention one – cotton."

He rose and pointed to England on his wall map. "Four million people, one in five of the English population, depend on the cotton trade for their survival. Imagine that. One in five. And that trade has for many years been almost wholly dependent on importing raw cotton from our Southern states. But now our blockade of the Southern ports has shut off England's supplies of raw cotton. Only the occasional shipment gets through. "

Stoddard left the map and sat on the edge of his desk, a frown on his face. "Because of this, the British Cabinet is under enormous pressure to intervene militarily in our war, at least enough to break our blockade and secure adequate supplies of cotton. And we believe they will intervene, or at least we have to assume that they will."

"Good Lord." Bartlett had never thought of England as an enemy, or as much of anything, for that matter.

"Correct," nodded Stoddard. "Having to fight England is a nightmare, but there's worse. Look at the South, now. It's good at growing things but not worth a damn at making things. If it can't export cotton and can't import everything it needs, everything from locomotives to needles, its industry will soon collapse. It won't be able even to put boots on its soldiers' feet this winter."

This image of frozen feet pleased him. "No boots on their feet," he repeated with satisfaction.

"So, if England breaks our blockade," Bartlett said, "the South can export cotton again and import everything it needs for its army. Guns, ammunition..."

"And ships. You're a quick study, Charles; it runs in the family." The famous smile flashed. "You see the enormous danger we're in from England."

"I suppose I do."

"Now, the English army is too small and too scattered to pose any kind of threat to us. That's obvious." Stoddard swept his arm in a sideways motion. "So the danger – any attack - will come from the sea. So you can see that we must learn as much as we can about the Royal Navy, and learn it fast."

"Then why not send a naval officer?"

"Two reasons: One, we need every one of our very few competent officers to train our crews and strengthen the blockade. Two, we know all about the British ships, but we know very little about their new ordnance - their new guns and ammunition – and as an artilleryman you're qualified to do that job. "

"To spy on their navy, you mean." He tried to keep the distaste from his tone.

"Call it reconnaissance, if that helps."

"And I have no training for a job like that, sir. Certainly not for spying. I wouldn't know where to begin or what to do."

"There is no training for the job, for Heaven's sake, and no army manual. It's what your initiative makes of it." Stoddard relented a bit. "The minister will tell you what *he* wants of you, which is basically information on our war that will persuade the English that we're sure to win and they should therefore stay the hell out of it."

Bartlett raised an eyebrow but said nothing. Stoddard smiled and went on. "And you'll establish relationships with the attachés from the important countries. Lots of socializing in store for you, some of which may be productive."

This made Bartlett even more nervous. Socializing was not one of his strengths. "I see. And the... reconnaissance?"

"You'll be guided by two men. Freeman Morse, the commercial consul in London, is first-class. The other is Commander Robert Jones, our attaché in Paris, who helped Morse set up our network in England."

"A naval officer?"

"Right. He works informally for me and formally for Henry Wise of naval intelligence. Very unconventional, very effective. He's senior to you, so look sharp when he's around."

Stoddard pulled out his watch. "I'll let him explain what he needs from you. I haven't the time right now." He gathered the papers on his desk.

Bartlett was beginning to like what he heard but his need to restore his pride, to restore it in battle, was still too strong. "It sounds tempting, I have to admit, sir, but I still would prefer troop duty."

"The war won't go away. It will still be here when you get back," Stoddard insisted. He advanced on Bartlett. "Charles, you have to decide now. I can order you to London, but I wouldn't do that to my sister's son. So, you have two choices. One, you can drill hayseeds in Spittoon, Kentucky, which any fool can do. And where your troops will learn soon enough that you're known across the army as the Hero of Bull Run." He watched Bartlett react to that. "The other choice is this posting to

London, where no one knows of your recent escapade and where you can do an important job of work for your country. Now, I'm far behind schedule already. Which will it be? Spittoon or London?"

Bartlett thought frantically. Could there be another choice? Was his uncle holding out on him to force him to choose the London posting? No. He

had no choice. Troop duty would have to wait. He turned and forced a smile. "London it is, sir."

Stoddard gripped Bartlett's shoulder. "Splendid. As of now, you are Military Attaché at the United States ministry in England. And *Major* Charles Bartlett. Congratulations. Only brevet rank, of course, but the extra pay will help and the English will pay some attention to you. Here are your promotion papers."

"Thank you, sir,"

"You sail tomorrow night from New York on the *Olympia*. You can convalesce on the voyage." He opened his office door and called to the waiting aide. "Lieutenant Lampson? Could you come in now, please, and bring that file for Major Bartlett?"

To Bartlett he explained "I *must* leave now, Charles, or face a court martial. Lampson here is one of about six people who know of your mission. He has your passage, your passport and your orders for London. He'll also brief you on the details - your official duties, reporting relationship with Minister Adams and so forth." He held out his hand. "The best of luck, Charles. We rely on you entirely to do your job well, and I know you will. I'll write your mother and tell her something about your posting."

"I seem to thank you every few minutes, sir, but once again. And good-bye."

"Good-bye, Charles. You'll find further instructions in your cabin on the ship. Give Jones every assistance." He trimmed his hat and turned to leave but stopped. "Oh, and Charles, if you're careful on the voyage there'll be some spare money in your travel allowance. Get yourself some decent uniforms as soon as you reach London, won't you? That one looks as if you stole it somewhere. Lampson has the name of my tailor, Fife's." Again the flashing smile, the half salute, half wave and he disappeared out the door.

To re-appear a moment later, saying "And for all of our sakes, Charles, stay the hell off a horse."

Chapter 5

France

Breakfast was never served before eleven at Napoleon's château near Compiegne, north of Paris. He and his Empress were still sipping their coffee at noon, hidden well away from their hundred guests for the long weekend.

Eugenie was complaining. "I do wish you wouldn't insist on dancing all night, Louis. It's bad for your insides, bad for my feet and almost fatal for those poor old people who can not leave until we leave."

Eugenie was no longer "the most beautiful woman in Europe", but she was stunning to look at. With her perfect profile, silken skin, trim figure and sleepy Andalucian eyes, there remained no doubt why Napoleon had surrendered to her.

"Few of those people would be any loss," he retorted. "So many Americans this year; how these democrats love the ceremonial of our court. But I promise I will try to... what is the program for today, my love?" He ran his hand through the wispy remains of his dark hair. With even less hair, blue eyes and a straighter nose, he would have been Morny's exact double.

She looked out over the formality of the small garden, where each tree and bush stood in precise alignment. That was how she liked to see things - arranged and orderly - in contrast to her husband's intuitive, almost haphazard, cast of mind. "More of the same. Riding and shooting this morning, a picnic lunch at two for those who want it, dinner at eight and then more of your wretched dancing," she sighed. "But La Beaugency insists that her smart friends will want to play at charades instead, so I've set aside the rose drawing room for them. The great cow."

He took her hand and patted it. "You look after our guests so well, my dear. I'm infinitely grateful to you." Eugenie didn't share his childlike love of their luxurious country weekends, where as a host he was at his best, where the dramatic costumes and the pomp of imperialism came close to realizing his adolescent dreams.

He put down his cup and rose to his feet, turning so she couldn't see him wince. The pain was bad today. "Speaking of difficult guests, I didn't see Morny last night."

"He declined at the last minute," she shrugged. "He must spend this weekend at Nades with his tiresome little Russian wife and her animals, so he says, or she threatens to join him in Paris." Morny was not a favorite of hers. He wielded far too much influence with her husband, influence she believed was rightly the due of the Empress.

"Horrors!" Napoleon mocked. "Now that *is* a threat to my gallant brother. Especially if she were to bring her wolf." He savored the image of the angry wife and her half-tamed carnivore cornering Morny in his library. Even Eugenie smiled. "It's annoying, though," he frowned. "I hoped to discuss the news from Mexico and America with him. Circumstances over there are moving in our favor at last."

"Well, it can't be helped," Eugenie said flatly. "The mighty Morny always does exactly what *he* wants to do." She brightened. "But Señor Hidalgo is here, just returned from Madrid. He will join us for tea today."

"Hidalgo again? My dear, people will begin to talk, if they have not done so already." He twisted the waxed end of his moustache, a favorite gesture when he teased her.

"What nonsense." Eugenie was always the last to see a joke at her expense; she was out of practice.

Napoleon gave up and rose stiffly. His short legs and long waist made him look taller when he was sitting, so he spent as much time as he could on a horse. He bowed and left for the stables.

*   *   *

"And was it frightfully hot in Madrid, Señor Hidalgo?" Eugenie asked the elegant Mexican over the silver teapot that afternoon. She sat back and fanned slowly. The château was not designed for hot weather, with its vast airless salons and lack of terraces. She longed for their usual summertime residence in their Biarritz villa, with its gardens and sea breezes. But Louis needed to be close to Paris for a few weeks more, so there they were.

After three years' attendance on the imperial couple, Hidalgo was at his ease. "Indeed, Your Majesty. My friends in the foreign ministry work only in the early morning and retire, gasping, to their villas in the hills by noon."

"But you managed to see all the right men in the ministry?" Napoleon asked sharply. He was not yet ready to trust everything Hidalgo reported.

"All but the foreign minister himself, sir." Hidalgo paused, knowing that his next few sentences were critical. "Spain is outraged, sir, by Mexico's suspension of payments on her debts. And she is decided. She will order her warships to Veracruz to enforce her demands. She is confident that England will join her and she prays that France will complete the expedition. She – Madrid, rather - has asked your humble servant to convey that message to you."

"I see, I see," said Louis. "Well, we've been talking about this expedition, for three years now. We now have the legal grounds on which to intervene and the military situation we've waited for. If Spain and England will move, then we will have the allies I have insisted are essential." He turned to Eugenie. "Do you agree, my dear?"

"Of course. Will you have more tea, Mr. Hidalgo? One of these cakes?" He took both. "You must be quite excited at these developments, my old friend?"

"Excited? Excited is hardly the word, Your Majesty! I have devoted fifteen years - ah, but you know all that." The Mexican subsided, abashed by his outburst. Napoleon disliked emotional talk.

But he wasn't listening. "The Americans will not, can not prevent us." He brought both hands down flat on the table. "Like Queen Isabella, I will await further word from Washington, but all our reports to date speak of panic and chaos in that city. Lincoln is paralyzed, our envoy says."

"The reports may exaggerate, sir. But even so, America will never dare to oppose the combined might of France, England and Spain." Hidalgo had recovered his aplomb, along with his conviction. "And when my people rise as one man to greet and salute their new monarch at Veracruz... why, not even Lincoln, the great democrat, will dare to interfere."

"You're certain of the popular support, Mr. Hidalgo?" Eugenie's instinct told her, more clearly than her husband could comprehend, that no European prince could long survive in a hostile Mexico. "He must know he can count on the support of the masses from the day he lands." For a man who himself sat on a shaky throne, Napoleon was obtusely slow to take in that elementary fact.

"I am certain of it, my lady."

It was time for France to select that European prince. Eugenie took great pleasure in the discussion that followed. If nothing else, she was determined that Isabella of Spain should have no chance to nominate any of her legion of unemployed, and unemployable, cousins. She also had vocal views on the religious and temperamental qualifications of the French and German noblemen they began to consider.

"The Duke of Auxerre?"

"Too old. And an Orleanist through his mother."

"The Duke of Modena?"

"Too old. And ill."

"Prince Paul Ernst!"

"A Protestant. And he turned down Greece."

"Count Otto of Harz."

"Too stupid."

"I have it - Aurillac's brother, the lame one."

"Too old *and* too stupid."

In the end, Napoleon and Hidalgo had to ask her the name of her candidate. "Really, gentlemen," she said, "it's too obvious: the Archduke Maximilian, Franz Joseph's brother. He is young, Catholic, married but childless, and he needs to make a name for himself away from Austria, where his brother stifles him. But I doubt he would be willing."

Hidalgo glanced at Napoleon and said, "The Archduke is known to be interested in Latin America, that is true. And one hears that his wife is..."

"Pushy. Very pushy," Napoleon took his cue. "Determined to make something of him after that fiasco in Venice." He stroked his beard and laughed. "He kicks his heels in his palace near Trieste and devotes himself to gardening and counterpoint. Hah! Can you imagine it?" He thought of his wife and quickly thought again. "But then, he is a Catholic. And he's the sort who might be receptive to suggestions from France."

Silence. Then, "Would he be receptive to a first approach from us? from my group?" Hidalgo assumed that Napoleon would prefer the initial contact to be unofficial; it would be less awkward if Maximilian refused out of hand. "With your approval, sir, I could leave next week."

"Excellent," said Eugenie. She addressed Hidalgo. "Perhaps I'm mistaken. Perhaps he will be willing. In fact, some presentiment now tells me that he will accept."

*   *   *

The sun hadn't yet penetrated the metallic Paris sky but it was hot on the edge of the Bois de Boulogne. It was the Count de Morny's custom when forced to remain in town in August to take his morning ride at seven, before his breakfast. He defied the heat with his fashionable black coat, white breeches and tall black hat. His companion was identically dressed, but he lacked the indefinable air that marks a man of true elegance. He also lacked Morny's easy grace in the saddle, the legacy of his years as a Lancer officer.

Morny looked with curiosity at his companion. He knew that Hidalgo had just returned from Trieste and reported to the Emperor, so he had agreed readily when the Mexican asked for an interview. "Tell me about this Mexican business. You have been to Miramar?" he encouraged.

Hidalgo had been a courtier long enough to slide through an opening when he was handed one. "You are most kind. As I had the honor to inform His Majesty, the Archduke Maximilian and the Archduchess received me with the utmost courtesy at Miramar. I found them surprisingly knowledgeable about my country and its present deprivations."

"Allow me to precede you here," Morny cut in. "There is a dangerous covered ditch we must avoid." He slowed to a walk and let his horse pick his way over a rough, overgrown patch of ground. Hidalgo followed him. "Carefully, sir. Well done. The Maillot Gate is just beyond those trees." They rode in silence for a time. "And then?"

"We talked for two days, the royal couple and I. Such an attractive pair, so kind, so unaffected. At length the Archduke intimated that he will consider with favor an offer of the crown of Mexico, subject to certain conditions, if the offer is made by men who can speak for the Mexican people."

"A reply phrased with typical Hapsburg caution. What are his conditions?"

"The main conditions are that the offer is first approved by his brother; that the crown is offered to him at the will of Mexico as a whole; and that his position is guaranteed by France and England. Guaranteed by an army and by financial support."

"No mention of guarantees or troops from Spain, eh? Odd." They had entered the fashionable section of the park and passed groups of stylish riders out for their daily exercise. Almost all lifted their hats to Morny; many of them also bowed from the waist. Hidalgo was impressed. "You have a wide acquaintance, sir," he observed.

"Yes, and some of these people are actually known to me." Morny turned his gaze to Hidalgo. "Well, I must congratulate you, it seems, on the success of your mission. The Emperor should be well pleased."

"The Empress is equally pleased, I may say," Hidalgo smiled. "It was her suggestion that I approach the Archduke. She is confident that he is the man she needs to shield Latin America from the barbarian Protestants of the north, as she charmingly describes them."

"Concerning these barbarians of the north, you and Their Majesties have no doubt weighed their reaction to France's intervention?"

"Of course, sir. Which is why I have taken precautions." Hidalgo explained the role that Robert Jones had accepted and why he had invited the American to take on that role. "I should emphasize that I have told Commander Jones only what my exile group is doing, nothing more. I have thus not thought it necessary to inform the Emperor that I am in touch with Jones."

"But now that France and, one could say, Austria are active..."

"Precisely. I will cease contact with Jones if you think I should do so."

"And whether I say yes or no, by telling me about him you have protected yourself against any accusation of duplicity." Morny smiled appreciatively, Hidalgo inclined his head. "Admirable. A tactic that one in my position always recognizes... and admires."

"Thank you, sir." Hidalgo was in no way abashed. "You will agree, I trust, that there is no need to inform the Emperor that I am using Jones'ss services?"

"That is a more complicated question, but yes, I do agree. And I see no need to cut off Jones now." Morny thought for a few seconds and asked, "You are satisfied that he is the right man for your purposes?"

"Oh, yes. Our former ambassador in Washington confirmed Jones'ss connection to General Stoddard and through him to Seward and General Scott."

"I know of the other two, but who is this Stoddard?"

"The rising man in the American army. A protégé of General Scott, who has made Stoddard the head of the board that fixes their army's long term strategy."

"I see. And has he replied to your first messages?"

"Yes, but only to confirm his willingness to use Jones as our private channel."

"Well then, I should like to meet this Commander Jones. Can you arrange it?"

"Nothing easier, sir. He is but a hundred meters behind us."

Jones was in fact closer than that, feeling foolish and conspicuous in equal measure. His uniform was hot and constricting on his hired horse, which was his equine double - short, dark, broad and foul-tempered.

When Hidalgo told him he had a chance to meet the illustrious Count de Morny, Jones understood that this would elevate him into the most perilous reaches of French diplomacy. He therefore told his new ambassador, William Dayton, about his dealings with Hidalgo and his messages from the Mexican exile group to Stoddard. Dayton, an amateur diplomat unfussed by protocol, went along and agreed that the same channel would be open to Morny if he asked for it.

So Jones had spent an hour that morning in a dutiful trot behind Morny and Hidalgo, doing his best to stay back one hundred meters, as instructed. Ah! There was his signal - about time, too. They had stopped and turned to look in his direction, their horses pawing the dusty ground. He threw down his cigar and started forward.

He was careful to maintain his same pace as he rode up to them so as not to appear anxious. Hidalgo made the introductions and all three, Morny in the center, continued at a walk toward the Allée des Acacias. After three years in France, Jones could 'defend himself' in the language, as his Mexican mother might have put it, but eloquence was beyond him.

"An honor, Excellency," he said.

"How providential that you are in the Bois this morning," Morny smiled amiably. "Mr. Hidalgo described his relations with you, I expressed the desire to meet you and *pouf!* there you are, as if by sorcery."

"*Pouf!* indeed, sir," Jones replied. "One of my better tricks." He examined his companion with open interest. "How may I be of service to you?"

"Valuably. You see, Commander, in my experience, the problems between nations - wars, even - are often caused by simple misunderstandings," Morny began. "Misunderstandings of a country's motives, of its intentions, primarily. We two are an example of this. The relations between our two countries are at present so precarious that we must all attempt to eliminate any misunderstandings." Jones said nothing and he went on. "To aid my attempts to do so, I would be grateful if I could take advantage of your direct links with the military authorities in Washington. In the same way that Mr. Hidalgo has done." He stopped and looked bemused. "My apologies for my directness."

"None are needed, sir. I welcome it," Jones said. "You would like me to pass on your messages to my superiors, as I understand you."

"Exactly," Morny smiled. "You understand that I speak only for myself, that in no respect can I speak for the government?"

"Yes. Nor can I."

"Others often think that I do, you see, and at times it suits me to let them think it." He gave a curious shrug of his shoulders. "But usually it does not suit me. So you will please tell General Stoddard, from me, the following: If France joins with Spain and England to intervene in Veracruz, there will be no military threat to your country, North or South. None. Our objective will be rigorously limited to the recovery of the sums owed by the Mexicans to our citizens."

"Sums owed by the Mexican government?"

"By the government and by banks, trading companies, citizens, everyone." Morny said. "But our forces will not pursue the individual debtors. They will simply take over the port of Veracruz and collect all the customs duties until the debts are satisfied. Then they will leave."

"Ah, I see. Then they will leave, as you say. But some European prince will remain as king, will he not? Supported only by the Mexican army."

Morny was unfazed. "*If* one is made the ruler, and that is far from established, he will be supported for a period by European forces. So much is obvious."

"So the intervention will not, after all, be limited to the recovery of debts, sir?"

"Yes, the *intervention* will." Morny enjoyed this fencing. "Whoever it is will be made ruler only if that is the wish of all the people of Mexico. In those circumstances the European intervention will, by definition, end when he is crowned." He smiled and spread his arms, dropping the reins. "The remaining modest forces will serve as a royal bodyguard." He paused for emphasis. "To return to the central issue, they will not, they *can not* pose any threat to America."

Hidalgo had been silent until then, admiring Morny's facile defense of the indefensible. Now it was time to take part. "If you will allow me, Excellency?" A nod from Morny. "Whoever is the new monarch, Commander, will be fully occupied for many years with the regeneration of my country. The idea of menacing the might of the North from Mexico is not realistic."

"True. The story of David and Goliath, though charming, is but a story," Morny observed.

They rode in silence for a few minutes. Jones sensed that Morny had said all he had to say. He drew up. "Excellency, I believe I comprehend your message, and I will forward it to my superiors immediately. As Mr. Hidalgo has seen, I can not guarantee that they will respond, but they usually do." He lifted his hat. "Good day, gentlemen."

Morny and Hidalgo remained in the shade of a grove of lime trees. "I like your Commander Jones," Morny said reflectively. "Direct, to the point. Is he reliable?"

"As far as one can tell. If General Stoddard replies, you will see that he also goes straight to the point." Hidalgo gave a Latin shrug. "More than that I can not say." He had accomplished what he had set out to do. He prayed that the Emperor would never find out.

Also satisfied with his early morning's work, Morny returned to his house, his breakfast and Henri's razor. Jecker would soon arrive to sign the papers drawn up by the notary. He had just time to thank Robert Jones, in a note that ended:

"I await the response to my message. Until then, my dear Commander, I shall be delighted to assist you however I can, with this matter or with any other.

De Morny"

Jones reported Morny's message of that morning in a coded letter to Stoddard. He saw no reason to mention the Count's note. It was personal.

But he took the note home to show Maria. He might not be in command of a frigate, he told her, but by all the saints he was consorting with the most powerful man in the land.

She was unimpressed. Another Frenchman more or less meant nothing to her, no matter how crested his writing paper. She said as much.

He was hurt. "But you have to admit, my pigeon, that I've made progress," he protested. "For a man who not long ago was on a leaky old fishing boat, up to my ass in herring, I've done pretty well."

"If you're so good," she snapped, "your great friends in Washington will need you back home. Why don't they realize that? Don't they know there's a war going on?" She flounced upstairs to see to Emily, who had reached her nightly fortissimo.

Maria might have been prescient. Jones ripped open the heavily sealed envelope on his desk the next day. In it was a coded letter in Miles Stoddard's briskest style:

> "Robert
>
> Bull Run woke everybody up to the prospect of a long bloody war. No quick, cheap win as most expected.
>
> The top men now agree that war will be won mostly at sea and that greatest (only?) real danger is intervention by England/France, for cotton, etc.
>
> To defend against English/French navies we now have rifled cannon and armor-piercing shells at the West Point works, but we need to know – God how we need to know – if the English now have them also. So, over to you. You know what to do.
>
> The sloop-of-war *Housatonic* will berth in the Thames late next month. Her captain has orders to transport you to Boston or New York or France as soon as you complete your mission.
>
> Major Charles Bartlett, newly appointed military attaché in London, has orders to assist you in every way you request.
>
> Miles Stoddard   Henry Wise
> Brig. Gen.   Commander"

Pinned to the foot of the letter was a short note from Stoddard to Bartlett that confirmed Jones's identity.

Chapter 6

Bartlett watched from the deck outside his cabin as the *Olympia* was towed up the Thames to her berth in the Lower Pool of London. Every ship in the world was in the Thames, it seemed, dwarfing Boston and even New York Harbor.

On their way up the Thames, at Greenhithe, the shipping was dominated by a black steam warship with a long, low profile and empty broadside gun ports. Hundreds of workmen crawled over her. A man of war, he thought, a battleship of the Royal Navy being fitted out. Huge, far larger than anything we have. It must be the *Warrior*, the Royal Navy's newest and most lethal ship, built entirely of iron.

The Atlantic passage had been quick and mercifully smooth. Bartlett's hospital pallor became a sunburn and the scar on his left cheek faded to pink. His shoulder responded to a rigorous program of exercise and he could now walk the deck without his sling and mostly upright.

A steward coughed at his elbow. "Your pardon, Major, the pilot brought a message for you from a Mr. Flanagan. He will meet you on the quay and help you with your luggage."

Mr. Flanagan was about twenty years old, long and thin as a rail, with a white face, bat ears and a shock of black hair. Bounding up to Bartlett as soon as he cleared the customs shed, he grabbed the briefcase and smiled. "I'm Flanagan, Major, from the ministry. Mr. Adams sent me to take you straight to your lodgings. No need for a hotel. You're to report to him tomorrow. I have a hansom waiting, so if you will please follow me?

He bustled about, saw to the baggage and handed Bartlett into the cab. Then he jumped in, shouted something to the cabbie, leaned back and grinned at Bartlett. "Do you know London at all, Major? Ah, it's a grand place. Except for the English, of course."

"This is my first trip. Ah, Mr. Flanagan, I'm grateful for your help, but tell me - who are you?" Bartlett asked.

"Just Flanagan, Major. No Mister, I fear. Don't let my polished manner deceive you. I'm the junior assistant dogsbody at the ministry - messenger, errand boy, file clerk, you name it and, from today, special assistant to you in my spare time if I ever have any which I doubt."

"I see. And where are we going now?"

"To your lodgings. In Rochester Place, quite close to the ministry. It's an old house that's being converted to rooms. Very nice, and cheap, too. One pound a week." Another grin.

Bartlett had expected to put up at a hotel for a week or so and to look for rooms himself. This was a most welcome development, as was Flanagan. He had never had an assistant before, even one like this.

"When did the minister know I was coming to London?" he asked.

"About a week ago. A letter in the diplomatic bag," was the reply.

They jolted painfully across the crowded London streets for the better part of an hour. Bartlett tried to keep his bearings but the sheer size of the city and the bewildering crush of people, carriages, carts and dogs were too much. He felt as if the entire world was coming straight at him. Suddenly, he was lonely.

"Here we are, sir, Lady Carra's home for gentlemen of regular habits," Flanagan said at last as the carriage rolled into a small tree-lined square and stopped before a row of handsome brick houses, each with four storeys and a white porch.

Flanagan paid the driver, lifted the baggage to the nearest porch and knocked. The door was opened by a small, grey-haired woman who squinted fiercely at them.

"Oh, it's you, is it, Flanagan? About time, too. And this will be the American major? Come in, sir, come in." She did her best to smile but could manage only a strange rictus. "You're in luck. Her ladyship is still here, putting everything in order."

As they entered the hallway, a slim woman in a plain grey dress came in from the other side. She smiled warmly at Flanagan and said, "Good afternoon, Mr. Flanagan. And Major Bartlett? I am Lady Carra, your landlady. Welcome."

Bartlett saw a pale face with high cheekbones, an arched nose and wide-set eyes of a vivid green, the most astonishing green. Her hair, the color of honey, was pulled back in a simple bun. Katherine Carra was a striking woman, indeed.

He bowed and stammered, "A great pleasure, Ma'am".

"Mrs. Mostyn will show you to your rooms, Major," Lady Carra said in a low, soft voice, "and perhaps Mr. Flanagan can bring in your cases."

Bartlett's rooms took up most of the ground floor. He found a fair-sized, light bedroom and bath at the rear of the house overlooking a garden, a large, comfortable drawing room with a dining alcove, a basic kitchen and a dark entrance hall. Bowls of fresh flowers brightened the bedroom and drawing room. It's perfect, he thought. Well done, Flanagan.

"I believe they will suit me well, Lady Carra," he said as she came in. "What are the, um, arrangements, if I may ask?"

"Of course you may." She turned to look him in the face and the glorious eyes rested for a moment on his scar. "The rent is one pound per week in arrears and your ministry has already paid for the first four weeks.

Mrs. Mostyn will clean the rooms and bring your breakfast each day, and if you would like a light supper you may arrange it directly with her. She lives in the basement."

"That sounds eminently acceptable," he said.

"Good. I might add, Major, that so do you - sound eminently acceptable, I mean to say. Mr. Flanagan has been telling us all about you." She couldn't quite suppress a smile. "I gather that you do not smoke, or swear, or spit or drink spirits and devote all of your free time to charity and to good works in general. Of course, I am not entirely certain of the source of his information, but until now I have had no doubts as to its substance."

"And now?" he ventured.

"And now... we shall see." She picked up her hat and smiled again. She had small, white teeth, slightly irregular, with a trace of an overbite. The effect was enchanting. "I must leave now, Major, but I live in the next house so we shall be neighbors. You will come to tea one day soon, I hope? Good-bye."

He bowed awkwardly. "Your servant, Ma'am."

Bartlett took another look around his new quarters, approving of the overstuffed furniture, the hunting scenes on the walls and the pale but formal curtains. The rooms had been done up recently, to judge from the faint smell of paint and varnish.

"Well, sir, what do you think?" asked Flanagan.

"I think you have done well, Flanagan. How did you find these rooms?"

"Mrs. Mostyn, the gorgon who lives downstairs - her sister is the charwoman at the Legation. But I meant what do you think of your landlady?"

"A charming woman. She lives next door, did she say?"

"That's right. She's the widow of some Irish lord and now lives with his uncle. Uncle owns a few houses in this row and she's converting them to apartments for him. This is the first one. She's his land agent, you might say, so you had better take care to pay your rent on time."

"You can depend on that," smiled Bartlett, not taking it all in. "Once she learns that everything you appear to have told her about me is false, prompt payment of the rent will remain my only hope."

"Well, I'll be off then," Flanagan said. "Here is a map I've drawn showing you the way to the ministry. We open for business at nine o'clock and Ambassador Adams will receive you at eleven. Good day, sir."

*   *   *

At eleven the next morning, Charles Francis Adams was leaving the office of the Foreign Secretary, Lord Russell, trying to hold his temper.

The news of the Union defeat at the Bull's Run Races, as Russell had insisted on calling the battle, had reached England and Russell happily taunted Adams with the details as reported in the London press.

"Surely it can not be true," he'd said, "as *The Times* would have it, that all of your troops dropped their rifles and ran back to Washington? That is a long way, I believe, and it must have been quite hot."

"Of course it is not true," Adams said thinly, running a hand over his trap-like mouth. "That damned newspaper never prints any truth about the rebellion."

They had discussed certain concerns that had arisen under the laws of neutrality, but looming behind them was the unspoken risk that England would break the Union blockade and secure adequate supplies of cotton. As *The Times* had written a few months earlier: "The destiny of the whole world hangs on a thread." A thread of cotton.

The South was certain that the need for its cotton would, sooner rather than later, force England into the war on its side. To bring England in became the overriding aim of Confederate foreign policy. To keep it out was Adams's only aim.

And I shall almost certainly fail, he admitted. Bull Run was a catastrophe. It proved to Russell and his friends that the Yankees won't fight. One more rebel victory will convince them that they can safely intervene against us. There are still a few months left until the stocks of raw cotton are drawn down to the danger level. Then they will only need some plausible pretext, or any pretext at all.

He headed glumly back to his legation in Mansfield Street. What more could he do to avert the disaster he saw coming? It was all in the hands of the Union generals and he had no confidence in them. He saw from his watch that he would be late for his interview with Major Bartlett, who he fervently hoped had brought better news of the war.

*   *   *

Bartlett's day began well. Mrs. Mostyn knocked at his door at eight o'clock, with her curious attempt at a smile on her face and a heavy breakfast tray in her hands. "Splendid, Mrs. Mostyn." Bartlett inspected the covered dishes. "Tell me... exactly what is this, please?" prodding his fork at an evil smelling piece of what might be fish.

"Finnan haddie, sir, a traditional English breakfast," she beamed, baring her teeth in a fractured grimace. "I'm sure you'll like it. Now, if you'll please leave the tray on the table when you finish, sir, I'll take it away when I clean."

He did not like it, not at all, but he was determined to try it again if it truly was as traditional as she declared it was.

His walk to the Legation following Flanagan's map was an unexpected delight. It took him through two leafy garden squares where the chestnut trees and lime trees were in blossom and dozens of shining-haired children were in full cry. Then around the top of Cavendish Square and up a few blocks to an imposing, formal house of weathered red brick.

"Ah, good morning to you, Major," cried Flanagan as Bartlett came through the open doorway. "Come this way, if you please, into the main office."

Bartlett followed into a large, light, crowded room. Flanagan led him to the corner in which the roll top desk, chair and floor safe he was to use had somehow been jammed. At least I have a window, he thought.

"This is it, Major, your very own corner. All the staff work in here, so it's a bit cramped, to say no more. The Minister's room is through that door. This ground floor is all offices and the family live in the upper three storeys."

Flanagan introduced Bartlett to the other staff members - Adams' earnest young son, Henry, who acted as a secretary; Mahan, a crabbed old man who was the senior secretary of the Legation; and Morse, the U.S. consul in London. Although their greetings were polite enough, Bartlett sensed an undertone of concern and suspicion.

After installing himself in his corner, he mentioned this to Flanagan, trying to be off-hand. The reply was "Of course, Major. They're not sure what you, a military type, will be doing here but they're afraid it will be spying, on them as well as on the English."

"Spying? Why?"

"Why not, sir? The London streets are heaving with spies - Northern, Southern, French, Russian, you name it. And you know what they say about military attachés, that they're gentlemen sent abroad to spy for their country. So it's to be expected if Mahan and the others look at you cross-eyed."

Around noon Bartlett saw a small, square, gray-haired figure dressed in black disappear into the Minister's office. Mahan followed him in and after a few minutes came out to summon Bartlett to the ministerial presence.

Adams greeted him with grave courtesy as he appraised Bartlett's worn uniform and obvious inexperience. He was disappointed. He was expecting an older officer, perhaps one with Mexican War experience, who could read the war reports, make sense of them for him and present them in the best possible light to the English officials.

"My apologies, Major, for being late," he said. "I was engaged at the Foreign Office, losing one of my periodic sparring matches with Lord Russell. Today it had to do with the laws of the sea. Do you know anything of the laws of the sea?"

"I'm afraid I do not, sir."

"Hmm. I suspect that no one really does." Adams gazed distractedly at his window. "Some day I might win one of these diplomatic jousts if I could once lead with some good news of the war. Do you bring me any?"

"None. The only real news is Bull Run, months ago."

"You were there, I think?"

"Regrettably, yes."

"Ah." Adams started to ask a question and changed his mind. "Well. Let us then turn to your work here." He scanned a paper on his table. "This says that you are to keep me informed on the progress of the war from your own official sources of information. That seems clear enough?"

"Perfectly."

"Next, you will establish a working relationship with the British military. This will also be under my control. I will arrange the appropriate introductions for you. Finally, you will keep your superiors in Washington informed on relevant developments in British ordnance." He glared at Bartlett. "Now I have considered those words and I must tell you this." His voice rose. "If, as I fear, it means spying, in any form and on any instructions, I want nothing to do with it, do you understand? Nothing."

"Of course. I...."

"You must tell me nothing of it, I say!" Adams broke in. "My over-zealous counterparts in Brussels and Paris have seen fit to organize a swarm of spies, first in Europe and now here in England. I tolerated it for a time but I have now demanded that Governor Seward put a stop to it immediately. It is too dangerous, insanely dangerous."

What a surprising statement, Bartlett thought. "Why so dangerous?"

"Don't be naive, Major." Adams said, his manner becoming agitated. "England is just waiting, or even hoping, for some pretext to intervene in the rebellion on the side of the Confederates. The discovery of a spy working in my ministry, with my evident acquiescence, would provide it with that pretext. Do you understand?"

"I do now." He had to be careful. Stoddard had warned him to stay on the good side of Adams, who was close to Seward, the Secretary of State. Seward was never happier than when meddling in military matters and he could break Bartlett's career on a whim.

"Bear this in mind, Major Bartlett," Adams said, recovering himself, "and conduct yourself accordingly. England is an enemy country. Their apparent good will in recent years was merely the result of their fear of our growing strength. Their real attitude has not changed since Doctor Johnson said Americans were a race of convicts who should be thankful the English didn't hang them all."

Bartlett was taken aback by Adams' vehemence. "You can rely on my discretion, Minister," he replied.

"Fine, Major. We'll let that be an end to it." Adams changed the subject. "Now, tell me - are your rooms satisfactory? Flanagan went to considerable trouble to locate them."

"Quite satisfactory. I admit, though, that I was surprised to learn that my lease is on a weekly basis."

"Those were my instructions. No need to take any financial risks. This legation is itself only rented from month to month. You must agree, from what I have told you, that that is but elementary prudence?"

Chapter 7

A week before Bartlett arrived on her doorstep, Katherine Carra had read a letter for the fourth time:

> "My dear sister,
> Wonderful news! My newspaper, the stodgy old *Pilot*, is sending me to England. I'm to be its European correspondent for two years, maybe longer. Can you believe it? I scarcely can. I'll be based in London but travel a great deal, mostly to Ireland to begin with.
> Can you put me up for a few weeks? Lord Carra won't mind too much, will he? I hope not. In any case, I'll come straight to you from Southhampton. I'm booked on the *Kincardineshire*, sailing next Monday from Boston, scheduled to arrive on 20th October.
> I calculate it's been twelve years since we last saw each other. Can it be? I can't wait to see you. And soon!
> All love,
> Owen"

My goodness, she realized with a start, October twentieth is tomorrow. Milly must clean the front bedroom and really clean it this time.

If they put Owen up, she thought, Lord Carra would grumble at the expense, of course. His generosity in allowing her to live with him was his unspoken excuse for his many small meannesses. But he would tolerate Owen for three or four nights, she calculated. After that, perhaps Owen could pay something if he meant to stay on?

Or better yet, he might rent the ground floor rooms in the adjoining house. She had just restored them to a livable condition. At enormous cost, or so Carra delighted to complain. She had half-promised it to the American legation for the use of their new military attaché, due in London any day now, but she had no faith in the assurances of any Yankees. That would be ideal, Owen living right next door and supplementing the meager Carra income. But probably too much to hope for.

*   *   *

"Well, that American army officer did turn up, after all," Katherine said as she entered her drawing room. "A Major Bartlett."

"Oh? What is he like?" Owen asked. He was of medium height, with sandy hair, light green eyes and a pleasant expression, but his features were somehow unfinished, lacking in definition.

"An agreeable surprise, I'd say. Not only financially, but personally." She sat at the small table which had been set for tea. "He arrived just as we finished tidying up next door. Well-mannered – lots of bowing and 'Your servant, Ma'am' and that sort of thing – but rather awkward. Shy, I think. Tea?"

"Yes, please."

"He has one arm in a sling and a fresh scar on his face, but he's quite nice looking. Tall, black hair, thin face. Looks a bit like a Red Indian, in fact." She grimaced. Mrs. Mostyn's tea was always unspeakable.

"Does he?" Owen grinned at her expression and took a slice of fruitcake. "Where in America is he from?"

"Does it matter? They have Red Indians everywhere, I believe."

"Really, Katherine! Not everywhere. Only in the west and the north. Like Canada."

She waved a dismissive hand. "Well, wherever Major Bartlett hails from, he's our first tenant and we must take care that he's satisfied. Lord Carra won't want to lose his pound a week in rent."

Wearing a plain grey dress, her hair gathered in a tight bun, she regretted that Major Bartlett's first impression of her must have been so... mousy. I look like a schoolteacher, she thought, patting her hair.

"Then be sure to keep him well away from Mrs. Mostyn's cooking, sister. Even a Red Indian doesn't want all his food burnt black."

Lord Carra entered the room. In his appearance the perfect caricature of the retired colonel, he had never served a day in the forces, a fact he was not quick to admit. He surveyed Owen with suspicion and turned to Katherine. "Tea, if you please," he said. "Now tell me, ah, um, Owen, how is your work coming along?" He still wasn't sure what that work was and hoped in this cunning way to find out.

Owen had wasted no time establishing the contacts he would need for his journalistic work. He told Carra of his meetings with prominent London Irishmen and his plans for his newspaper column. "I've even been asked to give a talk about Boston," he finished with pride.

"Sounds very Irish," Carra observed. "A piece of advice, young man. Have nothing to do with the Irish, if you can. A bad lot, by and large. Bound to mean trouble for you in the end." Suddenly he flushed a deeper red. "I mean the *Catholic* Irish, naturally."

"Naturally," Katherine smiled through clenched teeth. "Some fruitcake?"

Carra tried to recover the initiative. "Yes, please. And have you found a place to live yet?" he asked Owen. His meaning was plain.

Owen glanced at his sister. "In a way, sir." He cleared his throat. "I'd like to stay on here, if you'll let me, so I can be near Katherine. For a month or two, anyway." He hurried on to forestall Carra's sputtering. "I can pay you three pounds a week for room and board."

"Three pounds?" Carra gasped.

"Three pounds, yes sir. My employer is generous. And I expect to be away about half the time."

Katherine took pity on the torment visible in Carra's face. "And eventually Owen might rent the second flat next door, the one you plan to do up next on the first floor."

"Good idea!" Owen said. "What do you say, sir?"

Carra had to agree. He had recently bought an interest in a prizefighter, a huge West Indian who won several fights in devastating fashion but then began to lose his form. Too much attention from the ladies of London, his handler reported. The Barbados Bruiser had not dismantled the Orkney Giant that week, as expected, but had been stretchered away from his encounter with the Scottish gentleman, so his lordship's immediate cash flow prospects were uncertain. "Of course, young man. Anything to please Katherine. But payment in advance, that's understood."

$$*\qquad\qquad*\qquad\qquad*$$

A thin cold rain swept across the windows of the Prime Minister's library in Piccadilly. He poked at the fire without much hope and then pulled the bell cord beside the mantel. Dawson was the only man who could coax any heat out of the wretched thing, he admitted. And Russell was late again.

Henry Temple, Viscount Palmerston, was now seventy-seven and Prime Minister for the second time, the most terrifying Prime Minister, some thought, since Eric Bluetooth. Still reckless and domineering, he presided over a ramshackle coalition government that was kept in power by a distrustful alliance between the Tories and his own Whig-Liberals.

In recent years, England had humbled the Tsar, crushed the Indians and humiliated the Chinese. Now Palmerston scented the chance to put the Mexicans in their place and, much more important, to throw a scare into the Americans.

Lord Russell, his Foreign Secretary arrived with Dawson. He was a tiny man - as soon as he married a comfortable widow he was nicknamed "The Widow's Mite" - and a less than commanding physical presence. He and Palmerston, whom the Queen called "the two terrible old men", had once been enemies but were now reconciled.

He helped himself to tea and cakes while the servant heaped coal on the fire and fanned dutifully. The heat wafted the sickly scent of Palmerston's new hair dye across the room.

"Thank you, Dawson, that will do," Palmerston said. He turned to Russell. "And now, sir, let us have your news from Paris."

Russell sat down, his tiny legs dangling above the floor. "Our Ambassador in Paris met again with Thouvenel, who stated that the Northerns' defeat at Bulls Run and Mexico's suspension of payments have been enough to induce Spain to send troops to Mexico, to collect its debts. Spain has asked France to join it on the expedition and will soon ask England to join in. Isabella is determined on the expedition in any event."

"And France?"

"The Emperor is disposed to intervene jointly with Spain, provided that we do also. And that we three European powers undertake to help regenerate Mexico."

"'Regenerate'? What in blazes does that mean?"

"To the Emperor, it means imposing the European princeling of his choice on the Mexicans as their king." Russell looked angry. "I have stressed repeatedly that we can not accept any intervention in Mexico's internal affairs - that our aim is to collect what is owed to us and leave them to settle their own future."

"You propose a gentle little bondholders' war, then?"

"Exactly. A friendly little war, one might say. For us, it's an attractive course of action." He held up a hand and ticked off a finger. "First, we can prevent Napoleon from establishing a permanent base in the Americas. Second," another finger, "we put ourselves in position to help the Confederates - if that suits us - or to keep them out of Mexico if they win their war."

"And, third," Palmerston interrupted, "if we don't send troops, the French will scoop up every available penny out there and leave nothing for us." He paused and peered at the fireplace. "How much are we owed, by the way?"

"I don't have the exact figure. In the millions, though."

"Pesos?"

"Good Lord, no. Pounds sterling. Real money."

"That's enough. That will do very well." The Prime Minister studied Russell's face, clicked his teeth back into place and went on. "Let us understand each other. I don't give a curse for that witches' cauldron called Mexico, or for its effete and mongrel people. But we must keep that meddlesome mediocrity in Paris from setting up his stall in Central America."

"I agree entirely," Russell said. "Our position is strong. You remember that we have sent Juarez a list of our demands?" Palmerston grunted. "Well, I propose that, if he does not accept them within three weeks we go in along with the French and Spanish. For the three reasons we've stated. And provided, as I've said, that the French undertake to keep their dirty hands off Mexico's internal affairs."

"Fine," Palmerston said, "agreed. But what if Juarez *does* accept our demands? What then?"

"Why, we go in alone, of course. And straight away. Before the French and the Spanish can get there."

"Excellent," Palmerston broke in. "*We'll* occupy the customs house in Veracruz, and *we'll* keep Juarez in power. Whatever Napoleon attempts, however hard he tries to put his own creature on the throne." He sat back. "I like it, sir. I like it enormously."

He had every reason to like it. For twenty years he had wanted to punish the Americans militarily, and for twenty years he had been balked by his colleagues every time. This might be his best - and last - chance. If he couldn't leave office in clouds of glory, he would at least leave to the sound of trumpets.

*   *   *

The Tuileries, Paris

The Count de Morny sat back, drew on his cigarette and stubbed it out in the silver-gilt ashtray beside him. "You of all people, Louis, will know that I am rarely slow to give advice. And that before I give it I am always careful to make sure I understand the position." He paused. Napoleon III kept pacing in a small circle.

Morny clasped his hands on his chest, then with the hint of a smile slid his right hand over to touch the hortensia he always wore in his buttonhole. Napoleon hated this deliberate reminder of their brotherhood, hated any evidence of their mother's promiscuity because it might cast doubt on the legitimacy of his own birth. If any such reminder were to be given, he as the senior should give it, not his irreplaceable, infuriating half-brother. Irreplaceable because he was always right, infuriating because he was always right.

Eugenie sat silently at her needlework, presenting her cameo profile and matchless swan neck to the two men. She knew that her husband would decide at last to send troops to Mexico only if Morny led him to see that was what he really wanted to do. He needed Morny to help him order his thoughts. That was why she had invited her rival to the Elysee Palace that morning him. It had to be that morning. Time was short, and every evening of late Louis escaped to the arms of his Italian *puta*.

She had chosen the green room for their meeting. It was small enough for privacy but large enough to discourage any suggestion of real intimacy among them. "Do get on, Auguste, please," she urged him.

Morny glanced at her without expression and turned to Louis. "Let me see. You wish to establish a Central American Empire, based on Mexico, controlled from Paris. You wish to place Maximilian of Austria on that throne. You – "

"Yes, yes," Napoleon broke in. "This opportunity can never be repeated. Juarez has reneged on his debts; the Americans are at war; Maximilian is at loose ends. The timing is ideal. You know that Spanish America has always fascinated me. I can not miss this opportunity."

"You have chosen the Archduke in order to gratify Franz Josef, perhaps to the point that he will cede Venetia to you."

"Well, the Hapsburgs have contrived to lose two thrones in the last few years," Napoleon smiled. "It would be only neighborly of me to help them gain a new one."

"Quite. And there's the rub. Despite his proven lack of intellect, young Maximillian is shrewd enough to insist on the financial and military support of England as well as France before he bestirs himself from his seaside villa." Morny drew another cigarette from a jade case, lit it and sighed in satisfaction.

"And," Morny went on, "England swears it will not provide any support unless you swear not to intervene in the internal affairs of Mexico. But placing a Hapsburg by force on a Mexican throne that you will have invented only the day before might, I fear, verge on such intervention?"

"Most amusing, Auguste," said Napoleon. He checked his temper. "You are right, though. The English insist on non-intervention." He swung around and stopped. "Now the Spaniards threaten that they won't wait for us any longer, that if necessary they will occupy Veracruz on their own. And occupy it soon, with the army they already have in Cuba."

"I would take the Spanish at their word," Morny warned. "Isabella is stupid enough to believe her generals."

"So? So what should I do?"

"You, as Emperor of the French, must first place this Mexican question in its proper French context. And that is in the context of the Empire, the Empire you wish to pass on to your son." Napoleon stopped his pacing. "To do nothing is always a valid option. But you, after all, are the Nephew, the Nephew of the Uncle. So you must act. You can not be idle. An idle Napoleon is a contradiction."

"Oh, he's right, he's right, Louis," Eugenie said. "Listen to him, my love." She looked at Morny with gratitude.

"To preserve the Empire for your son, wars are imperative," declared Morny, "imperative to the people. These wars must of course be victorious, and as bloodless and inexpensive as possible. Mexico is a perfect example." He chuckled. "Who can say? It may even be profitable."

"It *will* be profitable. But you still miss the point, Auguste. How do we – I – persuade the English to join us on Maximilian's terms? With a British guarantee?"

"Simplicity itself. You lie."

"Lie? How do you mean?"

"Surely you're familiar with the word? And the concept?" He spread his hands wide and shrugged. "You lie. To the English."

"You must explain how," Eugenie said. "Tell him how." She sensed victory, but she knew how difficult it was for Napoleon to collect his thoughts. To collect new thoughts was for him like collecting a fog.

"All right," Morny replied. "You will write to Palmerston and you brush aside this trifling difficulty over non-intervention. You agree that of course you do not intend to intervene in Mexico's internal affairs. You intend only to collect your just debts and leave that unhappy country as soon as you can. But – "

"I must have an escape clause of some kind," Napoleon pleaded.

"Yes, yes, patience," Morny snapped. Now he began to pace, Napoleon's eyes following him around the room. "You add that, in exceptional circumstances and only if demanded by the legitimate elements of Mexican society, you may support those elements in their purposes for a brief period of time. In a disinterested way, naturally." He thought for a moment. "Yes, something like that will do. You can polish the phrasing in your own unmistakable style." He sat down with the air of a man who has done his country another great service but could do no less.

Napoleon looked at Eugenie, who nodded pointedly. The Emperor was a peculiar mixture of cunning and obtuseness, and he perpetually wavered between weakness and ill-considered rashness. This was his week to be rash. He understood that, unless he was honest with both Maximilian and Palmerston, each might go ahead on a false prospectus: the prince believing that Palmerston supported him with men and money, Palmerston believing the prince had been dropped. Well, he thought, he could straighten that out in good time, when it was far too late for either of them to back out.

Napoleon rose. "Thank you, Auguste, I will consider your advice. I think I'm inclined also to mention Maximilian – in passing, of course – in my letter." They shook hands and walked to the door. Morny bowed to Eugenie and started to leave, but his brother gripped his arm. "Tell me, Auguste, how much do you know of Mexico? I mean, really know of it?"

"Nothing, I fear. I have no interests there, and its politics concern me not at all. Except as they concern France, of course." He bowed. "But I have no doubt that you will come to learn all you will ever want to know."

Chapter 8

Secretary of State William Seward threw his cigar in the fire, leaned back in his shirtsleeves and swore bitterly, thus intensifying his facial resemblance to an eager bird of prey. Today Mexico was on his mind. Miles Stoddard had written that he had some news from Paris, and he was due any minute to report.

The elegant brigadier bustled in without ceremony. "Good morning, General." Seward extended his hand, smiling. He had considerable respect for his visitor. They had of late been thrown together on military matters by Lincoln's distrust of his War Secretary, Cameron, and his venal colleagues and by Seward's determination to act as unappointed Prime Minister to the bumbling President. "Sit down and tell me your news."

Stoddard set out the essentials of the latest message from Robert Jones in Paris. "France is sending an army to invade Mexico, collect what's owed to it and install some European prince as king. But Morny says their army will pose no threat to us." He paused. "It couldn't be more clear." He lit a large yellow cigarette and blew the smoke at the ceiling fan.

"Damn the Emperor! He's as mad as Palmerston." A long silence, broken by Seward's musing. "You know, Stoddard, I'm inclined to let the French into Mexico. Let 'em get bogged down there, chasing Juarez around. Less chance they'll try to break our blockade at the same time. Their people wouldn't stand for two overseas wars at the same time, would they?"

"I've no idea, sir, but what about the Monroe Doctrine? Can you ignore that?"

"No, certainly not." Seward began again to pace. "Damn! It's all down to Bull Run, you know. If only we'd won there, these yapping foreigners wouldn't dream of landing in Mexico with an army. But right now you have to reply to de Morny's message to you through Jones. That could be a useful channel for us." He tugged at a pendulous ear. "You might say, um, you acknowledge receipt of said message concerning France's peaceful intentions in Mexico, blah, blah, you appreciate the Count's frankness, but the Monroe Doctrine remains in full force and effect."

"All right. I'll write him tonight."

"Good. Good." Seward thought for a long minute. "We can't forget England in all this, you know. I've already had Lyons, their ambassador, in here a time or two. I've warned him that the French won't go to Mexico just to collect a few debts, tip their hats and politely go home. That they mean to stay there. But," he spread his arms, "the precious little sod pretends not to believe a word I say. Nor does he admit that the English have already thrown in with the French. And now we know that they have."

"It's a complex situation, sir," Stoddard sympathized.

"Yes and no," was the brisk reply. "We must never forget that the overriding aim of our foreign policy is to keep England and France out of *our* war, not out of Mexico. Our Mexican policy - if I can ever decide what it is - must be subordinate to that aim."

*   *   *

London

The next morning, chewing manfully on his finnan haddie, Bartlett reflected on his meeting with Adams. What a miserable old trout, he thought. Spies everywhere. England about to declare war. Renting by the month. No wonder his staff are jumpy.

He was more than a little nervous himself. For years, from the dreary frontier posts to his barren routine at West Point, he had dreamed of having his own command, of leading picked troops against a vicious enemy. Some dream. But after all this was his first independent command, and he had to find a way to carry it out successfully. He would be working on his own, in hostile territory, in a field he did not know. He suspected that his initiative and tenacity would soon be tested to their core for the first time in his career.

"You do this job well, and quickly," Lieutenant Lampson had said, "and the General will find you that field command. Do it badly, or slowly, and... who knows?"

He understood all that well enough. What he did not understand was the hand-written note from Miles Stoddard he had found along with his orders on board the *Olympia*.

> "Charles
>
> You have a personal credit of two thousand pounds at Bannerman's Bank in The Strand. You will find the bank discreet and helpful. This is the bank used by our military for funds required in England, so Mr. Bannerman is to be trusted.
>
> The money is for your personal use only in an emergency. Adams knows nothing of it.
>
> Destroy this.
>
> MS."

He needed to learn what that was about. He would look in at the ministry, visit Fifes', Uncle Miles' tailor, and then call on Bannerman's Bank.

*　　　　　*　　　　　*

Malcolm Bannerman was not at all what he expected of an English banker. In the first place, he was a Scot. In the second, he was much younger than any banker had the right to be. Not yet thirty, Bartlett guessed.

Bannerman & Co. had been established for centuries at its red brick building in The Strand. The ground floor was taken up with a regulation open banking floor and ranks of shirt-sleeved clerks. The Chairman's office, its paneled walls hung with portraits of disapproving ancestors, was at the river side of the second floor, with a wide and no doubt expensive view over a small park down to the Thames.

"Come in, Major Bartlett, come in," Bannerman called gaily when Bartlett peered around his door. Bartlett saw a tall, slim, elegant figure with an engaging smile. His face was round and pink, his protuberant eyes were a bright china blue and his tight blonde curls sprang off in all directions. He wore the dandy's London uniform, a blue frock coat, yellow waistcoat and heavy gold watch chain.

"If you will be kind enough not to look too surprised at my tender years, I shall overlook yours," he said, waving Bartlett to a chair. "And please don't worry. There is no mistake. I am indeed the last of the Bannermans, now Chairman and sole owner of this ancestral counting-house, bankers to the gentry."

"Ah, congratulations?" Bartlett queried.

"Thank you, but my position owes nothing to merit and everything to mortality. There were only two of our family in the last generation, you see - my uncle, who never married, for reasons I shall not dwell on, and my late father, who succumbed this last Christmas to an excess of plum duff. So, here am I, at your humble service."

Bartlett decided to plunge straight in. "I understand that the United States Army banks with Bannerman's in London and that a separate account has been opened in my name also, Mr. Bannerman, for use in, ah, certain circumstances." he began. "I would like to establish that I can have access to the funds." Was that banker-like, he wondered, or just pompous?

"Yes, indeed. Two thousand pounds, I believe, now resting comfortably on current account. You won't spend it all at once, I trust? We've grown quite fond of it."

"No, I don't expect that I will, but I may need to spend some of it in a hurry."

"In cash?"

"Ah, I don't know. Perhaps."

"No matter. I have the necessary documents right here." Within a few minutes the details of signature verification, payment instructions and the like were settled and signed.

"There," said Bannerman with a boyish smile, "you can be sure of access to your funds, as you so neatly expressed it. Even immediately, if necessary." He arranged the papers in a tidy pile.

Bartlett felt uncomfortable and rose to leave, but Bannerman stopped him. "Tell me, Major, will you be buying war material with that account? If so, perhaps I can offer advice with respect to your suppliers. Our bank has long relationships with the leading firms."

How do I answer that? Bartlett asked himself. He mumbled only that he had no instructions to do so.

"Well, if you do receive them," Bannerman pressed on, "I shouldn't delay, in your place. The rumor is that more Confederate agents will arrive later this month. But these are rumors, nothing more."

He knows more than he's saying, Bartlett thought. "What will they use for money?" he asked. "Their currency is worthless, isn't it?"

Bannerman shrugged a stylish shoulder. "Who can say? Perhaps they mean to pay in smuggled goods. Sugar? Cotton? They must think they have something of value to use as payment."

Bartlett was about to thank Bannerman for his help when the banker added, "One last bit of advice, unsolicited as always: Next time, tell Fifes' to give you more room in the collar. They *will* make their collars too tight." He was amused by Bartlett's surprise. "Nothing easier, my dear fellow. Fifes' coats are recognizable the world over. It's their cut."

Bartlett laughed ruefully. "I'll remember that, next time. But next time won't be until I've paid for this one."

"No, no – forgive me, I can't help myself - you mustn't pay for that one until you get the next one! If you pay off your account, poor Fifes' will think you don't like their work and that you're not coming back. Always leave at least one suit unpaid. At least one."

"I shall take care to do as you say, sir," Bartlett smiled. He rose and held out his hand. "Thank you for your help."

"It is my pleasure, Major. At Bannerman's, service is our watchword. Good morning, and good luck." A smile, a bow, and Bartlett was through the doors. Only to stop when his host called after him. "Oh, and Major, please give my kind regards to your neighbors, Lord and Lady Carra. Dear friends of mine."

*   *   *

Once he had dressed on Sunday morning, Bartlett needed fresh air so he decided to explore the streets and squares around Rochester Place. He stepped out into bright sunlight, Flanagan's map in his hand, and reached the pavement as Lady Carra and an older man opened the gate of the house next door. Both were dressed in black. Returning from church, Bartlett guessed.

They were arguing. Lady Carra's face was pink with anger. She began to reply to her companion but he snapped, "And we will do it my way, do you hear, or not at all. And where would that leave you, my dear, eh? eh? Where, indeed?"

She tightened her mouth, said nothing and began to follow the man through the doorway when the door slammed in her face. She raised the brass knocker but let it drop and then looked around distractedly. Seeing Bartlett on the pavement, she managed the beginning of a smile and walked toward him as if she were on her own way out.

Embarrassed, he raised his hat and walked on but she called his name. He stopped, they exchanged civilities and, when she learned of his plans for a walk, she asked him to accompany her to the nearby Sackville Square. There she meant to read the book she carried under her arm, which Bartlett saw was not a bible but a popular romance. "I simply cannot wait any longer to find out if she marries the scoundrel," she confided. "I do hope so."

So they walked on together. She tried to recover her composure; he searched for something to say. "This is a handsome row of houses," he faltered at last. "I'm fortunate to live here."

"So am I, Major," she replied. "Three belong to Lord Carra, whom I suspect you heard a few moments ago." She turned her brilliant eyes on him, now blazing anew with anger.

"Ah, yes, I believe I did. Your husband, Lady Carra?"

"Oh, heavens no! My husband's uncle." She saw his bewilderment. "My husband died a few years ago. We have no children so the title went to his uncle, along with his properties in Ireland and London. Among them are these houses you admire."

They walked a little farther and she stopped to look back at the row. "It's been quite sad," she said. "Both houses are empty. First my husband and then his uncle were too... preoccupied to look after them properly and let them. But now Lord Carra intends to do up all of them. In practice I will do the work while he provides the funds and, as you heard, the occasional suggestion."

"So that is what it was?" Bartlett ventured. He was curious why she had not inherited the houses.

She laughed, her usual serenity returning. "Nothing more than that, although vividly expressed, I grant you. His temperament is somewhat erratic, I'm afraid. Today he is persuaded that I should first do up the ground floors of all his houses and let them to others like you. But I think that I should finish one house before we move on to the next." She seemed to weigh the arguments. "Could I ask for your opinion on the matter, Major, as our first tenant?"

"I suppose it would be less expensive to finish each house in turn, would it?"

"I hope so. That would be a compelling argument with his lordship, I can assure you." She chewed her lower lip for a moment. "I must look into that with the builder."

"Who is he?"

"Oh, you'll meet Mr. Jenkinson soon enough. He's a dear man, pretends to be all business but he's quite soft-hearted."

"In my experience with builders, that places him in a group of one."

She searched his face. "I think I am looking forward to being your landlady, Major, or rather your landlord's agent. I must warn you, though, to pay your rent on the nail. I shall be ruthless about collecting it every week." She made as if to look stern.

"Thank you for the warning. You'll find me punctuality itself with my rent."

"Just as Mr. Flanagan promised you would be." She slowed her steps. "He also said you were wounded at Bulls Run, Major," gesturing at his sling. "Were you badly hurt, if you'll forgive my curiosity?"

"No worse than a few scratches and a bent shoulder, Ma'am," he said with mock bravery. "I was lucky." And he recounted a highly colored version of his struggles with Attila and then of his wild ride at Bull Run, on the wrong horse in the wrong direction with the wrong orders. She laughed with delight as he finished with, "Never again, Lady Carra, will you find me in a wagon with a dozen of your drunken countrymen. Next time, I shall walk, whatever my condition."

"We Irish are never at our best, sir, going *away* from a fight," she observed.

Bartlett feigned seriousness. "Their lack of respect for my lofty rank was total, shocking. A few of them, before they fell off the wagon, even accused me of being a rebel spy in disguise." Elaboration can only help a good story, he said to himself

He could see that Katherine was not merely listening, she was trying to visualize the crowded wagon in the chaos and panic of the retreat. But the image of the Irish troopers toppling solemnly off was too strong. She laughed again, showing her small white teeth. Bartlett was entranced. He started across a street crowded with traffic that was anarchical even by London standards, to be saved by her hand on his arm.

Her mind was still at Bull Run, it seemed. "But they weren't regular soldiers, were they?" she wanted to know.

"No, all ninety-day volunteers. All of them home by now, I reckon."

"But you are a regular soldier, Major?" To her faint surprise, she was curious about this man. "Is it a family tradition? To be a soldier?"

He shook his head, amused. "No, we don't have that tradition in America, not yet." He stopped well short of the next busy cross street. She seemed genuinely interested, he thought. "My father and grandfather were schoolmasters, hated the thought of war. I went in the army - to the Academy - because I didn't want to teach, or farm. I wanted to see the country, maybe something of the world."

"And have you?"

"Well, this bit of the world, London. Before that, after seeing more empty prairie and empty pine scrub than you can imagine, I ended up back at West Point, teaching. Greek, no less." He turned to her with a grin.

He's unlike any other man I've met, Katherine thought, and seems intelligent for an American.

She's not remotely like any other woman I've met, he thought. So intelligent, so charming, so spirited.

They passed through a wrought iron gate into Sackville Square. A vivid green in the sunlight, much greener than anything he had seen before, even in the hills to the west of Boston. Every blade of grass radiated color. The sudden quiet as they entered the square surprised him. There were fewer than a dozen children about. Why, he wondered, are there so few blond adults in London when all the children are blond?

"Isn't it lovely?" she said. "The colors at this time of year remind me of my home, of Ireland. I come here often to read or to remember our countryside. Do you like the country, Major?"

"Not much, Ma'am, I'm sorry to say. I've seen a great deal of it, as I said, and never found anything to commend it. All very flat. Lots of Indians."

"Ah, but our countryside is quite different. We have no Red Indians, for a start, so it's much safer. You must give it a chance. Perhaps one day I can show you some of it." She was silent for a moment. "But today I mean to read, and over there is a bench in the shade waiting for me."

He was dismissed, he knew. "Good afternoon, Lady Carra," he bowed. Strange, how bright the day had seemed until then.

Bartlett spent the rest of the afternoon pleasantly, poking into the crooked streets near Rochester Place, discovering the hidden churches and sudden green open spaces that gave London much of its charm. But the image of Katherine Carra stayed with him. He wanted to know her better, but somehow he doubted that he ever would. And he had forgotten to relay Malcolm Bannerman's greetings.

*   *   *

As Bartlett went through the ministry doorway the next day, Flanagan went to his desk, pulled out an envelope and handed it to him. "This was pushed through the door this afternoon, sir. It's addressed to you."

The address was "Bartlett - U.S.A. Ministry". The scrawled note inside read:

"Major Bartlett...

General Stoddard will have told you of me. I must see you urgently. I will dine at The Crown Restored in Bermondsey tomorrow evening and will look for you there.

Do not tell Adams of this note and do not wear uniform.

R. Jones, USN"

The Crown Restored had known far better days, and a great many of them. Lurking by the river in Shad Thames, almost in the shadow of Tower Bridge, it had been built in the last years of Charles I and defiantly named The Crown. Cromwell's mobs burned it to the ground a few years later and the proprietor, one Speek, took an early bath and retired hurt to Wapping.

On the return of Charles II in 1660, Speek's son, keenly sniffing the wind of public affection, was inspired to rebuild the tavern and give it a new name, one with its loyal double meaning. It soon prospered, becoming popular with naval officers, merchant seamen and the younger members of Charles II's circle attracted to rougher surroundings. In fact, Speek insisted that the King himself was an occasional incognito visitor, but no one believed him.

The establishment's fortunes declined remorselessly after the early 1800's. The ships, the docks and the sailors retreated eastward down the Thames as the ships' drafts became too deep for the upper reaches of the river. Since that time, The Crown Restored had survived on the custom of clerks and minor officials from the nearby Admiralty offices that had been left behind like seaweed at low tide.

It was now one large, dreary room with indifferent drink and dire food served by a sluttish waitress. Sitting here alone early in the evening was Robert Jones. He was holding a wine glass up to the light from a dirty window.

"Damn it, Molly, this glass hasn't been washed since the Black Death, which it probably caused. Bring me another one, and this time be sure it's clean." The waitress slouched away.

Jones wore his shapeless grey suit in his long-standing conviction that it would disguise him as a civilian. Bartlett was late, he saw from his ancient watch. That was annoying. He had other things to do after he dined with him.

Molly slammed down another glass and stalked off. Jones turned his head to protest but noticed a tall, dark-haired man advancing uncertainly into the gloom. Jones glanced at the nearest of several shabby men seated at a long table. The man nodded and raised his tankard.

Jones stood up and called, "It's Mr. Bartlett, is it not? Do join me, if you will."

Bartlett shook hands, sat down and ordered a whisky punch from the suddenly roguish Molly. Then he studied his host. He did not altogether like what he saw, so he said, "Look, Mr... Jones, before we begin. You plainly know who I am, but can you prove who you are? And what we're both doing in this slum?"

Jones laughed. "It's hardly the tavern of legend, with jolly tars and buxom serving wenches, is it? Hah! But it's close to where the ship I'm bunking on is moored. And I have friends here." He handed Bartlett a folded paper that was another note from Miles Stoddard. It said:

"Charles... This is Commander Jones. Kindly do what he asks of you. M. S."

The note was dated seven days before Bartlett had sailed from New York. The next order I get from Uncle Miles, he thought wryly, will be dated before Sumter.

"That is who I am, Mr. Bartlett," said Jones, "and we are in this place because it's quiet, discreet and, as I say, close to my ship. Your good health, sir," as the whisky arrived. "And you are Miles's nephew, I believe. He and I have been friends for years. A fine man, a first-rate mind. And flexible enough to see what few senior army people can see, that this war will be won on the water, not on the land." Jones waited to see how Bartlett reacted to this assertion.

With indifference, it seemed. "He said something about that. I can't say it made much sense to me, but then I'm not a strategist." He tried to see Molly. "Shall we order supper?"

"Of course, although the food here is dubious, at best. Speaking as a friend, I advise you to have nothing to do with anything on the list that died more than a few hours ago. Molly!"

After some thought, they both settled for bread, Stilton and a pint of bitter. Jones resumed his lecture, describing the high command's "Anaconda Plan" to squeeze the life out of the South by blockading her seaports and controlling the western rivers.

The Crown was emptying of customers as they ate. A desultory game of darts at one end of the room finished with no apparent winners. Most of the drinkers were clerks in the government and banking offices on both sides of the river, delaying their return to family and supper each evening in the late summer until darkness began to press in.

Molly was now the one woman in view. She brought candles to the table and took up a position in what she hoped was Bartlett's line of vision.

A while later, still chewing hard, Jones continued. "I was saying that we would win the war on the water. Although I confess it's not exactly what I had in mind, the British Cabinet has given us the chance to prove that assertion." Little noticed amidst the furor over cotton, he said, was the fact that the cabinet had the month before slapped an embargo on all exports of niter. "Saltpeter, the Brits call it. It's – "

"The essential ingredient of gunpowder. Yes, I know. Makes up eighty five percent of it."

"Miles said you're an artilleryman," Jones grinned. "Well, the Confederates managed to buy a full shipload – over a thousand tons – of the material and load it in a fast steamer, the *Bermuda*, the day before the embargo took effect. In fact," he laughed aloud, "they would have sailed that same day except that it was a Sunday and the skipper, a God-fearing Cajun, refused to profane the Lord's Day by sailing."

"Where is the vessel?" Bartlett asked idly.

"On the River Mersey at Liverpool. Under twenty-four hour guard. Hah! The English thought it was consigned to us, to the North, you see, so their embargo was aimed at us." Jones took a deep breath and leaned across towards his listener. "The South has no native source of saltpeter. The only sources in the world market are here in England. The material comes from India, but the English brokers have the suppliers all tied up. The *Bermuda's* cargo alone is perhaps *one year's supply* for the rebels."

"Good Lord!"

"Exactly. And that's exactly why we're going to sink her. And soon, before England declares war on us and revokes the embargo." The gleam in Jones'ss eye was unmistakable. He craved action, after years of shore-bound restlessness.

Bull Run had quenched Bartlett's thirst for action for some time to come. "We?" he stammered.

"But of course. I've not been in England for months, but my people in Liverpool have been busy. We have a good plan ready." He unfolded a sheet of paper with a rough map on it. "You figure in the plan, my friend. One might almost say you're the star turn."

"But – "

"This is a most important mission. That saltpeter must be destroyed."

"But my orders – I see that, but – "

"Look, Major, I don't want to have to report to Miles Stoddard that you declined to support me on our first mission. He – "

"All right. All right. You're on."

Chapter 9

Bartlett's new coat rubbed against his neck - a few days later - as he bent to examine the heavy brass knocker on the Carra door. It was in the shape of a broadsword, with coarse ornamentation on the hilt.

He had seen Katherine Carra for a minute in the morning as she swept up his staircase, a beefy man in a bowler hat in obedient tow. "Ah, Major Bartlett," she said, "what luck. I was this very minute speaking of you to Mr. Jenkinson." Bartlett and the beefy man exchanged doubtful nods. "His firm have agreed to remodel the first floor, to convert it to a flat much like yours. There'll be some noise and dust for a while, I fear, but he promises me faithfully to finish and clear up the foyer before six very evening."

Jenkinson excused himself and went on up the stairs. Katherine watched him for a moment and then smiled at Bartlett. "Can you come to tea this afternoon, Major? I do hope so. My uncle is anxious to meet you and I want you to meet another New Englander."

Bartlett muttered something appropriate and began to worry if his uniform had been pressed.

Katherine opened the door herself. She smiled to see him like that, then she pointed politely to the knocker as he straightened up.

"It's quite old, sixteenth century. It hung on the main door at Carra, my husband's house in Ireland, and his uncle insisted I bring it with me when I came to London. Everything else I left behind." She paused and seemed to look a long way over his shoulder. "But please come in, Major. We're all here now."

He followed her through a fine, pale yellow drawing room hung with green silk curtains and darkened portraits of variable quality. She waved her arm at them and observed, "We Irish have many accomplishments, but, as you see, painting is not among them. Perhaps it's because we don't often see the sunlight, as the Italians do, so we have no feeling for color."

Beyond her, in the garden, he saw that tea was laid on a white painted table in the shade of an elm tree. The garden was planted with climbing jasmine, roses and larkspur, all in glorious bloom, with flowering shrubs against the wall at the bottom.

Around the table three men sat on matching chairs. One, a pop-eyed, balding man, remained seated as they approached. That will be Lord Carra, Bartlett thought. The second was an elegant young man with protuberant blue eyes and wild blond hair, who stood with one raised eyebrow and a trace of a smile – Malcolm Bannerman, his friendly banker. The third man was unknown to him.

She made the introductions. "It's a great pleasure, Major," the uncle barked. "I rented that house for a period some years ago, and I've not been accustomed to tenants who speak proper English and pay their rent when it's due. Katherine says you do both; is that right?"

Bartlett was taken aback but recovered smoothly, he thought. "You must be the judge of that, sir, but I hope I can. Do both, I mean."

"And this is Malcolm Bannerman, a dear friend of our family."

Bartlett was caught in two minds – he was supposed to keep his funds secret, yet he did not want to lie to Katherine over a matter that did not affect her. He had never been a good liar and it seemed his clandestine life was going to be made twice as tricky by the close-knit nature of London society.

His mind was made up when Bannerman stuck a friendly hand towards Bartlett and said: "Mr. Bartlett and I have already met in a business context. A great pleasure to see you again, Major."

"I'm impressed, Major," Katherine interjected, "you really are making yourself at home. London's not such a big city after all, is it?"

"It's not that the world is small, Katherine, it is that the upper crust is thin." Lord Carra announced in a booming voice, pleased as punch.

Katherine was obviously less proud of this gross snobbery and quickly changed the subject. "And this is my brother, Owen Halliday, recently arrived from America."

Bartlett shook hands with the young man. "My pleasure, Mr. Halliday," Bartlett said, as they all sat down. "From New England, eh? From which part?"

"From your part of the world, Major - Boston."

"But you're not an American subject yet, are you, Owen?" Lady Carra asked, a hint of alarm in her voice.

"American *citizen*, Katherine. There's no king in America any more. I thought you knew that," he teased her. To Bartlett he added, "I'm Canadian, Major, brought up in Montreal. I moved to Boston last year to work for a newspaper there, the *Pilot*. They've sent me to England as their European correspondent."

"It's too wonderful," his sister said, handing Bartlett a cup of tea. "I haven't seen Owen for twelve whole years. "He'll live here with Lord Carra and me. And he'll write. And he'll travel to... oh, he'll travel everywhere, won't you?"

"Not quite, Katherine. England mostly. Ireland, of course, and maybe to France." Changing the subject, Owen pointed to the wall at the bottom of the garden, where Carra, who had stumped off a minute before, waved at them with his stick. "And now, my dear sister, we must both travel, all the way to the garden wall, and applaud the new tree - crab apple, is it? - that his lordship is so proud of."

"Please, Owen, it's a" - she tried to growl like Carra - "*micromalus kaido,* har'rumph: quite new to this country, of course. "

"How silly of me. My apologies to his lordship."

"To the crab apple it is, then," she said, rising. "Are you a gardener, Major? Do flowering trees fascinate you as they do us?"

"Of course they don't," Bannerman replied for him. "Major Bartlett's a soldier."

"What nonsense you talk, Malcolm! After all, Henry was..." she started to say. Then she took her brother's arm to stroll down to join Carra.

"What was that about?" Bartlett turned to Bannerman

"Rather rude of me, I'm afraid. Her husband - her late husband - Henry Carra was a soldier and he was mad about gardens. He only played at being a soldier, though, and she knows it."

"I see. You know the family well, then?"

"Yes, in a way. The Carras have banked with us for generations. When Henry married Katherine he came to see me to obtain my help in making changes to his affairs necessary upon his marriage. Sometime later I was on holiday in Ireland and visited the newlyweds at Carra. This was the first time I met Katherine and I instantly understood why Henry had married her inspite of her lack of dowry. Later Henry and I were in the Crimea at the same time. Although in different regiments, so we did not see much of each other. That's where he was wounded, you know."

"No, I didn't know. Wounded badly?"

"Quite badly, but in less than heroic circumstances, at Inkerman. The night before the big battle, in fact. The officers' mess tent was shot up, with Henry in it, counting out the regimental silver for a dinner that night. He was the mess officer, you see. He had just finished the spoons." He stifled a smile. "It was the only explosion he ever heard out there. Tragic."

"Yes, indeed. Tragic." His own antics at Bull Run did not seem so ridiculous now.

Bartlett noted the expression on Bannerman's face as he talked of Katherine, thinking it a look of admiration. He began to wonder if perhaps there was more between them than family friendship.

They discussed the weather for a few minutes and then rose to welcome the returning gardeners. Katherine still had her arm in Owen's arm and her eyes shone in the low sunlight as she argued mildly with Carra about manure, specifically the proper amount to apply. He favored the horticultural equivalent of the cavalry charge, whereas she advocated a gentler approach to plant nutrition.

Carra had, to his mind at least, conclusively won the battle of fertilizer and he now turned to squint at Bartlett. "Your rooms all right, Major? Hope so. God knows I spent enough on them. And now Katherine's talked me into doing up another floor."

"It's very comfortable, sir. And handy for the ministry where I work," Bartlett replied cautiously.

"That's good. Hah! Give you more time to help win your little war." He was off on a tangent. "And you had better win it soon, mark you."

What's the old boy on about? "We'll do our best, I assure you."

"Will you, indeed?" Carra snorted. "Win it soon, I say. Or you'll have to free all those blacks if you want to keep us and the French out of it."

Bartlett began to pay closer attention to his peppery host. So did Owen, he noticed. "What do you mean, sir?" he asked.

"It's obvious that Palmerston's looking for a fight - he always is, you know - and we need the cotton. They were all talking about it at the club last week. But he can't put his boot in if you promise to free those slaves. The country wouldn't stand for it."

"So we have to win soon," said Bartlett, "or promise to free the slaves, or be attacked by the English."

"That's about it. Don't you agree, Bannerman?"

"Yes. It's quite straightforward," Bannerman winked at Bartlett. "You'll have to win by Christmas."

"And that's quite enough politics," Katherine said. "Far too much, in fact. Will anyone have more tea?"

Bannerman said, "I will have more tea, Katherine, if I may."

As she reached for his cup Katherine said, "I do hope you write well for your readers, Owen. They'll want to read all about life in London and in Ireland, and you must make it amusing for them."

"Then I shall," Owen smiled. "You can be my muse. But what shall I be amusing about?"

"Well, when you're not reporting your beastly politics, you can tell them about, oh, about the theater, the concerts of course, and the opera. The opera, above all. The season begins soon. There are..."

"You're not serious, are you, Katherine?" Bannerman interjected. "For the denizens of the slums of Boston? The opera?"

"Well, they don't all live in slums, and Owen will make it interesting, entertaining, for them. Won't you, Owen?"

"I'll do my best. Somehow I don't think my stuffy editor expects pieces on the London theater scene from me." Owen thought of the flint-faced Boston Irishman in his waterfront office and laughed to himself. "He talked more in terms of Anglo-Irish relations, the Fenians, emigration conditions. Frivolous subjects like that."

"Then you must show him where he's wrong. Don't you agree, Major Bartlett?"

Bartlett had listened with half an ear, his attention fixed on the way the sun danced in Katherine's dark blonde hair. "Indeed I do. Just the thing.

A few reviews of Mr. Verdi's new works and I'll be surprised if the *Pilot* doesn't double its circulation."

"There, you see, Owen?" she teased. "And Major Bartlett knows Boston better than you do." She and Owen were delighted by their operatic fancy and chatted happily a while longer. There was some family resemblance, Bartlett saw, although Katherine's features were more precisely molded than Owen's soft profile. He watched her, fascinated by her physical grace and the intelligence that informed her words.

He found himself wondering how it was that Katherine had remained in Ireland while Owen had moved to Canada. Why had they waited twelve years before reuniting? What happened to the rest of her family? What an enigma this Lady Carra was. How he'd like to get to know Katherine better...

He realized that his fascination was all too visible when he saw Bannerman studying him. The banker's blonde hair was wilder than before, and the bulging blue eyes had a speculative look.

*   *   *

"Sit down, Bartlett, damn it!" Jones hissed, "I don't want to lose you over the side. Not yet, anyway."

Bartlett lowered himself with care to the boat's thwart. "It's this gunpowder," he hissed back, "not enough room for both of us on the seat."

"Make room."

It was four in the morning, an hour after high water on the River Mersey. Bartlett had met Jones off the late train from Euston Station and they had exchanged their Union uniforms for heavy workmen's clothes, boots and woolen hats.

They had assembled on the south bank of the river with Calder, a red-faced, middle-aged man who wore the evasive look of a failed alderman. He was in fact the senior clerk in the Port Captain's office and the top man in Jones's local network.

Calder had gone recruiting among the crew of a frigate that was laid up for repairs and had produced for the night's work a Scottish coxswain called Menzies, seven crewmen, eight oars and a ship's boat. The men were all seasoned hands, with tanned, seamed faces and the calm gaze of a man who expects nothing pleasant. Calder had told them only that their target was a foreign cargo vessel - nothing to do with any British flag - and that they would be in no danger.

"All Royal Navy hands, sir, the best there is, and only five pounds the man," Calder had told Jones with pride, "and ten pounds more for the boat. They'll speak only when spoken to. Cash, if you please, sir. Now."

Jones hadn't argued and peeled the notes off a thick bundle. Calder handed most of them to Menzies and disappeared into the windless, piercing cold of the night.

Moored to a small wharf, the boat was twenty feet long, light and broad-beamed. Resting on the stern thwart was a crude, open-sided wooden box that held four kegs of gunpowder, each weighing thirty-five pounds. On the top of the box were two eyebolts with two light ropes, each forty feet long, tied to them.

"You get aboard and sit there, Bartlett, there, next to the powder," Jones ordered. "Hold on to it and keep it balanced." The coxswain and the crew took their places on the first four thwarts and raised their oars. Jones sat in the stern sheets and took the tiller.

"Bear off forward. Out oars. Give way together," he said. The men fitted their oars to the muffled oarlocks and bent their backs. The oars dragged through the water, bit at the second stroke and pulled smoothly at the third. The acceleration caught Bartlett as he crouched to shift his weight and he had half toppled back onto Jones, earning his sharp rebuke.

"Easy now, men," Jones said. "The tide will do most of our work for us." The boat was moving downstream at four or five knots along the barren ground of Tranmere, just visible to port in the patchy moonlight. Bartlett sniffed the aroma of tobacco, hides, coffee, wet rope and mud that drifted off the bank.

After half a mile, Jones turned the boat and called, "Give way, now. We'll head out into the river, alongside this jetty, for a bit."

Bartlett saw the dim outline of the Tranmere Ferry jetty across their bow. The hands pulled harder and when they reached the end of the structure Jones steered around it. They glided into the entrance of the U-shaped Tranmere Pool.

"Easy port, give way starboard," and the boat swung left again, back towards the shore. "Back water," and it slowed almost to a stop, the tide taking it gently downstream.

Jones raised his voice. "We're at the mouth of the Tranmere Pool, boys, on its south side. Our target is a Confederate cargo vessel, the *Bermuda*, that lies on the north side of the pool. Her crew are all bunking ashore except for a small anchor watch on deck - three men, probably."

The hands muttered to each other and the coxswain spoke up. "Are they armed, sir? We wasn't told about any guns." He didn't sound at all worried.

"No guns; it's a merchant ship, not a naval vessel," Jones assured them. "Now, we'll slip along the inner side of the pool so we can't be seen, turn up to starboard and coast alongside her. Then we'll leave her our calling cards. My friend here" - pointing at Bartlett - "will go smartly up the ship's ladder and make fast these two lines" - holding up the ropes attached to the gunpowder box - "on her deck. Then..."

"What are you talking about?" Bartlett said. "Me? Up the ladder? You're mad, Jones."

"I'll explain - once," Jones said amiably. "If we suspend the powder from her deck, it will stay where we want it, hard against her side, right above her waterline. That's the only way to do it." He made a pushing motion with both hands. "If we just suspend it from the ladder, it'll swing well out from her side."

"Fine, fine, but why me?"

"Because Calder said that all these heroes here refused to do it. It's piracy, you see, a hanging offense. So that's them out of it. Me, I have to light the fuses. So," Bartlett could see his teeth in the malicious grin, "you're it. I hate to have to remind you, but I still report to Stoddard, and you wouldn't..."

"And I wouldn't want him to know I bagged it." What the hell, Bartlett thought, he'll get me killed sooner or later. It may as well be now. "All right."

They glided along in silence, with an occasional stroke to maintain steerage way. The river was a dark shadow, as unreal as the sky that Bartlett could only just discern. They ran into a strong eddy and Jones called the stroke, whispering "Hup!" every three seconds or so.

"That's your modern Naval Academy drill, is it?" Bartlett asked. "Hup! Hup!' Sounds like you're driving a team of mules."

"Quiet!"

Another few minutes and Jones steered to his right, with a touch on the tiller now and then to keep the boat on course for the far side of the pool. Then he saw it, or thought he saw it, a nucleus of deeper darkness on his port quarter, just where he expected the *Bermuda* to appear. "Easy, now," he whispered. The boat slowed and he let the tide take her to port. Soon the stern of a merchant ship loomed above them. "Port oars in. Give way, starboard. Easy, boys."

The wooden sides slid by them in the darkness. "Menzies," Jones called to the coxswain, "get ready to grab that ladder. Now, man." Menzies, a pained look on his face, reached out and took hold of the rusty ladder. "Starboard oars in." They sat in silence, rocking slightly, four feet from the ship they had come to destroy.

Bartlett realized that he was holding hard to the lethal box beside him. One hundred forty pounds of black powder, he thought, should make a respectable hole.

At length Jones said "All quiet up on deck, can't hear anything." He turned to Bartlett. "Up you go, my lad. Pull these lines tight, tie 'em to the stanchions either side of the ladder and get back down here in two minutes or less."

Bartlett grasped the two lines and stood up gingerly, reaching for the ladder. "Why two minutes?" he asked.

"That's when I light the fuses," Jones grinned. "Then we pull like hell for the next jetty, straight ahead of us, and get to the other side of it before the charge blows. Simple, eh?"

"And if it doesn't blow?" asked the hitherto mute Menzies.

"We wait ten minutes and then come back to try again. If it does blow, we wait three minutes and come back to make sure she'll sink." Jones glared at Menzies, daring him to object, then at the other hands.

Bartlett edged past the gunpowder box and took a grip on the ladder. It felt icy cold. "What if I don't make it in two minutes?"

"You wait for us. We'll be back, as I said."

"But..."

"Don't worry so much. Just get to the other side of the ship and wait there. She won't sink that fast." He and Menzies slid the powder box to the middle of Bartlett's vacant seat.

Bartlett put a foot on the lowest rung. "And, Charles," Jones whispered hoarsely, "don't forget you have diplomatic immunity - I think." He hoped that Bartlett wouldn't realize that the explosion would demolish the ladder. And hoped that he could swim.

Bartlett knew that he shouldn't look up, but he did anyway. Twenty feet straight up the icy iron to the deck, and above that to the overhanging spars, and then to the clouds that had begun to break up. He gasped and looked straight ahead, then down, then ahead. "Let's get this over with," he muttered and climbed faster.

At the top he dragged himself over the low rail and looked around. The moon gave enough light to see that the flat deck was bare and empty; no one in sight, no sound at all. No stanchions, either, but a rigging block just to his right and a large cleat farther to his left. Wrapping one line around his forearm, he pulled the other one taut, took three turns with it around the block and tied it off with two half hitches.

Still on his knees, he scrambled to his left, towards the cleat. Ten yards straight ahead was the paddle box that housed the starboard paddle wheel. The bridge extended out over the wheel. Was something moving on the bridge? He was still for a few seconds and then reached for the cleat. There was a line around it. He cast off the line and let it sag away toward the mainmast, scraping the deck. Again he was still.

"Even'n', cousin," said a soft voice behind him. He ducked to his left and took a hammer blow on the right side of his head and the base of his neck. Stunned, he lay flat, thanking God for the heavy woolen hat and thick jersey, sensing that if he twitched once he'd be hit again.

Something pulled hard at his left arm. He opened his eye a slit. A small man with a belaying pin in one hand was tugging at the line wrapped around his forearm. He worked it free, walked it slowly to the top of the ladder and peered down at the river and the boat.

Bartlett got to his knees, sank back to the deck from the agony in his neck and rose again, dizzy and sick. He saw that the man still leaning over the side was tiny, the size of a jockey, which did wonders for his courage. He stumbled toward the ladder. The man turned and raised his weapon, but Bartlett drove his good shoulder into his arm, taking much of the force from the downward blow. Then Bartlett kicked him in the stomach, pushing him out over the ladder. The man held on to the rope with one hand but dropped the belaying pin to seize the ladder with the other. Still he made no sound.

Bartlett swung his boot viciously into the man's chest. He gasped and slipped down a rung, clinging now to the ladder with one hand. Bartlett lifted his boot again and stared down at the ratlike face. "Yankee asshole," the man spat before the boot stamped his fingers from the ladder.

Down in the boat, Jones had heard the struggle on deck and was squinting upward when the belaying pin bounced off the seat beside him. He could see figures at the top of the ladder and guessed that at least one body would soon follow the pin down, so he barked at Menzies to hold tight to the powder box and pass him his oar. He pushed the oar against the ship's side with all his strength. The boat's stern swung slowly away from the ship, but the bow was held by the forward line up to the deck.

So he made barely enough room, but enough. The tiny rebel seaman, arms pin-wheeling, crashed onto the oar and slumped into the sea alongside the boat. The impact ripped the oar from Jones's hands. He picked it up, his arms numb, made sure the man was not Bartlett and shoved it brutally into his face, twice. The man sank without a sound, or even a bubble.

The rope from the powder box was tangled in the ladder, several rungs down from the top. Bartlett scrabbled down to retrieve it, fighting his weakness, and then climbed back up to the deck.

"Charles!" Jones called. "Make that second line fast on deck and get off the ship. I'm lighting the fuse *now*."

"But..."

"The others must have heard you. Watch out. Get to shore. I'll be back for you."

From a leather bag Jones pulled a knife, matches and fuses and placed them on the wet seat next to him. Calder says this powder hasn't been used since the Crimea, he thought, but it's all he could find. Not since

Trafalgar, is my bet. Let's see. The air is still, so slow match will burn at two minutes to the inch. I'll give it - two inches, to be safe. If they spot Bartlett, they'll be chasing him up on deck, not looking down here.

He fitted the slow match to the four kegs and tested the lines running up the ladder. Both were stretched taut, so he grasped one side of the box and nodded at Menzies. They lifted the box up and over the gunwale and lowered it gradually. It lay snug against the *Bermuda's* side a foot above the waterline, to Jones's shaking relief. The first match fired. He touched it to the fuse, checked his watch, studied the sparks for five seconds and sat down. The eight oars dipped in the water as he sat, and ten determined strokes propelled the boat fifty yards ahead. Three minutes more were all they needed to round the tip of the Birkenhead jetty and turn the boat around. Jones pulled out his watch and the matches. Less than a minute left.

Bartlett had at last tied the second line to the empty cleat and scanned the deck. One man in the bows, Jones had told him, and at least one at the stern. Where are they, then? He crouched and moved across the deck toward the foremast, reckoning that he would find the dockside ladder directly opposite the one he had scaled. His right arm and shoulder hung dead and almost useless at his side, and the pain made him gag. The same shoulder he tore up at Bull Run, he remembered.

A shadow slipped from behind the foremast to the other side of the cargo hatch ahead and to his left. He doesn't have a gun and he's alone, Bartlett thought, or he wouldn't be sneaking around like that. But I can't hope that he's as small as his late partner.

Trying to outguess his unseen opponent, Bartlett walked to his left, towards the paddlebox. No good; the shadow moved left with him, to a position behind another large, open hatch. Something tall loomed in the middle of the ship, to his left front - the mainmast, he thought, and the funnel. Risking all, he ran to the mast and looked for a spare belaying pin in the bitts. All were in use, holding the halyards.

The man stood up and moved straight at him. The moonlight showed that he had found his own belaying pin, which he shifted from one hand to the other. He was as silent as his shipmate, but bigger. Much bigger.

That powder will explode in less than a minute, Bartlett thought frantically. No point in mixing it with this gorilla, even if I had two arms in working order. He saw a companion-ladder by the funnel and stumbled up its steps to the bridge, which was no more than a rectangular walkway connecting the tops of the port and starboard paddle boxes.

Bartlett looked down, considered putting a boot in the furious face that was rising two rungs below him, decided against it and ran to the portside paddle box. There was no ladder down to the deck, so there was no way to reach the dockside ladder near the bow. He bent down, grabbed the rail with his only good hand and lowered himself painfully over the side. An eight foot drop, he saw. He also saw two uniformed men sauntering along the quay in his direction, nightsticks swinging.

He had no option, so he dropped. He wrapped his left hand around his right shoulder and rolled to his left as he hit, rolled in his own sphere of agony to a stop against a pair of high black boots. He stumbled to his knees and then to his feet, still clutching his shoulder.

"Well, well, what's all this?" boomed the uniformed figure in front of him, who was plainly no stranger to Liverpool ale. "Who're..."

Bartlett turned to look for the man from the ship, and the sky vanished in a blaze of light and noise. He was blinded and all the air was driven from his lungs. The three men fell to the ground, gulping air, waiting for the next explosion. At length Bartlett got up and stared at the ship. The foremast was gone, hidden by oily black smoke. The mainmast had broken off twenty feet above the deck and was leaning back against the funnel, which leaned aft against the bridge. The portside paddle box looked ten feet higher than it should. All the spars had snapped off and now dangled from their masts or lay in piles of rigging on the deck, which already was listing ten degrees to starboard.

"What in God's name was that?" breathed one of the recumbent uniforms.

"Cargo exploded, must have been," breathed the other, slowly rising.

"Saltpeter don't explode, idiot, it burns."

All three were on their feet now, red-faced, panting and surveying the damage. Bartlett read Harbour Police on his companions' blue caps. His heart turned over.

"Who're you, darling?" asked one, an edge in his voice.

"Jones. I've got the anchor watch," Bartlett found an answer.

"Oh, thought I knew all you boys by now," the edge still there.

"Got here yesterday. I was on the bridge, saw the bastards light the charge, in a boat, they were. I ran over here but fell and hurt my arm." He still held his bad shoulder.

"Forget about it, Frank," urged the other policeman. "We've got to rouse the crew, maybe they can save their ship. She's listing bad." To Bartlett: "Can you run?" Bartlett shook his head and pointed at his arm.

"Well, then I'd best get over to that place where they bunk, in case they haven't figured what that noise was. You stay here, Frank." He made off in the dark at a stately pace.

Bartlett knew he must get away before the crew turned out. And where in blazes was the other crewman, the man he'd run from on the ship? And Jones would be coming back in the boat about now. Maybe if -

"Have you seen - Waller? the other man on watch?" he asked, looking anxious. An indifferent shake of the head. "I have to get back on board; he may be hurt." Bartlett started for the portside ladder near the bow.

"Help yourself, mate," Frank said, "I'll stay here. I don't think any of your lot'll be stealing this hulk tonight."

The explosion seemed to have scattered the remaining clouds and the moon shone brightly now. Bartlett hadn't gone thirty yards when he heard a cry. He turned and saw the missing crewman - the gorilla - chasing after him on the quay, with the policeman following clumsily. He ran toward the ladder, to find it hidden behind a foremast spar that rested on the quay in a tangle of its shrouds. Disaster - the ship had listed enough to lift the bottom of the ladder, surprisingly intact, well out of his reach. Only one chance - the end of the fallen spar crossed the top of the ladder near the deck. He began to crawl up the spar, holding on for his life to the shrouds wrapped around it. If they came loose, he would fall into the water or at the feet of the chasing goon.

It was easier work than he'd hoped, helped by the adrenalin rush induced by stark terror. Up he scrambled, over the quay then out over the gap between the quay and the ship. Almost to the top of the spar, he felt it shake. The gorilla had reached the bottom and begun to climb. A last burst of strength and of agony in his shoulder carried Bartlett up to the ladder. He swung on to the deck, pushed hard on the spar and - it wouldn't move. He looked around, hands on his hips, where in his belt he found the knife that he'd forgotten about. His pursuer was twenty feet away, still silent, coming fast. Should he wait and knife him, or -

The spar, he saw at last, was not held in place by the ladder but by only one line that ran to the stump of the foremast. For the first time that night, Bartlett felt in control of events. He waved the knife at the gorilla, who stopped and pulled out his own. Then, with exquisite timing and pleasure, when the goon reached the point where he could drop only into the narrow gap between the ship and the quay, Bartlett cut the line. The spar rolled sharply and the gorilla duly dropped, still silent. Bartlett winced when he heard the splash. I never even saw his face, he shuddered.

The ship was now listing to starboard at twenty-five degrees, he estimated. He slid and stumbled down through the smoke and the twisted, blackened wreckage to the starboard ladder. Or to where the starboard ladder had been when he climbed it. Dummy, he thought, of course it was gone. He looked over the side, less than ten feet above the river, and spied a taut line that led aft from the anchor chain. At the end of the line was Jones, leaning from his seat to inspect the hole in the Bermuda's planking, through which the water was rushing at a satisfactory rate.

"Jones!"

"Ah! Well done, Charles! Anyone with you?"

"No, all gone. Come get me."

"Find a line and climb down. Give way, men. Let's pick him up."

That was a mistake. Bartlett's shoulder failed him halfway down and he slipped to his waist in the bitter Mersey water. Jones pulled him in over the stern of the boat, cursing rhythmically. Shaking from cold and fear, Bartlett responded in kind. They looked at each other and stopped. Then, together, they laughed until they could laugh no more. The crew shook their heads and rowed them back upriver to Birkenhead.

An hour later Bartlett had dried off by the fire in their hotel room and was obliged to listen to Jones'ss appraisal of his own skill and daring. "The charge was precisely placed, you understand, and that hole is twenty feet wide and ten feet high if it's an inch."

"So she'll have sunk by now?" Bartlett was so wrung out he didn't really care, his shoulder an agony.

"No, her mooring lines will keep her afloat for hours. But as the tide comes in," waving his hands about, "the lines will ease and she'll have more room to settle. In a day or two a thousand tons of prime Bengal saltpeter will have dissolved or washed away to the Atlantic."

"We did it, then?"

"We did it, by all the saints," Jones exulted. "The rebels won't recover from this night's work for a long time." His blissful grin became meditative. "Do you know, that was my first sea command? Would you credit it? After sixteen years in this navy?"

"Well, it certainly had all the traditional heroic elements: a stout ship, a veteran crew, the open sea, a crafty foe." A smugly self-satisfied Jones was an irresistible target.

"Yes, yes," Jones agreed, paying no attention.

"Historic, I'd call it," Bartlett persisted. "Almost Nelsonian."

They sat in silence for a time, drinking their coffee. As he relived the night's action, Bartlett realized with a mental glissade that he'd almost forgotten about the gorilla and the jockey, the two men he'd killed, the men for whom he felt no remorse whatever.

Day was breaking. They rose and made for the railway station. Bartlett noticed that Jones's slight limp was heavier now.

Their carriage was cold and empty. Bartlett supported his own bad arm and was almost asleep in his seat when Jones tapped his knee. "Charles, I want to say that you did well tonight - for an Army man."

* * *

The informal Cabinet meeting in Downing Street had ended but the Prime Minister asked his Foreign Secretary to remain. They faced each other across the long cabinet table, littered with teacups and cigar ends.

Palmerston had that morning received a delegation from the Cotton Supply Association of Liverpool. "These gentlemen told me," he said, "that the stocks of raw cotton in this country will run out in February or March of next year if the American war and the Yankee blockade continue. When they do run out, it's quite plain that millions of our people may begin to starve. The question for us today is: what action do we take?"

Lord Russell shifted on his cushion. "It's equally plain, Prime Minister," he said, "that we must examine how we can bring that war to an end. So I propose that we now consider issuing an ultimatum to both parties. In it we will set out the terms on which we demand that they make peace. And we will state that, if either party does not acquiesce in our terms, we will treat that party as an enemy. There is no doubt in my mind which party will not acquiesce."

"By which you mean the North, of course," said Palmerston. "And have you fully weighed the consequences of such an ultimatum to the North? What can that madman, Seward - what can the Northerns do if we issue this ultimatum?"

"Quite simple," Russell replied. "Attack Canada. That is what they can do. And what they will do, I believe. It's undefended, as you know."

"Yes, yes, I know all that," Palmerston said. "Yet I can not believe that Lincoln, however moronic he is, will allow himself to be dragged by one man, however belligerent he is, into drawing the sword against us. Still, perhaps this is our opportunity to put our swaggering Yankee cousins and their wretched democracy in their place, once and for all." In the last five years Palmerston had humbled the Russian Tsar, crushed the Indian sepoys and humiliated the Chinese Emperor. Now he had the upstart Lincoln in his sights. "But what then? What if we are at war?"

"Well," Russell said, "we could easily break their blockade. Then we would sweep their comical little navy off the seas and start to ship the cotton again. In English bottoms. Good for trade. And good for votes."

"Aren't we forgetting the French? What about them?"

"Oh, the Emperor would support us. As you know, he has long pressed us for joint action in America," Russell said with a dismissive wave. "France needs the cotton as badly as we do."

"Well, then," said Palmerston, "kindly draft your proposed ultimatum for consideration by the full Cabinet."

"Gladly. I hope we shall have the occasion to deliver it soon."

"Yes, perhaps the Northerns will give us a pretext."

"Never a pretext, sir," Russell corrected. "A *casus belli*. We can but hope."

Chapter 10

Malcolm Bannerman collected Katherine Carra, Owen and Bartlett at eight o'clock that Wednesday. Bartlett had inspected himself and the hired evening clothes in his mirror for ten minutes, praying that he and they would pass scrutiny. He was grateful for Bannerman's tiny nod of approval as he swept them into the waiting cab.

Bannerman had invited Bartlett to make up the numbers at the opera that night because Lord Carra was ill. "Too much brandy, I shouldn't wonder," his note had said. "Afraid it's evening dress, though. Do join us."

Bartlett sat opposite Katherine. He tried to keep his shoes off her dress and used this first chance to admire her without seeming to stare. Her evening dress and cape were of emerald green silk, her hair was piled high on her head and crowned with a lacy diamond tiara. Bartlett, bewitched, searched for something to say.

"I'm sorry to hear that Lord Carra is ill, Ma'am," was the best he could do.

"Not half as sorry as I am, Major," she smiled at him. "I confess he makes my life - mine and the servants' - a misery when he's ill. He is noisily convinced that his fever is the first in all of history, and that poor Mrs. Mostyn and I have no idea whatever of how to treat it."

"Anyway, Bartlett, it means you can make your first visit to the opera in London," Bannerman said. "And I'm sure you'll be better company than the dreaded lord."

"Do you know *Trovatore*, Major?" Katherine asked.

Bartlett had scoured the ministry's small library without success. "No, I don't," he said. "Something to do with gypsies, is it?"

"Oh, yes. The story is so romantic, tragic..."

"And absurd," from Bannerman, mildly.

"And quite absurd," she agreed happily. "I adore it."

"I saw it last season in Boston," Owen said. "It's the usual Italian melodrama, Major. The hero and his enemy are brothers but don't know it, a gypsy woman keeps throwing the wrong babies into the fire and at the end only the villain is left standing. In fact," he teased, "just the sort of thing to appeal to Katherine."

"Young people are so condescending these days," she giggled. "Don't you agree, Malcolm?"

"With anything you say, Katherine."

Bannerman's box at the Royal Lyceum Theatre was small but close to the stage. After some polite argument, he and Katherine took the gilt chairs in front and Bartlett and Owen sat behind them. When Katherine took off her cape, Bartlett saw the small gold cross on a chain around her slender neck, which seemed unexpectedly vulnerable.

The conductor bowed to the audience, the orchestra raced through the prelude and the curtain rose on the darkened palace of Aliaferia. Bartlett struggled to follow the story with the help of the program notes, then he gave it up and let himself melt into Verdi's glorious melodies.

Waiters brought champagne at the interval after the second act. Katherine sipped her wine and turned to Owen. "Well, my impertinent young brother, I do hope you're taking notes for your devoted readers. And you, Major, are you enjoying it?"

"I am indeed," he said brightly. "I'm no judge, but I think you're both right: the plot is a mystery and the music is wonderful."

"Isn't it? And in the next act you'll hear some real fireworks from the tenor. Although I find him a bit disappointing. Nervous, perhaps. What do you think, Malcolm?"

Bannerman studied the people below them in the stalls through his opera glass. "Look," he said to Katherine, "there are the McGregors, Alexander and his wife, near the front. And there's old Nicky Oppenheim. Haven't seen him in donkeys' years." He offered her the glass. "Do you see them?"

"I suppose so. I can't be certain because I don't know them," she said dryly and returned the glass.

"You don't? They're looking at you - staring, rather. By Heaven, so is everyone else." He put down the glass and leaned toward her proprietarily. "You must know them, Katherine," he insisted. "Everyone does."

"Everyone except me, it seems." She turned back to Bartlett as Bannerman resumed his examination of the stalls. "I embarrass poor Malcolm, Major, before his furiously fashionable friends." There was no regret, purely amusement, in her voice. "The fact is I know almost no one in London. I moved here last year, and Lord Carra dislikes entertaining, except at the Carlton Club with his political playmates."

The last two acts roared by. On the stage, eyes were rolled, breasts were beaten and singers rushed off stage and on to no discernible purpose. Bartlett shifted his seat so that his view of the action was in part blocked by more enchanting perspectives - the aquiline bend of Katherine's nose and the wisps of tawny hair from the nape of her neck.

She knows I'm looking at her, he thought. As long as she says nothing and I don't breathe all over her, I'll keep looking. Morse had warned that he was sure to fall asleep and off his chair. There was no danger of that, none at all. He couldn't help but notice that Malcolm Bannerman was also glancing at her more often than seemed necessary.

The final curtain came down and the singers took their bows to wild applause. Bannerman stood up, clapping and beaming. "I hope that pleased you as much as you'd expected, Katherine," he said. "I think they sang well."

"Oh, yes," she said, still dazed by the music. "The soprano, in particular. She sang the fourth act aria quite beautifully, I thought."

"I liked the ferocious gypsy woman more," Owen commented, "and I loved her last line: *Sei vendicata, madre* - 'Thou art revenged, Mother.' Strong stuff, that is."

Bannerman was seeing to their coats and paid no attention. "Some day, Katherine," Owen said softly, "you and I can sing *Sei vendicata, padre*. Or what do you think? Will we ever?"

"Don't be silly," she whispered fiercely and glanced anxiously at Bannerman's back. "Not here, for Heaven's sake." Then Bannerman held out her cape and she saw with relief that Bartlett had not heard Owen.

"You'll join us for supper, won't you, Major? Malcolm booked a table at deLancey's. It's not two blocks away, so we can walk if it's not raining."

"I would be delighted, Lady Carra," he bowed, and they began to move with the crowd to the main stairway. Bartlett had never seen so many elegant people at close range. Jewels, top hats and decorations everywhere, milling down the steps to the street. The odd well-bred bray marked the presence of a Guards officer.

Once outside, Bannerman took the lead with Katherine on his arm. Bartlett fell in with Owen. "It's not my place to ask, Mr. Halliday," he began, "but what did you mean back there about revenge?"

The pale eyes appraised him. "Call me Owen, Major, it's simpler."

Bartlett acknowledged this. He would not ask Owen to call him Charles; not yet.

Owen cocked his head and studied Bartlett again, as if he were judging his motives. Then he said, "There's no reason you shouldn't know. It's my - our father. He was killed by the English."

"Killed? How?"

"Well, not directly, I suppose." Owen slowed his step to fall farther behind his sister. "He and I emigrated to Canada in '49, forced out by the famine. When we reached Quebec the English agents threw us into the detention camp on Grosse Isle, even though we weren't sick." His tone was bitter now. "In a week we *were* sick, damn sick, with typhus. Father died without leaving the camp. They never gave him a chance. I survived somehow."

"I'm sorry," Bartlett said.

"Thanks. It was a long time back. And I was lucky. Father's cousin was stationed in Montreal with the army, and he more or less adopted me, so I had a kind of home."

"Why did you leave Canada?"

"I enlisted in his regiment when I was seventeen, so I'm a soldier, too; a corporal, no less. He was posted to India two years later," he stopped as they were jostled by a couple walking the other way, "and I didn't want to go with him so I stayed on for a year or so. Then this job with the paper came along and I decided I couldn't stick soldiering for another fifteen years. So I resigned."

Fifteen years in the army must seem forever at Owen's age. "Do you miss it at all?"

"Not for a minute. I like journalism, and the bonus is this chance to come over here. To see Katherine again." He dropped his voice. "And to see what I can do to…"

"Owen, please!" Katherine spoke sharply over her shoulder. She's been listening, Bartlett thought. Or did Owen want her to hear?

Owen's pale features flushed and he grinned maliciously at Bartlett. Leaning toward him, he whispered, "To see what I can do to strike at the English." He enjoyed the surprise on Bartlett's face. "Come now, Major. Admit it. That's why you're here too, isn't it?"

There was nothing Bartlett could say to that so he followed Bannerman and Katherine into deLancey's, which was dark, distinguished and filled with opera-goers. They were shown to the last table, where Bannerman called for the lobster supper he had arranged earlier.

Bartlett envied his host's easy authority. Is it Bannerman or is it all Englishmen of his class, he wondered as he puzzled over the daunting spread of silverware before him. He caught a sympathetic glance from Katherine, aware of his dilemma.

Bannerman raised his glass in Bartlett's direction, a wide smile on his cherubic face. "I think, Katherine, that we should drink to my two new friends from the great democracy across the Atlantic. Welcome to the home country!"

Katherine sipped and then looked from Bartlett to Owen, silently urging one of them to reply. At first Bartlett could remember only lewd toasts of the sort to be proposed at battalion dinners, but he rallied.

"And we, Owen, will drink to *our* new friend, for kindly including us this evening, as generous a host as he is eminent a banker." Not bad for a Yankee.

"To our new friend," Owen said and their glasses were drained.

"Yes, that's quite right, Malcolm," Katherine said. "You are so kind and generous to us. Do we deserve it, I wonder? You have done so much for Lord Carra and indeed for me since our arrival in London. It is hard to express one's gratitude and appreciation adequately."

"My dear Katherine, it is my great privilege." The broad smile returned. "Besides, when one is the sole proprietor and chairman of an ancient counting house - as I am, let me remind you - this sort of thing is expected of one."

"Then the bank prospers? I'm delighted to hear it," she replied, "because you once said..."

"It prospers mightily, I am glad to say," he interrupted smoothly. "In fact, soon I will - but forgive me, Katherine; it's rude of me to discuss business here."

Owen had been thinking. "Those were warm words about democracy, Mr. Bannerman," he said. "You won't mind if I say they surprised me?"

"You shouldn't be surprised, Owen," was the genial response. "I admire democracy, I do. In its proper place, that is, which for me is three thousand miles away, at the least." Bannerman stroked his chin to mask his delight at his sally.

"So you think it has no place here?" Owen pressed him.

"None at all. It would be divisive, serving to exaggerate the strains we already have in our society." He waved his glass. "Rich against poor, the English against the Welsh, the Scots..."

"And the Irish?" Owen asked evenly.

"And the Irish, of course. They are always with us."

"Really, Malcolm! That's most unfair, and discourteous to Owen and me. We *are* Irish, lest you forget." Now Katherine was upset.

"I am sorry, Katherine. I'm being rude once again." Bannerman sounded genuinely contrite. "I never think of the old Anglo-Irish families like yours as being Irish. I've learned my lesson now, I promise."

"I should hope so." She tapped his hand with her fan. "Tell me: Why is it that men think it rude to discuss business at table but perfectly acceptable to discuss politics?"

"Could it be," Bartlett asked, "because we know we should do something about business but can do nothing about politics?"

"Something like that, I imagine," Katherine said. "Take Lord Carra. He can blissfully review the iniquities of the Liberal Party for hours at a time, although I can't prevail on him to discuss new curtains for his flat for two minutes."

"That reminds me, Lady Carra," Bartlett said. "I've seen nothing of Mr. Jenkinson and his merry men. There's no trouble, I hope?"

"Ah. No, no trouble, Major," she replied. "Simply a short delay while we - while he finishes another job nearby."

That was not quite convincing. "I'm glad to hear it. So will Mrs Mostyn. I think she has her eye on poor Jenkinson."

The lobster arrived with suitable ceremony and the conversation turned to gentler topics.

*   *   *

Katherine bid Bannerman and Bartlett good night, closed the door and wheeled angrily on Owen. "What on earth do you think you're playing at, Owen? With all your wild talk of revenge? of Ireland?"

"What do you mean, wild talk?" Owen was astonished. "Have you forgotten? The English killed your father. And a million other Irishmen! Don't you want revenge?"

"Yes, of course I do." Then she shook her head hard. "No, I don't. Not as much as you do, anyway. It was a long time ago. I wasn't there with him." For years, she had tried her best to hate the English for the death of her father. But she couldn't: he had died in another world, another life.

"No, you weren't," Owen said, "still, I expected..."

"Don't you understand anything?" She grabbed his lapels and shook him. "Your crazy talk is risking my position here!"

"What? How?"

She let him go and said slowly, "By doing your best to anger Malcolm Bannerman, the single friend I have in England. What is worse, by goading Lord Carra, who lets me live in this house, his house."

"Lets you?" Owen smoothed his coat and pushed his hand through his hair.

"Of course! He doesn't have to give me a place." Afraid that Carra might hear them, she moved to the drawing room and began to poke fiercely at the fire in the grate. "He does so out of some dim sense of family obligation. Not out of affection, that's certain."

"But couldn't you live somewhere else? I assumed Henry had..."

"Henry left me nothing! Nothing." She whirled around to face him, poker in hand. "He was bankrupt. If his uncle asks you to leave, I'll have to leave as well. And I'll have no place to go, nowhere to live."

Owen was silent as he absorbed this devastating news.

"Now do you understand?" Katherine went on. "Beating your chest and crying for revenge may put me out on the street."

"I'm sorry, Katherine. Very sorry. I had no idea your situation was so uncertain." He slumped awkwardly into a leather chair by the fire.

"Well, it is. Highly uncertain. So you must promise me to mind your tongue around Lord Carra and around everyone else."

"Of course I promise," Owen said. "What you say about Henry staggers me."

"No more than it staggered me, I assure you." She was calmer now. "We can talk about that small surprise another time."

"All right."

She waved the poker at him. "I intend to hold you to your promise. Indeed, if I have to do so, I'll remove you from this house myself. Is that understood?"

"Yes." He rose from the chair.

She regarded him askance. Then she scattered the fire and they climbed the stairs by the light of the candlestick in his hand. Halfway up, she took his other hand and squeezed it hard.

Chapter 11

The soldiers came in the morning, a little after dawn. A platoon of Royal Scots Greys marched down the muddy village road, their rifles glinting dully in the soft rain. The platoon sergeant halted them at a one-roomed cabin, where a man with patched breeches and a tall black hat waited for them on horseback. The man nodded to the sergeant, who grunted a command to his men. They set to work without a word, ignoring the silent villagers who had gathered in the road.

Four soldiers climbed to the cabin roof and began tearing at the thatch and throwing it to the ground. Another six went inside and dragged out a young father and mother with three half naked, skeletal children. They were all gaunt and filthy, dressed in rags and shreds of clothing, with matted hair, swollen faces and hollowed eyes staring brightly ahead. Their bones protruded through their rags; they looked as if they had risen from the grave in their shrouds. Their cheeks sagged, their mouths hung open and on their faces was a look of apathy, desolation and death. They had passed through the agonies of starvation and now, silent and passive, they awaited the end.

The knot of villagers moved back as the little group crouched by the road. There were low cries of sympathy, but no offers of help. There was no help to give.

The soldiers tore down the roof beams, piled them by the side of the cabin and tried to set them on fire. Failing in this, they loaded the beams on a small cart and pulled it away.

The rest of the platoon attacked the two open windows and the sod walls with crowbars, quickly reducing them to rubble. They left standing only the chimneypiece at the far end of the cabin, a grisly monument to the family who had lived there. The rusty bedstead, a churn and two shovels - the cabin's only contents - were trodden into the dirt floor.

The sergeant gave a low command; the platoon formed up and marched back up the road. The man on horseback trotted off. The villagers dispersed, like specters, as quietly as they had collected twenty minutes earlier. In the rain, the evicted family huddled mutely by the road. They had nowhere to go.

The soldiers made little noise as they walked through the village, which kept as silent as when they arrived. There was not a cow, a sheep, a chicken or a pig. Even the dogs were gone.

On the edge of the village, the platoon stopped at a ruined cabin, one they had tumbled two weeks before. Here a scalpeen - a shallow hole in the earth covered over by a turf roof - had been dug in one corner, where the roof was supported by two beams propped against the low walls. A young private was sent to investigate. He kneeled and peered through the entry scraped in the ground but could see nothing. He removed one of the beams and half of the turves, then his head snapped back and he recoiled with his hand to his mouth. When he could speak, he called to the sergeant in a hoarse voice.

The sergeant tied a kerchief over his face and walked over. He knew what he would find, and he did. Sitting upright in the center of the dirt floor was a ragged young woman, her hair clotted with dirt and her face covered in sores. She stared straight ahead, seeing nothing, slowly chewing a dandelion stem. In her arms was a wretched tiny bundle, the body of a child. It was about four years old and clothed in rags like its mother.

The sergeant eased the child from the woman's arms and peeled back the rags. He gasped in horror as he saw that both legs and one ear had been devoured by the rats. He retched, dropped the bundle on the woman's lap and scrabbled back out of the hole.

Sergeant and private leaned on the ruined wall as they fought for breath. At last, the private could mumble a few words. "No, we'll leave it", the sergeant snapped. "What else can we do? If we bury it, the dogs will just get at it." And he began with care to replace the rude covering. When the last turf was in place, they rejoined the waiting platoon and resumed their march out of the village and back to their barracks.

The Greys paid no attention to the hilly country surrounding the village, which was called Kilveen. It was bog land, bleak, wet and undrained. The fields, separated by low banks of earth, were tiny, many of them less than half an acre.

The fields were planted in potatoes. A few weeks before, the plants had been in full, luxuriant bloom. Now, they were a foul waste of rotting vegetation, their leaves still bright green and their stalks scorched black. They gave off a sickening stench, which would grow even worse in a week or two as the fungus spread to the leaves and to the potatoes in the ground and they began to rot in their turn.

For this was the fifth year of the potato blight, the Great Famine of Ireland. Every year for five years, the famished peasants had prayed that the blight had left the Irish shores for good. Every year it returned, to destroy the crop that, alone, sustained millions of people.

Ireland was a country with almost no trade, no fishing and no factories; where the population had doubled in forty years; where every farmer's son wanted his own piece of land, however small, however high the rent demanded by his landlord. To be landless, to work as a farm laborer, was a disgrace. So the competition for land was desperate. The land had over generations been divided and sub-divided among the inheriting sons until the farms were so small that the family could survive only because of the potato.

The ordinary potato was a remarkable crop - nutritious, varied, simple to cook, suitable for animals as well as children. It was also the easiest to grow, needing no more than a spade and a patch of damp ground where trenches and lazy beds were made to receive the seed. An acre would feed the average family. The rest of the farmer's land could be planted in barley, oats, corn - whatever could be sold for the cash needed to pay an outrageous rent. A pittance was left over to buy oatmeal or other food for the family.

In Ireland, where "land was life itself", the potato was salvation.

But it could not be stored long enough, so even after a good crop one third of the Irish people were in a state of semi-starvation for half the year. They could buy no other food. When the crop failed, they starved. When the crop failed for five years, Ireland starved.

In the late summer of 1849, the crop failed for the fifth year. By the end, more than a million would die.

*   *   *

The rain was cold and heavy now, attacking from the northeast. The slim man in the black hat rode out of the village. He crossed the rotting fields and trotted up a long drive to a substantial stone house a mile away. His face was set. My God, poor Foley, he thought, they'll all be dead in a week. Thank heaven that's the last family I'll have to evict - ever. I couldn't bear one more. In ten days, I'll be away from this misery.

He was Desmond Halliday, a proud man of family, whose ancestor had crossed from England with Strongbow in the twelfth century. His branch of the Hallidays, resolute Protestants to a man, had owned farms near Kilveen and lived in the house since the late 1500's. Over the centuries too many horses, too few face cards and now the Famine had reduced the Halliday holdings to a few hundred acres.

Halliday was about 40, a barrister by training and by vocation, educated at Trinity College, Dublin, the Protestant citadel against the Catholic hordes. He had inherited from his father the remaining farms and a thriving small practice in Cork, a day's ride to the south and east of Kilveen. He was a forceful advocate and his practice prospered, despite his impetuous and sometime imperious manner.

With the incomes from his practice and from the Kilveen farms, Halliday, his wife Charlotte and their two children had led a comfortable, undemanding life. They spent most of the winter in a house they rented in Cork, a pleasant market town and seaport. Charlotte returned to Kilveen for the summer months with the children - Kate, now aged fourteen, and Owen, four years younger.

This easy existence had begun to crumble late in 1846, after the second attack of the potato blight. Halliday's clients, mainly the larger local landlords and merchants, were now less ready to risk the lengthy and expensive processes of the courts. At the same time, the agent who managed his Kilveen farms and four or five other properties began to report severe difficulties in collecting rents from even his strongest tenants. They in their turn could not collect the rents from their sub-tenants, all of whose tiny incomes now went to buy potatoes.

Charlotte died the following summer of typhus - the dreaded road fever - that followed inexorably behind the hunger. She had worked at a soup kitchen run by the Quakers in Kilveen and was infected by one of the filthy, louse-ridden skeletons who thronged the kitchen every day. She died in a week, and Halliday was not told of her sickness until she died. He never got over his loss.

His grief affected his work, and he lost more clients. To offset his drop in income from his practice and his farms, he began to borrow from his bank. At first, small sums to tide him over until the blight ended, as he was sure it must, and he could recover his unpaid rents. Then larger amounts, as the rents continued to dry up. Then the bank insisted on security for its loan, a mortgage on the Kilveen house and farms. He had no choice and granted the charge.

Then, calamity. The British Government, whose reluctant attempts to bring some relief to the starving had all failed, decreed that future relief must be paid for by the Irish, by means of much higher poor rates. Halliday and other landlords were forced to raise the rents they charged their tenants in order to collect the new higher rates. If a poorer tenant could not pay his rates, Halliday would have to pay them from his own pocket.

In desperation, Halliday closed his office in Cork. He sold Charlotte's jewelry, his pictures, furniture and books and removed with the children to Kilveen. There he soon confirmed what he had long suspected - that his land agent considered that he was entitled to half the rents he collected. Halliday recovered what he could and fired the man. Then he persuaded three of the other landlords to appoint him as their land agent. He became, in effect, a debt collector.

It was poisonous work, and he hated it. He spent his days face to face with human horror on a scale he could not comprehend. Once a man was no longer a tenant, his landlord paid no rates on that land, so Halliday's principals made him evict the poorer tenants if they could not pay their rent. To make sure that the man and his family stayed off the land, his house was tumbled.

Halliday saw that the west of Ireland would not recover from the Famine for many years, if ever. Perhaps the blight was in the soil forever. In any case, the land was ruined; the people were dying or bankrupt. There would be nothing left for him and the children. No future whatever. He began to think of emigrating, to England or North America, as hundreds of thousands had already done.

The thought of leaving the land and home that his family had owned for centuries, where he and Charlotte had been happy, that his children adored, made him physically sick. But he made enquiries and in early 1849 wrote to a cousin of Charlotte's in Canada. This was a Scot, Alastair Menzies, who commanded a battalion of the Highland Light Infantry, stationed in Montreal.

Major Menzies' response was prompt and enthusiastic. Canada was rich with opportunity for a professional man like Halliday, he wrote. Barristers were especially needed; at least two of his legal acquaintances had a place for Halliday if his qualifications were as Menzies described them. Living was cheap, by English standards, and the schools were adequate. Halliday must come as soon as he could and he must be prudent and bring enough capital to support his family for at least twelve months.

Halliday wavered for several months, then once again the British government made up his mind for him. It decreed that any property encumbered by a mortgage could be sold at auction on the petition of any creditor. His bank, Hughes & Co., lost no time in writing him that, to protect their own position, they would have to sell his Kilveen holdings at auction unless he brought his loan accounts up to date by the second half of August.

"You know perfectly well I can't pay off these arrears, Padmore," Halliday told his bank manager. "Who the hell could pay in these times? Who can even collect his rents?" He was in Cork to wind up with Hughes & Co. and to book his passages to

Canada. He knew his protests were useless, and he cared not at all how Padmore responded. He was finished with Ireland.

Padmore made soothing but determined noises. He had dreaded this interview. Not only had the Hallidays been customers of the bank for more than a century, they had notorious tempers.

"Anyway, who'll buy my house? Or my farms?" Halliday demanded. "No one here has any capital now and the tenants can't work - they're all starving to death. I suppose the English will take over on the cheap."

"You may be surprised, sir", Padmore smiled smoothly. "Some of the larger local landowners are buying, ah, distressed properties and consolidating them, with a view to growing corn. Your - the Kilveen farms may lend themselves to that purpose."

"Nonsense, Padmore. Who has that kind of money now? Fitzgerald? Lord Mallow? Perhaps. O'Brien - no, he's been drunk since '45. Wyndham, I suppose. Who else?"

"You've omitted to mention Lord Carra, sir."

"Carra? You're joking, surely. That old fool hasn't a pot to piss in."

Padmore shrugged. "That old fool has a new, rich wife and a sufficiency of pots. Capital is no longer a difficulty at Carra, Mr. Halliday. He also has a son with grand ideas. Very grand indeed."

Halliday walked two blocks to his other bank, where he had cautiously deposited the cash proceeds of his sales the summer before. He withdrew the entire balance, a bit over a thousand pounds, and strolled on to the pretty vicarage of St. Jude's Church.

Here he took tea with the vicar and his wife. Mr. Harding was a noisy, choleric clergyman whose Protestant faith was only a cover for his hatred of popery. Mrs. Harding was a sensible woman who struggled to disguise her husband's doctrinal excesses so that he did not lose his living or their position in Cork society. Their daughter Elizabeth and Kate Halliday were warm friends. Both had attended the Church of Ireland School in Cork until the summer before, when Kate was withdrawn.

Halliday had arranged that Kate would live with the Hardings after he and Owen sailed for Montreal. She would be comfortable, secure and supervised while he and his son risked the unknown in Canada and established a home for the family. She would finish her schooling and perhaps take her first steps into adult society under Mrs. Harding's careful eye.

Halliday was pleased with this arrangement. He expected it to last until the following summer, when he would come to fetch Kate to her new home.

He finished his tea, took out his wallet and said, "And now, Mr. Harding, here are two hundred pounds for Kate's expenses while she is with you. It's the amount we agreed on, I believe, but I must have your word that you will write to me if it is not adequate. This is my forwarding address in Montreal."

"And you have my word on it, sir," beamed Harding as he took the paper, "and I am certain that, bar some disaster, such as another Papist insurrection, this will more than suffice." Suffice to put meat on our table again, he thought grimly.

"Good. I hope it will not be inconvenient if I bring Kate to you a week tomorrow, in the early morning? Owen and I sail at noon." After an exchange of pleasantries, he left and hurried to the emigration agency in the docks.

At the agency he booked passage on the Liverpool packet and engaged two berths on the steamer *Aberdonian*, Liverpool to Quebec City. She was no coffin ship, such as those on which thousands of emigrants had died in the last two years. He and Owen were to travel in some style, sharing the Atlantic crossing with only eight others in their cabin. Meals would be served but the agent urged him to pack dried fruit and vegetables for four weeks. And a pistol.

A week later, Halliday, Kate and Owen dined at their hotel in Cork. The dinner was excellent - Dublin Bay prawns, the first roast lamb they had eaten that year and a bowl of fresh fruit topped with whipped cream. Good food was abundant in Cork, but very few could afford it. Nor could Halliday, for that matter, but he owed it to himself and the children, after months of privation, to have one decent meal together.

He patiently tried to convince Owen that they would not cross the Atlantic in a Royal Navy ship of the line, with seventy four guns at the least. Kate listened quietly. She had long since got over her shock and sorrow at the need to leave Kilveen and to live with the Hardings while her father and brother were thousands of miles over the sea. She was by now thankful to leave Kilveen and its hunger, disease and misery.

She happily contemplated living in Cork, going back to school, enjoying much greater independence. She would keep out of Mr. Harding's ill-tempered path and she would soon wind Mrs. Harding around her finger. She would see the Queen when the royal party visited Cork in a few weeks' time. She would learn to dance, she would go to balls, she would meet young men, as her friend Elizabeth had already done. Canada was far in the future, too far to think about.

Kate had left behind her adolescent angularity. How many hearts will she break before she's much older? her adoring father wondered. He reached for her hand and placed in it a small gilt box. "This is for you, my love," he said. "It was your grandmother's. I kept it back last year when I sold the jewelry and it's time I gave it to you. Open it."

She drew her breath sharply when she saw the thin gold chain with its small gold cross, set with emeralds. Tears in her lustrous eyes, she held it out to him and turned so that he could put it around her neck.

"Oh, thank you, Father, thank you, thank you," she whispered, looking down at the cross. "It's lovely, truly lovely. I shall wear it every day, and every day I shall think of you and Owen."

She leaned toward him, put her hands on his shoulders and kissed his cheek. "Every day," she said. "I promise."

Chapter 12

Charles Bartlett was settling complacently into a military attaché's routine. Performing the first part of his job, briefing the minister on developments in the war, was simple enough: there were virtually none. After the shock and disgrace of the first Bull Run, the Union Army devoted itself largely to recruiting, equipping and training the vast land army it could now see it would need to defeat the South. Apart from a few skirmishes in the west, nothing that could be called a battle took place. And apart from the real battles, of course: those among the general officers unlucky enough to command their units in the battle and who now clamored to shift the blame to other shoulders, any other shoulders.

There was little point in telling Adams every day or so that nothing of any importance had occurred two weeks before, certainly nothing that would help him persuade the British cabinet that the Union Army or Navy was a victorious fighting force. So a tacit understanding was reached, in which Bartlett would report only if some major event happened – a Union victory, or the capture of a Southern privateer or merchant ship.

Adams had, as promised, introduced him into the proper circles at the War Office, which in turn placed him on the list for the official functions that required an attaché's presence. Besides the usual parades, maneuvers and other flexings of England's military muscle, these included a surprising number of receptions and varied social occasions. At these, an attaché's real business, espionage, was conducted.

Conducted not well, perhaps, but with enthusiasm. Many a long secret report to headquarters was constructed on a chance remark overheard at the Guards Club punch bowl. Many an officer's career was blasted by his lack of attention at the same punch bowl.

Miles Stoddard had told Bartlett to be guided by Freeman Morse in his effort to learn the secrets of the Royal Navy's ordnance program, so he had consulted the laconic commercial consul soon after he took up his post.

Morse was willing but unhelpful. "Afraid I can't be of much help to you there, Major," he had shaken his head. "Naval guns? Armor-piercing shells? No, you see my people work on the commercial side – shipments to the rebels, the rebel purchasing agents over here, some recruiting. That's more our line. Robert Jones'ss people do all the military work."

Jones's last words to Bartlett had been had been to say that he would go back to Liverpool. "For a few weeks, probably. Other interesting things are going on up there. Some strange ships are being built, and they're not ours."

At weekends Bartlett had time on his hands. He didn't hunt, shoot or kill anything, so his army acquaintances thought it risky to invite him to their country houses. On fine days he widened his exploration of central London on foot. He found as he went that contemporary architecture began to interest him.

One Saturday afternoon he was approving the pillared facade of the new National Gallery, perched uneasily at the top of Trafalgar Square, when he saw that it was exhibiting its collection of paintings from English country houses. Curious, and anxious to escape the crowds and the pervasive stench of the Thames, he climbed the steps and went in.

The exhibition was small, ill lit and composed in the main of landscapes and portraits. He thought the landscapes dull, but the portraits were a revelation. These were not mere painted likenesses as he had seen in Boston; they were thoughtful expressions of the sitter's character or lack of it. Intelligence, wit, weariness, brutality - all the traits of humanity were presented with depth and clarity, and at times with compassion.

Admiring Reynolds's full-length portrait of a swaggering younger son, he stepped back to get a better perspective and heard a soft, amused voice.

"I'm not entirely sure about that one, are you, Major Bartlett? Even though it looks a bit like my husband." Katherine Carra was smiling at him, delighted to take him by surprise. She wore a day dress of pale yellow wool with lace at her throat. "Although Henry didn't shoot."

Bartlett bowed and, curious, examined once more the vacant-faced giant in the picture, draped in tweeds, guns and spaniels. He wanted to ask her about her husband. "Good afternoon, Lady Carra," he managed. "Yes, I do like it. He looks as if nothing could ever trouble him. I envy that."

"Perhaps he wouldn't know trouble if it rose up and bit him. That slightly vicious look suggests a sluggish brain," she said lightly. "But I think I see what you mean. I must study the picture with care on my next visit."

He walked with her as she moved down the gallery. "Do you come here often?"

"Yes, often. This is one of the few places where I can see fine pictures now." She turned her astonishing eyes on him and smiled sadly. "We had three or four in our house in Ireland, and they're all gone. One of them, in fact, is here, in the next room. Not one of our best. A portrait by an American, Rembrandt Peale. Do you know his work?"

"That question is an implicit compliment, Lady Carra. Thank you." He held open the door. "I have to confess that, apart from enforced youthful visits to the Fine Arts in Boston, my ignorance of painting is almost total."

"Ah, in that case you must learn while you are in London. I shall help you, here." She waved her arm at the picture-covered walls of the room, by now almost empty of people. Remembering, she added, "You made an impressive beginning with Italian opera, after all, for which I will take all the credit I can."

The Peale portrait, when they came to it, was disappointing. A study of a self-important New Englander with a high collar and high color, gazing loftily at the viewer as his mousy wife regarded him with suspicion.

"The coloring is excellent," Bartlett said, "but I find the figures a bit..."

"Wooden? Yes, they are," she said, "and his later work is better. But I admire the similarities with Dutch painting of the seventeenth. All those florid burghers with their white ruffs."

As they strolled along, she expressed a decided opinion on most of the pictures they passed. "I must apologize, Major, if I bore you with my views," she said. "One of the few benefits of widowhood, I find, is that I have the time to explore some of the things I ignored when I was married." She made a comic grimace. "And, living with Lord Carra, the incentive to go out to explore them."

"Is he so difficult, then?"

"He can be difficult at times, when I disagree with him. But he's a kind man at heart, and I have to remind myself - " She took a long breath. "Well, you'll know soon enough, I imagine: I live with him because I have no choice. My husband's estate is gone, sold by the bank to settle the debts he left, and Lord Carra took me in from a sense of family obligation. Some would say from charity," she added bluntly.

He didn't know what to say, or even if he should say anything. It was curious. Her admission of her dependence was endearing, as if her vulnerability - weakness, even - somehow made her seem softer, younger and no longer quite so, so unattainable. And it made him feel more capable and more protective. All in all, a new and welcome sensation for Bartlett.

New in London, anyway. At home he had considered himself a reasonable success with the ladies, allowing for the isolation of his postings. His uniform and his sunburnt, saturnine features did much of the preliminary work for him. In England, though, these seemed to count for nothing, so it was doubly agreeable to sense that his relationship with Katherine Carra began to show promise.

"It must be a pleasant change to have Owen with you now," he said, hoping for the right note.

She gave him what might have been a grateful glance. "Indeed it is, but he's begun to travel a great deal. The other day to Liverpool and he leaves for Ireland tomorrow. Chasing stories for his paper, I suppose."

Soon they had toured almost the entire exhibition. Bartlett was searching for some reason to stay with her when she exclaimed "Oh, look! Isn't it lovely? That flower painting at the end? I must look more closely."

When she came back to him, she laid her hand lightly on his arm and said, "Do let me apologize, Major. I'm afraid I sound like the most dreary woman alive, complaining every minute."

"Not in the slightest, ma'am," Bartlett replied.

"It's that I sometimes feel as if I'm - what do the suffragettes say about themselves? Condemned for life? Condemned to patience, petticoats and propriety."

"Well, they say that patience is a virtue. You'll understand that I can't speak either to petticoats or to propriety."

They recovered their coats and stepped outside into a steady rain. There was a cab rank at the foot of the steps and Bartlett persuaded Katherine to let him escort her back to Rochester Place.

"Tell me, Major, what does a military attaché do?" she asked as he settled back beside her. "I've droned on and on today about myself, and I realize that I know almost nothing about you or about your work."

"I'm still learning, but so far my duties seem to be largely ornamental. I stand around at receptions and dinners and try to look fierce. Civilized, but fierce."

She laughed gently and turned to face him. "And do you? Look fierce, I mean?"

"About as fierce as the Union Army, I'm afraid," he grinned. "No, to be fair, I can manage it for a few minutes at a time, but the strain on the facial muscles is intense."

She examined his face. Yes, she thought, with that black hair and angular jaw, he could look quite dangerous if he chose. "You must show me some time. Do I have your promise?"

"Certainly not," he replied. "I might frighten you."

"Indeed you might. And I can't believe that is all you do - stand around ornamentally." She was teasing him now, her good humor restored.

"No, I have other responsibilities. None so entertaining, though. I beg your pardon, Lady Carra, clumsy of me," he added, as he leaned against her when the cab swung off Piccadilly and up toward Berkeley Square.

The rest of the journey they talked about his rooms (very satisfactory), Mrs. Mostyn (difficult but reliable) and Mr. Jenkinson's builders (hopelessly slow but cheap).

He helped her out when the cab stopped in Rochester Place and was about to say good-bye when she put her hand on his arm and said, "Major – oh, this is awkward – but could I ask your advice? It's about Owen."

"Why, of course. Ah, I could offer you tea? Mrs. Mostyn is still here and she can produce tea, along with some elderly biscuits, if not much else."

She looked flustered. "No, thank you, I think perhaps –. Oh, why not? You're very kind. I place my reputation in your hands. And Mrs. Mostyn can protect me, if necessary."

The rain belted down now and the drawing room was quite dark. "You're my first guest here," Bartlett said as he poked the fire, "so please forgive the meagerness of my hospitality."

"Meager? Indeed?" Katherine laughed as she surveyed the frosted cakes Mrs. Mostyn had brought in. "You do well for yourself, Major."

She recoiled for an instant as the stewed tea assaulted her taste buds. Mrs. Mostyn prepared her tea the same way she cooked her finnan haddie - the same way she cooked all her food, in fact - long and hard.

They sipped in silence for a time and watched the fire. That is, she watched the fire and he watched the firelight play on her face, on the high cheekbones and fine arched nose. He was relaxed, at ease with her for the first time, so much so that he was not compelled to speak. He suspected that she was in the same mood.

"I like the changes you've made to the flat," she said at last. "You have a talent for making clever use of limited space. Most useful in your army quarters, I suppose?"

"I suppose so. And in childhood. There wasn't much space for children at our house." Damn it, he hadn't meant to say that. How pathetic it sounded.

"Was it so small?" she asked after a moment.

"No. Not so small, but we took in lodgers, you see."

Lodgers who came and went, lodgers who enabled his schoolmaster father to feed the widow and children of his dead brother. Lodgers who always seemed to occupy the chair he wanted, so that he spent much of his time in his own room.

Come to think of it, he had lived in cramped conditions all his life. As a child, at West Point and at his different army posts. Had they cramped his character? Who could say?

She changed the subject. "I had hoped to ask you to tea with me, Major, but Lord Carra is at home this afternoon, and I'm afraid that if I see him again right now I shall do something regrettable." She made a rueful face.

"Is he being difficult again?"

"He is being unspeakably difficult and has upset me again."

"I hope his bad temper is not due to my residence here?"

"It is, indirectly. He needs the rent you pay him and he wants more, so he needs new tenants. So he complains perpetually about how long Mr. Jenkinson is taking." She shook her head. "And about the cost of doing up the wretched flat. I'm the nearest target for his complaints."

"But that's not all," she said, looking at him from the corner of her eye. "Two policemen came for Owen this morning. They said they were reviewing his residence status. As a matter of routine, they said, for all American citizens because of your war."

"But Owen's not an American, he's a Canadian, a British subject. Isn't he?"

"Of course he is, and that's the worrying part. The policemen insist that he's American. He's to report to the police station as soon as he returns from wherever he is. Ireland, I think."

"I've heard nothing at the ministry about the police tracking down Americans, Lady Carra. I'll look into it on Monday, if you like." What more could he do? "Ah, is Owen in any sort of trouble?"

"None that I know of. No, I'm sure he's not. Although he always looks very tired – worn out - when he comes back." She couldn't admit how little she understood of Owen's work or his travels. "No, the trouble is with Lord Carra. You can imagine his reaction when the policemen came, searching for his mysterious nephew. Volcanic, to say no more, and I was in his line of fire." She looked at his reflection in the mirror over the fireplace. "Am I mixing my metaphors?"

"Delightfully."

"He's threatening to tell Owen to leave. He has never liked him, in any case, says he's impertinent." She sat down again on the fireside chair. "And if Owen leaves, I will have to leave, also. I couldn't stay here."

"But that won't happen, will it? Lord Carra can't be so irrational? Or so cruel?"

"Why not? All Carras are irrational and some can be rather cruel." She laughed shortly.

He was intrigued by this sudden intimacy.

The room was darkening and Mrs. Mostyn came in to light the gas lamps. "Will you have more tea, Milady?" she asked.

"No more, thank you, Mrs. Mostyn," Katherine replied before Bartlett could speak. Then she stood up and put out her hand to him. "And I must be going now, Major. Thank you so much. I've enjoyed our tea."

He took her hand and held it. "Do stay a bit longer, Lady Carra. Please." She wriggled her fingers gently and he let it go. "I haven't told you of – of, ah, my ideas for - your new flat upstairs. About your, ah, kitchen, for example. I've been thinking about it hard, you see, hoping my experience here would be useful."

She hesitated. She had no reason to go home and she would enjoy talking a bit more to this amusing, if awkward, American. The strange feeling had gone. "The kitchen? Very well," she said, sitting down again, "but only for a few minutes, and *only* if we examine the kitchen position with care. And please, no more talk about me. There's been far too much of that already." She turned to face him, hands in her lap.

Teaching Greek at the Academy had made Bartlett adept at extemporizing on subjects about which he knew next to nothing, so he floundered for only a moment or two before beginning to sketch the outlines of the ideal kitchen - oven, sinks, cupboards, roasting spit, tables and all. He did not fool his visitor for a second but she liked inventive humor and was content to share his with him that afternoon.

"For an unmarried man, your knowledge of domestic requirements is impressive," she said. "It must come from looking after your men on maneuvers." She hoped to make him talk about himself again.

"Ah, yes," he said, reaching for a cake, "the unrelenting demands of the army in peacetime. Kitchens, cook wagons, fire pits, latrines, I mastered them all."

"Come now, Major," she said, "you are plainly a man of diverse talents, admirably qualified for your work here." She was not even half serious, he could see.

"Immensely talented, yes, of course," he replied, "but London is so different and the people are so strange - to me, at least."

"Are they so strange? I wonder." Katherine tilted her head to one side. "I suppose they are, to me as well." She reached across and laid her hand for a second on his forearm. "It's still different to me, too. We shall just have to look after each other in this great city, it seems. If we can."

Keep calm, he thought, as his heart somersaulted. "Yes, indeed," he faltered, "I mean it would be - I'll try to do so."

"Don't look so purposeful, Major," she smiled. "I meant it as my hope, not as my challenge."

"So did I." That was it. He was hopelessly, irretrievably in love.

They chatted for half an hour or so and Katherine rose again to leave. This time, Bartlett let her go without protest, sensing that would diminish her evident contentment.

"Unto the breach once more, I fear," she said with a smile. "Good-bye." A pause. "Perhaps you'll invite me again?"

His mouth went dry. She means it, he thought. "Every day, if you like," escaped him. She drew back a bit and shook her head a fraction of an inch. He recovered. "Good afternoon, Lady Carra." Then, remembering, "And please don't worry about Owen," he said. "I'll find out what our legation knows of the matter."

Chapter 13

Palmerston pushed himself wearily back from the table where lay the letter he and Russell were studying. "Do you know, John, I sometimes believe the Emperor was put on this earth solely to torment me." He waved at the papers. "His letter contradicts itself. Look: here he writes the 'ostensible aim' of the expedition is *only* the redress of our grievances. And that we shall not intervene in Mexico's right to install its chosen form of government. Fine." He glared at the offending document. "But *here* he says that he has put forward the name of Maximilian as his candidate for the Mexican throne. Isn't that precisely the intervention we've said we won't accept?"

"Not really. He claims that, when we arrive at Veracruz, a national revolution will begin, Juarez will be thrown out and a new national assembly will establish a monarchy. His point is that this monarchy will be established by the Mexican people, *not* by the French. Who will not have intervened the least bit."

"I see. And the monarchy will require a monarch, and Napoleon will happen to have the Archduke up his sleeve, reaching for the crown. Clever." Palmerston nodded his great head reluctantly. "But what if this great national uprising does not occur, and Juarez remains in power, and no monarchy is established? What then?"

"Why, then we collect our debts and we all come home again." Russell smiled slyly. "But, debts can take a surprisingly long time to collect."

"Surprisingly. And the longer we stay, the longer we keep the Yanks' fingers out of the Mexican pie. Which is the purpose of the exercise." He smiled at Russell. "Fine. Let us sign their precious Convention. If the Navy can wake up we'll be in Veracruz by the new year."

$$*\qquad\qquad*\qquad\qquad*$$

Owen went to the Staunton Street police station as soon as he returned from Ireland and Katherine told him of his recent visitors. There he was interviewed by two detectives as well dressed and well spoken as he was and not much older. He told them who he was, where he lived and why his work as a reporter made him travel so much. They examined his Canadian passport with interest.

"We've not seen one of these before, Mr. Halliday," the darker one said, tossing the document on his desk. "Where did you get it?"

"As I've said - in Montreal. I needed it first to work in America, and then to leave America to come to England."

"It could be genuine, I suppose, Harry," the detective said to his partner, "but how can we be certain?"

"We'll have to ask Mr. Halliday to leave it with us," Harry said. "Unless you would object, sir?"

"No, I don't object," Owen said. "But what's the point? Even if it is a fake - and it's not, I assure you - that doesn't make me an American, and you told my sister you were concerned with Americans."

"With some Americans, Mr. Halliday, not all of them," Harry said deliberately. "With those that go to Ireland all the time. And those that spend their time in this country with the likes of the men you spend your time with." His voice held a practiced menace.

"I don't know what you're suggesting and I think it's time you told me. I go to Ireland because I report on Ireland for my paper's readers. As I've already shown you." He had filed enough stories from Ireland to satisfy his editor and now, he prayed, the English police, for whom he had brought copies. "That's hard to do from England."

"All we suggest, sir," Harry said, "is that you might want to be more careful, not knowing our country at all, about associating with men that could have different loyalties."

"Thank you for that advice," Owen said, recovering most of his nerve. They plainly had nothing on him but their suspicion. "I'm sure it's good advice, even for a Canadian like myself." He waited a few seconds and stood up. "Now, if there's nothing else you want to ask me, I'll say good day to you."

They did not rise. "Good day, sir," Harry said as he dropped Owen's passport into his pocket. "I'll return this when we're done with it."

"No, Katherine, I have not! I'll say it once again: I've done nothing to concern the police. Or to worry you." Owen stared out the window of the Carra drawing room at the dusk of late October.

"All right, Owen, I accept that. You must agree, though, that your wild talk about revenge for Father and striking blows at the English, and - oh, I don't know - gives me good reason to worry when the police come looking for you." Katherine stabbed her needle at the embroidery on her lap. This depicted the eagle from her family crest, a curious creature with a long blue neck and red beak that was known fondly as the Halliday Turkey. She took up the work only when she was angry or upset, so she spent half of her time unpicking her mistakes, but she insisted that it calmed her nerves.

Had she known the truth, her nerves would have needed much more than a needlework bird. Earlier that year, Owen had been sworn into the Fenian Brotherhood. The Fenians, so-called after the Fianna, a legendary band of Irish warriors, were the American arm of the Irish Republican

Brotherhood. To both, the English rule of Ireland was an evil tyranny to be overthrown by any means and at any cost. The Fenians could operate openly and legally in the United States but in Britain membership of the Brotherhood was a crime.

Owen had been recruited by John O'Mahony, a fiery émigré propagandist and a co-founder of the Fenian movement. He had come to Boston to raise recruits for the 49th New York, the Irish regiment that Bartlett would watch with awe at Bull Run. As one of the few Irish North Americans with recent military experience, Owen was a prime target for O'Mahony, who offered him the command of a company in his new regiment.

But when O'Mahony learned that the *Pilot* might send a reporter to England, he called on the paper's proprietor. A few polite questions about the terms of the fire insurance policies on his printing works persuaded that gentleman in no time at all that Owen was the only possible candidate for the assignment. O'Mahony's pale bony face, long jaw and wide-set crossed eyes were persuasive at close range.

Owen was delighted to go to England. He would see Katherine again and he would have the chance to avenge his father. His job as a reporter would provide ideal cover. He would not be tied to an office, he could travel freely (his proprietor had anxiously offered to be generous with his expenses) and he could mix with all sorts of people in Ireland without inviting the attention of the police.

Once settled in London, he had taken the time to file a few dispatches to his astonished editor. First, though, he had met James O'Connor, the Brotherhood's senior man in England, who was brief. "You work through our primary agents," he ordered. "One in Dublin, one in Cork, one in Liverpool. These are the names and addresses. Remember them." He handed Owen three slips of paper. "You will never meet any other men in the organization."

He stared hard at Owen. "You'll begin as a courier, carrying messages from me. And you'll carry something else - these." He held out a cast iron tube, six inches long with screw threads on each end. "Fuses. Time fuses. Our lads are having trouble setting their charges properly. They don't go off, or they go off too bloody soon. We've been losing arms, and men."

Owen stared at the innocuous grey pipe. "What are those markings?" he asked, his mouth tight and dry.

"Serial numbers. We lifted these from the army depot near Croydon. They're the best in the world. Nothing like them in Ireland."

"Shouldn't we remove the markings? Make it harder to identify them?"

"Any copper or soldier will know what they are, markings or no markings." O'Connor seemed to get pleasure from his implied threats.

Owen would carry the letters and the fuses to the three primary agents in turn. "Just one set, for all three, each trip," O'Connor explained. "The fewer fuses there are, the fewer the police can find." He reached under the bed he sat on and pulled out a package about ten inches square and six inches deep. "Here's the first set."

Again the coil of fear in Owen's gut. He was going to carry with him, on every trip he made, his own death sentence. It was just too dangerous. He would... And then, again, he remembered Grosse Isle, the quarantine station thirty miles down river from Quebec. Remembered the filthy fever sheds, where a thousand Irish patients groaned in a hospital with one hundred fifty beds. Where the nurses and priests appeared to be closer to death than did the sick. Where the English soldiers kept him away from his dying father's bed and then away from his dead father's burial. Where, robbed of his father's money, he was dropped on to the deck of another fever ship to Montreal, with only his uncle's name and regiment on a sign hung around his neck.

It was never far away, the smell of Grosse Isle, bearing with it the reasons he hated the English. I've been handed a chance to avenge my father, he reminded himself, and I *must* take that chance or kick myself forever.

*   *   *

His next trip after his interview with Harry and Dark Hair took him first to Cork and then to Dublin. Both the primary agents were enthusiastic about the new fuses.

"Work a treat, they do," affirmed Cork. "One street car and two bridges blown, but no casualties because we set the fuses for midnight."

Much the same from Dublin, except that one of his men had left an arm and most of a leg at a country bridge. "A tragedy," said Dublin, "but no great loss to us, to be honest with you. He never could do anything right, poor lad."

The overnight packet from Dublin Bay to Liverpool was jammed with passengers and Owen slept fitfully in his crowded, stinking cabin. Dirty and unshaven, his irritation turned to anger when a clerk who worked for his Liverpool agent met him on the quay and told him that the agent was away for five days on important business. "He said that you'll be sure to forgive him when he tells you what this business is, sir," the clerk insisted. Owen bit back all of his possible replies and shouted for a cab. Might as well push on to London, he thought bitterly.

His hansom drew up to the railroad station at the end of the morning rush hour, and he had to work his way in through the stream of men hurrying to their offices. He carried two small leather cases; the smaller, shabbier one held the fuses meant for Liverpool. He liked to think that in an emergency he could ditch it unobtrusively.

He was in good time for the train to London, so he paused at the entrance to the main hall to look for a place that served breakfast. Twenty yards ahead and to his right stood Harry, the ruder of the two rude detectives at Staunton Street, slowly scanning the hall. Owen froze, too frightened to look away.

Harry's eyes looked straight at Owen's - and straight through them. His gaze swept around past Owen and then back again until he was looking straight ahead. He jerked his head once and Owen saw the other detective, the dark-haired one, fifteen yards to his left. The man said something to a uniformed policeman at his side, who then moved off at a trot.

They're waiting for me, Owen thought frantically, they must be. Remembering his interview at Staunton Street, he felt weak with relief that one of his cases carried drafts of the kind of articles that he had told them he wrote in Ireland. Then reality hit him hard. That's all right, but I can never explain away the fuses in the other case. I must get rid of it. Blindly, he turned back toward the station entrance.

He risked one look over his shoulder. The dark-haired detective hadn't moved but Harry and the policeman were gone. Gone where? Probably following me. Have to dump this case somewhere. He inspected the station as he walked. No rubbish bin in sight, no windows low enough, only one exit to the street and they'll have that covered. In all of this damn great hall there is nowhere to ditch a small case.

Owen tripped over something and fell in an awkward tangle, his nose pressed against a large calfskin trunk, his own cases scattered, his senses jumbled. As he struggled up, he saw that he stood in the midst of a large assortment of worn leather luggage, plainly a family's, that a white-haired porter was piling on a cart. He grabbed his larger case and then, almost without thinking, snatched up another about the same size and shape as his smaller case. He apologized to the porter, held his nerve and altered course to make for the dingy eating-place he saw near the first platform. He ignored the little girl who had seen it all and now studied him unblinkingly.

Twenty minutes later, fortified by ham, bread and tea so strong that it gagged him, he walked toward his train. He had to pass by the dark-haired detective, who hadn't moved and who watched him take every step. As Owen came abreast, Dark Hair's eyes flickered for an instant and he raised his hat half an inch. Neither man spoke.

Gratefully, Owen slumped into a seat in an empty second-class carriage. I've made it, he thought. Then he thought some more. Where are they? If they came up from London to look for me, they must have known that I was in Ireland. Then why not pick me up when the boat docked? Why wait for me here?

The answer was obvious: So I couldn't drop my case in the river. So I'd have to drop it in the street or in the station. Where they could find it. He felt sick. They'll have the fuses by now. They'll have them for sure.

Chapter 14

The Bahamas

A few weeks later, Captain Charles Wilkes, U. S. Navy, provided Foreign Secretary Russell with precisely the kind of *casus belli* he hoped for. Commanding the steam frigate *San Jacinto*, Wilkes stopped and boarded the British mail packet *Trent* in the Bahamas Channel and carried off its two most distinguished passengers. These were James Mason and Charles Slidell, the newly appointed Confederate Commissioners to England and France, respectively.

Although jolted by the suddenness of their capture, the two Southerners very soon exulted in it. The North, through Wilkes, had violated the recognized shipping rights of neutral countries. And one of those countries was itching to find a reason to smash the Yankee blockade and turn around the tide of the American war. "This is just what Palmerston's been waiting for," they told themselves happily. "We'll soon hear Abe Lincoln howl.

$$*\qquad\qquad *\qquad\qquad *$$

Captain Wilkes' dispatches on his exploits in the Bahamas Channel reached Washington by special train late on a Friday. On Sunday, the news exploded off the headlines of every newspaper in the land. By Monday, the North was swept by a spasm of pure, fierce joy.

The fearless Wilkes had dealt a heavy blow, cried one overwrought but typical editor, at the vitals of the conspiracy threatening the North's existence. His capture of the arrogant slave-owners, Mason and Slidell, was one of those bold strokes by which the destinies of nations are determined, pronounced another. The *New York Times* demanded a new national holiday in his honor, plus gifts of silver services and the costliest of swords. And more, much more of the same in all the press.

The people rejoiced. To many, Mason and Slidell were men of exceptional abilities, capable of doing unlimited damage to the cause of freedom if they had reached Europe. To almost as many, Wilkes' sharp twist of the British lion's tail was sweet indeed, ample revenge for the insults and indignities suffered in the past.

For a populace that badly needed a hero, Wilkes was the man they needed. He was praised, feted and toasted on all sides. The Massachusetts Governor reflected the sentiment of his Irish voters when he avowed that the hero had crowned the exultation in the American heart by firing his cannon across the bows of the ship that bore the British lion at its head.

Navy Secretary Welles commended him for his great public service. Congress, never to be outdone, passed a joint resolution thanking him for his conduct and asking the President to give him a gold medal.

*   *   *

The *Trent* affair detonated the same shock wave in the British press and public as it had in America. Newspapers brandished their editorial swords across the Atlantic. The *News* railed at the wanton folly of an imbecile American government and demanded that ministers insist on complete and immediate satisfaction. The *Chronicle* cried that England was piratically outraged; the assault on the British flag was unendurable and must not go unchallenged

The public wanted more than satisfaction. It wanted war. Years of pent-up resentment and fear of the Yankee mobs erupted across England. The owners of textile mills, facing the ruinous prospect of shutting down their mills when cotton stocks ran out in two or three months, fanned the flames among the fifth of the island's population that depended on cotton for their survival. Every week, thousands more men lost their jobs; rumors of starvation had begun.

Pressure on the politicians grew by the hour. The Prime Minister was besieged by representatives of the cotton trades demanding that he take action, that he dispatch the North American Squadron from Bermuda to break the Yankee blockade for all time.

All of which fitted neatly with Palmerston's instincts and his global objectives. Smash the Northerns, he had convinced himself, and England would dominate the whole of the North American continent, the two weakened halves of America as well as Canada and then, in a year or two, Mexico.

At seventy-seven, he knew this was his last chance. So he lost no time. He called a meeting of the full Cabinet for noon the next day. All but Argyle, on holiday in France, were there.

"Gentlemen, you know why we are here today," he began. "To decide our response to this gross outrage against our ship and our flag. First, we must look to the legal aspects of Captain Wilkes' act." The crown law officers were unanimous, he reported, in their opinion that the act was illegal and unjustified by international law, because the *Trent* had not been taken to a United States port for adjudication as a prize of war. No mere naval captain, they agreed, could usurp the function of a prize court to decide the fate of passengers on a neutral vessel stopped at sea.

That being so, the next question was quite clear: Did the captain act under orders, or did he act on his own? The discussion, adroitly guided by Palmerston, soon came to the obvious conclusions.

"We are agreed then," he declared, "that our response to this barbaric act must be based on the presumption that the Yankee captain was under orders from Washington. And that this was a deliberately provocative action on the part of Lincoln, Seward and their advisors?" Silence. "And we are agreed that part of our response will be a communication to the Americans containing certain specific demands that we shall make of them. You have a draft for us, I believe, Foreign Secretary?"

Russell did indeed have a draft, whose main thrust he had agreed with Palmerston the night before. "Americans are dangerous people to run away from," he had said. He now read the draft aloud in his precise voice. It was in the form of a letter to Lord Lyons, the British minister in Washington.

First it set out, in elegant simplicity, the factual circumstances of the capture of the Confederate commissioners. Then it declared that the American government must know that the British government could not allow such an affront to its national honor to pass without full reparation. It ended by expecting that the United States would of its own accord offer the only satisfactory redress: the prompt delivery of the four captives to Ambassador Lyons and a suitable apology for the aggression it had committed.

Lyons was instructed to read the dispatch to Seward and, if he did not offer that satisfactory redress, to demand it from him.

It was, all things considered, the most gracefully crafted challenge to mass bloodshed in recent history.

And it was met by silence in the Cabinet Room. Russell, perplexed, peered at his colleagues and then at Palmerston. "Ah, comments, gentlemen?"

"Too weak, too weedy," snorted Somerset, the naval secretary, to approving growls from around the table. "If this was a punitive fleet action, I'd tell my opposite number exactly what I will do. That I will sink every flaming ship in his command if he don't comply."

"Even you must have grasped by now, sir," Russell said silkily, "that this is not a simple fleet action? We're talking about war."

"So we are," said Gladstone. "So why not tell the Americans that? As with our distinguished sailor here, they may not grasp it if you don't tell them."

Others agreed and a sharp discussion followed. Somerset still muttered about clearing his gunports but in the end Russell had won the argument. The unchanged ultimatum would be taken that day to the Queen at Windsor for her approval, or for the approval of the dying Prince Albert.

Palmerston closed the meeting. He could then, with sublime confidence, write to the Queen that, if the Federal Government complied with the demands in his ultimatum, it would be honorable to England and humiliating to the United States. Very satisfactory, he felt. If they refused to comply, England was in stronger condition than ever to inflict a severe blow upon the United States, one that it would not soon forget. That would be even better.

The Queen agreed. She later wrote to Palmerston that she looked forward to the utter destruction of the Yankees.

Finally, he sat back down to write to his pet editors at *The Times* and the *Morning Post* to describe the substance of the discussion. British public opinion was in flames. News of his ultimatum to the Americans would keep the fires nicely stoked.

Chapter 15

London

"Oh, you mustn't be so melodramatic, Owen," Katherine said at breakfast. "That man is out there in the street because Lady Kinnaird at number eighteen was burgled a few days ago. Her cook told Mrs. Mostyn all about it. Imagine! While she was upstairs in her bath!" She buttered her toast.

"So the cigar is meant to scare off the local burglars? One would have hoped his job is to catch them, not to warn them." Owen thought he knew why the man was there and it had nothing to do with burglars.

"It is. That's not the real reason you're concerned, though, is it?" She put her hand on his. "You've worn a rather haunted look the last few days, and I'm becoming concerned about you." She sipped her tea for a minute, then, "You must tell me everything."

And Owen did. That is, he told her the story he'd prepared weeks before in anticipation of this moment, a story derived from something O'Mahony had told him in Boston.

He said nothing about the Fenians or the time fuses. He claimed that on his trips to Ireland he was recruiting for O'Mahony's regiment. That O'Mahony expected, or hoped, that after the American war his regiment would form the core of an army of Irish veterans who would return to Ireland to drive the English off the island.

The Irish were emigrating to America in growing numbers, anyway, because of poor harvests, he explained. His job was to induce them to enlist in the Union Army as soon as they landed in Boston or New York.

This time she was silent for minutes. Then she asked, "What you are doing is against the law?" He nodded once. "And are you convinced these men you're helping to recruit will ever come back and fight to free Ireland?"

"I believe there's a chance that enough of them will." He grasped both her hands and looked her in her eye. "A small chance. They'll have good reasons to come back, and good reasons not to. That small chance is enough for me."

"Yes, I can understand why."

"But you will help me?"

"Why, of course!" she cried. "What did you think? You're my brother, and I love you." She gripped his hands hard. "I want to help."

She went to stand at the window, staring out at the softly falling rain. "Besides… Tell me about Grosse Isle, Owen. I've been thinking about it, ever since that night we went to the opera. I never had before, not really, I didn't want to think."

So he described the filth, the stench, the fatal overcrowding, the deaths, the mass graves, all of it. The worst, he said, was the offhandedness, the sheer indifference of most of the English doctors. "They didn't give a damn if Father died like a dog. And he did. They murdered him."

She turned to look at him. "It was horrible for you."

"Yes. I was numb for a long time after Grosse Isle, for months. And terrified. I cried every night. Then I got angry, and I'm still angry, very angry. At the English."

"We've a great deal to be angry about. Father, the famine, losing Mother, losing Kilveen and now you."

Owen had to smile. "My heavens! What a tigress you are, sister. How can we lose now?" She came back to the table and reality returned. "I have to get out of the country," he said flatly. "So I need a passport, a ticket and some money. There are about a hundred pounds in my account at the bank, so money is no obstacle. I have no idea how to get a passport or a ticket without announcing myself to the coppers."

"I can cash a check for you. Malcolm will cash one, I'm sure," she said. Her clear thinking surprised her. "And I suppose I can buy a ticket for you. But I have no idea how you can get another passport."

"Nor do I." Owen chewed on a knuckle. "Wait. Perhaps – Major Bartlett told me once, as a joke, that the Yankee army is enlisting Canadians so I'd better take care not to annoy him. I don't suppose – . What do you think? Could his legation enlist me and then give me a passport?"

She studied him for a moment and then went to her desk, saying, "I'll invite him to call this evening."

Bartlett was delighted to wait on Lady Carra when he returned from the legation. Once he'd recovered from Katherine's terse description of Owen's difficulties, he hadn't much to offer at first. Who would have guessed it - Owen a revolutionary!

His first impulse was to pledge the full support of the legation, but he checked himself and tried to think in practical terms. "I expect we'll want to do whatever we can, Lady Carra," he faltered, "but I'm doubtful about the passport. And you know how tense the relations between us and England are right now, because of this ultimatum the newspapers are full of." He thought aloud. "There might be another way. One of our naval vessels. If one calls in here, we may be able to get him aboard and out of England. But they have no schedule, and it may be weeks before one calls in."

"That would be marvelous, Major. Please, please try. That would save him." Her eyes brimmed with gratitude. "And that reminds me. Owen can't stay in this house, the police may come back at any time. Would you mind terribly if he moves in to the new flat above yours on the first floor?"

"How could I object, Ma'am?" Conspiracy is quite agreeable, he thought. "Do you know? The police haven't a chance against us. Not a chance."

*   *   *

The next day, the Republican Brotherhood in Dublin brought back from California the remains of a young Brother, a veteran of the great cabbage patch battle of '48, and gave the bones a martyr's funeral. After the body lay in state for a day, tens of thousands of mourners followed the coffin though the streets of Dublin to the cemetery at Glasnevin. The authorities panicked and the police followed suit, sweeping up every known Brother they could find in Ireland and England.

Bartlett had consulted Morse about Owen's situation, and later that week, the consul pulled Bartlett aside. "Damnedest thing," he said, "there's been a complete crackdown all over the country on this Fenian affair. You read about the funeral? You'd think it was Satan himself they buried." Bartlett nodded. "Well, it seems the police were ordered to pick up every Brother they could think of and they've flushed out some bigger birds than they expected. Including, they think, the head man, they thought was in New York."

"Have they got him?"

"No, but they're turning over every rock in the country and sealing off every port. My people are too scared to do anything, including talk. But –"

"Damn it," Bartlett swore, "just –"

"But," Morse continued, "one of 'em told me your man's on the list. Described as an American. Wanted in Ireland for conspiracy to murder.

Chapter 16

The Crown Restored had lost none of its shabby charm and none of its customers, whose indistinct features suggested that they spent their lives in its smoky recesses. Molly was gone, summarily sacked when a midshipman accused her of sexually assaulting him in the gents. What she tried to do and why he complained were never explained. Her replacement was the landlord's wife, a fearsome woman who prowled the bar quarreling with the customers she liked and insulting those she didn't.

The night of his return from Liverpool, Robert Jones was waiting for Bartlett at a table near the door. "We'll sit here in case she comes at us with a broken bottle," Jones gestured at the wife and explained, half-seriously, when he arrived. "And don't complain about the food or we're dead men."

"Just fine, thanks. Good of you to ask," Bartlett said, as he inspected the stains on his chair. "And how is Liverpool? Still standing?"

"Very dull, indeed, but challenging. There's a great deal going on up there in the shipyards, all of it bad news, but I'll tell you about that later." He looked into the distance for a second, shook his head and smiled broadly. "But this English ultimatum is good news, eh? If our president has the guts God gave him, the English are in for a surprise, a very nasty surprise."

"What do you mean?"

"We'll whip their lily-white asses. That's what I mean." Jones ordered two glasses of bitter from the scowling wife and picked up the greasy menu. "You'd better believe it."

"You're dreaming again, Jones."

"Am I? A lot has happened since you left. Our navy is now a damned formidable force." Jones explained that the North had perfected two entirely new weapons of war. One was the *Monitor* class warship – small, shallow draft vessels, built entirely of iron with eight inches of armor plate and armed with two nine inch Parrott rifles.

Bartlett sat up. "Nine inches? Hell, that must be, ah, one hundred eighty pounds of iron in its round!"

"Wrong. One hundred fifty pounds of iron plus thirty pounds of explosive. It's armor-piercing. Goes through eight-inch iron plate and teak backing like brown paper. The first and only armor-piercing explosive shell in history, my boy, the Holy Grail of weapons research. We have it. We call it the Taurus shell."

"Tell me more," Bartlett said slowly.

"We're building twelve *Monitors*, two for each of the main rebel seaports. They'll be on station in two months. They'll go right in the harbors and sink every rebel ship in sight. Then they'll wait for the Royal Navy to come over and break our blockade."

"Assuming we reject this ultimatum."

"We will reject it. Have no fear. The President knows exactly what we have waiting for the English. I can hardly wait for it." For an instant he looked like a boy with a brand new bicycle. "Anyway, once the war begins, the Admiralty will first dispatch its Bermuda squadron under old Admiral Milne. He has no ironclads, and he'll think he's going to fight the antique wooden cruisers that until now have made up our blockade fleet." Jones began to wave his hands apart, maneuvering his *Monitors* with skill. "He'll have a nasty shock. Our little ironclads will make matchwood of *his* wooden fleet in an afternoon. They'll do it with conventional shells, not the Taurus."

"But some of his ships will make it back to port, to warn the Admiralty about the *Monitors*."

"Correct, but not about the Taurus because they didn't see it. So in another month the *Warrior* and the *Black Prince* will turn up off our shores, looking for a fight. Enormous new iron frigates, nine thousand tons, fast, heavily armed – but with only four and a half inches of armor plate." Another evil smile on Jones's face. "To get at our ironclads, they'll have to come into shallow water, where they can't maneuver because of their length and their deep draft. They'll try to get very close, to have any hope of hitting our little turrets. When they get close enough, say three hundred yards, we'll change over to the Taurus shells. At that range, even our new crews can't miss. Two, three, maybe four hits will be enough. They'll never know what hit them."

"And that's the end of the Royal Navy," said Bartlett.

"And the end of the war." Jones sat back and stretched out his leg. "You can count on it."

Bartlett thought hard for a while. Everything Jones had said was plausible. The armor-piercing explosive shell had been the goal of weapons inventors for many years, and the West Point Foundry under Captain Robert Parrott had an outstanding record in research and development. But there remained one obvious question.

"Robert, one obvious question: Do the – "

"No. The English do not have the equivalent of our Taurus shell. They've been working at it for years, in particular a Captain Palliser, but they haven't cracked it. He's a genius, but his shell still breaks up in the bore about two thirds of the time."

He explained that the North had spies crawling all over the Woolwich Arsenal and Palliser's workshop in Norfolk, and that it sent observers to all the field trials – private and public – at the Woolwich and Shoeburyness firing ranges. "I've had them in there for two years," he said. "We pay them well, and they don't miss a trick. I talked to our head man at Woolwich yesterday, who reported no change in their test results. The Limeys are still a long, long way from having their own Taurus."

When the beer arrived they had again decided on bread and cheese. "Plain yellow cheese, please," Jones said. "No stilton." He looked shyly at Bartlett. "The last lot didn't agree with me, I found to my cost." He sipped his beer. "At least, we think they don't – have their own Taurus, I mean. So, to make certain of it, you and I are going to a party."

He pulled from his pocket an engraved invitation card and with due ceremony handed it to Bartlett. In it the Commandant of The Royal Arsenal at Woolwich begged Bartlett to present himself at the main gates of the Arsenal at 2:30 p.m. Wednesday to witness a test firing display of Royal Navy ordnance to begin at 3:00. A light repast would be served afterward at the Officers' Quarters.

"Well, won't you congratulate me?"

"Congratulate you on what?" was the waspish reply.

"For arranging your invitation to this firing display. What else? It took my people ten days to arrange it."

"Well, I have to admit I'm impressed. But you're not included. You intend to come along? To bluff your way in, do you?" Bartlett asked.

"Certainly. Stoddard and Wise have ordered me to get first-hand, eyeball proof that Palliser still doesn't work."

"You may need to talk yourself out of the brig in all three of your languages if the guards at the Arsenal don't like the cut of your jib."

"Confidence, Charles! Confidence is all in these missions. And think what an exciting evening we shall have! The Royal Navy will test some of its latest projectiles for you and me to marvel at."

*   *   *

For small gatherings, the Prime Minister preferred to play host at his home in Cambridge House in Piccadilly, where he had lived for years. The War Committee had finished their business and were draining his indifferent port while they gathered their papers.

The primary subject was the British response to the expected American rejection of the ultimatum and their invasion of Canada. The Americans had once attacked Canada with two thousand men; this time they could put forty- to fifty-thousand across the border.

The first British reinforcements had sailed for North America a few days earlier on the steamship *Melbourne*. Tonight the Committee had approved the dispatch of ten thousand more troops with artillery support. All of these men would have to make their way through the snow, on foot, from Halifax up across the northern tip of Maine and down to

Quebec. A fearsome journey but essentially a gesture because there was no pressing hurry.

"The Northerns will refuse our ultimatum," Palmerston had told them. "We will break their blockade in the spring, when we can adequately reinforce Canada. They can not attack it before then," he intoned with the utter self-confidence born of victory in the Crimea and in the Indian Mutiny. "I have told the Queen so."

Attention then turned briefly to Mexico. The French and the Spanish, Lewis reported, were each sending a force of about six thousand troops, plus artillery, which planned to arrive at Veracruz around New Year's Day. The small British contingent of seven hundred effectives would arrive a week or so later. No serious resistance was expected.

"How long will we stay there?" asked Gladstone.

"As long as we have to stay there, of course."

*   *   *

Bartlett was surprised the next morning to see Jones sidle through the ministry's front door and, while watching Adams's closed door, make his way slowly to the curtained corner that served as Bartlett's office.

"I don't think His Eminence saw me, thank God. Where's Flanagan?" he demanded. "I need coffee. Filthy weather." He removed his soaking coat, dropped it on Bartlett's only other chair and turned to stare out the window at the pelting rain.

Bartlett found Flanagan and came back. "This is a surprise, Robert. A welcome one, of course, but nevertheless – "

"Leave it, please. I'm here to make sure we're all squared off for tomorrow's jaunt to Woolwich. Ah, many thanks, Flanagan." He drank deeply. "Aagh. Filthy coffee, as well. What a day."

"Why the doubts? We take the one fifteen from London Bridge terminus. A taxicab will be waiting for us at the other end, you said."

"Right. Well, I should have told you. One of our sloops-of-war, the *Housatonic*, docked in the Thames yesterday. My very own personal transport. It will drop me off at Le Havre and then Captain Makin has orders to make all steam to Boston with my report on the famous Palliser shell."

"Boston?"

"Then the courier takes it on a special train to Washington – it's the fastest way. And it's that vital. Before it can respond to the ultimatum, Washington needs to know that the British shell is still useless."

"I understand. When do you leave?"

"Thursday on the morning tide, which leads me to my point: I think you should come with me to France." He told Bartlett in general terms of his work with the Count de Morny and Hidalgo and of its significance. "It's time you learned about all that."

He added that he had been promised the command of one of the new *Monitor* ironclads. "Hull Number Nine, by God! You can't imagine how long and hard I've dreamed of a sea command, and now I'll have one of the twelve deadliest ships afloat. I can hardly believe it, after all this time."

He would go back to take up his command as soon as she was launched. Provided, of course, that by then the North was at war with England. Otherwise, he would remain at his post in Paris. Another reason, he said, for Bartlett to learn something of his work in France. "You may have to take my place with Morny *pro tem* if I go home to the war and my replacement in Paris is delayed."

"Thanks. You said you'll leave on Thursday? Let me think about it. But that brings up another matter, an important one." Bartlett described Owen Halliday's supposed recruiting activities and his desperate need to leave England. "He's one of ours, you see, and I want to help him if I can. Can we get him on board the *Housatonic*, get him back to Boston?"

"For myself, I don't care one way or the other, but it's not my decision. It's up to Adams, as minister, since it involves a British subject."

"Damn. You're sure of that?"

"Yes, it's come up before. And since this particular subject is on the run from the police, I don't rate your chances at all. But you'll have to ask Adams." He held up a warning finger. "And remember, even if Adams approves, if the police follow Halliday to the ship and want to take him off, we can't protect him, because he's not a Yank. We'll leave him with the police." He poked the finger at Bartlett. "And the ship *will leave*, make no mistake. My report is that important to Washington."

"Fair enough. I'll tell Halliday that." Bartlett looked uneasy. He did not want to ask Adams for his approval.

"Another thought, my kind-hearted friend: If you've already been sheltering young Halliday, the police may charge you as well, for aiding and abetting a vicious criminal, or something like that. That will win *you* an easy twenty years in the slammer. At least." A malicious grin spread across Jones's Slavic features. "Now *you*, we'd have to protect. We may have to shoot our way down the Thames, of course, which would touch off the war with England that I'm hoping for. But don't worry about that – you'll get away."

Away, yes, thought Bartlett, away from London. Away from Katherine, but forever. A fine irony: To save her brother, he might need to abandon his hopes for her.

Once Jones had left, he approached the minister. The interview was brief. Adams stared at him for fifteen seconds before he exploded. "Did you not understand me, Major, when I said at our first meeting that I would not tolerate anything – *anything* – that could exacerbate our relationship, such as it is, with England? Which of my words did you not understand, I wonder, so that you can now propose to smuggle out a wanted Irish criminal on one of our ships? At a time when the prospect of war with England looms greater every day?" He paused to recover his control. "Explain yourself, sir."

Bartlett stood, bowed and left the office. Adams watched him for a moment, rubbed his jaw and then called in his secretary.

Then, although he suspected that he was headed down a dead end, Bartlett consulted the ministry's solicitor about his diplomatic immunity – or lack of it. Arthur Pettigrew was a large unkempt man who wheezed when he talked, but he liked a good fight and Bartlett took to him at once.

Pettigrew was ambivalent. "A tricky concept, immunity," he'd said. In principle, it shielded a foreign ambassador from prosecution; but, if it was a serious crime, perhaps not. In principle, it also shielded his staff; but, "What about his secretary? His clerk? His – ah - military attaché? Perhaps not."

The British had the broadest view on the issue, he said, because they had more ambassadors whose presence was unwelcome than any other nation. But there were few direct precedents and they were unclear, even contradictory.

He waved at the files that overflowed from his shelves to the floor of his office and steepled his fingers. "I'll have my junior review the precedents again, but I can say right now that if they try to deny you immunity we can take the issue to court and tie the matter up for years. Only think of it, Major. You'll be a footnote in all the textbooks."

*   *   *

It was the rarest of London evenings, clear, with an occasional visible star and the northerly wind blowing the stench of the Thames away toward Wandsworth. Although it was late, Bartlett decided to walk back to his rooms.

For several nights there had been no one standing in the shadows of his street and there was no one now. He went inside to tell Owen. The young man had been writing furiously to take his mind off his fears as well as meet his belated obligations to his editor.

He was still up, looking less gaunt than on the night he had come over the roof to his own flat. Three meals every day since then had made their mark and Bartlett remarked on his healthier appearance.

"Oddly enough, it must be because I worry less up here than I used to. I know," he interrupted Bartlett, "that sounds daft when I'm up here to hide from the police, but I'm not as worried. Scared, really." He recounted his experience a few weeks before with the two detectives in the Liverpool terminus. "Now that was a genuine, bowel opening scare," he said.

"And for what? I've a good idea of what you've been up to in Ireland, Owen, but I don't know why you do it." Bartlett waited enquiringly.

So Owen told him almost all his life story. Kilveen, Grosse Isle, the *Pilot*, the Fenians, the alleged recruiting. If Bartlett was going to smuggle him out of England, he deserved to know what he needed to know.

"You're wanted for conspiracy to murder. Did you know that?"

"Yes, I've been told. It's utter rubbish; the police in Ireland always accuse everybody of that."

Bartlett was silent for minutes. He believed Owen. How was he going to tell him that he couldn't take him back? The risk was too great. The risk that the police would follow Owen to the *Housatonic* and try to impound or detain the ship. And the risk that they would detain Charles Bartlett for aiding and abetting, which if nothing else would mean the abrupt, disgraced end of his career.

Now he stared at Owen and tried to think of a gentle way to break his terrible news.

Owen resolved his dilemma for him. "Wake up, Charles," he demanded, "and show a proper respect. As of today, my good man, I am your equal in rank as well as in popular esteem." He pulled a sheet of heavy foolscap from the left hand pile and flourished it at Bartlett. It was a brevet commission as a major in the Union Army.

"Sent to me on the USS *Housatonic* by a certain Colonel Kennedy of the Forty Ninth New York (Irish) Regiment. He invites me to join his rollicking band of cutthroats at my earliest convenience and no later than Christmas."

"How on earth did this happen?"

Owen smiled enigmatically, said, "Influence, sheer influence, but I won't tell you." He clapped his hands. "A remarkable military career, eh, Charles? From British corporal to American major in one breathtaking leap."

"Do you mean to accept the commission? And the posting?" Bartlett asked.

"Of course! Wouldn't you? If I can get back there." He hesitated. "This ship, the *Housatonic*, must have just arrived, Charles. Do you know anything about it? Can I get on it?" Bartlett saw in his face a glimpse of the terrified little boy at Grosse Isle.

"Ah, well, Owen..."

"Is it a navy ship? Is there a chance for me?" Owen pleaded. The image of an English jail now came to him like a knife. Bartlett was his best, perhaps his last, hope, but the American was plainly unhappy.

"I'm afraid not, Owen. I've already asked," Bartlett said. "Our minister forbids it. The risk that the police will follow you and pull you off the ship. The diplomatic consequences would be – well, it would be too risky for us."

"Can you not ask anyone else? The captain of the ship? The – "

"I'm very sorry. There's no one else. That's the last word."

Chapter 17

Bartlett and Morse assembled the pile of reports from their agents on the frantic British preparations for the defense of Canada. They had worked for a week to collate, assess and synthesize them into their joint paper for Stoddard and Henry Wise of the Navy. Now they signed it and sent it off by messenger to Captain Makin on the *Housatonic*.

Then Bartlett told Adams - still furious at him - that he was ordered to Paris, knowing that Jones would back him up if necessary.

He had never been to France and he sensed that Jones would be a first-rate guide and companion. He would meet some of Jones's important contacts. He could distance himself from Owen for a while, in case the police ran him down. Finally, he suspected that he hadn't heard the last of his role in sinking the *Bermuda*, and an absence from England might be wise.

He would pack that night and hope to see Katherine before he left.

*　　　　　*　　　　　*

This time, Jones was late. Bartlett paced along the dreary shops inside the London Bridge terminus, looking up every minute at the overhead clock, the station's solitary ornament. At last, stretching on his toes above the massed commuters on the platform, he saw Jones pushing toward him.

"Ah, Charles, right on time. Good. Our train leaves in four minutes. If we move up the platform we'll get a seat with less trouble. Look out for pickpockets; this station is stiff with them."

They found two facing seats in a first class compartment that filled with men who unfolded their newspapers thankfully as soon as they saw there was no threat of conversation.

There was more than a blast of winter in the cold, wet east wind that had blown since morning. Jones pulled *The Times* from a pocket of his greatcoat, elbowed some room for himself and opened it to the shipping news. Bartlett pushed his hands into his pockets and turned to look out through the rain sliding down his window as the train rattled across the shabby streets of south London and then over the Grand Surrey Canal.

He was excited at the prospect of seeing Woolwich, the great Royal Arsenal. As an instructor at West Point, Bartlett had needed to keep up to date with advances in gunnery. In his specialty, field artillery, the weapons and theory had changed little in the last two years, while the pace of change in naval gunnery had accelerated wildly. Many of the finest engineering minds of Europe and America were dedicated to this field.

The ultimate projectile - a rifled explosive shell that would pierce heavy armor and then explode inside the ship – had been the Holy Grail of gunnery. The United States now had one in its new Taurus shell; Bartlett and Jones would soon discover if the English had one.

The train pulled into Arsenal Station. "Ah, there he is," Jones said as they stepped off. He pointed his umbrella at the last taxi in the rank, which appeared to be the largest carriage in London.

They climbed in and the driver squinted at Jones. Bartlett saw a round face, piggish eyes and bad teeth. Jones said, "Security at the Arsenal is still loose, Wigan, so I don't expect any problems."

A short ride through the center of Woolwich village took them across an open square to the Arsenal's main entrance gates. A young lieutenant, resplendent in the uniform of the Royal Artillery, approached and saluted. He read Bartlett's invitation, consulted a list, saluted again and said, "Welcome to the Royal Arsenal, Major Bartlett. Your name was added to the guest list recently, so we're pleased you could arrange to be here. But I see no mention of your companion, who is - ? "

"Commander Jones, United States Navy. The Commander arrived from France this morning," Bartlett said briskly.

"I see." The lieutenant's face was doubtful as he looked from one to the other.

Bartlett tried for a lofty tone of voice. "There was no time to notify the Admiralty of his arrival, so I decided to presume on your courtesy and bring him with me. I hope there is no difficulty?"

"Please excuse me one minute, Major," and the lieutenant disappeared into the guardroom. He soon emerged with an even more resplendent Captain, who peered into the carriage, stepped back and said, "I am Captain Slater, officer of the guard, sir. This is most unfortunate but we cannot allow Commander Jones access to this afternoon's display. We are expecting some important visitors, the King of Sardinia and the Prince of Siam, and our orders -."

"Yes, of course, Captain," Jones interjected, "That must be His Majesty's party right behind ours. We seem to be blocking their way."

He waved at a superb black carriage, bearing what were plainly royal arms, that had entered the gate behind them. A grandly bemedalled reception committee that included at least one major general was forming up. A colonel beckoned fiercely at Slater.

Bartlett took his cue from this scene. "I believe you're wanted, Captain. To order out the guard, perhaps? We'll pull ahead, shall we?"

"Fine. No, I mean! No!" poor Slater shouted, his head swiveling back and forth. "Stay here until I get back."

"If we stay here," Jones said reasonably, "we'll block the King's progress. Why don't we go ahead and -"

"Certainly not!" But the colonel was now advancing on Slater, his face purple. "Well, if -"

"Thank you, Captain." Jones turned on his most winsome smile and rapped on the roof. "I hope we may see you at the reception?" The carriage bolted ahead. "When you want something done in the military," he told Bartlett with satisfaction, "and above all in the British military, fear is always the first lever to pull."

"We were lucky there," Bartlett said.

"Lucky? Why? Wigan knew what time the King would arrive. The rest was simple." Jones leaned out and called to the driver, "Go by the gun factories, Wigan. Then take the river route to the Select Committee Range."

The rain had stopped now. The carriage slowed to a walk and turned left in front of a large sundial. Jones took another look behind then sat back and waved his hand at the window. "Here you are, Charles, the mighty Royal Arsenal. One square mile, ten thousand workmen. The largest military establishment on earth."

Ahead on their left and right stretched vast buildings that were two, three, even four hundred yards long.

"On our right, part of the gun factory." Jones assumed the cadences of a tour guide, "On the left, the Royal Laboratory, which is another gun factory. Farther down on our right, that giant factory is where they make all their carriages."

They turned left and right again. They were now close to the river, and a mild tang of salt in the wind reminded Bartlett that the North Sea was not many miles to the east. A row of elm trees on his left bordered a park of dead artillery - fragments of guns that had burst in testing or in service. Some had been submitted by private inventors and failed their test; others had been tested to destruction. All were forlorn, shattered corpses.

They passed a scattering of smaller buildings and crossed over a canal ("They test their naval torpedoes in there," said Jones) and through a wall to emerge onto an open space. Bartlett estimated it was one hundred yards wide where they stood and about three quarters of a mile from their right to their left. Obviously a firing range, he thought, with the gun positions on the right and the targets on the left.

They turned left and stopped at a small brick grandstand set at a right angle to the range. It faced a row of target bays about one hundred yards in front and to the right. They climbed to their seats in the last row, shepherded by a self-important young officer. Bartlett had never seen so many different uniforms as there were on the fifty or so guests, but none from the Confederacy, he thought. Jones confirmed it.

After a few minutes the King's party arrived and were shown with practiced ceremony to chairs in the first row. A portly Royal Artillery colonel, extravagantly mustached, took his place a few yards in front of the King and, after a short speech of welcome, set out the business of the day.

"We will fire today, gentlemen," he announced, "at an eight inch *Warrior* type target, at a range of two hundred yards." Bartlett knew from his study of recent Woolwich test results that this target was almost twice as thick as the armor of H. M. S. *Warrior*, the long black ship he had seen on the Thames. It consisted of iron plates eight inches thick backed by eighteen inches of teak and a three quarter inch iron skin, held by iron ribs two feet apart. A supremely formidable defense, supported by wooden buttresses set into the bays in a wall of sand.

"This will be a display of different rifled shells," the colonel went on, "so we will use one gun, a nine inch Woolwich rifle. It will fire a battering charge of forty-three pounds of powder. The bursting charges will be small, between three and five pounds of powder. The bugle will sound one minute before each round. Thank you."

"This is heavy iron, indeed," Jones said quietly as he eyed the Russian naval officer beside him, "heavier than I expected. But at two hundred yards and with a heavy battering charge, eight inches of armor plate will be a fair test. Hold onto your hat."

The bugle blew and the small knot of artillery officers down near the target scrambled for safety into a casemate to one side. Along with the rest, Bartlett trained his field glasses on the broad black target and held his breath.

There was a deep, rolling boom of the gun behind them, followed immediately by a shattering CRACK as the first shell struck. Despite his years on artillery ranges, Bartlett dropped the glasses.

Jones surveyed him with amusement. "Not quite like your army popguns, eh? These are real guns, my boy, naval guns."

The officers from the casemate inspected the target and reported to the mustachioed colonel, who called in a ringing voice, "Round Number One was a steel shell on Mr. Alderson's pattern. Muzzle velocity 1,340 feet per second. Damage to target: indent fifteen inches across by twelve inches; penetration eight to nine inches." An excited murmur from the grandstand. "No damage visible at back of the target." The murmur subsided.

"Not bad," Jones conceded, "but it exploded backward. It would have done no damage to the ship."

Again the bugle sounded, again the silent wait and the shattering noise. This time the colonel's report was carefully neutral. "Round Number Two was also a steel shell, made by Firths on the Ordnance Select Committee pattern. Muzzle velocity 1,335 feet. Indent twelve inches by twelve inches. Penetration seven inches. The head of the shell was buried in the armor. Damage to back of target - none visible."

Once again, the bugle, the wait and the noise of the gun. This time, cries of surprise from the stand. Looking through his glasses, Bartlett was stunned. The shell had struck one of the eight-inch iron plates in the center. It had cut clean through the plate and its teak and iron backing and had then exploded. The plate was not buckled in the least, so that all the shell's energy had been used to punch its hole. The explosion had torn a great hole in a stone wall twenty feet behind the target.

The colonel reported to a hushed audience. "Gentlemen, that was a cast iron shell on the Palliser model. Muzzle velocity 1,330 feet. Indent twelve inches by twelve inches. Bursting charge three and one-half pounds. As you can see, the target was fully penetrated, with substantial damage to its other side."

A patter of applause from the grandstand. Bartlett saw that Jones did not applaud; he was scribbling in a tiny black notebook. "That's the one we've come to see. Would you call it promising?"

"I didn't know they had anything remotely like it," Bartlett said in a subdued voice. "It's not in any of their published reports, although you and General Stoddard both mentioned it." He felt foolish. He should have expected the English to have a projectile like it, and he should by now have known much more about it.

"Of course it's not published, it's still too experimental. Now, the real question is: how will it perform on its next two rounds?"

Another five shells, all different, were fired at the same target. None pierced the plate and two bounced off it, to the entertainment of the King of Sardinia and his aides. The colonel then announced that the same eight models of shell would be fired a second time, in the same order.

The two steel shells performed no better than the first time. Conversations died away and the tension tightened as the second Palliser shell was being loaded behind the grandstand. The bugle sounded and the target observers ambled to their casemate.

The thunder of the gun swept over the crowd, but there was no CRACK from the target. Instead, a storm of iron fragments rained on the target and the nearby casemate.

Bartlett examined the target area through his glasses and exclaimed, "That round must have broken up in the barrel! Fragments everywhere."

Jones was punching the air and beaming like an excited child. "Thank you, Lord! Holy Mary, thank you too." he said under his breath.

The colonel announced the unhappy results. Another seven rounds were fired without incident. Some missed the target, some passed through holes made by other shells. None did serious harm to the eight-inch plates. The assembled officers shifted their bottoms restively as the two steel shells were fired for the third time. The King did not bother to raise his field glasses.

Then it was the turn of the third Palliser shell. This time the audience was plainly uneasy and as soon as the bugle blew the observers hurried into the casemate.

Several muted thuds from the target followed the gun's roar. The shell had broken into five large fragments, all of which struck the target, two after bouncing off the ground.

"Well, so much for your friend Palliser," Bartlett said as he put down his binoculars. "Two failures out of three is a trifle risky, I'd say. Unless of course the Royal Navy thinks that what it needs is a big shotgun, say a nine inch shotgun."

Jones agreed. "Far too risky. For the English. For us – the confirmation we need. The damn thing still doesn't work!"

It was dusk when the firing ended. Deafened, Bartlett and Jones filed slowly down from the top row, impressed by the dozen different languages being spoken around them. They found their carriage and Jones instructed the impassive Wigan to take them back the same way. They were the last to leave.

"Well, Mr. Gunnery Instructor, what did you think of that?" Jones demanded.

"I think I'm more impressed by the Arsenal itself than by the test firing," Bartlett said. "From what you've said, the English are still far behind us. Palliser may be a genius, but his shells have a worrying tendency to break up in the bore."

"They sure do. Isn't it grand? When Stoddard and Wise read my report, that will be all they need to know. I -"

Suddenly Jones rapped on the roof with his umbrella and shouted to Wigan to stop. He got out of the carriage. Bartlett followed him and studied the surroundings.

They had covered half a mile from the grandstand and were once more close to the river. Around them rose a group of low, small brick buildings, each with a single lantern over its main gate. On their left rose the cylindrical tanks of the gas works.

"Wait here for a minute, Charles," Jones said and was lost in the gloom.

He was soon back, looking animated. "We may be in luck." Then to Wigan: "How much time do we have?"

Wigan grinned. "Twenty eight minutes, by the clock."

"Fine. Move the carriage off the road and wait for us between the first two gasometers on the left."

To Bartlett: "Come with me." Bartlett, startled, followed him along the side of the first building, where they turned right and soon stopped between the building and a stable.

"This is one of the Shot and Shell Stores," Jones said. "Number Three. I think the test shells are kept here. We're going inside to get a good look at a Palliser model."

"Are you out of your mind, Jones? What if we're caught inside? It's an act of war. The English will be shelling New York in three weeks. And shelling it with Palliser rounds."

"We won't be caught. You heard Wigan. The watchman won't clock in here for over twenty minutes."

"Wigan? What does he know?"

"Everything. He works here, as a watchman." Then, "The hell with it, there's no time to argue. You stay here, I'll go in. First, open the catch of that sash window. I can't reach it."

Bartlett knew an order when he heard it. He managed to move the catch to one side with his umbrella. Together they pushed up the lower sash.

"Bend down and I'll get up on your shoulders," Jones growled.

"Stay off the left one. It's still sore."

Jones pulled himself up to the open sash, said, "Rap on this window if the watchman comes," and was through.

Bartlett saw a flare as a small lantern was lit inside, but it quickly disappeared. He paced in a tight circle, his mouth dry.

"Bartlett?" Jones called in a low voice. "Success! Wait - there's a door here. I'll try to open it." After a few dull blows a wide door opened in front of Bartlett. "Nothing easier, one small bolt. Do come in."

Once inside, Bartlett could see that the storeroom was vast, much larger than he had thought. Rows of upright shells reached in all directions.

"You found them? How?" He was whispering for no reason

"Quite simple. I walked down each row until I saw a group of shells painted black, white and red. They're over here. Still wet from the rain and not even bagged yet."

They were surprisingly small, eight of them squatting in the dark on wooden planks. About two feet long, Bartlett guessed, but weighing more than 170 pounds. Their noses were ogival curves, sharply pointed. They were deadly, threatening, waiting.

"We'll take four," Jones announced.

"They'll spot that at once!"

"Nonsense. Look at that slate there. No one will inspect these for months. Not until December 10th, which must be the next test firing. By then no one will know if there should be eight of them or eight hundred.

He could be right, Bartlett conceded. Chalked on the slate was:

9" Palliser Model II - 8X, Move to No. 1 Store, NLT 10 Dec 61

"A haphazard method of stock control, eh? I'll just change that 8 to a 4." Jones stepped back from the slate, a piece of chalk in his right hand, and squinted at Bartlett. "Right. We'll use that ammunition wagon there and that lifting cradle and we'll have them in the carriage in no time."

Bartlett was trapped. If they were caught by the watchman, he would be as guilty as Jones of common theft. If they weren't caught and he had refused to help, his career would be finished. Stoddard would make sure of that. He had no real choice. He knew it, and Jones knew it.

Two minutes before the watchman was due, they had manhandled the four shells up to the carriage floor. Wigan laid lengths of a heavy mooring hawser around and between the shells and then threw a thick horse blanket over them. They were out of sight and, Bartlett prayed, stable, because he would be sitting on twenty pounds of gunpowder. He now understood why the carriage was so large. Even so, it seemed to squat on the track when they climbed in.

Jones told Wigan to head for the Royal Artillery headquarters, slapped Bartlett's knee and laughed. "We'll still be in time to drink our share of the Queen's champagne."

Bartlett ignored him. His shoulder throbbed. He gripped the window strap, planted both feet on the blanket and peered into the gloom. So he was the first to see a solitary lantern coming at them beside the road. He watched it as they passed by.

Jones saw it, too. "We had two minutes to spare. No need to worry."

Bartlett asked, "What if the watchman had seen us?"

"His body would now be under your feet. Wigan would have killed him," Jones said flatly. "Or I would have. Or you, if necessary. Your knife and mine are in my pocket." He patted it.

Bartlett was silent, so Jones slapped his knee again and said "Don't worry about it now. You did well. Your uncle will be told." He chuckled. "There was a moment, though, in the Shell Stores when I thought you were going to wet your smalls, but you didn't. Did you?" Bartlett gave him an icy glare.

They stopped at the gates by the entrance to the Royal Artillery headquarters and climbed down. "We'll wait to make sure Wigan gets through the gates," Jones said as the carriage moved on.

Bartlett had recovered some of his nerve. "Can you trust him that much? Where's he going with the - ?"

"He helped remove the goods, didn't he? And he'll get ten pounds from *Housatonic's* captain for each item he delivers tonight. We can trust him."

The sentries did not even look at the carriage as it plodded sedately past them. "Fine. Just the way we practiced it," Jones said. "Shall we join the party? There are some people here you should meet."

Chapter 18

Bartlett paid off the cabbie a few blocks from Rochester Place. He opened his street door and saw the envelope on the floor. The note inside read:

"My dear Major,

Would you be kind enough to call on me tonight? I shall wait until nine. Explanations when (as I hope) I see you.

Katherine Carra"

Surprise, curiosity, excitement; all crowded across his mind. He looked over at the Carra house where a light glowed in the fanlight. It's beckoning me, almost, he thought and laughed at the fancy. He went into his rooms.

A few minutes later, he stood in the Carra drawing room, holding his breath. Katherine looked ravishing. She wore a swirling silk dress of cobalt blue, her hair fell to her bare shoulders and the long green eyes appraised him favorably. Her only jewelry was the gold and emerald cross on the delicate chain around her neck. A fire danced in the grate and a crystal decanter with two glasses waited on a table in the window. It was probably just the lighting, but Bartlett was somewhat taken aback by the look on Katherine's face. He couldn't quite put his finger on it, but he'd never seen this expression before.

"Thank you so much for calling at this strange hour." She smiled warmly, that look – whatever it was - disappeared in an instant. "Lord Carra is up in Yorkshire, shooting. Or, more likely, he's amusing the local birdlife. He's not managed to hit anything all season." She paused. "Malcolm Bannerman has just left and Milly is ill, so I'm quite alone."

"I do hope that you are not too lonely."

"No, indeed, I love having the house to myself. In fact, I was hoping you might help me navigate Lord Carra's extensive collection of brandies."

"Oh, I couldn't. Are you sure?"

"Nonsense. I insist that you have one glass. And you mustn't worry about my reputation; it was probably lost when I opened the door to you." She seemed to float towards the bar, where she picked up a gleaming decanter and glasses. "I've heard Lord Carra tell his friends that this brandy is rather special." She returned to Bartlett and stood close in front of his chair. "Will you pour a glass for yourself and one for me?"

He was truly shocked by her request; previously the strongest drink he had shared with Katherine had been Mrs. Mostyn's tea, and even that had been accompanied by the beady eyes of the aforementioned Mostyn boring into the back of his head.

"Please suggest a toast, Major. I would very much like to try some of this famous brandy."

"To friends and neighbors."

"Oh, I like it. Friends and neighbors."

They clinked glasses and both took hesitant sips; Bartlett because he was unsure of the correct etiquette in a situation like this, Katherine because brandy was clearly not something she drank regularly.

After a brief interlude, Katherine turned to Bartlett with a serious expression: "I'm anxious to ask you about Owen – and Mrs. Mostyn told me you were packing to go away."

"Yes." He tried to avoid her unspoken question. "I shall be away for a time – in France – we sail at dawn tomorrow - and I'd like to pay my rent in advance." He reached in his pocket and handed her six pound coins.

"That's most thoughtful of you." She counted the coins. "You mean to be away for six weeks?"

"Well, it depends if there's a war or not." That sounds very offhand and soldierly, he thought with satisfaction.

"A war?" She looked incredulous. "Malcolm said that is most unlikely."

"Did he? He may be wrong. You see – I say, Lady Carra - you don't object to talking about politics?"

"I object only when Lord Carra insists on rubbishing my opinions."

"Does he? He's a brave man, indeed," Bartlett teased. Maybe she truly didn't object. This seemed almost too good to be true – a beautiful, intelligent woman with whom he could sit, drink brandy, and bore with his political opinions.

Well, you see, England thinks its navy can destroy any other navy," he began, "so it thinks it can threaten any country it pleases. But we believe there's every chance that our navy can destroy England's." Why was he telling her this? What the hell, it was time he got a chance to blow his own horn. "In fact, we now have the proof of that, which is why I'll leave London for a bit."

"And why you've paid six weeks' rent in advance," she smiled at last. "His lordship's bank manager would wish you well in your work, anyway." She studied his face. "And now you have this famous proof? What happens then?"

"It will go immediately to Washington, and Washington will reject the English ultimatum. There will be war, a naval war, and - we will win it." It sounded quite simple and quite convincing.

"You'll win? Nonsense!"

"We will."

"Dear Lord! That means - poor Owen!" she whispered. "Were you able to get permission, permission to take him with you? That is what I meant to ask you." He shook his head sadly. "No? Oh, dear." She held her head in her hands. "Well, I feared it was impossible."

"I am so sorry, Lady Carra," Bartlett said. "I..."

"You did as much as anyone could have done, I'm certain, and you were wonderfully kind to try."

Bartlett studied his hands. For the first time he felt that he was with Katherine, the woman, and not with Lady Carra, the charming, the elusive, the unattainable. He'd been with her when she was emotional, even a few times when she was vulnerable, but never when she was so - womanly.

She was silent for a time, taking the occasional sip of her brandy. "My poor Owen. He will take this terribly hard."

"Yes, he will."

"And now I must tell him that the detective, that odious Mr. Crawford, was here again this afternoon."

"What did he want?"

"He said he wanted to give Owen back his passport, but he really was snooping hard. Where is Owen? he asked, and I lied again and said in Ireland or Liverpool. Then he asked me about the next house, your house: do you still live there alone, and have we finished redoing the first floor? I told him that is none of his concern."

So she didn't know that Owen was charged with conspiracy to murder. "Good for you," he said. "He's only trying to frighten you."

"Well, he's making a fine job of it, I assure you. He terrified me. He was so... so matter of fact." She shivered.

Bartlett shifted uncomfortably when he saw the tears in her eyes, which she tried to blink away. She's too proud to wipe them away, he thought.

"I seem to bring you nothing but bad news, Lady Carra. Can I at least pour you another brandy to make up for it?"

"Yes please. And don't worry yourself about being the bearer of bad news. I am no stranger to bad news and – in your case – you are only the messenger. The cause is always this wretched Commander Jones of yours." She laughed shortly, drinking a large slug of the brandy. "I see him with horns, red eyes and a pointed tail. Am I right?"

Beginning to feel the effects of the brandy, Barlett felt like embellishing somewhat. "Exactly right, and with a Russian accent. But Jones isn't the cause; he doesn't care if Owen sails with us or not, so long as he isn't caught. It's Minister Adams." Katherine looked surprised. "He was terrified that Owen would get caught on our ship and cause a diplomatic uproar." He grinned and shook his head. "That would be the end of my career. The minister would destroy me. He'd make sure of that."

"Oh? Surely not."

"Afraid so. No question about that!"

"And Owen can't travel on a regular ship without his passport." She was almost talking to herself. Bartlett saw in her face the expression he had glimpsed when he had walked in the room, a sort of desperation that he didn't think possible in such a strong, independent women. Perhaps she was human after all?

"Even if he could travel, the ports are still being watched," Bartlett pointed out. "No, I'm afraid his best hope remains to get aboard another one of our ships. Perhaps his only hope."

"But you'll be at war, you say. When will this war begin, do you think? Soon?"

"I expect so. I should say in about three weeks," he said. "That's for President Lincoln to reply to the ultimatum. The war can begin any time after that."

"Only three weeks? My goodness." She bowed her head in dismay. When she looked up, the firelight brought out the golden glow in her hair and then the emerald in her eyes. "And then your ships will stop calling here."

For some reason, this fragility made Katherine all the more attractive. Maybe it was the alcohol, but at that moment he would have done anything in the world to bring a smile to her face, to make that melancholy disappear. Which is why it was so hard for him to say:

"Yes, of course."

"I see." A long pause. In fact, the longest pause Bartlett had ever experienced. He watched her face intently as every thought was telegraphed in her continually morphing expression. It seemed to go from disappointment, to sadness, to thoughtfulness, to determination, and onto a meek and seductive look. Possibly with more expressions lost in the transitions.

"We must drink another toast, then, to great triumphs to come in your chosen field. Please excuse me while I see if I can track down a different decanter of brandy. I believe I have heard Lord Carra waxing lyrically about some Cognac of his."

She tottered slightly as she disappeared off into the dining room, leaving Bartlett to examine the endless portraits of unprepossessing Carras who had been staring down at him from the walls all evening. She was soon back, with a practically over-flowing glass of brandy in each hand.

Bartlett felt the need for another toast. "To an entente cordiale between our nations and a swift end to the war."

"And to your speedy return."

Either the exertions of the last few days were catching up with him or the brandy was surprisingly strong, because he soon felt the irresistible call of the sofa in front of the fire. As he eased himself down into his seat, struggling to appear dignified, he realized that he was beginning to feel quite at home in London and in civilian life

Katherine was soon perched delicately on the sofa next to him, staring off into the distance, lost in thought. After a short while, she turned to him and whispered, "You know, Major, I was getting quite used to having you around."

His head really was spinning now; in the last few days he committed piracy, killed two men, broken into a military warehouse and more. Now the woman he was infatuated with was whisterping sweet nothings into his ear. It was almost too much to bare. "Yes?"

"Yes..." the word drifting off into nothing.

Katherine snapped out of her reverie and turned to face him. "Will you come back before then?" she asked softly.

"As soon as I can." Although his head was swirling, he managed to find his most magnetic smile. "Unless they need me for some heroic mission in France, one that requires stealth and low cunning. In my own quiet way, I've become an accomplished criminal."

"I don't doubt it, sir. I said once that you are plainly a man of many talents," she smiled back. "A man who can look civilized and fierce at the same time can do almost anything, I imagine."

He inclined his head. "You are too kind, Madam."

"It's peculiar how one can doesn't appreciate something until it's almost gone," she said enigmatically.

He turned to face her, gently placing his hand on hers and whispered in her ear, "Sometimes things won't go if they are truly appreciated."

Was that the best he could come up with? Why weren't the words forming in his mouth?

She turned to face him, gazing up into his eyes. He returned her gaze, but was distracted by her full, red lips. He edged closer to her, like a cat creeping up on a mouse, afraid of startling her. But she didn't back away, but rather held his gaze until their lips touched.

What happened after this was all a haze, except a snippet of conversation.

"Charles, how long will your war last?"

"Once we whip the English? Oh, another year or so, I'd guess. Why?"

"What will you do after the war?"

"I've never really thought about it. Stay in the army, I suppose. All American field marshals are expected to stay in." His fingertips traced the line of her fine golden chain.

She pressed herself against him. "Will you ever come back to England?"

"Yes, if there were - um - a good - reason - to come back - then, possibly."

"Could anything prevent you from leaving in the first place?"

"Hmm - That would be more difficult, but possibly..."

*   *   *

The fury in England was mirrored in the North. The storms of defiance that had blown across the northern states in the wake of the *Trent* capture were beginning to abate when the first news came of the English ultimatum and its likely arrogant contents. To the people, the English demands for the release of the rebel emissaries and for an apology were intolerable.

Then came the telegraph reports from Newfoundland of England's rapid preparations for war. "WAR FEVER HIGH IN ENGLAND", "MORE TROOPS TO CANADA" and "AN IMMENSE ARMAMENT IN PREPARATION" ran the headlines, and the mood of the populace ran to violence, to war with England.

Seward found the President lying on the sofa in his office, leafing through English newspapers. He wore his favorite carpet slippers and a patched pair of grey trousers. "Ah, come in, Governor, come in. Just the man I need," he said without rising.

Seward was once again struck by the change in Lincoln, who had aged ten years in ten months. "I see you're busy, Mr. President, but I've had a visit from Lord Lyons and I..."

"Fine, fine, in a minute. First, I need your help with a particular problem. It's this - " he waved at the pile of journals - "the English papers are in some difficulty deciding precisely what form of higher primate I am." He grinned at the distance that Seward's jaw dropped. "*The Times*, here, would have it that I am an ape. The *Chronicle*, on the other hand, and a few other respected journals insist I'm a baboon. Now, what is your opinion?"

"Sir..."

"I'm leaning to the ape camp, myself," Lincoln said meditatively. "The name itself, 'ape', bespeaks - what? - solidity, reliability, even a certain - ruggedness, dare I say it. Yes, you can always count on your ape."

"Sir, don't you think..."

"Your baboon, now. There's a foreign flavor to it - to the name, not to the creature, of course. A certain unpredictability, perhaps even a hint of menace in the name. Baboooooon. I wonder." Lincoln relished Seward's glassy stare. "Yes, a menace. A threat. That decides it. In these troubled times, a threat is more effective with our English friends than simple reliability." He sat up and crossed his long legs. "It's a baboon I will be,

Governor, a baboon. Ask Mr. Adams in London to see to it, if you please." A pause. "Governor?"

Seward at last caught the laughter in Lincoln's eyes and, playing the game, promised blandly to write to Adams that day. "I'll tell him to be polite to the editors but firm."

He went on to report his interview with the British minister. Lord Lyons, he said, had followed his orders to the letter and had brought no papers with him to Seward's office. He'd been instructed to tell Seward that he was to ask for the prompt delivery of Mason and Slidell to England and for an appropriate apology from the American government for its action. These instructions represented the much-trumpeted English ultimatum. Lyons indicated that he could wait a week for a reply and that, if none was received or if the reply was negative, he would demand his passports and return to England.

"He's a timid little swine, behind that cold arrogance," Seward commented," so I was able to persuade him to send me a copy of his instructions. That'll take a day or two, and then I'll ask for another delay before the clock starts to run."

"So that's all?" Lincoln asked. "No threats? No warnings?"

"None, but don't be fooled. His departure would be a formality, no more. They mean war." Seward was in no doubt.

"I suppose they do, damn them. And all this fuss over two senile secessionists who, if we'd just let them be, would have promptly got up the nose of every Englishman and Frenchman they met." That reminded him. "The French, have you heard from the French yet?"

"I have." Seward pursed his lips. "Their ambassador told me this morning that the Emperor is backing the English all the way this time."

"So much for our diplomacy, Seward. We've got the two strongest nations on the planet against us." Lincoln stood up and began to pace the room. "So we have at least a week to reply. That's something. It might even give us enough time to decide *how* to reply."

"It's primarily a military question, isn't it, and I've brought with me General Stoddard, whom you know, Commander Wise, head of naval intelligence, and Captain Ericsson, the inventor and builder of the *Monitor*-class batteries. Shall I call them in? They know why they're here."

Lincoln nodded. Once again Seward was assuming the responsibilities of the War Secretary, Cameron, which was annoying. But not as annoying, he had to admit, as listening to the venal Cameron, whom Lincoln had once described as a man who would steal anything except a red-hot stove.

There followed a protracted technical discussion of the advances in ship design and naval gunnery that had convinced Lincoln's interlocutors that, if war came, the Royal Navy would go down to crushing defeat. At the close of the meeting, Ericsson took the floor:

"Sir, you must understand what a revolution in warfare we're going to make with my ships and our new Taurus shells." He jumped up and ran to the wall map. He slapped a hand over England and declared, "The Royal Navy, sir, has one hundred forty nine first class warships. In two weeks' time, when my first ship is launched, all but two of them - *Warrior* and *Black Prince* - will be obsolete. Useless, against us. A few weeks later, those two will be on the bottom.

Lincoln said quietly, "Thank you, Captain. I trust you won't object if I ask you a more general question: Is there anything wrong with your ship? Anything at all?"

"Well, Mr. President," Ericsson admitted, "I still have a problem with the heads. The problem is with the reverse water pressure, that can blow a man up off the toilet seat? I can't..."

"Well, sir, I'm sure you'll put that right in no time at all," Lincoln interrupted. He wanted to move on before the Swede's plumbing difficulties took over the discussion.

Lincoln turned to Wise. "Tell me once more, Commander. How many hits will it take to sink the *Warrior* - honestly?"

"Honestly, sir? One. Just one. You can count on it."

*　　　　　*　　　　　*

When Bartlett was eventually able to pry his eyes open the next morning, he found himself lying face down in his bed, still fully-dressed from the night before. He couldn't be sure, but he was fairly convinced that a small animal had died behind his eyes. On top of that, his tongue was stuck to the top of his mouth, he felt like he was on a rocking boat, and someone was spinning the entire room around his bed.

Once he had recovered sufficiently to crawl towards his jacket lying on the floor, he checked his fob watch. At first he thought that the watch must have stopped, but the ticking was soon sounding like a hammer to his head. That meant that it was, indeed, ten o'clock in the morning. Which meant he had, indeed, missed his boat. This meant he was, indeed, in deep trouble.

Having splashed some cold water on his face and stuffed anything he could find into his two cases, he staggered next door and knocked at the Carra's. When Mrs. Mostyn eventually opened the door, Bartlett practically collapsed onto the poor woman.

After the requisite apologies (him) and witheringly stern looks (her), Bartlett was able to ask "Have you seen Lady Carra this morning?"

"Her Ladyship's gone up north, to Yorkshire, so Milly told me," was the reply. "Took an early train, she did."

*   *   *

Later that day, Bartlett received a letter at the ministry.

> "Paris, 11 December
> Charles
> I suppose you can explain some day why you missed my ship.
> Young Halliday didn't, though. Turned up at five am, wearing a major's uniform, waving his commission, asking for me. Nobody had followed him that we could see, but we made him sit on the quay until 1 minute before 7. Then he ran up the gangplank and we were off. Still no sign of the law.
> A brave lad. I told him that we'd hand him over to the police instantly if they came looking for him. Now he's on his way to Boston. He said to thank you. (For what, pray?)
> No need for you to come to Paris just now. If it's war, I go back to take command of my ironclad when it's launched. If it's not, I may find another war for us.
> R. Jones
> Lt. Cmdr. USN"

Stunned, Bartlett read it again. That little bastard! he thought. The tricky little bastard. He did it by himself, and wearing one of my uniforms. Lucky for him I didn't get there. I'd have – Lucky? Was it luck, by God? Could Katherine –

Freeman Morse came over and leaned on his desk. "There are two detectives here waiting to speak to you, Charles," he said in a low voice. "The Minister asked me to look after them until you arrived and to find out what they want, but they're not saying anything."

"Good Lord, what next?" Bartlett held his head in his hands.

"Well, remember that you're accredited to this ministry and therefore may have immunity. Also, Adams would remind you that he will tolerate nothing that makes our relations with England even worse than they are. A familiar topic, is it?"

"Yes, indeed."

"So you're to tell these two whatever they need to know." He paused. "That's the official line, anyway."

"And your line?"

"Don't tell them any more than you want to."

Both detectives, Harry and Dark Hair, were young, well dressed and well spoken. They were investigating certain matters, they said as they sat in front of his desk, that may have involved persons known to Bartlett, and they would welcome any information he could give them. Was it true, for example, that Bartlett had recently attended an official test firing at the Woolwich Arsenal? And, if so, was he accompanied by Commander Robert Jones of the Federal navy?

"Yes to both," was his reply.

"Major, several rounds of an experimental cannon shell were taken from the Woolwich storehouse that day. And Commander Jones arrived at the Royal Artillery reception long after the other guests. Any connection between the two?"

"None."

"Or that Commander Jones sailed the next morning on a ship that was waiting for him?" This was the dark-haired one, so far nameless.

"I know nothing of his movements since that reception," Bartlett snapped, his anger showing.

This was only the beginning. Over the next hour, they grilled Bartlett hard. First, about Owen Halliday, his landlady's brother, a Republican terrorist with an outstanding arrest warrant for conspiracy to murder, who lodges with his sister in Rochester Place.

"I know Owen, yes. We've shared a house for several months."

"And what is his occupation?"

"He's a journalist. For a newspaper in Boston, United States. *The Pilot.*"

"An Irish paper?"

"I believe so. He reports on Irish affairs in Britain."

"So he does. And travels a great deal? Ireland and Liverpool, mostly?"

"I think that's right. He says there's a large Irish population in Liverpool." Bartlett let them see that he was bored with this line of questioning.

"Does he ever carry small, heavy cases in or out of your house?"

"Not that I've seen."

Until then, Dark Hair had asked all the questions, while Harry fixed Bartlett with what he thought was a dark, threatening stare. Now he said, with heavy sarcasm, "So Mr. Halliday lives a very quiet life, a man we suspect and the Dublin police are certain is an American Fenian, a sworn enemy of the Crown. And, since two small boys were blasted to bits on a bridge, a murderer."

"Rubbish."

And so on for another few minutes, until Bartlett said, "That's all I have to say, gentlemen, on the subject of Owen Halliday. You're repeating yourselves. Are we finished?"

"Not yet, sir." They moved on to the Mersey, where a Confederate cargo vessel had been blown up and the next day two Americans, their descriptions fitting Bartlett and Jones, had left Liverpool on an early train for London.

Bartlett denied everything, with a calm and persuasiveness that impressed him. At length the two men left. Going out the door, just before Flanagan slammed it shut, Harry said, "Thanks for your time, Major, if not for your frankness. We'll be back soon."

"Good day, gentlemen," Bartlett said. Then he leaned back and thought hard. What were Harry and Dark Hair playing at? Why tell him they were suspicious of Jones and himself? Obviously, to persuade him that it was too dangerous to operate against the Confederacy in England. Even to persuade them to leave England. His instinct recoiled from this line of thought. But, then... And Owen? Could he be a murderer?

Flanagan coughed and cleared his throat noisily. "The old man wants to see you in his office, sir. Now."

Adams managed to look outraged and satisfied at the same time. The two detectives had brought a letter from the Commissioner at Scotland Yard that explained why they wanted to question Bartlett. It lay open on his desk. "Irish terrorists I knew about," he exclaimed. "But theft of naval ordnance? Sabotage of Confederate shipping? What's this all about, Major?"

"I've explained to you about Owen Halliday, sir, and I can swear I will have no more to do with him. As to the other matters, there is some sort of mistake. I – "

"Let us hope so," Adams warned. "Now if they file charges against you, you may have immunity, but I must have the power to send you back. Therefore, I'll ask Secretary Seward to get General Stoddard to authorize me to do just that, at my sole discretion. I hope it will not be necessary, but for the time being you are on formal notice."

"All right, sir. Is there anything else?"

"No."

*   *   *

Arthur Pettigrew was more forthcoming this time, and he was less optimistic. "There are two issues, as I see it, Major," he said from behind his littered desk. "First: Can you be prosecuted for harboring a man you knew to be a criminal? Second: if Lady Carra is prosecuted for that offence, can you be compelled to testify against her?"

"That sounds right."

"As to the first, we have discovered an alarming pattern in the jurisprudence." He placed his hand on a stack of books for effect. "This is that the judges tend to respond to the political pressures of the day, and those pressures appear to be strongest when a threat to the Crown is involved. The Republican Brotherhood is plainly a threat to the Crown, in Ireland at least."

"So - "

"So, I calculate that there is an even chance that you will not be protected by diplomatic immunity if you are prosecuted."

"My God."

"As to the second issue, the chances are higher – substantially higher – that you will have to testify. That is because denying you immunity does not of itself place you, personally, at risk."

"Hah! 'Of itself.' And it sure as hell places Lady Carra at risk. But – " Bartlett held up his hand – "I take your point, Counselor. Tell me, if they prosecute Lady Carra and she's found guilty, what sort of sentence would you expect?"

"Anything up to twenty years in prison, because Halliday is a Fenian, a threat to the Crown, not some common thief. But she has a clean record, I assume, so perhaps only ten years."

Bartlett rose to go. "Thank you, Mr. Pettigrew. May I consult you again if necessary?"

"Of course. How else can I pay my bills?"

*   *   *

"Milady's away until after Christmas, sir," Milly told Bartlett. "With Lord Carra's cousins in Yorkshire. I've just sent her a trunk with her clothes, like she wrote and asked me to do."

"Christmas?" Bartlett repeated dumbly.

"Yes, sir." She giggled and covered her mouth with her hand. "She says Lord Carra has at last found birds that are slow enough for him to hit, and he means to stay there until he's killed them all."

Chapter 19

Christmas? Christmas was ten days away. Should he write to her? No – what could he say, ask? Perhaps she would write to him.

A long, painful week later, she did:

> "My dear Charles
>
> You will have guessed by now what I did. I woke Owen and told him that your ship, his last chance to escape, was sailing at dawn and that Commander Jones might let him on board.
>
> It came to me that night that what you had said about a war – that now you have the proof you needed it will begin in three weeks – meant that poor Owen would be trapped here for years. His only chance was on one of your ships, and if there's a war there won't be any ships, will there? And so he'll be called a traitor and hunted down and even hanged.
>
> Can you ever forgive me? I knew I was putting your career at risk, and I knew you would be furious, but against that was Owen's whole future, and perhaps his life.
>
> Please try very hard to forgive me.
> Affectionately
> Katherine
> PS. I hate to ask you, but please could you telegraph me at Normanby House, near Salton, Yorkshire and say if Owen escaped? Thank you, thank you. K."

That's too much to ask of me, he thought angrily, too damn much. Although he could sympathize with her motives, he couldn't help but feel like he'd been used by her. He was totally enamored with the woman, yet he had no idea how she felt about him. Kissing her might have been one of the best things that had ever happened to him, but only if the feeling was mutual. What made matters infinitely worse was his hazy memory of all that had happened. Why couldn't he remember more?

He thought of cabling her that he didn't know but discarded that as unworthy. In the end, grudgingly, he wired:

> "JOURNALIST ALL RIGHT STOP
> CHARLES"

If he ever spoke to her again, he'd say that he didn't mention Owen or brother or Boston in case the police were reading his cables. Meanwhile, let her suffer, let her stew in poisonous uncertainty, like him. What's more, let her suspect that he was doing this to her deliberately.

*   *   *

Christmas Day in Washington was rainy and mild. The elusive Vice President was at home in Maine, but the rest of the Cabinet, plus General Winfield Scott, had been summoned to a formal meeting at the White House after their church services. The meeting would decide on the United States response to the ultimatum from England.

Before then, though, the President met with Secretary Seward, Miles Stoddard for the Army and Henry Wise for the Navy. Their purpose was to decide, on all the evidence, if the Royal Navy did or did not possess an armor-piercing naval shell the equal of the North's new Taurus shell. Their decision would be crucial to the President's recommendation that morning to his Cabinet and then to the nation's response to the ultimatum.

Wise summarized all the earlier intelligence reports stating that the English had not discovered how to cast their shell so that it did not break up in the bore. "You and we are familiar with these reports, Mr. President," he said, "but a few days ago we got the final, irrefutable proof." Three of the Palliser shells shipped from England, he said, had been test fired at the West Point Foundry proving grounds, and two of them fragmented in the bore. Palliser was no closer to cracking his problem. "The English shell simply does not work," he finished. "And that's a fact."

"Who, ah, sent you the projectiles?" Lincoln asked in his high, reedy voice.

"Commander Jones, our attaché in Paris, and Major Bartlett, our attaché in London."

"Bartlett? Sounds familiar. Something to do with Bull Run, was it?" Lincoln's curiosity about the men who served him was a constant nuisance to his staff.

"That's right, sir," replied Stoddard. "Went the wrong way with the wrong orders, and so forth. But a good officer."

"Ah, yes, I remember. And Jones?"

Wise sketched Jones's background and career. "Also a good officer, sir."

"H'mm. Mexican, Russian. Speaks French too, I suppose?"

"Indeed, sir," said Wise, anxious to get on with it. "So you see that our *Monitors* will have nothing to fear from the Royal Navy."

"You are all agreed on that?" Seward and Stoddard nodded firmly. "And the *Monitors*. What news of them?" The President looked sharply at Wise.

"The first ship has passed her sea trials in fine shape, sir. Mounting her guns improved her stability, and the few leaks have been fixed by redesigning the fittings."

"Has Captain Ericsson solved his plumbing problem?"

"Ah, I believe not, sir."

A long silence. Then the President asked slowly, "Do any of you believe that there is more than a tiny chance that we will *not* destroy the Royal Navy when the time comes?"

"No, sir," they replied.

"Well, then, thank you General Stoddard, Commander Wise. You have been most helpful," Lincoln smiled as he stood up. "Governor, will you have a cup of coffee with me before the Cabinet?"

As the military men left the room, they overheard Lincoln say, half in jest, "When all this is over, Seward, I'll want you to explain how the fate of our country came to rest in the hands of one officer who came up short at Bull Run, another officer who's half Russian and half Mexican, and an engineer Swede who can't even fix a toilet."

*   *   *

Bartlett passed a gloomy Christmas season, lightened only by a happy Christmas Eve dinner with Freeman Morse and his young family. The oldest son, nine years old and a gifted mimic, did a shockingly accurate imitation of Charles Francis Adams in full, angry flow.

"The minister caught young Frederick here picking flowers in the legation garden last summer," Morse explained, "and let him have both sides of his tongue. Fred's been refining his act ever since, but he hasn't quite caught the Boston accent."

"Or the sneer," said Bartlett. "But he will in time, I have no doubt."

"Time?" asked Mrs. Morse, a pale woman with worried eyes. "What time, Major? We won't be here another month, will we?"

"Probably not," Bartlett agreed.

*   *   *

The sun emerged one morning as Bartlett reached the street outside his door. Only to leap back on to his porch as a black hansom swept past him to deposit Katherine Carra on her doorstep, followed by half a dozen cases and Lord Carra.

"Morning, Major," the little peer called. "We're just back from the north."

"Good morning, sir. Madam."

Katherine turned an anxious face to him. He bowed, she nodded and rang the bell for Milly. Without thinking, Bartlett walked across to her and in a low voice asked for a word with her.

"Now?" she asked, a wary look in her eyes.

"Now - please."

"I can't, not now – oh, very well." She looked at Carra, then at Milly. "Milly, please show the driver where to put my cases. I'll be back in a short while." Then to Bartlett, "Shall we walk to the gardens? It's not too cold."

Bartlett took her arm, nodded again to Carra, who stood open-mouthed, and led Katherine down the street. "You're very early," he said.

"Yes, we spent last night in St. Albans with friends. Did you get my letter?" she asked gently.

"Of course. And my telegram?"

"Yes. Did it mean that…"

"Owen's safe in New York or Boston by now."

"Thank God."

"Thank yourself, you mean. You saved him. If you hadn't kept me away from that ship, he'd still be here." He took a deep breath. "Of course, the fact that you might easily have destroyed my career didn't matter to you at all. Nor that you risked causing a serious breakdown in my country's relationship with England." He didn't try to mask his bitterness. "None of that mattered to you. Only Owen's safety."

She was fighting back tears. "You're unfair. It *did* matter to me. But not as much as Owen's safety, or his life." She stopped to wipe her eyes. "I wrote you that I was sorry – am sorry. Don't you believe me?"

"I suppose I do. But still – " They had reached the gate to the little gardens. He put his hand on Katherine's waist and steered her through the gate and around a vast puddle. Only patches were left of the indomitable English grass, still green when by all rights it should be brown, scattered among the few acres of grey mud. A gust blew a sodden leaf into Bartlett's face and he wiped it off.

"Look," he said, "I can understand why you did what you did. Understand, I say, not forgive. It's hard to forgive someone who would happily have me sent home in disgrace. Not now. Maybe some day. I'll try." He stopped and turned to face her. "Katherine," he said, "did you mean anything you said that last night? "

"Must we talk of it?" Faintly. "Now?"

"We must, I'm afraid, and now. We can't pretend it didn't happen."

"Why not? "

"Because there's something I have to know."

Her tone hardened. "Oh, dear, the ever-curious male. And what is it that you have to know?"

"When did you decide to wake Owen?" He looked stricken.

She had been dreading this question for weeks. Her anger at its implications had partly dissipated and she had prepared different answers. She would leave it to her mood at the time to choose one. Her mood was now resentful, but sad as well, so she temporized. "What? Oh, I can't remember. Is it important?"

"To me it is. You must see that. Stop teasing and tell me. Please."

She walked on a few yards and then turned to him, eyes glittering. "I know why you're asking, Charles, and I'm angry that you need to ask. You're insulting me, and I won't have it."

"You're angry?" He was stunned. "You betrayed me, you might have done enormous damage to my country and now *you're* angry? It's beyond belief!"

"Is it, indeed? That is too bad. But what I did is in the past. It can't be helped. What you're doing now, by asking me, is about right now!" She began to weep. "Whatever my answer is, you're spoiling the present. And you're destroying our..."

He put his hands on her shoulders. He searched her face and saw her pain in her eyes. "Destroying our what?"

"Our... my hopes for... Nothing." She glared at him through her tears. "Katherine!"

"You have asked me an insulting question, sir. Now take me home, please."

"Katherine, please! I..."

"Home."

At her door, he tried once more. "Katherine, I know I sounded insulting and I beg you to forgive me. I won't trouble you again. Good night." He waited a moment, then he bowed and turned away. That had definitely not gone as planned. He had hoped to have a grown-up conversation about what had happened, but he had barely managed to get any words out before she had begun her offensive. What was more, he still had no idea how four glasses of brandy could have caused such memory loss. After years in the army, he was no stranger to hard liquor.

Chapter 20

The footman showed Morny straight through the waiting rooms to the Emperor's office. He stopped in the doorway to examine the scene.

Napoleon sat hunched at a broad desk strewn with papers. Across from him sat his Empress, holding in one hand a bundle of papers and in the other a lock of hair that she pulled abstractedly. Both were reading aloud from their papers; neither was paying attention to the other. Behind Napoleon a wide map of Mexico was tacked to a curtain, beside it a smaller map of Veracruz and its environs. The maps were studded with colored drawing pins taken from the pile at the Emperor's right hand.

May God help France, Morny thought, I'm looking at her Supreme War Council. "Good evening," he announced himself. "Louis. My dear Eugenie."

"Come in, come in, Auguste," Napoleon cried, "sit down here. No, there. Anywhere. We're reading the first reports from Veracruz. They're from Admiral Jurien and Saligny, our ambassador out there." He waved Morny to a seat and turned back to the paper in his hand. "Militarily, it goes well. The Spanish arrived first, before New Year, then the English – only seven hundred men – then our forces, then the rest of the Spaniards. About nine thousand men in all, a third of them ours. That should take care of the Mexicans, eh, eh?" He looked up at Eugenie.

"This is from Jurien, Auguste," he went on. "He says the risk of yellow fever is so high that the troops can not remain in the *tierra caliente*, they call it, the hot lands along the coast. They'll move up to higher ground at – " he scooped up some pins and moved eagerly to the map of Veracruz – "here, here and - here." A blue pin pierced each village. "It's cooler up there, you see, safe from the fever." He stood back to admire his work.

"A neat pattern in blue, but surely we need men in Veracruz itself?" Morny, a former soldier, was skeptical.

"No. There has been no fighting. The garrison vanished when they saw our ships." A contemptuous snort. "As we expected. So we hold the custom house and are collecting the import duties."

Eugenie plowed on. " - five Commissioners. Admiral Jurien and Saligny for France, Wyke and Dunlop for England, General Prim for Spain. They take all the major decisions. And," she finished, "They all plainly despise each other."

They looked at each other. Morny spoke first. "A divided command never succeeds, Louis. You must make Jurien understand that Saligny speaks for you in all but strictly military matters. This is, after all, a political venture."

"You're quite right. I shall do so tonight."

They returned to their papers. At length, "Listen to this!" Eugenie exclaimed, blue eyes glittering. "The commissioners have drafted a grand proclamation to the Mexican people. In it, they deny any hidden plan of conquest or intervention. Instead, they declare they have come, and I quote, 'to preside at the grand spectacle of your regeneration.'"

"What utter rubbish!" Napoleon cried. He stroked his pointed beard in agitation. For the last decade he had dreamed of a Latin American Empire stretching from Mexico down through Central America and out to Cuba and the other principal Caribbean islands. An empire controlled by France, by a Napoleon, by the Nephew of the Uncle. Now at last he had what he needed - the political opportunity, the *casus belli* and in Maximilian the princely instrument - an ideal combination for action. Which looked on the verge of political disaster because of the pusillanimous fools he had placed in command of the expedition.

"Eugenie," asked Morny, "has Saligny presented our formal demands on the Mexican government? For the money?"

"No."

"Good. That means that there may still be time, Louis, to rescue the position. Time to get new instructions to Saligny to demand full payment of all our claims, and then to enforce our claims with troops if necessary."

"Auguste is right, Louis," Eugenie urged. "You must – "

Morny faced his half brother. "Send your instructions by the hand of someone senior to Saligny. Send them by his superior. Send Thouvenel." He paused. "It is that important, Louis."

Napoleon reacted badly to this kind of pressure. "No, I can't spare the Foreign Minister just now. I need him to deal with the Austrians."

Then his brain cleared. Morny was right: it *was* that important. (Damn him, he was always right.) The success of the Mexican venture might depend on his choice. And not only the venture – the Mexican Empire. And possibly even the future of the French Empire. The Empire he so badly wanted to hand on to his son.

"There is only one possible candidate, Auguste," Napoleon forced a smile, "and that is you."

"I? What nonsense! I couldn't possibly go. I – "

"Have too many commitments? What nonsense, to quote you. The legislature doesn't sit again for months. Your businesses run themselves. Your mistress is in Naples for the winter." Napoleon laughed aloud. "You're a free man, by God! I wish I could – "

Morny let his silence stretch out for a minute or two. "Very well. Very well. Again, France calls; again, I respond. I will leave for Veracruz in seven days, Louis, if you're certain you want me." Napoleon nodded once. "And if you can deliver my instructions to me tomorrow morning." Another nod. "And if you, my dear Empress, will commend my mission."

"Of course," she said.

"Then I cannot fail, can I?"

After he left, Emperor and Empress eyed each other. "I have complete confidence in him, my dear," he said defensively. "He's the one man in France who *always* does what he says he will do."

"No doubt," she replied. "He never fails. What concerns me is that he often does what he has not said he will not do."

*   *   *

In the morning, the ministry staff - Morse, Flanagan and the three secretaries - were all gathered around a table covered with newspapers. The minister himself could be seen through his open door squinting at *The Times*.

"What's happened?" Bartlett asked Flanagan. "Is it war?"

With a look of supreme disgust, Flanagan handed him two of the papers.

Every headline screamed that the United States had accepted the ultimatum from Her Majesty's government. In their editors' opinions, this was either a craven surrender or a statesmanlike recognition of the principles of international law. Take your pick. In any case, it was a matter of righteous rejoicing for the English people and of eternal shame for the blustering Yankees.

"Oh, no," Bartlett said. "Those miserable – "

Adams waved Bartlett in, beaming with delight. He was already contemplating a long and peaceful tenure in London, one that should be more productive than his grandfather's had been. "My copy of Seward's reply to the English cabinet arrived last night." He shook his grey head admiringly. "Masterly stuff." He smiled again. "*Without apologizing,* he offers to turn those rebel commissioners over to the British. He finishes by saying how pleased he is that England is at last accepting the same principles of international law that we advanced decades ago. Some nerve, eh?" He came close to an outright laugh. "Pure claptrap, of course, but masterly."

"Yes, sir."

"So there'll be no war, thank the Lord. I'm told the President listened to all the arguments, said, 'Gentlemen, we must be content with one war at a time,' and that was the end of it."

Bartlett turned to leave in black disgust. "By the way, Major," Adams said, "I'm summoned to Lord Russell this morning, so we'll postpone your briefing until next week." The smile vanished. "Thereafter, we'll resume our old schedule of briefings on Monday and Friday."

*   *   *

The New Year was not a good year for Bartlett. He sipped another brandy, slumped back on his sofa and contemplated his little world as it crashed around him.

Put not your faith in Presidents, he thought. There would be no war. So there was no need for Owen to escape so soon; no need for Katherine to betray him, Bartlett; and no need to suspect her, insult her and drive her away, probably for all time. It had all been a bitter, ironic waste.

His work bored him, there was no prospect of action like the *Bermuda* sinking and there was little chance of having a real war even to report on until spring arrived in the Border States. What was worse, Adams distrusted him and showed signs of making his job difficult or sending him back.

The police would pursue him for aiding Owen Halliday, the alleged murderer. Of that he was certain. At the very least – and he had to face it – he would be compelled to testify against Katherine, when his evidence would be fatal to her case. His choice would be to lie on oath or to condemn her to prison, and he was constitutionally incapable of lying on oath.

He had helped to sink the *Bermuda* and to steal from the Woolwich Arsenal. Those actions would, sooner or later, come back to put him in the dock. The police seemed destined to play a large part in his life, to Adams's fury and his own terror.

And again there was Katherine. Or, there had been Katherine. He'd insulted her, that much was clear, and now she hated him. He still adored her, but he was completely unclear as to her feelings and the black shadow of suspicion hung over his love. And it would stay there, he feared, until he knew the truth, if he ever knew it.

That was enough. He would ask Stoddard to transfer him back, to a regular line regiment if possible, but to somewhere, anywhere that was not England.

*   *   *

As Bartlett thought Jones to be in France, he was somewhat surprised, on his return from the Ministry one day, to find him awaiting him in his rooms.

"You do well here for yourself, Charles." he observed. "And the luscious Lady Carra lives next door, does she? You're doubly lucky."

"Do you know her?" Bartlett tried to keep the surprise from his voice as he poured the whisky. He resented his guest's ability to catch him off guard each time they met.

"No, alas, but young Flanagan at the ministry described her to me. The poor lad's in love, I fear." He raised his glass in silent toast.

"When did you return to London and where are you staying this time?" Bartlett asked.

"With a friend near Regent's Park, in great comfort. No ship's bunk for me this time. Arrived last night, sent you that note and here I am, at your service."

They talked for a while about Lincoln's acceptance of the English ultimatum and what a waste it was of America's best opportunity to destroy the Royal Navy. And the waste of their own work and talents, Bartlett said.

"Those are politicians for you," said Jones, "gutless, every one of 'em, even Lincoln. I should know; I spent twelve years fighting them before the war."

And more in that vein. Then he clapped Bartlett on the back and said, "Enough of that. It's all in the past. I've come to tell you about your future - in Mexico!"

From Le Havre, he said, he had gone to Paris under orders from Stoddard. "Washington knew that the French and the English were preparing to attack Mexico, so he told me to get close to Morny again. I saw him once, but he went down to his country place for the month and couldn't see me again until ten days ago. By then the French force had sailed. He was quite pleased – the so-called informal channel to Stoddard that I'd set up for him was working well. Then he surprised me. He expected to go to Mexico soon and he invited me to go with him, as a 'neutral observer.'"

Bartlett reflected. "Which means – "

"Which means that he wants me to report to Stoddard by cable from Mexico that the French intentions are honorable. That they intend only to flirt with the *señorita*, not to rape her. This is very important to him. He doesn't want Lincoln to send a couple of divisions to Veracruz to chase him back home." Jones rolled his Rs with relish. "I told him no, because I meant to get back to Washington as soon as I could to take up my new command."

"Ah, yes, the long-overdue sea command."

"Then I reconsidered," said Jones. "I decided to wait a few days to see if there would be war with England. If there was, I'd head for home to take up my command. If there's no war, I'd come here to tie up a few things and find you." An evil Slavic laugh.

"Me? Why?" Bartlett frowned. Then, "Oh, no!"

"Yes, indeed. Mexico calls, my son. It's the land of opportunity for any army officer who's under a cloud. Or many clouds. Like you."

"Ridiculous."

"Not at all. Now look. Morny called me in three days ago and said the Emperor had just appointed him Lord High Admiral or something of the French forces in Mexico. We're sailing from Le Havre on Tuesday. That gives you plenty of time to finish up here and cross with me on Monday."

It was Bartlett's turn to reconsider. He did want to leave England, but not permanently. Katherine still meant too much to him. Besides, to ask Stoddard for a transfer home so soon would naturally annoy him, even though Bartlett had accomplished what he had asked. The chances that he could find a post in a regular regiment were slim – the stain of Bull Run was still on him – and the chances that he would end up training shit-kickers in Kentucky were high.

He could play along with Jones as far as Le Havre. If he didn't like the look of this Morny fellow, he could bow out and go back to London. Jones wouldn't stop him.

"You know, Robert, I just might go with you," he allowed. "I could consider..."

"*Consider*, nonsense!" Jones punched his arm. "You're dying to go, admit it. You've nothing to do here until the war starts up again in the spring." The smile became a crude leer. "Except toadying to Adams and lusting after your landlady."

I'll ignore that, Bartlett thought. "I might consider Mexico," he repeated, "but I'd need new orders. To show Adams."

"When you have the broad array of talents that I have," Jones declared, "a sensible superior will give you a number of supplementary orders and leave you to choose the ones you need. Stoddard is nothing if not sensible. So - " he leaned far back in his seat, "he cut an order that authorizes me to take one Major Charles Bartlett to Mexico with me as my deputy. At my discretion, of course."

"I don't believe it."

"Believe it, *amigo*, believe it."

After Jones left, Bartlett told himself: Face the facts. You're no closer to redeeming yourself from Bull Run than when you arrived. And Jones could be right about Mexico. After all, the presence of three European armies over there, no matter how small, must constitute some sort of threat to the North, and maybe he and Jones could put a spoke in their wheel. At worst it was more promising professionally than Kentucky, that was plain enough. Besides, the Europeans will collect their Mexican debts quickly. I expect I'll be back here in three or four months.

He made up his mind. Jones had almost persuaded him to go with him, and this analysis decided him. He *would* go to Mexico. He could do some real damage there, he hoped. He would inform Adams tomorrow, as soon as Jones gave him his new orders.

But first he had to try to square himself with Katherine.

Bartlett fingered the crisp notes in his pocket as he stood on the Carra doorstep. He had always paid his rent in pound coins, one for each week, but paying with notes would make this fifteen-week prepayment more formal, somehow. He smiled at Milly when she opened the door and strode into the drawing room.

"Ah, Major!" called Lord Carra from his lair by the fire. "Good to see you. Will you have a glass of wine?"

"Thank you, sir, but I can only stay a minute."

"Haven't seen you for some time. That was quite a turn-up in the Mersey the other day," Carra persisted, "that Southern ship sinking at her mooring. Nothing to do with you, I suppose? Ha!"

"I'm afraid not," Bartlett said, "but I wish I could claim the credit." He turned to Katherine, whose eyes were wary. "I've come to pay my rent for the next fifteen weeks, Lady Carra. I'll be gone much of the time and I – "

"Fifteen weeks?" Carra interrupted. "Where are you off to, then?" He came over to them.

"Mexico, sir. I – "

"Mexico, eh? A bit late, aren't you? Our men have already landed there. And the fearless French." He took the three notes from Bartlett's fingers and pocketed them.

"Yes. My invitation was slow to arrive." Bartlett looked for an escape and behind Carra's back pointed to the front door and mouthed the word, "Walk".

She shook her head scornfully. He thought for an instant. "Ah, Lady Carra, as you once asked me, I do have a few ideas for alterations to my rooms. Would this be a convenient time to discuss them?"

"That's a good idea, my dear," said Carra, "from the horse's mouth, so to speak. Why not go along with the Major?"

"It seems I must. I'll get my hat and coat, though. It's cold outside. You'll excuse us, Uncle?"

It was cold and windy. Without speaking they again walked in the direction of Sackville Square.

"Look, Katherine," he began.

"So you're leaving again, and so soon?" she said. "Hoping to start another war, I presume? You Yankees are relentless, I'll give you that."

The icy air had flushed her cheeks and turned her matchless eyes more green than ever, their unique, astonishing green. "No," he said, "I've given up that line of work. It turned out that I wasn't much good at it."

"The English can sleep easy in their beds, then."

"Oh, yes, for some time. Meanwhile, I try to be your ideal tenant; I pay in advance and stay away."

"Yes," she said, "ideal. At least Lord Carra thinks you are."

They walked on. The wind rose and she moved closer to him. They walked farther and he said, "Before I leave, I want to apologize - for what I said the other night."

"Please, Charles, let's not – "

"No, you *must* hear me. You apologized for what you did, and I accept it. I accept that your reasons were strong ones, even good ones. As to my other question – "

"For heaven's sake, Charles,..."

"That was a matter of vanity, painful male vanity, if you will. I'll have forgotten all about it when I return." He would never forget it, and he knew it.

"Return? Oh, yes, Mexico. I must wish you Godspeed." She showed him that she was making an effort to be pleasant. "It sounds most exciting. What will you do there?"

He tried for a light-hearted tone. "Besides escape the English winter? Why, I'll be engaged in diplomacy of extreme delicacy. And at a very high level."

"I never doubted your delicacy, or your importance. When will you leave?"

"On Monday. I go first to France to meet Robert Jones. "

"Not him, again? He is a guarantee of trouble, from what you've told me."

"Yes, it does seem to follow him about." He laughed. "But not this trip. This will all be innocently peaceful."

"And frantically diplomatic, of course." She could almost smile.

There seemed to be no more to say. They looked sadly at each other and walked back to her house. Despite herself, she began to weep softly.

He bowed and started down her steps. Through her tears she watched him. She started to say something, but caught herself before any sound escaped her lips.

Chapter 21

Two days later Morny led a group of chilled and befurred men along the quay at Le Havre. "There she is, my friends," he smiled, pointing to a topsail schooner moored half a mile out in the harbour. A brilliant white hull with a gold stripe along her side, the glint of brass everywhere on her deck, a thoroughbred beauty. "My *Isabella*. Thirty five meters long, two hundred horsepower, single screw." A massive shrug. "I quote her master; these details mean nothing to me. I only know that she is mine, and that she will give me a fast passage to Veracruz."

One of his companions lowered his scarf long enough to ask, "Russian built, did you say?"

"In Saint Petersburg, yes. A Christmas present from Sophie, my wife. Lovely, don't you agree?" A nod from the other man. "And built entirely of various woods from her family's estates up there. But designed by a Frenchman. Russians are proficient with an axe in their hand, but not so skilled with a drawing pen." He laughed. "And, trust a Frenchman, the first flush toilets on any private vessel at sea."

The men were a selection of Morny's political and business associates. The politicians would remain on *Isabella* only until Brest, where they would be dropped off to make their way back to Paris and their intrigues. The businessmen would be carried as far as La Coruna or Vigo in the west of Spain. Morny told them all to be ready to sail at three o'clock that afternoon and hurried to his suite to greet the American, Commander Jones.

Who waited inside with another officer, a tall dark-haired man with a diffident manner and the uniform of the Union Army, whom Jones presented as his colleague, Major Bartlett. "Washington knows how important my work with you may prove to be, Count," said Jones, "so they took it upon themselves to order Major Bartlett to go with us. But only with your approval, of course."

Morny saw that to refuse Bartlett would cripple his own credibility in Washington, and he welcomed him warmly. "*Isabella* can accommodate twelve of us in some comfort," he said, "but I trust you will not object to sharing a cabin for two or three nights? Good. I must excuse myself now. Shall we meet downstairs after lunch, then? At – " he consulted a thin gold watch – "two o'clock."

The cold front had passed through, leaving behind it a fresh northerly breeze on *Isabella's* beam as she drove southwest towards the tip of Brittany at a steady twelve knots. A sudden gust staggered her, green water tore along her lee rail. The crew eased the sheets, the quartermaster luffed up a point or two and then resumed his course. The master, Captain Carbonnel, studied her sails from his position near the mainmast. He decided not to shorten sail, at least not for another hour until sunset. This was *Isabella*'s first real test, her first cruise in any sort of wind, so he was uneasy, but she had sailed well for twenty four hours and had shown no sign of excessive strain in her rigging.

Morny and his political friends occupied the dining saloon, lounging around the long oak table, smoking their cigars relentlessly. Little had been seen of them. The businessmen pondered their papers in their own cabins.

In theirs, Jones was giving Bartlett his first Spanish lesson. "You *must* learn it, Charles," he had insisted before they left London. "We'll have two weeks at sea, plenty of time. I'll teach you myself."

At heart, Bartlett didn't object. He had some facility for languages, he liked to think; he'd read Latin and French at school, he'd even taught a form of Greek at West Point for two years. To be taught by Jones placed him in an inferior position, especially when Jones turned out to be an excellent instructor, but that was better than working in Mexico without a word of Spanish.

"What do you suppose Morny and his political pals talk about all day?" he asked.

"Riot and revolution, I reckon," Jones said. "You know that Morny organized the *coup* that eventually put Napoleon on his throne? He was Minister of the Interior. One night after the opera he met with Napoleon and the others and they decided the time was right. Then he gambled at his club until dawn, went home, put on his uniform and came out on the streets to lead his police force as they shot down the opposition." He shook his head in admiration. "Quite a man."

"Quite a man." Bartlett returned to his vocabularies.

Isabella anchored in Brest just long enough to deposit the two politicians on shore, she turned south into the Bay of Biscay and ran with the northeast trade winds toward Spain, all sails spread and full. The sun came out, the thermometer rose and the passengers began to risk the sloping deck from time to time. But mostly the group – two mining engineers, two bankers, one geologist, one land speculator *cum* property developer – gathered with Morny in the dining saloon, where they pored over maps and geological reports.

Morny explained to Jones that his spectacularly successful mining investments had attracted to him promoters of mining ventures around the world. "Copper, diamonds, zinc, cobalt – whatever it is, or may be, they come to me. And I listen to them all, fools, rogues, charlatans, even bankers. Why? Because something in my heart insists that somewhere out there is my next big strike. It is the curse of the mining investor, and it will not let me go."

That afternoon Bartlett took a turn on deck with his first regular verbs. "I *amo*, thou *amas*, he *ama*, we *amamos*, you/they *aman*," he said dully. "That's easy enough, like Latin, but I'll have to stick to the present tense at first."

Morny and two of his guests walked toward him, heads bent, leaning left to keep their balance. Morny smiled and nodded at Bartlett, then went on with what he was saying. "No, no, gentlemen. You will not persuade me that there is any ore in that formation. It needs a banker to find any ore there."

"But, Count – "

"You need an expert, not an amateur like me." They passed out of earshot.

His daily submission to Jones's tutelage, combined with Morny's treatment of Jones as the senior of his two American guests, was resented by Bartlett and he tried to hit back.

"Tell me again, will you," he said at dinner in their cabin, "just why we're on this tropical cruise. What with all the excitement of meeting the great Morny and his Lucullan concept of ocean transport, I confess I've lost the plot." He held the second bottle of burgundy up to the lamp to confirm that it was indeed empty. "We're going to save Mexico, is that it? Who from?"

"I've explained it to you often enough."

"Explain to me why I'm missing all that excitement in London – my bi-weekly briefings with Adams, arguing strategy with that pompous son of his, the – "

"You could be back home, you know. Think about that."

"I do. I'd probably have a battalion by now. Maybe a battalion of those new Parrott rifles. Twenty five pounders."

"Hah. You'd have a battalion of Kentucky farmers to train, who don't know their firing pins from their foreskins. And you'd train them through the cold and the snow and the mud, all winter long." He waved a hand at the birch-panelled walls. "You wouldn't want to trade all this for a winter in Kentucky."

Both were silent for a time, then Jones went on. "Besides, when you think about it, we *will* be where the action is."

"How is that?"

"There won't be any fighting, real fighting, at home until the spring. We're not ready, the rebels aren't ready. And for me, my ship's still not ready."

"So meanwhile you take a cruise in southern waters, like Morny's poodle?"

Jones snorted. "Some cruise. This mission is important, Charles. If the French, which in practice means Morny, show any sign of grabbing a piece of Mexico, or setting up some sort of puppet government there, we have to get word to Stoddard immediately. The same goes for the English, although Washington thinks they're a much smaller risk." He brought a hairy fist down on the table slowly. "We must not let any European power get a foothold in Mexico."

"That makes no sense, Robert. You say that Morny takes us along so we can warn Stoddard and ruin his own plans?" Bartlett's confidence in Jones's grasp of their situation was fast eroding.

"We're along to keep Washington persuaded that Morny's only objective in Mexico is to collect the money owed to France. But I'm sure that he means to trick us, so we'll need to be alert and see it at once when he does, ah, widen his objectives." He grinned hugely. "And once we've foiled his evil plans, I'll go back and claim my new ship."

"I see." Bartlett folded his napkin and began a tour of the cabin, head bent, an uncharacteristic cigar in his hand. This was their third night at sea and, despite the opulence of the vessel and their accommodations, he felt cramped. He had the inexplicable sense that time was running out. But that was silly. Time for what? There was no schedule to meet, no deadline. Maybe it was only the recurrence of that feeling he'd often had the year before, the feeling that someone else – in this case, Morny – was pulling his strings, deciding what he would do next. That he was not in control of his career, or of his life. Guardedly, he said something of the sort to Jones, who admitted that at times he also felt a bit like a puppet.

"I can understand why you feel it more, with your record," Jones joked harshly. But after a moment he went on. "I wasn't going to mention this until later, but – look, Charles, we know the official reason for our being on this trip, but I hope we can do more, much more."

"Like what?"

"Like we find a way to drive the Europeans out of Mexico. They're a military threat to the Union, whatever they all say, so let's show them their way home."

"Sure, sure. The two of us will force ten thousand troops to turn tail and run. Sure we will." A long pull at the bottle, followed by a longer pause. "But, you know, you may not be wholly mad," he allowed. "They're allies, and history proves that allies always fall out, sooner or later. Maybe we can accelerate the process." He stopped pacing and turned to Jones. "You're sure that Stoddard would want us to do that if we can?"

"No, I'm not sure, but how could he object?"

"I don't see how. And I don't have any idea how we can do it. We'll just have to hope for an opportunity."

"Or try to make one. We'll keep this objective in mind all the time." Jones reached across and squeezed Bartlett's knee. "Agreed, *amigo*?"

Bartlett nodded a silent agreement. He calculated that his career was still in the hole. He *must* find a triumph of some kind in Mexico. He must.

Meanwhile, all he could do was to learn Spanish. He pulled down his books and turned up the lamp. Jones went out on deck.

The sullen knot of miners and their bankers were dumped on the rain-swept quay at Vigo. Short of shaking their fists at Morny, their displeasure could not have been more plain. They came away with nothing, not even a promise. He watched them struggle with their luggage, a tight smile on his lips, and then turned with a broad grin to the watching Bartlett and Jones.

"At last, gentlemen, we are rid of those tiresome men and their flattery, which they hoped to turn into gold at my expense. Phut! I shall ask the captain to make for Veracruz with all possible speed. And for you, Major, the steward will move you to another cabin, where you will be more comfortable."

Bartlett's French was just good enough to understand all this, but not good enough to reply except with a smile and a bow. He went below, back to his books.

In a flat calm, *Isabella* left the shabby little port under power, her single screw pushing her hard at nine knots. Once outside the harbour, one topsail was set to stiffen her and she steamed southwest towards the Windward Passage east of Cuba. Captain Carbonel expected to cross the Atlantic in twelve days, with any luck and a reasonable wind.

The days grew longer and the sun grew hotter, and now the trades blew steadily over the starboard quarter. Under full sail, *Isabella* rose and fell with an easy rhythm that belied her speed through the water. All was as content as only a calm sea passage can be. Bartlett and Jones were on deck most of their time, Bartlett reciting his lessons and Jones correcting him patiently as they circled the main cabin. Their lunch was served on the stern, on a linen-covered table placed up against the taffrail. They seldom talked, absorbing the sun and watching *Isabella* lay down her white wake on the dark blue sea.

Morny disliked the hot sun, he said. "I saw too much of it in Africa." So Jones was surprised one evening, six days out from Vigo, when his host joined him on the bow to watch the red disc fall into the sea dead ahead. "Glorious, is it not, Commander? This is a new experience for me, and I envy you of the navy for whom this must be a routine sight."

Jones was embarrassed to admit how seldom he had put to sea, so he didn't. "Yes, glorious, sir. You can expect more evenings like this as we go farther south."

"Captain Carbonnel estimates Veracruz in six or seven days. How accurate can he be, do you think?"

"With your horsepower, sir, I'll be surprised if he's wrong by more than twelve hours. Barring bad weather, of course."

"Fine." A long pause. "Oh, my belated apologies to you and the Major. I've neglected you, I fear."

"Not at all. Your business must come first."

"It is not business. It is that as we left Vigo I had a brilliant idea for a play, a comedy, and I simply have to finish it before we arrive." Jones and Bartlett had seen Morny, through the portholes of the saloon, dictating to his secretary and had wondered what he was writing so intently. "I have almost finished – the last act still needs revision – and I am quite pleased with it." He grasped a shroud to steady himself.

Jones would learn later that writing dramatic fiction was the only talent that Morny lacked, that he lacked it absolutely, to the delight of his friends, and that he refused to admit it

"We must confer, you two and I, before we land," Morny said. "I will explain how you will be kept informed of developments among the three allies. It is in our best interest, without doubt, that you be kept informed, so that you in turn can keep Mr. Seward and your General Stoddard informed. And keep them happy that our intentions are as we have stated - peacefully to collect our just debts and then to return to our countries." He tapped Jones lightly on the shoulder. "It would never do, would it, for two such eminent men to lose any sleep over our tiny forces in Mexico?"

Chapter 22

Montgomery, Alabama

Captain James Dunwoody Bulloch was of Scottish ancestry and Savannah birth, and had served in the American navy for fourteen years, rising from midshipman to the command of a mail steamer. He had then moved to New York to build a successful private career as a ship captain and builder of merchant ships. But the day after Sumter he wrote to the Confederate government in Montgomery to offer his services in the conflict.

He was summoned by Stephen Mallory, the Confederate Secretary of the Navy, who was an able man with long experience in naval matters. He was blunt, as well.

"I am glad to see you, Captain Bulloch," he said now, "I want you to go to Europe. When can you start?"

Bulloch lost no time either. "I have no impedimenta and can start as soon as you explain what I am to do."

That settled, Mallory began to explain, studying his guest as he did so. Not yet forty, Bulloch was an imposing figure – tall, and wide shouldered.

"I am charged with the creation of a navy, from scratch," Mallory declared. "But I am like a chieftain without a clan. The Confederate Navy today consists of one small steamer than can be converted to a ship-of-war. One. We have one large dockyard, at Norfolk, but even if we could build ships there they would never reach the Atlantic. The Yankee blockade would sink them. The other dockyard at Pensacola is not one for construction, and it too is shut off by the blockade, and by the Yankee forts at the entrance."

He paused for effect, fixing Bulloch with a pair of steel grey eyes.

"What of engines?" Bulloch asked. "Iron plates? Cannon? Ammunition? I have been in the North for so long that I am not in touch with our industry."

"What industry?" said Mallory. "There is not one mill in the country that can roll a two and one half inch iron plate, if we had any iron; only one shop that can turn out a good marine engine; only one shop that can cast or forge a heavy gun. And virtually no saltpeter without which we cannot produce ammunition."

"Indeed. And, as is obvious, we perforce lack the skilled men in all of the relevant trades. Ordnance stores, medical supplies, food and clothing are all scarce, as well." Another pause. "In short, sir, we are, at this moment, incapable of building and equipping a single cruising ship of moderate offensive power. Not one."

"I see. Hence, Europe?"

*   *   *

That interview had taken place the year before and Bulloch had made his way to England, where he had settled in Liverpool. He was now perhaps the most dangerous Confederate agent alive. He was responsible for obtaining ships, munitions and other war supplies in Europe and shipping them to Southern ports through the Yankee blockade.

This mission was what had brought him to Bannerman's Bank. Through his spies Bulloch had discovered that the bank was in a perilous financial situation. So, although he knew that Bannerman's was also the Union army's bank in London, Bulloch realized that Malcom Bannerman was probably desperate enough to help him obtain the large quantities of the saltpeter the Confederates so badly needed. Under normal circumstances Bannerman would probably not have even considered such a dangerous scheme but these were far from normal times and he realized that if he could pull this off it would save his bank. Equally, Bulloch and the Confederates would not normally accept such uneconomical terms had they not recently lost a year's supply of saltpeter in a mysterious explosion on the Mersey.

Bulloch's proposal was to trade Southern cotton for Indian saltpeter. He asserted that one or more Southern ships would be able to slip the blockade and reach Liverpool, loaded with bales of raw cotton, within the next month. He was authorized to sell up to five thousand bales of that cotton at six pence per pound. This was equal to the pre-war market price and less than one half of the current Liverpool price for the few bales that were occasionally traded there. The buyer of the cotton would pay spot cash to Bulloch on delivery and would then be free to resell the cotton at whatever price it could obtain. Bulloch wanted Bannerman's Bank to be the buyer.

There was, inevitably, a catch. Bannerman's would also have to supply Bulloch in Liverpool with at least one thousand tons of saltpeter. Bulloch was prepared to pay up to forty-five shillings per hundredweight, he said - well above the market price. His orders were in fact to pay any price for the material, so desperate was the South to get it.

"But you understand, Mr. Bannerman," Bulloch had drawled softly, "that I can't deliver the cotton to you until I see your saltpeter on the quay. At the risk of sounding discourteous – no saltpeter, no cotton." They were sitting in Bannerman's office over a lunch of cold chicken and hock.

A man still in his thirties, Bulloch had a broad, open face, little hair on his head and enormous sideburns. His integrity was well known: as soon as the Charleston guns fired on Sumter, he had insisted on returning the merchant ship he was commanding to its northern owners and returning to offer his services to the Confederates.

Bannerman had been recommended to Bulloch as a banker who could lay his hands on the cotton purchase price and who, as the Union Army's banker, would know where to find the saltpeter in the required tonnage. His bank was also known to be in serious financial trouble.

"That's a devil of a lot of saltpeter, Mr. Bulloch," Bannerman sighed.

"That's a devil of a lot of cotton, sir. And one hell of a lot of profit for your bank." Bulloch waved a drumstick. "I'd assemble the saltpeter myself you understand, but I haven't the time and besides those Yankee spies keep a close watch on me. I need a middleman, someone with the money, the contacts and the time to put together the tonnage we require."

The truth was that Bulloch was out of money and couldn't hope to get more from Richmond for at least another couple of months. Without cash in an English bank, he had to trade for his saltpeter with cotton – cotton that hadn't even been loaded at a Confederate port.

For his part, Bannerman calculated that the bank's profit on four thousand bales of cotton would be at least seventy thousand pounds. Enough to pay off his creditors. Enough to free him from the sinking dread of the future that had lain coiled in the pit of his stomach every day for the past year. Enough to marry Katherine Carra.

Finding the money to pay for the cotton was easy. He would use the Union Army's sixty thousand pounds now resting in current account at his bank. He would replace it as soon as he resold the cotton. As for the saltpeter – it amused him to think that the Union's own suppliers would find it for him. All he had to do was to bribe them not to deliver it but instead to hold on a month or so for the price of forty-five shillings per hundredweight that he would pay them. No broker he knew of would turn down an offer like that. He would only break even on the saltpeter, which was acceptable. His profit was all in the cotton.

He would have to think hard about the difficulties in the Southerner's strange offer, but even before Bulloch had left his office after this first meeting, he was halfway to accepting it.

Chapter 23

The trade winds held and *Isabella* swept westward, with Cuba a green smudge over the starboard rail. The days grew longer and hotter. Bartlett battled unequally with the irregular verbs until Jones could bear it no more. "*Fui*," he sighed, "*yo fui*. I went." Then, "Never mind, Charles, you're doing fine, just fine, but for now you'd better stick to the regular verbs."

"And the present tense?"

"And the present tense, if you must." Jones squinted up to admire the precision movements of the crewmen racing aloft to shorten sail. "Look at them," he said admiringly, "did you think you'd ever see that sight again?"

In time, one bright morning the lookout sighted land, a few points off the starboard bow, a thin green line with the hint of mountains and high clouds beyond.

"Mexico at last," announced Morny gravely when he appeared on deck, "about ten miles north of Veracruz. The Captain calculates that we will anchor in the harbor in two hours." He breathed out with satisfaction. "Ahhhh, such a pleasant voyage," he said, "once we disposed of those importunate miners. I am convinced that this is the only way for me to travel, in the warmer latitudes at least. And such pleasant company in you two gentlemen." Another deep breath. "For myself, I have finished the last act – it is now truly splendid – so I must find a way to get it to my publishers without delay."

Isabella approached the coast slowly under mainsail and jib, her engine adding perhaps a knot to her speed. Guarding the entrance to Veracruz harbor, the fortress of San Juan de Ulloa rose from its reef, dark, silent and empty. The Mexican army, convinced that the three hundred year old structure could not withstand the modern gunfire they assumed would be directed at it, had abandoned the fort when the European warships first appeared before it.

As they left the fort to windward, *Isabella* turned into the harbour, rising to the slight swell. Bartlett and Jones, standing in the bows, surveyed the town ahead of them through their telescopes. Veracruz looked smaller than they expected of the main port of Mexico, a place of steeples and domes, all clear white, as if made of marble. Far inland they saw the deep blue of the mountains, with the snowy peak of Orizaba soaring in their center. Along the waterfront, the white customhouse stood out by reason of its size and the flags of France, Spain and Britain that snapped above it in the stiffish breeze. The town's only pier jutted out into the sea from the customhouse. A few small boats tacked about close inshore, but the overall impression was peaceful, even somnolent. "Must be lunchtime," Bartlett said.

Suddenly a hum, a snick and a four inch circular hole appeared in the jib.

"Christ! We're under fire," cried Jones. "Where in the devil - ?" They scanned the waterfront, then looked back at the fort. "There!" they said as the wind tore away the smoke from the upper parapet of the massive structure. "Looks like a short gun." The second round smashed into the mainmast, directly above the gaff boom, bounced off a shroud and fell smoking at Jones's feet. "That's damn good shooting," he allowed as they ran aft. Then Captain Carbonnel was ordering the watch to lower all sails and demanding full power from the engine room.

Morny emerged from the main cabin, looked around once and listened to Carbonnel. "But, Captain," he said, "surely it's dangerous for the men to lower the sails? That gunner is good. Perhaps they should be told to go below, where it's safer. Will we lose speed if we leave the sails up?" The third round hit *Isabella* amidships, burying itself in her white side despite its shallow angle of impact. Owner and skipper eyed each other.

"No. The engine will add a knot or two, sir," Carbonnel said, "but your point is well taken."

"I suggest you make due south, Captain," Jones urged, "along the coast. That gun's in the northwest corner of the fort and can't bear on us much longer."

Carbonnel peered at Jones and at the fort. He nodded, bellowed his new orders and then returned to the other three.

"Well, Commander Jones, what do you think of all this?" Morny asked, a slight smile on his lips. *Isabella* began to surge ahead as her propeller bit hard.

"This mission's already more dangerous than I expected, sir," Jones laughed. "Any chance of a raise in pay?" He studied the fort through his telescope. "Good shooting, that is, at over a mile. Hey! Get down, here comes an - " There was a small splash sixty yards ahead of them.

Bartlett sighted his glass on the parapet. Four or five men, he thought; not in uniform, no hats, one with bright red hair. "Down again, gentlemen," he called. They all ducked, but this round lost itself in the waves. They stood up, and Morny smoothed the wings of dark hair at his temples. The grey-blue eyes were amused.

"They've lost the range," Jones said, "and at this speed we should be out of shot in a few minutes. Wait a minute. They're leaving the fort, at the double." He lowered his glass and shook Carbonnel's hand. "Well done, Captain." To Morny he said, "I'll recover that round for you, sir. A twelve pounder, I think." He went forward.

Carbonnel heaved himself aloft, concluded that there was no danger of losing the topmast, lowered all sail and reduced his revolutions. *Isabella* turned around and steamed back into Veracruz harbor at a stately, almost regal, pace, one that befitted the grandeur of its owner and principal passenger.

That grandeur, as Carbonnel and his signalman soon found, was not easy to communicate with flags to the officer of the day at the Custom House. "They seem to think you're either the Emperor himself or your wife, sir," Carbonnel fumed. "What a confusion."

"At least they know I'm French," Morny laughed. "Just spell out my name and title. That will be sufficient."

Jones presented Morny with a flattened lump of warm lead. "Thank you, friend Jones. In Africa I was under fire many times, but never did I see what had almost hit me."

Bartlett looked at Jones with interest. "But it's your first time under fire, isn't it, Robert?"

"Yes," Jones admitted. Deflecting the conversation he went on, "Not yours, Count, you say?"

Carbonnel toadied in smartly. "The Count was a hero in Africa, gentlemen, decorated for valor in saving the life of a general. He was hit four times, the Count was."

"Very noble of you, sir," Bartlett said. "Most of the soldiers I know wouldn't – "

"Nobility had nothing to do with it," Morny smiled, "he was a terrible general. I just wanted the Legion of Honor."

At length the detachment on shore stopped running around and a launch put out in the direction of *Isabella*. Morny peered at it through Carbonnel's telescope and then told him, "Unless that boat contains Admiral Jurien or Ambassador de Saligny, I'll not receive them, Captain. Please tell them who I am, if any doubt remains, that I am here to represent the Emperor and that I will need at least one floor of the best hotel. Or the governor's quarters if the hotel is not suitable."

"Yes, sir."

"Then, tell them I shall go ashore at six this evening, when I shall be pleased to receive the general and the ambassador in my suite." Carbonnel hurried aft and Morny turned to Jones. "I hope you and the Major will go ashore with me, Commander." Jones nodded dumbly. Morny's eyebrow lifted, then he called, "Henri! Lunch, please, you peasant. I think a chicken."

It is still not known what inducement Ambassador Saligny was forced to offer the Spanish administrator of Veracruz, but it was enough. That worthy judged that the Hotel Magnifico, though peeling in many places and cursed with erratic plumbing, was better suited to the Emperor's brother than any alternative accomodation. Its location was ideal, right on the Plaza de Armas, the main square. The second floor was vacated, scoured, fumigated and whitewashed in time for Morny's arrival. Bartlett and Jones trooped along in his train, trying hard not to look like hangers-on. He saw them installed in tolerable rooms, insisted they join him for a cognac after his dinner and retired to prepare for his official guests.

"Well, Charles, what do you think of the Rich Town of the True Cross?" Jones asked as he drained his coffee after dinner.

"Where's that?"

"Right here. That's what the Spaniards called Veracruz when Cortes got here. In Spanish, of course."

"No!"

"Back in Texas they'd say we're living in tall cotton here," Jones went on. "Light duty, a soft bed, cheap food and – "

"And a million mosquitoes," Bartlett complained. "Back in Texas they'd say we'll be lucky to live another week if we stay here. This coast is stiff with malaria, you know, and yellow fever, and God knows what other delights."

"Courage, *mon brave*, a good mosquito net and a barrel of quinine are all we need. Then we'll stick close to our man, keep our eyes open and find some way to get our reports to Washington." He dropped his napkin, stood up and stretched noisily. "I may not have mentioned that the telegraph line from Monterrey to California, to the Presidio, is reported to have been cut by the Juaristas."

"What else? And the line from here to Mexico City and then to Monterrey?"

"Intact, I think. We can confirm that in the morning."

Morny seemed distracted when they joined him later in his quarters. He remained standing when they settled back with their brandy and cigars; he even paced a bit, fanning hard with one of the palm leaf fans Henri had found for them. The reason for his agitation he soon made known.

"It seems, Commander, that - " He stopped himself, turned to Bartlett. "But how rude of me, Major Bartlett! I have neglected to ask if you understand French."

"A little, sir, but don't worry yourself," Bartlett blushed. "Jones explains what I fail."

"No, indeed," Morny beamed. "What luck! This will give me the chance – no, it will oblige me – to practice my English. I lived in England until I was nine, you know." He said this last sentence with obvious pleasure and the trace of a Kentish accent. From then on he spoke to both of them only in English.

"Well, it seems, gentlemen, that France, Spain and England have assembled this formidable force and transported it to Mexico only to place it under the command of three donkeys. After one month here, our esteemed Commissioners have so far managed to produce - a proclamation! And a proclamation of stunning fatuity, at that. They have rolled back the limits of human stupidity, those three." He coldly rattled off the document's main points. "Imagine! That is all these donkeys could think of to do, except to do what they do now, which is nothing except await the response of the Mexican government."

"Who will not respond?" Jones guessed.

"Exactly! You have the mind of a Latin politician, my friend." Morny sat down with a crash. "Why would Juarez respond until he knows why we are here?"

Bartlett looked around the suite. Henri had transformed it in no time. Pots of fiery bougainvillea stood in the corners, the windows were draped in fine netting and an array of oil lamps blazed on the side tables. Best of all, he had found the kind of flowers whose nighttime scent nearly overcame the stench of Veracruz that seeped through the closed windows.

"And so," Morny continued, "in two days time the allied Commissioners and I will meet to prepare our formal demands on the Mexicans. I shall sit with them in place of Admiral Jurien, but they can be in no doubt that I will convey the explicit wishes of the Emperor. And that he expects action: The delivery of our demands to the Mexicans and our offer to discuss them with Juarez or his representative within ten days."

"Or else?" It was Jones's turn.

"Or else —who knows?" laughed Morny. "You must know that one discloses one's negotiating position to no one in advance. Besides, I have told you too much already."

"But, sir – " Jones started.

"I know, Commander. I undertook to keep you fully informed, so that your masters in Washington do not worry about our intentions here." He drained his glass of brandy. "And so I shall, but only with respect to military matters, which after all are your only concern. And Washington's." He did not tell them that he was acting in strict accordance with the Emperor's new orders to Savigny. He would let them think that he alone was deciding French political strategy and, if it came to that, French military strategy.

*   *   *

Two days later

"Twelve million?"

"TWELVE MILLION DOLLARS?"

"Absurd!"

"Preposterous!"

These were the first spontaneous comments made at the conference of the Commissioners in the Custom House, and they came from the soul. Sir Charles Wyke, the English ambassador, felt as if he'd been kicked in the chest. Of all those present, he was the most determined to reach a peaceful settlement with Juarez.

Saligny was of nervous disposition and he looked uneasy as he repeated himself. "Yes, twelve million dollars. That figure comprises the total French demands resulting from events before July of last year." He sat back, glanced apprehensively at the still figure of Morny beside him and exhaled deeply.

Wyke recovered enough to say to Saligny, whom he loathed, "You presumably verified each of these claims before you presented us with this stupendous figure?"

Then it was the turn of Prim, the Spanish force commander and Commissioner. The thin-bearded general, an austere Catalan nobleman with far grander personal goals in Mexico than Wyke or Saligny, felt it was time to take control of the conference, as he had taken control of Veracruz. "We and the English have taken pains to examine all the claims of our citizens, and we are satisfied that our demands are fair and accurate. Can you say the same?"

"No, of course not," blustered Saligny. "Every other Frenchman in Mexico has presented a claim of some sort. It would take years to examine them all. A total waste of time. So," he pressed his fingertips together and tried to look confident, "so, I was instructed to name a round figure."

"A round figure?" exclaimed Wyke. "I don't believe what I'm hearing."

"Yes, within a million or two," said Saligny. "Less, perhaps."

"As I said before – preposterous," Prim said. "Your 'round figure' is far larger than the claims of Spain and England combined. It can not be considered serious."

"I assure you, General," Morny spoke for the first time, "it is serious."

"Serious or not, Count, England can not accept your figure," said Wyke.

"Nor can Spain, needless to say. And," Prim paused for effect, "it is obvious that if we put it forward with our claims, Juarez will never accept it."

"And if you do not present *our* claim, gentlemen, you may not present your *own*." Morny spoke sharply. "To do so would violate the terms of the

London Convention." He brushed his moustache approvingly. "We are allies, after all, are we not?"

Confusion in the ranks. Prim lit a vast cigar and waved away the smoke; Wyke chewed his fingernails; and Morny waited a few seconds longer to drop his bombshell. "I must tell you, gentlemen, there is more," he said somberly. "A matter of which Ambassador Saligny is not aware." He described the loan Jecker had made to the Mexican government and the bonds that the government had in exchange issued to his bank.

No cries of outrage this time, but a shocked silence. Then Wyke managed a weak, " Thirty million dollars?"

"Exactly, with the interest included," said Morny. "For a grand total of – "

"Forty two million," Prim supplied in a low tone. "Forty two million."

"But this Jecker is a Swiss," Wyke protested. "I know of him. In Mexico he's notorious. A Swiss swindler."

"He is now a French citizen, a most loyal one, and a respectable banker," Morny corrected him. "And the Mexican bonds that he has deposited for safekeeping with our Foreign Ministry are incontestably genuine. You must accept my word on this." He waved his left hand idly, to make it plain that never had any man not accepted his word.

"Bonds issued by a displaced government, signed by a disgraced President," sneered Prim. "What are they really worth?"

"You know as well as I do, General Prim - their face value." Morny was indignant, almost genuinely so. "That is an old question with an old answer: No government could function if its obligations could be disowned by its successors." Pause. "Not even yours."

Saligny found his courage at this point. "There you have it, my friends – genuine, prime government bonds. Validated, in effect, by the Mexican government."

"Precisely," Morny agreed. He spread his hands and said to the stunned Wyke and Prim, "Gentlemen, what Ambassador Saligny and I have told you this morning has doubtless come as a surprise, an unsettling one. You need to confer, in private, so with your permission we shall take a stroll along the waterfront to afford you some time." With a nod to the other two, they rose and left the room, which was until recently the office of the Collector of Customs.

"What do you think, General?" Wyke was now seething, all his tribal hatreds of the French boiling to the surface. He had always opposed England's participation in a joint expedition with allies, any allies, but Russell had not even acknowledged his dispatches. Maybe the wee bastard would listen to him next time.

"What can I think, Sir Charles? The same as you." Prim blew a cloud of bluish smoke at the ceiling. "Morny will not be moved, that much is clear.

So we can not present France's claim with our own claims, and so we can not present our own claims." He paused, shrugged. "It makes one wonder why we are here at all, does it not?"

"And what we can say to the Mexicans, who will also be wondering. And laughing their filthy heads off, I shouldn't be surprised."

After another brief exchange, they agreed that their only dignified course was to ask their governments for new instructions, which they knew would take weeks to arrive. They sent a Spanish soldier to invite the two Frenchmen to return to the table.

Prim stretched, rose and said, "I only hope that a few of my men will survive that long."

"Yes," assented Wyke, "and that you and I survive that long."

Chapter 24

Veracruz, Mexico

One evening Bartlett and Jones sat sprawled on the veranda in front of the hotel. Shadows cast by the palm trees on the sea front slid across the square as they contemplated their situation with the help of a bottle of the local dark rum, a potion known to all on that coast as *Matacura*, the Priestkiller.

The wide-roofed veranda was dark and cool, lined with massive, exhausted wooden chairs and tables. It was the best place from which to observe life on the square and in the cafes and coffee houses set into the arches that lined its sides. But there was little life at this time of day, the residents waiting until the sun went down before beginning their twilight promenade. A stolid waiter stood silent in the far corner. Otherwise, the two men were alone.

Their mood was somber. Morny had just warned them of the long delay likely before the English and Spanish commissioners received their new orders. The day before, Admiral Jurien had confirmed that the telegraph line between Monterrey in northern Mexico and Fort Presidio in San Francisco was out of action. "It could have been cut by Juarez' people," he shrugged, "or by your southern rebels. Who knows?" And who cares? was his silent signal. He was angry at Morny's order to keep the American officers informed so they could relay his troop dispositions to Washington.

"So, what now, Robert?" Bartlett was asking. "You're the senior officer; I'm your admiring deputy." A short laugh. "Go ahead. Be brilliant."

The rum softened Jones's annoyance, and besides he had become accustomed to Bartlett's recourse to sarcasm when he felt under pressure. "It's obvious that the first thing is to get the telegraph line fixed. The army laid the line after the war in '48, you know, so by now even they should realize it's out of service. Stoddard will have to get it fixed."

"So you propose to do nothing?"

"Did I say that? We'll have to do something ourselves, that's plain enough, but maybe we'll get some help. That's all I meant." Another meditative pull at the rum. "You know, I haven't thought of your Uncle Miles for a while. How is he, anyway?"

"Scheming, as ever." Bartlett stretched, yawned and picked up his glass. "I'd forgotten that you and he are old friends."

"Yes, we go way back. To when we were lieutenants on the planning staffs, trying to convince the brass hats that a civil war was coming and that, when it turned up, it would be nice if we had some semblance of an army and a navy. Hah. We got nowhere. But we made some good friends. Winfield Scott, for one. Miles has been his blue-eyed boy for years. Gave him the job of running that long term strategy board, in fact."

Bartlett sat up. "I didn't know that."

"Oh, yes. There's no need to worry about Uncle Miles. He has powerful friends, and he knows how to look after himself. He'll be in the top bunk when the flood comes, you can count on it."

"Besides," Jones added, "he always has his women to console him."

Bartlett laughed. He liked and admired his uncle, who he suspected had rescued him from the tedium of Fort Pickens and worked his transfer to West Point. Silence descended for a time, along with the rum and the sun. At length, Bartlett yawned and said, "I'm told that *cantina* two blocks west of here can be pretty lively this time of day, and that they serve a decent roast chicken. Shall we try it?"

They picked their way along the narrow unpaved street, avoiding the goats and the reeking stream of water down its middle, which served the residents as a sewer. Vultures, protected by the law, hopped in the open gutters.

People were heading for the main square now, the men in rusty black jackets and loose trousers and the women in long colorful shawls with their hair done up. Some were plainly the descendants of the African slaves brought in to work in the cane fields and the shipyards. A few were pure Spanish beauties, walking in pairs, who wore black mantillas that covered the lower part of their faces. All crossed the street and dropped their eyes when they saw the two Americans coming.

El Caribe was no cleaner or brighter than any other café in town. The tables on the street were taken so Bartlett and Jones, after tripping over a bootblack who was hard at work, maneuvered with care to a table at the back, near the smoky open kitchen. They looked around, nobody objected and they sat down.

Soon a pair of sumptuous breasts appeared beside Jones, closely followed by a barmaid in a low cut shirt and a kittenish mood. She was Conchita, she announced in passable English, and what did the gentlemens want? That what she wanted was a closer acquaintance was left in no doubt. They settled for chicken and beer, Jones rattling away in Spanish to Conchita's delight, and sat back to observe the scene.

But not for long. "Bartlett! Charles Bartlett, by God!" came a shout from the street. "What in the world – " and a tall, thin man with fierce red hair forced himself through the crowd to their table.

Bartlett laughed, stood up and gripped the man's hand. "By God, indeed, Pancho! What a surprise. How are you? Sit down, won't you? Join us." Bartlett turned to Jones. "Robert Jones, meet Pancho Laffan, horseman extraordinary and the first Mexican to get through West Point." They shook hands.

"Irish-Mexican, if you please, Charles," Laffan corrected. "My apologies – *Major* Bartlett." He looked back over his shoulder. "My sister's outside. I'll bring her in, if you don't mind."

Carolina Laffan was a rangy redhead with light blue eyes, a wide grin and an easy manner. It seemed that the Celtic genes dominated the Laffan blood line. "I'll just have a lemonade, Eufemio," she said to her brother.

"Eufemio?" Jones asked.

"Eufemio Rigoberto Laffan Montealban, at your service," Laffan intoned with a bow and a sweep of his arm. He winked at Bartlett.

"Nobody at the Point could begin to pronounce Eufemio, least of all the instructors," Bartlett explained, " and they thought *all* Mexicans are called Pancho, so as soon as he arrived..."

"Pancho I became."

"But not to me," Carolina sniffed. "I think it's degrading."

Laffan raised expressive eyebrows. "As you like," he said. "But now, a toast to – what? To Mexico!" They raised their glasses and drank. "And now," he went on, "tell me what two shiny American officers are doing in this fever port. You're not here with these European bandits, are you?"

"Yes and no," Bartlett said, his eyes flicking to Jones and back. He and Jones were the American military attachés in London and Paris, respectively, he said, and were assigned to Veracruz to observe the European expedition. The Europeans had objected, he lied, but couldn't force them to leave.

"How did you get here?" Carolina asked. "Not through the southern states, surely?"

"Ah," Jones replied, "we traveled in grand style, in the yacht of the senior Frenchman. It's, well, it's a complicated – "

"You were on that white schooner? The one that arrived three days ago?" Laffan cried. "Hah! I lobbed four or five shells at you. From the fort." He smiled broadly.

Bartlett remembered the bright red hair on the parapet. "I might have guessed that was you. I saw the red hair, and for an alleged artilleryman you never could hit anything."

"I put a couple of rounds up your backside, my friend, before I took pity on you."

"You didn't tell me this, Eufemio," Carolina said. "Why did you shoot at them?"

"Out of pure shame, my dear sister." He turned to the men. "Would you credit it? Not a shot was fired when the Europeans landed here. Not one. We had troops all around the town, thousands of them, and every man jack of them legged it to the hills. Shameful."

"Disgraceful," Carolina agreed.

"So somebody had to make a show of resistance. National pride and all that. Lucky I picked on you. You couldn't shoot back."

Conchita brought the roast chicken at last and they ordered more beer. She lingered at Jones's side, appraising him, and then sauntered off. The *cantina* was full now, mostly with men but here and there a gaily-dressed woman held court. A violin, trumpet and accordion appeared near the door with three *nortenos* who were plainly threatening to play them.

"Oh, do stop them, Eufemio," Carolina implored. "I've heard them at the hotel and they're dreadful, truly dreadful."

Laffan obediently rose and moved towards the trio. To Carolina, Bartlett said, "Robert here has a background like yours, Miss Laffan, if I remember rightly. Your father is Irish and your mother Mexican, right?" She nodded. "And you lived in Texas when it was part of Mexico?" Another nod. "So you became Texans when it declared independence, and then Americans when Texas joined the Union. Which is how Pancho got to West Point." He attacked a drumstick.

"I too have been a Mexican, a Texan and now an American, Miss Laffan," Jones said, unfurling all his Slavic charm, "but my father was Russian."

"It's Carolina, please, gentlemen," she smiled. Her voice rose and fell in the Mexican manner.

Laffan rejoined them and raised his glass. "I have to report bad news on the orchestral front: they've already been paid to play and they're men of honor."

In reply to Bartlett's question, Laffan told his story. He had been commissioned two years before Bartlett, just in time to catch the last months of the Mexican War as a staff officer to Winfield Scott. He saw action – "a few skirmishes" – around Mexico City. Then at the battle of Churubusco the turncoat San Patricio Battalion of Irish-American soldiers fought on the side of the Mexicans, and the promotion prospects of every Irish-American officer evaporated.

"We were all under suspicion. Even General Scott couldn't help me," he said. He was transferred to ever more remote outposts on the western frontier, ending with three years at Fort Bridger in the Utah Territory. "The army was shrinking in size, my chances of promotion were zero or worse and I'd had a bellyful of Indians." He shrugged. "So I resigned as soon as I could. Still a lieutenant. Kept my uniform and went home."

Homes, in fact: a vast cattle ranch in Sonora and a fruit farm down in Colima. His father, a mining engineer from Galway, had done well. Young Laffan divided his time between the properties. "Good riding country but the life was dull as hell."

Then Juarez rose in revolt. As a landed gentleman, Laffan fought at first with the Conservatives. "Overnight I was a major." He soon became ashamed and disgusted by his companions – arrogant, stupid and cruel, he said, and priest-ridden. Then Juarez became President, which put Laffan in revolt against the elected government and in real danger of hanging. He resigned and again went home. But the fighting dragged on, so he joined Juarez to help put an end to it. "Overnight a colonel. I outrank you, Charles, so I'll look for a lot more respect from you."

The fighting was almost over by then, but he'd been in a few battles. Nothing heroic, he said, only survival. Then the Europeans landed at Veracruz. Juarez was stunned. Laffan soon persuaded him that, with his training and languages, he'd make a first-class spy.

"That's why I'm here in plain clothes, not sweating in a uniform like you two," he finished. "My mother's sister lives here, and Carolina and I look after her. For me it's a useful front."

The trio of musicians had tuned up and assaulted their first number, a dirge that dwelt at length on the infidelities of a certain Indian lady. The man strangling his trumpet was their leader and plainly determined to be heard on the Plaza de Armas.

Carolina winced and said to Bartlett, "But my aunt will leave soon for the hills, to escape the fever. The fever season will be here any day."

"That's right," Laffan said, "what they call the black vomit. Unattractive but descriptive. And you foreigners are very vulnerable. Have you seen the European hospitals, by the way?"

"No."

"You should. They've taken over some of the warehouses and they're full of sick soldiers. And dying soldiers." He laughed shortly. "I may tell El Presidente that he needs only to wait a month and the fever will drive the thieving scum back over the sea."

After a while and promises to meet again in the next day or two, Jones called for the bill. Conchita presented him with a scrap of paper as she deployed her formidable pectoral assets at him. He started back in surprise and grinned wolfishly at Bartlett.

"That's a quick conquest, Robert."

"She responds to my sensitive, brooding features," Jones said as he reached into his pocket, "all women do."

The next day, Bartlett and Jones were perforce thinking of clothes, specifically the light, cream-colored linen suit and wide straw hat worn by Morny, who sat and sipped a coffee on the Magnifico veranda as a Spanish platoon practiced close order drill in the square. Henri's search for the traditional hortensia having failed, his buttonhole today was two bougainvillea blossoms. Their bright splash of scarlet gave Morny the raffish air he deemed appropriate to his present latitude.

"You're looking terribly tropical today, sir," Jones smiled. "I envy you." He checked himself; he had taken care until then not to address the Emperor's brother informally.

"There is no need for envy, Commander," Morny replied, sensing Jones's unease. "The indefatigable Henri has found a tailor who promises to reproduce this suit in four different shades in two days. You and the Major can do the same, extract yourselves from all that heavy blue serge."

Bartlett caught Jones's mood. "A splendid idea," he said. "We can design our own hot weather uniforms, Robert, one for the army and one for the navy.

"Yes, something in white duck, I think. With epaulets, of course."

"Of course. And a sash? I've always fancied myself in a sash."

"Excellent, dear boy!" cried Jones, mimicking the bray of a Guards officer. "Just like the, ah, Old Unspeakables. Won the right to wear them at Waterloo, don't y'know, old fruit."

"Most entertaining," Morny said dryly. "I'll ask Henri to advise you; he is the expert on gentlemen's dress." He lit a long cigar. "Tell me, what is the cause of all this frisky chatter?"

"Boredom, sir," Bartlett was quick to reply, "boredom, pure and simple. We have weeks to wait, as you said, for the English and Spanish to decide their next move. And we have no way to send a report. If we had anything to report." He explained about the telegraph breakdown.

"I see. I see." Morny stared out over the square for a minute. "Now, those Spanish troops march well, do they not?" The Americans nodded. "Can you see anything wrong in their formation? No?" He looked disappointed. "Well, that is a platoon, which in the Spanish army is commanded by a lieutenant and a senior sergeant. But that platoon is led by a corporal, and a young corporal at that."

The penny dropped. "Yellow fever," Bartlett said. "They're in the hospital."

"Or dead," said Jones.

"Exactly," Morny confirmed. "There are in Veracruz seven thousand five hundred soldiers from the three nations. Of those, almost two hundred and fifty are dead and six hundred are in what we are pleased to call our hospitals." He let that sink in. "Admiral Jurien reports that the men are going down at the rate of ninety every day."

"And the fever season hasn't even begun yet," Jones said.

"Not yet. The scale and immediacy of the problem are clear. As is the solution: move inland to higher ground."

Morny opened a map of Veracruz and the surrounding country. His finger moved to three villages halfway up the mountain range that lay eighty kilometers to the west. He named them: Orizaba, Cordoba and Tehuacan. The troops must be moved up into the sierra to those villages, he said, and soon, or they would die.

"I – and you if you wish – can retreat to the relative safety of *Isabella,*" he said, "but our soldiers can not. They must move to higher ground." He waved a hand. "Even the English and the Spanish can see that. It's the one issue on which we all agree."

But the villages were occupied by Mexican soldiers, and their commander, a General Doblado, refused to let the Europeans move inland until they specified exactly what they wanted in Mexico. "And as we can not yet agree what we want, we can not specify it. And so we can not move inland."

They sat for a time and pondered the intractability of the European position, Morny with anger, Bartlett and Jones with silent satisfaction.

Suddenly Bartlett heard himself saying, "Count, I have an idea that may help the situation." Why on earth did I say that? he asked himself, half in shock. The merest trace of an idea had flickered across the back of his mind and he had to blurt it out. "But I need to make a few enquiries first," he stammered, trying to think. Morny raised an eyebrow but said nothing. Jones looked startled. "It would mean leaving Veracruz for some days. You would have no objection?"

"None whatever," Morny said, "provided Commander Jones remains here. To make sure that in your absence I do not perpetrate some vile treachery."

"What are you playing at, Charles?" Jones demanded after they excused themselves and left Morny.

"Trust me, Robert, can't you?" To do what, exactly? Well, he had a day or two to think of something.

"It seems I'll have to."

*   *   *

"That's not good enough, Malcolm. We must have our money. Every penny, and now! Plus interest, of course."

Bannerman tightened his teeth. Christ above, how he hated his cousin Sydney! His mother's cousin, in fact, of the Derbyshire branch of the Arbuthnott family. He sat stiffly by the fire in Bannerman's office with a face like a cliff, demanding the impossible, glancing from time to time at his two allies, Primrose and Keith.

It was quite simple. The Bannerman bank owed the banks owned by each of the three men something over thirty thousand pounds – plus interest, of course. Malcolm's father and uncle had plunged disastrously in the new railroad companies that sprang up during the '50s. Not all of the roads had failed, but four, one of them the notorious London to Brighton line, had gone spectacularly bankrupt, leaving their debenture holders to whistle for their money.

In desperation, the Bannerman brothers turned to cousin Arbuthnott for an advance to make up the huge hole in the bank's accounts. He brought in the two other banks and together they loaned Bannerman's enough for it to stagger through its crisis. But after that the brothers could not even make a dent in the loan. They somehow managed to stay current with the interest payments, which kept Arbuthnott and his cronies at bay for several years, but the three began to close in when Malcolm's father died. Now time had run out.

Malcolm knew none of this when he inherited the bank. To him, banking was a leisurely, comfortable profession where he would take his proper place when the time came. It offered short hours, long congenial lunches and much longer congenial weekends with the hunting and fishing that all gentlemen required. Much like the peacetime army, in fact, which he had adorned in the years after the Crimea, but with more money.

Hence his horror when he discovered that his chairmanship of the bank was to be a bed of nails. He came to understand the reasons for his father's surliness in later years and to suspect that his uncle's suicide was not, after all, due entirely to his fondness for younger men.

And, like them, he found no way to reduce the debt. He cut back the bank's staff, he tried to attract business from the 'new men' coming to prominence in industry, he even made loans at high rates to the solvent railroads. Nothing helped.

"And I repeat, my dear Cousin Sydney," he now said, "I cannot pay you now. I must have more time."

"No."

Bannerman played his last card but one. "Or, I shall at last have to go to the Bank."

Bannerman didn't know himself if he was bluffing or not. Nor did his three listeners. They all knew, however, that the Governor of the Bank of England would not sit on his hands when he learned that one of England's oldest banks was going to the wall. With a wave of his cigar he would force Arbuthnott and his two friends to stretch out their loans for years, for long enough to give Bannerman's a fair chance of eventual survival. Their bankers' souls winced in silent pain at this prospect.

With another wave, the Governor would strip Malcolm of all authority in his own bank and install one of his creatures as its master. Malcolm could stay on as chairman, if he liked, but he would soon find himself with a great deal of time on his hands and damn few invitations with which to fill it. And no money. And so no chance at all of winning Katherine Carra.

Therefore, impasse. But the three creditors were prepared for this threat – they had feared it for years – and had agreed that they could not risk it, not yet.

"You don't want that, Malcolm, and nor do we," said Arbuthnott. He waited.

"There may be one alternative, gentlemen." Bannerman said at length, having already decided how much to tell them. "I have received an offer, an unusual offer. I can say only that it involves America. If the venture succeeds, I expect to be able to see the back of you three and your poxy banks by Christmas."

"And if it does not succeed?"

"Then I must call in the Governor.

This afternoon's meeting with Cousin Sydney and his two friends left him with no choice at all. If he was to save his bank, he would have to do a deal with Bulloch. He was out of his front door moments after the three lenders departed his office.

It was a short ride from the bank to the Warburton, Bulloch's hotel, where - as instructed - Bannerman dined in the smaller dining room on the first floor. Then, trying to look like a man retiring to his room for the night, he bought an Evening Standard and climbed the stairs to the fourth floor. Bulloch and a large brandy were waiting for him in Room 404.

After brief pleasantries, Bulloch opened his hands and said "Well, sir. As the Carolina judge said to the defendant: What do you bring me?"

Any remaining doubts in Bannerman's mind had evaporated since leaving his bank. "First, can you confirm your offer?"

"I'm happy to do so," Bulloch replied easily. "As I told you, I was given a free hand in this matter when I left Charleston. And I've received no instructions to the contrary since we first met."

"In that case, I am pleased to accept your proposal, with one proviso."

"And that is?"

"That I can terminate the arrangement if your cotton is not on the Liverpool dock by the end of next month."

Bulloch didn't hesitate. "Agreed, provided that I have the same right on your saltpeter."

The remaining details were settled. As he put on his coat, Bannerman stopped and asked "Tell me, Captain Bulloch, as we're going to be partners: Why are you ready to sell the cotton to me at a price well below the market?"

Bulloch smiled for the first time. "I'm sure you'll see why, sir. It helps to get me the saltpeter which is the main objective of this mission. We have a great deal of cotton but very little saltpeter. Also the price of cotton may fall before very long."

"Fall? How?" Bannerman suddenly felt vulnerable. "With the Northern blockade? And your embargo on cotton exports?"

"Don't you know? There is no official embargo. None at all. Nothing more than a lot of loud official talk. But it will suit you and me to keep that a secret, won't it?" He handed Bannerman his hat and gloves. "As for the blockade, why, we're counting on you English to break it for us. You'll have to, sooner or later."

"Perhaps."

"Not perhaps, Mr. Bannerman. For certain. Or you'll have revolution on your hands. So my advice to you is to get that saltpeter together right soon. Good night, sir. "

Chapter 25

The sun vaulted into the hard blue sky and lifted the temperature on the desolate plain into the nineties. They had hoped to reach Tehuacan the night before but Bartlett could ride no farther and they camped overnight. His thighs burned, his buttocks were agony and his soul was a pit of self-disgust.

"Sorry, Pancho," he repeated, "but it's been a long time since I sat a horse." Not since Bull Run, in fact. He had loathed all horses from childhood, but first Bull Run and now this long ride over the steaming scrubland elevated his loathing to a new and unimagined plane.

"So you've told me – often enough," Laffan said, sitting his horse as if welded to its saddle. "But don't worry, old man, only fifteen miles to go. We'll be there for lunch."

It had been easy to persuade Laffan to take him to General Doblado's headquarters in the foothills, once the lanky redhead grasped why it was vital to everyone to repair the telegraph line.

"I think I have this straight," he had said. "You and Washington need the line open so you can keep Washington informed what the Europeans are doing. This almighty Frenchman of yours needs the line open so you can tell Washington what the French are doing." A slow smile. "And you aim to persuade Doblado that *he* needs the line open so you can keep Washington informed. Sounds simple enough."

"It will be if he has any sense. He should be able to see that, if the Europeans stay peaceful, Juarez will want us Americans to keep out of it. But if they attack, he may want us to send him some help. In either case, Washington will need to know what's happening down here."

"Eminently logical, Charles, as always. Of course, I don't know how logical this Doblado is. I've never met him."

"Oh? You didn't mention that detail."

"I didn't? Well, let's hope for the best. He's our latest minister for war."

Now, Bartlett ground his teeth against the pain as they plodded across the stony, shadeless landscape. He hadn't told Laffan his second objective: to persuade Doblado to allow the European forces to move inland to a cooler, fever-free altitude. Fifty miles inland was fifty miles closer to Puebla and to Mexico City. Doblado would doubtless object but Bartlett hoped to show him that the alternatives were more dangerous for Mexico.

But first he had to reach Tehuacan. On a horse. "The two finest animals in the state," Laffan had announced when he produced them the morning before. "A joy to ride."

Bartlett had not told Jones where he was going or what he hoped to accomplish. He suspected that he needed to accomplish something on his own to earn – regain? – Jones's respect and confidence.

They rode up to a line of scrawny banana trees and found enough water in the stream to relieve the horses. They dismounted. "All right?" Laffan asked as he unscrewed his canteen lid.

"Just about. Two hours more?"

Laffan nodded, eased up into the saddle and headed west towards the light green foothills that now began to take a solid shape. Bartlett fell in behind him, looking as if he'd broken a tooth.

The band of horsemen behind them reached the stream fifteen minutes later. All, horses and men, drank deep. They were nominally soldiers attached to Doblado's division, but no action and no booty in the uplands had led them to look for freelance work down on the coastal plain. A bad choice so far, but things were looking up. Two gringos, one of them in a white military uniform, spelled ransom, a big ransom to be paid by one of the European armies that infested Veracruz.

They had picked up the trail early that morning and tracked the two easily. Their leader, a stringy sergeant known as El Chino because of his oriental features, decided that they had ridden far enough from Veracruz that no European search party could find the captives if his men hid them well. Time, therefore, to take the gringos captive.

They rode south at a canter, sweeping wide around their prey to wait for them in the forest of stunted pine trees where the road began to climb up to Tehuacan. There they dismounted, tethered the horses and waited.

Soon enough Bartlett and Laffan rode slowly into view and then straight towards them. It was too easy. El Chino nodded and pointed right and left. His half dozen men rose from their bushes in a half circle and aimed straight at Bartlett's dirty white coat. Their rifles were scarred and battered and wobbled in their hands, but there were enough of them that there was no escape. Bartlett decided to let Laffan talk them out of what looked like serious trouble.

This was a mistake. Laffan demanded to know what the hell they were playing at. He used the voice of a colonel berating a useless sergeant, which, given the bandoleers and the scraps of uniforms that his captors wore, was a natural error. He even identified himself as a colonel in the army, forgetting that as a spy he carried no papers. El Chino was having none of it. He knew a panicky lie when he heard one. He hawked and spat heavily in the dust. His men closed in. They stripped Bartlett and Laffan of their side arms, tied their wrists to their saddle horns and led them up into the forest.

Bartlett's new white uniform puzzled them. "Yo Americano," he said, pointing at his chest, "Americano army." But he couldn't fool them. El Chino had fought the Yankees at Contreras and Churubusco, and he remembered with certainty that they all wore dark blue uniforms and blue hats. No, this was some fancy European officer from the invaders at Veracruz. Not Spanish, but French or English, for sure, and that meant a pile of gold for his ransom.

"We'll keep this one," he told his men, "but we'll kill the Mexican. He could be trouble if we keep him." He himself would go into Veracruz to bargain for the gringo's ransom. He licked his lips.

Bartlett understood most of this and looked at Laffan in alarm, but Laffan reasoned that nothing he said then would help them. He shook his head, a signal Bartlett missed. They sat silent for an hour or more as their horses climbed the steeply tilted path towards Tehuacan.

At length El Chino judged that they were far enough from Doblado's headquarters to avoid being spotted by his scouts and far enough from Veracruz. "We'll eat first, boys," he said, "and then we'll take care of these two."

Laffan moaned, and his head sank to his saddle horn and rocked from side to side.

"God, he's pissed himself," sneered one of the men. Sure enough, the dark stain spread down Laffan's leg. The others laughed and fell on their beans, salt fish and tortillas, ignoring their prisoners.

When he had sucked the last bit of grease from his fingers, El Chino belched, stood up and looked over his men. "You, Romero," the man closest to him, he commanded, "and you, Chaparro," by far the shortest, "you two take our smelly Mexican guest over behind that hill and don't bring him back. Oh, and take the gringo, so he'll see what happens if he tries to run." He snorted. "Let him dig the grave, but bring *him* back."

Bartlett was sick with horror. He had tried desperately for an hour to ease the leather bonds on his wrists but he could not even get his fingers to them. He looked again at Laffan, who was still slumped lifeless over his saddle horn, groaning feebly and praying. Bartlett could just make out his words: "*Santa Maria, Madre de Dios...*"

Chaparro and Romero led the horses by their reins over the hill and began to descend. "This is far enough," Romero said, dismounting. "You know, Chaparrito, I'm sick of all these dirty jobs. Why is it always me?" He prodded Laffan's back with his rifle. "Get down, *amigo*, let's get it over with."

Shaking violently, Laffan was incapable of movement. Romero prodded again, then he reached his knife across the withers to cut Laffan's bonds. With a smooth backhand stroke, Laffan's right hand slashed across

Romero's throat. It held a knife, and Romero was dead when Laffan's left hand ripped the rifle from his hand. Both men fell to the ground.

Bartlett saw this but Chaparro, standing on the far side of Bartlett's horse, could not. Bartlett instinctively rolled off the horse on to his feet on the near side, which gave Laffan a clear shot under both horses at the unlucky Chaparro's crotch. The first round tore away the tiny bandit's manhood; the second, his life.

"Mount up," hissed Laffan. "Walk." He thrust Chaparro's pistol in his belt and led the way down the hill and into a shallow valley at the bottom. Here he cut Bartlett's bonds and let out his breath. "We're not out of this yet. Follow me and *stay on that horse*."

Laffan figured that El Chino would assume that the two shots had killed him and that Bartlett was now digging his grave. He hoped the bandit wouldn't guess that they were making for Doblado's headquarters. If he did, his band would wait for them in the pine forests near there. To throw them off, he headed north for almost an hour at a medium canter. Bartlett clung grimly to one rein and the saddle horn and let his horse follow Laffan. This was his only chance to stay aboard because, as Laffan guided his mount around the pine trees, bushes, tree stumps and fallen logs in their path, Bartlett's horse dutifully tracked every move.

They halted again on the south slope of the first real mountain, about three thousand feet up. Laffan pulled a telescope from his saddlebag and sighted south, then east and west. "Nothing," he said. "Hear anything?" Bartlett shook his head, his lungs heaving for air. He was exhausted; he had needed all his strength just to stay upright. His legs were on fire.

Laffan smiled. "I told you these were the finest horses in the state. They'll run away from anything. But," he raised a finger, "those pricks are still after us. After me, so I won't report them; after you, so you can make them rich." He held out his canteen to Bartlett, who waved it away. Then he pointed to the southwest. "There. See that smoke over the second hill? That's Tehuacan, that's where we're going."

"Five miles or so?" Bartlett guessed.

"About that. We'll take it slowly. Speed's not important now, but noise is."

Bartlett studied him. "Pancho, how in hell – "

"Later, my friend. Plenty of time later." He flowed up into the saddle. "Let's go."

They trotted down that hill and around the base of the next with no sign of their pursuers. The track began to climb more sharply and the horses' breathing became labored. Again they stopped, sighted in all directions and listened but heard only a warm wind from the seacoast. The sun was dropping now, with no more than an hour to dusk, and had lost its heat. The closer they got to their goal, the more tense they grew.

Bartlett shivered. One more foothill to work their way around, then safety. Laffan waved an arm and they set off.

The pine branch over Bartlett's head exploded. The second bullet clipped his horse's left ear. "They're behind us," Laffan cried and spurred to a gallop, aiming for the ridge line a few hundred yards ahead and to their left. Bartlett dropped the reins, leaned forward and gripped the bridle with both hands. The horse needed no orders. It leapt after its fellow, with Bartlett swaying wildly but staying aboard somehow. Laffan looked back, saw Bartlett was in trouble and slowed to help him. They rode saddle to saddle and Laffan gripped Bartlett's shoulder to steady him, or at the least to keep him from falling off. They heard no more shots as they raced up through the pines and around the last hill and down to the mountain stream that a few hundred yards farther up bisected the dreary village of Tehuacan.

There was no bridge. "Of course not," Laffan swore. He measured the gorge, looked right, then left and galloped up the hill to their right. His instinct was correct and their luck was in. Two minutes later they presented themselves to the guard at the tall outer gate of the hacienda that Doblado had commandeered.

Laffan helped Bartlett down and steadied him as he tried to straighten up. Then he turned to the slovenly guard who watched with his mouth wide open. "Tell General Doblado, corporal, that Colonel Eufemio Laffan presents his compliments and requests an immediate interview."

"Colonel who?"

"You salute when an officer addresses you, soldier," Laffan snapped. "Colonel Laffan, damn you, with an important guest. Now move." The corporal did, looking over his shoulder at Laffan's soiled trousers.

Laffan dragged a pair of trousers out of a saddlebag and moved behind the horses. "Keep an eye out, will you, while I change these trousers." After a minute or two he stepped back into the light, fastening his belt. "I'm a new man now. I expect I smell no worse than this Doblado."

Bartlett laughed. "You're the first man I've met, Pancho, who could piss on demand. And after two days in the desert."

"It's a useful talent at times. Got me out of the classroom often enough." He took in Bartlett's admiring stare. "Oh, it was easy enough. I always have a knife in my sleeve – a trick I did not learn at the Point – and they stupidly crossed my wrists when they tied me to the saddle horn. The knots were easy."

"So you just had to wait for the right moment."

"Correct, and hope they'd send us off to be killed with only two or three men."

A short, thick young cavalry colonel appeared with the corporal, who held a basin of water, and introduced himself. He brought General

Doblado's invitation to supper for Colonel Laffan and his distinguished guest, but perhaps they would first prefer to clean up? His men would see to the horses. They would and did. The water seemed clean. The colonel meanwhile smoothed his extravagant moustaches, then he led them through the outer gates of the hacienda.

It was barely light enough to see, but they made out the stables, a chapel, storerooms and a granary. Another set of gates gave on to a vast courtyard with splashing fountains and trees. Along the low verandas there were birdcages with vividly colored parrots and rows of potted flowering plants. The large, rectangular stone house in the center had barred windows, loopholes in the walls and fortifications at the corners.

"This is built to stand off a siege," Laffan said as he surveyed the house.

The colonel led them in past the guards at the entrance, along a veranda facing a central courtyard and then into what looked like the main dining room. Clustered at one end of the massive table were General Doblado and three staff officers. They were most of the way down a decanter of brandy.

"Thank you, Colonel Diaz," Doblado called. He held out a hand and a wide smile. "Colonel Laffan, I have heard the President speak of you. This is a singular pleasure." Laffan saluted and they shook hands. "And our guest is?"

Laffan presented Bartlett as an old schoolmate, a close friend, a major in the Union Army and the special representative in Mexico of Brigadier Miles Stoddard. Doblado shook hands and introduced his staff, who all bowed. "Welcome on all four counts, Major," he said in English. "I believe I, ah, encountered General Stoddard at Chapultepec in forty-eight. A fine soldier."

"Thank you, sir," Bartlett replied. "He asked me to send you his compliments if I met you," he added imaginatively.

Doblado raised an eyebrow, smiled and waved them to seats next to him. Far from smelling, he was neatly dressed, almost dandyish, with a high forehead, full lips and calm, intelligent greenish-brown eyes. This man's no fool, Bartlett warned himself.

They declined supper, pleading exhaustion, and asked only for a bath and a bed, which were duly promised. After further formalities involving the brandy, Doblado told them he was at their service and asked them to tell him in plain language what they wanted from him.

Laffan nodded and Bartlett accounted for his presence in Veracruz. Without naming Morny, he explained that he was attached to one European leader, and he hinted at a second, who relied on him to allay any American fears that the invaders had "a wider objective" by reporting their military movements to Stoddard in Washington.

"A heavy responsibility, Major," Doblado said.

"Yes, sir, but one I have been unable to carry out." The telegraph cable from Veracruz to Mexico City, he pointed out, and from the capital to Monterrey was in good order. But none of his telegrams had reached the Presidio in San Francisco. "There's a breakage, or a disconnection of some sort this side of the border, sir. The cable's been checked on the other side." He prayed that it had been.

"How do you know that?" Doblado asked sharply.

"From our embassy in Mexico City." Another flat lie, but it couldn't be helped.

"Your reports are in code?"

"Of course, sir."

"Perhaps that's the reason. Perhaps our people refuse to transmit messages they can't read."

Laffan broke in. He set out in Spanish the reasons why Bartlett, and he, believed that allowing the reports to go through would benefit Mexico. "To help persuade the Americans to stay the hell out if they're not needed, but to send help *quickly* if they are. That could be an immense benefit to us," he urged. Bartlett understood most of this and nodded his approval.

After a long pause, Doblado sucked his teeth and replied. "That all makes sense, Colonel, but it depends on the accuracy of this man's reports."

"I will be in Veracruz and I will make certain –"

"Ah! And will the Major allow you to read his reports?"

"Sorry, no. I could not do that." Bartlett lifted his chin and looked noble. "It would betray the trust the Europeans place in me."

Doblado was not wholly persuaded. It would be a simple matter to cable his counterpart in Monterrey to do whatever was necessary, but he hesitated. Was there a need to consult Juarez? No. He had extracted from the President, before accepting his present position, full authority to negotiate with the Europeans, and this matter of the telegraph fell well within that authority. He would think about it.

"Gentlemen, this is an important proposal you bring me. I shall have to consult my staff in the morning. And now, may I suggest one last brandy before Colonel Diaz shows you to your quarters?"

Laffan shook Bartlett awake the next morning. "Good news, Charles, good news, old man!" Doblado had called him in an hour ago. He would do what they asked. He would cable General Monroy in Monterrey today to get that cable repaired and report back to him. "What's more, he'll notify me when it's fixed."

"That's splendid, Pancho. Good work." Bartlett held out his hand.

Laffan shook it. "Just put in a good word for me when you Yanks take Mexico again." He paused. "There is a price for this, though, and I've paid it. He made me vouch for your integrity, swear that your reports will be accurate."

"Oh. Well, that's no problem. Is it?" He started to get up and fell back with a cry. His inner thighs were afire. "Is it?"

"Well, I'd – " Laffan changed his mind. "No, of course not."

After breakfast they called again on Doblado, Laffan to report their encounter with his renegade soldiers the day before, Bartlett, limping badly, to thank him for his help with the cable and to ask for one more dispensation. He had devoted much time over the past three days to polish his arguments for his second request to the Mexican army.

"Allow them to move up to the foothills, to those three villages?" Doblado was almost angry. "Really, Major, you presume too much on the courtesies due to a guest in our country." He shook his head and stood up to examine a map on the wall. The three villages were too small, he said, and would be swamped by the numbers of the foreign troops. They were fifty miles closer to Puebla and Mexico City; could Bartlett guarantee that the Europeans would go no farther inland? Of course he could not. The brown eyes were cold.

"Besides, Major, we have no clear idea of what they really want in Mexico. We know they are stealing – collecting, they call it – our customs duties. But for how long? And they issued a high-minded proclamation about helping with the so-called "regeneration" of Mexico. What can that mean? Insulting rubbish."

"I understand, General, and – "

"If they would tell me honestly and clearly what they want here, I could consider permitting some of their troops to move up to a safer altitude. *Consider*, you will note. Can you tell me what they want?"

"I can not speak for any of the three forces, sir." The critical point was reached. "But I can give you my personal opinion as to what they *don't* want here, and that is a fight."

"And your professional opinion?"

"The same. A fight is the last thing the three commanders want to face *here*, in Mexico." Bartlett arranged his thoughts. "But the last thing they want *anywhere* is to be forced by the fever to scuttle back to Europe. To be defeated by the black vomit, humiliated by a disease." He laughed harshly. "You can imagine, sir, the reception they would get from their superiors and from their rulers. The disgrace. They would be humiliated, ruined." He began to admire his own eloquence.

"Yes, I can imagine it. I would not want to face either the Emperor or Lord Palmerston in those circumstances." Doblado rubbed his thin beard and lifted his wide-set eyes to the ceiling. "I'm told their men are sickening by the hundreds and dying by the dozens, and far worse is to come."

"That's right. They soon must make their choice, I believe," Bartlett said. Was his argument taking hold?

"A clear-cut choice, yes," Doblado said. "To return and face the Emperor and Palmerston in disgrace, or to stay and fight me and my thirty thousand men." He turned to Laffan. "Colonel, in their place which would you choose?"

Laffan replied crisply, "To die like a soldier in battle with the Mexicans, sir." Doblado didn't see his wink at Bartlett. "No doubt in my mind."

"Or not to die in that battle," Doblado corrected. "But I have to concede your point." He reviewed the facts. His ragged, untrained army of less than ten thousand was no match for the veteran, well-armed European regiments in an open battle. If the Europeans attacked with determination, he could not keep them out of the foothills; he probably would not even try to keep them out. So, militarily his decision was plain. Politically, he would have to consult Juarez, who, as the gods would have it, was expected in a day or two. He was coming to Tehuacan to see for himself.

There was no need, though, to tell the gringo major that the decision was not his alone to make. "Your arguments are well presented, Major. And Colonel Laffan. I will consult my staff and my unit commanders – it will take a day, perhaps two days – and let you have my decision in due course." During that time, they would be his guests. He prayed they would enjoy whatever amusement they might find in the hacienda or the village. Now, if they would excuse him?

Two days later and boredom had closed in. After he had done his duty and described El Chino and his men to Colonel Diaz, Laffan busied himself by reporting on the strength and dispositions of the European forces. "Acting like a proper spy," as he told Bartlett, who felt bound not to inspect the Mexican troops camped in and around the village. To do so would betray his honor as a guest, he believed. Laffan confirmed this. "We Mexicans like to say 'My house is your house,' and we mean every word, but while you're in it we don't want you to act like one of our own thieving cousins."

It was after lunch and they were lounging on the veranda in the shade, half hidden from the main entrance by two wicker cages in which four *papagallos*, the gaudy local macaws, harshly disputed their ration of bananas. Against the low background noises of an army camp, there came a rush of horses and shouting at the main gate. Half a dozen men in dusty black suits and broad hats hurried into the hacienda and made for the dining room. In their center was a short, dark Indian with a smooth head, cropped black hair and saurian eyes.

"Juarez," whispered Laffan, "El Presidente himself."

Juarez, indeed. He had passed the morning with his troops. He inspected the soldiers and then addressed their officers on the need to throw the Europeans back into the sea if diplomacy failed and they marched on Puebla. Now he wanted his lunch and a discussion with Doblado about this ominous request from some Yanqui officer.

An hour later Laffan greeted his new friend, Diaz, who hastened towards them. "What's up, Porfirio? Why the rush?"

Juarez wanted to see Colonel Laffan on the double. With a knowing smirk at Bartlett, Laffan marched off proudly after Diaz, leaving Bartlett to wait and wonder.

Soon enough Juarez and his suite bustled out of the house and Bartlett was summoned to the presence. Laffan stood in the background. "Please sit, Major," the general said. He straightened up in his chair and fixed his gaze on the Yankee. "Now, for purely humanitarian reasons, I will allow the Europeans to move up to Tehuacan, Orizaba and Cordoba." Bartlett breathed out heavily. "I will move my formations to the north, to make certain there are no accidental encounters with the Europeans. That could have unfortunate consequences."

"That's good news, General," Bartlett said, "I..."

"Yes, yes. But, there are three conditions." He held up a hand with the fingers spread. "One," he bent back one finger, "I must have a written request to this effect from Sir Charles Wyke within three days, along with his personal assurance that no villager will be harmed. Two," another finger bent, "the Europeans will not move up here before the last day of this month. And finally, all of their sick will remain in Veracruz."

Bartlett began to stammer his thanks but Doblado stopped him. "The request must be signed by Sir Charles, whom we respect. We don't know the Spanish commander, and we know Saligny too well to trust him at all."

"That's fine, sir – I think."

"It must be." Doblado relaxed back in his chair and crossed his arms. "I regret we have so little time together, Major." He asked a number of general questions about conditions in Veracruz, especially the medical facilities, all of which Bartlett felt able to answer honestly. Then: "I'm told there is some French grandee in the town who has commandeered the hotel and is lording it over everyone. The Emperor's cousin, is he?"

"His half-brother, the Count de Morny."

"A magnificent personage to send five thousand miles to collect a few trifling debts, don't you agree?"

"Ah, perhaps, sir." Bartlett paused, went on. "But his presence supports my opinion that the French would refuse to leave Mexico in disgrace, that instead they would fight to gain the foothills."

Chapter 26

They left at dawn the next day, determined to make Veracruz by sunset and escorted by Diaz and a squad of outriders who made El Chino and his associates look like cherubim.

But they didn't reach Veracruz that night. They were forced to camp a dozen miles outside the town. Laffan told Diaz it was because the Europeans sent out armed and nervous patrols in the area and he didn't know the password, but the reality was that Bartlett could not ride another mile. He was defeated by two long days in the saddle, aching so badly that Laffan suspected he'd come down with yellow fever and refused to take any chances with him. Diaz, his mind on the Veracruz cantinas after weeks in the outback, agreed with bad grace to the delay, taking care to show his contempt for the effete Yankee.

So it was a surly squad of men that gathered for coffee the next morning, their resentment running high. Oblivious to the general mood, Bartlett set his sidearm on a rock ledge when he removed his uniform coat. It was a new Colt that Chaparro had found in someone's holster. A scruffy, pockmarked soldier picked it up and held it out in the sun as if to admire it. Bartlett reached across to retrieve it but the soldier turned away. Shrugging, Bartlett asked Laffan, who was watching this tableau, to intervene. At his sharp command, the soldier spat, tossed the revolver at Bartlett and snarled, *"Chinga tu madre, pendejo."*

Bartlett, now furious, wheeled on Laffan and demanded what the man had said.

"Well, old boy, it was a bit of a paradox, but then most Mexicans like a paradox. I think it has something to do with their Indian – "

"What did he say, Pancho, dammit?"

"First he urged you to - ah, accommodate your mother. But then he implied that you're not physically equipped to do so. As I said, a bit of a paradox."

"Right. Can I shoot him? Just a little? In the foot, maybe?" The soldier was only yards away. Bartlett cocked the pistol and aimed.

"By all means. However..."

"I must advise you against, Major," Diaz cut in smoothly. "This man he one of four brothers who fight for the cause of the liberty and the justice in Mexico."

"So what?" snapped the enraged American.

"So, the other three are standing behind you."

"Oh."

Bartlett maintained an impassive dignity as they rode on to Veracruz, despite the occasional stifled guffaw from Laffan, who at length decided to ride well ahead. His mood brightened, though, two hours later when they rode into Veracruz and he could find Jones and tell him of his exploits in the foothills.

"You told General Doblado *what?*" Jones cried. They were again sitting, Bartlett most thankfully, in the massive chairs on the hotel veranda.

"That the Europeans will fight their way inland if they have to, to escape the fever. What else?" Bartlett smiled loftily.

"What on earth made you think they will?"

"Won't they? I have no idea. It sounded convincing at the time, though." Bartlett began to laugh, Jones caught his eye and joined in and at once they were doubled up.

Jones gasped, wiped his eyes and said, "God Almighty, what a nerve." He stifled another laugh and thought for a moment. "But, do you know, you just may be right. The way I see it, though, is that, if they have to, these boys will fight their way back onto their own ships, not up into the hills."

"The English and Spanish, yes, but not our master and his fellow Frogs. They'll fight to stay here. They're after big game, we know they are."

"Speaking of whom, I think you – we – owe the Count the courtesy of a call to relate your recent triumphs."

They duly formed up to Morny in his sitting room. It was now filled with flowers, and Henri had contrived to rig a vertical fan made of painted canvas, a sort of Indian *punkah* suspended from the ceiling. Relays of small boys worked the fan with ropes that ran through the windows to the ground outside.

Morny looked up from the latest draft of his third act. "The fan machine makes no difference to my comfort, if truth be told," he said with good humor, "but it pleases Henri and allows me to help a few poor children." He listened to Bartlett's tale and then asked several questions about Doblado's appearance, attitudes and intelligence, nodding in appreciation as Bartlett replied. Finally he shook Bartlett's surprised hand with warmth, saying, "Remarkable, truly remarkable, Major. The expedition owes you its gratitude."

"And Colonel Laffan, sir, you mustn't forget him."

"Indeed I will not." He was delighted, he said, that the telegraph line should soon be repaired and asked to be told when they transmitted their first report. "I can not inquire *what* you report, but as you are here as my guest I may properly insist that you tell me *when* you report it. No?" They could only agree.

"Now, as to General Doblado's three conditions: First, I'm certain Sir Charles Wyke will be only too happy to request a move to the uplands.

Second, I doubt we will be in a position to move before the end of the month in any event. Third, to leave all of our sick in Veracruz. That could be a difficulty. Perhaps we can send the worst cases to Cuba." He rubbed his chin hard. "We shall see, but in the end we will take up the general's offer. To refuse it would be to murder our own men."

After a few minutes discussing the terrain and the roads into the foothills, Morny rose and brushed his coatfront. He need not detain them further, he said. He would call on Sir Charles Wyke that morning to relay Bartlett's report, but first, "I should like to meet your Colonel Laffan - immediately." He looked around for Henri. "I prefer not to disclose your role in this matter, Major Bartlett, for obvious reasons. I propose to tell Sir Charles that General Doblado's message was brought to me by Colonel Laffan, so I must first persuade that officer to permit me to do so."

Bartlett glanced at Jones, who just rolled his eyes and shrugged. "I understand, sir, and I expect Laffan will, also. I'll find him and send him to you."

"He's quite a man, is your Count de Morny," Laffan drawled. It was that evening at Veracruz' best restaurant. Carolina, Bartlett and Jones listened with care as he told them of his meeting with the Frenchman earlier in the day. They had finished the speciality of the house, roast kid, and now, sitting in the candle-lit garden, they drank the sweet Mexican coffee from earthenware cups. "Quite a man. *Very* convincing. Can talk almost anyone into doing almost anything, I would bet."

"So you'll go along with his story to Wyke?" asked Jones in a low voice. The other tables were filled with Spanish and French officers. The English were confined to their ships.

"Of course. We can't let the English think that the Count is negotiating with Doblado on his own, can we? Wouldn't suit anyone's book."

"Is there any chance, Eufemio, that this - intervention can be resolved peacefully?" Carolina sounded doubtful.

"Every chance, Miss Laffan," Jones interjected, "sorry – Carolina." A half bow. "Provided, that is, that the Mexican army doesn't attack. And I don't think they will."

"Well, I'm in the Mexican army," said Laffan, "and I sure hope you're right. I aim to retire to my ranches as a colonel, not die near here as a general."

"Very wise, Pancho," Bartlett agreed, "if not very warlike." He called for another coffee and only Jones joined him. "But, tell me: Wouldn't you find it, um, uncomfortable fighting for Mexico, for Juarez? You had no trouble fighting *against* the Mexicans in forty eight."

"That's easy. I wasn't really a Mexican in forty-eight, you see. My Mexican mother died when I was nine, my father was Irish and I was raised in Texas, where Mexicans were foreigners.'

"And now?"

"Too obvious. All I want is peace, so my lands aren't stolen from me by the bandits on one side or the other."

*   *   *

In London, the usual mid-winter thaw had lasted longer than expected. Katherine, sitting in the window of her drawing room, looked up from her needlepoint and out over the sunlit garden. She searched apprehensively for the first crocus or daffodil to show a bright green leaf. Another two or three weeks yet, she hoped, and that's only if it doesn't freeze over again. She was relieved, in a way. She disliked gardening and each spring had to find a way to put off the day when she must begin to prepare the flower beds for Lord Carra's equinoctial assault on them. He had sacked his gardener some years ago and nothing could persuade him that he lacked all trace of horticultural talent.

Katherine was lonely. She missed Owen, more than she foresaw when he fled back to Boston. She knew that she might not see him again, ever. He would risk his life if he slipped back into England. Or he might be killed in the American war. His regiment had pulled back from the Canadian frontier, he wrote, and was now training in Brooklyn, but they would be moved to the front in the coming springtime, the season of battles.

Charles Bartlett... she missed him as well. She could not deny it. Even before they became... intimate, a term she hated, she had been reassured by merely knowing that he was there in the house next door. Perhaps the physical presence of any man younger than forty would have had the same effect, but she doubted it. His long frame, angular features and awkward manner were somehow comforting, even protective. Perhaps... She picked up her needlepoint.

*   *   *

"VERACRUZ MEXICO
FOR BRIG GENL M STODDARD
REPORT NUMBER ONE
PARA ONE STOP TOTAL EXPEDITION TROOP NUMBERS APPROXIMATELY SEVEN THOUSAND FIVE HUNDRED OF WHICH SPANISH FOUR THOUSAND FRENCH TWO

THOUSAND FIVE HUNDRED ENGLISH ONE THOUSAND STOP STRONG BUT UNCONFIRMED RUMORS OF IMMINENT FRENCH REINFORCEMENTS OF PERHAPS FOUR THOUSAND MORE STOP
TWO STOP YELLOW FEVER SPREADING FAST STOP WE ESTIMATE THREE TO FIVE HUNDRED DEAD SIX TO EIGHT HUNDRED IN MAKESHIFT HOSPITALS STOP PEAK OF FEVER SEASON EXPECTED IN TWO TO FOUR WEEKS STOP
THREE STOP MEXICAN GENERAL DOBLADO WILL ALLOW EXPEDITION TROOPS TO MOVE INLAND THIS MONTH TO ESCAPE FEVER STOP SPANISH TO ORIZABA FRENCH TO TEHUACAN AND CORDOBA ENGLISH UNDECIDED STOP DOBLADO AND SPANISH GENERAL PRIM MEETING NOW AT LA SOLEDAD TO ESTABLISH DETAILS OF MOVE STOP WILL REPORT RESULTS WHEN AVAILABLE STOP
FOUR STOP NO SIGN YET OF POPULAR UPRISING AS EXPECTED BY FRENCH STOP NO SIGN YET OF FRENCH ATTEMPT TO INSTALL EUROPEAN AS KING STOP
PLEASE CONFIRM RECEIPT STOP
XZ"

Laffan had reported three days earlier that the line from Monterrey to the border was repaired. Every message was to be encoded with Bartlett's one-time pad and go to Stoddard, who after decoding would pass it on to Henry Wise at naval intelligence.

"VERACRUZ MEXICO
FOR BRIG GENL M STODDARD
REPORT NUMBER TWO
FURTHER TO REPORT ONE STOP PRIM RETURNED TODAY FROM LA SOLEDAD MEETING WITH DOBLADO. ESSENTIALS OF THEIR AGREEMENT FOLLOW STOP
ONE STOP ALLIES RECOGNIZE MEXICO NEEDS NO HELP TO PROTECT ITSELF AGAINST INTERNAL REVOLT STOP

TWO STOP ALLIES WILL MAKE NO ATTEMPT
AGAINST SOVEREIGNTY OF MEXICO AND
WILL NEGOTIATE ALL THEIR CLAIMS WITH
MEXICO STOP
THREE STOP ALLIES WILL OCCUPY ORIZABA
CORDOBA AND TEHUACAN UNTIL
NEGOTIATIONS FINISH STOP
MORNY ANGRY AT ABOVE TERMS BUT
FORCED TO ACCEPT THEM AS FAIT ACCOMPLI
BY PRIM STOP OUR SOURCE REPORTS JUAREZ
WILL RATIFY TERMS STOP
KINDLY CONFIRM RECEIPT THIS REPORT AND
REPORT NUMBER ONE STOP
XZ"

"*Morny angry*? Apoplectic, more like," Jones observed as Henri left for the telegraph office with their encrypted cable. "I never saw French royalty spitting nails before."

"He should have gone up to La Soledad, then," said Bartlett as he poured a beer. He stacked the discarded drafts of their report that littered the table and made a space to set down the glass. Then he settled with care back into the nest of cushions that Conchita had arranged for his aching buttocks.

They had established the *cantina* as their headquarters. Morny now spent much of his time in *Isabella's* stateroom, polishing his play and escaping the worst of the nighttime heat. He had invited them to use a spare bedroom in his hotel suite as their office but they declined. They preferred El Caribe for its liveliness, its colder beer and – Bartlett suspected – the accessibility of Conchita, whose implacable pursuit of Jones showed no sign of flagging. Or of success, if her prey could be believed.

"No, there was no chance he would go up there," Jones corrected. "He expected Doblado to demand some sort of rubbish about the dignity and sovereignty of Mexico, and he wasn't going to put his name to it. Let that pompous Spaniard, Prim, take responsibility for it, he said."

They lingered at the table for another hour or two, Jones bantering with Conchita. He wore one of the new non-regulation uniforms he had picked up that morning. Henri's tailor had used up all his white duck on Bartlett, so Jones had to make do instead with some dark tan material. When he and Bartlett entered the cantina, Conchita promptly and loudly christened them *café con leche* – coffee with milk. The regulars at the bar thought this hilarious, the gringo officers brought down a peg or two.

Bartlett let his mind drift far from Veracruz. He thought of London. Then he pondered once again why he had let Jones persuade him that this trip to Mexico would restore him to the esteem of Miles Stoddard. Granted, he had done well on his mission to Doblado, but would Stoddard ever learn of it? And if he did, would he appreciate the obstacles that he, Bartlett, had to master before he could do so well? Not bloody likely.

Then he looked across at Jones, obscured in part by the abundant form of Conchita on his knee. Overhanging both his knees, in fact. The poor devil. He was also stuck in a tropical barroom while the goal of his professional life, a deadly new ironclad gunboat, took shape two thousand miles north in a Brooklyn shipyard. Sympathy for his companion diluted Bartlett's own self-pity somewhat, but not much.

*   *   *

"WASHINGTON DC
FOR JONES BARTLETT
CONFIRM RECEIPT YOUR REPORTS NUMBER ONE AND TWO STOP WELL DONE STOP
SEND REGULAR REPORTS ON INTENDED AND ACTUAL TROOP DISPOSITIONS STOP ALSO REPORTS REGARDING OBJECTIVES OF POLITICAL AND MILITARY COMMANDERS WITH SPECIAL REFERENCE TO FRENCH COMMANDERS STOP AM CONCERNED BY OBVIOUS RISK THAT TROOP MOVEMENTS INLAND NOT ENTIRELY DUE TO FEVER RISK STOP
STILL NO SIGN OF EXPECTED POPULAR UPRISING BY NATIVES QUERY
STODDARD"

Seward handed the cable back to Stoddard. "As a diplomat, I suggest you change 'natives' to 'Mexicans', but otherwise I think that covers the ground commendably, General," he smiled.

"I'll send it today." Stoddard put the paper in his coat pocket. "I'm relieved they finally fixed that telegraph line," he admitted. "Jones and Bartlett would be of scant use to me without it."

Seward was reflecting on the wider scene of the war. To him and to all of Lincoln's cabinet, war was no longer a strange concept. Battles had been fought. Greater battles would be fought soon.

The North intended to capture the Mississippi down to New Orleans and break the South's back. The South built formidable defences along the great river, neglecting the other river invasion routes. The North struck first at Fort Henry on the Tennessee River, then at Fort Donelson on the Cumberland. Shiloh, on the Tennessee, was only a month away.

These victories proved that at last the North would fight, could fight well and could win. So now Seward could warn France off. The victories on the western rivers had made that possible. He said he had instructed Dayton, his man in Paris, to stress to the French foreign minister that the United States could not look with indifference upon any armed European intervention for political ends in Mexico.

"A shot across Napoleon's bows, eh?" Stoddard said.

"Yes, but it will need much more than that to warn him off. He's a determined cuss, you know, when he wants something badly. People forget that; they think he's just a jumped-up adventurer." Seward leaned back and crossed his arms, the sign that he wanted to chat for a time. He reminded Stoddard that Napoleon had twice mounted an armed *coup d'etat* against Louis Phillippe. "Once he led a platoon of soldiers against a barracks in Strasbourg, helped by an army colonel who wanted to sleep with his mistress. The second time he rented a pleasure steamer in England, filled it with fifty amateur revolutionaries and sailed over to Boulogne. Both attempts failed immediately, came to nothing and made him a laughing stock. The second time they locked him away for life in Ham fortress, but he escaped, dressed as a workman and carrying a plank of lumber. Two years later he was President of France."

"Yes, I know the story," Stoddard said, "but Mexico's a long way from Paris."

"Of course, but what you may not know is that he's been obsessed with Latin America for years. Years!" Seward jumped to his feet. "He believes it's where the future lies. And he'll be hard to shift out of there. Damned hard."

*   *   *

Henri delivered Stoddard's cable to Jones and Bartlett about five o'clock the next afternoon. It instructed them to show it to Morny, so Bartlett pocketed it and left to look in the hotel for their host, taking the longer route along the seafront for some exercise. He walked quickly, anxious to escape the clouds of mosquitoes that began to patrol at dusk every day. The easterly wind had dropped away so he was treated to the full measure of the Veracruz stench, a noisome combination of rotting fruit, smoke from the mangrove fires and the town's open plan sanitation system.

The narrow, empty beach was littered with coconuts. The boys who collect them are either sick or up in the hills, he said to himself, and so are the people who used to throng this stretch of the *malecon* at about this time. The street vendors, purveying everything from stuffed iguanas to sharks' teeth to tortoise-shell combs, had folded up and gone. A few bands of black Chasseurs loitered about, looking for girls and trusting to their African ancestry to protect them from the mosquitoes. Otherwise, the front was bare of soldiers, the rest of them on the sick list or restricted to quarters.

As he approached the municipal bathhouse, Bartlett looked out over the bay and the reefs and saw that Morny's launch was rowing in from *Isabella*. Morny himself stood upright in the bow, his bald dome glistening in the sunlight as he fanned hard with his planter's hat. Bartlett decided to meet him on the pier that jutted into the sea from the customhouse.

In a town whose most prosperous industry was smuggling, it was fitting that the customhouse was by far the grandest structure. Its façade was a series of tall arches and pillars that fronted the vast storage rooms behind them. Bales of cotton, stacks of hardwood timber, bags of rice and pieces of machinery were being moved around by somnolent porters. At one side lay what looked like most of a steam locomotive.

The invaders had trimmed the personnel roster, but Bartlett saw rows of clerks bent over their ledgers in the offices that lined the central passageway that led to the pier. He pushed past the Spanish guards and walked out to the end of the pier as Morny's crew tied up his launch. Morny soon followed them up the ladder, on his face a look of thunder.

"Good evening, Count," Bartlett announced himself. Morny returned only a glance of recognition and a faint smile, so Bartlett hurried to explain his mission and hand him the cable.

Morny studied it as they walked along, started to hand it back and then read it once more. "Not very subtle, your foreign secretary, is he? Still, if one's only club is as frail as your famous Monroe Doctrine, I suppose one must wave it about as noisily as possible, hoping thus to scare off the natives." Bartlett did not reply, and Morny added, "Henri tells me you keep him busy with your telegrams. Have you sent another report today? No? Then it seems I am up to date. As, I trust, are your superiors in Washington."

Bartlett murmured his assent, fearing to say anything to annoy his companion. He's obviously furious about something, he thought, and I'll press him a bit. "What brings you ashore this evening, sir, if I may ask?"

"Yet another conference with the Commissioners," was the angry response. Then, "I suppose I'm obliged to tell you more, am I? Well, we have all received our new instructions, and we have to consider the implications of this wretched La Soledad agreement."

"Yes, it appears to limit your freedom of movement," Bartlett ventured.

"To put it politely, yes it does." They passed through the customhouse and out into the square before their hotel. Few people were about. Morny swore softly. "Damn that Spanish cretin, that Prim. I've never trusted him. His wife is Mexican, you know, and is said to spend much of her time in this country" He looked up sharply at Bartlett by his side. "You will repeat none of this, of course."

"Of course."

Morny seemed to have mislaid his discretion. "Prim is like the man who went out to buy wool and came back shorn." He shook his head in annoyance. "But he's man of great common sense, Saligny assured me before we sent him up there alone. Never choose a man for his common sense, I replied, it's the first thing to go when he's under pressure. How right I was."

They walked into the hotel to be met by the fretting Henri, anxious to move his master to the safety of his suite with its overhead fan and heavily netted windows and doors. "Do stop clucking, Henri!" Morny snapped. "You're a worse nuisance than the mosquitoes."

Chapter 27

Napoleon III had converted a corner of the Green Room into his operations center. A large map of Mexico, dotted with paper flags, hung on the wall behind his desk. On a table lay sketches of his own designs for the new uniforms in which his troops would, he was confident, cope with the coastal heat.

His Empress, in a vivid blue dress, sat to one side, with Hidalgo directly in front of the imperial desk. Tension was high. Hidalgo shifted in his seat and coughed. Napoleon turned away from his map and smiled at the Mexican.

"We must welcome you back," he said. "A pleasant journey from Mexico?"

"Most unpleasant, sir, but rapid." Hidalgo laid a thick envelope on the edge of the desk. "I have prepared a written report for you, sir, but for the present I would prefer to touch on one aspect only of the situation." A nod of the imperial head. "And that is the absence thus far of any sort of uprising by my people in support of a new monarchy." He drew a deep breath. "This lamentable state of affairs has arisen because there is no outstanding leader among our Conservatives, there is no clear-cut, visible purpose to the expedition, and there is – "

"No support from the expedition, from its Commissioners," finished Napoleon.

"Indeed. They quarrel among themselves as their men die around them. They negotiate with the usurper Juarez when they should attack him. The Conservative forces in Mexico can see nothing to rally to, sir, and they can see no hope of success if they do rise."

"Well, the Commission have been hamstrung by this disgraceful agreement of La Soledad, negotiated by that traitorous Spaniard, Prim." Napoleon tossed his cigarette at the fire.

"Yes, the Count de Morny explained that he was forced to accept those terms only so that his troops can be moved up to healthier altitudes."

"You saw Morny?" Eugenie asked.

"I did, and he asked me to give you this "humble offering", as he called it." Hidalgo handed Eugenie a Veracruz *serape*, a long shawl made of fine goat's hair and dyed a striking geometric pattern in red, black and green. Morny knew of Eugenie's recent passion for Mexican decorative arts, and he had chosen well. She was delighted and not too shy to display her delight. She wound the shawl around her shoulders as she made for the nearest looking glass.

"What do you think, Louis?" she asked without turning around.

"Enchanting, my love. Every lady in Paris must soon have one or perish of shame." He lit another cigarette, waved away the smoke and said to Hidalgo, "You saw my brother? Is he well?"

"Very well, sir. Waiting for the reinforcements he requested."

"*Requested*, indeed. Demanded, rather. And he'll get them. I'm sending him General Lorencez and a brigade of four thousand men." This was said with satisfaction.

Eugenie spoke softly to her husband. "Señor Hidalgo is too polite to remind you, Louis, that what is also needed is the man to lead the popular rising. Is that correct, Mr. Hidalgo? And that he is needed in Mexico now?"

"Quite correct, as ever, Madame," Hidalgo smiled.

"What? What?" asked Napoleon. "Ah! I see. Of course. Almonte."

General Juan Nepucemeno Almonte was said to be the natural son of Morelos, the liberal priest who led the Mexican forces in the revolt against colonial Spain. He became a soldier, fighting with Santa Anna in the Texan wars and ten years later commanding a large force against the invaders from the United States. Juarez' predecessor sent him as Minister to Paris, where he met Hidalgo, gained the confidence of the Emperor and stayed on in Paris as a resident member of the imperial court.

Almonte had been Napoleon's obvious choice to inspire and lead the uprising on which so much depended. A choice enthusiastically endorsed by the rich Mexican émigrés in Europe, most of them in France. They had formed a Junta composed in traditional Latin style of no fewer than thirty-five of their number. These had then set up an inner junta, which they called with commendable optimism La Regencia, and placed Almonte at its head.

"Has he returned from Miramar?" Eugenie asked. "Did Maximilian accept him?"

"His visit was a remarkable success," Hidalgo said excitedly. "He and the Archduke agreed on everything." He produced another sheet of paper. "The Archduke named the General as his sole representative in Mexico."

"Almonte is an inspired choice, Mr. Hidalgo, our congratulations." Eugenie sounded almost as excited as the Mexican.

Napoleon looked at his watch. "I don't suppose they agreed about Almonte's expenses, such as who will pay them?"

For the first time, Hidalgo looked uncertain. "I believe not."

"Then we can guess who will pay, can we not?" No reply. "I'll see General Almonte with you tomorrow morning, if you would be kind enough to arrange it. Tell him I expect him to leave for Mexico as soon as he can. We can send him over with Lorencez."

Napoleon made his brief excuses to Eugenie and Hidalgo and hurried out. His doctor was waiting – the pain was more severe than usual today – and then La Italiana was expecting him before dinner.

As he left he heard Eugenie tell Hidalgo, her voice faltering, that the Pope had at last given his blessing to Maximilian's installation as monarch of Mexico. All of Italy is with us now, he grinned to himself. How can we fail?

*   *   *

A few hours later, the Prime Minister sat slumped in his Piccadilly study by a fire that was for once hot enough for him, listening as his Foreign Secretary relayed the reports from Paris and Mexico. They were all bad.

There was now no doubt that Napoleon himself had originated the idea of placing Maximilian on the Mexican throne and that the Archduke would accept the throne when offered to him. It was also plain that Napoleon had assured him that England had guaranteed him, militarily and financially, as he had required.

There was more. General Lorencez would soon sail for Veracuz with four thousand more men, and the French money demands on Mexico were on the order of forty million dollars.

Palmerston groaned. "That is grand larceny, not policy," he said. "And they'll be in Mexico for *years* to extract that sum. Or," the thought struck him, "they'll use the debt as their excuse for military action."

"I fear you're correct," said Russell.

"But we can't withdraw. We can't. That would suit Lincoln down to the ground, to see England turn tail and run for cover. So – and I trust you'll agree, John – we will remain in Mexico at all costs, we will negotiate all our claims at great length. We keep our spoke in the Emperor's wheel and we find some way to strike at the Yanks."

Russell smiled grimly. "I'll instruct Wyke to stay on at all costs."

"At all costs. Make sure he understands that in no circumstances can we leave Mexico until after the French leave – all of them."

*   *   *

In Hampton Roads, two ironclad ships fought the most momentous naval engagement in history. John Ericsson's ugly *Monitor* and the Confederacy's rebuilt *Virginia* hammered each other with solid shot for hours, at ranges as low as a few yards. Both ships retired undamaged, their armored sides and crewmen's pride both intact.

The historic naval supremacy of England vanished in the Chesapeake smoke, as *The Times* of London reported: "There is not now a ship in the

English navy, apart from *Warrior* and *Black Prince,* that it would not be madness to trust in an engagement with that little *Monitor.*"

$*$ $*$ $*$

In Veracruz, three weeks had passed - three weeks of heat, boredom and pestilence - while the Commissioners waited for new instructions from their masters in Europe.

One third of the allied soldiers lay dead or lay gasping in the filthy makeshift hospital wards, tended by the nuns from the town's three convents. Mounds of red earth and white wooden crosses lined the low hill outside the city wall near Fort Santiago. President Juarez had decreed that any Mexican who helped or traded with the invaders was to be prosecuted, so all the gravediggers downed tools and the soldiers had to bury their own.

Small groups of horsemen in ragtag uniforms patrolled the savannah around Veracruz. Often now they rode under the walls, never staying but never hurrying. The rumor was that General Doblado, furious at the repeated postponements of the negotiations called for in the La Soledad agreement, had ordered his commanders to reconnoiter the allies' troop dispositions. And to indulge in light harassment of those troops if they felt like it. Three French Zouaves were found knifed to death at the top of an alley one morning, whether by Mexican soldiers or by their own comrades was never established. To the allied officers, it was inevitable that a minor confrontation between the two sides would lead to a skirmish, then to a battle and then to a shooting war. Doblado also spread the report that he was assembling all his forces in the mountains around Orizaba and that they were thirty thousand strong.

Meanwhile the allied commissioners argued fiercely over where to send their troops and when to send them there. Morny left no doubt that he wanted Tehuacan for the French units already on site and he wanted Cordoba for the reinforcements Napoleon was sending him. Tehuacan was a mile high and boasted a railhead and a telegraph station, rare amenities in the region. Cordoba was lower and hotter, but closer to Veracruz. General Prim, spitting oaths that did not become his station, in the end agreed. He would move up to Orizaba and Jalapa. The English chose to remain on their ships.

Leaving behind a small detachment to maintain order and collect the customs duties, the Spanish marched out bravely on a Sunday morning. The French, leaving behind a detachment that included Morny, Henri, Jones and Bartlett, looked even braver when they left two days later.

These four watched them go. Then Morny swabbed his bald head with a scarlet bandanna, patted his hat back in place and smiled at the two

Americans. "Well, my friends, by Friday my poor soldiers should at last be safe from the fever. Thank God for that."

"That's if the Mexicans don't kill them on the way," said Jones. "There're a lot of them out there, Count. And not many of them are friendly, from what we hear."

"True, but Doblado will never risk an attack on us. Not when he must be thinking that he can stall us and stall us until we leave out of sheer boredom." He looked at his watch and saw that it was time for his afternoon swim. *Isabella's* crew had scrutinized the water around her hull since they anchored and, other than one stray barracuda, had spotted no aquatic predators, certainly no sharks. The troop of small boys who swam daily from the ramparts of Fort Juan de Ulloa also reassured them, and Morny.

The Americans accepted his invitation to dinner aboard that night and he took his leave. "Until eight, gentlemen. We shall drink champagne in large quantities, to toast the safety of my soldiers. Come, Henri."

Bartlett and Jones sloped off to El Caribe to compose their report to Stoddard on the French movement. By now they were quite skilled in the use of the one-time pad, and after they encoded the report they amused themselves by encoding other, preposterous messages to Stoddard by way of practice. In one, the German fleet anchored off Veracruz harbor and leveled the town with its big guns. In another, the Mexican army tore the Spanish invaders to pieces in a set piece battle near Orizaba. In the last, Jones ran off to Tampico with the wife of the chef at the Hotel Magnifico.

Jones screwed up the practice papers and threw them in the fire as he rose to leave. "I'll take our report to the telegraph office and then I'm off to ride with Carolina. Want to come?"

This was a standing joke. He knew that Bartlett detested horses. But he had prevailed on Bartlett to teach him a few of the finer points of horsemanship that he had painfully acquired in the western prairie. He reminded Bartlett of all the time he spent teaching him Spanish and Bartlett's sense of obligation did the rest, as Jones knew it would. They borrowed horses from Laffan and Jones turned out to be a fast learner.

"With Carolina again?" Bartlett asked, unsurprised. They rode together most late afternoons. She thought that he protected her on their rides but Jones knew she had it backwards: as the sister of a colonel in the Mexican army, she protected him.

"Yep," Jones replied evenly. "Laffan has six horses here and he likes us to exercise them all. You won't come, then?"

Bartlett laughed and waved him away. It struck him that he hadn't seen Laffan for four or five days. The Mexican now spent less time in town, saying that there was no action there and he had other jobs to do along the coast. What they were he never said.

The *cantina* began to fill up and he asked for a beer. Conchita had been persuaded by Jones that serving two American officers did not put her at risk of execution, so she was happy to produce a glass of the coldest beer in the bar for him. She had begun to despair of netting Jones but Bartlett, now that she inspected him at her leisure, looked promising.

Then Gomez, the owner, appeared at his table wearing his usual cheesy grin and his burlap and leather sandals. Bartlett had observed that Gomez was most friendly when his other customers were not and that he understood more English than he let on. Today they exchanged banalities for a minute or two and Gomez went back to his kitchen.

Bartlett sat back and watched as other customers filtered in, all of them avoiding his eye although he knew many of them well enough to exchange greetings with. It's as if they expect something to happen, he thought. Should he alert Jones? No, he could look after himself. And Carolina.

The focus of his thoughts shifted. Jones and Carolina – what was going on there? They were in each other's company often enough, and probably more often than he knew. Jones had taken to disappearing from time to time with only a muttered excuse of some kind. And he had denied all knowledge of a wife when he first met her.

His relationship with Jones was subtly changing. Jones had long been the senior partner in their ventures because of his rank and his closer professional relationships with, first, Miles Stoddard, their superior officer, and now with Morny, their only client, so to speak. But more than that, Jones had a definite manner, a manner that declared that he was in charge of things and that nothing would stop him from performing his mission. It also declared that he expected Bartlett to go along with him and that he would not be too upset if he didn't.

From the time he first worked with Jones on North Star, Bartlett's reaction to this relationship had been one of tolerance mixed with mild resentment, punctuated by moments of hatred when Jones exposed them both to real danger. A resentment underlain by jealousy – jealousy of Jones's self-confidence and single-minded pursuit of his goal, jealousy even of his easy success with women. First Conchita, and now Carolina? While he, Bartlett, was left only with his memories of Katherine Carra. And his worries.

He recognized that he often now felt the need to compete with Jones, compete on their professional level, that is. He was equipped to do so: his Spanish was adequate; his knowledge of Veracruz and the hills was better than Jones's; Morny treated them as equals; and their one success – the concessions he had extracted from Doblado – was his alone. But, as in any joint venture, competition could lead to simple obstruction for its own sake. Of this he was aware, as he was aware of his instinct to complain and dig his heels in when under pressure.

God, he thought as he wiped his forehead, life gets complicated, even on a simple job like this one. And we still have no idea how we can possibly induce the allies to go back home. What a pair we are.

He declined another beer from Conchita. It was time to dodge the mosquitoes and bathe and dress in the shelter of the netting in his room if he was to be on time for dinner on *Isabella*. Civilian dress tonight, he thought, Morny won't mind.

Another French fleet had anchored outside the harbor in the night. Now, in the blistering light of early morning three dozen transport ships lay close to the shore and alongside the pier. Soldiers filed on to the pier from the ships, formed up and marched ashore through the wide gate of the customhouse. The decks of the transports in the harbor and farther out near the fort were jammed with bright uniforms waiting their turn to reach the pier.

Bartlett and Jones observed them through telescopes from the balcony of the customhouse. Jones snapped his glass shut. "I'd say it's a full brigade, about four thousand men, just like Morny said."

They had all slept late on *Isabella* after too much champagne at dinner. A young French officer came aboard with a message from the flagship for Morny and was forced to wait for an hour while Henri shaved and dressed the count and served him his breakfast. After a brief conference, the officer left on his gig and Morny summoned his two guests.

He first enquired after their health and their breakfast. "Henri has yet to discover a reliable source of fruit, I regret, but we make the best of what we can find along this wretched coast." Then he got down to business. "As I expected, the Emperor has reinforced me with a brigade of infantry, with a section of light artillery, under the command of General Lorencez. The general will assume military command of all French forces in Mexico, replacing Admiral Jurien. The brigade will move inland to Cordoba as soon as possible – in two or three days – to avoid the risk of fever," he beamed, looking quite pleased with himself. "You will kindly report this development to Washington. You will doubtless add that the brigade's movement conforms to the La Soledad convention and is required to protect the men's health." They sensed he was anxious to be rid of them so they assented, thanked him for dinner and went ashore.

From his post on the balcony Bartlett continued to study the French transports through his glass, first the ships in the harbor and then the dozen anchored under the fort. His eye was caught by a white eight- oared launch that steered for and then tied up alongside *Isabella*. Its lone passenger stood up and with care began to climb the ladder. Bartlett nudged Jones and said, "Quick, the *Isabella*."

The passenger was now on deck – of middle age, tall, sallow skinned with abundant black hair and an erect carriage. The officer of the deck evidently asked him to wait while he went forward to consult some one – Morny? The man looked around the yacht and then raised his gaze and looked straight at the customhouse. Jones whistled. "Good Lord! It's Almonte, General Almonte."

"Who?"

"Wait. I want to see this."

The officer of the deck hurried back and escorted the man forward to the main saloon, where he was met and ushered inside by Morny with great formality. They could see no more.

Jones shut his glass and told Bartlett all he knew about Almonte. "He and Hidalgo are thick as thieves, everyone knows that, and I got the impression when I was in Paris that the Emperor thinks highly of him, as well." He began to pace the stone floor. "What is he doing here, now – that's the question. And we'd better have the answer damn soon. Stoddard will want to know."

"We can ask Morny."

"We can ask him," said Jones, "but he'll deny the man's even here."

"Then we'd better not ask him. Why let him know that we've seen Almonte ? Why show our hand, such as it is?"

Jones paused. "You're right, but we'll give him a chance to tell us. We'll visit the great man at his afternoon swim."

They climbed *Isabella's* ladder about five that afternoon. On the same side of the boat, her two launches and a borrowed skiff formed a line astern about fifty feet away. Their crews, armed with rifles, scanned the water around the enclosed space. Inside it Morny and Henri swam a stately breaststroke, their heads held high, as they completed their twenty laps.

"No sharks today, Count?" Jones called when Morny grasped the bottom rung of the ladder.

"Good afternoon, gentlemen. This is a pleasant surprise, indeed." Morny reached the deck and held out his dripping arms to put on the enormous robe Henri had waiting. "No, no sharks, thanks to Henri. His frantic splashing frightens the poor creatures away."

He offered them tea, which they refused, so they remained standing on the teak deck. Bartlett explained that they would soon draft their report to Washington on the arrival of the French brigade and merely wanted to know if there were any changes or additions to the information Morny had given them that morning.

"Changes?" Morny raised his eyebrows. "No, none. General Lorencez's brigade will be fully disembarked tomorrow and will leave for Cordoba the following day. That is all."

Jones wanted to keep the conversation going but could only think to say, "We counted sixteen transports that have yet to unload, sir. Does that sound about right?"

Morny looked at him coldly. "I haven't the remotest idea, Commander, and why should I?" Then he relented. "But I suppose so. And, if you're counting, don't overlook the ship with all the horses."

Another five minutes of embarrassed generalities and they crept down to their waiting boat. "Think he saw our hand?" Jones asked bitterly.

As they walked back to the Magnifico, Bartlett said, "Another French brigade. Almonte. Things are heating up. They're going to make a move of some kind, and we sit here like dummies. We have to do something."

"You're damn right." Jones slapped Bartlett on the back. "I've been talking to Carolina about an idea she had. I'll tell you more soon."

Chapter 28

"Who is this fellow, Almonte?"

Seward told Lincoln what his department knew about Almonte, with emphasis on his standing among the conservative forces of Mexico. "Now, sir, why has this man returned? What is his objective?" He held up a warning hand. "Obviously, to organize and lead the conservatives in an uprising against Juarez."

"Which we don't want."

"Correct. We don't want any uprising at all. We want to keep things just as they are – going nowhere – for as long as possible." He prepared for the obvious question.

"I sense another of your ambitious plans, Governor," Lincoln said with a doubtful smile. "Please tell me we're not going to invade Mexico again."

"Better than that, much better," Seward gloated. "We're going to *buy* Mexico. Or a great chunk of it." He sat back, pleased with the effect that had. Then he hurried to explain himself. He was negotiating a treaty with Juarez under which the United States would pay off all of Mexico's legitimate debts, paying directly to the three European creditors. Mexico would repay the same amount to Washington within six years. The loan, to call it that, would bear interest at six per cent per annum until it was repaid. "Totally uninteresting, I hear you say," he smiled. "But, hear this: the loan will be secured by a specific lien on all the public land and the mineral rights in the states of Baja California, Chihuahua, Sonora and Sinaloa."

"Good Lord," Lincoln exclaimed, "that's half of Mexico!"

"Not quite, sir. Just the northwest third of it. But the richest third." He drew a deep breath. "We estimate we'll have to pay out between ten and twenty million dollars to the Europeans. And we know that Juarez hasn't a prayer of paying us back. He can't even pay his soldiers. He may not survive six years. Anything can happen, but one thing is certain – Mexico won't repay the loan. We'll simply wait six years and the richest part of the country will just fall into our lap."

"So that's why we want the Europeans to stay down there, to put financial pressure on Juarez."

"Exactly. The longer they press him for their money, the harder they'll push him into our kindly hands. He'll have no choice but to accept our loan."

They were silent for a time, contemplating the consequences of annexing such a vast stretch of land. Half a dozen federal territories could be carved out of it, all of them free of slaves. The country's Pacific coast would be extended and protected. Lincoln and Seward would be hailed and praised in American history books for all time. Their vision was literally breathtaking.

"And that is just the beginning for us, Mr. President," Seward urged. "We can – we must reach up to the pole and down to the tropics. That *must* be our objective, as I've said many times. From -"

Lincoln had heard enough. He was as hungry for territory as any other statesman of the day. "That's all fine, Governor, very fine indeed." He aimed a bony finger at his interlocutor. "Mexico. That would be a magnificent prize. You get that stretch of Mexico for me – for us, that is - and then we can think about the rest, the pole and the tropics and the rest of it."

"Consider it done. All we need are three or four more months of calm down there. Three or four months of the Europeans stalled, fighting among themselves. Juarez will have to accept our terms and in six years one third of Mexico will be ours."

*   *   *

While Lincoln and Seward were dreaming of invasion and victory, Malcolm Bannerman in London was dreaming of financial salvation, his own. The first sign that it might be at hand came in the form of a telegram from Captain Caleb Huse, who was deputizing for James Bulloch. The telegram was in the simple code Bannerman had devised.

"PROSPERO LYING IN MERSEY RIVER WITH THREE THOUSAND TWO HUNDRED SEVENTY FIVE UNITS OF CORN FOR DELIVERY TO YOUR NOMINEE STOP KINDLY ARRANGE FOR DRAFT ON FRASERS BANK IN AMOUNT OF POUNDS STERLING FIFTY NINE THOUSAND FIVE HUNDRED STOP WILL COMMENCE DISCHARGE OF CARGO UPON YOUR PRESENTATION OF ABOVE DRAFT AND SATISFACTORY CONFIRMATION THAT YOU WILL DELIVER TO PROSPERO ONE THOUSAND TONS MINIMUM OF FLOUR WITHIN SEVEN DAYS AT AGREED PRICE STOP MATTER IS MOST URGENT END
HUSE"

So Bulloch had not lied. Over three thousand bales of middling Orleans cotton were waiting for him in Liverpool. All he had to do was take the cotton purchase price from the Union Army's account with his bank and transfer it to Fraser in exchange for their bank draft in the same amount. That, together with the sight of at least one thousand tons of saltpeter piled on the Mersey wharf, would secure the cotton for him.

First, though, he needed to be sure that he had his cotton buyers ready to go. He called his agent in to discuss the price.

"The price? The price is – you won't believe this – the price is fifteen pence per pound at dockside." The agent sat back proudly. "That is, of course, before our commission," he added "Plus our expenses of..."

"Hang your expenses." He paused as if in deep thought, stroking his chin. "All right the price is agreed." Agreed? Jumped at was more accurate It was tuppence a pound higher than the last recorded sale; the buyers must mean to hold the cotton as a speculation. A speculation that couldn't miss; three spinning mills had shut down in Manchester alone that week.

Bannerman shook his head thoughtfully, smoothed his yellow hair and went to work. He called in his clerk and dictated telegrams to the saltpeter brokers he was paying to hold their stocks for him. He told them to draw up their sales documents and to move their material to Morpeth dock in Liverpool by Friday of that week.

Then he strolled over to Fraser's Bank in Cheapside. There he arranged to buy a sight draft in favor of the Confederate cotton shipper and to pay for it with the Union Army's money, which he kept on overnight deposit with Fraser's. He would fix the exact amount the next day as soon as he heard that the cotton had arrived and was of a good quality.

He couldn't work the next day. He could think of nothing but the vast profit that would be his – his bank's, anyway – in just a few days. He would resell the cotton for over one hundred thirty thousand pounds, net of agents' commission. After replacing the Union's sixty thousand he could pay off Cousin Arbuthnott and his friends with thirty thousand and be left with around forty thousand, free and clear.

Forty thousand pounds! He would save his bank. He would save his name. No more cutting corners, or sacking staff or doing business with third-rate names. He would restore to the Bannerman Bank and to the Bannerman name, their historic dignity.

Then he could marry Katherine Carra. How could she turn him down now? He knew how precarious her future was. And then he might buy a small estate in Ireland, perhaps Katherine's old home, Kilveen. She would love that, even if they went there for the fishing and the hunting alone.

His reverie was interrupted that afternoon by the arrival of a telegram from his agent in Liverpool announcing that the quantity and the quality of the cotton were exactly as declared. Bannerman dispatched a note to Fraser's confirming the face amount of the sight draft and that he would collect it at opening the next day. Then he went in search of a decent meal, a theatre and some compliant feminine company. A very good day for the Bannerman's, he thought, with still better to come.

When his train clanked haltingly, as if lost, into Liverpool the following afternoon, Bannerman remembered how much he hated the city. On his one other visit, a few years earlier, he and his uncle Horace had tried to salvage something from the financial wreckage that had been the Great Cumbrian Railway Company. The railroad had gone under, taking with it the best part of Bannerman's twenty thousand pound loan. He, his uncle and the other creditors had picked forlornly at the corporate corpse for a week and come away with nothing but a deep distrust of anything that ran on rails and hooted.

But this time would be different. He left his case at the waterfront inn and went to call on Captain Freelove Townsend. Barely five feet tall, the Captain had a gaunt, pitted face, a black beard down to his breastbone and immaculate manners. The son of a fundamentalist preacher whose views on hellfire were considered extreme even by the inhabitants of his Louisiana bayou, Townsend was a notorious for his piety as for his skill in slipping the Yankee blockade.

"I have all the papers right here. The bill of sale, inspection certificates and so forth are yours. And you have for me, I imagine, a draft on the good folks at Fraser's Bank?" With a solemn flourish, Bannerman handed him the draft he had bought with the Union Army's money.

Captain Townsend regretted that he couldn't allow Bannerman to take delivery of the cotton until he had sight of the saltpeter on Morpeth Dock. "The South needs that saltpeter the way you English need my cotton, I'm told. And I believe Captain Bulloch stipulated – how shall I put it? - no saltpeter, no cotton?"

"He did indeed," Bannerman acknowledged.

"Well then, sir, nothing could be simpler. I'll unload my cotton here on Friday, slip across the river to Morpeth Dock and load your saltpeter on Saturday." He beamed amiably at the banker, who saw that there was no more to be said on that topic.

Then Bannerman accepted Townsend's offer to view his cotton in the holds. Bannerman whistled when he saw the rows and rows of cotton bales stacked six high down the length of the holds. Townsend chuckled at his obvious surprise. "It is quite a sight, no doubt about it. One thousand tons. The biggest shipment of cotton to reach Liverpool since last winter. One of the few of any size, come to that."

"How did you get past the blockade?" Bannerman was now deeply impressed by the little southerner.

"That's a professional secret, Mr. Bannerman," Townsend said. "And all I can tell you is that when there's no moon and a heavy rain those Yankee sailors get mighty lazy." He laughed. "And that my owners told me I needn't even think of returning to port if I didn't get through."

The following Saturday Bannerman stood on the dock thinking that this must be what a merchant prince feels like, as he watched the bales of cotton rise from the holds and vanish into the waiting rail wagons. He imagined himself as a Mongol khan, lolling on cushions as his slaves loaded the endless line of camels with silks and spices. Was it camels, he wondered, or was it horses? No matter; a mere banker doesn't often feel like this.

However, he found himself thinking, watching twenty thousand bags of saltpeter being loaded is deeply boring if one makes no profit whatever on each bag. Twenty thousand bags by nil shillings profit per bag is a total profit of nil shillings. Still it was a central part of his scheme to save the bank and, viewed in that light, oddly gratifying.

At last the counts were confirmed, the sales documents were stamped and exchanged. On behalf of the Confederacy, Captain Huse pressed a bank draft for fifty two thousand pounds into Bannerman's hand. He feigned a close examination of the document, endorsed it over to his agent so that he could pay the other brokers in cash. Bannerman's Bank was in and out of the Saltpeter deal in seconds.

As he said farewell to Huse and Townsend the following day he thought, "I've done it. It was damned difficult and I pulled it off. Father would be pleased with me. I'm pleased with me."

*   *   *

"And for you, Primrose, ten thousand four hundred sixteen pounds and eight shillings, also. There." Bannerman pushed the draft across the table and sat back. He had repaid all three loans, with interest, in full.

"So that American venture paid off, did it, Bannerman?" he said. "Another one like that comes along, don't you forget your friends at Primrose's, eh?" Bannerman bit his lip and said nothing.

Sydney Arbuthnott was torn. On one hand he was relieved to recover in full what was to him a large bad loan and to his fellow Directors conclusive proof of his incompetence. On the other hand, he hated to lose his sense of domination over his glamorous young cousin. In his confusion, he began to stammer about bygones, his hope for friendship in the future and the like.

Chapter 29

"It's Almonte, all right, no doubt about it." Jones looked pleased with himself as he brushed off the dust and grime from his journey in the open rail car. They were in his room at the Magnifico. He had taken the asthmatic, jerky train up to Paso del Macho, the end of its line, and then ridden south to Tehuacan. His trip was at Morny's invitation. The Count was pleased to let Jones inspect the French troops bivouacked there and report to Washington that there was no sign that they were going any farther.

Bartlett grinned from the room's only chair. "I know it's Almonte."

"Oh." Pause. "How do you know, damn it?"

"Simple. I asked Henri who Morny's visitor was. Nobody had told him to keep quiet."

"That's fine, just fine. I had to flog all the way over to Cordoba and bribe a couple of French sergeants to find out. These frogs don't come cheap, either."

"We have to cable Stoddard about Almonte."

"I already have, as soon as I got back here. Also - and hear this, *amigo* — he left today for Puebla with a small bodyguard. He'll get there tomorrow," he drawled, "if the creek don't rise."

Jones is transforming, or reverting, to a Tex-Mex before my eyes, Bartlett thought. The slow drawl, the rustic figures of speech, the longer hair, the new rakish angle of his hat. Any day now and he'll turn up wearing boots, spurs and a guitar.

"Stoddard hasn't replied," Bartlett said. "Maybe tomorrow."

"Well, I'm off now to see Morny to tell him that the situation up there was peaceful as a prayer meeting back home, just as he said it was. Meet you at the *cantina* after the mosquitoes have gone home?"

It was another routine night at El Caribe. Gomez was his smiling attentive self as he waved Jones to their regular table at the back, where Bartlett waited. The listless little band played their standard tunes very badly. After a supper of grilled red snapper, Bartlett and Jones practised their encryption for a time, using their alternate system based on the date of the month. Then, earlier than usual, they started on a game of pinochle and a bottle of the Priestkiller. The other regulars all ignored them. Conchita was in a sulk, which Jones put down to his lack of attention to her and Bartlett to his. Both men were bored and short tempered.

"Spades aren't trumps, Robert, clubs are," Bartlett sighed. "That's the third time tonight. Try to keep up, will you?"

"Sorry. My mind's not on it." He peered at his hand. "Let's make this the last deal. When I win it you'll owe me four and a half million dollars."

"Sure, sure." This annoyed Bartlett and he wanted to retaliate. "How is Carolina these days?"

Jones stared at him meditatively over his cards. "She's fine," he said evenly. "We're riding together in the morning, and afterwards I'll give you a full report if you're so interested." He played a card, melded and stared at Bartlett again.

His stares annoyed Bartlett further. "Does she still believe you're not married?"

"That's no concern of yours, is it?" Jones flushed. "Or am I missing something here?"

"Well, her brother is an old friend of mine, after all, and I'm not sure I shouldn't..."

"Warn him about me? Listen well, *amigo*, I'll - " Jones drew a long breath and collected himself. "Ah, it's not worth getting angry over." He reached across and slapped Bartlett's shoulder lightly. "Look, she and I are just friends, no more, no less. I like the company of a woman, especially a handsome one and especially in this dump, that's all."

Bartlett lifted an eyebrow. "That's all, you say?"

"That is all, I swear. And you wouldn't be so everlasting gloomy if you did the same. Why don't you find – "

"Find what, Charles?" Laffan boomed, appearing behind Jones. "A drink for me? Excellent idea. Make it a very cold one, please." He sat down and stretched his long legs into the aisle. "Mind if I join you?"

His face was weary and gaunt, his trousers torn, his boots thick with dust. He was just back from Alvarado, he said, a village on the coast a few dozen miles south of Veracruz. One of his agents had reported that a party of Conservative exiles from Spain would put ashore in its bay and make their way to Mexico City, so he had tried to intercept them. "I am a spy, after all. Remember?" He drained half his beer and belched contentedly. He had perched on the cliff that overlooked the bay for four days and nights, he said. "I haven't had so much fun since the dog died," he snarled. "And not a sniff of the bastards. A complete waste of my time." He spotted Conchita and cried, "*Conchita, mi amor, vente.*"

She wandered over to the table and Jones asked for a beer and another bottle of rum. "My treat," he said to Laffan. Unimpressed, she swished off, easily avoiding Laffan's grab for her bottom.

"So, Pancho, how is the spying business these days?" asked Bartlett. "Pretty slow, I expect."

"I can't complain. That new French brigade at Cordoba keeps a few of my men busy. Juarez wants a report every hour, it seems."

"Tell him to rest easy. They're not going anywhere, not for a while, anyway," Jones asserted. "I've just come back from there myself."

"I know," Laffan grinned. "But why are they up there? They don't intend to sit around scratching their ass for a bit and then go home." He favored Conchita with his most winning smile as she dropped the beer and rum on the table, looked idly around the emptying bar room and took up station at a nearby table.

"Part of their mission is simply to even up the numbers with the Spanish," said Bartlett. "There's some sort of conflict between the French and the Spanish which we haven't figured out." The rum was getting to him.

The evening unrolled before them. Laffan cleaned himself up and told stories, almost entirely untrue, about the siege of Veracruz in the so-called Mexican War a dozen years earlier. Jones countered with the recent exploits of his agents in France and England, and Bartlett wasn't too shy to parade his prowess against the Cheyenne on the plains out of Leavenworth. Fellowship burgeoned, confidences multiplied. Bartlett forgot his irritation with Jones. Jones forgot his TexMex drawl and lapsed into a rich Slavic bass. Laffan forgot his weariness, swore off beer forever and joined them on the rum bottle. Conchita tossed her head in disgust and kept well clear.

At one point Laffan scooped up a sheaf of scribbled notes and demanded to know what they were. Bartlett snatched at them but Laffan held them out of reach, giggling, and asked again. Jones tried to explain that they were practice notes, and that they were learning to use a different encryption system. "Hell, you're a spy, Pancho, you must know all about codes."

"Robert, my old friend, most of Juarez' people can't even read Spanish. Why would I need a code?" He spread the papers in front of him. "Hah. If these are your secrets, your work here must be damn dull."

Bartlett tried to explain that the system was partly phonetic. "But we have the real thing here." He pointed vaguely at Jones, who pulled from his breast pocket a sheaf of papers that he spread on the table.

"This week's reports," he said proudly, "all coded and correct. I keep 'em for a week and then burn them all." He pushed them at Laffan. "Look all you want, you can't read them."

Laffan leafed negligently through the papers, stacked them and tried to get up. His boot caught in a chair rung and he sprawled over the table, knocking the stack to the floor. "Whoops!" he cried. "Sorry, Robert, just dizzy from the sun. Be right back," as he got up and lurched out towards the privy.

"Now, gentlemen," he announced when he came back, "tonight's the night I promised you." They looked at him with interest and then at each other. "The night that the best kept secret in Veracruz, so secret that not even the priests can find it, is revealed to you." He pointed out the door. "I refer of course to Madam Melinda's, the house of an English gentlewoman who reserves her chaste young treasures for the delectation of a few selected visitors. Follow me, chaps!"

*   *   *

General Prim welcomed Sir Charles Wyke to his Veracruz quarters, a high-windowed house near the southern wall, the next night. The two men were markedly dissimilar. Prim's thin frame, pale freckled face and reddish hair contrasted with Wyke's bulk and dark complexion. But they had become, if not friends, allies. Allies against the French.

Wyke accepted a brandy and a cigar and they retreated through the netting into Prim's study. Prim said that as both had received new instructions it was time to co-ordinate their negotiating positions for the next Commissioners' meeting on Thursday. "And then," he said, "I have some news which will interest you."

Their instructions echoed each other. Both emphasized that their forces were to remain in Mexico until their mission was fully accomplished. They were ordered to negotiate all points at issue with General Doblado and to adhere to the terms of the London Convention among the Allies. At all costs they were not to let the French steal a march on them.

"It seems we'll both be here for some time yet, General," Wyke said ruefully.

"Yes, it seems so. Now, we may not be as one on the next point," Prim warned, "which is the absurd amount of money the French are claiming." Queen Isabella's financial experts, he said, had confirmed that the deplorable Jecker bonds, so-called, were undoubtedly valid claims on the Mexican treasury. "What an inexcusable business it is, but my instructions are precise: I can go as high as twenty millions for all of the French claims, including the bonds."

"My limit is twenty five million, so we have ample room to maneuver. I look forward to making Saligny sweat for his miserable millions."

"You may watch Saligny sweat if you like, I will watch Morny," Prim retorted. "I suspect he has much more to do with those bonds than we know."

Wyke asked for Prim's interesting news. "Almonte," the general said. "He's here. The French smuggled him in and he's up in Cordoba, unless he has already left for Puebla, under their protection."

Wyke considered this. It was disturbing but predictable. The Emperor badly needed a Conservative revolution against the Juarez revolution, and he counted on Almonte to spark it off and lead it. But to escort Almonte to the interior and protect him with French troops, he said, was a clear violation of the London Convention, which prohibited the signatories from interfering in the internal affairs of Mexico.

Prim gave a short laugh. "Yes," he said, "to protect and promote the leader of a party that is in open rebellion against the Juarez government could be said to constitute such interference. But I will now give you a document that is much more important than even the movements of General Almonte."

He laid two sheets of crumpled paper before Wyke. One was in English, the other in code. Wyke read:

"VERACRUZ TWELVE APRIL
URGENT FOR GENL STODDARD
REPORT NUMBER TWELVE
HAVE TODAY INTERCEPTED FOLLOWING MESSAGE FROM GENERAL LORENCEZ AT TEHUACAN TO SALIGNY AT VERACRUZ
QUOTE
IN ACCORDANCE WITH YOUR ORDERS AM PREPARING PLAN TO PROCEED MEXICO CITY AND PLACE IT UNDER MY CONTROL STOP PLAN WILL ASSUME DEPARTURE FROM THIS POSITION WITHIN SEVEN DAYS OF RECEIPT YOUR FINAL ORDERS TO PROCEED STOP MY DEPARTURE WILL BE TIMED TO COINCIDE WITH ARMED UPRISING IN PUEBLA TO BE ORGANIZED BY GENERAL ALMONTE STOP TO MINIMIZE CHANCE OF CONTACT WITH GOVERNMENT FORCES WILL BYPASS PUEBLA ON DAY OF UPRISING AND TAKE NORTHERN ROUTE NAPOLACA TLAXCALA TEOTIHUACAN STOP
WILL REVIEW MY DETAILED PLANS WITH YOU IN VERACRUZ ON 26 APRIL STOP TRUST YOU WILL THEN HAVE LATEST INFORMATION ON MEXICAN TROOP DISPOSITIONS STOP
LORENCEZ
GENERAL
UNQUOTE
WE BELIEVE THIS A GENUINE MESSAGE STOP NOTE CONFIRMATION ALMONTES PRESENCE

HERE STOP WE AWAIT YOUR INSTRUCTIONS
STOP
XZ"

"As an example of military prose, the Lorencez telegram is lamentable," Prim said, enjoying Wyke's stunned expression and open mouth, "But its intent is all too plain." Wyke still said nothing. "The other sheet before you is the encrypted version of this same telegram. The American officers sent it yesterday from Veracruz to Washington."

"And you're satisfied that both messages are genuine?"

"Quite satisfied."

"May I ask you why?"

"Of course. In fact, you may ask the source of the messages himself. Excuse me." Prim opened the study door, went out and returned with his hand on the shoulder of an officer in the Mexican army. "Sir Charles, allow me to present my nephew, Colonel Eufemio Laffan."

After the usual civilities, the three men sat down and Prim went on. "Eufemio is really my wife's nephew, the son of her sister. But he is also the husband of my own niece, Carolina. Our connection is therefore close. And his uniform is not necessarily indicative of his ultimate loyalties, which are to his family and to his properties in Sonora and Colima. Now he will tell you the origin of the papers before you."

It was really quite simple, as Laffan described it. He and the two Americans were friendly, they had all met in the cantina the night before and they had all drunk more rum than was good for them. The Americans treated the cantina as their office and they often laid their papers on their table, as they had last night. It had been easy for him to glance at them to see if any were important. Disregarding those in code, he had at once seen the importance of the message that quoted Lorencez and Saligny.

"Those two names demanded my attention," Laffan grinned. That paper was sticking with beer or rum to another, encrypted sheet, so he had stumbled, slid all the papers to the floor, stuffed those two papers under his coat and gone out to the privy. He could see that the two sheets were a match in terms of word count and format, so he kept them in his coat. When later they left the bar to look for more robust entertainment, he had still not found a way to disguise his theft. But his luck was in. Jones, the naval officer, wadded up all the papers on the table and tossed them in the cooking fire without a word. He watched them burn and said to Laffan: "We experienced spies always burn all our papers."

"He was drunk?" asked Wyke.

"At the time, yes."

Prim took up the story. "Eufemio brought the papers to me this morning, so I sent my aide to interrogate the telegraph clerk. He confirmed that he had transmitted a coded telegram for the Americans yesterday afternoon. He couldn't verify that it was the same message as the one that Eufemio showed him, of course, but the length was about the same."

Wyke was off balance. They were discussing a potentially fatal blow to the allies' expedition with a de facto representative of Juarez. He had no idea what to say, so he temporized. "I notice that the handwriting on the two sheets is not the same, Colonel," he said coolly.

"One of the Yankees drafts the message, sir, and the other encodes it. It's their invariable practice." He anticipated the next question. "The encryption is consistent. That is, if A replaces B in one word, it does in all the other words."

"And you're certain, are you, that they didn't palm these off on you? Arrange for you to spot these sheets and take them?"

"As certain as I can be. I've asked myself that question all day."

"What would be their purpose in that?" Prim wondered. Laffan looked inquiringly at Prim, who nodded and inclined his head at the door. Laffan rose, accepted their thanks and left. Prim went with him.

"We can believe Eufemio," Prim said with satisfaction as he came back in. "To make doubly sure, another source has verified his story, my best agent on this coast." He rubbed his hands rapidly. "Now, Sir Charles, we have in our hands two useful but dangerous cards. How shall we play them?"

"With great care. The situation is awkward, but promising." Wyke pressed his palms together and looked over them at Prim. "Our prime objective must be to prevent any French move on Mexico City or Puebla."

"Quite right. That would violate every agreement and destroy our expedition. At all costs, we must prevent it; we certainly can not stop it if Lorencez once begins to move."

"So," Wyke continued, "I think our point of attack on Thursday should be the presence of Almonte and his protection by the French. It violates the basic undertakings between ourselves and violates our agreement with Juarez. We must make Morny understand that Spain and England will - simply - not - tolerate it."

"Yes," said Prim, "we should exaggerate Almonte's importance and use it as a negotiating lever. We must threaten to leave if the French do not cease their protection of Almonte, and we must be ready to leave if they do not."

"Yes. We may only need to imply such a threat, not to state it, but we must make it a real one. And if we leave the French will of course be forced by the London Convention to leave with us. They will have no choice. They can not act alone."

"But you appreciate, of course," Prim mused, "that for us to leave Mexico would contravene our instructions, which are to stick it out here."

"But *we* would have no choice," Wyke retorted. "We could not remain and be implicated in what the French have in mind here."

Prim twirled his glass slowly and stared into it. "Do you know, I still find it hard to believe that the Emperor – and Morny and Saligny are merely dancing to his tune – will risk so much for – for what? For money? Thirty or forty million is an enormous amount, but -"

"Money is his secondary motive." Wyke interjected. "His overriding aim, his dream is to put Maximilian on the throne of Mexico, under his protection and guidance. And I don't think he *will* risk his dream just to protect one expendable Mexican exile like Almonte."

"So we have a strong hand to play on Thursday."

"Yes, indeed. I am confident that, if we press hard enough, Morny will abandon Almonte."

*   *   *

The village of Orizaba is a mile above sea level, and the air was cold when the allied leaders arranged themselves around the carved table in Prim's office. Speaking in French, he welcomed them to Orizaba, apologized for the poverty of their accommodation and got to the point. He and Sir Charles, he declared, thought the time had come for frank explanations of the policies of France in Mexico. In particular, they could not reconcile the presence of General Almonte in the French ranks with the London Convention or with the La Soledad Preliminaries.

"Nonsense, General," spat Saligny, to whom this accusation came as a nasty shock. "If there has been any infraction of the Convention, it has nothing to do with General Almonte and everything to do with the excessive consideration you and Sir Charles have shown to the Mexican government." Take that, he thought, you conniving Iberian fraud.

"We can not agree," said Prim. "Almonte has actually been proscribed by the Mexican government. For you to bring him to these shores and to protect him is, beyond any possible doubt, your interference in the internal affairs of Mexico. How can it be any other?"

"Quite simply." Saligny's voice now had an edge to it. "Our protection is no more than the protection of the French flag, which, unlike many" – here a glance at Wyke – "will never fail the exiles of any country."

"Commendable, to be sure," countered Prim, "but not when extended to a man whose stated aim is to overthrow the government of the country where you protect him."

"The Juarez government is impotent and we treat them like heroes," Saligny said. "That is our only mistake."

"I am informed, sir," Wyke sneered, taking the offensive, "that you have said that you consider the La Soledad agreement to be worth less than the paper it is written on. Is that true?"

"What is true is that I have no confidence whatever in anything signed by a man as faithless as Juarez."

General Prim's anger at Saligny's evasions was as plain as it was great, and he had a personal grievance to explore. He demanded of the Frenchman a straight answer. Was it true that Saligny had publicly accused the general of being hostile to Maximilian's candidature because he himself aspired to the crown of Mexico? Yes or no?

"Yes, of course," Saligny smiled. "But I only stated what is public knowledge. You yourself once declared that, although the idea of an Austrian prince as ruler here is absurd, there might be a chance for a distinguished soldier." He gave a short laugh. "Whom did you have in mind, General?"

All gloves were off now. Accusations, recriminations, insults, all the animosities carefully nourished in the last three steamy, pestilential months boiled up and over. At length, Prim stood up and held out his arms in a bid for calm.

"M. Saligny, we ask you once again: Will you return General Almonte to Veracruz and convey him back to France?"

Morny spoke for the first time. "The protection of the French flag," he said, "once given, can never be withdrawn. Never. It is a matter of national honor."

Silence for a time. Then from Wyke, "Do you understand, Count, that neither Spain nor England can be associated with such protection?"

"My answer to your question must be yes." Morny had concluded that it was time to take control of the discussion.

"And that your refusal to remove Almonte may constitute France's unilateral abrogation of the London Convention?"

"How presumptuous of you, Sir Charles." Morny was now coldly furious. To be lectured by some Foreign Office functionary was intolerable. "I understand no such thing, and nor do you."

"What Sir Charles meant to say, Count," interposed Prim smoothly, "was that your refusal could be considered *by us* to abrogate the Convention?"

"Thank you, General, but I need no lessons from either of you on the London Convention. In this matter, how you choose to consider whatever you choose to consider is of remarkably little interest to me."

Stunned, Prim tried to backtrack. He could not allow Morny to damage the allies' relationship so badly that he and Wyke would be forced to withdraw their forces. No, they must reserve that choice for themselves.

He said he hoped Morny would not object if he and Wyke conferred outside. Morny waved him at the door and sat back.

Prim and Wyke returned. Prim had reminded Wyke that he had ten times as many troops in Mexico as did the English and so he would speak for both of them. "Gentlemen," he began, "we withdraw the word 'abrogate'. But we insist that your protection of General Almonte violates the Convention. As you have confirmed that you have no intention of removing such protection, we have no choice but to retire from a position which would implicate us in such violation."

He turned to Wyke, who weighed in with his allotted speech. "England and Spain will withdraw from this country with all possible speed, but we do not – can not – withdraw from our alliance under the Convention." He looked from Saligny to Morny, who raised a dismissive hand at him and his English splitting of hairs. "The Convention remains in full force and effect. I remind you that it specifically contemplates a *combined* expedition and *combined* operations by the three powers, so that it prohibits unilateral action by any of the three. Therefore – "

"Therefore France must withdraw along with its allies in this expedition," Morny finished for him. "As I have said, Sir Charles, M. Saligny and I need no lessons from you in respect of the Convention, which we agree remains in effect. Do not fear. France will comply with its obligations under the agreement. *As she has always complied.*"

"Then you will withdraw?"

"Sir Charles, I say what I have to say only once. Good day to you." Morny rose, bowed and left the room.

Chapter 30

The English left first. They buried their last few dead, bundled their sick out of the convent and on to their crowded ships, looked around once for deserters and sailed for Bermuda.

Wyke went with them, composing his final report for Lord Russell in his tiny cabin. He was confident Russell would agree that, in the face of such French treachery, to quit Mexico with dignity was the only possible course for men of honor on a mission of honor. At least, he certainly hoped so; otherwise, Lady Wyke would not accept his abrupt retirement from the Foreign Office either happily or silently.

Morny himself was off in a few days, to the Yucatan in *Isabella* to explore a few Mayan ruins. Pancho Laffan had excited his curiosity about the Mayans with a few scraps of description, mostly bloody, of their extinct civilization, which were supplemented by three volumes in the cathedral library. It was a convenient time to be away from Veracruz. The Spaniards would not go so quietly, or he didn't know Prim.

"I shall see Uxmal and Zayil," Morny said, "but we haven't time to reach Tulum. It is too far down the Atlantic coast."

"A dangerous trip, sir," observed Bartlett. He and Jones were in Morny's suite the day before he sailed.

"No, Admiral Jurien has loaned me a dozen of his Marines. I shall be quite safe, thank you, Major." He tapped his cigarette ash into the enameled bowl held out by Henri.

"I mean the fever, sir, and the rain. The rainy season has begun out there and from what I hear it's not like anything your crew will have seen before." Bartlett had been listening to the talk in El Caribe.

"Ah," Morny gave the curious flick with his right hand, "I'm confident that Captain Carbonnel can avoid or surmount any difficulties with the weather. In any case, I am determined to go to the Yucatan." His manner became animated. "I have an instinct that I may find there the elements for another play. Ideas already form in the mind."

He had instructed Saligny and Jurien to tell the Americans whatever they needed to know, he said. He would have invited them to join him on his cruise, but he knew that their duty required them to stay close to the allied forces. "Keep sending those telegrams, my friends, or General Stoddard will worry about me." They didn't see him again for twelve days.

The Spanish battalions came down from the hills the next day, along with a swarm of refugees, brand new wives, prostitutes and peddlers of all the goods that young men five thousand miles from home might need. Veracruz was overrun, swamped. The troops on shore drilled and drilled and drilled again, but discipline was ignored as the commanders fought to get their men on the waiting ships as quickly as they could. The quay and the single pier were jammed with wailing women who had begun to suspect that their dashing new husbands, now skulking aboard a transport, would not after all carry them off to a life of ease in Mother Spain.

El Caribe offered a dependable refuge from the clamor in the streets. After a series of bloody fights with the machete-wielding locals, all uniformed Spaniards were barred and the ambiance was almost back to its somnolent normality. Except for the rain, which had arrived on schedule. Rain such as Bartlett and Jones had never seen, a driving, thundering, gully-washing, turd-floating wall of water that scoured the streets of filth and drove even the pigs to shelter. It also drove El Caribe's regulars away from the open street side and back into the packed kitchen area, so that the Americans could no longer count on their regular table, try as Gomez might to hold it for them.

Laffan and Carolina joined them early one evening, the first time Bartlett had seen either of them since the night of Madam Melinda's. Carolina was explaining to Bartlett how the plot had taken shape. "Robert would not stop complaining, Charles, on all our rides together, of how bored he was here, how he longed to go back to Washington and take up his new command. So I decided to do something. Just to shut him up, if nothing else." Bartlett shot a look at Jones, who hadn't given Carolina much credit for the scheme.

It was quite straightforward, she went on: Jones couldn't go to Washington until the French left Mexico, and they wouldn't leave unless the Spanish and English left. But, if those two left, the French would have to leave with them because of the Convention of London, which every educated Mexican knew by heart. And the surest way to force those two to leave was to convince them the French had violated the Convention. "Very circular," she smiled, "and very neat."

From there it was a simple matter to persuade Bartlett and Jones to prepare the phony telegrams and for Laffan to steal them in the El Caribe. "And I had to make sure that Prim's pet spy saw me," Laffan confided, "to confirm my story."

Bartlett whistled. "Who's that?"

"Why, who else but – " he stopped and nodded at Conchita, advancing on them with a tray of coffee and sweet cakes. She placed it on the table, waited expectantly with hand on hip and then swayed off.

"Can't be!" Jones said.

Laffan shook his head. "No doubt about it, none at all." He looked after her. "From the day after Prim arrived."

Silence for a minute. "So," Laffan went on, "be careful what you say here." Another pause as they remembered a good many of their indiscretions at that same table. "Anyway, on with my story. I delivered your two fake telegrams to General Doblado – rode all day while you two slept it off – and he used one of his agents to get them into Prim's hands."

"Who swallowed them whole?" Jones asked doubtfully.

"He surely did. Then the big allied chiefs met in Orizaba a day or two later and they had an enormous bust-up. A real dogfight. They all stormed off and made ready to leave our sun-kissed shores."

"As we've seen," said Bartlett, waving at the commotion in the street. Then, "I've been thinking, late as usual. We took a huge gamble. What if Prim had shown those telegrams to Morny?"

"He would not have done it," replied Laffan. "A Spanish nobleman can not admit he's read another man's mail."

"Sure, sure, but what if he had?"

"Morny would have said they were fakes, a dirty American trick to split the allies, and Prim could not have proved otherwise."

"You're right. It *was* worth the gamble," Jones declared.

"Absolutely," said Laffan, patting Bartlett's arm. "It worked, you'll be out of here before you know it, so stop worrying and cheer the hell up. Let's all have a drink. Champagne! We'll toast my clever little sister, whose idea it was." He started for the bar, calling, "*Conchita, luz de mi vida!*"

Isabella dropped anchor in Veracruz harbor one afternoon and Morny swept ashore in full regalia to find Prim before the rain came. He had timed his return nicely. Except for a small rearguard, deployed on the pier with loaded rifles to keep the new wives at bay, all the Spanish troops had re-embarked and were already seasick. Morny's borrowed Marines cleared a path through the women and escorted him to Prim's headquarters, where the staff were packing their files and his extensive library.

Morny had sent word to Saligny to join him there, and Prim received them both with unconcealed caution. "Welcome back, Count," he managed as they sat around a heavy table. "Your expedition was a success, I trust?"

"Yes, it was, thank you, fascinating in many ways. I would urge you to make the same trip if your duties in Havana ever allow you the time."

"Ah, perhaps one day," Prim sighed. "One day. But back to the present, if we may. M. Saligny will confirm that we have handed over to you the administrative functions we have performed since we arrived. Including the telegraph service of which your American, ah, associates have made such enthusiastic use." Saligny's head bobbed up and down. "For myself, it only remains to embark with my staff tomorrow on the flagship. We expect to sail by noon."

"I have explained to the general that our troops will begin to arrive the following day" Saligny said. "The units at Tehuacan first, as they have been up there the longest." Morny lifted a graceful eyebrow. "We thought it best to wait until our Spanish friends left, Count, to avoid the possibility of, ah, conflict between the soldiers."

"And to clear out the itinerant rabble loitering on the streets, perhaps?," Morny asked. "I must say, General, that your troops appear to attract the most unusual types, and in such numbers. The scene on the pier just now was extraordinary."

"Ah, yes. Well," and Prim launched into a long excuse for the rabble in question. When he finished he tried to go on the offensive, asking in peremptory terms how soon the French forces would leave Veracruz.

"As soon as we are ready," Saligny said with a shrug. "It can not be any sooner."

"And when do you think that will be?" demanded Prim

Saligny glanced at Morny, who ignored him, and said "Ten days? Two weeks?"

"And General Almonte will return with you?"

"Of course. We – "

"You need say no more, M. Saligny," Morny broke in. "I have made my statement on this matter once, and once is enough." Prim started to object but Morny cut him off. "And I have a question for you, General: You do realize, don't you, that you have been in Mexico all these months and you have never told the Mexicans why you are here?" Prim's pale face turned paler. "How will you explain that to your good friend, Queen Isabella?"

Saligny's tea in Morny's rooms was followed by a large measure of Morny's best brandy and then by his own departure on shaking legs.

"You saw the poor man's face, Henri?" Morny crowed. "When I told him that we are not leaving, that we will stay and that in time we will conquer this wretched country?"

"Yes, sir, I saw it. I was right here, remember?" Henri kept on clearing the tea service.

"I'll inform our military men tonight." Morny exhaled with deep content. The English already gone, the Spanish to leave tomorrow. Now he had what he wanted, what he'd planned for: Eight thousand armed men and a free hand. "Well, Henri, that is only the first step, but well executed. Think of it, just think of it, you villain. If the rest of my plan goes as well, Mexico City and ten million dollars – *ten million* - will in not many months be mine."

Chapter 31

London

Malcolm Bannerman had been invited to tea by Katherine Carra at Rochester Place and his good humor was quite restored when the cab dropped him off there. His humor had most certainly been in need of restoration, as he thought about just how close to disaster his bank had come.

The parlor maid had brought the candles and lamps into the drawing room but it was still quite dark, the portraits on the walls fading into obscurity in the corners. Katherine wore a day dress of smoke-colored silk and no jewelry but the golden cross, and the effect was oddly severe. Even her eyes lacked their usual intensity.

"Where is the dreaded lord today?" Bannerman asked, picking up his teacup. "He is heeding my advice, I hope, to save his diminishing savings and to raise more income."

Katherine replied that work was almost complete on the new flat next door. Lord Carra had been persuaded by her artless charm and the prospect of more rent coming in every week.

She had already found a tenant for it who would move in as soon as the flat was ready.

"You say he's a Belgian?" Bannerman asked.

"Who?"

"The new tenant, the chap next door."

"Oh. Yes, he's with their embassy."

"Should be good for the rent, then. A soldier, like Bartlett?"

"No." She again thought of Charles Bartlett, again remembered with a shiver that night of brandy and so much more. But, he was now thousands of miles away across the sea. He was also unsuitable in every practical sense. He might never return. He might still hate her. Still, he wouldn't quite go away. Not yet, anyway.

She was still as conflicted about her feelings towards him as she had ever been. He was undoubtedly a good man, a man of honor, but the odd lapses into crude sarcasm and the occasional signs of uncertainty were unsettling. It seemed that he wasn't fully prepared for the faintly sinister military responsibilities he carried, whatever they were. That he wasn't quite sure of himself. But there was something attractive and endearing about him, something she missed.

But he was also so heavily entwined with all that had happened with Owen and the police. Did she feel guilty about what she had done, was that it? It was what any sibling would do; yet she couldn't stop thinking about it, which made her think of Bartlett even more.

She snapped back to the present when Bannerman asked:

"Won't that mean more work for you, Katherine? "

"Yes, it will, but not a great deal more. Besides, it makes me feel useful to him. And it helps to fill my day." The last had slipped out unbidden.

"My poor Katherine," said Bannerman, surprised by this sign of unhappiness, the first she had ever let escape, "are you very bored here?" He inclined his large blond head in her direction.

"No, not bored, exactly. I - " I – why? She wondered. Why should I want to tell Malcolm anything about my personal life?

When he had come to visit them at Carra shortly after Henry's death she had found him to be a great help in sorting out the difficult situation in which she had found herself. When she had arrived in London he had soon become a good friend, attentive, reliable and generous. In the last months, she had come to believe that he wanted to be more than a friend. He never asked her about herself. Now he had asked and she was reluctant to answer. But to Charles Bartlett, almost a stranger, she had freely talked of her life without embarrassment. Why? Was Malcolm somehow less sympathetic than the American officer? Of course not. So why not answer his question?

"Who am I fooling?" she laughed. "Yes, I am bored, I confess. But I've taken up drawing again. More tea, Malcolm?" He shook his head "and if it goes well I hope to begin to paint."

"Do you take lessons?" He'd not known that Katherine had artistic inclinations.

"Goodness, no! I have first to see if I have any talent and the signs are not promising." She surveyed the darkened room. "Do you see those lilies in the vase in the far corner? Quite ordinary lilies? In my work they appear as lobsters, with claws for the petals."

"Ah, perhaps you're right. Lessons can wait," he teased. "But, Katherine, I -"

"No more about me. Tell me about you, please. How does it fare at the ancestral counting-house?"

"Well - " She seemed genuinely to want to know. "It fares well, as you ask. I begin to think I may not be entirely hopeless as a banker."

"Malcolm," she giggled, "the idea of you as hopeless at anything is too silly for words."

"Thank you, madam, but then you never knew me as a subaltern." Was this the opportunity he needed? "In fact, I have finally managed to resolve a minor, ah, situation at the bank that's been troublesome and can how look ahead with more assurance, even confidence." He turned to face directly at her.

"I'm so glad. I'd sensed at our last meeting that something was wrong at the bank," Katherine said, sounding pleased.

"It was, but I've put it right. So now -"

"So now, are you rich? I do hope so. Terribly rich? You're the kind of man who should be."

Her chatter was meant to delay his apparent intention to declare himself and to give herself time to prepare for it. Also, to her surprise, she wanted him to tell her just how rich he would be, so she would know better how to answer his declaration. I'll have to discourage him if he can't afford to give me what I want – what I need, she thought. Heavens, what a mercenary woman I've become, without even suspecting it! I've been too poor too long.

Bannerman suspected the reasons for her question and despite himself he admired her. "You're right I should be very rich. Deserve it. Not yet, I have to confess. Soon."

"I'm so glad," she said reflectively.

"And in a position now, at last, to ask you – to tell you -"

"To tell me what?"

"To tell you how fond of you I am," was the best he could do. What's happening? He asked himself. I should be in charge here, I should be controlling this conversation and she has me pinned on the back foot.

"Of course you are, dear Malcolm, such a good friend to me." I'm beginning to seem willfully dense, she told herself. This is quite entertaining, this maidenly fencing, but am I going too far? I'll let him have a chance, now. "And I am fond of you."

Bannerman hid his disappointment. Why couldn't she be as serious as he plainly was? "Don't tease me, Katherine, Please," he said slowly. "I'm trying to tell you – it can't be a surprise – that I'm absurdly fond of you, perhaps even in love with you - that I hope - some day you can..."

She had to stop him. The quick, overwhelming joy at glimpsing her release, glimpsing her escape from her circumstances, gave way as quickly to doubts. Doubts about his finances, about Malcolm himself, about marriage itself tumbled across her mind. It was not so entertaining any longer. She felt alone, and frightened.

"Oh Malcolm," she whispered, "don't say..."

"I will, Katherine. I must tell you," he said. "I want to marry you, Katherine." He seized both her hands.

She took a deep breath and sat back, leaving her hands in his. She recovered enough to remind herself wryly that he still hadn't asked her, despite all the melodrama. He had only told her what he wanted. At least I don't have to answer him, she thought, with a trace of amusement.

"Are you sure that is what you want?" she asked at last.

"Very sure." He was remarkably calm.

"Ah, how can you be? I couldn't be sure, and I've been married. Perhaps if I'd been happier then, I could know what I want now, but I don't." And if she had loved Henry at all, perhaps she could love Malcolm now.

"Don't answer me now, but -"

She couldn't resist. "Answer you? My dear man, you haven't asked me anything!"

He threw back his head and laughed with delight, his pink face turning red. "I haven't, have I? What a coward!" Dropping her hands he wiped his eyes with a handkerchief. "Well, then: Don't answer me now, but will you marry me? Some day?"

"Why shouldn't I answer you now?"

Chapter 32

Veracruz, Mexico

It was a perfect evening in the harbor. The moonless tropical sky had exploded with stars. The onshore breeze blew more briskly than usual, and the few mosquitoes it did not discourage were kept at bay by the fine Havana smoke that drifted downwind from the three cigars glowing on *Isabella's* transom. For the first time in many weeks, the strains of marimba bands from the seafront promenade were heard and even the occasional gust of laughter.

"The town's come back to life," observed Jones. "They're celebrating. And so should we." The news had come through to them of the ferocious fighting at Shiloh, near the Tennessee River. It had ended as a stand-off, but the battle was seen to end the South's chances of fighting on even terms in the west.

"Why not?" said Morny, standing beside him at the rail. "And these people have even more reason to celebrate. The Spanish and the English have left, and our own men are eighty kilometers away, most of them." He signed to Henri, who was in attendance, to fill their brandy glasses.

"And when will you leave, sir?" Three large brandies accounted for Bartlett's daring to ask the question which, he remembered too late, annoyed Morny profoundly.

"*Et tu*, Bartlett?" Morny snapped. Then he relented. "I have given the necessary instructions, Major. That is all I will say on the matter." After a short pause he resumed his description of the Mayan ruins he had inspected in the Yucatan. It was plain that they intrigued him, that he had seen nothing to match their antique emptiness, not even in Africa.

At length he tossed his cigar over the rail, turned to his guests and said, "If you will excuse me, my friends, I shall retire to my office." He looked pleased. "I think I mentioned the possibility of a drama to be set in those ancient cities? I may claim that it goes well, very well, but I regret that it demands my attention now."

Bartlett and Jones began to make departing noises but their host stopped them. "No, no, I insist that you be my guests on board *Isabella* tonight. Henri has brought out everything you need – he tells me, by the way, that you travel with astonishingly little – so there can be no thought of returning to that odious hotel tonight." They looked at each other, shrugged happily and picked up their glasses again. "Henri will look after you. You must tell him if you want anything. Good night."

They were alone on deck except for Henri at a discreet distance and the anchor watch in the bows. "Well, ole buddy," Jones drawled, "again I have to wonder – "

"- what the poor people in the world are doing tonight. Very amusing, Tex." Bartlett stepped off a few paces back and forth. "What I wonder is what *we're* doing tonight. Here, on Morny's boat."

"That's easy: smoking his cigars, drinking his *fine champagne* and all in good time bunking down on his downy beds."

Their host had gone ashore early, Henri informed them at breakfast, and had urged them to remain on board as long as they liked. "The Count has a complicated day," the valet said, "and may not return until the dinner hour."

"If then," Captain Carbonnel corrected when they found him on deck, a fat yellow cigarette in his fingers. Three months in the fetid tropics had done nothing for the skipper's attitude or his waistline, which struggled to stay inside his stained shirt. But his beard was still tightly trimmed and the expensive cologne was still evident. "He's taken his launch for God knows how long, and the other boat's gone for supplies, so I wouldn't hope to get ashore soon, if I were you." He glared at them for a moment, heaved his belly around and stalked off to the bows.

Jones lifted an eyebrow and turned to Bartlett. "Pinochle? I saw some cards in the main cabin."

"I wonder what's for lunch," Bartlett mused as they headed below.

"We have to face it, Robert," said Bartlett as he wiped the bordelaise sauce from his chin and folded the linen napkin, "we're going nowhere. We are prisoners."

"Too right, partner, but let's just make sure. Let's find Carbonnel again."

The captain was if anything less forthcoming this time. "All I know, gentlemen, is that my orders are to see that you are comfortable here on board until the Count returns. Comfortable and safe."

"Safe?"

"Yes, that you don't attempt to swim in the sea." A hint of a grin. "It's dangerous, you might say. If the sharks don't kill you, the sewage will."

"Most considerate of the Count, to be sure," Bartlett said. "Thank you, Captain."

Carbonnel touched a forefinger to his cap and left them on the stern. Instinctively they looked around the harbor at the French warships and transports that lay at anchor inside the fort. The nearest vessel was a quarter of a mile distant; Morny insisted on his privacy. "Sharks, sewage or the crew's rifles. Those are our choices if we swim for it," said Bartlett.

"And we can assume that all the crew – they're down to about a dozen, would you say? – are armed. And can shoot."

"What a hole, and we walked right into it." Jones kicked a stanchion. "And I was getting quite fond of the bald-headed bastard."

"You're correct on all counts – excuse the pun," Bartlett laughed. "He really is a bastard, remember." His smile faded. "Well, at least we kept Washington informed that the Spanish and English have left. Or did we? You did send that last cable to Stoddard that we drafted?"

Jones nodded. "Yesterday afternoon. That job's done, anyway. And, yes, the codebook's safe with me." He paused. "You know, Charles, maybe we should forget about escaping. Why not lie back and enjoy all this luxury at Morny's expense for a few days? I don't think he means to kill us when he gets back. Do you?"

"You must be joking," Bartlett flared. "It's our duty, our – "

Jones raised a hand. "Just testing you, Charles. Calm down, old man." The denial was not wholly convincing. "Let's analyze this," he went on. "The crew are armed, and there will always be at least one of them watching us, guarding us. So in daylight we can't swim for it or get near a boat. Or get near a boat at night, for that matter."

"So we swim at night. From our cabins, so they can't see us get wet."

"Hm'm. Sharks? Barracuda?"

"They don't feed at night." A pause. "Do they?"

"I don't like that word 'feed'. It suggests a leisurely, contemplative grazing on my extremities. Why not just 'kill'?"

"Whatever." Bartlett waved an impatient hand. "There are two elements missing from your analysis, though. One, Carbonnel will have come to the same conclusion. Two, how do we cut our way out of our cabins, at night, at the same time?"

"Details, details." Jones tried to sound confident. "We'll think of something. Plenty of time."

"I'm afraid you're right. Plenty of time." Bartlett pondered for a minute or two. "But I have a question for you, Robert: Why are we joking about the trap we're in? Why do we take it so lightly, both of us?"

"It's a well-known reaction, a form of relief." Gone now were Jones's Texas vowels. "After months of sitting around and functioning as no more than clerks, we suddenly find we have to function with initiative and skill if we're to get out of the trap. The danger adds excitement, and we welcome the excitement."

"Do you have any idea what you're talking about?"

"Of course. We learned about this at Annapolis. It just shows how ignorant *you* can be when you set your mind to it."

It began to rain, hard, and kept it up for two full days. Belatedly, they found that Henri had left them their sidearms but had pocketed their bullets. They played pinochle in the main cabin, Jones tried to read Morny's library of French histories, Bartlett practiced his irregular verbs and they both regularly kicked the walls.

Morny appeared on *Isabella* in late afternoon on the third day. His riding clothes were rumpled; his boots were muddy; he was plainly hot and angry. The wings of hair above his ears stood out, and for the first time the Americans could see a film of sweat on his face. Carbonnel and Henri met him as he came over the rail and the valet took him to his suite, where a quantity of hot water awaited him. He emerged an hour later in a creamy linen suit and striped cravat, every inch the cool boulevardier they knew so well.

He at once took on the role of the generous, thoughtful host, inquiring after their comfort, the performance of the chef and the solicitude of the captain and the valet. They replied with courtesy and tempered enthusiasm and waited for him to get to the point. Which he did in due course.

"I must ask you to remain on board as my guests for some time." There was no generosity in his tone now. "You will be as comfortable as one can be in this latitude, in this maddening rain, and you will be well looked after. I can not say when – "

"We're prisoners, Count, say it," interjected Jones.

"My guests, Commander, involuntary guests if you like, but my guests nonetheless."

"Count, you have made us prisoners. That is an act of war," Bartlett said.

"That is nonsense. Face the facts. It would be an act of war only if your country knew of it and were in a position to protest effectively." He flicked out his right hand. "Forget about war, gentlemen, and make the best of your - limited circumstances."

"When do we get off this boat, Count?" demanded Jones.

"As soon as possible," said Morny. He said no more to them and went ashore in the morning. Henri and four large cases went with him in the launch.

"Good news, gentlemen," beamed Carbonnel later, rubbing his hands. "The Count fears that you may become bored if we merely lie at anchor here, fascinating as this harbor is, so he instructed me to sail up the coast for a few days to give you a change of scene." He laughed shortly. "And so I can make sure that our engine was truly repaired."

"I think Morny means to kill us and drop us gently in the sea," Bartlett said.

"No. Why would he want us dead? It would be just another complication for him." Jones tried to sound positive.

"Why would he want us alive? We've done what he brought us here to do."

Jones looked up sharply and slammed his hand against the bulkhead. "You're right, damn it! Exactly right! That bastard!"

"What's that all about?"

"You saw Henri take four cases ashore with him, didn't you? Four cases. That means they're staying here. They're not leaving; they're *staying*!"

"But the English and - my God!" Bartlett stared at Jones.

Jones grabbed Bartlett's sleeve. "And we've done precisely what he brought us here to do – get the English and the Spanish to leave. The prick!"

"Wait a minute." Bartlett pulled his arm free and held up his hand. "That's ridiculous. How on earth could he expect us to accomplish that?"

"He didn't expect it. He hoped for it. He's no fool. He guessed that we'd try to get them all to leave. They're a threat to the Union, don't forget. And he'd lose nothing if we failed."

"So we've done his dirty work for him." The bulkhead took further punishment as Bartlett tried to think. "But, hang on, Robert. At least we got rid of two of the three expeditions. Stoddard should thank us for that."

"And left the French with an open field? Is that better than all three of them here squabbling like children and not moving from their bases? I wonder. If it's not, partner, we can expect all kinds of grief when we get back home."

"Not me, *partner*," Bartlett forced a smile. "I'll blame it all on you, as my superior officer." After a moment he added, "Just kidding, of course."

"Of course." Jones smiled sourly. "We need to get to a telegraph line."

"And get out of Veracruz, or we'll die with the rest of them."

The glass continued to rise and at noon *Isabella* steamed slowly south, out past the fort and the anchored rows of French ships. "Talk about boredom," Jones said, pointing his chin at them, "the poor devils in those crews have been stuck out here for months. One week on, one week ashore is their routine, I'm told."

"Our own crew has almost doubled," said Bartlett. "I make it about twenty men."

"But still only twelve rifles."

"'Only'?"

They stayed inside the Sacrifice Islands and the beached wreck of a three-master. Then they swung southeast, keeping a distance of about one mile from the black reefs that shielded the brilliant white beaches. The shoreline was flat and uninteresting, with thin grass, scrubby vegetation and the occasional tree or mangrove plantation. There were few villages but many small bays, one that widened into a respectable lake.

At sundown they anchored in the lee of three fair-sized islands that stood half a dozen miles off the coast. The cloud cover had vanished and off to the west the mountains stood out vividly as the sun sank behind them. The big volcano, Orizaba, towered over the other peaks. Bartlett and Jones watched from the rail as dozens of two-man boats draped with nets threaded the channels through the dark reefs. The tide was out and the reefs were starkly visible above the white water at their bases.

"I wonder if at high water they can ride straight over those reefs," Bartlett commented.

"Why take a chance," replied Jones, "when they can find their channels blind-folded?"

They looked at each other. "Right," said Bartlett, "they may be our best bet. But when?"

"The first chance we get." Jones shifted closer and dropped his voice. "We have to put our uniforms, pistols, codebook, money and anything else we'll need in a box, or a barrel, or whatever will keep them dry. When we get our chance, we must be ready."

"Aye, aye, Skipper."

They sailed slowly south and east over a lively sea for two more days. The weather held, the coastline became flatter, the mountains dropped back and the reefs shrank to nothing. Then without any notice Carbonnel reversed course and headed back north, still along the coast, towards Veracruz. It was their fourth day of captivity and they had seen not the ghost of a chance to escape.

Time crawled by. One afternoon about four o'clock Bartlett and Jones were at their usual post at the weather rail, watching the fishermen work their nets. A light breeze blew over the starboard quarter and Carbonnel had set the mainsail, foresail and two jibs. *Isabella's* deck rose and shuddered from the pressure of the sea and her rudder. "Those boats are closer inshore than they were last time," commented Bartlett.

"That's where the fish are, obviously." Jones was in a black humor. "Or," he looked at the sky, "might it be," he turned around and stared out to sea, "might it be because of the weather?" He pointed in that direction and Bartlett scanned the ocean sky, not knowing what to look for. But he couldn't miss the smudged, black horizontal bar that lay about ten degrees above the horizon, with towering thunderheads piling up behind it.

"That, my friend, unless I'm wholly mistaken," Jones breathed, "is a squall, a line squall. A bad one. Very rare in these latitudes, so Carbonnel and his lads may not recognize the signs."

"I know them," Bartlett said. "They come down from the north on the waters near Boston."

Without another word they went below to Bartlett's cabin on the starboard side, which gave a view through its porthole out to sea. Jones planted himself in front of it and whistled. "This one's coming from the northeast, and coming fast. Look at all those small boats running in from it. These squalls can cover forty or fifty miles in an hour, you know."

A dozen larger fishing boats, all with a single triangular sail and a crew of two or three, were flying across the darkening water towards a point of land a mile ahead of *Isabella*. Those farthest out were reefing their sails or dropping them altogether. Sunlight flashed from their oars as they began to row. "They know what's coming," said Jones.

"This may be our chance," Bartlett ventured. "Sharks?"

"The waves will drive them deeper – I think. And if we can get on one of those boats, or at least hold on to its side - " Jones left the cabin and returned in a minute. "Carbonnel woke up at last. They're taking the jibs down but leaving both mains up. Idiots!"

Bartlett pocketed his pistol and put his boots in the wooden keg that already held their uniforms, papers, codebook and gold coins. Jones came back from his cabin and did the same. Bartlett nailed the round wooden top into place and then nailed three lengths of rope to its sides. "We both have to hang on to this. It might keep us afloat, and we'll need what's in it."

"Right," said Jones. "Now when this thing hits us, which I estimate," peering through the streaming porthole, "will be in five minutes, all hell will happen on deck. Every man in the crew will be needed to get those big sails down and it'll get dark. Nobody on deck will be looking for us. So we'll get to the rear door of the saloon and slip over the leeward side."

"The helmsman will see us!"

"Can't be helped. And a dollar to a dirt fly he won't care. He'll be fighting to bring her up into the wind. Ready?"

Bartlett nodded. No rebellious instincts this time.

A vicious sea was already running. The temperature dropped ten degrees, the waves swelled and *Isabella* began to pitch steeply. Harsh cries from the stern, bare feet running, more loud cries and she heeled hard to port. It got colder still, the cabin grew dark and the noise of the wind in the rigging rose to the whine that meant rising weather. The main engine kicked into life and the boat began to vibrate as the propeller bit.

A lifetime passed and the storm hit with full force, laying *Isabella* well over. When she struggled back up, the watch raced up the ratlines to drop the sails and other crewmen eased the halyards, but a block was jammed and the foresail refused to come down. Jones and Bartlett crept to the door of the saloon and squinted aft through the spray. Bartlett almost didn't recognize the deck, which slanted violently to port under a tangle of lines and sails. A wild-eyed Carbonnel stood braced on the foredeck bawling orders to the men battling with the halyard.

The helmsman and the quartermaster, lashed to the wheelbox, fought the wheel but the pressure on the foresail prevented the boat from heading up into the wind. She lurched sickeningly to port and the propeller raced as a wild gust staggered the hull.

"If they don't get that sail down she may broach in the next gust," Jones shouted over the wail of the storm. They felt a vacuum in their ears and a blast of wind, cold sheeting rain and hailstones raked the deck. Then a ragged comber came crashing aboard and raced the length of the open deck. In reaction, the men at the wheel shielded their eyes with their hands.

"Go!" cried Jones and they slid down into the warm sea boiling over the leeward rail. The quartermaster looked up, saw them and raised a hand in slow salute. They shoved out from the hull and kicked frantically to get away from the propeller.

As soon as *Isabella's* transom slid by three massive waves drove them deep and left them gasping each time they surfaced, still clutching the wooden keg. The hailstones peppered them, the rain and salt spray blinded them and for a time they were disoriented. They couldn't find the shore over the waves. They saw *Isabella* as she drew away. But they couldn't make out if she had contrived to swing up into the wind and out to sea, so they didn't know whether to swim after her or away from her. Then Jones saw that her foresail was down. "She's heading out!" he cried. Another enormous wave, another ducking, another choking recovery.

Bartlett tightened his grip on the keg and wiped his sleeve across his eyes. He spotted four of the fishing boats out to windward with scraps of canvas on their masts, making line astern for the reef on a course that would bring them within a hundred yards. Bartlett pointed at them and shouted, "Make for the first one!"

Together they dragged the stubborn keg across the eight-foot waves, riding the crests and kicking hard in the troughs. Every yard was a battle against wind, rain and wave. Luckily the four fishing crews were concerned only to stay afloat, and the oars they had extended from the sides helped to steady their boats, not speed them to shore. Bartlett and Jones saw they had every chance to intercept the first boat if they could only keep going.

But when they had swum desperately for twenty minutes they began to suffer for their months of tropical indolence. Jones grasped the keg to his chest and stopped, treading water. "Go on, Charles," he gasped. "Stop a boat with your weapon and slow it. I'll be right behind you."

They rose abruptly to the crest of a wave and saw that the first boat was about eighty yards upwind and would cross twenty yards ahead of them. The fishermen still hadn't spotted them. "You talk too much," Bartlett croaked. "Let's go."

He plunged ahead. Jones rested his chest on the keg and kicked hard but could not keep up. Bartlett let go his line to the keg and with the last of his strength paddled ahead, to find himself two yards from the bow of the first boat, still unseen. He wrenched the pistol from his pocket, ducked under the extended oar and surfaced with the pistol almost in the face of the man at the tiller. Who stared at him impassively and didn't react. Stunned, Bartlett forgot his Spanish and lost his nerve, as the boat glided past him.

The next boat was twenty yards away, heading slowly at him. The skipper saw Jones at last and cried out to his crewman. Bartlett waited, dived under the boat and came up on the other, starboard, side, pistol still in his hand. He grabbed the gunwale with the other hand and waved his weapon at the man in the stern. He remembered his regular verbs. "*Parar!*" he shouted. Again, no reaction, but the second man started to raise his port oar to shove it at Bartlett. It wouldn't release and, looking down, he saw that Jones was draped across it and aiming at his chest. The keg bobbed beside him.

Jones spat a mouthful of seawater, retched and commanded, "*Vamos! Andale!*" He reached in over the gunwale and pulled out a machete, which he dropped in the sea. "Look for the other one, Charles!" he called. Bartlett found its mate in a sling under the skipper's seat and tossed it overboard.

"I reckon they're wondering if our weapons will fire," Jones said casually. "I'll reassure them." There followed a rapid exchange of coastal Spanish, after which the Mexicans grinned and shook their heads in astonishment. "I explained that both of them work just fine, that we're here to save their boat for them and that, once they get us ashore, we'll be on our way."

"They believed you?" Bartlett gasped.

"Of course. Wouldn't you?"

The boat was about fifteen feet long, with a narrow beam, a rudimentary centerboard and a deep hold piled with nets and a few small fish. The weight and drag of their bodies and the keg had slowed it so much that the third and fourth boats, now a quarter of a mile astern, gained on them rapidly. Jones pushed the keg over the gunwale and into the hold, but he told Bartlett to stay in the water and try not to be seen. Another volley of Spanish told their hosts what they could expect if their comrades made any trouble. The grins vanished.

The squall was largely spent by now. The hail had stopped, the rain had diminished to a tropical downpour and the wind had dropped to thirty knots. But it needed all their strength just to hang on to the boat. They decided not to try to scramble on board because that would unbalance it, and by remaining in the water they helped to keep it upright. Jones fought his way forward, ahead of the crewman with the oars, so that his unseen pistol was a deadlier threat to the man's back. Bartlett held his weapon steadily, much of the time, on the skipper, who showed no sign of mutiny.

The waves still rose high and crashed over the reefs that lay dead ahead. The channel they steered for was marked by a lower band of white surf and the occasional glimpse of green water. Jones had regained some of his customary assurance and felt compelled to instruct the skipper on his approach to the channel's entrance. The skipper bore it for a minute but then took both hands off the tiller and offered it to Jones, who subsided with ill grace. "Our friend here may try to scrape us off on the reef when we go through," he said to Bartlett, "better keep your legs up."

In the end, their passage down the channel was uneventful. The skipper rode the waves through the chute with practised skill and the American legs were never in obvious danger. The surf surged and roared around them, spilling off the reef and rocking the boat violently sideways, but their four legs, two heavy bodies and two oars in the water kept them upright.

Once inside the reef the waves subsided to about three feet as the water shoaled, but they and the wind had enough power to propel the craft over the water ahead of the last two boats. Jones waved his pistol and told the skipper to head for the closest beach, and five minutes later the boat ground up on the seashells that composed most of it. They staggered ashore. Jones shook hands with their unwilling rescuers and delivered a short speech to the skipper, who gave a soft giggle and looked bemused. Bartlett ventured a nervous wave at them.

Bartlett and Jones strode slowly inland with the keg between them. Their backs and arms ached like fire, the shells cut their feet and their throats were parched. They sat on the first fallen palm they came to, opened their mouths wide and leaned back to drink the rain. At length Jones shook his head and said, "I told them I'm a Mexican and you're a Yank and we've escaped from that European scum who invaded their country. They may believe me and not come after us, at least until Carbonel puts a boat ashore and bribes them to bring us in."

"Sharks," said Bartlett. "You know, I forgot all about them."

"Like I said, the waves drive them deep."

"Right."

They watched as the last two boats drew up on the beach and the six fishermen conferred excitedly, looking often at the path Jones and Bartlett had taken. At length they all shrugged and set to work pulling out their nets and fish before overturning their boats.

"We need to get to Puebla and a telegraph office," said Bartlett, wiping the rain from his brow.

"Right," agreed Jones, "but we need horses to get there, and the only horses I know of are back in Veracruz, in Laffan's stables."

"I make that ten miles. Twelve? Straight up the beach."

"Right. If this damned rain ever stops, we can stop for the night."

Chapter 33

"What in the name of God?" Laffan's astonishment was almost comical. "Robert? Charles? Come inside! Quickly."

The two men, wearing only their shorts, undershirts and side arms, stumbled across the doorstep of the house of Laffan's "aunt". They clutched makeshift satchels fashioned from scraps of canvas and rope.

"Carolina, come here!" Laffan called. "Our Yankee friends need a bath and dry clothes."

"And a whisky," Jones added. "Please."

One bath, two whiskeys and oven-dried clothes later, they lounged gratefully in the high-ceilinged drawing room and told of their escape from *Isabella*. Rain pounded at the tall windows. A footman stood ready in a corner to refill their glasses.

Bartlett first described their swim and their ride ashore in the storm. Then Jones took over, at length. "It was quite simple, really," he finished. "The rain washed away our tracks, and we only had to walk inshore to avoid the squad that Carbonnel sent in to round us up."

"*Isabella's* anchored in the harbor now," Carolina remarked. "She lost the top of her front mast and that pole on her bow." The candlelight was doing something to her reddish hair and softening the planes of her face.

"Bowsprit," Laffan supplied. "There are very few French left in the city, by the way. They've moved up to the hills."

"To escape the mosquitoes, I suppose," grunted Jones. He took up the tale. "We slept last night in a hole in the sand that we covered over with palm branches. We reached the grove of palm trees near the Fort Santiago gate about noon today and lay up until dusk. Then, we just walked in under the guard tower, trying hard to look like Mexicans. The guard was drunk or asleep. And here we are." He raised his glass to Carolina. "And delighted to see you again."

"What are your plans now?" asked Laffan. "Can you stay the night?"

"Thanks, Pancho, thanks very much," Bartlett said, "but we want to get to Puebla – to the telegraph office there – as soon as we can. We'll leave tonight."

"Then we must have dinner right away," said Carolina, rising from her chair. "I'll tell Quesada." As she passed behind Jones, she dropped a hand lightly on his shoulder. "It's good to have you here, Roberto," she said. Jones grinned with delight, missing the tiny wink she gave Laffan.

"Ah, Pancho," Bartlett said, "a great favor to ask you. Can you lend us two horses?"

"Of course we can," Carolina replied as she left the room. "Take Milagro, the bay mare, and – "

"Take a couple of mules, she means," smiled Laffan. "Remember, my sister, we're dealing with two certified equiphobes here." He turned to the startled Bartlett. "Only joking, old friend. By all means, take two horses. Carolina will choose them for you."

"That's generous of you, Pancho."

"Not at all." Laffan stretched lazily. "Just return them – how will you return them, by the way?"

"Ah. Let's see. Can we send you a bank draft instead? In dollars?"

"Of course not. You – "

"The solution is obvious," Jones interjected. "To get back to Washington when we finish in Puebla, we must ride through either Mexico City or Veracruz. If we go through here, the problem solves itself. If we go through the capital, we'll have our embassy get the horses back to you." He sat back, pleased with his logic.

"You're a genius, Robert. Much underrated. I've always said so," Bartlett smiled. "Pancho?"

"Fine, fine, anything you say. Just get my horses back and don't get yourselves killed before then." He went to a desk against a wall and pulled out a creased document. "Do you have a good map? Take this if you need one."

"We have the best, thanks to the unwitting generosity of His Excellency le Comte de Morny," Jones said. "It's drying upstairs."

"Well, have a look at this one. I'll tell you how to go." Laffan unrolled the map on a table and arranged more candles around it. He tapped it with a poker. "Now, pay attention, class. You should wear plain clothes when you start. The French will arrest you if they identify you."

"He's right," Bartlett declared. "Morny will send a platoon after us when he hears we left *Isabella*. He can't let us run around loose."

"Morny's up in Orizaba," Laffan said. "He won't hear about you for a day or two." He surveyed them. "Can we get back to the map now?"

"So the French *are* staying on," Jones said bitterly. "We thought so. Damn Morny."

"Are they, Pancho?" Bartlett asked. "Maybe we're wrong."

"For God's sake, Charles," Jones said. "They'll either stay in Veracruz to collect the rest of their money or they'll strike for Mexico City." He paused to see the effects of this on the other two. "And I'll bet on Mexico City."

"Well, he did say that they were obligated to pull out by their treaty and that they would."

"No, he only said that he'd given the necessary orders," Jones corrected heatedly. "He didn't say what they were."

"Now, now, boys," Laffan interceded, "calm down, both of you." He signalled for the footman. "Another whisky and think for a moment, if you're able." They looked at him in silence. "Look," he went on, "whatever your noble friend is up to, you two need to get to that telegraph office in Puebla pronto. And I'm just the man to tell you how to do that, so gather 'round this nice big map again."

They did so. Laffan told them to take the route north of the mountains. They were to leave Veracruz by the Puerta Nueva and take the road that led to Jalapa, but to bypass Jalapa itself because a few French units were still stationed in the area. Stay on the road north of the second mountain, he said, the Cofre de Perote, which was well to the north of Mount Orizaba, the big volcano. After rounding the Cofre they would turn southwest towards Puebla. That terrain was flat, easy riding country and they couldn't lose the route.

Bartlett looked up from the map. "How many miles in all?"

"Oh, one hundred sixty to seventy. Four days' steady ride."

"And if we get into trouble?" Jones asked.

"I'd ride south of Perote, between the two mountains. You'll find no trails in there, but follow the river valleys up to the crest and then head west down to the flat lands. Then southwest until you hit the Puebla road. The country up there is rough, but you should lose any patrols that come after you. Mexicans don't like going up there, and if you put on your uniforms they won't chase you too hard."

"What about French patrols?"

"They don't go up there. They're scared of the Mexican army."

They set off about nine o'clock that night, dressed like Mexicans and hiding their pistols in their pockets. Jones rode Milagro, the easy striding mare, while Bartlett perched uncertainly on a creature that had all the characteristics of a mule except docility and announced its intentions with a savage bite at his knee. Their saddlebags held all their gear: food, water, ammunition, uniforms, boots, Morny's map and woollen serapes for the cold in the hills. Bartlett had thought of asking Laffan for rifles but decided in the end not to push their friendship that far. A decision he would regret.

All went well the first night. The rain had stopped. They cleared the Puerta Nueva without a glance from the guard and followed the road northwest towards Jalapa for almost twenty miles. They saw little traffic and no patrols, Mexican or French. The road was not much more than a broad, potholed track, marked every two or three hundred yards by a small, candlelit shrine. Jones explained that each was a monument to a man murdered on that spot. Bartlett stopped counting them after an hour or so.

About midnight they stopped at a bathhouse in a dark village and persuaded the sleeping caretaker that a few pesos were enough to buy hammocks, baths and breakfasts in the morning.

Stiff and sore from the unaccustomed hammocks and queasy from their breakfast beans, they set out at dawn the next day. The road was now busy with farmers, peddlers and laborers on foot between the villages, which consisted of two-roomed adobe cottages scattered around a peeling church. Gaudily costumed peasant women squatted outside the cottages grinding corn. Bartlett and Jones came upon the occasional passenger diligence or mounted Mexican army patrol on the road. Dressed as they were, they attracted inspection but no audible comment as they passed by.

The road rose steadily. They estimated they were at four thousand feet when they stopped to dismount a few miles before Jalapa and stretch their legs. The town lay in a valley beneath them, flanked on both sides by a steep ridge. Rubbing his buttocks hard, Jones said, "Laffan warned of French patrols around here. What do you reckon – do we go north or south of the town?"

Bartlett studied their map. "Pancho forgot to tell us that a river runs through Jalapa, and this map doesn't show any other bridges across it. And, besides" – he surveyed the terrain again – "we could spend hours climbing up one of those two ridges and then find there *is* no bridge on the other side. My instinct – "

"Right," said Jones, "straight through the middle of town it is. To hell with the French."

It was the correct choice. A party of mounted African Chasseurs, splendid in their white uniforms and black skins, followed them closely until they were a mile outside the pretty town and then turned away. "I think they're harmless," Jones muttered at one point, "They don't have an officer, and no mere corporal will take the risk of shooting a native."

Now they were well into the mountains and the road climbed steeply. On their left, the Cofre de Perote lifted its chopped-off summit far above the snow line. And forty miles to the south the magnificent white volcanic peak of Mount Orizaba towered nineteen thousand feet into the deep blue evening sky.

They passed another night at another cheap, clean bath house, this one with a fire that burned all night and eggs and tortillas for breakfast. Bartlett left a generous tip for the cook and Jones objected. "Don't you go spoiling the peasants around here, Charles, you'll ruin a good thing. And pick up the pace, can't you?"

"Does it look like it?" Bartlett was having his usual difficulty with his mount. "This - thing has a mind of its own, and right now it's decided it wants to walk." A brisk kick in the animal's ribs had no effect.

As they circled the northern approaches to the Cofre, the road levelled off at seven or eight thousand feet. When it turned to the southwest, in the direction of Puebla, they saw a broad, flat empty plain all the way to the horizon. The semi-desert slopes of the first day had changed into wide green fields of corn, beans and tomatoes. "About eighty miles to go," Bartlett said as he looked up from the map. "We'll be there tomorrow night, if we're lucky."

They pulled up to a walk and then stopped to dismount and water the horses in an icy stream running down from the mountain. Bartlett climbed a small rise and scanned the plain ahead of them through their telescope. Then he idly turned to look back down the road. He tensed, wiped the lens and looked again. "Could be trouble, Robert. We will soon find out if those Africans are as harmless as you said they are."

Jones grabbed the glass and raised it. "Damn it! They must be after us. Why else would they be on their own so far from Jalapa?"

"How many? Have they seen us?"

"Six, seven – no, eight. One's an officer. They're at a sharp trot, about a mile away."

"Have they seen us?"

"No. We're still screened by these trees." Jones gnawed his fist in indecision. "We have to assume they're looking for us, to take us back to Jalapa. To hold us, not to shoot us. Morny must have got word to them somehow."

"Well, we can't outrun them," Bartlett said. "They'll catch up sometime today. So..."

"If we can't run and we can't stay here, there's only one way to go." Jones pointed up the mountain. "Up that *barranca.*"

Bartlett looked up where he pointed. The narrow, densely wooded ravine snaked on a diagonal up the mountainside for half a mile before it disappeared over the crest of a jagged ridge. Beyond it was a grassy slope covered with boulders, and above that was a series of winding valleys that seemed to lead in all directions. He remembered that Laffan had advised them to head into the upper valleys if necessary, but he had meant the valleys that lay between the two main mountains and they were north of both.

What the hell, he thought. Laffan had also said that the French wouldn't go into the mountains, but despite that his general advice was sound and, besides, there was no other option. They would have to walk the horses much of the way, but, if they could get high enough and stay out of the Africans' sight, they stood every chance to avoid capture and reach Puebla in the next day or two.

And we *must* get to Puebla, he told himself. We *must* warn Stoddard that the French are still here. And that they mean to stay. If we don't, our whole mission will be a failure.

The sky had got much darker, as cumulus clouds rushed to join each other above the next range to the west. Rain would help our chances of escape, he thought. Or would it? These Africans are said to be tough and determined soldiers. But maybe Jones is right, maybe they don't mean to kill us.

They slipped into the trees at the foot of the ravine and walked the horses straight up it as far as they could. But soon enough the undergrowth forced them to dismount and lead the horses on foot. Jones scanned the road beneath them every few minutes and at last, after they crossed a ridgeline, reported that the Africans had reached the foot of the ravine. They tied the horses in a copse and crawled back behind a rocky ledge to observe their pursuers. They were a thousand feet above the Africans.

"They're looking in all directions," Jones muttered, his glass to his eye. "Our tracks just end where they've stopped. It won't take them long to figure out we must have headed up here."

But the Africans surprised them. Their lieutenant, distinguished by an extravagant gold headgear, sent two men farther along the road and another two out across the fields to their right, all four at the gallop. Then he sat down to wait.

"You know, there was a story going 'round about our friends down there," Jones said, chewing on a straw as he sat. "One of their sergeants was murdered last month in a village near Veracruz. He may have been fooling around with someone's wife. Or he may not. In any case, they say his mates went back the next night and killed every man in the village."

"That's your subtle way to warn me not to shoot at them, is it?" Bartlett was nervous and needed to say something humorous. Jones grinned in sympathy.

After half an hour both patrols cantered back, shaking their heads and shouting. The lieutenant rose and studied the ravine through his telescope. Then he scanned left and right along the ridge. Jones and Bartlett froze and prayed that their horses would behave. The lieutenant shrugged, shook his head and remounted. The patrol moved forward at a fast trot along the road and within minutes were out of sight around a long sweeping bend to the left.

The Americans eyed each other in silence. At last Bartlett said, "I think they'll wait for us down the road. They figure we have to come down some time and they plan to sight us when we do."

"Makes sense," Jones grunted. "They'd be right. So, what do we do? Suppose you be leader today."

Was that an admission of error? Bartlett asked himself. Not likely, but certainly a grudging request for help. "We keep going," he said grimly. "We can't go back and we can't go down yet. Sound familiar? So we keep going at this level, or a bit higher, and hope to slip past them in the night."

"Some hope, but the only one we have. I agree. Let's go."

They crept slowly across the mountainside, keeping well in the trees and leading their horses all the way. Cover was adequate except for the two hundred yard traverse of a clearing littered with boulders. Reluctant to leave the tree line and unwilling to circle above the clearing, their dilemma was solved by a burst of driving rain. They crouched behind a rock and peered down through the mist. "Quick!" urged Jones. "Run for it!" When Bartlett failed to respond, he shouted, "Our friends will be taking cover from this. They won't look up. Let's go!"

The ground in the clearing was clay or smooth rock, and Bartlett slipped twice. Only his frantic grip on the reins kept him on his feet. He knew from his Indian fighting days what a bullet sounds like when it ricochets off a rock, and for the last fifty yards he hunched his shoulders, lowered his head and waited for that sound. It never came. Jones was right, and he got across first.

"You showed a nice turn of speed there," Jones allowed, panting hard, "at the end, anyway." He swung his telescope along the road beneath them. "Nothing. I reckon we keep going. You?" Bartlett nodded and started off along the same line as before.

After another half an hour the rain had stopped and they had still seen nothing of the Africans. Jones pulled up alongside Bartlett and said wearily, "We haven't seen those black bastards for at least four miles. They must be well ahead of us now."

Again Bartlett scanned the road. This time he held a hand up sharply, passed the glass to Jones and pointed down the mountain. A white-uniformed back could be discerned through the trees at the base of the mountain. Then another. Both troopers smoked long yellow cigarettes and rested against a tree, looking out over the plains before them. Bartlett and Jones waited fifteen minutes but no other Chasseur appeared, so they resumed their trek through the dripping pine forest, edging upward as they went.

It was not long before they sighted two more Chasseurs squatting by the road, now five hundred yards below them, almost out of earshot in the cool breeze blowing up the slope from the west. Bartlett deduced the obvious, that the lieutenant had split his men into four squads of two and was leaving a pair of them by the road every half mile or so. He would probably remain with the last pair, the one with the greatest chance of intercepting the Americans.

The third pair were easily detected because each man was pulling hard on the handle of a large brass canteen and screaming at the other. The last group were tucked into the trees fairly well, but the setting sun struck the lieutenant's magnificent headdress at an angle that reflected its rays straight up to the Americans as they picked their way through the formidable underbrush.

"I think we should camp here for the night, keep an eye on this bunch," Bartlett breathed.

"Right." Jones seemed content for the present to let Bartlett take the decisions. They unsaddled the horses.

They passed the worst night of their careers on the Cofre de Perote. The cold bit through their wet uniforms and thin serapes. To make a fire was out of the question, and the beans, bread and cheese barely unknotted their stomachs, aching from hunger and the cold. They forced themselves to stay awake past midnight, beating their arms and legs regularly, and then they stood two-hour watches. Not a sound reached them all night, from the Africans or from the trees. There was no talk, no attempt to make the time pass in conversation. They simply endured until daybreak. Then they forced down a breakfast of beans, bread and cheese.

"Who packed our food?" growled Jones.

"The Laffans' cook, I suppose."

"She must have thought we were a couple of field hands, damn her soul."

"Speak to Carolina when we get back."

Jones grunted and secured his saddlebags. There came a loud shout from the Africans hunched around their fire below them and another white-clad figure cantered into view back down the road. Jones and Bartlett dropped to the still wet ground. Through the telescope Bartlett watched him ride up, salute the officer and give him what was plainly an important message. Important enough, at least, for the officer to slam his headgear to the ground and gesture with his fist up the mountain. The new arrival shrugged, spoke again and dismounted. The officer took a long look with his glass in the direction of the Americans, prodded his finger where he looked and screamed at the messenger. Then he jammed his golden hat back on his head, spoke sharply to his men and set off at a slow trot back towards Jalapa. They kicked out the fire, leapt on to their saddled horses and followed him.

"What do you make of that?" Bartlett asked.

"The same as you. They've been ordered back to base. Something came up that's more important than us." Jones kept his tone level to hide his relief.

"We might just make it to Puebla after all."

"Sure enough. Let's go, but we'd better stay high for another mile or so, to make sure."

An hour later, with no trace of the Chasseurs, they started down the slope towards the road. They soon came to the head of a small but spectacular waterfall that sprang out from a dense grove of trees and crashed fifty feet below in a burst of spray. As they circled above it, a low harsh voice spoke from the thick brush on Bartlett's left: "*Buenos dias, Señores.*" A shabby figure stepped out from the gloom, rifle pointed at Bartlett's belt buckle. At the same time his twin, similarly armed and aimed, emerged on Jones's right.

Blast! Bartlett thought as he lifted his hands. It was El Chino. But maybe...

But no such luck. El Chino did recognize him, and happily. "*Fíjate, Pulido, es el pinche gringo quien mato a Romero y al Chaparrito.*"

Chino was not really a happy man, though. Business was bad. Revenues were way off and profits down to zero. His eight-strong band of brothers had dwindled to just two. Death, desertion and disease had accounted for the other six.

The truth was that Chino was not good at his trade. His fragile connection with the Mexican army had been severed, and not by his choice, so he was angry, as mean as a junkyard dog. And no longer constrained by the niceties of international relations, so everyone was fair game, especially Yankees.

"He recognizes you, says you killed his partner," Jones hissed.

"It wasn't me, tell him. It was Laffan. Tell him!"

"*Hablas español, gringo?*" Chino demanded of Jones.

"*Soy tan Mexicano como tu, amigo.*"

There followed a rapid-fire exchange in Spanish, too fast for Bartlett to understand, although the shrill note in Chino's voice suggested that he wasn't buying Jones's explanation.

"He doesn't believe you. He says he'll kill you later," said Jones evenly. "Better do something, and quick."

The two bandits stood in front of their captives and shouted at them. Jones said, "Drop your weapon, Charles, and slowly," as he drew his own from its holster. Bartlett dropped his in the longest grass near him. As Chino bent to pick it up, he lowered his eyes to look for it. Bartlett, expecting this, dropped to his knees, lunged for Chino's left boot and lifted hard, hard enough to spoil his point blank aim as he fell backward and fired. He fell on his gun hand, which Bartlett pinned to the ground just before he brought his right knee viciously down into the Mexican's groin.

Pulido had turned to fire at Bartlett when Jones's knife leapt out of his side pocket and hit him in the left shoulder. He stumbled, turned back toward Jones with his pistol and caught Jones's boot in his teeth. Jones picked up the pistol and shot the bandit once in the foot, which dropped him screaming to the ground. Then he recovered his own weapon and stood over Bartlett and Chino, who were thrashing violently in the wet grass. Chino still held on to his rifle and was trying to throttle Bartlett with it.

"Shoot this bastard, Jones!" croaked Bartlett.

"Oh, it wouldn't be fair," Jones said. "Besides, you're doing all right."

In fact, the two were evenly matched. Bartlett was much heavier and stronger, but Chino offset this with his stunning body odor, a distillate of wet goat and horse manure, and his eye-watering breath of pure refried beans. Together, they packed a vicious punch.

Bartlett at last pushed the rifle above Chino's head and wrenched it from his hands. Or he thought he did. As he reached for a large rock, Chino swung the butt into his ribs. Bartlett fended off the next swing and smashed the rock on Chino's forehead. Stunned, Chino tried to raise and fire the rifle, but he took another rock on the head and lay back. This time Bartlett did free the rifle and in a cold fury tossed it to one side, where Jones picked it up while he kept Pulido covered.

All of Bartlett's fears of the past three days surged away and, in his relief and rage, he lost his senses. He grabbed Chino's left leg from behind and pulled him up on to his other leg. Then he half pushed and half pulled the desperately hopping bandit to the rim of the gorge carved out by the waterfall. There he kicked out the Mexican's right leg, rolled him on his back and forced the filthy head back and down.

"You'll kill me, will you? Can you see that, you greasy little turd?"

Chino could not see what Bartlett could see – a broad ledge twelve feet below them. "Take a closer look." He loosed his grip and rolled his enemy over the edge. Chino dropped howling for a second, then Bartlett heard the thud of his body on the ledge and the muffled snap of a tibia. He looked over the rim of the gorge. Chino was sprawled on the ledge, eyes open but not moving.

An unwelcome spasm of regret and sympathy hit Bartlett. He walked back past the open-mouthed Jones, snatched the coil of rope from Chino's horse and dangled one end of it by Chino's face. The Mexican raised one hand and extended its middle finger in Bartlett's direction.

"Ah, yes," said Jones from Bartlett's side. "The traditional Mexican salute of the vanquished to the victor."

Bartlett shrugged and, expressionless, dropped the rope so that Chino could see it hit the ledge by his side and slide off, down to the stream below.

Pulido had recovered somewhat and lay terrified and moaning at Jones's feet. Bartlett sank to the grass nearby and hid his head in his hands. After a bit he raised his head and gasped, "That knife again. You're pretty handy with it. Like Laffan."

"All well-bred Mexicans are handy with a knife. We learn young."

Bartlett took that in. Then he pointed at the Mexican and said, "Why did you shoot him?"

"Why did I – what? You almost killed a man in cold blood, and you ask me why I shot a man who was about to kill you?" Jones was as curious as he was angry.

Bartlett didn't answer. He had no answer. He couldn't even explain it to himself.

Jones sensed that. "I only shot him once, in the big toe. A man can't walk without a big toe, I read somewhere."

"He'll die here, then."

"And *you're* worried? No, we'll leave him on the road. Someone will find him in time. They may even come back here for Chino."

They rounded up the horses, helped Pulido onto his mare and made for the road. There they pulled him off, remounted and rode west, each with a bandit's horse on a lead.

Bartlett had much to think about. He'd meant to kill a man, the third in a few months, and he still felt no remorse. Why not? And why had he dropped them in the water? Some sort of atavistic curse? Nonsense; just bad luck. For them. They had crossed paths with a gravity killer.

As they bedded down for the night in a sleeping village, a full day's ride from Puebla, Jones said, "Charles? I just want to say that what you did – to Chino - is all right with me." He coughed heavily. "Ah, in fact, ah, you're doing - you're doing all right."

Chapter 34

Washington

"URGENT FOR GENL STODDARD

REGRET DELAY STOP NOW REPORTING FROM
PUEBLA STOP ENGLISH AND SPANISH FORCES
HAVE FULLY EMBARKED FROM VERACRUZ
AND NOW PRESUMABLY RETURNING TO
HOME PORTS PARAGRAPH
FRENCH FORCES HAVE NOT REPEAT NOT
EMBARKED AND ARE CONCENTRATED
ALONG CORDOBA – ORIZABA LINE STOP
WITH ESTIMATED ONE THOUSAND MEN IN
VERACRUZ HOSPITALS WE ESTIMATE FRENCH
STRENGTH AT ABOVE AREA AT SIX
THOUSAND FIT FOR DUTY STOP MORNY
REPORTED IN ORIZABA WITH FRENCH FORCE
COMMANDERS PARAGRAPH
MEXICAN DEFENCE FORCE OF FIVE
THOUSAND EFFECTIVES INCLUDING ONE
THOUSAND CAVALRY AND TEN LIGHT FIELD
PIECES ARRIVED PUEBLA TODAY STOP
GENERAL IGNACIO ZARAGOSA
COMMANDING STOP OUR PRELIMINARY
OPINION IS THAT MEXICAN TROOPS ARE
INEXPERIENCED AND BADLY ARMED STOP
FRENCH OBJECTIVE ASSUMED TO BE MEXICO
CITY AND IF SO THEY MUST FIRST TAKE
PUEBLA PARAGARAPH
WILL REPORT AGAIN AFTER CONFERENCE
WITH ZARAGOSA EXPECTED LATER TODAY
STOP
END
XZ"

"URGENT FOR GENL STODDARD

FURTHER TO OURS OF THIS MORNING STOP
GENL ZARAGOSA CONFIRMS THAT FRENCH
FORCE OF ABOUT FIVE THOUSAND UNDER
LORENCEZ LEFT CORDOBA-ORIZABA LINE

ONE MAY AND IS MOVING WEST TOWARDS
PUEBLA ALONG MAIN EAST – WEST ROAD
STOP MEXICANS HAVE OFFERED NO
RESISTANCE AND HAVE CONCENTRATED ALL
AVAILABLE TROOPS IN PUEBLA STOP
ZARAGOSA HAS REQUESTED REINFORCE-
MENTS OF TWO THOUSAND STOP FRENCH
FORCE EXPECTED TO REACH AMOZOC
FOURTEEN MILES EAST OF PUEBLA IN NEXT
COUPLE DAYS STOP AWAIT YOUR
INSTRUCTIONS STOP
END
XZ"

"So the French are staying in Mexico, are they?" Lincoln mused. "Isn't
that exactly what we don't want? And I thought they had to go once the
English and Spanish left, under the terms of the London Convention.
Doesn't the convention prohibit unilateral action?"

"Ah - no," said Seward.

Lincoln cocked an amused eye. "You see? The English and Spanish
needed more lawyers. Or better lawyers." He straightened up, a hand
pressed to his lower back. "You can't spend too much money on lawyers,
I've always said." He became serious. "So what went wrong down there?
Why did the English and Spanish leave?"

Seward let Stoddard field that one. "We don't know for sure, sir. Some
sort of violent disagreement with the French, it seems. We're trying to
find out."

"Please do." Lincoln regarded Stoddard with a frown. "General, what
will Morny try to accomplish now, with only five thousand men who can
fight?"

"It's difficult, sir. He's probably aiming to take Mexico City, so he needs
to take Puebla first. And with his five thousand tough veterans against
five thousand recruits, he'll surely take it. But he must see that he can't go
on to take Mexico City with five thousand men. So – "

"So," Seward jumped in, "he must be counting on a massive popular
uprising in support of France. Mass defections from the army, the
Catholics taking up arms, politicians switching sides, the Juarez
government paralyzed and so on. But," he raised a dramatic finger, "to
date there been no sign of anything like that. None."

"That's right, sir," Stoddard began, "but if the French win at Puebla,
that victory alone might be all it takes to spark off an uprising. Then the
French, with their Conservative allies, could grow strong enough to defeat

Juarez in the field. If they do that, they can occupy the capital and control the country."

"And let me write the next act for you," said Seward. "Napoleon will first put Maximilian on its throne. He will then feel secure enough to strike an alliance with our Southern rebels."

"What?" Stoddard couldn't stop himself.

Seward smiled grimly. To Stoddard he said, "You should know that Jefferson Davis would do almost anything to persuade the French to recognize the Confederacy. He reckons that when they do they will be obliged to attack us. He's offered Napoleon cheap cotton, he's offered to send troops to Mexico to support him, offered to recognize Maximilian's crown when he gets it, offered everything but his own wife - as far as I know."

He let them absorb that and then went on. "But the Emperor is too wary of our strength to take the bait. So far. But if – or when – France does recognize the rebels, the English won't be far behind them. In that event we would face three allied enemies, not just one."

A long pause, then Lincoln said, "Time enough to discuss that little problem if the French win at Puebla." He fixed his eye on Seward. "Still on the subject of Mexico, Governor, how is that loan project you mentioned the other day?"

"Well, the circumstances have changed, obviously. We're working hard on it, but we won't have the months of stalemate I wanted."

"I understand. Let's move along, then," Lincoln said. "Secretary Chase is due here any minute to tell me once again that we can not possibly finance our own war."

They all stood up. Lincoln thanked them and then said, almost to himself, "Well, we must pray, gentlemen, that our Mexican friends find the strength they will soon need. If they lose at Puebla, we just might lose our own war."

*   *   *

Bartlett and Jones had straggled into Puebla late the night before, bone tired, thirsty and thankful to have avoided any more dangers. They had entered Mexico's second city on the new road from Veracruz, across the Christmas Bridge and into the old town. The streets were dark, and Bartlett could barely make out the parks and open squares as they walked by. A decent hotel near what turned out to be the Episcopal Palace offered low-lice beds and a rusty iron bath, but first they needed the three glasses of beer and the fried beefsteaks they found at the inn around the corner.

"Looks like a nice town," Jones said as he stretched out his legs, "an improvement on that rat hole, Veracruz."

"And no mosquitoes,"

"No, we're about seven thousand feet up here. Too cold for the buggers."

"Right," said Bartlett. "Well. A good night's sleep, we find that telegraph office, then we sit back and wait for orders. Sound good?"

"Sure, as long as we don't – what the hell?"

A volley of shouts from the doorway, two or three shots and a dozen soldiers erupted into the bar area. The seated diners did not delay in rushing out to the street. Bartlett and Jones looked at each other, dropped a coin on the table and headed for the kitchen, conscious of their uniforms. They dashed for the door to the side street and rounded the corner by a tree-lined plaza.

A small group of Mexican officers, dressed in blue coats with brass buttons, advanced on them. Bartlett recognized Porfirio Diaz, the young colonel who had befriended Laffan when they visited General Doblado. His exuberant moustaches and staring, deep-set eyes were unmistakable, even in the near darkness. Another, larger group of officers followed at twenty yards' distance.

And Diaz recognized him. "*Es un amigo Yanqui,*" he said to his group as he saluted and shook hands with Bartlett.

Bartlett responded as well as he could and introduced Jones, whose Spanish took over their side of the conversation. He explained what he and Bartlett were doing in Puebla. Diaz told his followers to go on to the inn, where their sergeants had just found tables for them.

He was now a general, he told the Americans, and commander of a brigade under the great General Ignacio Zaragosa. He and his men had arrived that day and Zaragosa would lead the rest of his forces, five thousand strong, into Puebla the next morning.

"The French will try to capture Puebla," he said to Bartlett. "They move in this direction now. So you will meet General Zaragosa and say him everything about the French. Everything you know."

Jones protested that they were neutrals and could not assist either side, and besides they knew almost nothing of the French dispositions or intentions.

Diaz listened with obvious impatience. "You want use the telegraph? Yes? The only telegraph in Puebla? Yes? So, you will meet the general tomorrow, quick as he gets here. Take this" – he scribbled a note – "to the telegraph in the morning and they will help you. Without this, they will not. Then wait at your hotel." He hurried away.

The Americans looked at each other. "We were right," Bartlett said. "The French did stay on."

"Yep. They sure did. All we can do now is help Morny to regret it."

Next day, they did as they were told. The telegraph clerk cleared his office of reporters and sent off their first telegram to Stoddard quickly, despite its encryption. Then they strolled back to their hotel.

Puebla de los Angeles, as they soon saw, was a city on a plain, a lovely city of flowering parks and squares, fountains, graceful churches and an ideal climate. The tower of the cathedral, the largest in Mexico they were told, dominated the eastern half of the city. Mountains of different heights and different colors could be seen in all directions. The streets were broad and clean, with the pigs, dogs, chickens and buzzards of Veracuz notably absent.

An hour later and they were back on the street, walking again to the telegraph station. The interview with Zaragosa in his office had been brief and to the point. The defender of Puebla was young – younger than I am, thought Bartlett – with a round, clean-shaven face, short dark hair and incongruous wire-rimmed spectacles clamped on his nose. A military man all his life, he resembled an intelligent schoolmaster, but a schoolmaster with a most determined jawline. He had been Minister for War the year before and his wife had died four months earlier, so he was well accustomed to despair.

Once Zaragosa told them that their future use of the telegraph was conditional on their cooperation, Jones told him all he could about the French forces – their numbers, training, apparent state of readiness, commanders, even their diet.

"But you must know all this already," Jones observed, "if your spies are half as good as they should be."

"They are almost half as good, so every bit you have helps me. Thank you," said Zaragosa. "The French are on the march. Lorencez means to attack Puebla, that much is obvious, and will probably camp tonight near Amozoc. I must know all I can. He may attack tomorrow."

The Americans saluted and prepared to leave. Zaragosa looked up from a paper in his hand and asked, "Where is the Count de Morny?" They didn't know, they said. "You must understand his motives well, despite your claim to neutrality. Would you expect him to go forward with his troops, with Lorencez? I've heard he had a good military career."

They looked at each other. Jones replied. "He'll be tempted to run things, but he'll stay well back," he said. "Morny won't run any risk of danger to himself. You can count on it."

A messenger came in with a telegram. Zaragosa read it, threw it to the floor and stared out the window. "Mother of God! Two thousand men," he cried, "that's all I ask them for, and those cretins can't even find me two thousand men." He remembered his visitors, turned and waved them out of the office.

The telegraph office, hidden on the top floor of the town hall, was again packed with reporters, but the scrap of paper from Diaz worked its magic for the second time. Pleased with their morning's work, Bartlett and Jones then decided to reconnoiter the city.

The streets were crowded now with troops under orders to bivouac where they could, which was usually in a park or a side street. Even in a city of eighty thousand, the arrival of five thousand soldiers led to a severe shortage of usable space. Most were infantrymen wearing brown trousers, squared-off hats and a kind of frock coat. "See the rifles they carry?" said Jones. "They say the English captured them from the French at Waterloo and then kindly sold them on to the Mexicans."

Unable to make headway on the streets, they retreated up the bell tower of the cathedral. The sky was clouding over but the view was magnificent. The palaces, churches, bullrings, barracks and hospitals stood out among the flowered squares of the town. The two volcanoes, Popocatepetl and Ixtacihuatl, towered in the south and west. To the east, the mighty peaks of Orizaba and Cofre de Perote reminded them of their escape from the Chasseurs.

A smaller, purplish mountain rose closer in the northeast. "That one's called La Malinche," said Jones, pointing, "after the Indian girl who was Cortez' mistress and betrayed her people for him."

In the same direction, but less than a mile from the city, rose a saddlebacked, east-west ridge with a white fortified church on the hill at its eastern end and entrenchments on the hill at its western end. Gun emplacements and army units were visible at both points, but their numbers were impossible to estimate through the copse of sycamore trees at each fort. Bartlett and Jones studied the terrain and their map.

"Those two forts on that ridge will be important if Lorencez attacks from the north," Bartlett commented. "The one on the west is called Loreto; the one to the east, the church, is Gua – da – lupe. Suitably holy."

"Well, he certainly won't come from the north, and if he comes from the east he'll attack farther south, down the old Veracruz road. There – do you see it? The third road over."

"I see it. So you learned infantry tactics at Annapolis, did you?" Bartlett snapped shut the telescope. "Why, there's just no end to what you picked up there. And I had you pegged as a simple sea dog."

Jones wasn't amused. "Tactics are no mystery, just common sense."

"We'll see tomorrow."

But it wasn't tomorrow, when nothing happened. Except that Jones went off after breakfast, saying something about a family errand. Then at noon, when Bartlett sat with a beer and a newspaper in a shady square near the cathedral, he saw Jones and a young girl walking slowly under the trees on the far side of the square. Two nuns, heads bowed, walked ten paces behind them. They turned the corner and came towards him. He instinctively felt that Jones did not want to be seen, so he moved to a table just inside the door of a bar and shielded his face with the paper.

They were speaking Spanish as they passed by, the girl with vivid animation, her hands flying and a broad smile flickering on her lips. She was perhaps sixteen, with brilliant black hair, white skin, grey eyes and a wide mouth. She wore a dark, straight shapeless dress that didn't suit her. Jones looked as if he was trying to stand as erect as he could, while he bent over her so as not to miss a word she said. Once he started to put his hand on her shoulder but withdrew it before he touched her. His eyes wouldn't leave her. He looked immensely proud and immensely sad.

Jones stopped and said a few words to the nuns. One of them shook her head once, Jones raised and dropped his shoulders and the little group moved on. At the far corner of the square they climbed into a waiting closed carriage and set off to the west.

Bartlett sat for a minute or two and tried to understand what he'd just seen. Jones will tell me, he said to himself, but Jones didn't.

It was early in the morning of the next day when they were summoned to meet Diaz at Zaragosa's headquarters.

"Should we go?" asked Bartlett. "These Mexicans have no authority over us, and we're neutrals, after all. We're getting too close to taking sides."

Jones sighed. "Shall I quote Stoddard's latest orders – 'Report often.' By telegraph, need I add?" A pause. "Let's get the horses."

"All right, but we must do something to show that we're neutral."

"I have it – our uniforms."

"Our uniforms? The whites? Good thinking."

Snowy in their Veracruz best, they were escorted back in to the same office. A grim Diaz stood in a corner as Zaragosa dictated a telegram to a weary clerk. "I must have the two thousand men I respectfully requested. Stop." Jones translated in a whisper. "Lorencez camped last night at Amozoc and his patrols reached Los Remedios at dawn today. Stop. I expect him to attack this morning along the Veracruz roads at the eastern sector of the city and have posted my five divisions and cavalry accordingly. Stop. I expect heavy street fighting later today. Stop. Send me the men I requested and I personally guarantee that I will defeat the French. Stop. With the greatest respect, etcetera, etcetera." Jones finished and looked anxiously at Diaz, who ignored him and advanced on Zaragosa's desk.

He angrily demanded something from his superior, who replied with a long and emphatic refusal. Jones later explained that Diaz wanted to deploy all their cavalry on the plains around Puebla, but Zaragosa ordered five hundred lancers to move far to the south to prevent a renegade Conservative general and his army from joining the French. Diaz shrugged, saluted and hurried out.

It was nine o'clock. The first French patrols were reaching the slope that led up to Guadalupe, the fortified church on the ridge to the north.

"You come with me," Diaz said over his shoulder. "Zaragosa want you come with me." As soon as he mounted his horse, a huge grey, he abandoned English. He explained to Jones that the commanding general wanted the two Americans to stay by him during the battle. Their knowledge of the French units could be useful. In addition, he grinned at Bartlett, the army man, "He think maybe you stop me do crazy thing. He think I half crazy."

Zaragosa had divided his command into five brigades of equal strength. One, supported by artillery, occupied the two forts on the northern ridge. The second barricaded San Francisco Square, south of Guadalupe; the third took up a position in San Jose Square. Diaz' brigade and another infantry brigade guarded the eastern approaches to the city along the roads from Veracruz, the point where Zaragosa confidently expected the main thrust of the French attack.

But Lorencez swung his infantry around to the north, moved his artillery forward at eleven o'clock and began shelling the two forts on the ridge.

Chapter 35

Puebla, Mexico - May 5, 1862

The French infantry massed at the northern foot of the ridge while their artillery raked the defensive line between Fort Loreto and the fortified church of Guadalupe. Zaragosa realized that he was wrong - the first assault was coming from the north. He moved a second brigade and artillery support from the center of the city up to that line.

At half past eleven the French attacked. A wave of four thousand veteran troops advanced steadily up the bare slope towards Guadalupe, kneeling and firing massed volleys as they came. The raw defenders wavered under the vicious fire, but suddenly the regiment in Fort Loreto charged out of the smoke that enveloped the fort and fell on the French right flank. The French faltered, rallied and then withdrew in good order back down the hill. The first attack had failed.

Bartlett, Jones, Diaz and four of his field officers were packed in the windows of a seventeenth century campanile, a mile to the south, watching the action through their telescopes. An enormous roar rose from them all, even the American observers. Diaz pounded his guests on the back and roared with the rest.

Zaragosa now had three brigades, reinforced by two rifle battalions, holding both forts and the line along the crest of the ridge between them. After a brief artillery barrage, the French came up the hill again, this time in three columns. Two columns attacked Guadalupe fort, the third pounded the center of the ridge. The third column was thrown back. This allowed the central defenders and the light artillery in Fort Loreto to enfilade the second column as it struggled up. The effect on the French was devastating. The Mexicans in the chapel now rushed the shaken enemy and fought them hand to hand. They used their side arms, bayonets, grenades, machetes and even rocks in the bloodiest fighting of the day. Again the French retired down the body-strewn slope, their ranks shredded.

Not even the jubilant shouts in their flaking bell tower could drown the noise of battle for the Americans. There was not much artillery fire now, but the rattle of small arms fire, the cries and screams of the wounded and the occasional thump of a field piece reached them clearly. To Jones, the scene was shocking. To Bartlett, it revived harsh memories of the carnage at Bull Run.

Diaz needed to be available for new orders, so he scrambled down the tower steps, shouting at his staff to follow. He had positioned his brigade along the two Veracruz roads, crouched in the windows of the adobe buildings and behind makeshift barricades. Most of his men had seen some fighting in the north of the country, but they had never faced an enemy as experienced and well armed as the French were said to be. The Mexicans were lightly armed and some of their uniforms were random affairs, topped off with non-regulation broad straw hats. But they could see that their companions on the northern ridge were giving the French all they wanted, and a sense, not yet of confidence, but of resolve grew in their ranks.

Zaragosa rode up on a splendid mare, trailed by two staff officers. He told Diaz to feed his men and then to anchor his line on the bridge and wheel it to face north, keeping his cavalry squadrons out on the right wing. In the tower Jones translated for Bartlett, "Zaragosa expects the French to hit this sector next."

"We'd better go down," Bartlett said.

An hour later the French came once more, stepping over the bodies of their dead comrades. This time their only objective was Guadalupe and the hill it commanded. Again they were fought off, so their two columns turned slightly to the south, searching for an entrance to the city itself. They made good ground at first, as the defenders on the ridge lost their fields of fire, and advanced quickly on the left of the sector held by Diaz' brigade.

Jones had never faced an enemy army in battle; Bartlett's experience at Bull Run was brief. Both were astonished at the speed and ferocity of the French advance on the open ground across their front. The French were a terrifying but colorful sight – the tight ranks of blue and red coats of the regulars; a cavalry squadron with drawn sabers; two platoons of Nubians; a company of Zouaves in their scarlet pantaloons; the African Chasseurs in white; even a unit of Turks in short skirts – all firing, all screaming as they hit the Mexican lines.

Both brigades held their ground behind the houses and barricades, but then Diaz' center began to buckle. He had two rifle battalions positioned there behind wooden barricades and they were hit hard by cavalry and regular infantry. They fell back a yard at a time, their ranks crumbling slowly in the fierce fighting. Diaz rode up behind them and looked around. He saw at once that if his center collapsed his entire right flank could be rolled up and the battle lost.

Bartlett and Jones had taken care to stay at least two hundred yards behind the fighting to preserve their neutrality as well as their skins. But now Diaz waved them forward frantically.

"The hell with him," Bartlett shouted over the rattle of rifle fire, "I'm staying here."

"Coward!" replied Jones with a smile.

"Damn right! And a neutral. See my white suit?"

"Ah, let's just see what he wants. A matter of courtesy to our host."
Jones spurred his reluctant horse forward.

"Get the major here!" Diaz greeted him. "I want his advice."

"He won't – all right!" Jones waved hard. Bartlett couldn't lose face in
the midst of a battle so he cantered up to the other two, his head well
down between his shoulders.

Diaz swept his arm over the battlefield in front and Jones translated.
His center was cracking open, his men staggering back, and he had only
two infantry battalions and two light cavalry squadrons in reserve. What
should he do? he demanded. Should he reinforce the center or attack the
French flanks? What would they say at West Point?

What *would* West Point say? Bartlett had no idea. He was too confused
by the noise and smoke to recall anything he learned there. His horse
reared wildly and almost threw him. Wait – wasn't there a doctrine that
you didn't use your reserves to shore up a weak point; you only used them
to exploit a success? Or was it the other way around? Hell, he couldn't be
sure. But he was advising a wildly excited Mexican, the French had been
hammered all day and the odds must favor – "Attack, general, attack with
every man you have! Hit them on the left with the infantry and out on the
right with your lancers!"

A vast grin lit Diaz' powder-streaked face. He clapped Bartlett on the
knee and started to turn away.

"And tell your lancers to hit the base of their column, not the middle."
That much Bartlett could remember from his Indian fighting days, or
hoped he could.

"Zaragosa shoot me if you wrong, gringo!" Diaz called in English as he
rode to join his staff. "But first I shoot you!"

Bartlett and Jones beat a stately retreat up a leafy avenue and
dismounted. "Well, Hannibal, you'd better be right," Jones laughed. "He
wasn't joking." He looked up and held out his hand. It was wet. "Rain's
coming." Black thunderheads were massing over Orizaba Peak to the east
and sliding towards Puebla.

Diaz did as he was told. His center stiffened as the French shifted to
their right to defend against the onslaught of his reserve battalions. To no
avail. "These people can fight!" Jones cried in admiration as the French
right began to buckle under heavy fire from the houses on the edge of the
city. The collapse became a general retirement to the east and then almost
a rout when Diaz' cavalry began to carve into the rear of the French
column.

The Mexicans inflicted appalling casualties in the open field now, and
only the legendary discipline of the French soldier kept order. It was their
third retreat of the day, but the first time they were threatened with

encirclement by cavalry, which always quickens the step. This was not to be their day; perhaps tomorrow.

"Let's move up and follow them, Charles," Jones urged, telescope at his eye. "I can't see them clearly from here."

Exhilarated by the success of his tactical advice, Bartlett forgot his reservations and remounted. "Good idea. We'll stay a couple of hundred yards behind the infantry." They set off at a fast trot. It was late afternoon and the sun was sinking behind a black wall of cloud.

Diaz kept his foot soldiers a respectful distance from the main body of the retreating French, while his lancers cut up the stragglers. The Mexicans had won the day, and he would not risk losing it if the French turned and rushed them. He would not do anything crazy, he told himself. The Americans stayed on the road well behind them, even when Diaz rode by and suggested forcefully that the real men were farther forward.

When they had covered half a mile from the edge of the city, a French regiment retreating from its last failed attack on Guadalupe straggled over a rise in the ground and joined the retreating column. The French slowed, stopped and wheeled to face Diaz. Bartlett and Jones heard a flurry of French commands and to their astonishment the mass of infantrymen reformed and advanced back up the slight slope, rifles at the ready. They were a formidable force, fifteen hundred men and still full of fight.

The Mexicans halted and began to edge backward, as did the two Americans. "These Frenchmen don't know when to quit," Jones complained, "and they outnumber Diaz by a half." He and Bartlett slanted off to their left as they withdrew, to the side of the Mexican formation. The firing was light and steady, not enough to drown out the screams of rage and pain from both sides.

The French advance and the Mexican retreat picked up speed. Then the sky lit up twice, followed by a ferocious CRAAAAAAK of lightning and then another. The bitter cold rain hit them with fury, then a thunderclap that rolled and rumbled over the volcanoes. The rain turned to hail, and hailstones the size of walnuts raked the ground and all the combatants. Within fifteen minutes the ground was blanketed in icy white pebbles, the wind howled and the sky was black.

Everything had stopped. Silence took over. The Mexicans under their broad straw hats suffered less than the French troopers, but neither side could do more than keep their heads down and cower in self-protection. Jones's horse, the stolid Milagro, stung by the hailstones, leapt to one side when two larger stones hit her ears. When she landed on the road both right legs slid out from under her, she dropped on her side and Jones fell off and out on to the road. Milagro heaved back up, skidded sideways and took off down the hill at flank speed, leaving Jones stretched out on the road.

He looked badly hurt, perhaps dead, as he lay inert. Bartlett dismounted with care and picked his way to his side. "How is it?" he asked. No reply. "Robert! How is it?"

Jones stirred, gulped wordlessly and pointed at his left knee. "Something wrong there. Help me up." Bartlett's animal decided he liked the noise of battle no more than did Milagro and cantered after her, slowing only to aim a kick at his quondam master as he bent over Jones.

Jones couldn't stand on his left leg or walk. Bartlett held him up as he studied the battle scene. The rifle fire had picked up again, and the French had pushed Diaz half way back to the city, well past where the two stood. But the French counter attack was stalling. The hail and rain had already made the ground too slippery to walk on and neither side could move. Horses fell in the slop and slid down into the ravines, pulling their wagons after them. Soldiers of both armies stumbled across the slope if they could stand; they couldn't make any ground up the slope. The hail eased off but the rain tipped down harder than before.

It looked to Bartlett that the French were digging in where they lay, but it was too dark to be certain. The one certainty was that he and Jones had to move farther off to the side before their white uniforms looked like unmissable targets to some rifleman.

A lightning flash revealed a row of huts not far to the side. Without a word, Bartlett knelt and hoisted Jones over his shoulder, keeping the damaged knee to the front. "It's about fifty yards," Bartlett gasped, "so keep quiet." Jones did so. Bartlett kept his boots close to the ground and shuffled through the mud and hailstones all the way without slipping.

The huts were pigsties. That was undeniable when they stopped in the doorway of one, but they were empty. "The farmer has all his animals in his house so the French won't steal them," Jones said weakly as Bartlett helped him lie down inside. The pain was getting the better of him. "My first battle and I fall off my horse," he fumed.

"So did I," Bartlett consoled him

Jones's face was dead white. "What's next, *compadre?*"

"It's dark. I think we're here for the night." Bartlett had considered their situation. "When the firing stops, we could make for the Mexican lines, but they might shoot us because our uniforms don't look like theirs." He rubbed his eyes. He was more tired than he had any right to be. "I don't know how far away the French base is, but I don't like our chances of a friendly welcome there, either."

"You're right," said Jones. "I'm no doctor, but I don't think my leg is broken, it's just that my knee was bent back when the horse rolled on me. I'll pack it in hailstones. That'll help it." He took off his coat.

"Let me." Bartlett filled a sleeve with hailstones and Jones wrapped it around his knee.

With only their sense of smell as a guide, they found places near the open doorway to lie down. The noises from the battlefield a hundred yards away diminished and then died out, except for the whimpers and screams from the dying. It's strange, thought Bartlett, I hear those terrible sounds but it's as if they had nothing to do with me, as if they come from another world.

Then another sound grew louder, the crunch of wheels on the hailstones. It was the noise of carts collecting the wounded, presumably the French wounded. He heard loud French oaths, and they came closer. Then came the sound of footsteps on the hailstones and the light of several lanterns at the hut next door. Bartlett moved farther into the hut, but Jones could not. He was in his same spot when the lantern beam fell on him from the doorway. A French sergeant stooped and came in, exclaimed at the reek and called for his officer.

Who came in brandishing a bigger lantern and a revolver. "*Merde!*" he exclaimed, handing the lantern to the sergeant and jamming a handkerchief to his nose. He bowed uncertainly. "Commander Jones? Major Bartolett? What luck. I bring you an invitation to dinner from Monsieur the Count de Morny."

Chapter 36

But they were too late for dinner that night. Jones couldn't possibly sit a horse and had to ride, propped up and cursing, in a bloody two-wheeled cart that had been used to recover the French wounded and dead from the field. The ground was littered with bodies and the road was mainly mud, so by the time they reached the French base at Amozoc their illustrious host had retired for the night. He had left orders for the doctors to attend Jones's injury as soon as he arrived and for Lieutenant D'Urfe to see that his guests were made as comfortable as possible. They would join him at breakfast, he hoped.

"How did he know I was injured?" Jones asked.

"My sergeant and I were detached to watch you during the battle," D'Urfe replied loftily. "A clerk's job. Your white uniforms made our task easier than we expected."

The next day Henri escorted them, Jones swinging jerkily on crutches, through rows of tents to a linen-clad table under a pine tree where Morny was sipping coffee. He welcomed them with extravagant courtesy, sent Henri for a doctor to examine Jones's knee again and began to praise a certain kind of Mexican bread roll.

"It is called a *bolillo*, my friends," he said as he poured their coffee, "and it is unsurpassed even in France. Henri discovered it for me. I have at least one every morning, and when I return to France I shall capture a Mexican baker and take him with me." He held up a nondescript crusty roll. "This will change the French breakfast for all time. Henri will bring you one when he returns. Meanwhile, do help yourselves to the fruit. I can commend the melon."

A jovial, unapologetic Morny discoursing on baked goods was not what they expected to meet that morning. After all, at their last meeting he had kidnapped them, and yesterday his army had been shattered by a ragged assortment of recruits and a few horsemen. They searched his face for any evidence of regret or sorrow and found none. As the day passed, Morny never referred to their escape from *Isabella*, and nor did they.

They discussed yesterday's battle. Morny was eager to learn how it had developed from the Mexican side and to have their opinions on the quality of the Mexican soldiers and officers, especially their cavalry.

"Other than to state the obvious, Count, that they fought well enough to defeat a veteran European army," Jones said with emphasis, "we can't offer any opinions. We're neutral, remember? "

"A veteran army weakened by disease, fatigue and shocking leadership," Morny corrected, "but I take your point. And I respect your neutrality." Then the doctor arrived, and they watched as he manipulated Jones's leg.

"Well, Doctor?" Morny said.

It was as he had suspected the night before, the doctor reported. He had removed his apron, bloody from the evening's work, but his tunic was smeared with red and his eyes exhausted. "The knee was badly over-extended and at least two ligaments have been torn. I can immobilize the joint now, but this man must go wherever he can receive proper treatment. Immediately." He set to work with splints and a roll of bandage.

Morny waited for him to finish and then asked, "How many, Doctor?"

"Almost five hundred dead, three hundred wounded, only a few taken prisoner. A sad day, sir."

After he left, Bartlett echoed him. "A sad day."

"Bah! A sad day for the French army, to be sure, but a splendid day for France," Morny declared. He laughed harshly. "My word, look at your expressions. You think I'm mad, don't you?" He drained his coffee and lit a cigarette. "You are both short-sighted, gentlemen. You lack strategic vision. I've noted it before and have wondered if it is an American trait."

They waited in silence, aware that he needed no prompting to develop his theme. Jones adjusted his strapped-up leg on the chair Henri had brought for him.

"We must first absorb the lessons to be learnt from yesterday's debacle." Morny struck a professorial pose and waved his cigarette about. "And the first lesson is that to defeat Juarez France will need many more than five thousand sick men. Many, many more. I estimate thirty thousand. With much more artillery and cavalry."

"That seems obvious," ventured Bartlett.

"It is if you think about it," Morny agreed. "But the second lesson is less obvious: that the French can not depend on a massive popular uprising in their favor." He gave his short laugh again. "Poor Lorencez. The esteemed General Almonte convinced him of his vision, a vision of being carried through the streets of Puebla by an adoring mob of tens of thousands of smiling natives. Hah!"

"Is that why he attacked from the north?" Bartlett asked.

"That is why - is one reason. He believed he had only to take Fort Guadalupe and the Juaristas would desert to a man, would drop their rifles and join the throngs waiting to throw flowers at him." Morny shook his head in disbelief and amusement. "He tried three times to take that fort, so I suppose we must credit him with determination, at least." He shook his head again. "And Almonte is discredited now. For all his good qualities it seems the leading Conservatives will not support him. He has been away too long and has become far too grand, far too French for them."

Morny pulled out his watch and rose. "But now I fear I must receive General Lorencez. He wants to remain here to induce the Juaristas to come out for another fight, but I shall dissuade him."

He walked a few steps and turned. "I almost forgot. I have named a new military advisor to our army. I've asked him to make himself known to you."

He walked over to a large blue tent, where heavily braided uniforms stood waiting for him. Their dejected demeanor was markedly different from Morny's, whose stride was almost jaunty. He led them inside.

"So he lied to you in Paris – about the limit on French objectives here," said Bartlett to Jones.

"So? You want me to challenge him on that? It's not too clever to tell the most powerful man in France that he's a liar, especially when he has an army with him."

Bartlett looked for another line of attack. "You do realize, Robert, that we've been kidnapped again." Jones winced as he shifted his weight. "That there is no chance he'll let us get near a telegraph line. And that once again we're dancing to another man's tune?" He finished his *bolillo*. "That's not bad, you know." He asked Henri for more coffee. "First it was Morny, then the Mexicans, and now Morny again. I blame you entirely, by the way. Where have we gone wrong, o leader of men?" He counted on Jones to see that he was joking, mostly.

Jones was too weak to take offence. "You have a point, but I can't – "

"Can't what, Robert? Ride a horse? Hell, we all knew that." It was Laffan, standing behind Bartlett, dressed like a *charro*. He clapped Bartlett on the back and squeezed his shoulder. Then he stood beside Jones's extended leg. "I heard your horse – *my* horse, I suppose – rolled on you before it ran off. And yours, Charles?" A broad grin at Bartlett. "Up in the hills somewhere, is it?" Bartlett nodded, trying to hide his surprise. "Well, let's see, two horses and two saddles – send me an army draft for two hundred dollars when you can." He sat down and surveyed them cheerfully.

"It's good to see you, Pancho," said Bartlett as he shook hands. "but what, ah, brings you here? Spying hard, are you?"

"Hardly. Didn't His Worship tell you?" He paused to enjoy their reaction. "I'm now the chief military advisor to the French army in Mexico." He sounded proud of himself. "Almonte is out. I'm in."

"I thought you were with Juarez," said Jones, his mouth open.

"No, never. I spied for him for a time, but that was just a way to get close to Morny. Jose Manuel Hidalgo – your old friend from Paris, Robert – introduced me to Morny, and I needed a reason to stay in Veracruz to get to know him, to see if he's the man Mexico needs."

"And is he?"

"What do you think? I'm here, am I not? You're damn right he is. He's going back to France in a few days to get the Emperor to send reinforcements here. Twenty five to thirty thousand men, I've said are enough. More than enough, if we do it right this time." He jumped up and leaned against the pine tree. "He'll get the men, I'm certain of it, and, we'll drive Juarez and his thieves and murderers into the sea."

"And then?" Bartlett was intrigued by the change in Laffan. Or, more likely, the revelation of the real Laffan.

"And then? Your servant, General Eufemio Laffan Montealban, will command the new Mexican army. The faithful defender of the new royal government, destined perhaps for even greater things!" He slapped Bartlett's back again. "Who knows, eh?"

"Great stuff, Eufemio, and you so young," Bartlett teased.

"Old enough, Charles, older than both Zaragosa and Diaz, the best the Juaristas have."

He was right, Bartlett saw with a shock. Men his own age, fighting over a nation, while he fretted over a telegraph line. He suspected Jones was having the same thought.

"I have to do this, Charles," Laffan went on, his eyes glittering, "get rid of Juarez and his gang of thieves. They want to take everything from every one who has anything." His hand swept along the horizon. "Land. They'll take the land, both ranches my father's worked forty years to build. I can't let that happen. I can't let some wretched little *Indian* come along and steal his life's work. And my future. And I won't."

"Your lands are forfeit if he wins," Jones said. The morphine was at last taking effect, and he looked healthier.

"They're forfeit now sooner or later. It's my *life* – and Carolina's – that's forfeit if Juarez wins."

"Where is she?"

"In Veracruz with her aunt." He turned to face Jones. "By the way, she's my wife, not my sister."

"Ah. Why – "

"Just for a joke. We look so much alike, and we enjoy the game. Especially when someone gets interested in her."

Jones said nothing and fussed with his strapping.

Laffan looked from one to the other, relishing the surprises he had given them. "I'll be off," he smiled. "Have to find a couple of decent horses now. Until we meet later." He was plainly a happy man.

"Hold on, Pancho," said Bartlett, almost without thinking. "One question: those coded cables, the cables that you said you gave to Doblado. You gave them straight to Prim, not to Doblado, didn't you? You told Prim, not Doblado, that you'd stolen them from us." Now he saw the implications. "You were working for Morny even then, weren't you? You knew that he *wanted* the English and Spanish to leave, because he'd already decided that the French would stay on alone. He – "

"That's only half of it, Charles," Jones interrupted. "The whole trick with the cables was Carolina's idea, remember? Which means it was Laffan's idea. Or Morny's idea. Take your pick."

"So we were used, we were played like a couple of - guitars by you and Morny. From the beginning. Is that right, Pancho?"

"Figure it out for yourself, Charles. It's pretty obvious. *Hasta luego.*" Laffan sauntered away, his spurs ringing.

They slumped back to their chairs, stunned. "Let's agree on one thing, Robert," Bartlett said at last, "we keep very quiet about this. Very quiet. Forever."

"Right. We don't even let Morny know that we know."

The sun was high now and Henri moved their table to keep it in the shade of the tree. Bartlett looked around the camp. They were in the officers' section, small blue tents set out in rows in the pine grove. The hospital tents, marked by a long line of men waiting for treatment, were placed at the end of the grove but despite the distance he could hear the cries of the wounded inside. The enlisted men's quarters, larger tents with a cooking fire in front of each, were in the open. Except for the dogs that ranged for scraps, there was scant visible movement anywhere, and an air of defeat hung over the camp. He would be glad to leave.

Morny returned soon afterward, looking like a man who had just issued a stream of important orders to unwilling subordinates. He conferred with Henri for a few minutes, smoothed his moustaches and turned to his guests. "Can there be anything more sensitive than a French general's pride?" he wondered as he took his seat. "I think not." He looked at them benignly. "May I ask, Commander, if your orders are unchanged, and if you are anxious to telegraph Washington?"

Jones allowed that was correct.

"Excellent. Tomorrow we leave for Veracruz, where you can send your cable." He gave his curious flick of the wrist. "But in any case General Stoddard - all of Washington, in fact - will know of our defeat in a day or two, from the Mexican press or from your minister in Mexico City."

"I suppose so."

"The following day, we leave for France, and I hope to have your company on *Isabella* again. And that of Major Bartlett, it goes without saying."

"Is this an invitation, Count, or another kidnapping?" Jones's resentment was undisguised.

"An invitation, what else?" Morny's voice was unruffled. "But consider this, Commander. Only one or two American ships per month call at

Veracruz. And who can know if they will be bound for your east coast, and not for, ah, China?" He reached across to pat Jones on his arm. "So you can sail with me in the accomplished care of Henri, or you can rot indefinitely in the heat of Veracruz under the care of a Mexican surgeon, for I will see to it that no French doctor attends you."

Jones had no choice. That was plain enough. "Your hospitality is overwhelming, Count, as always," he conceded. "We are delighted to accept your offer."

"Not as delighted as I am, I assure you. Your company will be most welcome on the voyage." Morny stifled a smile. "To me, at least. I'm not sure how pleased Captain Carbonnel will be to have you aboard again."

They rattled cautiously down to Veracruz at dawn the next morning. Morny had commandeered the three-car train and filled it with a platoon of riflemen for his protection. Jones was in reasonable comfort; the swelling had gone down and the morphine was working well. He and Bartlett sat at one end of a car and contemplated their futures.

"No matter how I look at it, Charles," he observed, "going back to Paris with Morny doesn't make sense for me. I need to get this leg into an American hospital pronto. Besides, I need to be handy, and back on my feet, when Hull Number Nine is launched in Philadelphia. I can't miss my chance at a *Monitor* again."

Bartlett had to agree. Whatever happened next, the job did not require both of them, he said.

"Good. So I'll ask Morny to put me off with our blockade fleet at Charleston or Norfolk. They'll get me back to Washington somehow."

Veracruz was a shock after more than a week in the crisp, scented air of Puebla and the mountains. The reek of the open sewers and the steaming coastal heat almost overcame them and they made for the relative safety of the Hotel Magnifico.

In their rooms each found a surprise. A stack of new clothing that included two uniforms in a light duck material and cotton shirts and trousers in the correct sizes to replace what they had lost in their saddlebags. It could only have been Henri, and it was, as he smilingly admitted. Their tailor had put all his vast family to work the day before, he said, and was as good as his word.

They were a gift from Morny. "So that you can feel frisky once more," the Frenchman said. "I regret he could not find the silk to make suitable sashes for you."

That was after he had agreed without hesitation to deposit Jones with the blockade squadron off Norfolk. "Carbonnel says it will add a day or two, at most, to our journey," he said.

"You understand, Count," Jones said, "that I will report everything you have told us, including in particular your aim to send massive reinforcements to Mexico."

"Naturally. It is your duty. But it makes no difference, now that England and Spain have left. If Mr. Lincoln even *thinks* of supporting Juarez with troops, the Emperor will threaten to recognize the southern states, with all that implies, and Mr. Lincoln will have to think again."

Chapter 37

Captain Carbonnel had learned to keep *Isabella* in perfect condition. The brass gleamed, the varnish shone, the teak decks were holystoned and the crew were shaven and mostly sober. All women had been banished sulking to the shore. Morny inspected her with pride. "Well done, Captain." Carbonnel nodded and stared straight through Bartlett and Jones.

Henri had been busy in the Veracruz markets. He filled Morny's larder with sacks of vegetables and fruit and, after threatening Carbonnel with a mutiny if he didn't shut up, installed a dozen chickens in the compartment under the transom. Even Morny balked at this experiment – "What next, villain? Goats?" - but he relented after Henri made the appropriate vows concerning noise and sanitation.

Laffan came aboard at sunset. He conferred with Morny in the main salon for an hour and then joined the Americans on deck for a farewell glass of champagne, miraculously chilled. His bearing was formal and he looked older. Even the red hair seemed restrained.

"*Bon voyage, mes amis,*" he said. "Who can say when we meet again, or in what circumstances?"

"You've definitely thrown in with Morny?" Jones asked him. "What if he's not all you think he is? What if he's all hat and no cattle, as we – "

"…say in Texas," Laffan finished for him. "There's no chance of that. He is Napoleon's brother, remember? He'll bring back those reinforcements, no doubt in my mind. At least twenty five thousand men, with cavalry and artillery."

"He's coming back himself?" Bartlett asked sharply. He hadn't yet come to terms with the fact that both Laffan and Morny would in the near future be his enemies. Or were already.

"He hasn't committed himself, but I expect he will." He read their minds. "And you can warn the boys in Washington, Robert, not even to dream about intervening to help Juarez. We'll drive him into the sea in sixty days."

In the silence they heard the nightly music and laughter from the plaza. With almost all the alliance troops gone, as well as the mosquitoes, Veracruz had soon recovered its tropical tempos, customs and vivacity.

"You'll say good-bye to Carolina for us?" Jones said.

"Of course." Laffan drained his glass and rose. "You won't forget that dollar draft, now. Send it to me care of the Banco Oriental here." He held his hand out to Jones first.

"And you promise not to shell us as we leave."

Laffan grinned, shook hands and went over the side to his waiting skiff.

"An impressive young man," Morny observed as he walked towards them. "He will do well here for me – for France." He tossed his cigarette over the side. "But in one thing he is mistaken. I shall not return to Mexico. I have fulfilled my obligation to the Emperor and must now look after my own affairs." Dinner was ready, he told them.

This time their route took *Isabella* north of Cuba. They picked up the Gulf Stream in the Florida Straits and followed the brisk southwest wind around the Keys and north along the Florida and Carolina coast towards Norfolk. The sun shone, the heat was dissipated by the steady breeze over the stern and the food was excellent. The crew rigged a canvas awning from the mast and, while Morny struggled in the salon with his latest play, Jones and Bartlett sprawled in the shade and drafted their report to the War Department.

"Come on, Robert, we have to finish this," Bartlett urged. "Now, what are our recommendations about Mexico?"

"Let the French have it. Except Puebla. I liked Puebla."

"But you were a Mexican yourself."

"Yes, and I'm now a Texan. There's a big difference."

"Fine, fine, but what do we recommend to Washington?"

"I'll think about it." Jones lay back and tipped his hat over his eyes.

They kept to their agreement and did not admit to Morny that they knew how he had used them. They seldom saw him in the day, but at night Henri served them all dinner on deck. Morny had fallen in love with the sea, he claimed, perhaps because his experience was limited to tranquil days on a handsome yacht in calm waters.

"Tell me about the squall," he asked them one night. They did so, magnifying the horrific elements of the storm and their escape through the reefs. Another night they told him of their brushes with the African *chasseurs* and then with El Chino and his friend. Morny wore a look of dismay. "How do you manage to take part in all these affairs?" he asked. "I was in Mexico exactly as long as you were and knew only one moment of possible danger - when Colonel Laffan fired at us from the fort."

"You must get out and about more, Count," Bartlett joked.

"No, my chance has passed. I fear I am condemned to an old age of surpassing dullness."

The weather and the wind held steady and Carbonel flew the topsail and two headsails with confidence. One day they spotted the Union squadron that blockaded Charleston, about a dozen ships in all, most of them anchored in the shallow waters. Morny asked Jones if he preferred to be taken to one of them, but Jones demurred. He calculated that he could get to Washington sooner if *Isabella* took him to the Norfolk squadron.

His knee improved remarkably fast. The swelling was down and he could walk at a reasonable pace with one crutch, but he doubted that he would be fully fit by the time Hull Number Nine was commissioned.

"For God's sake, Robert, stop worrying," Bartlett complained. "As you've said, Stoddard's a man of his word and he's given you his word. You'll get your ship." He adjusted the slope of the awning.

"You're right. I'll get it at last." Jones cheered up. "What about you, though? You'll no longer be under my so-called command, poor fellow. What will you do?"

"Go back to being a military attaché, I suppose. Damn dull work unless you turn up, I've learned."

"Yes, it must be. So if Stoddard dreams up another unconventional assignment, you won't mind if I recommend you for it?"

"Why not, although I'd rather have a battalion." Bartlett had worked with Jones, on and off, for half a year, and that was the closest Jones had come to a compliment on his work. Bartlett was about to acknowledge it as such, but discretion stopped him. To do so might embarrass Jones.

Jones changed the subject. "It's time I alerted you to something in Paris." He swiveled his head to be sure no one heard him. "You remember I told you I had built up quite a network of agents in France?" Bartlett nodded. "Well, just before I left I gave an important assignment to two of them. They hadn't done the job when I left, so I briefed my replacement, Major Preston, and asked him to write a private letter to you in London if they turned up anything of interest. With a copy to me in Washington."

"Fine. Go on."

"I don't know Preston well, but he struck me as intelligent. He can't say much in his letter – if there *is* a letter – but read it carefully and if he suggests you go to Paris, go there quickly."

"You can count on it."

Carbonnel dropped *Isabella's* sails and maneuvered her under steam to a position two hundred yards to leeward of the anchored Union sloop-of-war *Niantic*. The crew lowered Jones to her boat and rowed him across to the warship, where he was helped up the ladder and received a salute from the watch. He hadn't looked back.

"We shall miss him, both of us," mused Morny. "An unusual man, wouldn't you say? And an effective one. It was a good day for me when we met in the Bois." He laughed aloud. "There was something about him, a sort of directness, that convinced me he was quite reliable. And so he is."

Was there a hint of condescension in that "reliable"? Did it mask his satisfaction that Jones had done precisely what he, Morny, had chosen him to do? Perhaps. Probably, in fact, and in that case Morny's condescension included Bartlett.

Isabella turned northeast and headed out to the North Atlantic. Soon enough, she was met by a wild blast straight out of that quarter. Carbonnel lowered sail and hammered into the steep seas under power. Morny ordered all possible speed and retired to his cabin, where he was attended only by Henri. Bartlett took his meals alone in the lurching salon and speculated whether Morny's romance with the sea would survive the storm.

He also wondered why he was such a good sailor. This was his third Atlantic crossing and he had not yet been forced below. It couldn't be genetics. His forebears had all been schoolmasters and doctors who lived near the sea but never on it, as far as he knew. There were no admirals or merchant princes in the Bartlett line. Or any money, either.

After five days they struggled out from the storm and found a broken sea and the expected westerly. Morny surfaced at dinner, looking wan and wasted, much worse than Bartlett expected. It was not only the mal-de-mer, he explained as he picked at his chicken breast, but a chronic intestinal complaint that attacked him from time to time. Taken together, the two afflictions had laid him low.

In the background, Henri nodded meaningfully. He had yet to inform his master that, because of the storm, the chef would be offering no more omelettes, only a broad array of chicken stews.

Morny admitted that he had put aside his Mayan play. He had built the tension in the third act to an acceptable level, he said, but could find no archaeologically correct climax that did not involve the spilling of large quantities of the princess's blood. The Parisian audience, he felt, especially at the elite theaters that ran his plays, was not yet ready for so much gore. He needed to rewrite the first scene and go on from there.

One night Morny said he wanted to review the Puebla debacle, or "first act" as he called it, with a professional soldier. He touched a wing of hair and smoothed the formidable moustache. "Poor Lorencez," he said. "He had complete faith in the assurances of that Frenchified mountebank, Almonte."

Bartlett merely stated the obvious. "From what I saw, Count, he still could have taken the city if he'd attacked from the east, or maybe the south. The north was suicide."

"Quite possibly. And he wanted to attack from the east." A broad smile. "I pointed out that the east meant fighting in the streets of Puebla. This would have led to intolerable losses among his men and among the civilians gathered gaily in the streets to welcome him. Whereas on the northern side, he had only to take and hold those two forts on the hill."

Bartlett understood. "From there he could pound Puebla into submission."

"I neglected to warn him, of course, that if he failed to take the two forts he would be defeated. But I would expect any graduate of Saint-Cyr to see that by himself, wouldn't you?"

"I would, indeed." They laughed together. For both, it was the first time for days. "And you did this, sir, so that your army would lose? So that France will have to send massive reinforcements to Mexico?"

"What else?" Morny shook a not so playful finger at him. "What if Lorencez had won at Puebla? Where could he go? To Mexico City, with only five thousand men? Ridiculous! Stay in Puebla amidst a hostile populace? Almost as ridiculous. Juarez would soon concentrate enough troops to wipe him out. His only possible move was back to Veracruz, where at least he could escape if he had to."

"And by losing now, he has no choice but to fall back on Veracruz."

"Precisely. I've saved his army from his own foolishness, you must admit. And I've prepared it to be reinforced."

Bartlett leaned back in thought as he took in the extent of Morny's treachery. Morny read his mind.

"Talleyrand – my grandfather, Major – was a great man and a great Frenchman." Morny straightened his back. "He was often accused, correctly, of disloyalty to one colleague or another. His response was that he may have been disloyal to Minister X or General Y, but he was *always* loyal to France."

It was a moonlit, windswept evening, with *Isabella* bowling along at a dozen knots, when they sighted the Lizard light off the port bow. Morny joined Bartlett at the rail. "Well, Major, here we are," he said, pointing. "The captain tells me that, if this wind out of the south holds, we will make Le Havre a day or so earlier if we can put you off at Plymouth instead of Southampton. Every day is important to me, as you know, so I hope – "

"Whatever is most convenient for you, sir," Bartlett said. "Plymouth will be fine and may, in fact, save me some time to London."

Morny studied his face, as if to predict his reaction. Then he said, "You know, do you not? About your coded cables?"

"Yes, sir. We know all about it."

"And you do not complain?"

"At first, yes, but they say all is fair in - war."

"I have never agreed with that."

After a minute or two, he went on to say again how deeply he regretted the end of their professional relationship. As he had explained, he had no further need of an informal channel of communications with Washington, and Washington had no further need of private reports on his activities. "In France it will all be in the public eye, you understand, and Washington will have many sources in Mexico – Mexican newspapers, Yankee reporters, even your own ambassador if he ever shows himself." The non-appearance of this functionary was notorious.

"I agree completely, sir, and besides it's time I went back to work. But *Isabella* has spoiled me. I don't think I can tolerate my usual forms of transport any more."

"I trust this will not be your last voyage on her." A wave of the hand. "And that you can forgive the inconvenience I caused you and Commander Jones aboard her last month. It was a necessary, ah, digression."

"Diversion." Bartlett renewed his thanks. Morny replied with flowery assurances of esteem. Each retired for the night feeling pleased with himself.

Bartlett stumbled, fully dressed for departure, to his cabin door at five the next morning. In the doorway was an envelope and in the envelope was a note:

> "My dear Charles Bartlett
> I sincerely hope that the presumed end of our professional relationship will mark the beginning of an equally warm and productive personal relationship.
> Please call on me at any time for any assistance you consider I may be able to render. It will be my privilege to render it.
> I suggest you retain this note to remind you of my offer.
> With my highest personal regards, I am, sir,
> Charles-Auguste, Count de Morny"

Chapter 38

Robert Jones was lucky. The captain of *USS Niantic* was an Annapolis classmate who took him at his word and hustled him back to Washington on a coaling vessel. Three days after he left *Isabella* he was in Stoddard's office with his report. That afternoon Stoddard proudly gave him his orders to take command of the still-building Hull Number Nine.

Then he said, "Robert, Henry Wise and I want to talk to you again about the circumstances in which the English and the Spanish left Veracruz. And, ah, to get your views on whether Morny will return to Mexico or not. Shall we go see Henry now?"

"Of course. Why not?" said Jones.

*   *   *

Well, Major, it's kind of you to drop by from time to time and tell us of your adventures," said Adams with a frozen smile. The minister was much less on edge these days, thanks to Hampton Roads and the Union Army's victories on the western rivers. These had halfway convinced Palmerston's ministers, and Russell in particular, that the North could fight and win, and that any rush to recognize the Confederacy must therefore be restrained. Adams thought he even detected the occasional hint of respect in Russell's attitude, which was gratifying after the despair of the year before. He could now afford to be easier on this vexing fellow Bartlett and his endless absences.

"Where was it this time – Cuba? Morocco? Bali?" he asked, referring to Bartlett's sunburn and his creamy uniform.

Bartlett had gone directly to the ministry from the station. He felt oddly blameless and was not put off balance by the false geniality of Adams's welcome. So he wasted no time. "Close, sir – Mexico," he replied and launched into a shorter version of the report that he and Jones had agreed to give their superiors.

"Interesting, most interesting," Adams allowed. "I've read a good deal about this man, the Count de Morny, and I suspect he is even more powerful in France than you imagine." He reflected for a minute. "I'll see if your relationship with him can be useful to me here, but I believe we must leave him to our people in Paris."

"My orders to attach myself to him are still in effect," Bartlett volunteered. "He told Jones and me that he no longer needs our services, which is why we left him, but if he asks me to go back I suppose I'll have to go."

"Probably, but this time pray tell me what your orders are *before* you go wandering off, if you please."

"Of course, sir."

Adams had heard that at their last meeting, so he reminded Bartlett at some length just why he had been so angry. The police, he said, had not to his knowledge pursued their inquiry into Bartlett's activities, but there was no reason to think their file on him was closed. "And, Major," he finished, "I now have written authority to return you to Washington, at my discretion, if you again jeopardize our relationship with the government." He glared belligerently at Bartlett, thrusting out his trap-like lower jaw. "So watch your step, sir."

It was a glorious early summer evening when Bartlett walked from the ministry to his lodgings in Rochester Place. The sun was still high, the grass and trees along the streets and in the small parks he crossed were their most brilliant greens. They made a striking contrast to the baked browns of the Mexican landscape and the timeless slate blues of the Atlantic. He had never really felt at home in London, but now on his return it began to seem familiar, almost welcoming, to him. It was good to be back, and much better than that to see Katherine again soon.

But she was away, Mrs. Mostyn told him as she banged the pots in his kitchen later on. "She's in Ireland, sir, in Cork, second time in a month. Don't know what takes her there, I don't."

*   *   *

"He's back, Milady, that nice American officer came back when you were away." Milly sounded excited, perhaps because she sensed that her news was important to her mistress. She carried Katherine's case up the stairs as Katherine took off her hat.

Dear God, another complication, was her first thought. She had re-examined her relationship with Malcolm Bannerman, the man she was engaged to marry. And now Charles Bartlett, whose attractiveness had diminished in his long absence, had returned to give her emotional pot another stir or two. Well, she would deal with him when circumstances required.

Which was around six o'clock that same day, when he called to pay his overdue rent, an excuse he had used before. They stared openly at each other as Milly showed him into the yellow drawing room. She had hoped that seeing him would dispel the thoughts that had been going through her head these past months, but she was immediately thwarted. He was better looking than she remembered. His dark suntan, with the scar only a pale line now, combined with the straight black hair to impart a faintly exotic look to the flat planes of his face.

This is not good, she thought to herself. What about Malcolm? What about security? Pull yourself together, woman.

"Good afternoon, Major."

She was every bit as stunning as he remembered her. The honey-colored hair, the arched nose and incomparable green eyes matched his visual memory exactly. The small gold cross was as ever around her neck. But as they talked he discerned a new directness, less elusiveness, in her manner.

After what seemed like a lifetime in Mexico, Bartlett was now unsure of where he stood with Katherine. He had decided to play it casually with her and the way she had referred to him as Major - not Charles - made it clear that she was not going to mention 'the night' or even their confrontation on her porch. In that case, nor would he.

"Ma'am."

After some pleasantries and a cup of stewed tea he needed to explain his presence. He resorted to his stock excuse for visiting her: "I calculate it's five pounds I owe you, ah, Lady Carra, with my most humble apologies." He pushed the coins across the table to her.

"Thank you, ah, Major. I'll hide those before Lord Carra sees them." She dropped them in a drawer. "He returns tomorrow from Bath, where he will swear that he's been taking the waters."

"But really..?"

"Taking losses on the flat races, I shouldn't wonder."

"But at least he's given up the prize ring. Or has he?"

"Oh, yes, just before it ruined him. No more Barbados blasters for him." She straightened the silverware on the table. "And, Charles, you must come to dinner with us on Saturday, if you're free."

Ah, some hope! he thought.

"I am. I will, thank you."

"Eight for eight thirty, then. Lord Carra will want to hear all your adventures in Mexico, and I'll wait until then to hear them. You did have adventures, didn't you?" She surveyed him coolly. "You can't have been there all this time without some adventures."

"A few. I'll elaborate on them as necessary to keep his lordship entertained. Lots of insulting stories about the French."

"Oh, good. He'll love that."

Bantering about Lord Carra's failings had in the past helped them to relax and it worked again. There was still a frostiness in the air, but it ws definitely thawing. Then after half an hour of random chatter about the weather, Owen (Katherine had a recent letter) the American war and the British political situation, Bartlett took his leave.

"I'm sorry to be so late with the rent, Lady Carra, I'd no idea I'd be gone this long." He opened the front door and stopped. "And you're not at all ruthless about collecting your rents, you know. Do you recall telling me once that you would be ruthless?"

"Of course. I remember telling you many things." She smiled sweetly at him. "Good night, Major."

Chapter 39

Paris

The Count de Morny, wrapped in a brocade dressing gown, lay on a sofa in his library. He was ill. His face was thinner, and it was fast losing the sunburn acquired on the passage from Veracruz. Henri fussed in a corner and made clucking sounds. A footman announced the arrival of Doctor Jolliffe. "The Count will see him," Henri said.

Dr. Jolliffe was a fixture in the higher strata of Paris society. An Irishman, he had been drummed out of his profession at home for criminal incompetence and fled to Paris, where medical standards were less demanding and titled ladies more willing to try his seductive pills. A man with such a benign manner, distinguished grey hair and apostolic exterior must be a capable physician, they told each other. And there were all those orders and degrees, and all those medals from sultans and princes. And finally, there were his magical pearls – pills whose secret working ingredient was either cocaine or arsenic. Once having taken them, no patient could do without them.

Morny knew the man was a fraud, but the pills did ease his intestinal pain, and the doctor's failure rate was something less than one hundred per cent. He counted on Jolliffe's acquaintance with basic chemistry and his reluctance to lose a profitable patient to keep himself alive.

After a few solicitous questions and sympathetic murmurs, Jolliffe turned to the subject of his visit. At Morny's suggestion, he had scouted the French seashore searching for the ideal site to create a new watering place, a summer retreat to be built for the select of Paris. He had found it, he claimed with pardonable excitement. "Near Trouville, sir. Constant sun, sandy beaches, safe bathing, and the waters..."

"Excellent, Doctor," Morny said. "New châteaux. A casino, of course. Race course. Real property. Inaccessible to all but a few. It will be my triumph."

Jolliffe was delighted by Morny's approval but anxious about his health. "Ah, what shall we call it? There is nothing at all there now."

"You mentioned the waters? Then why not D'Eau Ville?" A short laugh. "Yes. I like it. Deauville it shall be. My triumph, but your project to erect. Very exclusive. The old watering places are now so crowded." He eyed Jolliffe closely. "I shall recommend it to my friends. Now get out."

Jolliffe started for the door but stopped when his patient demanded another prescription, explaining that he had an audience with the Emperor that evening. "That is too many, sir, it is not safe," he objected.

"You don't think I believe your pills are curative, do you?" Morny said. "I know the danger, but they're safe as long as I know what poison they contain." He sighed. "And I don't intend to live as long as possible; only as long as necessary."

*   *   *

Napoleon's manner when Morny arrived was gracious but reserved. Eugenie would join them in a few minutes, he said. After Morny gave a brief account of the last meeting of the Commissioners, he described how he and Pancho Laffan had maneuvered Prim and Wyke into a political corner from which they could only escape by taking to their ships.

"Bravo, Auguste," applauded the Emperor. "You forced two major powers out of Mexico with a bit of paper. And a forgery, at that. Bravo." He inclined his head. "And this Laffan? He sounds resourceful. Where is he now?"

"Awaiting reinforcements. He will raise and then command the royalist forces."

"Reinforcements? Ah. We shall discuss that in due course, but first I want you to show me how we lost at Puebla. Here."

He spread out a map of Puebla and watched as Morny sketched the progress of the battle. Even he could see the futility of the attacks on the fortified hills north of the city, and he pressed Morny for Lorencez's reasons for that tactic. On the surface, Morny's replies placed most of the blame for the debacle on the bad advice from Almonte, but they also made sure that the French general would be discarded along with the Mexican.

Eugenie had drifted into the room unnoticed, wearing a simple dress of black silk and her Mexican shawl. "Welcome back to Paris, Auguste. You have had an eventful trip."

"Eventful, yes. And encouraging. I mean to say, it was encouraging to discover how simple it would have been, with a larger force and a competent commander, to reach the capital."

"Lorencez is not competent, then?"

"I fear not." Morny sat down again. Then briskly: "I spoke of reinforcements. To eject Juarez, to control Mexico, will require reinforcements of twenty-five thousand men. That is the unanimous opinion of myself, Lorencez and Colonel Laffan, who knows the strength of Juarez' army intimately."

"Twenty five thousand!" gasped Napoleon. "We couldn't find *ten* thousand. We have forces scattered across the world. The Far East, Africa... "

Eugenie cut him off. "You must find them if you mean to install Maximilian. If you mean to honor your pledge to install him."

Morny had never seen Eugenie so determined. "The Empress is right, Louis," he said gravely. "To send fewer is to send too few, and we learned at Puebla that too few means a disaster. Now, if it's the cost of the expedition that concerns you, I'm confident that I can convince the Deputies to approve the funds."

"No, it is more than that, Auguste, more than that!" cried Eugenie, her face alight. "Of course! *You* must command the expedition. "

Morny sat back and thought for a moment or two. Then he shook his head. "No. Not again. I have done my duty to France. Impossible."

"She's right, you know," Napoleon weighed in. He studied his brother. "I could not trust anyone else to accomplish our purpose there."

"And your reputation, Auguste, as the man who can do anything, the man who never fails." Eugenie scored a palpable hit. "You can restore it, you can –"

"I - did - not - fail, Madame," Morny glowered. "I simply did not finish."

"Those are the facts, we know that, my dear Auguste, but history deals only with results, not facts." She had skewered him and she knew it. "History is cruel to those who do not finish."

Morny searched for excuses: His health; the Mexican heat and mosquitoes; his young family. "I am not well, as you know, Louis."

"You will recover at once if you escape from that Irish charlatan and his magic pearls."

"Consider, Auguste." Napoleon's eyes searched Morny's. "You will have the chance to accomplish something truly grand, something truly noble, for France. And for the family."

"For Maximilian, you mean."

"At first, yes. But over time? You can be sure I will never let him or Austria really control Mexico. We've discussed this already, you and I." He waved his arm grandly upward. "And in time, who can say? An empire for my son? For your son? Everything is possible."

"Yes, everything is possible," said Morny. "Even my return to that pestilential country, for you are both most persuasive. Most persuasive, indeed." He rubbed his chin and smoothed the wings of hair. He seemed to revive a bit. "I would insist, of course, on the twenty five thousand men. All French." Pause. "And my choice of commanders." Pause. "I could not leave in less than ninety days."

"Fine. It will take that long to mobilize the divisions you will lead."

"Then I shall think about it carefully. You will allow me a few days?"

"As long as you need."

"Very well. If I go, this would be the second time you have persuaded me." Morny stood up and kissed Eugenie's hand. He held his hand out to the Emperor but, as if on impulse, said, "Ah. There is just one more thing, Louis."

"Name it."

"You once made me an offer, a most gratifying offer. It was five years ago, if you can recall. I chose to decline it at the time. But, now..."

Napoleon stared stonily at him for ten seconds and then said, "Yes, I believe I do recall. You would like that now?"

"Now, if you please." Morny bowed and left the room.

*   *   *

As the only yankee military man in London, Bartlett had a certain curiosity value at the receptions and balls he attended in the course of duty. The string of Union victories at Forts Henry and Donelson, Shiloh, Hampton Roads and New Orleans did wonders for his standing with the other attachés. He had made few real friends but many acquaintances at these affairs, and his social life revived rapidly once he made known his return. All in all, he was reasonably content.

Except for one thing: There was no word from Stoddard in Washington. Bartlett agonized. Had Jones told Stoddard how they had helped to drive Spain and England from Mexico? Did Stoddard blame them that France was left there with a free hand? How did he rate Bartlett's performance in Mexico? Would he, Bartlett ever know the answers to these questions?

*   *   *

Katherine had arranged the flowers herself in the living room and dining room. She had little talent for it, but in the spring and summer she thought it one of her more pleasant duties and she did her best. She loved flowers around her, the sight of them more than the smell. A country girl with no country skills, she said to herself.

She placed Bartlett at one end of the dining table, opposite Lord Carra, with herself in the middle. Her hair was up and she wore her favorite green silk dress, the one that showed off her shoulders. She had made Carra swear that he would not mention Malcolm Bannerman, improvising that he and Bartlett had once disagreed violently over a banking matter. With this off her mind and with her new, more tolerant attitude to Bartlett, she expected to enjoy her little party.

And she did. Mrs. Mostyn was not on peak form in the kitchen but the food was digestible, Carra was generous with his wine and the talk was light-hearted. She told Bartlett that she wanted to hear all about Mexico and, sensing her new mood, he contrived to be amusing as well as long-winded.

The one difficulty was that Carra perversely refused to understand just what Bartlett had been doing in Mexico, and Bartlett could not fully explain his role without revealing that he had been, in effect, a spy. A spy approved by his target, but a spy nonetheless.

"You mean to say you just *watched* 'em fight at this Poobla? You didn't get stuck in yourself?" Carra shook his head in wonder.

"I was a neutral, sir, an observer. If I'd got stuck in, as you say, I would have violated international law, which would have led to an exchange of diplomatic notes, then to certain war with France and Russia." Bartlett ignored Katherine's frown and warning hand. This was fun.

"I don't understand any of that," persisted his host, "but I can tell you this: If I were an army officer, I wouldn't have missed any chance to shove a bayonet up a Frenchman's - fundamental, I wouldn't."

"Of course you wouldn't, Uncle, and nor would I," Katherine soothed, "I've always longed to do just that. But Major Bartlett was there more as a diplomat than a soldier." She turned brightly to Bartlett. "Although his credentials as a diplomat, in my experience, are – what is the judicial term? Not proven."

This was all too much for Carra, who eyed Bartlett with lowering suspicion the rest of the evening.

"You must give me another opportunity to display them, Lady Carra." Bartlett sipped his wine. "You are not being fair. In fact, if truth be told, my diplomatic skills saved my skin several times in Mexico." He told a severely edited version of his clash with the Mexican soldier who had questioned his manhood. "And so the Colonel said 'His three brothers are standing right behind you.' At that point my mastery of diplomacy came to the fore. I lowered my pistol, smiled benevolently on all concerned and returned to my breakfast."

"I see," smiled Katherine. "You did not press your advantage unfairly, as others might have done, but let your prospective opponents retire with dignity."

"Exactly."

"Talleyrand himself would be proud of you."

"Odd you should mention him. The Count de Morny is rumored to be - Ah, but that would be gossip."

"I do hope so. And?"

"And, another time, a most unpleasant Mexican with Asiatic ancestry tried to separate my friend Laffan from his horse. And his life. My diplomatic ability to sit quite still and not scream and offend the Mexican was crucial to Laffan's escape." More wine. "That, and the fact that Laffan is a dead shot."

"Shoots birds, does he?" asked Carra.

"No, sir, Mexicans." Bartlett told the story at some length and with a shameless amount of embroidery.

Katherine was mildly impressed. "It sounds as if you and your friends – the ineffable Commander Jones among them, I assume – were determined to wipe out the natives."

"No, indeed," Bartlett countered, "we were usually running for our lives. Or swimming." He recounted their escape from *Isabella,* making much of their wild ride on the fishing boat through the reefs.

"And did your pistols work after that time in the water?" Carra wanted to know.

"We never fired them. Strange. I forgot about the water," Bartlett mused, "even when the Chasseurs chased us up into the hills." Another long story followed. "Something of an anti-climax," he finished lamely. "They never even saw us after we got above them."

Katherine asked Milly to take the coffee into the drawing room. As she rose, she observed, "Riding, yachting, swimming and shooting. Mexico was just one long holiday for you, Major."

"Yes, I'm surprised that I'm so glad to be back here." He tried a meaningful look in Katherine's direction but she deflected it.

Carra wanted back in the conversation. "Your chaps in the north are doing rather better over there now," he said. "Winning on all those rivers with the most extraordinary names, and now this ironclad gunboat business."

Bartlett had plowed through the reports from Washington that had stacked up in his absence. "Yes, sir, and we believe that Hampton Roads, where our ironclad beat their ironclad, is the most significant. It means that we can control all the water around the South, which is in effect an island." He turned to Katherine. "I learned that grand strategic concept from Jones, who, incidentally, should by now be in command of one of the *Monitors.*"

"Your very own Cochrane, I'll warrant." Katherine's low opinion of Jones still in full effect. "That's if he doesn't -"

"Tell me, Major, why don't these iron ships sink?" Carra wanted to know. "The men at my club can't explain it. It doesn't seem right."

Bartlett wasn't sure of the answer so he rabbitted on about Archimedes, water displacement and specific gravity until Carra's eyes glazed. Then he diverted his host's attention back to the war. Katherine gave him a grateful half-smile.

They soon agreed that the Union would prevail by Christmas, and Carra drew out his gold hunter and announced that he was for bed. Bartlett made a tentative move to leave, but Katherine motioned him back to his chair. Goodnights were exchanged and Milly brought in the good port and two glasses.

"It's kind of you to give me dinner, Katherine," said Bartlett. "And tolerant. I'm past all that, all that doubt and suspicion."

"I'm glad." She sipped her port and was silent for a time. "And the truth is I missed you, with Owen gone and only my uncle and Mrs. Mostyn to talk to."

"And my new neighbor, the Belgian statesman?"

"I scarcely ever see him, although he seems amiable enough."

"Well, my life is as quiet as yours. It needs to be livened up." He would push his luck now. "You must allow me to take you to the theater. And the opera. I enjoyed our one venture to the Lyric. And the National Gallery. We owe ourselves another visit there."

"All this culture, Charles! Are you up to it? I mean, your being an American and all," she teased.

Ah, she had called him Charles again, not the dreaded 'Major;' it was a small victory, but it gave him hope. "Try me."

"Talk is cheap, sir, but I will. For myself, I'd like to travel. Around England, or to Ireland again. I went back there again a few days ago and I loved it." She poured him another glass. He glanced at the clock behind her and nodded his thanks. He wanted to be sure not to outstay his welcome.

"You should begin the real traveling you spoke of."

"Yes. I'm desperate to see some of the continent. You know, I've never left the British Isles. I'd so love to see Paris."

"Really?" What the hell, in for a penny - "As it happens, I have to go to Paris for a few days sometime soon."

The letter from Major Preston, Jones's replacement in Paris, had awaited Bartlett at his rooms when he arrived from Mexico. In guarded terms it reported that Jones's agents had turned up something 'most interesting' and urged Bartlett to come to Paris to inspect it. He, Preston, could not measure the discovery's importance, but from what Jones had told him he was confident that Bartlett could. Cryptic stuff, Bartlett thought when he read it, but it was what Jones had predicted on *Isabella* and definitely worth a trip. Besides, he'd never been to Paris.

"And you hope I'll go with you? Impossible, my dear Charles."

"Well, I'll now make a fool of myself again, but suppose I can arrange matters so that there is absolutely no question of any impropriety?"

"I don't believe you can arrange it, but -"

"But you'll consider it?"

"*Pourquoi pas?*"

Chapter 40

The buzzing sound came from inside her head, from a spot just behind the sharp pain. That knowledge, along with her parched mouth and the spinning room when she lifted her head from her pillow, made it child's play for Katherine to conclude that she was suffering from a surfeit of port.

This time it was Katherine's turn to have been bitten by the Hound of Hangover. It was all that fine old claret last night, followed by two glasses of port with Charles Bart – oh, dear God. Charles. She had talked far too long with him, far too loosely. Like a loose woman, in fact. *Pourquoi pas*, indeed! That was crass, shameless. I know him, he'll become much too excited by a few careless words. I must set him straight right away. A letter; he'll see it tonight. I'll write it when my hand stops shaking.

> "My dear Charles,
> I did enjoy your company last night, and you were so kind to his lordship. But I fear that my enjoyment – and the wine - led me to be indiscreet and, what is worse, to encourage you unfairly, for which I must apologize. The sad fact is, and you must see it as clearly as I, that I could not possibly accompany you on a trip outside London. A pity, because I long to see Paris and I believe it looks its best this time of year.
> Please forgive my thoughtlessness, and please do call on me when you think you can withstand a cup of Mrs. Mostyn's unforgettable tea.
> *A bientôt*,
> Katherine"

There. That will make him see that Paris is out of the question but that he is not.

*   *   *

That morning Bartlett opened the larger of the two heavy envelopes with French postmarks that lay on his desk. It contained one magnificently engraved card from the Mayor of Clermont-Ferrand, capital of the Auvergne. This invited him with elaborate courtesy to attend the ceremony on July sixth next at which His Imperial Majesty would graciously confer on Charles-Auguste-Joseph, le Comte de Morny, a Dukedom.

Bartlett asked Freeman Morse to confirm his reading of the florid French. Then they both read the equally magnificent card in the second envelope. "My God, Charles," said Morse, "you didn't waste your time in Mexico, did you?" For the prospective new duke invited Bartlett to a ball at his château near Clermont on the night of his accession.

Bartlett didn't at first notice Morny's card pinned to this invitation. Morse deciphered the handwritten message on it:

"My dear Major,

You will be the only representative of your country, so you must attend. Duty demands it, I demand it. Bring your wife or the most beautiful woman you know.

Morny."

As he slipped the card back in the envelope, he saw a brief scrawl on the blank side. "What's this now?"

Morse tried to make it out. "It's signed Henri, I think, and it says something like: 'Dear Major, it is of supreme importance that you attend, in the name of God. I must see you. You must save Monsieur. I await you in private at the Petit Bourbon on 4 or 5 July. Henri.' He stared hard at Bartlett. "What's that all about?"

Bartlett was mystified, intrigued. "I have no idea, but whatever it is I'm going to Paris." He picked up the invitations. "Excuse me, Freeman, I have to see Adams. Wait till he reads these."

The Minister was suitably impressed by the grandeur of his attaché's social connections and objected not at all to his proposed visit to France. "Just wish I could go with you," was his parting shot as Bartlett went out his door. That, you old trout, will be the day, Bartlett said to himself.

Next he drafted with care a telegram to Major Preston in Paris. He suggested they meet on the morning of the third of July to review the material mentioned in Preston's last telegram. He also asked Preston to notify Henri, with total discretion, of his visit and to suggest the valet call on him at his hotel on the fourth. Finally, he asked Preston to book him into a hotel near the ministry. "Regret imposing on you like this," he finished, "but believe valet's business important." He gave the draft to one of the secretaries to encode and send to the Paris legation.

Then he sent a messenger to Rochester Place with a note for Katherine: "Very good news. Must see you this evening. May I call at six?"

The prospect of taking part, however modestly, in the celebrations at Clermont-Ferrand appealed to Bartlett's sense of history and of theater. His curiosity about Preston's discovery and about Henri's demand that he save Morny was irresistible. And the chance of seeing Paris with Katherine was delectable. In his imagination, Bartlett was approaching a state of bliss.

But paradise looked like being postponed when he went home and read Katherine's first note. A heavy blow, but the pain eased when he read it again and marked her open invitation to tea, and it disappeared when her second note declared, a bit ungraciously, that she would call on him at six o'clock or thereabouts and please could she have some lemonade?

Higgins & Daughter, the local fruiter, was still open, so freshly made citrus juice awaited Katherine when she knocked on his door. "I've brought you these," she announced as she thrust a straggling bunch of wet flowers at him. "From our garden. It's just begun to rain. Can you produce a vase of some kind?" He found one on a top shelf and she fussed with them. "There, that's better, I suppose, but I do wish I had some trace of talent with flowers."

He had decided to ignore her first note, and she was content to go along. He told her with some excitement of his invitations to Morny's festivities. "So that's your 'very good news', is it?" she asked when he finished. "A dukedom! Fancy that. It all sounds too splendid, and I trust you won't miss it."

"Oh, I'll be there," he said loftily. "But let me read you the best part, from Morny's own card: 'You must attend. Bring your wife or the most beautiful woman you know.'" He raised his eyes to hers.

"Well, you're not married – or are you? – so who is the lucky woman?" Unusually for her, Katherine had suffered an emotional day. Her feelings for Bartlett had been stretched in all directions. So in a curious way she almost resented him and the choice he was now presenting to her. It was a most attractive choice, but an emotionally complicating one and she didn't need any more complications.

"Why, you, of course." Bartlett had hoped for a more positive response despite the sharp tone of her first note. "I don't know a more beautiful woman, and you said last night that you wanted to travel to France."

"And this morning that I couldn't go with you. But I'm grateful for the compliment."

"I'm hoping to change your mind." He grabbed her hand. The fact that she had already said no once made him feel that he had nothing to lose, and that he might as well press her more forcefully. "Look, Katherine, this is the invitation of a lifetime. Imagine the splendor, the excitement of these occasions. I can't imagine why Morny wants me there, but he does and it's no accident." He took hold of her other hand and leaned closer. "He's the supreme gentleman. He'll make certain that we're well looked after, and that you enjoy yourself."

She looked doubtful. "I expect you're right, but..."

"You would have nothing to worry about. Not from me, anyway. Your reputation will be safe." He was thinking fast. "I'll go there before you go and come back after you. We'll stay in separate hotels and, if you like, we'll meet only at these formal - occasions."

She sipped her lemonade, sighed and sat back on the sofa. She began to visualize a dazzling ball in a splendid ballroom, the women in glittering gowns, the men in full dress. She still had one gown that might do. "It does sound tempting," she conceded, "like something I've never seen, or will see."

"It will be."

"And of course Paris itself. I'm longing to see it." She looked at him from under her eyelashes, "Will you be engaged all the time you're in Paris?"

"No, only once or twice. I'll be available to you whenever you wish, but remember that I'm no guide. I've not been there either."

She was silent for a time. "No. Dear Charles, I fear that it just wouldn't look proper, going off to Paris with a gentlemen friend, as they say." She patted his hand. "However proper that friend promises to be."

He wanted to ask why she cared how it looked but he controlled himself. Instead he said, "Nonsense, Katherine." Suddenly, a promising thought. "That's it." He turned eagerly to her, still holding one hand. "Don't say no, not yet. Let me try to arrange something for you. I should know by tomorrow night if I can."

The telegram from Preston arrived at ten the next morning:

"LOOK FORWARD TO MEETING YOU AT MINISTRY MORNING OF THIRD JULY STOP YOUR VALET FRIEND NOW PREFERS YOU CALL ON HIM AT HIS HOUSE IN MONTMARTRE DISTRICT STOP EYE HAVE THE ADDRESS HERE STOP HAVE BOOKED YOU INTO HOTEL MONTGUYON FORTY THREE AVENUE ST ETIENNE STOP MRS PRESTON AND EYE HOPING YOU CAN DINE WITH US EVENING OF THIRD OR FOURTH TO CELEBRATE INDEPENDENCE FROM LOATHSOME KING GEORGE STOP PLEASE ADVISE.
JOHN PRESTON
MAJOR USA"

Preston was married. Just what he needed to know as he drafted his careful reply.

Preston's response came quickly. He and Mrs. Preston would be delighted to put up Lady Carra for as long as she cared to stay in Paris and believed she would be comfortable with them. If Major Bartlett would kindly let them know when she planned to arrive?

Chapter 41

Katherine had spent another near sleepless night, although not this time due to too much port. As she tossed and turned she tried to analyze her feelings for Charles Bartlett. This inevitably led on to an examination of her emotions and her conscience, the cause of this particular examination being Malcolm Bannerman. She could not keep him waiting longer unless she meant to marry him. It was a matter of honor and of simple courtesy. But what reason could she give him? As she tossed and turned she eventually reached the conclusion that truth was better than falsehood, even if it caused pain at the time. The one definite conclusion she reached was that she could not let Malcolm Bannerman continue to think she would marry him. It was not fair to him or to herself. So she must go and see him as soon as possible. At his office – that was best.

*   *   *

Bannerman remained standing at his window when she left. He had kissed her on each cheek and said nothing more when she held out her hand in good-bye.

He had behaved well, he thought. He'd expected something of the sort for weeks, so there was no surprise, and he was grateful that she had told him in the privacy of his office. Breeding always showed, even Irish breeding.

She's a desirable, enchanting woman and a woman of character. Will I find another like her? Perhaps but first I need to get over this pain.

While Katherine was visiting Bannerman, Bartlett called round with Preston's invitation. "Milady is out shopping again, sir," said Milly, a look of surprise on her face. She let him in to attach his card to Preston's telegram and leave them for her ladyship to find when she returned.

The card had a simple message composed at the ministry with the advice of young Henry Adams, who reluctantly admitted that he was shaky on the subjunctive. It read:

"*Voila! Tout est arreglé. Il faut absolument que vous venez.*
Charles"

Katherine smiled when she read it and took it up to her bedroom to think.

She found Bartlett's card and wrote on it "Yes, please" and signed it K. She would put it though his letterbox after he left in the morning. She would let him wait all day to find it.

*   *   *

It would be Bartlett's only good news that day. The bad news came in two envelopes on his desk at the ministry.

The first, with a War Department seal, held two letters. One, signed by Miles Stoddard, revoked his earlier order to deputize temporarily for Robert Jones in his mission as neutral observer for Count de Morny in Mexico.

The second letter was a personal note from Stoddard:

"Charles –

I've asked Robert Jones to explain informally what this is about. Until further notice, better stay away from Morny. In fact, better stay away from France altogether. MS"

Angry and mystified, Bartlett ripped open the other envelope, to find Jones's letter:

"Charles

Afraid I've dropped you in the mire.

You have to understand that everyone here is furious – and scared – that the French didn't leave Mexico with the Brits and the Spanish. For this reason, Stoddard and Wise weren't satisfied with my first report on our Mexico trip, which glossed over certain details, as you remember. They demanded a complete report, which I gave them, omitting nothing. Then they asked a lot of questions about you. So I built you up, maybe even exaggerating your role: how you persuaded Doblado to let the French and the others move up from the fever zone that would have killed them. How you were a close friend of Laffan – who we couldn't have known would turn out to be an enemy – and how that led to our trick with the cables that induced the Brits and the Spanish to leave. (I couldn't swear that the original idea for the trick wasn't Morny's.) How your advice saved Diaz's brigade at Puebla and won the day for the Mexicans - which as it turned out suited Morny's book.

They wondered why you went back to England on Morny's yacht, but I explained that it was your only way back and that you were trying to find out if Morny intended to return with the French reinforcements. (I hope you were.) This is an important question, as a French army in Mexico is much more of a threat to us under Morny than under some ordinary French general.

So – well, you get my drift.

Very sorry about all this, but I'm sure if you sit tight it will
blow over in a few months.
Saludos
Robert
PS. I can't be sure, but I suspect Seward's hand in this.
Adams is close to him. Have you annoyed His Eminence
more than usual? About young Owen Halliday, maybe?
RJ"

Bartlett threw the letters on his desk and jumped up. Damn Stoddard!
Damn Wise! Damn them all! Even Jones, whose letter didn't quite ring
true. He bruised his toes on the wall and stormed out to the garden.

So this was his reward for his good work in Mexico, and his good work
with Morny – suspicion, doubts about his loyalty. Damn them all! He'd –
what would he do? He'd go to France, anyway, that was certain. Just to
show the bastards. Besides, he couldn't back down on his promise to
Katherine.

He barely knew Wise, but Stoddard? His uncle? What on earth had led
him to *his* doubts? Jones might be right, Seward was behind this. Which
meant Adams had reported something critical to Washington. Which
could only have been... Owen Halliday, of course, his request to Adams
months ago for passage for Owen. Jones must be right. *Damn* Adams.

Who might have been reading Bartlett's thoughts. "No, Major, I cannot
permit you to go to Paris on official business," was his icy response when
Bartlett told him his final travel arrangements.

Bartlett tried to look astonished. "But, sir, I don't understand. A few
days ago you said you wished you could go with me."

A thin-lipped smile. "I did, indeed, but circumstances have changed. I
am now advised that your temporary orders as deputy to Commander
Jones have been revoked," Adams said with satisfaction, "and that you are
requested to have no further contact with the Count de Morny."

"That is correct, but – "

"That, to me, means quite clearly that I must deny my permission for
your proposed visit to France on legation business."

Is that a hint? Bartlett asked himself. "On official business, I believe you
said, sir?"

"I did."

"In that case, I will take a week's leave. I've had none since I came to
London."

"I see. So you will go to France?"

"That, I believe, is *my* business, sir." He left the office, his head as high
as he could manage. I'll go to Paris, he thought, with Katherine, to see
Morny. And to find out if he'll return to Mexico.

Adams was pleased with himself. His troublesome, insubordinate military attaché had rushed into his trap, he thought. He reached for pen and paper.

*   *   *

Major Preston had chosen well. The Hotel Montguyon had belonged to the eponymous family for generations, until their political instincts failed them and they underestimated Louis Phillippe. The Citizen King urged the vicomte of the day to go tend his vineyards in Tuscany. After selling the property to a thrusting young hotelier from Rennes, he did just that.

The building stood in the middle of a shady block in the sixteenth arondissement, a few hundred yards from the American ministry in the rue de Presbourg. Bartlett arrived at sundown and, while he absorbed a long whisky punch in a lounge off the dining room, his clothes were laid out and his bath was run for him. Dinner was excellent, his cigar was soothing and he was in bed by eleven o'clock.

Major Preston, the next morning, was something of a novelty. In his forties, short and plump, with spectacles falling off his nose, he resembled a Pickwickian clerk more than the master spy Jones had painted: "Next to Gringo Wise and me, the smartest man in the service, and the meanest." Preston read Bartlett's look of surprise, chuckled, ushered him to a leather chair and offered coffee.

"Excellent, excellent, Major Bartlett. A pleasure to meet you at last. Robert Jones left me a short memorandum about you, the gist of which was that I'm to trust you without question." He rubbed his hands hard. "One can not make that statement about every man in our army, I fear."

"No, I suppose not."

"And Lady Carra arrives this afternoon, I believe? My wife and I look forward to the pleasure."

"Yes, this afternoon sometime. She was vague about her schedule." 'Vague', indeed; clam-like, rather. Infuriating. "No, Charles, I do not need to be met at the station," she'd insisted.

"It's most kind of you to put her up. She's my landlady, you see, and not used to travelling alone. I'm afraid I'm imposing on you."

"Not in the slightest. And you'll both be with us for dinner tonight? Excellent, excellent." Preston then described his colleagues in the ministry: Dayton, the amateur diplomat who was proving a success as a minister; Bigelow, the Consul with long experience. "And your humble servant. We like to claim that not since Franklin, Adams and Jefferson were posted here together has there been such a concentration of talent at our Paris legation," he said.

"I can well believe it." Bartlett drew his chair closer. "Now, Major, you said you'd found some interesting things?"

"Yes. How interesting they really are, only you can tell." He crossed his arms on his desk. "Robert Jones assembled a first-class network here. Many of his people are professional thieves - safecrackers, forgers, pickpockets and the odd second-storey man. He used them on an ad hoc basis, paying them by the job and paying them well."

"We have one or two like that."

"Before he left here, Jones assigned two of his top people, a safecracker and a burglar, to take a long look at the files of Auguste de Morny, whom you know well, and Jose Manuel Hidalgo, whom you don't. Their object was Mexico, only material relating to Mexico." He reminded Bartlett who Hidalgo was and how he was connected to Morny. "Jones told his two men to take their time, to follow every lead to Mexico they could find and to report to me every week. On Hidalgo, they turned up nothing of value. His files held no surprises for us. I looked at a few of his papers but had them put back."

The little major sounded competent, Bartlett acknowledged, once he hit his stride. "Morny, as you can imagine, is a much harder case. He has so many enemies that he leaves almost no tracks – paper tracks, that is – and those he leaves are scattered around Paris and the Auvergne. Well tucked away."

"In his houses? His offices?"

"Both, and, as we eventually learned, in his servants' rooms." He pushed himself up and twirled the knobs on a wall safe. He placed a leather folder on his desk and opened it with an air of drama. "This," he announced, "was found in the safe of his valet, Henri. The safe, a large one, is behind a kitchen cupboard and hadn't been opened for months. You will agree that a valet's kitchen isn't the first place one expects to find a heavy safe."

He spread two identical parchment-like documents on his desk. "These we think are interesting. Here are the translations." Two more papers appeared beside them.

Bartlett picked up one document and its translation. He read slowly, then faster. He compared the second translation to the first. Then he sat back and pulled at his chin. "Are they genuine?" he asked.

"The paper and ink and the engraving are original, high quality work, according to our best forger. They are not copies, we're sure of that," Preston grinned. "Whether they are what they purport to be is another matter."

"Why would the valet keep forgeries in a safe?" asked Bartlett vaguely.

"Why, indeed? If he knew they're forgeries."

"Ah." Bartlett calculated how much to tell his host. Everything, he decided. "If they're genuine – *if*, I say – do you understand their significance?"

"I can guess at it."

Bartlett explained.

"Good Lord," reflected Preston. "There have been rumors about their relationship. But then Paris would have far too few rumors if it weren't for the imperial family."

*   *   *

When Bartlett arrived at the Preston's tall house that evening, Katherine was cornered on a sofa in the drawing room by the ebullient Priscilla Preston describing the schedule she had planned for the next day. "Notre Dame and Sainte Chappelle, of course. Then the new Louvre, then a ride along the left bank to a delightful restaurant we know right on the Seine. Oh, you'll just love it, Lady Carra."

Slight and dark, Mrs. Preston was a Peabody from Boston and the money in a marriage in which her husband was the brains. She was thrilled when he was assigned to Paris and had been thrilled ever since. The prospect of a day or two revisiting her favorite Paris landmarks with a titled stranger to the city was intoxicating and she was going to make the most of it.

Katherine looked a bit stunned, but game. Her trip from London was trouble-free, she told Bartlett primly, she was right not to bring Milly, the porters were so helpful and Mrs. Preston made her feel right at home in this beautiful city.

"This torn-up city, I'm afraid," Preston lamented. "You've seen that Paris is one huge construction project, Lady Carra. It's all the work of this Baron Haussmann, who seems determined to raze every other old building to make room for his new boulevards. Which, you'll be interested to know, Bartlett, are designed to make it easier to move troops around the city."

"I've heard that," said Bartlett. "The French royalty have always been terrified of the Paris mob."

"With good reason," Preston agreed. "Ah, here we are," as the butler bore in the champagne and glasses. "You have to imagine that it's 1776, Lady Carra, and that you're a colonist. First, we'll wish confusion to King George, and then long life to General Washington and then *Sante* to our gallant French allies."

These formalities over, the conversation turned again to the sights that Katherine must be sure to see. Bartlett waited through dinner for an opportunity to insinuate himself into her plans but it never came. He had to be content with the assurance that Preston had booked them on the same train to Clermont and into the same inn there.

Over cigars after the ladies left them, Preston asked, "Have you thought any more about those documents?"

"Of nothing else, and I still don't know how best to handle them. Maybe I'll learn something from Henri tomorrow."

Preston handed him a slip of paper. "There's his address, in the northern end of the city. About eight, tomorrow morning, in civilian dress. Your hotel will find you a cab."

Bartlett was slowly losing the feeling that he was engaged in something illicit. They discussed the progress of the war, so far away that it lacked reality for them, stubbed out their cigars and moved back to the drawing room.

*   *   *

Henri's little white house stood at the top of a narrow street in Montmartre, overlooking the tiled roofs of the houses that sloped down towards the center of Paris. He and his beloved Clemence, who worked at the Tuileries for the imperial family, were seldom there together for long, and every square meter was precious to them.

"A thousand apologies for your long trip up here, Major," said Henri as Bartlett stooped and entered. They clasped hands in a friendship that had grown over the months on *Isabella* and in Veracruz.

"You wrote that it was important, Henri, so I had to see you." He took the offered chair in the tiny living room. "Thanks. Now, what's it all about?"

He spoke in slow English in the knowledge that Henri could understand most of it. In turn, Henri spoke in slow French, hoping that Bartlett would get some of it.

"It is about Monsieur, Major. He must be stopped. I must stop him and you are the only one who can help me. You understand?"

Bartlett nodded. "Stopped, you say? From what? Why? How?"

Henri held up a hand. "Monsieur desires to be King of Mexico, and more. He goes back to Mexico with a new army, but not to win it for Maximilian. No, he goes back to win it for himself."

"How do you know this?"

"Hah! How do I know everything about Monsieur? I am his valet, am I not? You have seen me, always at his side. I see everything. He tells me everything."

"Does the Emperor know this?" Bartlett saw how foolish this was before he finished it.

Henri looked at him doubtfully. "But no, of course. Monsieur tricked Le Moustache to order him back to Mexico. He thinks my master goes to win Mexico and hold it for the young fool Maximilian."

Bartlett didn't respond so Henri went on. "Monsieur wants to be ruler of a big country, to have his own country to pass on to his sons. He wants to show his brother that he is the better man."

Even Bartlett's limited grasp of geopolitics perceived that a Mexico with Morny as ruler would be a far greater threat to the Union than a Mexico with the puppet Maximilian at its head. Henri's next statement confirmed this.

"A big country, Major, bigger than Mexico. He meets each day with Mr. Stone, who speaks for the American Southerns. And with Mr. Slidell, who speaks for Mr. Jefferson Davis of Richmond. They make grand plans together."

"What plans?"

"Army plans. The Southerns will send soldiers – thousands and thousands of men – to Mexico when the new French army arrives at Veracruz. Together they will squeeze Juarez between them." He made as if to squeeze a lemon. "And together they will march down through Mexico and down to South America. To Brazil, maybe."

"Good God! You've heard all this?"

"Did I not say I hear everything? Hunh! Then together they will place Monsieur on the throne of his new empire, the Empire of Middle America." Henri tried to gauge his effect on Bartlett. "And by then Le Moustache can do nothing to stop it."

The effect was considerable. He had to get this news to Stoddard. No, he had to stop Morny. No, first he had to get more information. "Henri, why do you tell me this? Why do you want to stop the Count?"

"To save his life. If he goes back to Mexico he will die. It is certain. Six months, no more." He told Bartlett of Morny's diseased intestines and of Dr. Jolliffe and his lethal magic tablets. "If Monsieur stays here, with his wife, he will now be treated by a proper doctor. He has sworn it to Madame Sophie, and he is a man of his word." If he went to Mexico, he would die from either the disease or the tablets he would take with him.

"Your concern is commendable, Henri, as is your courage in telling me this."

"Courage? Pah! I have served this man from the age of ten, Major. Forty-five years. He has a young foreign wife, four young children and many enemies. What will happen to them if he dies soon?"

"I see."

"He is a great man, of great accomplishments, who has served his country well for many years. He should live out his life in peace with his family. I must make sure that he can." Henri's eyes were wet and Bartlett himself was moved.

"I agree." Bartlett gathered his thoughts. He must take care not to offend Henri. "I will help you if I can. My reasons are obvious. What do you suggest?"

Henri had given it much thought. The only man who could stop Morny's return to Mexico was the Emperor, but to reach him directly was impossible. The only route to Napoleon's ear that Henri knew was through the Mexican, Jose Manuel Hidalgo, and he explained why. Hidalgo would certainly object to Morny's replacing Maximilian. And Hidalgo, he continued, had known Robert Jones well and would receive Major Bartlett if he were asked.

"I'll get our minister to ask him. Today. As soon as I can get back."

"I must be included in the meeting."

"Of course. You're the star turn. Will you stay at home? I'll send a cab for you."

"Good. It must be today or tomorrow. Señor Hidalgo will not be at the celebrations in Clermont."

Bartlett left, figuratively shaking his head. If Henri knew what had been taken from his kitchen safe, he gave no sign of it. But that wasn't conclusive. Maybe he did know and had written to Bartlett as a direct result.

Did it matter? In all events, Morny had to be stopped. Not to save his life, as Henri intended, but to save Mexico from the French and the Confederates, and to protect the United States from a new, powerful and threatening neighbor to its south.

Minister Dayton acted fast. As soon as Preston and Bartlett told him of Morny's plan and what they needed, he wrote a fastidiously polite letter to Hidalgo, mentioning Commander Robert Jones, and sent it off by messenger.

Bartlett began to draft a report to Stoddard about Morny's plan, angrily confident that it would end all speculation in Washington about his loyalty. But when Drayton told him that the next post was scheduled five days ahead, he put the paper in his pocket. He would finish it and send it after he'd seen Morny himself. That would give it more authority.

Hidalgo answered within an hour. Any colleague of Commander Jones was welcome at any time, he wrote, but he was most welcome at twelve o'clock that morning. The ministry driver was dispatched to pick up Henri and carry him to the Hidalgo mansion, and Bartlett filled in the details for Preston, whose twinkly impassivity slipped when he took in the enormous scale of Morny's ambitions. Bartlett left him shaking his head as he studied the globe in his office.

Bartlett went into Hidalgo's study first, leaving Henri to gaze at the Toltec stone heads along the walls of the entrance chamber. Hidalgo was as Jones had described him, large, brown-bearded, brown-eyed and charming. He rose from behind a marquetry desk and extended a vast paw at Bartlett, who took it cautiously.

Hidalgo asked after Jones, whom he remembered fondly, he said, and expressed his pleasure that Jones was now at the helm of one of the Union's deadly new ironclads. "Those ships will win the war for you, I'm sure of it," he observed. "The French know it, too, if they have any sense, which is always an open question."

He knew that Bartlett and Jones had accompanied Morny to Mexico and pressed his guest about Lorencez's tactics at Puebla. "That tallies with what I've heard from the Emperor's ADC," he said at last. "Almonte had it disastrously wrong. He is back in Paris now, trying to blame Lorencez and everyone else, but as far as my Junta are concerned he is finished." He looked through the French windows into his garden for a moment, as though trying to erase Almonte from his memory, then he asked: "And how can I be of service to you, Major? You realize of course that your government supports the Indian Juarez, and that we intend to rid our country of him?"

"I know that, sir, but I have information that is important to your movement. It concerns the Count de Morny, and on this question we may find ourselves on the same side."

"Anything that concerns the Count will interest me. What is this information?"

Bartlett's memory was precise and detailed. He told Hidalgo what Henri had told him that morning, almost word for word. Hidalgo did not comment until he finished.

"So this valet, Henri, tells you his master's supreme secret, his supreme ambition, in order to prolong his life. And you believe him?"

"Yes."

"And he begged you to tell all this to me, so that I will tell all to the Emperor and he will forbid Morny to return to Mexico?"

"Yes."

"The Emperor will forbid it because he wants to place Maximilian on the throne of Mexico? And, because he knows that Morny, when ruler of his new empire, would never let Maximilian replace him and would soon rival even the Emperor himself?"

"Yes."

Hidalgo seemed to be miles away in thought. "What you tell me is logical. It makes sense, the combination of Morny and your rebellious southern states. Their agents here are intelligent and active." He traced the borders of the new empire on the globe behind his desk. "It is well known that Jefferson Davis and his friends have for many years looked for a way to expand to the south. The timing is favorable for them. They now have an army. They may well be confident that an alliance with Morny and his French army will achieve their result."

Bartlett found himself holding his breath.

"That much is clear." Hidalgo said. "It is Henri's motive that I do not yet accept. I will talk to him. Bring him in, please."

His charm put Henri at ease within minutes, and his familiarity with the fraudulent Dr. Jolliffe helped him to understand when Henri explained his alarm about his master's health. Hidalgo sympathized. "I did not know that the Count is so ill; he hides it well. This Irish mountebank is a dangerous man, and you are correct, my friend, to fear that his pills will kill the Count."

Hidalgo was trying his best to hide his joy. "I believe you. I'll do it," he said at last. "I would be derelict in my duty to Their Majesties if I did not warn them of what you tell me." He looked at the clock on his desk. "This afternoon. I see the Empress at six o'clock, to talk of old times. His Majesty will not be far away."

Bartlett and Henri left after Hidalgo promised to send word to Bartlett's hotel that evening. "My note will be carefully worded, but you will understand it. Goodbye, Major, and goodbye to you, noble Henri. It is a fine thing you are doing."

Bartlett and Henri never imagined that Hidalgo dropped to his knees at once and said an intense prayer of thanks for their visit. They had made the Mexican a supremely lucky man. Weeks earlier, as soon as he had learned of the debacle at Puebla and the disgrace of Almonte, he raced to Maximilian's villa on the Adriatic and offered himself as Almonte's replacement. The compliant Archduke was soon persuaded to name Hidalgo as his sole representative before the Mexican people. This was the equivalent of naming him as his regent, to rule in Mexico after Juarez was deposed and until Maximilian crossed the sea and claimed his crown. It was a position of power for which every dedicated Mexican exile would cheerfully strangle his wife, mother and mistress.

And now Morny's valet and an unknown American officer had, by divine chance, warned him of a plot by Morny, the one man who could possibly displace Maximilian and thereby displace his regent, Jose Manuel Hidalgo. He had unlimited respect for Morny's talent and his influence over his half-brother. Once in power in Mexico, Morny would never be removed by Napoleon. That was a given. He, Hidalgo, had to make certain that Morny never gained power, that he never even went back to Mexico. He would make certain that afternoon. Eugenie would be his instrument. He, not the Count de Morny, would rule in Mexico.

After a fervent handshake with Henri and a promise to report to him in Clermont, Bartlett told the ministry coachman to take the valet home while he headed for the ministry in a hansom. He was anxious to tell Preston about Hidalgo's offer to intervene with Napoleon. Because of the extensive roadworks in that section of the city, the return trip took far longer than he expected and it was three o'clock before he knocked on Preston's office door.

The major was a good listener. He had the right questions ready, and by the time Bartlett finished his story he was fully in the picture. "I expect Hidalgo will protect his backside and present Henri's tale to Eugenie as a threat that needs to be verified," he remarked. "The only man who can verify it is Morny himself, so he needs to be asked a direct question. What if he lies?"

"He wouldn't. He would say that he's been working up this scheme with the Confederates and intended, when the time was right, to present it to Napoleon as an alternative to Maximilian."

"Quick thinking, Charles."

"Wasn't it? You can bet that Morny would be even quicker. So we need a fallback plan."

"We have one: the documents in my safe."

"Blackmail, you mean."

"What else?" Preston looked pleased with himself. "I called in my number one forger today. He swears on his son's life that they're genuine." Seeing the alarm on Bartlett's face, he added, "No, he didn't see the names. I made sure of that."

An hour later they decided that they still didn't need to decide what to do with the documents. There was plenty of time and in any case they had to wait until they knew the results of Hidalgo's intervention with Napoleon.

As Bartlett reached for his hat, Preston said, "By the way, Priscilla has reported in. She and Lady Carra are exhausted from their tour and would like a quiet night at home. Will you forgive them if they decline your invitation to dinner tonight?"

"Damn," said Bartlett. "Do I have a choice?"

"Of course not."

Hidalgo's note, delivered with a flourish in Bartlett's hotel dining room, read:

> "Interviewed by both IM's. Positive reception, I believe.
> Further talk tomorrow. Come see me on eighth.
> H."

Chapter 42

Bartlett and Katherine, dressed in their best, leaned over the balcony of their hotel and watched the crowds gather in the Place du Jaude. It seemed that every sentient being in the Puy de Dome district had converged on the ancient market town of Clermont-Ferrand for the big day. The biggest day for hundreds of years, in fact; the last time a French crowned head had deigned to visit the Auvergne was in the sixteenth century.

The trip from Paris in a first class rail car the day before was tolerable, given the heat, noise and engine soot. Katherine chattered away at an impressive rate about her tours of the Paris sights. Bartlett had seen almost nothing of Paris and slightly resented her endless descriptions of pictures and cathedrals. If she's like this after two days, he grumbled to himself, what will she be like after a week? For Priscilla Preston was so taken by Katherine that she insisted her guest spend another week with her after Clermont. Katherine accepted for two more days, but Bartlett had no doubt that they would extend to a full week.

Their hotel in Clermont was an old coaching inn that had grown by haphazard accretion over the centuries. Their bedrooms were small and, by Bartlett's instructions to Preston, as far apart as the architecture permitted. Katherine acknowledged his thoughtfulness with a lift of her eyebrows and an enigmatic smile. For dinner, the owner admitted that his chef was already too drunk to cook, so they ventured across the square to a bistro owned by his brother. Later they agreed they were unlucky that his cook was still sober.

They chatted with each other easily now. Paris gave them much to talk about, and Bartlett's time in Mexico had stiffened his self-confidence and relaxed his tongue. Even the occasional silence was comfortable. Katherine appeared to have forgotten that terrible scene in the winter when he had come close to accusing her of seducing him for her own purposes.

The crowds swelled, the sun rose in a cloudless sky and the white dust rose to their balcony. The Place du Jaude was transformed by banners, bunting and merchants' booths selling cold drinks, photographs, biscuits, chocolates and everything else. Before the prefecture a covered grandstand, festooned with colored streamers, had been erected with a raised platform in front of the dignitaries.

And from all over the people came in their thick black suits and dresses, the squat, broad-shouldered men and women of the region, all united by their affection and respect for Morny and all ready to dispute on any other subject. They were drinking his wine and the disputes tended to be noisy.

One group below the balcony were quarrelling with gusto on the main topic of the day: what title would their new Duke assume?

"He will be the Duc de Nades, beyond any doubt," shouted one, referring to the village of Morny's château.

"You know nothing," countered another, "he will keep his own name as the Duc de Morny."

"That is not even his name, brother," snorted a third. "His name is – "

"It's too obvious, you fools," cried the youngest, "it must be Clermont, the Duc de Clermont. What else?"

"His name is – "

The cathedral bells exploded into song, cannon thundered and the imperial train rolled into the station. The escort composed of the Cent Gardes from Paris, a detachment of local hussars and the town brass band, thirty strong, formed up. The procession struck out from the station for the Place. It was followed by representatives of the provincial trade associations and then, resplendent in the state carriage, the Emperor and his Empress, who waved languidly to the people in the stifling heat. Bartlett and Katherine rushed downstairs and across the Place to take their assigned seats in the grandstand.

There, Katherine looked around with intense interest. "I'm trying to calculate just where we – you, I should say – rank among the Count's guests," she observed. "Assuming that the reddest faces belong to the local notables and the laciest hats to the Parisian visitors, I'd say we're about midway between them."

"You mean that we're the salt of the earth but still quite grand."

"Exactly."

The imperial couple reached the grandstand and, escorted by the Mayor, strolled to the center of the platform. Patriotic, banner-waving cheers from every throat. Then Morny came on, to an uproarious cheer. The brothers faced the crowd together. Napoleon, anxious to escape the heat, raised his hand for silence. This had no effect. He said something to Morny, who raised his hand to instant silence.

The Emperor spoke well, praising Morny for his public roles and for his work as the district Deputy. Then he talked of the Auvergne, of the schools, highways and railroads that he would bring forth in the region. In all, he spoke for an hour. He finished by announcing that, in tribute to the region, he was making the Comte de Morny the Duc de Morny, thus settling innumerable local arguments.

Not to be outdone by any Emperor, the Archbishop maundered on for an eternity. Then Morny rose. In a short speech graceful by even his standards, he thanked Napoleon for coming to the countryside, "where Bonapartism is not an opinion, but a religion." He thanked Eugenie, "who has made Grace mount the throne and who makes Charity descend from it each day." He accepted his dukedom in the name of the people of the Auvergne.

The red-faced notable next to Bartlett breathed onion over him as he commented, "You know, the Duke told his brother he would not accept this title unless he came to Clermont to award it." Bartlett nodded knowledgeably.

"Where is the Duke's wife?" Katherine wondered in English.

"At home," smiled her fashionable neighbor, fanning delicately. "The heat. A difficult birth."

It was over. The imperial party left the platform, the band worked its way into a march and Bartlett steered Katherine through the press and back to their hotel. She bought an iced drink and a box of chocolates on the way. "To eat on the balcony," she said. "I want to watch the people."

The crowd dispersed in good humor, as they had gathered in the morning. "They're fascinating to watch," Katherine commented, leaning a bit too far over the railing. "Do you know they're the first really large crowd I've ever seen? What a sheltered life I've led – or haven't led!" She turned to Bartlett, a broad smile on her face. "They all look the same, and they all look so different. It's amazing. You must take me to see many more crowds, Charles. I rely on you."

"Anywhere you say, Katherine. Hyde Park, Stepney, maybe even Ramsgate."

"Don't be facetious. I mean Vienna, Rome, Prague."

"Well, I hear Stepney is glorious this time of year, but I'll think about it." He pulled out his watch. "And now, Madame, it's time for you to rest before the Duke's ball. Henri promised to send a carriage for us at half past nine."

"Katherine, you look fabulous. Stunning." She took away Bartlett's breath as she came down the stairway of the inn. She wore a trailing dress of some flimsy stuff, pale grey with a hint of blue, of a severe, slender cut and a décolletage low enough to make Bartlett uneasy. The thin gold chain and cross were as always around her neck, but she wore jeweled earrings, bracelets and combs in her piled-up hair that he had not seen before. The effect was heart-stopping, and he told her so again.

"Thank you, Charles, so gallant." She fluttered her eyelashes extravagantly. "But tell me truly, is it too obvious that these are every single bit of jewelry I own? The impression I want to give is that these are just a few simple things that I wear to rustic affairs in the provinces."

"Whatever impression you want to give you are giving, believe me."

The carriage made its way through the outskirts of Clermont and took a winding road through the still sunlit countryside towards the château. At the top of a slight rise the coachman stopped and pointed behind them.

All the public buildings in Clermont were illuminated and a fiery cross rose above the unfinished cathedral. Around them, higher up on the mountainsides, bonfires had been lit in all directions. Some of them made the extinct volcano of Puy de Dome look as if it had come back to life.

Katherine clapped her hands. "Wonderful! All those fires! How imaginative!"

Morny had built his château at Nades in the fashionable style, a mixture of Renaissance and Gothic. Constructed of red and white brick, with battlements and castellated towers, the house stood on a terrace carved out of the native rock, with a fine view over a garden and then over the hardwood forests to the volcano.

Bartlett and Katherine walked up the torchlit outside stairway to the entrance doors at precisely ten o'clock. A few minutes later they were announced to the new Duke and a lovely young woman at his side who must be the Duchess. Fair haired, slender, with large dark eyes, she wore an emerald-studded tiara and a necklace with pearls and diamonds; Morny's only decoration was the Cross of the Legion of Honor.

"Bartlett!" he cried. "*Amigo mio*! How splendid. And Lady Carra. A great pleasure, my dear." He presented them to Sophie, who tried to look interested. "This is the American I've told you so much about, you know, from Mexico." Sophie smiled sweetly as Bartlett made his leg in approved West Point style. To Katherine Morny said, "The Major is always the most considerate guest, Lady Carra. I ask – no, I instruct - him to bring the most beautiful woman he knows and, as ever, he obliges." Sophie pulled at his sleeve, he made a resigned grimace and released Katherine's hand.

"Goodness!" breathed Katherine as they walked toward the main salon, where the guests were assembling. "I see what you meant, Charles. The charm is overwhelming."

A waiter presented flutes of champagne and they looked around the room. There were fewer people than Bartlett had expected, fewer than two hundred, he guessed. Many of the men were in uniform, each sporting every decoration he could find in his closet. Bartlett's four campaign medals that represented a total of two dead Indians betokened, he hoped, the manly modesty that most became an American officer in wartime.

Then they were shepherded into the ballroom, a vast, two-storied room that had been transformed into a garden. It was hung in green silk with golden trellises and ivy superimposed. Medallions painted in the style of the eighteenth century were hung at intervals around the room. There were blooming flowers everywhere one looked, and marble statues and bowers of green bushes were dotted about. Vast crystal chandeliers with hundreds of candles lit the room, while the illusion of space was magnified by a series of tall mirrors placed around the walls.

Bartlett heard the opening strains of the national anthem and Napoleon III and his Empress entered the room, arm in arm with Morny and his new duchess. The thirty-piece band played for all they were worth as the two brothers and their wives stood beaming at the assemblage.

Then the band played the traditional opening waltz. First Morny and Eugenie, then Napoleon and Sophie whirled away to the music and Katherine formed up to Bartlett.

"Can you manage a waltz in that uniform, Charles?"

"Watch me," said Bartlett with more assurance than he felt. One-two-three, one-two-three, he counted to himself. Right, and away they went.

They didn't get far around the room, but they contrived to stop at almost the same time as the music. "Wonderful, Charles," said Katherine, a bit out of breath. "Next time, though, please try to remember that we're on the same team."

"Oh yes?" said Bartlett, turning to accept two glasses of wine from an assiduous waiter. "I'll – "

But an elegant young officer with lots of white teeth had emerged from nowhere, smiled and bowed at Katherine and carried her off in the next waltz. Her merry laugh did nothing for his self-esteem as he took another drink.

"When you are with a woman that lovely, my friend," said a familiar voice at his elbow, "never turn your back on her." A heavy brown beard and a broad smile materialized at his side.

"Good evening, sir. That is good advice, but too late." He tried to mask his surprise; Henri had said Hidalgo was not invited.

"*Je regrette*," said the Mexican, "but I also have good news." They were standing on the edge of the dance floor, in front of a mirror, so he guided Bartlett by the elbow into a leafy bower. "This is more private. As one who spends too much time with the couple, I have grown sensitive to passing eyes and ears."

"I'm not surprised." Bartlett brushed aside a magnolia branch. "Your news, sir?"

"Ah, yes. I spoke first to the lady, and she called him in. Both reacted as I'd hoped." He paused, a reflective smile on his lips but not his eyes. "She is furious at our friend's betrayal, as she puts it, but above all because of his presumed lack of interest in the, ah, spiritual side of the matter."

"In the church?"

"Yes. She is certain that the other runner is much sounder in that respect." His gazed swung slowly around their corner of the room, as if checking for eavesdroppers or lip readers. "Himself is every bit as furious. He swore that he will put an immediate stop to our friend's adventure. In himself's case, it is the flagrant ambition of our friend to rival him that maddens him most."

"Are you sure he will stop him? The implications for my country are as obvious as they are enormous."

"Himself swore that he will stop him, and I am confident that he will. As I say, he is furious."

"I would guess himself must also feel foolish to have let our friend trick them into begging him to go back." Bartlett felt silly trading anonymous names with Hidalgo.

"You would be right. By the way, himself might want to question you or your source while he's here, which is why he brought me along at the last minute."

"Question me?" Bartlett squeaked.

"Don't be alarmed," Hidalgo grinned. "It probably won't happen. But he knows your name."

Hidalgo made a slight bow and began to move away. At the same time, Katherine's partner handed her back to Bartlett, flashed her a winning smile and melted into the crowd.

"Ah, Katherine, there you are," said Bartlett. "May I present Sr. Hidalgo? Lady Carra, sir."

Hidalgo bowed, recited a few formalized compliments and, when the band leapt into another waltz, offered her his arm and swept her away. She looked a bit dazed but managed to twiddle her fingers at Bartlett over her partner's shoulder.

He was too absorbed in Hidalgo's good news to take much notice of her for an instant, and she marked it. She gave him her best pout and smiled hard at Hidalgo's profile.

"It's Charles Bartlett, isn't it?" He couldn't at first place the central European accent as he looked to his left. A thin-faced, handsome man in sleek uniform and sleek hair held out his hand.

"Good Lord, Andre. What a pleasant surprise! How are you? What brings you here, of all places?" Andre Mariassy, a talkative Hungarian in the Austrian army, was one of the few attachés in London whom Bartlett could call a friend

"I'm well, thank you, and I'm here because I've been posted to Paris and our radiant new duchess is my cousin. She likes to have her family around her, you see." He shrugged heavily. "It's difficult. She loathes the imperial court, it's all too common for her. Amateurs not sure of their parts, she calls them. She prefers to sit with a few compatriots in her apartments, smoking hard and singing Russian songs with a balalaika."

"It's hard to feel sorry for Morny, but – "

"Oh, she's good for Morny – four children she's given him – and he's besotted with her. Or so she says. My Snow Fairy, he calls her."

"A handsome woman."

"Indeed. And you? This isn't your usual social milieu, I imagine?"

"It could be." And Bartlett gave a fanciful account of his association with Morny. Mariassy believed not a word but was too well bred to show it.

"Ah!" he breathed. "My word, Charles."

The music had stopped and Hidalgo and Katherine joined them. Hidalgo kissed Katherine's hand, bowed to Bartlett and Mariassy and said, "Do please let me know, Major, if you are in Paris next week."

Bartlett bowed and presented the openly admiring Mariassy to Katherine, who took a few deeper breaths. "Your Mexican friend is what I would call a determined dancer, Charles. My goodness, I need a rest."

"If you will forgive me, Madame," Mariassy said easily, "what you need is a" - a crash of opening chords from the band – "a mazurka!" He held out his hand, she took it and Bartlett was alone again.

And so it went. Every ten or fifteen minutes Bartlett was joined by a couple who wanted to meet their first American, or by a uniformed dandy who asked about his time in Mexico with Morny – "Auguste said I must ask you about Puebla" – or about the war in America. Katherine came back to him with her partners on about the same cycle, so they found some time to converse between introductions and good-byes.

"Are you enjoying yourself?" she would ask.

"Well -"

"That's nice. Oh, yes, I would love to."

As time went by, he noticed that more and more men followed Katherine around the floor with their eyes. And then that Morny himself was doing so. It was no surprise, therefore, that his host's arrival at his side coincided with the end of a polonaise and Katherine's return.

"Ah, Major, I hope you are enjoying yourself?"

"Well – "

"Excellent, excellent. And Lady Carra? Why, here she comes." Morny's sleepy eyes seemed more catlike than usual, Bartlett imagined, the moustache and pointed beard seemed fuller and the lips redder. I have a predatory duke on my hands, thought Bartlett, I never saw him like this in Mexico. Katherine needs my protection from this man.

Katherine needed no protection from anyone. She would be delighted, she told Morny, the next waltz. "What a marvelous dance, sir, what handsome people, what a kind host!" She was enthralled, she went on, with everything and she couldn't decide whom to thank first, her host or her escort.

"Always your escort, Lady Carra," smiled Morny. "It is he who takes you home."

There was a stir and the conversations around them fell away. Napoleon and Eugenie were making a tour of the room, stopping here and there for a few pleasantries with friends, and they were drawing closer. Napoleon loved to dance and was proficient despite his short legs. Eugenie at thirty-five was just beginning to show her age and that she colored her hair. They had warned Morny they would not stay for breakfast, so this was their last round of the night.

Morny approached the Emperor, into whose left ear Eugenie whispered fiercely. Napoleon paled, gathered himself and led Morny by the elbow to a gap in the crowd. Four hundred ears strained to hear what the brothers said to each other but only Bartlett and Hidalgo could guess with any accuracy.

Morny, looking distracted, nodded and returned to Katherine's side. "The Emperor wants to leave inconspicuously quite soon," he said, "and he demands my presence at noon tomorrow. What a nuisance."

"Surely no one can 'demand' the presence of a duke?" Katherine said.

"Oh anybody can, but only an Emperor tries. But not even an Emperor, Lady Carra, could keep me from the next dance with you. But before then, a quick word with Major Bartlett, if you will excuse us, Madame."

They stepped aside for a few minutes and then returned to her. The band struck up. It was the elder Strauss again, the rhapsodic strains of a waltz. Bartlett saw that Morny, his small feet flashing, was an accomplished dancer.

"Thank you so much, Madame," Morny smiled when it was over. To Bartlett he said, "At ten o'clock, then. My coach will fetch you." Another smile and bow at Katherine and he was away.

Bartlett turned to Katherine and gave her his most winning smile. "Well you have most definitely been the belle of the ball. The world and his wife have been lining up to dance with you." His smile turned to a mock pout. "I just feel a little put out that no-one seemed to want to dance with me."

"Why, Charles, I've been yearning to dance with you all evening. I thought you were occupied with important matters of state."

He held out his hand and led her to the dance floor. A sense of wellbeing overwhelmed him, not only because he was dancing with the prettiest girl in the building, but also because that pretty girl had called him Charles.

*   *   *

As he led Katherine out of the coach and into the inn, with her clutching, with both hands, his upper arm, his sense of wellbeing was slowly replaced by anticipation. He had grown used to her fickle behavior with him, but knew that tonight might be his best – possibly his only – opportunity to find out how she really felt about him. He was to return to London any time now and Katherine was talking seriously of staying on for a while in Paris with Priscilla Preston.

"Charles, I've had the most delightful evening. What a happy coincidence that we were both in France at the same time." She gave him a knowing look.

"A happy coincidence indeed. And quite lucky that we were both invited to yet another Ducal Coronation, or whatever these things are called. I go to so many, but I forget what they're called."

"Oh, I know. It's hard to keep track of them all."

"Do you think the salons of London society are currently swept with gossip about our impropriety? What with your chaperone nowhere to be seen."

They were let into the inn by the innkeeper's son, who had obviously been asleep seconds before, and slowly made their way up the stairs.

"I don't think so. As you say, it was merely a coincidence that we were both at the same ball. You kindly agreed to accompany me back to my inn, defending me against marauding highwaymen."

"That makes sense to me. Well, this is your room, so I'm glad that I've got you back un-marauded."

There followed a silence that seemed to last an eternity, as Katherine gazed up into his eyes with a sleepy fascination.

Those same eyes flickered for a split-second as they took in a glance at his mouth. She looked from side to side, up and down the corridors.

"Sometimes the idea of being marauded isn't so bad for a girl."

A step forward. "Really?"

"Sometimes -"

Another step. An arm around a waist. A door opened. A door closed.

Chapter 43

Bartlett was able to creep back to his room before the staff had arisen to save Katherine from too much chance of scandal reaching the salons of London. It was thus that he was able to make it appear like yet another happy coincidence that he too had chosen to take his breakfast at exactly nine in the morning.

"My, Major Bartlett, these crescent pastries really are delicious. Have you tried one?"

"They are even better with some butter and strawberry jam."

"Butter! They consist almost entirely of butter already. How can you add more?"

"I always say that you can't have too much of a good thing."

"Stop it, Charles," she whispered urgently, kicking him under the table, "you really are incorrigible."

Katherine sipped her coffee in silence as Bartlett tried to regain feeling in his leg.

"Anyway, I have been thinking and have decided that I need to taste more of the Paris's delights. Mrs. Preston has invited me to stay on with her in Paris and it's too good an opportunity to pass up."

"Oh." Bartlett felt deflated and let it show on his face.

"Do not misunderstand me, Major Bartlett. There are still many things for me in London, but I am hoping they will still be there when I get back in a few weeks."

His heart lifted, Bartlett stood up and gave Katherine his most military of West Point bows.

"You can rest assured that I and Union Army of the United State of America will make it our upmost priority to ensure that you have something worth coming back to London for. On that note, I must bid you au revoir, as I have an appointment with Le Duc."

*   *   *

Morny's face showed signs of wear and tear. It was pale, thinner and had a faint bluish cast to it. The effects of last night or of his illness, Bartlett thought as they shook hands.

Whatever it was, Morny seemed in his usual mode of contained ebullience and greeted his guest with warmth as he lead him to the library in a wing of the château. "Coffee, Major? A cigarette? No? To business, then, if we may. I see the Emperor at noon."

He would make Bartlett a proposition, he said, a challenging proposition. It involved Mexico and had grown from their work together in that country.

"As soon as I returned to Paris," he said, "I demanded of the Emperor that he immediately send twenty five thousand troops to Veracruz to reinforce our army and that he send a competent general to replace Lorencez. He agreed, with one condition: That I also return and take command of the expedition. I may tell you that there are personal reasons against my accepting, but I said I would consider it."

At about the same time, he was approached by two Commissioners of the Confederate states, men with whom he had often discussed possible French assistance to their rebellion. They proposed an alliance. The South would send thirty thousand troops across the Texas border into Mexico. Together with the reinforced French army in the south, they would squeeze Juarez like a lemon and spit him far out to sea.

Then both parties would establish a new nation, the Empire of Middle America, which would in short order annex the Central American states, Cuba, Jamaica and several other Caribbean islands. He, Morny, would be installed as the *pro tem* ruler of the new empire, to be replaced in time – "When I eventually choose to retire, that is" – by the candidate of the Southern partners.

This announcement excited Bartlett - Henri's story confirmed by Morny himself. Now he could finish his report to Stoddard and send it off. It might be faster to return to London and send it from there. He'd cable Morse about it. In any case, this would certainly quash any doubts about his loyalty. He'd try to lead Morny on, learn more of his plans.

"This is a most ambitious project," Morny said with satisfaction, "but we live in the age of ambitious projects. Look at the westward expansion of the Americans; look at Italy, at the German states. And I am convinced mine can succeed, for a perverse reason: The South will lose your war. And lose it very soon."

"Why is that?" Bartlett was intrigued. Candor from Morny was a new experience.

"Look at the map. The North controls the western rivers, most of the Mississippi and all of the Atlantic and Gulf coasts. It has won the last four or five major battles. The rebels have no industry, no foreign trade, no navy and no hope. No hope at all. It will all be over in three months time." He dismissed the Confederacy with a wave of the hand.

And as soon as they lost the war, the rulers of the Confederacy would look to the south, to Mexico, to recoup what they were about to lose – their land, their slaves, their way of life, their independence. Jefferson Davis's closest friends had long coveted Mexico. Now was their chance to take it. They had the veteran armed manpower and they would use it, no question. There would be no shortage of volunteers.

Morny's confidence was persuasive, Bartlett conceded. And there was more. "The amusing aspect of this scheme is that it makes your celebrated Monroe Doctrine irrelevant. Even assuming the United States wanted to intervene in a Mexico controlled by sixty thousand French and American soldiers, how could it attack its own citizens?" And by the time those citizens became citizens of the new nation, he added, it would be too late to intervene.

Finally, he said, there was the question of Mexico's foreign debts. The southerners were to grant the new empire enough dollars to pay off those debts, even though in law it would have no responsibility for them. In addition, they would lend it enough dollars to retire the so-called Jecker bonds at par.

"What are those?" asked Bartlett.

"Oh, some dollar bonds issued by the previous government to a Swiss bank."

There was a pause. Bartlett looked expectantly at Morny, who seemed to be working out his next step. Should he ask a question? No need. "Now, Major," Morny said at last, smoothing the moustache, "I wanted you to have the full picture against which to measure my proposition to you, which is this."

"My task in Mexico will be a most difficult one," he went on, a note of concern in his tone. "I will need at my side a senior military aide-de-camp on whom I can rely utterly." A little flourish with the right hand. "His responsibilities will be broad. He will liaise with the southern forces in the north. He will liaise with the Mexican conservative forces who, this time, *will* rally to our support under the leadership of Colonel Laffan. He will, if requested, give me military advice. He will carry out other important assignments as the need arises. I want that man to be you, Major."

Bartlett did not take in all the implications of this last statement, and he still thought he needed to keep Morny talking. "Sir, that's very flattering, but I'm a serving –"

Morny held up a hand. "I know, but do let me finish, please." He looked up and out the tall window. "It's a glorious day and after the exertions of last night we both need fresh air. Shall we inspect the gardens? I think my wife's wolf is locked away. We should be quite safe."

It was indeed a glorious day. As Bartlett fell into step with Morny, he thought of Katherine, who planned to sleep as long as humanly possible and after breakfast visit the Clermont historical museum, which he assured her was widely held to be unmissable. "That's if one is an Auvergnat peasant," she yawned as he left, "but I shall take a chance. Don't be late." They were booked on the four o'clock train to Paris.

"I want that man to be you," Morny repeated, "for good reasons." Bartlett's integrity was undoubted. His all-round ability – witness the deal he struck with General Doblado that saved the French troops from the fever; his, ah, escape from *Isabella*; his fighting journey to Puebla. He was an American who could work with the Southern commanders, despite their recent differences. He already knew Laffan, the language and something of the country. "To top off these impressive credentials, Major, you're unmarried and you speak some French." He stopped to admire a flowering tree of exotic colors. "Lovely, is it not?"

"Sir, I'm an officer in the army of the United States," said Bartlett stiffly. "We're at war with the same Southern politicians you're inviting me to help. You must see that what you suggest is impossible."

"As I once remarked in Mexico, you must learn to take the longer view. Your war will be over in three or four months, when the cold weather hits the ragged Southern troops in the field, or even sooner. You can then resign your commission, as thousands have honorably done already." He resumed his leisurely stroll. "You have fifteen years' service, I believe?"

"Fourteen."

"There you are. You have no impediment to resigning. Or, better still. Your orders for Mexico remain in effect, so you can properly go with me to Mexico on those orders, see how your war goes and then resign if you are convinced it is the right thing for you to do." He held out both arms in appeal.

I'll say nothing about my orders, Bartlett thought, I want to hear more. "Well, I suppose – "

"What are your prospects for advancement in London? Be honest with yourself. Or in America, in what is left of the war? Or indeed after the war? More long years in Kansas, or Florida? Pah!" He pointed a finger at Bartlett. "History teaches that the first casualty of victory is the winning army."

He's relentless, Bartlett thought, and, if I'm honest with myself, he's right. He's right about me, and if he's right about our war ending soon...

"Then, to be practical, there is the financial aspect." Morny *was* relentless, by God. "We would triple your present pay. More important, a country emerging from a war offers to those in command countless opportunities for large returns, most of which are quick and do not require any capital."

Bartlett was forced to think again of Katherine, of his need for money before he could even hope to marry her. Morny knew about her, of course, he must know how he felt and how poor he was. The man's a master. He'd hate to be on the – MY GOD! He'd lost his mind. What was he thinking of? Morny was not going to Mexico. He was not going anywhere. Henri and Hidalgo and he had seen to that, blast it. Or so

Hidalgo had said after he talked to the Emperor. Maybe the Mexican was wrong, though, or lying. He had to hear this out. It was tempting as hell, the ideal assignment for him. He now almost hoped Hidalgo was lying.

Henri came around a camellia bush and coughed meaningfully. He wouldn't look at Bartlett. Morny consulted the thinnest watch in France. "I must leave you for a while, my friend. The Emperor awaits me at the Prefecture." Bartlett would be served luncheon in the garden, in that shady corner over there, and his host would return as soon as he could. "Please think about what I've said. You're important to my plans."

Bartlett watched as two burly footmen prepared his table. Lunch consisted mainly of broiled fish, wine of the country and quantities of fresh fruit.

He was unable to think clearly, logically. There were too many variables, too many unknowns. Would the Emperor squash Morny's grand ambition today with a word? Or would Morny talk him around? What if he accepted the offer and Morny died in Mexico? What if... but there was no end to them. The only sensible conclusion was that he must wait for Morny's return. Meanwhile, he would close his eyes for a minute and think of Katherine.

After a night of exuberant carnality and paradise in a lumpy bed, he was no closer to understanding her. How she could be so womanly in bed and so elusive at other times. He would try to persuade her to pass another night in Clermont. Perhaps she would reveal more of herself. All he really knew now was that she was determined to spread her wings. For how long? Long enough for him to go to Mexico with Morny, make up his mind and return to London to resign?

Morny stalked around the corner of the house, a cold-eyed Morny, with Henri and a tray of coffee close behind. Henri still refused to look at Bartlett. Morny sat, Henri poured and Morny stared unblinking at Bartlett.

"I know everything," he said thinly. "Henri, you, Hidalgo – everything. The Emperor no longer begs me to return to Mexico. He *forbids* it." A long sip of the coffee. "He fears that I intend to establish an empire overseas to rival his own, and that I will leave it to my sons. To *my* sons, not his son."

His lip curled. "Why, Major?" he spat. "Why did you betray me? Henri did it to save my life, as he thought. That I understand, and that I forgive. But you?"

Bartlett had had enough time to reply with some control. "Sir, I did not betray you." He took a deep breath. "I did my plain duty as an officer of the army of the United States. Henri told me that you and the southern rebels intend to carve up Mexico and conquer all of Central America. The presence of a large rebel force in Mexico would be an undeniable, serious military threat to my country while it's at war with the Confederacy. *As an officer*, I am obliged to try my best to stop your plan. How could you expect me to act otherwise?"

Morny listened, his eyes intent. "I see. You choose your words with extreme care, Major," he replied. His tone softened. "All right. You probably acted correctly in the present circumstances – as an officer. I concede that much. But," he pressed his palms together before his face, "the circumstances, I again insist, will change."

He rose and traced a small circle in the grass for a minute. Then he went back to his seat. "I will ask you something. I ask you to assume for the moment that the American war ends in, let us say, ninety days. I am then ready to depart with my twenty-five thousand men, and I make the same offer to you." He paused. "How do you respond?"

"The war is over? Well. I can't be certain, but I would be inclined – strongly inclined - to accept your offer. Provided always that I could resign my commission with no stain whatever on my record."

"You can take that as a given," Morny allowed himself a cool little smile. Now he sat back, lit another cigarette and surveyed Bartlett with some confidence. Bartlett just managed to hold his air of relaxed interest.

"But I must ask you, sir. Your health?"

"Is not an issue. What Henri did not know is that I promised my wife that I will take with me to Mexico a physician who is a specialist in my condition. I will live for many years, I assure you."

"I see."

"*Eh bien*," Morny said at last. "You say you would be strongly inclined to accept. Fine. My offer stands. It will remain open until fifteen days before the reinforcements sail for Veracruz. If you accept it before then, conditionally, you will have a letter from me setting out the terms of our eventual agreement. You will accompany me to Mexico and have thirty days in which to decide finally.

He laughed curtly. "If you choose to reject it before then, you will have the courtesy to inform me at once. Understood?" Bartlett nodded. "Your hand on it, then." Morny had a strong grip. "We must hope, both of us, that your Generals Grant and Sherman meet with continued success."

Henri at last deigned to look at Bartlett, a sly glance accompanied by a long wink and a quick thumbs up.

"Sir," ventured Bartlett, "not to intrude in your private affairs, but isn't this discussion a trifle premature? You did say earlier that the Emperor forbids you to return."

"Quite right. I must attend to that straight away." Morny sounded grateful to be reminded of the matter which had put him in a cold fury only an hour before. It was a straightforward problem, he said, he had changed the Emperor's mind for him many times.

First, he needed to discredit Hidalgo's story, which meant to discredit Hidalgo himself. That was easy. Hidalgo had sold out to Maximilian and agreed in writing to act as his regent in Mexico. "I have a copy of their memorandum. It replicates the deal that the little Archduke signed with that fool Almonte." He smiled at Bartlett. "Don't look so surprised, my friend. Your Robert Jones is not alone in his employment of agents in Vienna."

"The Emperor will accept that memorandum as written proof of Hidalgo's reason to discredit me. He's never fully trusted the Mexican. The Empress will be harder to convince. She dotes on him. But I will succeed, of that there can be no doubt." Morny was becoming more animated every minute. He plainly enjoyed his plotting, and he laughed at Bartlett's incredulous look. "This, Major, is what is known as statesmanship."

But Their Majesties would still insist on hearing Henri and Bartlett, in person, deny that they had ever even talked to Hidalgo about Morny's return to Mexico.

Henri had undertaken to tell the royal couple just that, with touching indignation. Alas, Henri was his valet, Morny said, and might be suspected of lying to protect his master. Bartlett, on the other hand, was independent, the representative of a foreign power, and as such a reliable witness. All Bartlett had to do was confirm Henri's testimony when face to face with the imperial couple.

"They can be quite amiable," Morny said, "nothing for you to fear from them."

Bartlett listened to this monologue with growing horror, as it became evident that it would end with Morny's finger pointed straight at him. When in a tight spot, temporize.

"You want me to deny to them that I ever discussed your return to Mexico with Henri or with Hidalgo."

"Correct. I hoped I'd made myself clear."

It was Bartlett's turn to walk in circles on the grass. His instinctive reaction was to say no, but he forced himself to think. He must at last take the long view, he thought, he must look ahead, to his life after the war. Morny's offer was incredibly tempting, and at all costs he must not throw it away on nothing but instinct.

So *think*: If the war were over, and if he were a private citizen, he would plainly have no obligation to resist the establishment by Morny of his Central American Republic. He would, in fact, be quite free to take part in it alongside Morny. If the authorities in Washington then decided to invoke the Monroe Doctrine and throw the invaders out of Mexico, he could not, as a citizen, resist them, but he would be under no obligation to help them.

Try to think like a civilian, he told himself, because that's what you will be. As a civilian, there is no ethical or official bar to accepting Morny's offer, only your instinctive, personal bar. And how important can that be, measured against the opportunities he is holding out to you? Be sensible, for once in your life. Be sensible, for God's sake.

"I - I can't do it. I won't do it." It escaped before he could stop it.

"What are you saying? Of course you can. I'll arrange the interview. It will take ten minutes."

"I'm sorry, sir. I won't lie for you." It was so clear to him now.

"For me? For you, you mean. For your future. Have you forgotten all that?"

"Of course I haven't forgotten. I know what I'm saying and what it means for me. But I can't lie." He looked to Henri, hoping that the little valet would approve his stand, but Henri stared at him impassively. "It's not because I'm an officer, sir, it's because I just don't lie. Not in anything important, anyway, and this is damned important."

Morny said nothing for a minute or two. Then he jerked his head at Henri, who vanished in the direction of the stables.

Bartlett said, "I'm sorry, sir, but that's it."

Morny almost lost his temper. He stormed at Bartlett, promised him more money, cautioned him on the consequences of his refusal and at last subsided. "Very well, so be it." His face was ashen. "I shall try to convince the Emperor on the basis of Henri's testimony alone. I may very well succeed."

Bartlett shook with relief. "I'm truly sorry, sir. I can't wish you well yet because our war is not over, but, when it is, I will." He extended his hand. "Now, if your coachman can – "

"Sit down, Major Bartlett," Morny hissed. "I have changed my mind. You will go nowhere."

"I beg your pardon? I think we've finished. It's been most interesting, but -"

"Must I always need to repeat the obvious to you? You will not leave here."

"You'll kidnap me? Again?"

"Don't play the fool. Hidalgo told the Emperor who you are. When I take Henri to the Tuileries, Napoleon will want to talk to you as well. You will tell him what I instruct you to tell him." This was a new Morny, cold, determined, frightening. "Until then, you will stay here, in this house. You and Lady Carra."

"She has nothing to do with this. You know that."

"Nothing yet, but she will come to look for you, and she will report to your legation that you were last here with me."

"You're mad."

"Hardly. I've sent a carriage for her. She will be here in half an hour."

He means it, Bartlett thought, unless *I* change *my* mind. "How long will you keep us here?"

"Until you have talked to the Emperor and convinced him that Hidalgo is lying about me. Until then, Lady Carra will also be my guest, and her stay with me will not be - pleasant, I assure you." His face and expression showed no emotion at all. "You understand me."

That's plain enough, Bartlett said to himself. He means it. And this is the man who had hundreds of Parisians shot in the streets before breakfast.

He turned cold inside as he realized that, if Morny kept him prisoner, his absence would convince Stoddard that he was disloyal, that his prime loyalty lay to the Frenchman, Morny. Even if Morny released him after a time, he might never persuade them otherwise. He would almost certainly be cashiered, drummed out of the army in disgrace.

He had to get out of there. He had to keep Katherine away from Morny

Time to play his trump card. And it had damn well better be a trump card, or it was lights out.

"There is something you should know," he said. "In the safe of the American minister in Paris are two documents that you must hope never reach the Emperor." Bartlett pulled a folded bit of paper from his breast pocket and began to read in Spanish:

"We, the undersigned, Ministers of the General Treasury of the Mexican Republic, do make known: whereas the National Congress of the Republic of Mexico, did on 14 October 1850, issue a Decree for liquidating and adjusting definitively the Foreign Debt of the Republic; which Decree His Excellency the President of the Republic did sanction…"

"You lie," whispered Morny.

"In that safe lie two dollar bonds issued by the government of Mexico to the Jecker bank and endorsed to one H. Demorny. Two bonds that will destroy your reputation and your life."

"You lie."

"Each in the face amount of fifty thousand dollars, each signed by former President Miramon." Bartlett's voice trembled only a little. "Your partner Mr. Jecker took no chances."

"Impossible," Morny hissed.

"They were issued in July 1859 and mature in June 1865. The interest rate is eight per cent."

"All right," said Morny, barely audible, "enough." He rose from the table and looked out over the garden towards the old volcano. "You have the bonds. They mean nothing."

"These two are numbered 401 and 600. At fifty thousand dollars each and with at least six hundred bonds, that is at least thirty million dollars, the full amount of the bond issue. Of which two hundred bonds, worth ten million dollars, look like your share."

"Ridiculous. I'll – "

I'm betting you have all the rest of them – everybody's share – in a safe somewhere."

"Prove it."

"Oh, the Jecker bonds are well known to our Paris ministry. They are confident Mr. Jecker can be found and... induced to tell the Emperor who he transferred his bonds to. Especially if the Empress is informed how important his testimony is."

"All right. Enough." Morny kept his head high as he glared at Bartlett, but inside he was crushed. "What now?"

"Now they stay tucked up in the minister's safe and your carriage takes Lady Carra and me to the station. We can still make our train."

"I can keep you here. You saw how the local people adore me. *They* will not betray me. No one else will know you are here."

"The Minister in Paris will see that I'm not *there*. He is instructed precisely what to do in that case." Bartlett began to believe for the first time that he and Katherine might yet escape. "He'll allow you twelve hours to release us or he will personally deliver one of the bonds into the hands of the Empress. I hear she reads Spanish well. Can you doubt that she will use them to destroy you with the Emperor?" He took a very deep breath. "I suspect he won't be pleased to learn that your purpose in returning to Mexico is not only to set up your own empire but to steal ten million dollars."

Morny swung around to face Bartlett. He looked ten years older and worn out. "Imbecile! You have no idea what you're doing! What you are throwing away!"

"I know what I'm doing. I hate to do it, but I must. It's a matter of honor."

"'Honor'? You? Pah!"

They sat in silence in the garden for ten minutes. Then Morny said, "So it is over." A long, sorrowing sigh. "History will not commend you, Major Charles Bartlett."

"My superiors will. And history need never know."

Another silence, and Bartlett asked, "Who is H. Demorny?"

"Henri, of course. He is my brother, my foster brother."

"Ah."

"Those two bonds are – were – his pension. I shall have to make other arrangements."

Chapter 44

"What a charming man," Katherine said as they rode down the drive. "Charming. But I'm sorry not to have seen the duchess to thank her again for that marvelous ball."

"She was playing with her animals, I believe," said Bartlett in a muted voice.

"Are you all right, Charles? You sound depressed."

"Do I? No, I'm fine."

The last two hours with Morny were already taking on an airy, dreamlike quality, as does any totally new and unexpected experience. Had he really turned down a magnificent career opportunity for a moment of ethical satisfaction? He had, indeed, and he sensed he would regret it all his life.

But he still had a life, one that had hung in the balance a few minutes earlier.

"What did he mean, though, when he said good-bye? He said something about – "

"He said, 'Remember, Major, that the Mexicans invited me first, before the Austrian.'" Bartlett shrugged. "Oh, it's just the last line of a private joke."

*   *   *

Bartlett huddled with the Minister and Major Preston the next morning. "I don't want to keep those bonds here," Dayton said. "Morny can hire the same safe cracker we used, and he'll know where to look. I'll send them to Washington as soon as I can."

"It's quite satisfying, but nevertheless strange," commented Preston, "to know that we have the most powerful man in France by his testicles."

"Which is more or less where he had me," said Bartlett. He finished his report to Stoddard and sealed its envelope himself. That should put an end to any doubts about my loyalty, he thought. My own uncle. I wonder if I'll ever get an apology from him.

Then, true to his word to Katherine, he went back to London on the overnight steamer without her.

Part 2

"Aficionados [of the Civil War]… are strangely ignorant about what happened in Europe or on the high seas. Yet it was there that the fate of the Confederacy was determined. Not Antietam or Gettysburg or Vicksburg decided the destiny of the United States as a nation. The decision was made in the chancelleries of Europe, and, except for a few major battles, the outcome was influenced more by what happened on the sea than on the land."

Philip Van Doren Stern
Introduction to: *The Secret Service of the Confederate States in Europe*

Chapter 45

After all the excitement and glamour in Clermont-Ferrand and Paris, Bartlett felt his life crashing back to normality as he entered the consulate on a typically overcast Monday. It had been a struggle to motivate himself out of bed that morning and the demeanor in the office was not helping. It was not that there was anything particularly depressing about the office – it was just so mundane. Clerks scribbling away in their ledgers, office boys scuttling around, endless meetings about meetings – were things ever going to change?

To think, he could have been aide de camp to the future Emperor of Mexico and Beyond. He could be commanding armies and accumulating embarrassing riches. Instead, he was struggling over the correct diplomatic language for his report.

It was for this reason that he was delighted when Freeman Morse stopped by his desk at noon and suggested they have a drink at a little hotel nearby. "We have a problem you should know about right away, Major."

"I'd be delighted," Bartlett accepted. He began to gather his papers. "If you want to go ahead, I'll be a few more minutes here."

Morse ordered two whisky punches from the lone waiter. The hotel catered to families up in London from the country so on Mondays it was quiet. The small dark lobby was deserted except for the waiter and a tweedy mother and son who had missed their train home and now argued viciously what to do next.

Bartlett began to relax and exchanged the usual civilities with Morse, who was a pleasant enough companion in his brisk way. He confirmed Bartlett's impressions of their co-workers; in his view no more could be expected from amateurs.

"Careful what you say, Morse, I'd still consider myself an amateur," Bartlett said, "but I hope to grow into my job quickly." He sipped his drink. "You mentioned a problem?"

Morse quickly brought Bartlett up to speed on the growing menace that was James Dunwoody Bulloch. Although the Union had not picked up on his presence in Britain in time to intercept his sale of cotton or his acquisition of saltpeter, they were very much aware of him now. He was now doggedly pursuing his primary objective, which was to buy naval ships for the Confederate war effort.

"How does he do it?" Bartlett asked. "The neutrality law must prohibit him from building these ships."

"He's sharp as a snake and he has a lawyer who's even sharper," replied Morse. "You see, the Foreign Enlistment Act makes it an offence to arm or equip or fit out a ship in Britain for a combatant, that is, to equip it for war. It is not an offence to *build* one for a combatant. So when his ships leave Liverpool they'll leave under a British flag, with a British master and crew and without a single item of military equipment on board – no guns, no powder, not even a musket or signal gun."

"How do you know?"

"Know? Our people have crawled all over that first ship, the *Oreto*, since they began building her." His pause was meaningful.

"A clever bastard. But how does he get away with this? We must have protested; the English must realize that he's breaking their laws?"

"We protest, all right. Adams screams at Lord Russell every week, in person and on paper, and all he gets back is a lofty silence." He drained his glass and checked his watch. "Must go. But consider this: Bulloch's work here suits England down to the ground. It means more work in the yards. And it will help to weaken our blockade and let some cotton get through. And it will cripple our shipping fleet, and we're England's strongest competition."

*　　　　*　　　　*

Flanagan came skipping into the legation on Monday, full of news of his weekend in Liverpool with his Uncle Patrick Burnett and Mrs. Patrick. "Ah, it's good to have some family in England, sir," he had said to Bartlett. "I can visit them anytime, he told me. A fine man, he is. And such a fine house."

Patrick Burnett had grown rich from his import business, Flanagan reported. Mostly jute from India, with occasional cargoes of timber and hides from Hong Kong. He now owned four ships outright and commanded enough credit to charter others whenever he spotted an opportunity. But what had excited Flanagan was his offer to get Flanagan and Bartlett aboard the *Oreto*. He was confident that one of his captains could arrange it. He was anti-slavery and anti-English, and he wanted to help his nephew Kevin in the war he said was coming between the North and England.

"Why's he so sure that war will come?" Bartlett had asked.

"Because he's in Liverpool and Liverpool's in the middle of the cotton trade, isn't it? He can see the results of our blockade around there. Mills are closing right and left. People are starving. Sooner or later, he says, Palmerston will have to break the blockade, and you know what that'll mean."

"Fine. We'll go up there. You'd fancy another trip to that fine house, I expect? Cable him that we'd like to call on him, let me see, Friday morning. And ask him to book two rooms for us near his office for Thursday night. Some place quiet; no drunken sailors."

Flanagan coasted off to the telegraph desk and Bartlett entered Adams' office to brief him on the few developments in the war at home. When he came out, he saw that Morse was pointing at the small conference room, so he walked across the main office. The consul spoke briefly to Flanagan and closed the door behind them. "I heard what young Flanagan said about his uncle. I agree that it's a fine idea to get a good look at the *Oreto*. Adams is going to make a full dress protest to Russell about Bulloch's work. He has legal opinions, piles of sworn affidavits, the lot, but what he doesn't have is direct evidence from any of his own staff." He spread his arms. "I've offered to go up there, but he thinks I know nothing about ships. Which I don't."

"And I do?"

"More than I do, for sure. The point is that he wants credible direct testimony from some one he can blame – and sack – if he's wrong."

"I see. Fair enough." Bartlett scratched his head, trying to clear his thoughts. "This *Oreto*. What's her status now?"

"She was launched at Lairds over two months ago and moved to a graving dock where her boilers and engines were installed," Morse recited flatly. "She made her first trial run last month, and I'm told she'll be ready for commissioning in a few weeks' time."

"Good Lord! As soon as that?"

"Better get your skates on. I've told Flanagan not to cable his uncle just yet."

"Thanks." Bartlett was suddenly abstracted. "Ah, Freeman, maybe you should see this. Delivered to my rooms last night, by hand." He pushed a sheet of heavy writing paper across the desk.

> "My dear Charles,
> In the spirit of our continuing partnership, I report that I am reliably told that the English have made great strides with their Palliser armor-piercing round. News of your Taurus shell (You see? No secrets) evidently made an impact and Palliser now rides high, indeed, with all facilities at the Woolwich grounds at his service. At the latest proofs, ten days ago, reliability of his heaviest sample was ninety five per cent.
> More proofs scheduled next month. Do try to obtain their results. And don't forget your
> Uncle Andre"

Morse looked up at Bartlett and shrugged. "Who's this?"

Bartlett explained. Andre Mariassy was the Austrian military attaché in London. Very late one night, just after pledging eternal friendship, they had also pledged eternal solidarity in their espionage into England's naval ordnance programs. "Here he's saying that the English will soon have their own wonder weapon, a rifled armor-piercing explosive shell. You can see the implications of that."

"I can."

"Why didn't we know about this?"

"Well, our best man at Woolwich, Wigan the watchman, is locked up and Adams has cracked down hard on our networks. Cut off their money, except for our agents in Liverpool."

"Because of Bulloch's ships. Damn! This letter is very bad news. I'll report it to Stoddard today."

"And to Adams?"

"Ah - no." Bartlett's mind was divided. "He'll demand proof, won't he, and we don't have it yet. And I'd have to tell him all about our Taurus shell and God knows what else." He looked at Morse full on. "Don't you agree?"

"I suppose so. But this news from your Hungarian friend makes your trip up north more urgent."

"I'll leave tomorrow. I say, Flanagan," he called, "about that cable!"

Chapter 46

Wednesday was one of those impossibly clear days that England sees perhaps five times a year. At Euston Station, Bartlett and Flanagan found two seats in an empty first-class compartment and settled back.

"I should know more about your famous Uncle Patrick, Flanagan," Bartlett said after they cleared London, "if I'm going to accept his help."

"He's my mother's oldest brother, Major," Flanagan replied. "He and my father and mother emigrated to Liverpool in '48, after the rising, taking me with them, thank the Lord. They had to leave Ireland in a hurry. The police were about to find out that they were mixed up in the rising."

"What was that?"

"The grand insurrection of Young Ireland in 1848?" Flanagan snorted derisively. "The greatest farce in our history, it was. A genuine comic opera, Irish style. The so-called leaders went from town to town, trying to raise the people to attack the English, but most people left the rallies when they saw there was no food being handed out." He raised his arms in mock despair. "In the end, they assembled about twenty rifles, a few pikes and thirty or forty men ready to throw stones. Can you imagine it? Pikes and stones against the Fusiliers?"

"I suppose the army cut them down?"

"No fear." Flanagan suppressed his giggle. "All the desperadoes surrendered to a couple of Irish coppers in the Widow McCormack's cabbage patch. Saved them from dying of shame, I expect." His face tightened as he studied the scenery through the window. "Pa and Uncle Patrick weren't in the cabbage patch, you understand. They'd cut out the day before, when they saw how things were going. But somebody gave their names to the police so they had to do a runner."

"Sounds as if they were lucky."

"We all were. We hid in a ditch outside Cork for a week before we found a ship to Liverpool. I'll never forget it." He shuddered. "We were to go on to Boston, all of us, but the money ran out and my uncle had to stay in Liverpool. He stayed lucky, too, I guess. He's made a lot of money. You'll see."

*   *   *

Patrick Xavier Burnett was as tall and thin as his nephew, but the resemblance ended there. In his early fifties, Bartlett guessed, with pale ginger hair and moustache. His chin and forehead both receded so sharply that they seemed to be racing each other to the back of his head, around his enormous ears. Flanagan's mother can't possibly look like this brother of hers, Bartlett sniggered, or he would never have been conceived.

Burnett received them in a large, dark room crowded with large, dark furniture. Bartlett had the impression of lace, feathers and dried flowers everywhere. Their host was seated in a red plush armchair with one bandaged foot perched high on a matching stool. He greeted them cordially enough, but it was plain that his gout did nothing for his disposition. He made a few routine enquiries about their journey and turned to the subject of their visit.

"Kevin has told me of your concern for Captain Bulloch's work up here, Major, and I have told him that I may be able to help. It will please me if we can."

He leaned forward as if to pat Flanagan on his shoulder but winced and sat back again. "Madeira, gentlemen. It's the damned Madeira that's done this to me. Would you credit it? I've treated that toe with affection and respect all my life, and now it's turned on me."

Bartlett made sympathetic noises and started to respond but decided it would be wiser to hear Burnett out. Maybe I'm learning to listen, he thought.

One of Burnett's ships was in dry dock, he said, and her captain, Francis O'Hara, was in Liverpool, working with Bartlett's enemies. He grinned at his guest's surprise and explained that O'Hara had applied for the command of the *Oreto*, built by John Laird & Sons. Everyone in Liverpool knew that the real owner of the ship was Captain Bulloch, and everyone knew that he had built her on behalf of the Confederate Navy.

"So everyone knows that her first captain's job will last just as long as it takes to stick her cannons in her on some island somewhere. But that suits a few of the candidates, and O'Hara's one of 'em. His wife's pregnant with their first."

"Can he get us on board her?" Flanagan asked before he thought.

Half of Liverpool, Burnett said, and every foreign agent in the city had inspected the vessel at some stage of her construction. He could, in fact, lend Bartlett a report made for him by one of his own men after the *Oreto* was launched. It described her interior design in some detail but was of limited use otherwise. "Except to prove that he actually got aboard her."

"As to O'Hara," he went on, "I expect he will. Unless it would hurt his chances of getting that job, I think he'll be willing to get you aboard somehow." He chewed a finger. "I'll send word to you at your hotel tomorrow."

Burnett was as good as his word. At noon the next day, Bartlett and Flanagan, the former also in a civilian suit, met Captain O'Hara at the entrance to the vast shipyard of John Laird & Sons at Birkenhead, upriver and on the opposite bank from the center of Liverpool. O'Hara, short and broad, looked little older than Flanagan.

A Friendly Little War

Bartlett asked after the health and parturient schedule of Mrs. O'Hara and then insisted that they call off the visit if it might prejudice her husband's chances of being named master of the *Oreto*.

"Ah, don't you worry, Major," the Irishman grinned. "Anything to help Mr. Burnett. Besides, it'll only prejudice me if they rumble you, and if they do that skipper's job will be the least of my worries."

Bartlett was taken aback. "But..."

"Don't worry, I said. I've told the foreman that you're my Flanagan cousins from Waterford, both of you joiners who've always wanted to see a ship under construction. He's a County Kerry man himself, so he won't mind as long as you don't get in the way."

"Will Captain Bulloch be here?" asked Flanagan.

"No, he's away. Besides, he usually comes in the evening, when he says all the spies have gone home to have their tea."

The grace and elegance of *Oreto's* lines as she lay in the Laird dock were striking even to a landsman like Bartlett. They walked beside her from the stern to the bow, dodging the hurrying workers, O'Hara making quiet comments as they moved along.

"Two hundred twenty feet long, a beam of thirty two feet, a bit over a thousand tons." Then, "Bark rigged, as you can see: fore and main masts almost ninety feet, long lower masts; steel rigging." Both visitors struggled to absorb all this as they walked, and O'Hara had to point often. "Retractable propeller to eliminate drag when under sail. No, you can't see it from here." Finally, as they came to a halt and peered straight up at the bowsprit, "A beauty, eh? Shall we go aboard?"

"Fine," said Bartlett, "but why is she all wood? No iron that I can see."

"These raiders are built to cruise the world, remember, and won't have a home port. If they get shot up, they can repair the damage to a wooden hull in any port, but an iron hull can be repaired in only a few."

They trailed up the gangplank behind O'Hara and stepped on deck feeling conspicuous. Four crews were fitting the main deck skylights with iron grills; a dozen men were aloft in the shrouds with paint and tar brushes; another dozen clustered around the single funnel; and four more lowered a Turkish carpet down to the Captain's quarters in the stern. The noise was loud but orderly.

O'Hara found the Kerry foreman, who genially invited them to tour the main deck but asked that they stay out of the lower deck. "We're fitting the big condenser and tank today and it'll be a mite dangerous." He explained. "Sorry about that, but you couldn't see much today anyway." Out of courtesy, he asked a few questions about the joinery trade in Waterford. Flanagan fielded these with skill, Bartlett muttered incomprehensibly and he left them to it, pleading urgent work. "You know your way around by now, Captain, so I'll leave you in charge."

"Damn," breathed O'Hara, "I'd hoped to take you below. But we can see parts of the lower deck through the openings in the main deck."

They were level with the mizzenmast. "Look!" he commanded. "Down the gangway. That's called the gunroom on the construction drawings." He anticipated Bartlett's surprised question. "No, I don't have them. The foreman let me have a quick look once, that's all."

Farther along towards the bow and down another gangway. "You can see both engines, larger than normal for a ship this size. Each three hundred horsepower nominal, maybe closer to a thousand combined actual. She'll make fifteen knots in a breeze."

They picked their way forward through the knots of workmen, who ignored them. O'Hara showed the coal bunkers ("enough coal for fifteen days' cruising.") and, at last, he pointed guardedly at two lower bulkheads just visible through a skylight. "See there? That thick bulkhead? Three layers of lead in it. The shell store's behind it."

"Where are the cannon?" asked Flanagan, a bit bewildered by now.

"No cannon, not yet," O'Hara whispered as he looked round. "She'll have three thirty two pounders broadside, plus a hundred pound pivot gun in the bows and maybe one in the stern as well. The broadside gun carriages will be about where we're standing, I reckon."

They took a quick turn around the bows, admired the towering bowsprit again and returned to the gangplank. O'Hara thanked the foreman, who had reappeared, and they descended to the dockside.

"Well, Major, what do you think? Is Captain Bulloch getting his money's worth? Forty eight thousand pounds?"

"If she's as fast as you say and carries those guns, no merchant ship has a chance against her, that's certain. I suppose it will all depend on her luck in finding them."

"Yes, I'd like to try my luck at it," O'Hara sighed, "but at best I'll have her for two or three months. If I get the post. I'll know in a week or so."

His ambition was palpable and Bartlett wished him success. "I don't suppose I could have a look at those drawings?"

"No chance. I won't see them again unless I'm made skipper."

O'Hara escorted them through the main gate along the north wall towards a cab rank. As the passed a smaller open gate, he pulled at Bartlett's arm and stopped him. "Look there, Major," he pointed, "at the far end of the yard. See those two ships being built there? You can see that half their backing is down. I bet they'll be laying teak next month."

"What are they?"

"Hulls 294 and 295, that's all I know for sure. Rumor has it, though, that they're ironclads. Big ones."

Chapter 47

"That's fine, Major," Adams said, pulling at his square jaw. "Good work." He laid Bartlett's affidavit on his desk.

Flanagan had drafted the paper on the train from Liverpool the night before and by noon it was edited, transcribed, sworn and notarized. Not bad for a novice spy, Bartlett said to himself. To Adams he said, "Your appointment's at four, sir?"

"Correct. We will leave here at half past three. The streets are impossible with all this construction work."

The two would see Lord Russell to demand yet again that he take action against Bulloch for what Adams insisted were criminal evasions of the neutrality laws. Bartlett's affidavit, sworn by an officer of the United States government, would carry more weight than its predecessors, sworn by paid spies and dockside hangers-on. Adams had another surprise for Russell, as well.

The grandeur of the Foreign Office was almost overwhelming, as it was meant to be. Generations of dusky ambassadors had been quelled by the towering ceilings, the dark paneled walls and the impenetrable arrogance of the grandees whose portraits were spaced along them, gazing tolerantly down at the supplicants.

Russell welcomed them to his office with his invariable courtesy. He soon made it plain that he was weary of the constant whining and badgering by Adams on this matter and that Bartlett's affidavit, though doubtless honest and complete, was insufficient evidence for any action. "My dear sir, as I have said so many times – bring me legal proof of an offence under the Foreign Enlistment Act and I shall take the appropriate steps. But I need proof, and I do not have it." He turned to Bartlett. "You quote here, Major, your unnamed guide to this *Oreto*. He told you that on the construction plans one area of the ship that you saw was described as the gunroom and another as the shell store. Did you see these plans yourself?"

"No, sir."

"Did you see any guns? Any shells?"

"No, sir."

Russell held up his hands. "You see, Minister? What can I do with this?"

Adams snorted. "Too obvious, I'd have thought. Have your customs surveyors demand to see those drawings."

"They have of course already done so. On their first inspection of the vessel, as I recall." He looked for confirmation to his elegant secretary, Carruthers, who nodded and resumed taking notes.

Russell folded his hands on his desk. "To repeat: I need proof that an agent of the southern states is engaged in equipping, furnishing, fitting out or arming a ship in Britain for the purpose of taking part in a war. Our customs officers have inspected this ship monthly and have found no such proof. Provide me with the proof and I will do what the law requires."

If he hoped that was the last word on the subject, he was disappointed. Adams produced another pile of affidavits. "These, sir," he pronounced, "are sworn statements, all to the same effect: that Captain Bulloch and his English associates are recruiting English seamen to sail in the *Oreto* with the intent of preying on American merchant vessels. That must be a breach of your laws."

Russell hefted the papers and passed them to Carruthers. "Interesting. A new line of attack. I shall read these with care." He stifled a smile. "Perhaps they resemble the affidavits we receive concerning the alleged recruiting practices of your consuls in Ireland. These assert that thousands of foolish young Irishmen are being deceived into volunteering for the American army. A grave offence if it can be proven, don't you agree?"

"If it can be proven, which of course it can not be." Adams held Russell's eyes.

It cost him, but Russell kept his anger in check. "I will pass these papers to the law officers of the Crown," he gritted at last. "More I can not – and will not – do at this time."

Bartlett was impressed by the ferocity of these exchanges, and on the way back to the ministry he said with admiration, "You were quite forceful with Lord Russell, sir. Are you always so frank?"

"The forcefulness of my remarks is in exact proportion to our success on the battlefield at home." Adams grinned without any humor. "Our recent victories have enabled me to take a more - robust line with his lordship than previously. Quite a change, as you can imagine, from my line after Bull Run."

"One of the skills of diplomacy, I suppose."

"What skills? Diplomacy, Major, is the art of saying, 'Nice doggy! Nice doggy!' while you reach for a club. Nothing more."

*　　　　　*　　　　　*

Washington Navy Yard was a drab, slapdash establishment, thrown together on the east bank of the Potomac after Sumter. There was an air of impermanence about the place, accentuated by the strange ship moored at the main wharf and the damp sailors lined up in their dress whites alongside her. A cloudburst that morning was putting paid to any sense of occasion, and the crew wanted only to get back aboard.

This was USS *Nantucket*, ex-Hull Number Nine, a Monitor-class ironclad, Commander Robert Jones commanding. He shook hands with his sullen predecessor, had his executive officer dismiss the ship's company and hurried across the wharf to the administration building.

There waiting for him was Miles Stoddard. He had made good on his promise that Jones would take command of this ship and he thought it fitting to attend the brief handover ceremony.

They exchanged congratulations and heartfelt thanks. His obligation to Jones had weighed on Stoddard for months, for just as long as Jones had wondered if he would really get the promised command.

They stood and looked out at the rain. "I stayed in here because it's dry, Robert," said Stoddard, "and because this uniform would have been too conspicuous at a time like this."

"Thanks. The man I replaced is a classmate. He's convinced, as are many others, that I got this command because I have political influence. He made that plain enough."

"Too bad, but there you are."

"I can't blame them." A massive Crimean shrug. "I disappeared for months to no one knows where and reappeared on a luxury yacht owned by some French Nob. Not exactly fighting your savage war at sea, is it?"

"Some day you'll publish your memoirs and your exploits will make them all feel like idiots," said Stoddard. He may not have been joking.

"I may even have some exploits by then. I sail tomorrow to join the blockading squadron off Savannah. Maybe a reb or two will try to slip past me. I hope so."

"Or maybe the English will."

"Hah! Some chance. The English won't try anything. They're our great friends now."

"There's been a development." Stoddard repeated what Bartlett had written him of Mariassy's revelations about the Palliser shell. "And the English still need the cotton, don't forget."

"Forget? That's the reason I'm heading for Savannah. If I can figure out which end of my ship is the bow, that is." Jones started to clap Stoddard on the back but remembered discipline just in time. "Four or five months of gentle relaxation in the southern sun, my friend." He grinned broadly. "Thank God for political influence, say I."

Stoddard shook his hand and watched him trot towards the *Nantucket*. Then he climbed into his waiting coach to return to work. Well, he thought, I suppose he does deserve a less demanding posting, for a while, anyway.

* * *

When Bartlett returned from the Ministry that afternoon, he was delighted to see Katherine arriving at the same time. It took all his self-control to stop himself from running up to her and picking her up in his arms. Sadly, but sensibly, decorum won out, so he strolled purposefully enough to catch up with her and give a courteous tip of the hat.

"Lady Carra," he declared, with a sly wink and a glimmer in his eye.

"Major Bartlett," she replied, but without any hint of charm. In fact, she seemed to be avoiding his eyes. Uh oh, he thought, a return to pre-Paris Katherine. What had he done?

"How was Paris, Katherine? Did you have a wonderful time? Are you now a fully-fledged Parisienne?"

She was clearly uncomfortable with this use of her first name and she cast a glance around her, in an evident effort to detect eavesdroppers. She barely looked at him as she placed her key in the front door.

"Most educational, Major. I am afraid that I really am most busy. Perhaps we can converse more at a future occasion?"

Stunned by this brush-off, Bartlett resorted to his stock-in-trade conversation starter – his tardy rent.

But even this secret weapon was obviously firing blanks when she responded: "No, no. Keep it, if you will, until next week, when you can pay me for two weeks. That will be simpler."

"As you wish, ma'am." He lifted his hat. "Good day. I look forward to conversing with you more fully at a future opportunity."

As the door closed behind her, Bartlett stood on the doorstep vowing to put thoughts of Katherine out of his mind and focus it instead on this Bulloch fellow.

Chapter 48

Bulloch had found himself trapped in Savannah for months by the Federal blockade. Months of teeth-grinding frustration and anger passed. When he finally managed to run it, his ship had one engine, was badly found for the North Atlantic and was perilously short of coal. She limped into Queenstown burning bunker sweepings mixed with rosin and the spare spars cut into short lengths. Two days later Bulloch stepped off the train in Liverpool.

He was just in time, as it happened, to watch the Oreto sail out from the Mersey to the open sea under the British flag, her reputed Italian owner revealed as one James D. Bulloch, Esq.

And just in time to cheer as No. 290 slid down the ways at Messrs. Laird's yard, her graceful hull named *Enrica* by the lady who christened her. Bulloch had a weakness for Mediterranean names.

*   *   *

"Allow me to take a few minutes of your time, Foreign Secretary," Adams said, a touch of ice in his tone. This time he had not asked for an interview. He had simply stormed over to the Foreign Office and demanded to see Lord Russell in a tone that could only be obeyed. "I have here a statement from the captain of the USS *Adirondack*, patrolling off the Bahamas these last six months, which you will find relevant."

"Will I?" Russell sighed again as he sagged back in his chair, his feet inches off the floor. "Will I, indeed?"

Adams ignored the implications of that question. "The British ship *Oreto*, out of Liverpool, owned by Bulloch himself, anchored in Nassau harbor recently and took on new officers. Among them was a southern rebel who talked freely to an officer of the port; so freely, in fact, that the Governor seized the ship and charged in your Vice Admiralty Court that her owner and agents were in violation of the Foreign Enlistment Act." Adams paused here and then added, "The first time that a rebel vessel has been dragged into court, so to speak."

Carruthers nodded when Adams lifted an eyebrow at him. "Fascinating," the little man murmured, "do go on."

"The Court in the end released the ship, citing 'insufficient evidence', just as you have done many times."

"There will be a lesson for me here," Russell smiled thinly, "I sense its arrival."

A grimace from Adams. "The *Oreto* promptly made for Green Cay, some seventy miles distant in the islands, where – can you credit it, Foreign Secretary? – she found another British vessel, the, ah," he searched the paper in his hand, "the *Prince Albert*. And by chance this obliging vessel was loaded with cannon, shot, shell, powder, rams, sponges. Everything that a brand new commerce raider might need for a long voyage of destruction."

"All of which, one may assume, was transferred to the *Oreto*?"

"Of course, in daylight, under the eyes of the officers and crew of the *Adirondack.*" Adams's fury began to show himself in the pink spots on his cheeks. "Then there was some sort of ritual on deck, your ensign was lowered, the rebel flag was raised and she was renamed the CSS *Florida*. It was a commissioning ceremony of some sort."

"Obviously."

"Our captain's statement, sworn before a Nassau judge, was forwarded to me by Secretary Seward. Along with a report from our Navy Department to the effect that, as of sixteen days ago, the *Florida* had sunk or captured seven American merchant vessels. With substantial loss of life."

"I am so sorry to hear that. But – "

"I will not repeat the Secretary's instructions to me, but you can imagine what they are." Adams drew himself up as far as he could in his chair. "There can be no doubt whatever that this was a single, coordinated enterprise. With British ships, British armaments and British crews. A single enterprise conceived, planned and carried out wholly in England by a resident of England, James Bulloch."

"But..."

"A single enterprise aimed to attack American merchant ships. To engage in warfare against a country friendly to England. To violate your so-called neutrality laws."

"So *you* claim, Minister."

Adams was in full flow. "Bulloch will now violate your neutrality laws in precisely the same way with his second ship, this *Enrica*. Of that there can be no doubt, either." He paused to regain some composure. "You must seize that ship, sir, as your laws require you to do, and seize it now, before it escapes. You can no longer do nothing."

It cost him, but Russell kept his anger in check. "I will pass these papers to the law officers of the Crown," he gritted at last. "More I can not – and will not – do at this time."

Adams rode back to his legation in profound gloom. He could see no hope. The English had no intention of stopping, or even of hindering, Bulloch's operation in Liverpool. Russell and his Cabinet colleagues appeared to have no conception that their conduct would inevitably lead to conflict. Experienced, sophisticated men, every one of them, but they acted as if they were morally and politically blind.

*   *   *

Flanagan handed Bartlett a cable form. "From Uncle Patrick, sir."
"OUR FRIEND OBTAINED THE POST HE APPLIED FOR ON SECOND VESSEL STOP HE EXPECTS IMMINENT DEPARTURE DESTINATION WEST INDIES STOP PATRICK BURNETT"
"Delphic but intelligible," Bartlett observed. "O'Hara's skipper of the *Enrica*. Tell me, Flanagan, why do Captain O'Hara and your uncle take such risks to help us?"
"They're Irish, sir; they hate the English. And they hate slavery. That's reason enough."
Bartlett then told Adams that an independent source expected the *Enrica* to sail soon, probably to the Bahamas. Adams growled that he would write at once to warn Russell but that Russell would do nothing to stop her.

*   *   *

In this he was not quite correct. James Bulloch had the covert means of knowing with certainty the state of the discussions between Adams and Russell about his ships. So he had been warned that day by his source in the Foreign Office that Russell wanted the customs surveyors to make a thorough sweep of the ship on the Monday and to find something – anything – on which duty was payable but unpaid. That would be enough to detain the vessel until the law officers could report on the new affidavits from Bartlett and from the master of the *Adirondack* off Nassau.
Bulloch was not the man to take needless chances. He directed O'Hara to coal the ship, put all her stores on board and ship several more hands for a voyage to Havana. They would sail on the Monday tide, and he told Messrs. Laird that he would run a rigorous, all-day trial in the open sea on that day. Then he dispatched a series of telegrams to his agents in London.
Monday morning was fine and breezy. The *Enrica* left her dock early and anchored off Seacombe. There she was boarded by dozens of special guests, Bullock's friends and business colleagues with their families, who were invited to go out for the trial trip. The crew had dressed her with flags and bunting, a brass band played marches and the wine was Liverpool's best. The steam tug *Hercules* came along as a tender.

Once at sea, they ran a number of times from the Bell buoy to the northwest lightship and back to the buoy. The sea was calm, the breeze had turned light and the passengers promenaded on the main deck after a lunch of cold meat and salads. Bulloch was at his genial southern best, chatting with the wives, praising the daughters and showing the youngest sons how to steer the ship. But he kept a close watch on her performance and noted with satisfaction that she averaged almost thirteen knots over the smooth surface.

At mid-afternoon, though, he announced that the trials were going so well that he had decided to keep *Enrica* out all night to complete them. His guests would all return to Liverpool on the *Hercules*, and he hoped to meet them under equally agreeable circumstances before long. They crowded around him with exclamations of pleasure and were soon escorted aboard the tug and heading home.

Bulloch stood at the stern and waved until *Hercules* was half a mile away. Then he called to O'Hara. "Captain, a word with you."

O'Hara, exhilarated by the performance of his new command, bounded up to the quarterdeck and saluted her owner. "A splendid ship, sir – fast, handy and well found. Where in the West Indies shall I take her?"

"You will take her to the Azores, Captain. Do you know the island of Terceira?" O'Hara nodded slowly. "You will shape a course for the Bay of Praya on that island."

O'Hara looked puzzled. "Not the West Indies, then?"

"No. Terceira." Bulloch handed over a letter. "These are your detailed instructions, sir. You will follow them exactly, word for word. I cannot over-stress their importance."

O'Hara began to read the letter but Bulloch held up a hand. He explained that a Federal frigate had been cruising in the waters around Southampton for several weeks, presumably waiting for the *Enrica* to leave the Mersey and snap her up. Just before he boarded his ship that morning, a telegram had arrived to warn him that the frigate had left Southampton and would probably make for Queenstown, on the south coast of Ireland.

"She'll be looking for us?" O'Hara asked.

"Quite possibly. Your normal route to the West Indies would take you down the Irish Sea and close to Queenstown. We can expect the frigate to lie off that coast, or somewhere in that channel, and look for you there."

"So I'll go north about?"

"Yes. I've consulted the pilot. He knows the route well. Carry on, sir."

O'Hara saluted and went down to give the pilot his orders and to read his own. As he studied them, a low whistle formed in his mouth and was released when he finished. It would be an interesting voyage.

A Friendly Little War

They were under way by midnight under steam alone, straight into a near gale and driving rain from the northwest. By the morning the wind had dropped, so they set all sail and scudded along the coast of Northern Ireland at fourteen knots. As the sun sank, they lowered sail and steamed into a small cove near the Giant's Causeway, where Bulloch and the pilot went ashore in a fishing boat.

By the time they reached the shingle, *Enrica*, carrying one light at her masthead, was just visible through the gloom as she beat to the west. They found shelter in a primitive hotel, whose owner unearthed a bottle of ancient brandy. Its quality was adequate to the many toasts they raised to the ship's future in the shipping lanes of the world's oceans.

The next morning, a nondescript bark of four hundred tons, heavily laden, slipped down the Thames with the tide. Once into the North Sea, her captain opened his orders. He too whistled. It would be a long and interesting voyage.

*   *   *

The report of the Chief Inspector of H.M. Customs, Mersey District, reached Russell's desk that afternoon. The Chief Inspector had in person led the team that went to inspect *Enrica* the day before, only to find that the ship was gone. She had left to undergo her last trials, with many notable guests aboard. She was due back the next day, he wrote. Then she would be inspected as thoroughly as the Foreign Office had specified. The Foreign Secretary could be entirely confident of that.

Adams seemed impatient on Monday morning, shifting papers around on his desk while Bartlett briefed him on the developments in the war. There had been very few. Apart from a series of skirmishes in Virginia, where the Confederates were plainly up to something, little had happened in the week ended fifteen days earlier. Bartlett was soon finished.

"Thank you, Major," said the minister. "Now, if you would call in Mr. Morse, I have a matter to discuss with you both." Once the consul was seated, he went on. "You may not know that not every Member of Parliament is hostile to our country. Some, in fact, actively support us." He crossed his arms and sat back, bouncing a bit in his chair. "I make it my business to meet as many of them, on a social basis, as possible and have become friendly with - a few. Last weekend, at his estate, one of these men handed me this." He slid a three-page document over the desk. "It's a copy, but a true copy, I'm assured."

It was the draft of a contract between Messrs. Laird Brothers, shipbuilders, of Birkenhead, Merseyside, and James Dunwoody Bulloch, ship-owner of Liverpool. Under its terms, Lairds would construct two iron vessels with stated specifications:

Length:	230 feet
Beam:	42 feet
Loaded draft:	15 feet extreme
Engines:	2 x 350 horsepower nominal
Speed:	12 ½ knots
Tonnage:	1850

for a price of £93,750, payable in five equal installments, for each fully equipped ship.

Both ships would be built wholly of iron, simultaneously, by crews working two shifts, seven days per week. The details of the masts and rigging and the deck plans were to be specified in the drawings that would form part of the final contract when they were accepted by both parties.

Bartlett and Morse read this far, looked in surprise at each other and then at Adams and read further.

The ships were to be armored along the waterline with a belt of iron plate on teak backing having a maximum thickness of four and a half inches amidships, tapering to two inches at the extremities, reaching three and a half feet below the waterline. Each would have a large iron extension projecting from the bow under the waterline. Morse pointed at that clause and raised an eyebrow at Bartlett.

"To ram the enemy, I suppose," Bartlett said.

The contract required Bulloch to furnish within one month the drawings of the two revolving turrets each ship would carry. It was understood *pro tem* that each turret would mount two guns of the heaviest caliber practicable, in parallel four to five feet apart. Any major changes would be reflected in the purchase prices.

There followed the standard boilerplate clauses dealing with the applicable law, force majeure, notices and the like.

"Well?" Adams demanded. "What do you think of that, eh?" he looked pleased with himself but somewhat apprehensive, as if he feared that he had been tricked. His weekend host was certain, he said, that the draft was genuine. That gentleman had refused to disclose how he came to possess the document, but he'd said that he might obtain further information on the transaction.

"Sounds like the source is a lawyer," Morse volunteered, "a Liverpool lawyer, bent like all the rest of 'em."

"I saw those two ships," Bartlett said. "In Lairds' yard, when I went aboard the *Enrica*." He told them what O'Hara had said about them. "I'm no expert, but the hulls looked well along to me."

"Ah!" Morse exclaimed. "Because this document, even when it's signed, is no more than a letter of intent. However, if Lairds have begun construction – "

"The final contract must have been signed," Adams interrupted, "and I was told Bulloch has made the first payment." He gave a dry cough. "The obvious question is: What should we do now?"

"Show that to Lord Russell right away," said Morse.

"I can't do that. In the first place, our pettifogging little friend will dismiss it as an alleged copy of an unsigned draft, of no evidentiary value whatever. In the second place," he coughed again, "it would be a mistake to give him proof that we – I engage in espionage here."

"I don't agree, sir," Bartlett blurted. "Your first objection can be overcome by a visit by Customs to the yard, where those two iron ships can not be hidden away. Second, this is not espionage at all. It's not obtained by paid spies from an enemy; it is information about a private citizen given to you by a friend."

"A friend whose identity must be protected."

"Certainly."

"I take your point, Major, but you know how I deplore anything that smells of espionage. Using this document in that way seems wrong to me, somehow underhanded." Adams looked uncomfortable.

Bartlett made a tiny gesture of annoyance. "Well, as to the Foreign Secretary, the choice is yours. I have no choice. I must report this to Washington at once."

"This is serious?" asked Morse.

"I learned a bit about our own ironclads from, ah..." he recalled that Adams hated Jones "...when I was in Washington. These ships are bigger, faster and more heavily armed than ours. This is serious."

"We must get our hands on the drawings, then," Morse said. "Minister, can your friend help?"

"I'll ask him. And I'll ask about the final contract."

"Fine, sir." Morse was taking charge. "Charles, you and I should leave the minister to it now." He jerked his head at the door.

Outside he went on, "We have to get the contract and the drawings. I'll cable our people up there. Any other ideas?"

"One, maybe."

*　　　　　　　*　　　　　　　*

James Bulloch made a rare trip to London to see his banker. He needed more money and he needed it soon. The foreign currency that Richmond scraped together from its occasional successes in blockade running had many hands reaching for it. Navy Secretary Stephen Mallory was an accomplished political infighter who always got his share, small as it was, but he then had the difficulty of transferring the money to London. The last transfer was two months overdue.

Bulloch liked and enjoyed London. The greatest city in the world, he told himself on each visit. Handsome, dignified people; grand architecture; booming industry and commerce, especially seafaring commerce; close to the Continent. Perhaps he would settle here if the South lost the war. And it might well lose the war if his trip was a failure.

He turned into The Strand and into the doorway of the familiar brick building. The doorman touched his cap, gave him a respectful, "Good afternoon, Captain," and showed him up to the Chairman's waiting room.

"Good day, Captain. Come in, come in," called Malcolm Bannerman through the open door. They shook hands. "Please – this chair, if you will? Will you have coffee? Tea?"

After the saltpeter for cotton deal that had worked out so satisfactorily for both men they had formed a mutual admiration for each other. Bulloch for Bannerman's courage under intense pressure and Bannerman for Bulloch's willingness to risk all on his own responsibility.

"Nothing, thanks," said Bulloch. He had already decided how to play the few cards he held. Frankness was the only way to deal with Bannerman.

Bannerman opened the bidding. "So, Captain, how is the construction of the two new, ah, merchant vessels proceeding? Well?"

"Well enough, after a slow start. Lairds are not as experienced at iron ships as they want one to believe. And I suspect they're a trifle concerned that the next installment on the purchase price may not be paid on time."

"Surely Fraser's can give them the necessary assurances?" Fraser's Bank was the Confederacy's main bank in England.

"They do. And I've paid the first two installments on the nail. But they know I'm not rolling in cash and, to be fair, there is some uncertainty about this project, financial uncertainty."

"So, how can we help?" Bannerman was prepared to listen sympathetically. He wanted the South to win its war – was he jealous of Bartlett's closeness with Katherine? - and their previous deal had proven most profitable.

"I need a loan of thirty thousand pounds, repayable in full in sixty days. To be secured by a first charge on my interest in either one of the two construction contracts for Hulls 294 and 295. Interest at market rates. And I need it soon." That can't have come as a complete surprise to him, he thought. Let's see how he responds.

Bannerman was not at all surprised, and the amount was less than he expected. "That's a lot of money, Captain," he said.

"Each ship is a lot of ship, on which over sixty thousand pounds will have been paid."

"The next transfer from Richmond - when do you expect to receive it?"

"Could arrive any day now. It's about one month overdue."

"Can I take it that, if those funds arrive before the sixty days are up, they will go to repay the loan?"

"Of course." In practice, Bulloch would, when the time came, hope to negotiate an extension.

The bargaining that followed took a few minutes only. Bulloch tried to get ninety days, not sixty, but Bannerman held firm. "We'll see how sixty days works out this first time." Bannerman hinted he would not approve the loan unless his bank had a first charge on Bulloch's position in both contracts, but Bulloch would not be shifted. "You can have either ship, Mr. Bannerman, but only one of them." Bannerman spun a coin. "Hull Number 294 it is, then."

Another ten minutes of details and Bulloch rose to grasp Bannerman's hand in both of his. "I'm much obliged to you, sir. This money is vital to our cause."

"Delighted to help. If you'll drop by tomorrow afternoon, Captain, we'll sign the agreement."

Chapter 49

For several weeks Bartlett had been concerned about Flanagan. The young man was not his normal ebullient self about the office and carried out his ill-defined duties listlessly and with at least one eye on the wall clock near the main door.

It also seemed that Flanagan went to Liverpool almost every weekend. That was an expensive trip for an assistant dogsbody, as Flanagan styled himself, so from time to time Bartlett sent him up there on a fabricated mission and the ministry paid his fare.

He once asked Flanagan about the cost of his trips, to be told that because the Burnetts put him up for the weekend it was cheaper than hanging around the pubs in London. "And safer," he said.

"'Safer?' What does that mean?"

"It means, sir, that as I'm Irish and most of the men in the pubs are English, that the occasional harsh words are exchanged, you see. And the occasional fist."

"And you're not exactly built like a heavyweight, are you?"

"More like a pipe cleaner. I'm tough as hell, of course, sir, but lacking in - substance. And punch."

"And numbers."

"Aye, but it's the other way around for me in Liverpool, so it's much safer."

Despite this reassurance, Bartlett took it upon himself to make known his concern to Burnett.

Burnett replied by return of post. He and Mrs. Burnett thanked Bartlett for his interest in their nephew's well-being, physical and emotional, and were pleased to allay any fears he might have. "The truth is," wrote Burnett, "that Kevin has taken a fancy to a young lady who lives nearby, the daughter of friends. We suspect this is the first time that he has been so attached, as they say, and therefore hasn't much idea of how to deal with his emotions. All will be well in the end, though, we are confident."

Then, presumably in return for Bartlett's concern for Kevin, Burnett had added a post script: "The attached sketches will be of interest, I'm sure. They were made by the man who gave me the drawing I gave you of the *Enrica's* deck plans. You may want to reward him when next you're in town."

Bartlett unfolded the creased sheet, which was headed 'HULL NUMBER 294 per Construction Drawings'. Below it were two precise sketches in brown ink, one sketch of the ironclad's hull and sail plan, the second of her main deck plan.

"The rams," Bartlett breathed. "The old rascal's done it!"

To his beginner's eye, 294 looked at first like any conventional screw steamer. She was bark rigged, like the *Enrica*, with iron lower masts supported by three large shrouds on each side. But the bowsprit was hinged so that it could be turned inboard when the ship was to ram the enemy with her twenty-foot below-waterline ram. She had a single smokestack amidships.

Then he noticed the two revolving turrets, mounted fore and aft on the centerline, each showing two guns. An arrow on the drawing led from a turret to a tiny box, in which was written: "2 x 9" Armstrong guns, 11 tons each. Projectile 240 lbs."

That's a hell of a battery, he thought; almost one thousand pounds of iron. Plus, he saw at last, a seventy-pound Whitworth pivot gun mounted at bow and stern.

He took the sketches to one of the ministry secretaries and asked him to make two copies, one for the minister and one for Washington. Then he dashed off a note of profound thanks to Burnett and knocked on Adams's door.

Ten minutes later he emerged and cornered the other secretary to take down his report to Stoddard.

* * *

James Bulloch remained in Northern Ireland for a week after the *Enrica* made her escape. On his return to Liverpool he found, as he expected, a bewildered manager at Lairds and an apoplectic Chief Customs Inspector, the latter demanding furiously to know where the ship was and the former professing total ignorance with total honesty.

"The *Enrica* has left England, gentlemen," said Bulloch calmly, "and I doubt she will ever return. She is my personal property, fully paid for and mine to do with as I will, as Lairds will verify. No law has been broken but, as you evidently suspect otherwise, Chief Inspector, I suggest you call on my solicitor. Here is his card. I have authorized him to deal with all my legal matters. You will find him most helpful, I'm sure."

The Lairds man repeated his firm's denial of any responsibility for anything that might have occurred anywhere, while the customs officer raged and studied the card he held. Bulloch excused himself and retreated to his hotel.

The end game in England was near, he admitted to himself. That was certain. He had explained to Richmond that he expected the Cabinet to interfere with any attempt to slip the ironclads out of England when they were completed. Adams was pressing hard to induce it to take action, he wrote, and the extent to which the Union's system of bribery and spying was practiced by its agents was scarcely credible. Ordinary messengers and clerks, and now the French and English post offices, were no longer secure means of communication. Even a portion of the police in England had been converted into secret agents of the North.

But there was a solution to his problem, and it lay in France. The Confederate Commissioner in Paris, John Slidell, had urged Stephen Mallory to transfer his European shipbuilding program to France, where the government was still much more sympathetic to the Cause than the faithless English. Mallory had jumped on this idea and concocted a scheme to send the Laird ironclads to Bordeaux, where they would be finished, loaded with supplies for the French army in Mexico, cleared for Veracruz and then delivered to the Confederacy in the Azores.

Bulloch had reservations about this plan, but Mallory had become a desperate man. "We all here agree with your assessment that the two ironclads nearing completion could sweep away the entire blockade of the enemy," he wrote Bulloch. "Our early possession of these ships in a condition for service is an object of such paramount importance to our country that no effort, no sacrifice, must be spared to accomplish it. I suggest you run over to Paris and consult our Commissioner, Mr. Slidell."

That's clear enough, Bulloch thought. Time to visit Paris.

*   *   *

John Slidell's Louisiana charm had in no time acquired a slight French patina. They met at his large house on the edge of the Bois de Boulogne the night that Bulloch reached Paris. There he soon put Bulloch, a rather reserved man, at ease over a fine bourbon and impressed him with his knowledge of the Laird rams and the solution proposed by Mallory.

"But that dog won't hunt, Captain," he said with a regretful shake of the head, "begging Stephen Mallory's pardon. It's a bit too complex, I'm afraid, and it depends on the good will of the French authorities, who get nothing in return." He splashed a drop or two into Bulloch's glass. "I have a different proposal, which I'll set out for you. But, first, how much time do we have?"

"Almost none. Both ships are nearly plated and can be launched in three or four weeks, I'd judge. Another week or so to install their engines, their screws and shafts and so forth, plus two days to coal and to ship the crews– say six weeks at the outside. But," he held up a warning forefinger, "The government can move in at any time before then."

"To amend the law? No, that requires an act of Parliament, does it not?"

"To evade the law. With an Order in Council they can override the ordinary rules of the law without bothering Parliament. At any time."

"So we don't really know how much time. I see. We'll just have to move as fast as we can." Slidell smiled and rubbed his hands. "Fortunately, Captain, I am in close contact with maybe the one man who can help solve our difficulty. We'll meet him tomorrow at ten. I'll collect you at your hotel at half past nine. Explanations then."

Slidell's bearing the next morning showed a mixture of enthusiasm and confidence. In France, he explained to Bulloch, it was vital to have the support of influential figures – "Politically influential, I mean, as all major decisions are taken in the Palace." – if any important project was to prosper. The man they were going to see was undoubtedly that. In fact, he was the source of controversy: many argued that he was more powerful than the Emperor, others that he was second to the ruler. "Only the French can take such lasting pleasure in a debate of that nature," Slidell smiled.

Slidell had been consulting their host since his arrival in Paris. The Frenchman was sympathetic to the Confederacy and had favorably received the few proposals that Slidell had put to him. "We've discussed cotton any number of times, but although he wants to get involved he doubts he can convince the Emperor to break the blockade. Not yet, anyway. Too risky, and I can understand that."

In recent weeks they had reached tentative agreement on a much more ambitious plan, one that would if implemented radically change the scope and balance of the war, but of late he had appeared reluctant. "He seemed to go cool on the plan overnight, for some reason. Says the timing's not yet right. But I have hopes of bringing him 'round again."

The fact was that the French government, like all governments, was nothing if not practical. It had to be on the winning side. The string of Union victories in the spring had damaged the South's standing in the marble halls of French foreign policy. "If you can call it a policy. It's more like pragmatic opportunism." Except for the Duc de Morny. He could take, and invariably did take, the longer view.

Their carriage drove past the entrance to the grand circular driveway of the Petit Bourbon and turned up the next side street. Bulloch looked expressively at Slidell as they went by and nodded his recognition of the obvious splendor of the man they were to see. A door in the side of the building opened as they stopped and a short square man with short grey hair stepped out into the sunshine and greeted them.

"Monsieur asks that you come straight up to his quarters, Mr. Commissioner," he announced. "If you will come this way, please, we can avoid the rabble waiting downstairs." He led them up a paneled stairway and then down a corridor to a painted doorway. He knocked and without waiting for a response ushered them into the de Morny's dressing room. There, wearing only trousers, shirt and embroidered slippers, the Emperor's half brother received them.

He looked pale and distracted, but he did his best to conceal whatever troubled him and greeted them in English with genuine interest. "Ah, Commissioner, always a privilege. And this is the notorious Captain Bulloch, of whom one has read so much? He looks quite peaceful, don't you agree, Henri?"

Henri didn't trouble to respond to this solecism and busied himself with the coffee. Morny recovered his aplomb and showed his guests to seats on an oriental sofa. He was delighted, he said, that they could come to him so soon. He had been looking into the suggestion that Slidell had put forward a week or so ago and was pleased to report that it seemed feasible.

"I can confirm that our government would look with favor on almost any project that would strengthen your navy, gentlemen," he began. "Informally, of course. You know that our neutrality law forbids any subject to cooperate in any way in the equipping or arming of a warship for you or the North."

"Which is why I went to England, sir," commented Bulloch.

"Naturally. But our government is more - elastic than the English." Morny spread his fingers expressively. "I shall be frank. The Emperor hopes the South will win your war. Why? Because he – we prefer to face two rival republics on your continent, not one, and that one pledged to resist any French advances in Mexico. Or elsewhere."

"That makes sense," Slidell said, careful not to seem eager.

"So any project to strengthen your navy will be quietly encouraged." You can not of course expect to be given any formal assent to it, but no obstacles will be offered and certain facilities will be extended." He laughed unexpectedly. "And if you could arrange to have your next ships built in French yards – which are superior to their English competitors, I am assured – then some financial inducements may also be considered."

"That is good news, indeed, Excellency," said Slidell, hiding his surprise. "We are most grateful to you."

"Oh, I can claim no credit for this propitious situation. It merely reflects the objectives of our foreign policy, of which by now you must have gleaned some understanding, Commissioner."

"An inkling, no more."

"That is more than anyone else in France. You must be content." Morny looked around for Henri. "The cravat now, I think." He stood up. Henri advanced on him with a plum-colored silk cravat in the fingers of one hand and set to work on the ducal neck.

"Now, your plan, as I remember, is to send the ships to France – Bordeaux was mentioned – as soon as their engines are installed. There their cannon would be fitted and crew put aboard. They would be coaled, provisioned and made ready for the Atlantic crossing. The objective is to get them out of England at the earliest possible minute."

"That's right," agreed Slidell.

"As to her cannon, will they be made in France or brought from England?" Henri stood back to inspect his work and Morny waved him away.

Slidell deferred to Bulloch. "They will almost surely be brought from England, sir. I have narrowed my choice to two, the Armstrong and the Whitworth models, and it will be difficult, if not impossible, to select a French replacement in time."

Morny was admiring himself in a full-length mirror, turning first left and then right. "But in either case your ships will be superior to the American ironclads, I take it."

"Absolutely," affirmed Bulloch. "They're bigger, faster, more heavily armed. You see, sir, the *Monitors* – "

"I know quite enough about the *Monitors*, Captain. I learned a great deal from an... acquaintance, a man who by now should be in command of one."

"Oh?"

"Yes, indeed." Morny smoothed an eyebrow with his thumb. "And your ships will leave Liverpool unarmed?"

"Yes. English law prohibits me from arming them anywhere 'in Her Majesty's Dominions'."

"English lawyers have always had a flair for the grandiloquent," Morny observed. "And their silly law will leave your two ships at the mercy of any Northern frigate that happens by, will it not? Or how will they defend themselves?"

"With their armor plate, their speed and with their rams," said Bulloch. "But you're right, sir. It will be a risk."

"A risk to which my idea addresses itself." He sat back down, lit a cigarette and waved away the smoke. "I suggest, my friends, that Captain Bulloch sells his two vessels to a French company, their ownership to pass to that company immediately they are ready to put to sea. That company sails them to, let us say, Bordeaux, under the flag of France and therefore unmolested by any Yankee frigates. There it equips them and arms them. Then – "

"But, Excellency," interjected Slidell, "that would defeat the entire -"

" -purpose? No, it will not, as you will see if I may continue." Slidell had the grace to look abashed. "Then, as I was saying, the company sells the ships back to the good Captain here. Or to your government. As you choose." He smiled indulgently, proudly.

The two Americans looked hard at each other, each hoping the other would spot the flaw that Morny's scheme must have. "What would be my sales price to the company?" Bulloch asked at last, conscious that he personally would be the seller.

"It is not important. The company could pay you a nominal price and resell them for that price plus a small profit to cover its expenses, lawyers and the like. Or," he thought further, "it may be better to pay you a full commercial price and resell them at the same small profit."

"I'd prefer the second. It would help if I ever had to attest to the *bona fides* of the deal in an English court," said Bulloch. He was beginning to admire the plan. "The buyer should also be me personally, don't you think, Mr. Slidell? Much easier to handle the paperwork if the Duc's company and I are the only two parties to the transactions."

"Certainly. I don't have the necessary authority, and I believe you do." Slidell was content to be a spectator at this stage play.

Morny stood to receive his coat and insert his buttonhole. "Excellent, excellent. Now I must leave you for my official duties, trivial as they are." He pointed to the door and Henri went to open it. "But first I must introduce you to Mr. Armand Bravay, of Messrs. Bravay & Cie., the leading shipbuilders of Bordeaux. I have had with him precisely the same talk I have just enjoyed with you, and his company is prepared to act as the French company we have been discussing."

Bravay, fiftyish, tall and fair-haired with a slight limp, declared his pleasure at meeting such illustrious Americans. Morny took his ceremonial leave after asking them to report to him on the progress of their negotiations. Henri shut the door behind him and vanished somewhere.

In erratic but businesslike English, Bravay proved that he understood Morny's scheme, approved it and was more than willing to act as the French counterparty in the sale and repurchase transactions. He had read in the French press about the looming legal obstacles the Confederate Navy faced in England, he said, and the opportunity for French shipbuilders that they opened up. He did not disguise that his primary interest in Morny's scheme was not to earn a small profit for shuffling contracts but to demonstrate his yard's proficiency in building and arming modern iron warships. "This market will grow quickly, we think," he said, "and we want to be on the hot floor."

All this suited Bulloch's book. He had with him the specifications for two small, shallow-draft ironclads for river work and four fast wooden corvettes. There was no hope of having them built in England now,

France was the next best choice and Bravay's was the only shipbuilder he had met.

They quickly agreed that the money amounts in the purchase and resale of the rams would be nominal; that dual contracts in English and French were needed; that when drafted they would be signed in Paris; and that it was time for lunch.

Bravay was a generous host and their talk in the pretentious restaurant nearby was soon convivial. Slidell bragged about his Cajun relations and Bravay bragged about the wonders of his family shipyard. Bulloch, whose humor tended to the sarcastic, began to suggest that the yard could not possibly be as wonderful as all that and Bravay lunged for the bait.

"Ah, Captain," he proclaimed, "you must come to visit us in Bordeaux. Come to see for yourself that what I say is true, all true. Come soon." He called for the bill. "I return to Bordeaux tomorrow. You will come later this week, *hein*? You have only to telegram us in advance and we meet you off the train. Here is my card."

Bulloch accepted the challenge with relish. "I'll be there, sir. I need to take some time tomorrow with the Commission's lawyers, get them started on these contracts, but I should be free to go down to see you on Thursday, if that would be convenient."

"But of course. You have only to advise me before."

They parted on excellent terms, all of them with a vision that their immediate problem may have been solved and that their requirements in the future could be met.

Chapter 50

It was a wild Saturday afternoon in London, wet, windy and cold. Bartlett dropped more coal on the fire in his drawing room and began to read again the few dispatches that had arrived the day before. There was little to read because now there was little happening in the war. The occasional skirmishes in Virginia had frightened the politicians even more than the soldiers who fought in them. The West was almost completely quiet. There's nothing here to help the minister with Lord Russell, he thought, no more evidence that we can fight and win.

Although Bartlett was bored, he was guiltily grateful for the rain because it meant he did not have to look for something to do outside his flat. He hadn't shaken his childhood training that men didn't stay indoors in daylight hours if they could go outdoors. He tossed aside the dispatches and was reaching for *The Times* when Mrs. Mostyn edged around the door, the death's head grin in place.

"May I clean in here now, sir?" she said. "I won't be a minute." A loud knock at the front door. "Excuse me, sir, I'll just see who's there."

Katherine Carra came in a moment later and Jenkinson the builder, bowler in hand, trailed in after her. "I must apologize for descending on you like this, Major. Mr. Jenkinson and I have inspected the upstairs flat. We think the building work is – at last - almost finished, and finished so well, I must say." Here an admiring glance at the beaming Jenkinson "But before I bring in the decorators, there are one or two matters on which I need an expert opinion. A bachelor's opinion." She gave Bartlett a strained smile and waited, but he had no idea what she wanted him to say; her manner on the doorstep the previous week had left him incapable of second-guessing her motives."

"*Your* opinion, in fact."

"Why, I'll be delighted, of course, ma'am, if you think -"

"On a few things." She moved to the doorway. "Which way this door should open, for example, where the bookcase should go, and the cupboards in the bedroom. Perhaps you'll be kind enough to make other suggestions as well."

"I am at your service, Lady Carra. Shall I go up there now?"

"Thank you, but would this afternoon be too inconvenient? I could accompany you then." He didn't respond, so she went on. "May I come back at shall we say four o'clock?"

"Four o'clock will be fine."

"No, on second thoughts, I might disturb you. Perhaps you could knock on my door whenever you're not occupied?"

A Friendly Little War

Disturb me? What does she think I do on a rainy Saturday? he wondered. Get out the opium pipe? Bring in the girls? But he smilingly agreed and showed his visitors to the door.

Although he had mostly succeeded in putting her out of his mind since their doorstep encounter, he was still confused by her frostiness then. This time she had seemed different again. Although not the relaxed and romantic girl of their time in Paris, he did sense that she wanted his company. Four o'clock seemed an age away.

He held out somehow and it was half past four when he rapped with the ancient Carra door knocker. A long wait and the door was opened by a young and flustered parlor maid, who mumbled that Milady was ill and begged him to excuse her. He was turning away, puzzled, when Katherine came out. She crammed a bonnet on her head, breathed, "Good afternoon, Major. Shall we go?" and led him, now even more puzzled, back to his house.

He followed her wordlessly up to the new flat where he could look at her. She had been weeping, she still had tears in her eyes and her face was pale and pinched. Her look dared him to comment on her distress and he had wit enough to ignore it.

"I've been considering your questions," he said, "and I believe this door should open into the drawing room because the passage is a bit, um, restricted."

"I think you mean because it's criminally small, Major. But I agree. And the bookcase? Have you thought about that?"

"Why, of course. About nothing else. I suggest two bookcases, one on each side of the fireplace, instead of a large one against the opposite wall."

"Excellent. And that would allow me to hang my husband's great aunt Patricia on that wall. Her portrait, I mean. She's too wide to go anywhere else and I long to see the back of her. She's hideous, poor thing."

"If she's as you say, you may want to wait to hang her until after the flat is let."

"That could be tricky. A tenant of a sensitive disposition might object."

"Perhaps, but not for long, if you were to insist in person. No man of any sensitivity could deny you."

"Ah, Major Bartlett, how silly of me. I had forgotten how forward you colonials can be. Quite different from what one expects of you."

Once again, he was astonished how quickly Katherine could regain her good humor. The tears and the pallor were gone, the matchless eyes shone, the smile hovered. What an enigmatic creature she was.

Another twenty minutes and they completed their tour of the new flat. Bartlett offered his opinion on everything from the height of the window seat to the color of the wallpaper.

"I am most grateful for your help, Charles," Katherine said as they descended the stairs.

He saw an opportunity. "Would you care to join me for a repeat of our previous tea party?"

"I suppose Mrs Mostyn can act as my chaperone once again. Thank you."

Once the interminable ceremony of tea pouring and cake offering were dispensed with, Katherine folded her hands in her lap and turned to Bartlett. "I must apologize for my behavior this afternoon, Charles," she said, hesitating. "For having Milly send you away, I mean. It was as rude as it was unnecessary."

"Please don't apologize. It makes me feel guilty." He had a question for her. "Is his lordship in one of his moods again?"

"I'm afraid so. In fact, he's been in quite some mood ever since I returned from Paris. Ever since - ever since he discovered that I was not to marry Malcolm Bannerman."

Bartlett's stomach suddenly did more cartwheels than a Russian circus gymnast. Marry Bannerman? Not marry Bannerman? This was both the best news and the worst news he had ever heard.

"Not marry Bannerman?" he managed to splutter.

"Ah yes. I may not have mentioned that. Anyway, Lord Carra had his heart set on my marrying into the Bannerman fortune. He's so angry that he is threatening to eject me from the house and send me back to Ireland. I'm afraid that is why I have been so unfriendly to you... and everyone recently."

"But that won't happen, will it? Lord Carra can't be so irrational? Or so cruel?"

"Why not? The Carras are all irrational. And they can be cruel, at times. Like his brother." She laughed shortly. "Like his nephew."

"Your husband?"

Bartlett wanted to hear more. He pressed on, even though he knew it was rude. "He was cruel to you? I..."

She came back to the present. "Yes, he could be cruel. At times." She sighed. "He was - he was a swine, I'm afraid." There, she had said it aloud. It was such a release that she said it again. "An old-fashioned kind. Only in his last few years, after he came back from the hospital in Turkey. He was horribly wounded, you see, so his cruelty was his tragedy, but not his fault."

Katherine nodded. She was remembering. It was strange, she almost never thought of Henry now, but she felt an impulse to confide in Charles Bartlett.

"Yes, my husband, Henry. I seem to have been remembering my life at Carra frequently since my return from my stay in Paris. It was comfortable and tolerably pleasant. We lived in the new east wing and took our meals with his father and stepmother. We entertained frequently and I learned to tolerate the local county society which was of more than ordinary mediocrity. I even learned to hunt, and hunt well, in part to tease Henry, whose solemnity I often thought tiresome.

"To me, he was polite, distant and undemanding. Children did not arrive, for which I was thankful and perhaps even responsible; I could never be certain. Henry and his father were often away to inspect their own properties and to search for new ones, and when he was home Henry liked to plan his flower garden. I think his garden was for him an unconscious representation of the vast holdings that he was accumulating, and almost as important.

"As the years passed and Henry and I grew further apart, I became closer to his stepmother, Henrietta who was twenty-five years older than I and quite eccentric. She had inherited a large sum from her first husband, a wool merchant from Belfast, and as custom required she had used it to trap a title and the husband who came with it. This she had accomplished easily because Lancelot Carra valued money more and valued a title less than any man in Ireland. She brought him less money than he had hoped for and he had even less charm than she had hoped for, but they appeared to rub along amiably enough.

"I knew that Henrietta was lonely, but did not seem able to get closer to her. Eventually she confided in me her fearful secret: she was a closet Catholic. Not a practicing Catholic, of course, but an aspiring one. Henrietta was hazy on the subject and she thought that discovery would lead to the loss at least of her title, if not of her life."

"Good heavens," said Bartlett, "Is it still such a terrible sin in Ireland to be a Catholic in 1862?"

"Probably not for most people but most certainly for the Carras and their neighbors."

"Do continue with your story, Katherine, if you wish to." Bartlett was trying to speak as little as possible as he feared if he interrupted she might change her mind and stop telling him her story.

"In the beginning I wrote to Owen every two or three months and he replied as often. I heard of his first unhappy years with the Menzies cousins and then his acceptance by Major Menzies' regiment. But as he grew older his letters came less often and told me less. My memory of my young brother began to fade beside that of my father.

"The Carra estates expanded steadily and within a few years Lancelot and Henry held more than twenty thousand acres, stretching to Rathmore and Ballydesmond. They were content, their bankers were content but hundreds of their former tenants were starving on the road or were buried beside it. Not of course that I was aware of that at the time.

"I realized that I was probably never going to see my brother again and that I had to adapt to my lonely life with my husband, who appeared to despise me, at Carra. But then the war in the Crimea came along. Henry rejoined his regiment, the 45th Foot, an undistinguished unit attached to the Fourth Division, which soon embarked for the Black Sea. He went dutifully, unemotionally and mainly to appease all the bankers, patriots to a man, who held his notes."

"What did you do in his absence?"

"I became closer to his stepmother, whose secret I by then knew and I continued to hunt and socialize with the local gentry. It was a boring but bearable life – actually I admit it was more bearable without Henry.

"Once in the field Henry, not a warrior born, was made regimental mess officer. He was soon wounded, at Inkerman, counting out the regimental silver. He lost both feet and lay in a suffocating hospital at Scutari until he was sent home in the spring of 1855. He was a man destroyed, either by the horrors of the Crimea or by bottomless despair at his future as a cripple. He never recovered, he never walked and he was never sober again. To me he was by turns dismissive and abusive. Worst of all, he wouldn't believe that I wasn't attracted to other men. It was horrible. Unbearable. It reached the point where I had to... do something. So I... and my friend... oh, never mind. I must forget about that. I must. He was furious at what he thought was my willful failure to bear a son. To his father and stepmother he was wholly indifferent. Only in his garden did he ever seem peaceful, but he did not plant a single new rose bush."

Bartlett wanted very much to hear what it was she had been about to say but was still afraid to interrupt her narrative.

"Three years later, Lord Carra died suddenly of what his doctor chose to call apoplexy. The potato rot had come back, land values were sinking from sight and his bankers were sharpening their knives, so whether his final seizure was owed to his deplorable finances or to his discovery of Henrietta's popery was never established. For her part, when the lawyers convinced her that the money she had brought was gone, and gone several times over, she took to her bedroom and her rosary and reappeared solely on Sundays, dressed all in white."

Katherine's tone became distant and she appeared to be on the brink of tears as the remembered the bad times that had come back to Ireland, ten years on. Blight, starvation, disease, evictions, death and bankruptcies all followed the same inexorable pattern.

She continued: "The banks panicked, called in their delinquent loans and once more found themselves landowners on a massive scale. The bankers explained to me that the Carra family owed them everything I had thought it owned. This is when I first got to know Malcolm Bannerman who came to visit and advise us.

"Alone and untrained, I fought to save what lands I could while my sodden husband sneered from his bath chair. Our old friend, Mr. Padmore at Hughes Bank, with his own job in the balance, was my single ally. For a year I thought we could save Kilveen, at least, but that too went in the end."

Bartlett could not think of an adequate response to this sorry tale. All he could manage was: "How did it all end? How do you come to be living here in London with your husband's uncle and what happened to your husband?"

"We were desperate and I had no idea what I was going to do next. Henry seemed not to care what happened. Then, one misty morning in April 1860. Henry was found face down in the shallow garden fountain, his overturned bath chair behind him. He had been abusive but coherent at dinner the evening before. 'You bitch! You filthy bitch! You want to leave me, do you? But I'll see you in hell before I let you run off with Dunn and his damned dogs!' were the last words he ever said to me as I fled the table.

"After a perfunctory investigation by the county police, the coroner had no trouble bringing in a verdict of death by misadventure.

"'I'm very much afraid that this is the end, Milady,' Padmore, my bank manager, said to me at the funeral. 'Everything is gone'.

"That night I talked long and earnestly with Henry's uncle Hugh, who inherited the title. Henry had never thought to change his will and his Irish estate came to me, but I wanted his uncle's agreement before I sold it all at auction to pay the Carra debts. All, that is, but some family portaits and the silver Hugh smuggled past the bailiffs when he left to take ship at Cork."

"Oh you poor woman. You have had so very difficult a life. It is remarkable that you manage to remain so cheerful after such adversity." said Bartlett.

"I had little jewelry besides my father's golden cross," she fingered it as she spoke "but I took what I had when I followed Henry's Uncle Hugh to London a month later. I never saw Henrietta again but I heard she retreated to Belfast, where she helped an older sister and her husband run their public house into the ground. But this may be a rumor. I do sometimes wonder what happened to her and how she managed to be a closet catholic in Belfast, if that is indeed where she went."

Now she had said far too much and embarrassed herself. Why did she talk so freely to this man? She'd say no more about Henry.

Emboldened, Bartlett said, "Please forgive the presumption, ma'am, but I have to tell you that the thought of any man being cruel to you is intolerable."

John Sherman

"I could not agree with you more, Charles," she said lightly. "The thought was in the end intolerable to me, as well."

At last, he thought, a definite resumption in their intimacy. Just as he was having this happy thought she got up abruptly and left without a word. Undoubtedly she was embarrassed to have confided in him. This was understandable but left him feeling even more confused than before about his relationship with this woman with whom he was falling more and more in love.

Chapter 51

The failures in the field of McClellan and Pope persuaded Palmerston and Russell that it was time to do what they had long wanted to do: recognize the independence of the Confederacy. Russell wanted first to offer England's services as a mediator in the war and to declare that if mediation failed – as they knew it would fail – England would recognize the Confederacy. Palmerston agreed and suggested mediation on the basis of victory by the South and its recognition by England. Both knew for a certainty that recognition would lead overnight to war with the United States, and both were determined to press ahead.

Adams knew most of this. He asked Russell if he should pack his carpetbag and his trunks. Russell had just been told by Palmerston that they must continue to be mere lookers-on until the war took a more decided turn, so he replied bitterly that the Minister could keep his traps in his basement for the present.

*   *   *

At the Bay of Praya on the island of Terceira in the Azores, the *Enrica* made her long-planned rendezvous with the *Agrippina*, the nondescript little bark from the Thames. Captain O'Hara followed his orders precisely. He placed the carriage for the eight-inch gun on the quarterdeck, the carriage for the seven-inch rifle forward of the bridge and the carriages for the broadside guns opposite the sideports. The shot was put in its racks; the shells were put in the shell room, spherical shells to starboard and elongated shells to port.

A day later Captain Raphael Semmes and his Confederate crew pulled into Terceira in a steamer chartered by Captain Bulloch, who thought it prudent to accompany them. Proudly, Bulloch watched as the armed and manned *Enrica* was commissioned into the Confederate Navy as CSS *Alabama*. She then set out on the first cruise of her career as the most feared commerce raider in naval history.

*   *   *

At Birkenhead, Hulls 294 and 295 were fully plated and their engines installed. Lairds put on a third shift during weekdays and erected sheds over the hulls to protect the workers from the constant rain. Bulloch inspected them one windy evening and reported to Richmond that he believed they could escape to Bordeaux in another two weeks.

John Sherman

Robert Jones was unhappy, deeply unhappy. He had at last brought the officers and men of USS *Nantucket*, himself included, to a passable level of efficiency in the Savannah blockade squadron when he was yanked off his command and carried to Washington in a fast sloop.

"Sorry, Robert," soothed Stoddard, "but we need you up here. It's important." Henry Wise added his endorsement.

"More important than…?" Strange, he'd never noticed just how icy Stoddard's blue eyes could get. "Right, sir, I'm here. What's up?"

"For you, London." Stoddard explained what was up, ignoring Jones's instinctive groan. "You leave tonight. Major Lampard has your orders for you."

"I blame you, Charles," Jones exclaimed. "If you hadn't shipped those drawings of Hull 294 to your Uncle Miles I'd still be cruising idly off Savannah. Sinking the occasional rebel rowboat, flogging the watch now and then, fishing for mackerel, and catching up on my sleep. Instead your uncle sends me back to cold, rainy, dreary London."

Bartlett was caught off guard by the belligerence of his old comrade. Why were all his friends treating him like a stranger? First Katherine, now Jones? He decided two could play at that game - "Perhaps you needn't stay long, Commander. When can you leave?"

"Leave? Hah! I'm here to stay for a bit. While my executive officer does his best to ruin my crew." He calmed down. "But I'll save it for Adams. When can we see him?"

"I'm at your service now, Commander," said Adams behind him, holding the letter from Seward that Jones had delivered. Adams regarded Jones with the distaste of one who had first condemned him for spinning his web of agents and now had to use that web to do his job.

They filed into the minister's office and he closed the door. "Welcome, Commander," he tried to smile. "Secretary Seward writes that you bear important news?"

"Yes, sir, and all of it bad. Shall I begin?" Adams waved him to a seat. "First, the South has a new ocean raider, the *Alabama*. She's bigger, faster and throws more weight of shot than *Florida* and she was built right here in England. You saw her, Major, when she was called the *Enrica*."

Jones described the rendezvous in the Azores with the *Agrippina* and the commissioning ceremony that took place as soon as *Alabama* cleared Portuguese waters. "We'll hear much more of this ship before the war's over."

Adams leapt up and called for his secretary, on his face a curious combination of anger and satisfaction. "That does it," he fumed, "I'll write to the Foreign Office to demand a meeting with Lord Russell. This time I'll – "

"Wait a minute, sir, just wait." Adams, halfway to his door, turned and stared at Jones's impertinence. "Sorry, sir, but there's more, and it's worse." Adams subsided growling into his chair.

"When we saw your report on the Palliser shell, Major," Jones went on smoothly, "quoting your friend from the Austrian Army, I reactivated an old contact of mine at their embassy in Washington. Have you heard any more about that shell, by the way?"

"Not a word. We've no one at Woolwich Arsenal any more, as you must know, and I've not been invited there myself." Bartlett was embarrassed, almost ashamed, that he hadn't found a way to confirm Mariassy's information.

"Well, it seems that Captain Palliser has cracked it at last. He's found a way to cast his armor-piercing shells, half in sand and half in cold, so that they don't fracture in the bore anymore. And they go clean through the *Warrior* target. Twelve out of twelve last month at Woolwich."

"With the Armstrong cannon?"

"Yep. The nine-inch model."

"Christ!"

"Yep." Jones remembered Adams. He explained the destructive power of the Palliser shell and its implications.

"I think I understand, Commander, but I don't see how this English projectile is relevant."

"Bear with me, sir, and you will. Now, as to Hulls Number 294 and 295, the Laird rams." He drew a long breath. "Our naval architects have studied the papers you sent us, Major, and they've come to a unanimous conclusion: That is, *that these two ships can win the war on their own.*" With grim satisfaction he watched their faces fall. "On their own."

"What? Nonsense! How?" in a rush from Bartlett.

"We think they'll be good sea-boats, with fifteen feet of draft, and as easily handled as ironclads can be, so the Atlantic crossing should present no obstacle. Once in Southern waters, they can probably sweep our blockading squadrons away, in turn, from the Virginia Capes to the Sabine Pass."

"*How*, man?" repeated Bartlett, incredulous.

"With their speed, their armor and the firepower of the Palliser shells, they can destroy our *Monitors* one by one, we think. If they can't sink 'em with their cannon, their speed means they can ram them."

John Sherman

"But we were sure the *Monitors* could sink the *Warrior*, and these ships are no *Warrior*, far from it." Warrior was England's enormous armored frigate, the most powerful ship afloat.

"First, *Warrior* draws almost thirty feet, so it can't go in after the *Monitors* in the shallow waters off the southern Atlantic ports. These rams draw only fifteen feet, and they can. Second, I said the *Monitors* would sink *Warrior* if they were armed with the Parrott rifle and our Taurus armor-piercing shell. They're not."

"They're not? Why not?"

"Because Commodore Dahlgren, the ordnance chief, decided in his wisdom to arm them with his own huge smoothbores, not the rifles, and the smoothbores can't fire the Taurus, only round shot." Jones's disgust was plain to see. "The most idiotic decision of the war."

"Well, we can change their guns to Parrott rifles, damn it! Excuse me, sir." Adams, intent on their argument, didn't hear him.

"Too late. The *Monitors* make eight knots, at best, and in a heavy sea maybe four or five. Plus, they're likely to founder. Think how long it would take to move them, one pair at a time, from New Orleans, Jacksonville, and the rest back to Norfolk or Philadelphia, fit the rifles and move them back to their stations." A sad Crimean shrug. "We'd finish by Christmas – maybe."

A gloomy silence from Bartlett and Adams.

"And the Laird rams will be off our coast in, how long? Thirty days?" Jones asked.

"Longer," said Bartlett. "Our people think they'll take to the sea in two weeks, and then their guns have to be fitted somewhere."

"Anyway, they'll be on us long before we can be ready for them." Jones sounded certain.

"Commander," interposed Adams, "it's obvious that sinking our blockading ships will be an enormous victory for the Confederacy, but why would it be a mortal blow? What will these rams do then?"

"They can cruise freely up and down the coast and prevent any systematic interruption of rebel shipping. The South will then export all the cotton it can ship and buy whatever it needs for its armies with the foreign exchange. Our greatest strategic advantage will vanish in a few months."

"I see, I see," said Adams, drumming his fingers. He began to plan his attack on Russell. In his heart he knew that, once the rams had destroyed the blockade, England would declare war on the North.

"Well, we may still have some hope." Jones added. "The Austrians *think* Bulloch is in contact with Palliser and has already bought a shipment of his new rounds. But they can't be certain that he has. If he has, there's no contest. None. Those two ships will rip all our *Monitors* apart in no time." He shrugged. "But, if he hasn't – "

Appalled silence from Adams and Bartlett. Then Bartlett objected. "Bulloch is watched night and day, or so I'm told." He looked at Adams. "Can we get Mr. Morse in here, sir, and ask him about this?"

Morse was loitering near Adams's office and was quickly produced. He confirmed that Bulloch was under surveillance every day. None of his agents had reported a meeting between Bulloch and Palliser, whose description Morse had circulated as a matter of routine late the year before. "When you explained these wonder weapons to me." He would go back over his records, though, to make sure. "Of course," he added, "Bulloch could have met with Palliser's representative, not the man himself. Or, now that I think of it, Bulloch wouldn't buy ammunition from Palliser; he'd buy it from the Royal Navy, or from a manufacturer."

"In which case - " said Adams slowly.

"In which case, we'd probably not know about it," Morse said slowly. "It could be anyone Bulloch met with. Such as the cannon founders. He's been talking to the Whitworth and Armstrong firms for months."

"Well," Jones observed, "we can be sure of one thing: The Armstrong people will have told him all about their success at Woolwich with the Palliser shell."

This time no one could think of an intelligent comment. It was all too obvious. And so were the consequences.

Adams spoke. "Gentlemen, this letter from Secretary Seward directs me to use every resource of this ministry to stop those two ships from leaving Liverpool. That is an order from the President himself. I shall protest vigorously to Lord Russell. You, Mr. Morse, will review your files, as you said, and give new instructions to your people in Liverpool. Perhaps the Liverpool Post Office is important now?"

"Correct," said Morse.

"Major Bartlett and Commander Jones will have their own orders, I assume?" Two earnest nods. "What will you do, Commander? No, don't tell me. Though you will make sure it's legal, won't you?"

"Yes, sir."

"This ministry will help you whenever it can. And you will all kindly keep me informed." The meeting was over.

"Well, what do you think of that?" Jones smiled. "I expected His Eminence to try to give me orders, but he doesn't even want to know what I do."

"You'll go to Liverpool, I assume? I'll see what I can find out here about Palliser."

"I go up there tomorrow. What I didn't tell Adams is that our navy is sending over two frigates to deal with these rams when they leave the Mersey. I have to make contact with them."

"Why didn't you tell Adams that? He'll be furious."

"I was told not to. Seward wants him to think for the moment that Russell is the one man who can stop them leaving."

"What's the point? They won't be armed. Our frigates will stop them."

"Maybe not. They may not get here in time. And those rams can fight without their guns. They're armor-plated, remember; they can make fifteen knots; and they have those long rams. How would you like to see one of them steaming straight at your wooden waterline?"

*   *   *

"Dear me," sighed Lord Russell as Adams paused for breath. "The Azores, did you say? A pattern seems to be emerging."

"*A pattern*? 'Emerging'? A proven conspiracy, you must mean. Why -"

"How do you know that all this took place in a remote bay in a remote island?" Russell tried a diversion. He was on the defensive because Adams knew that his plan to recognize the South had been vetoed by Palmerston.

"From the United States consul in Ponta Delgada. He has a large budget, and the islanders are poor."

"I see. Well, what you tell me, Minister, is serious, most serious. Kindly let me have a copy of your consul's report and I shall forward it to our law officers for their urgent review of Captain Bulloch's activities on British soil."

"Another review, eh. Good. But not good enough." Adams's tone was quiet but as menacing as he could make it. "Those rams must not leave port, Foreign Secretary, and I want your word on it."

"My dear Minister, you know quite well that I can act only if our laws have been breached. For that I must rely on the law officers, who, I assure you – "

"Foreign Secretary, I see I've not made my instructions clear. I shall try again: If either one of those two ironclads leaves port, *that - means - war.*

*   *   *

"That means war, eh?" Palmerston repeated. "Do they mean it?"

"Definitely, in my opinion," said Russell. "They mean it. Seward is cock-a-hoop these days because of all their victories."

"Until this last one," bumbled Somerset, the First Sea Lord. Russell had brought him along because he had news that was relevant to the American question.

378

"Cock-a-hoop," said Russell icily, "and he's persuaded President Ape that with their new ships they have nothing to fear from us. Lincoln still longs for a Canadian Empire, according to Lyons, so it all fits."

He had told the Prime Minister that he and Somerset needed to see him after cabinet and they were now gathered around the end of the long cabinet table, still littered with papers and dead cigars. It was night time and again Palmerston lamented the inadequate lighting in the room.

At seventy eight, Palmerston had few ambitions or illusions left. He would die, he sensed, without punishing the Americans. Still -

"Well, what do you recommend, Foreign Secretary?" he asked.

"The Laird rams will not be in condition to sail for another two weeks or so," Russell said crisply, "which gives the law officers enough time to find a valid reason to detain them. We can do that with an Order in Council, as you know."

"Yes, yes. But why detain them? Why submit to a crude threat from Seward?"

"Canada, sir," said Russell and Somerset in unison.

"Of course. Canada. Those benighted colonists won't defend themselves and we can't. They're hostages, plain and simple."

"And the First Sea Lord has another excellent reason, which he will now explain." Perched high on his cushioned chair, Russell bowed in Somerset's direction.

"Could be important news, Prime Minister," the latter said. "This fellow Palliser – the army officer with the armor-piercing shell, you'll recall – has come up with the goods at last. He's been testing at Woolwich, and the results are extraordinary. Damn things go through four or five inch plate like paper and then explode."

"Every time? Isn't that the problem?" Palmerston was stirred from his apathy by this development.

"Every time, or as near as dammit. We're putting his new shells on *Warrior* and *Black Prince* now. Makes them unbeatable, even by those funny little American ships they're so proud of."

"Very interesting, I'm sure, but what has that to do with - ah, I see!" Palmerston crashed his fist on the table. "I see. If we can get *our* hands on these rams we can put the new shells on them."

"Exactly," said Russell. "They would be supremely formidable."

"The Royal Navy can certainly use them, Prime Minister," Somerset chimed in. "They're big enough to cross the oceans and small enough to fight up rivers. They can go up the Rhine, the Danube – "

"The Seine?" smiled Palmerston. "What wouldn't I give to see the Emperor's face when these ships cruise past his window in the Tuileries, eh? Eh?" The smile died away. "But how do we get 'em away from their owners?"

"We buy them. We pay the Southern navy what they will have paid for them, which is around one hundred thousand pounds each." Russell chose not to point out how many low bridges crossed the Seine before it reached the Tuileries.

"Sounds a lot."

"It's cheap," Somerset corrected, "dirt cheap. But the main thing is, it's quick. We can have those two ships, armed and equipped, in a month or so. To design, negotiate and build their equivalents would take at least a year, more like fifteen months."

"And they will sell them to our navy because, if they don't, our law officers will by then have found the reasons for us to detain them." Russell's tone was almost triumphant. "Of course, the South could always fight us in the courts, but in our courts that would take time, would it not? A great deal of time, which they may not think they have."

"So we present them with two alternatives, with only one real choice: Sell or sue." Palmerston now enjoyed this as much as the other two.

"Yes, Prime Minister," they chorused.

"I'll tell the Chancellor to find the money."

*   *   *

James Bulloch's source in the Foreign Office wasted no time in alerting him to the gist of Russell's letter to the law officers, and Bulloch was just as quick to cable Slidell in Paris. He used the standard diplomatic code of the Confederacy:

> "AM RELIABLY INFORMED CABINET INTENDS DETAIN LIVERPOOL CONTRACTS WITHIN TWO WEEKS STOP IMPOSSIBLE REMOVE THEM BEFORE THEN STOP CAN YOUR FRIENDS HELP QUERY PLEASE ADVISE SOONEST STOP
> BULLOCH"

Slidell did his part with equal dispatch:

> "COME IMMEDIATELY STOP MEETING OUR FRIEND WITH THE BELL WEDNESDAY MORNING STOP
> SLIDELL"

It was almost the same drill as before. Henri again met them at the side door of the palace and led them up the stairs to Morny's dressing room, but this time their host was being shaved by a man with a broad, open face.

Morny greeted them with grave courtesy and begged to be excused his shave. "This young fellow with the razor is Henri's nephew from the

Auvergne, who aspires to replace his uncle when the old villain at last releases me from his grasp and retires."

Coffee was served them on an ebony table. The nephew finished his work, admired it and left. Morny surveyed his image in a gilt mirror, patting himself with a sigh under the chin, put it aside and went straight to the point. Time was short, he said, and an emergency solution was imperative. He was confident that he had one.

It was self-evident, he said, that the core of the problem was that the two rams, when completed and paid for, would be the property of Captain Bulloch, an acknowledged agent of the Confederacy which was a combatant in the American war. The Captain's contract to sell the ships to Bravay and Cie. provided that title to them would pass once they were delivered to Bravay in Bordeaux. Until then, they were for all practical purposes intended for a combatant. The English law officers had presumably found a way, or soon would, to translate those practical purposes into legal purposes in order to apply their neutrality laws.

"Therefore, the solution finds itself with but a little thought: the two rams must *immediately*, tomorrow, become the property of a French person or company. France is not a combatant in any war, as we know, so the dreaded English neutrality law does not apply to any of her citizens or her enterprises. *Voila*." He awaited congratulations.

He got puzzled silence instead. At last Slidell asked, "Brilliant, sir, but would Mr. Bravay still be a party to all this?"

"But of course." Morny gave a wide smile. "Forgive me, I thought that his participation would be understood. I have consulted him by telegraph and he is enthusiastic."

"And I or Richmond would repurchase the ships as before?"

"Again, of course. The difference is that you will not sell him the ships; you will sell him your positions in the two shipbuilding contracts. Mr. Bravay assures me this is not an unusual procedure."

"Yes, it's quite common." Bulloch had been thinking through the consequences of Morny's proposal. "It's a standard form of agreement. The price is usually whatever the seller has already paid the shipbuilder on the contract." He had at once seen the attraction of the deal and could think of only one flaw. "The English will want to know why Bravay is buying the ships – sorry, the contracts."

"Ah. He has the best reason: he has a customer who will pay him a large sum for the ships when he has completed and equipped them." Morny paused for effect. "And that purchaser is - the ruler of Egypt, Ismail Pasha!"

"Who? Really?" Slidell shook his head in admiration. "My word, Duc, you and Mr. Bravay have been busy."

"No, it is simpler than you imagine, Commissioner," Morny said graciously. "The Bravays have done much business with the Pasha and his predecessors for generations. They are often in the market, not always actively, for warships, so his name came to Mr. Bravay's head at once."

Bulloch was unconvinced. "Will the Pasha really buy these ships?"

"If asked, Mr. Bravay will say that he will, even though it is nobody's business but his own." Morny chuckled quietly. "And the Emperor will say, if asked impertinently, that he has known Bravay for many years and that his close relationship with the Pasha's family is well established. But," he held up a warning finger, "he will say no more than that."

The Emperor, he explained, was willing to help because, besides the geopolitical reasons mentioned earlier, Mr. Bravay was a political ally. He was a Deputy for the Gironde. He was decorated in his shipyard by the Emperor, who told him at the time that if he built ships for the Confederates they could leave French ports under French flag if he had any plausible cover story.

"He warned the Emperor there and then that he planned to build ships for trading between San Francisco and Japan. They needed to have great speed under steam or canvas, and they needed to be well armed to protect them against pirates in the Eastern Seas." To the Emperor's credit, Morny said, he managed not to smile at this.

"So you see, gentlemen, many things are possible in France if the project is presented correctly." They laughed at this, chatted a bit and then Morny rose and said, "We are agreed, then? Good. Captain, Mr. Bravay awaits you in Bordeaux with his lawyers. You know the way there and I urge you to take it at once. Mr. Commissioner, a great pleasure, as always." They shook hands. "On that other matter we have discussed, your proposed joint venture, I have a few thoughts. Can you call on me next week?" Slidell smiled and nodded.

As soon as they cleared the palace, Bulloch turned to Slidell. "He's quite a man, your friend the Duc. Will all this happen?"

"You can be sure of it. In France, what Morny wants, Morny gets."

"So I can ask you: Do you know what he wants by helping us?" They found a hansom and climbed up. Slidell would accompany Bulloch to his hotel and then to the railway station.

"Oh, I know all right. But I can't tell you yet, I fear. Just be grateful."

Once in his seat on the express to Bordeaux, Bulloch opened his brief case and pulled out several blueprints. They were the preliminary drawings of the ships he wanted Bravay to build for him: Four wooden clipper corvettes of one thousand five hundred tons, with four hundred horsepower, armed with twelve six-inch French rifles. For the Far Eastern trade. The United States's trade, that is. These would finish it off.

Chapter 52

Katherine Carra received few letters other than bills from local tradesmen and their subsequent demands for payment, so the large stiff envelope with a Cork postmark rested on her breakfast table until she finished her coffee. What could it be?

It proved to be Messrs. Cunningham & Cunningham, Solicitors, of No. 9, The Broadway, Cork. One of the Messrs. Cunningham wrote in a jerky script:

"My Dear Lady Carra

We act for the estate of Henrietta, the late Dowager Lady Carra of Carra, who died in Belfast recently. In her will Lady Carra bequeathed certain properties to you under specific conditions. If it should be convenient for you to call on me at this address in the near future, I shall be pleased to explain the position to you at greater length.

Yours, etc

Patrick Cunningham"

Henrietta. For Heaven's sake. Her scatty mother-in-law. No, her scatty stepmother-in-law, Henry's father's second wife, the rich widow. Her money had financed the Carra property empire in southwest Ireland at the beginning. In the end, all she had left was the Carra title she had snared with her money. Or so Katherine and everyone else had believed.

"Certain properties?" "Specific conditions?" What could they possibly be? Henrietta had nothing to leave. A vague sense of curiosity, excitement and hope began to form in her chest and her heart beat a bit faster. She would go to Cork to see this Messr. Cunningham. She would leave for Cork tomorrow and telegraph the solicitor today, asking him to book a hotel for her. Meanwhile, she would do her best to stifle her imagination. After all, "certain properties" probably meant two acres of potato bog.

*   *   *

Patrick Cunningham turned out to be a vast, youngish man in tweed with a brown beard and bear-like charm, a copy of his father, who pushed his bulk around his son's door to greet the titled young lady from London. After the formalities and a cup of Darjeeling, Patrick opened the limp file on his desk and extracted a last will and testament.

"My father acted for the late Lady Carra from the time she married her first husband," he rumbled. "He was a rich man, much older than she was, and she wanted to be properly looked after when he died. My father made sure that she was so she came to him again when she married your father-in-law, Lord Carra. He was of course a poor man who had once been rich and she wanted to make sure he couldn't ruin her." He studied Katherine's face to see if his frankness offended her and saw that it didn't. "He tried his best, as you know, but he didn't succeed, because," he paused for emphasis, "because we had bought for her three fairly large farms and put them in a kind of blind trust. A trust he could never find and, even if he did, could never touch." He leaned back and waited for questions but none came. Katherine, her mouth half open, was in a state of semi-shock. He poured her more tea.

"To come to the happy point, Lady Carra, my father and I are the trustees of this trust and our client's will instructs us to dissolve the trust and distribute its assets – the three farms – to you." He paused and grinned broadly. "Free and clear, that is. There are no debts in the trust or attached to the properties."

"Dear heaven above," Katherine gasped. "I never imagined – "

"Yes, it's the stuff of Dickens, is it not? The half-forgotten relation, the large bequest when most needed, the – I beg your pardon, Ma'am," he flushed, "if that sounded overly familiar."

Katherine waved this aside. "*Fairly large* you said, Mr. Cunningham'? How large? What are the farms worth?" She held her breath.

"I could only guess at their value, I fear. You would need a professional valuation. But I can tell you that the farms are all let and that the net rents to the trust are two thousand pounds per year, plus or minus a few pounds." His pleasure in Katherine's astonishment was written on his face. He related further details about the lease agreements and the tenants, the locations and the acreage, none of which she could take in.

TWO THOUSAND POUNDS! It was a fortune. It was freedom. It was… "Tell me, Mr. Cunningham, what are the 'specific conditions' her will mentions?" She had come back down to earth in a hurry.

"Ah, those. Let me see." He ran his thumb down the second page of the will. "Yes. It seems that Lady Carra converted to the Roman Catholic faith some years ago. Nevertheless she wished to be buried in the Carra family plot, next to her husband, and her bequest to you is conditional on her being so buried." He looked embarrassed. "It seems that, although she did not fully trust her husband, she loved him enough to insist on, ah, lying next to him."

Katherine had to think for a moment. "I think that's right; she did. It means that I must now persuade the present Lord Carra, who is her brother-in-law, and the vicar of St. Margaret's church here in Cork. A Protestant church."

"Will that be difficult? The will does not specify burial according to the Roman rites."

"I don't know."

The vicar, as it happened, was a willing conquest. He had loathed old Lancelot Carra, for doctrinal as well as monetary reasons, and was not rabidly anti-Rome. So he was pleased to approve a funeral ceremony that Lancelot would have fought to the death, as it were. Shaken by the charm Katherine unleashed on him, he told her that he required only a letter from Hugh Carra asking that Henrietta be planted in the family plot. He would square his bishop himself.

With the vicar well in hand, Katherine and Cunningham took the rest of the day to make the other arrangements for the proper disposal of Henrietta on the following Wednesday. They assumed that Lord Carra's request would be received by then.

"If you'll cable me when his lordship agrees, Lady Carra, I will instruct all concerned and count on his letter arriving in time." It was late. They were back in his office as dusk fell.

"Oh, I'll bring it myself. One can't rely on the Post Office." This surprised her; she hadn't thought of returning for the funeral until she said it.

He drove her to her hotel in his fashionable brougham, a conveyance he delighted in driving with considerable dash. As he escorted her to the entrance, he asked, "I say, Lady Carra, would you allow me to take you to dinner? Perhaps here in the hotel, if you like? Excellent food, especially the prawns."

She almost said no automatically but stopped herself. Why not? She was a free woman, she was hungry and he had been kindness itself to her all day. She could think of nothing nicer, she said. If he would excuse her for a minute, she would go to her room and change her clothes.

Only this morning, she thought as she hurried up the stairs, I doubted I could afford to have dinner here, or anywhere. And now -

"I've ordered champagne," he said, rising when she appeared, "I hope you don't mind." She shook her head happily. "And our first toast must be to the late Henrietta Carra!"

They drank and she raised her glass. "And now, to Hugh Carra."

"Who?"

"The present Lord Carra. He of the family plot."

"But of course. Who better?"

*   *   *

John Sherman

Back in London his lordship turned out to be a tough nut to crack. "Henrietta? That fruitcake? In the family plot? Is this a joke, Katherine?" were his opening observations.

She gradually wore him down. She had to concede that Henrietta's grip on reality may have slipped from time to time, but it was undeniable that she had loved her husband deeply and surely such a love should be respected. The Carra family was known across Ireland, she lied, for its strong family feelings, and to exclude the widow of the head of the family for the odd mental lapse would fly in the face of that noble tradition.

He retreated grimly under this kind of fire and at last gave his consent, upon which Katherine felt obliged to point out that Henrietta had died a Roman Catholic.

"A Popish fruitcake? Never!" He beetled away from her and slammed the door.

More powerful arguments were needed and to Hugh Carra nothing was more powerful than money. She suggested that if Henrietta were buried according to her will, she, Katherine, would come into a modest sum of money, part of which might accrue to the household exchequer in the form of a weekly rent.

The rent must be a matter for negotiation. After a few sharp exchanges they settled at three pounds a week, which she remembered was what Owen had paid. And a small price to pay for her legacy.

In no time she had written his letter to the vicar of St. Margaret's and placed the pen in his hand. Grumbling no more than normal, he signed and her heart flew up. Still, she didn't let herself believe it, not until she saw all three farms and Henrietta was well and truly in the Protestant earth.

She hurried to the post office and sent the cable to Messr. Cunningham Junior. He replied within the hour to congratulate her and to offer after the funeral to accompany her on a tour of her new properties. They were near her old family estate at Kilveen, he wrote, and could be seen in one day.

Of course I'll see them, she said to herself, but I'll wait until tomorrow to reply. I must not seem too eager, it's unladylike.

*　　　　　*　　　　　*

It was astonishing. The sun shone on Cork for the first time that month; the vicar was as good as his word and dispatched Henrietta with due ceremonial and not a hint of her apostasy; and an unexpectedly large number of friends from Katherine's days at Carra turned out. On Cunningham's advice and on his credit, she had at the last moment laid on a banqueting room at her hotel and there the post-entombment frolics went with a swing. No one pretended it was an occasion for sadness.

Every one at the burial and dozens more were there, including many of her old admirers, redder, louder and slower than she remembered them. The master of the hunt, Jeremy Dunn, who had pursued her with more doggedness than skill, still had hopes and still smelt of his damned dogs. Oliver Whiting, the new owner of Carra, hovered close by. Cunningham Junior showed no sign of a wife and somehow managed to give her his full attention and control the flow of food and drink. "Everyone's here who had a clean collar," he told her, smiling. She could not remember when she had enjoyed herself as much.

The next day, another fine day, the visit to her three farms was another splendid surprise. Accustomed to the dilapidation and squalor of the countless farms ruined in the second great famine, the pestilence that destroyed the Carra empire, Katherine found it hard to understand how the tenants of her own properties had survived and prospered.

"They were never in debt," Cunningham had explained, "not they or the trust. So they could pay their taxes and most of their rent and still have enough to eat." He stopped their carriage on a hill that overlooked the two larger farms. It was a magnificent vista. Ireland had never looked so inviting. To the northwest Katherine imagined she could see the wood that formed one of the boundaries of Kilveen. She decided she did not want to go there. That could wait for another time. Today was a day for happiness only.

"We – the trust – bought the three properties from the same estate," he went on. "Two are let to James Reilly, who is slowly paying off his small arrears." He pointed to the west with his whip. "The third farm lies down that valley. It's let to a young Scot named Hamilton, who we think will become a significant owner in this section."

Katherine was to leave the next morning and Cunningham promised to complete the transfer papers as soon as he could and post them to Rochester Place. Then he returned her to her hotel and drove away slowly, leaving her with much to think about, some of it disturbing. Her sudden affluence would allow her to examine her relationship with Charles Bartlett.

Chapter 53

This time they met at Palmerston's gloomy house in Piccadilly. Russell and Somerset looked subdued, the Prime Minister thought. It was out of character. They probably bore bad news of those Liverpool ironclads, when he'd assumed that the situation was well in hand.

He was right. "It's bad news, I'm afraid, Prime Minister," said Somerset, slumped in his overstuffed armchair and pulling at his whiskers. "I sent Captain Hoare of the Navy up to Liverpool to talk sense to this Bulloch fellow, offer to buy those two ships as we'd agreed. But he had no luck at all."

"What happened?" Palmerston asked. Blast it! he said to himself, this American war is the most frustrating business. Opportunity after opportunity comes along to do real damage to those Yankees and they all come to nothing. What now?

"Captain Hoare wrote a full report. Easiest if I read you bits of it." Palmerston didn't object so Somerset produced three pages of manuscript, cleared his throat and began:

"I met with Catain Bulloch and John Laird of the Laird firm at the latter's offices in Birkenhead. Both maintain that Bulloch had sold his positions in his contracts with Lairds for the construction of Hulls Number 294 and 295 (the two rams). The buyer is a French shipbuilder based in Bordeaux called Bravay & Cie. The new construction contracts between Lairds and Bravay have been signed and Bulloch has been paid out, so the two vessels are legally the property of Bravay. Bulloch's only connection with them now is that he is acting as technical consultant to Bravay until they are delivered to Bordeaux."

"Damn! Damn. Damn." whispered Palmerston. "Another one gone."

"There's more," Somerset admitted, "and it's worse:"

"Captain Bulloch naturally insisted that he is in no longer in a position even to listen to my offers to buy the two ships. 'At any price,' were his words on that score. He said he understood informally that Bravay have one or more buyers lined up to take the ships off their hands, but they might still listen to an offer from the Royal Navy."

"The guns," Palmerston said. "Does he mention their guns, or their ammunition?"

"Yes, but I'll revert to that subject later, if I may," Somerset said nervously. "To continue:"

"I therefore sent a telegram to Mr. Bravay asking for an interview and was invited to visit him at his works three days later, on the 18th of this month. I traveled to Bordeaux by way of Paris and met him on the appointed day.

A Friendly Little War

Mr. Bravay listened with care when I set out the purpose of my visit. He then confirmed what I had been told in Liverpool, namely that his firm now own the two ships outright. I offered him up to £120,000 for each ship, fully armed and equipped in his yard, and he declined the offer. It was not a question of price, he said. When I pressed him, he at first refused to expound on his refusal of my offer, saying in effect that it was no business of the Royal Navy what Bravay planned to do with their property. Then he relented and said that, in view of my wasted journey and the friendly relations between the French and British Navies, he could reveal one fact. That was that in these transactions his firm is acting as undisclosed agent for Ismail Pasha, the ruler of Egypt. The Pasha, on behalf of the Egyptian Navy, is the true owner of the two ships."

"What rubbish!" Palmerston blurted.

"It sounds like rubbish," Russell spoke at last, "but he convinced Captain Hoare, who expressed – with more delicacy, I trust – the same disbelief when he heard it."

Somerset said that Bravay had shown Hoare extensive files of correspondence, including orders, from the Egyptian Government in recent years. "No papers relating to these two ships, of course, but enough to persuade Hoare that Bravay has done a lot of business with the Egpyptians."

"Mr. Bravay also suggested that if it became necessary – referring I assume to proceedings before an English court – the Emperor himself would attest to the close and long-established relationship between the Bravay firm and the Pasha's family." Russell sighed. "That would be trouble that we don't need right now, Prime Minister, in view of the Emperor's position in Mexico."

"Sod the Emperor," Palmerston bluffed, "it's the Pasha I'm worried about."

"Who has already named his two new ships: the *El Tousson* and the *El Monassir*, if you please. Rather previous, one might think." Russell disliked needless haste in any enterprise.

"I still say it's rubbish," snapped Palmerston. To Russell he said, "Send one of your people to Cairo to verify this story."

"He left yesterday," Russell replied smoothly. "But we won't hear from him for at least a week, and that is only if the Pasha will see him straight away."

Palmerston pondered that for a minute, when Somerset ventured: "You asked about their cannon, Prime Minister. They're nine-inch Armstrong rifles, according to Bravay, to be delivered to Birkenhead soon."

"In England? But that would violate – "

"The neutrality laws? No, sir; France and Egypt are not combatants." Russell had verified this earlier.

"Worse and worse," Palmerston muttered. "Next you'll tell me they'll be armed with these new Palliser projectiles that you think so much of."

"Hoare attempted to find out, sir," Somerset said, "but Bulloch would only admit to having heard of them. He and then Bravay said it was a matter for the Egyptians."

"Indeed!" Palmerston felt it was time to take action. "Gentlemen, in a few days we shall witness two new, exceedingly formidable warships, designed by British engineers, built by British hands, sail serenely out of the Mersey under the French flag. Two ships that the Royal Navy wants, that it needs, that when armed with these new British projectiles can destroy every other foreign ship afloat. We cannot allow that. You must detain them, Foreign Secretary. Immediately."

"I will, just as soon as the law officers have constructed a plausible legal argument to detain them. The change from the Confederate Bulloch as owner to Bravay as owner – ignoring the Pasha – has weakened our case." Russell reveled in the legal quiddities of the neutrality law, and Palmerston feared that he was more concerned with the process than the results. "Add to that the possible need to satisfy the Emperor as to the merits of our case and – "

"Foreign Secretary," Palmerston said, measuring his words, "surely by now we can all recognize that we must act outside the neutrality law, by an Order in Council? The law officer must merely provide reasonable cover for our action."

"Ah. Another problem, I fear." Now Russell felt the first flushes of panic. "The responsible law officer was taken to hospital yesterday. A mental hospital; he's gone insane, temporarily they think. He was on the verge of a nervous attack, in any case, from the strain of building a plausible case against Bulloch, and the entry of the French firm pushed him over."

"Great Lord in Heaven! What next, damn it?" Palmerston fought for his poise. "Well, is there no other law officer capable of the work?"

"No, it's too specialized. And all the papers are at his house. We are looking for them now."

Palmerston let out a long breath. "Gentlemen, I'm weary of the endless difficulties in this exercise. I'll put it to you straight. One way or another, *those ships will not leave England.* Or I will hold you two directly responsible."

Chapter 54

Soon after Katherine's return from Cork she was sifting through the few letters in her post. The usual bills, two invitations and a letter with an Irish postmark She knew the handwriting – Patrick Cunningham, agent of her sudden wealth.

> "My dear Lady Carra," it read, "I have received a disturbing letter from a barrister in Dublin, one Harry Gilsenan. He claims to be the son of the late Henrietta Lady Carra by her first husband, Lawrence Gilsenan of Belfast. I have no reason to doubt this claim but have put in hand the usual enquiries in Dublin and expect a reply within a day or two.
>
> Mr. Gilsenan asks me to forward to him a copy of Lady Carra's will. Assuming he is her son, that is a legitimate request and I shall have to oblige him after a suitable delay while we attempt to ascertain the purpose of the request. In my experience, close relations who ask to see a will which has left them nothing never have the best interests of the major beneficiary in mind, so I expect trouble of some sort.
>
> If you can tell me anything of Mr. Gilsenan, please do so as soon as you can. I shall of course keep you apprised of any developments.
>
> Yours, etc.
>
> Patrick Cunningham"

Gilsenan? Katherine realized that she had not known even the name of Henrietta's first husband. And she had never mentioned a son. Despite her erratic and at times disturbing behavior, Henrietta had been, it seemed, unusually close-mouthed about her past.

Were there other children? Would they cause her any trouble? It came to her with a shock that she herself did not have a copy of the will, had never read it, in fact. She would write to Patrick to ask for a copy and tell him she knew nothing of any Gilsenans. She cleared a space on the table and found a pen.

Patrick Cunningham's second letter crossed Katherine's reply to his first. After noting that he had not yet heard from her, he went on:

> "According to my solicitor friends in Dublin, it seems that Harry Gilsenan is indeed the only son of the late Lady Carra. He is aged about thirty and engaged in the private practice of criminal law in Dublin. Much of his work, I am told, is concerned with the defense of Irish

subjects accused by the Crown of various offences under the sedition laws, and four of his clients will be sent for trial later in this year.

Having delivered to his office a copy of Lady Carra's will, as I was obliged to do, I was not surprised when he wrote to ask for an appointment. This meeting took place in my office today and I hasten to relate the substance of it.

Mr. Gilsenan did not indulge himself in critical or vindictive remarks against the mother who disinherited him. It was about what he expected of her, he said, as they never 'got along', to use his expression. He hinted that his late father bequeathed him some property in Dublin in anticipation of just such an action by his widow. 'How right the old boy was,' he said.

I began to hope that the interview would be as brief as I desired but he started to ask questions about you. I confirmed only that you are alive and therefore a beneficiary under his mother's will and that you live at 12 Rochester Place, London. I did not reply to any other questions and he as a lawyer did not really expect me to do so, but I began to think that he meant to alarm me.

Which proved to be the case. In an elliptical fashion, he let me know that he believes that the death of your husband was not in fact an accident, that you were somehow involved in his death and that he has evidence to prove it.

At this point he dropped all pretense of amiability and, I regret having to report, threatened you, through me. He swore that he can and will obtain further evidence and that he might then be minded to take that evidence to the police in Dublin.

I was of course silent during his exposition. When he finished, I reminded him that blackmail is a criminal offence and if that was what he contemplated I would report him to the police directly he left my office, which would take place before he could even find his hat.

He denied any such intent. He was merely suggesting, he said, that I forward the substance of his remarks to you and ask you to consider how important your legacy is to you.

He was in the street moments later, his hat following as he picked himself up. I doubt he will bring a charge of battery against me but I made no friend today.

I do not mean to alarm you, but Mr. Gilsenan plainly aims to make trouble. I have no idea how serious his threat may be. I can advise you, though, that convicted criminals can not in law benefit from an inheritance or legacy.

I will continue my research into Mr. Gilsenan's past and present in order to try to weigh the gravity of his threat. Meanwhile, perhaps you will be good enough to let me have your reaction to this regrettable letter.

Yours, etc.

Patrick Cunningham

PS.

On reading the foregoing, I fear I have not made it plain that, if for whatever reason you can not inherit under Lady C's will, the assets in her trust, i.e., the three farms, will go to Mr. Gilsenan as her closest surviving relation.

PC"

Katherine read the letter twice. She still held it as she slumped on her bed and lay back, tears sliding down her cheeks, her breathing short and harsh as a weight pressed hard on her chest.

"Dear God. Dear God in Heaven," she sighed after a few minutes.

When Milly admitted Bartlett that evening, Lord Carra spotted him as he moved toward the drinks tray and pressed a whisky on him.

"I hear you're doing well in the prize ring, sir," Bartlett said politely, sitting down. The room was brightly lit and a fire blazed under the Adam mantel.

"*Was* doing very well, you mean, blast it," Carra growled, glaring at his drink. Petulance was one of the few indulgences left to him. "Brought this big nigger over from Barbados, don't y'know, and he beat all comers for months. Now the damn fellow's gone soft, got too much attention from the ladies. Lost his last two bouts."

"Perhaps he needs a rest."

"Not as badly as my bank account needs one." The peer drained his glass, wiped his chin and stood up. "Here's Katherine, now." Looking pointedly at Bartlett, he asked, "Dinner at the usual time, my dear?"

At the table, Bartlett and Carra reviewed the war, interminably. Every day Carra read three newspapers, each with a special correspondent who maintained he was in the thick of things, so he knew every battle, every commander and every cannon ball, or so it seemed to his guest. And to Katherine. Why are men so insistent on details? she asked herself. First it was France, now it's Tennessee.

At last his lordship tottered upstairs to bed. Katherine's eyes followed him from the room. She turned back to Bartlett and gave a helpless shrug, half a smile on her lips. "You are very good company for him. He loves to talk about your war and other masculine things, and I can offer only feminine irrelevancies." She smoothed her skirt and looked up at him. "And now, I must tell you how my circumstances have changed."

"Tell me, please."

Briefly she told him of her legacy, of Henrietta, her three farms, Cunningham Junior and her two thousand a year. Not knowing if he had a view on Catholics being buried in a Protestant churchyard, she left that part out.

Bartlett was delighted for her. "Lady Carra, that's wonderful for you. Now you can really travel, go wherever you want to go."

"Yes, it is quite wonderful. I haven't yet grasped what it means for me now." She sighed and then frowned. "But my extraordinary good fortune is leading me into trouble."

She told the stunned Bartlett of her letters from Cunningham and Gilsenan's threats. She was calm now, but she still found it hard to assess her danger objectively.

Bartlett could scarcely take in what she was saying, but after a moment he recovered something of his poise. His immediate task, he thought, was to bring to bear some masculine logic. "That is dreadful, Lady Carra, truly dreadful, but think for a moment. You are innocent. What could this cretin, this Gilsenan, possibly know? What evidence could he possibly have? Nothing, nothing at all." He was persuading himself as he went along. "He's just trying to frighten you."

"I suppose you're right. And he's succeeding. I don't know why, but simply the thought that a man I don't know is threatening me like this is unsettling, it makes me feel - well, almost as if I were guilty."

*   *   *

On reflection, Katherine saw that Bartlett was of little help to her. Who else could she ask? Only Malcolm Bannerman. She knew no one else.

Bannerman, when she went to see him, was in an expansive mood. The banking business was good, his money troubles were well behind him and he had not given up hope of winning Katherine back. That she was now consulting him, and not the boorish Yank, Bartlett, over a genuine danger in her life could encourage him to think that she would soon be back, figuratively, in his arms for good. He was clutching at straws, he knew, but he still felt a small glow of optimism.

His advice to her was unexpected and had nothing to do with the law. "Look, my dear," he said, "the first thing you must do is to accept that you have an enemy, a declared enemy."

"All right," she said slowly. Then, "I do."

"Good. Now any man with military experience," he searched her face but saw no reaction, "will tell you that the next thing is to learn as much as you can about your enemy. What his objectives are, his capabilities, his weak points and so on. Especially his weak points."

"I know almost nothing about him. What Mr. Cunningham has written, that's all."

"Leave that to me. I have friends in Dublin. We'll soon know all we need to know about this Harry Gilsenan." He spat the name with lordly distaste, like a mouthwash. "I'll let you know as soon as I hear from them. Leave it all to me."

Chapter 55

It was now Robert Jones's turn to be bored. His trip north to Liverpool had so far been quick and successful. Now he could only wait, and the dreary Welsh seaside town of Holyhead offered little in the way of comfort, much less amusement. He sipped his ale disconsolately in the dim public room of the tavern and thought about the day before.

Dudley, the American consul in Liverpool, had hired a boat to carry them out into the Mersey to inspect the Laird rams. They ran past the long grey hulls of 294 and 295 moored side by side in the Birkenhead float. No chance of getting anywhere near these two from the river side, Jones concluded. We'll have to take them on at sea.

He saw that the armor plating of both ships was in place, all engines and condensers were installed, the funnels, the masts and the rigging looked complete and the turrets were centered. Dozens of men still worked on the turrets, though, fitting the extra-heavy armor to their circular sides.

"Any sign of crews for these two beauties?" he asked.

"We think so. The *Florida* put in to Ostend a week ago and disembarked about sixty men, who made their way to Calais and then disappeared. My men have spotted a few southern seamen in the local taverns, and I assume there's a lot more of them around here and that they're here to take these ships out as soon as they're ready."

In reply to Jones's question, Dudley said there had been no sign of cannon or ammunition and he didn't expect to see any. To mount the cannon or load the ammunition would violate the neutrality law.

"So they can rig the turrets and stay within the law, but not the ordnance?"

"Crazy, isn't it? The turrets alone do not 'arm or equip' a ship, unquote. All the fanciest lawyers agree on that. But just one round of ammunition does."

Dudley and his men had watched over 294 and 295 since their keels were laid, and Dudley claimed to know every rivet personally. On the equally slow return trip in the boat, farther out from the ships, he pointed out details of design and construction that Jones, a naval architect, would have missed.

When Jones had seen enough they repaired to Dudley's cramped office on the Liverpool side. They agreed that the two rebel warships could, in theory, leave at any time – if their engines worked. "They've run no sea trials, you know, but they've fired up the boilers twice and nothing blew out," said Dudley. "They could make it to France, for sure, if the English try to detain them here."

A Friendly Little War

Jones's primary mission was to meet the two Union warships that were storming across the Atlantic to intercept and sink the ironclads once they left the Mersey. The ships had been pulled off their stations along the Carolina coast and ordered to coal in Bermuda and make all speed to Holyhead, where Jones would be waiting for them with their final orders.

Holyhead was seventy five miles west of the mouth of the Mersey; far enough, Washington hoped, to avoid the Confederate spies and close enough to reach the Mersey in six or seven hours if need be. It also had a telegraph line that Dudley would use to tell Jones about the status of the rams. And if the telegraph failed it was no more than two hours away by rail. That the town was dreary beyond description couldn't be helped.

Dudley had tried to sympathize. "It's not that bad, Commander, and the Yardarm's a decent tavern. The food's not up to much but the rooms are all right."

*   *   *

Liar, Jones swore, when he surveyed his tiny bedroom under the eaves. But at least I'm close to the telegraph office here. Dudley would cable him every six hours and at once if the rams raised any steam. The two telegraph clerks were routinely bribed to take well-paid twelve-hour shifts.

Before heading for the evening train to Holyhead, Jones had first cabled Bartlett to join him there as soon as possible. Unless Bartlett had other urgent business, he'd added. Urgent business, indeed, he thought, Bartlett has had no urgent business since he got here.

Then he had gone to call on Patrick Burnett, who received him with a glass of sherry and cautious courtesy in his vast overstuffed drawing room. "I merely wanted to express the thanks and gratitude of the American navy, Mr. Burnett, for all the help you've given us over the past year or so." A pretty speech, he thought. Should he mention that he was asked to deliver it? No, there was no point.

His host seemed oddly relieved by those words, as if he'd expected something else. He inquired in formal tones after Charles Bartlett's health and well-being.

"Please give him my regards, Commander. He's been kind to my young nephew, and I was glad I could arrange for him to inspect that cruiser. Which I hear, by the way, is doing some damage to your merchant fleet."

"It is. We should have tried to damage *it* before it left Liverpool."

"Hindsight's a fine thing, they say." Burnett winced as he shifted his gouty foot away from the fire.

"Well, we know better now," Jones declared. "We have to, if we're to win this war."

"Will you win it, d'you think?"

"You can count on it – provided we can keep those two ironclads out of it. And it's thanks to you that we know just how dangerous they are."

"Not dangerous to you, though. Not any more."

"Oh? How do you mean?"

"Captain Bulloch – or the Confederates – doesn't own them now. He sold them to a French yard. Got a good price, too, I'm told." He looked at Jones with disdain. "Good Lord, man, don't all those spies of yours tell you anything?"

Stunned, Jones thought hard. What should he do? He had no idea. Only one, that he must ask Burnett for one more favor: that he say nothing of this to Dudley or any of his people.

Burnett agreed, having guessed Jones's reasons and expected his request. "Happy to be of service. Anything I will do anything that serves to end slavery."

"I'll drink to that." Jones clinked his glass against Burnett's, and soon afterwards he shook Burnett's hand with both of his and was on his way to the seaside.

*   *   *

It was a brilliant day, warm, no cloud, no wind. So perfect that it virtually announced itself as the last fine day of the year. So perfect that Katherine took herself and her latest novel off to her bench in Sackville Square. She counted on an hour or two in the sunshine, to herself and away from her troubles with the law.

The book's villain was behaving vilely, just as she'd hoped, when she noticed a man walking towards her from the direction of Rochester Place. A young man, perhaps thirty, tall, fashionably dressed. Too fashionably, in fact; the coat was an inch too long, the cravat an inch too wide. He passed by, stopped and walked back towards her.

She scarcely had time for an icy premonition when he said politely, "Have I the honor of addressing Lady Carra?"

She looked up to see a pleasant, open face with blue eyes, black hair and an attractive smile. No matter; she knew who he was. "Yes," she said firmly. "Who are you, sir?"

"Gilsenan, Lady Carra, Harry Gilsenan at your service. I've been admiring your houses in Rochester Place, and your maid said you might be here."

A flat lie. Milly would never say that to a stranger. He'd been watching her. She kept silent.

"I spoke to your solicitor, Mr. Cunningham, a few weeks ago and I believe he wrote you about it?"

"He did." She folded her book and began to rise to escape but thought better of it. She was sure she was in no physical danger and it was wiser to learn from him what he had to say than from another source.

He read her thoughts. "Good. Now if you'll allow me to impose on your time for five minutes, I'll state my business and leave you in peace."

"Go ahead."

"May I sit down?"

"Not near me."

"So be it," he smiled and took up a position six feet in front of her, crossing his arms. "When my mother died," he began, "she left me, her only child, nothing. Only her clothes and books. And her diaries. That was all right, I thought, that was all she had, because that old fool Carra had lost every last penny she brought to their marriage. I asked the older Cunningham if she had any other assets and I believed him when he said no. Technically he was correct: the three farms in the trust were not her property, they were the property of the trustees. He tricked me, deliberately. I never even read her will, more fool I."

The bitterness in his tone was unmistakable and, to Katherine's surprise, deserved some sympathy. She stayed silent, though.

"So when a clerk in the Dublin courthouse told me that she had left three farms to you, and you no relation to her at all, I demanded as a legatee to see a copy of her will. Sure enough, her trustees were instructed to distribute the farms to your husband, to Henry Carra."

"To me, you mean!"

"Hah! Cunningham didn't tell you that, did he? I thought not." Gilsenan sensed an advantage here. "No, Lady Carra, my mother left those farms to your husband, and to you only if he didn't survive her. Ask Cunningham. Tell him to send you a copy. You'll see I'm right."

"I've asked him for one."

"Well, read it carefully, if I may suggest. You'll see I'm right. Plain as day."

"Why didn't she change her will when he died, then?"

"I don't know. Just forgot, I suppose, and Cunningham saw no need for her to change it."

"Will this take much longer, Mr. Gilsenan?"

"I'll try to hurry." He assembled his thoughts.

"Please do."

"All right, Lady Carra, my cards on the table," he hissed. "Fair and square. It's about your husband. About how he died."

She felt him watching her closely as she fought to keep her nerve. "Good day, Mr. Gilsenan." She stood up and started away, looking straight ahead.

"I did some digging," he said slowly as he kept by her side. "I went to Cork and then to Carra, talked to people, some of your old friends around there. A few of them hinted they think you killed Lord Carra, or more likely had him killed. But they don't blame you. A real pig, was he?"

She stopped short, her face dead white and blank. "What rot," she breathed. "You're mad, Mr. Gilsenan, and insulting."

"Am I? You should read my mother's diaries. I did, at last. You all thought *she* was mad, didn't you?" He sounded genuinely angry. "Well, she wasn't. She liked you, she kept her eye on you all the time and she kept her conclusions in her diaries. She wrote that you wanted him dead, and that there was more than one man hanging around you who would have done him for you. They were with you the night he died, in fact, when she heard some very strange talk."

"A pity she's not here to repeat her fantasies."

"Your servants were witnesses. And there are the star witnesses – you, Lady Carra, and your Irish friends Dunn and Lord Whiting."

"They wouldn't say one word to you, Mr. Gilsenan."

"I know. But they'll talk to the police. They'll have to. And it's to the police I'm going next. The police will be glad to see me, you can bet on it."

"Then you must be on your way to them."

"I will, you can be sure of that, unless you and I can settle this business out of court, so to speak." He smiled with an almost childlike appeal.

"Explain yourself."

"It's too simple. If you make over those three farms to me, free and clear, then I forget all about your husband and whoever helped him on his way. I swear I'll drop it for all time. All I want are those farms."

"Good day, Mr. Gilsenan." Katherine started walking again.

He walked beside her despite her grimace of repulsion. "I swear I'll never say another word if you do."

"I've had enough of this insult. I'm calling a policeman."

"Oh, I'll leave you now, Lady Carra. But remember one thing: in Ireland, a convicted criminal can't inherit anything. Nothing. So those farms will go to me in the end, when they put you away. Better to accept my offer now." He paused, shrugged. "I'll give you a few days. A very few days. Cunningham will know how to find me."

He bowed and left her, standing rigid on the edge of Sackville Square. There was still no cloud in the blazing blue sky.

* * *

She returned home immediately in a state of shock and she sent Milly round with a note to Malcolm Bannerman, asking if she could call on him at his office again to bring him up to date. His reply came back with Milly, inviting her over that afternoon.

"My Lord, Katherine, that is a truly horrible story. Poor you." Malcolm Bannerman was at his most comforting. "That's everything he said to you?" She nodded. "And you've spoken to no one else about this?" Another, more vigorous nod. "Good." She hadn't turned to Bartlett. After all that had taken place between himself and her, she believed that he was the only man who could help her. And he would.

He had found that in these circumstances the fatherly approach was best, and he was good at it. "Poor you," he repeated, "what a ghastly experience. But don't worry. It can't be as bad as you think it is. More tea? No?" He waved away the clerk who held the teapot in the doorway and came around his desk to sit beside her on the sofa.

She smiled feebly at him. "You're so kind, Malcolm. I'm dreadfully sorry to trouble you."

"It's nothing, my dear. You know I'm always here to help if I can. Now, the more I look at what he said, the less worried I am for you. So we should look at Gilsenan himself, for a change." He rested his hand on her shoulder and moved confidently back to his desk, where he extracted a folder from the central drawer and opened it.

"Gilsenan does have some strong points, according to my friends in Dublin. He has money of his own, no one knows from where. A surprisingly successful barrister for a young man, with a reputation for getting Republican thugs off." He looked up at her from the paper in his hand. "And some weak points, as well. The police know him as a chancer, who's been accused of tampering with criminal juries and, at least once, of trying to bribe a High Court judge. They would like to remove him from circulation but so far they have nothing solid on him."

"Good Heavens! To think he's the son of poor, dear Henrietta!"

"And the late Mr. Gilsenan, don't forget, of whom we know nothing." He pulled at his chin. "Anyway, I haven't told you the worst about his son. It seems that before he set up his practice our friend was known as a hard man, on the rougher fringes of the Republican Brotherhood. The rumor is that they paid his way to the bar in gratitude for some of his earlier, ah, accomplishments."

"Such as murder?" she asked weakly.

"No, such as the occasional broken arm and broken head. Nothing too serious."

"How can you say that?" Her hand was at her throat in alarm.

Bannerman ignored her. "So if he persists with his threats - or even if he doesn't - I suggest we fight fire with fire, have him frightened off."

"I won't hear of it!" She wasn't sure she meant that.

"Precisely. You'll hear no more of this, ever. Just leave it to me. Please."

"What will you do, Malcolm?" She was frightened now, but curious.

"Perhaps nothing, but whatever it takes to persuade Mr. Gilsenan to leave you alone." He held up a hand. "If necessary, my dear, only if it's plainly necessary. I promise."

She was silent for a time, her thoughts straying from Gilsenan. "Odd, isn't it? I would never have dreamed that I could sit here and listen to what you've said without running away." A sad, deep sigh. "It just proves how much my farms mean to me. If I can keep them, I'll be free, you see, and I can do with my life what I *want* to do, not what I *have* to do because I'm penniless. Does that make any sense to you, Malcolm?"

"I suppose it does."

She guessed at the anxiety and confusion in his mind, but she made no attempt to dispel them..

Chapter 56

Detective Crawford was proud of his air of quiet, unblinking menace and it showed. He drank his tea in the approved manner, kept his voice low and calm and accepted Bartlett's presence in the Carra drawing room with indifference. He explained that this was the first, routine stage of the station's enquiries into allegations made by a private citizen to the police in Dublin

Katherine had told Bartlett of her confrontation with Gilsenan in the park, the reason for his hatred of her and his threat to continue investigating Henry's death. This interview was obviously his doing, she said. Bartlett had insisted that he wanted to help her, and he could only help if he was in the room with her. At the least, he could prevent Crawford from bullying her.

"I'd rather hoped you'd say that. I prefer you to hear all of it, because if you don't you may become suspicious yourself."

"Of you? What a joke."

"Ah, so you say now, but who can tell what dark secrets I hide in my past?"

"I can't wait to hear them."

Crawford gave him his second most intimidating stare and opened his notebook. Expensive leather, Bartlett noted. Crawford pushed his teacup aside and faced Katherine. Acting upon information received, he began, the Cork police had opened an investigation into the death of Henry Lord Carra. He, Crawford, had been selected to visit Cork to consult the police there. It would save them all time, he said, if he began by reciting the background to Henry Carra's death, welcoming any comments Lady Carra cared to make, and then went into the questions that had arisen thus far.

"Fine," Katherine said brightly, "fire away, Detective."

Crawford skipped quickly over Henry's marriage to Katherine, his wounding in the Crimea and his subsequent 'fondness for drink', the death of his father and his eventual bankruptcy. By that point, he observed slyly, Katherine must have believed that she faced a bleak future as the wife of a penniless alcoholic.

"You're out of line, Crawford," Bartlett warned as he half rose from the sofa.

"Don't be upset, Charles," Katherine said. "The detective wants to provoke me and see how I react, that's all. Do go on, Mr. Crawford."

He did. Katherine was fortunate, he said, in having many friends in the county to support and console her in her difficulty. There was Mr. Doolan, for example.

"Our solicitor," Katherine said

"Mr. Padmore."

"Our banker, poor man."

"Lord Whiting."

"A neighbor. Really, Mr. Crawford, shall I list all our friends for you?"

"Mr. Dunn, Jeremy Dunn."

"Joint master of the Kilcarroll Hunt."

"And a frequent visitor."

"Yes. He taught me how to ride properly."

"And was his frequent presence an irritation to Lord Carra?"

"What do you think? Henry couldn't ride and he so, of course, was jealous of our rides together."

Crawford waited a moment or two and then described what he plainly expected to be met with astonishment – Henrietta's diaries. These, he said, had been turned over to the Irish police but he had been allowed to review them and make notes. Katherine received this impassively. Bartlett looked concerned as he glanced at her. Her profile told him nothing.

Henrietta, Crawford said, wrote a full page in her diary every day of her life after her husband died. It may have been one of the few consolations left to her, he surmised. She was fond of the present Lady Carra and wrote at length about her daily activities.

"Her style was, ah, ambiguous, shall I say, and at times almost incoherent. She used pet names or code names for people. For example, you, Lady Carra, were often called Butterfly. Does that surprise you?"

"Nothing Henrietta did surprised me. She was ever so slightly mad, I always thought."

Milly came in to turn up the gas lamps, throwing Crawford a steely glare as she passed behind him. Katherine pointedly did not ask her to bring fresh tea and Crawford took note.

Henry Carra had closed the wing of Carra House in which his father and Henrietta had lived, to save the cost of heating it, and Henrietta moved to the east wing with Henry and Katherine. "This," said Crawford, "was a great boon to her, because she had remarkable powers of hearing or of imagination. Or both. Her diary became concerned, Ma'am, with you and Lord Carra. Intimately concerned, if I may say so."

This riposte to the snub he had just perceived pleased him. That was as obvious to Bartlett as to Katherine. He looked a question at her and inclined his head at the door. She shook hers firmly.

"She was also preoccupied with her will, according to the diary," Crawford went on, disappointed at the lack of any outburst from Bartlett. "She had placed some property in a trust and made Lord Carra its beneficiary. She writes that she often told you that she was minded to make you the beneficiary instead. This was often after Lord Carra had taken more drink than he could manage."

"She never said one word to me about that trust. I only learned of it after she died." Katherine glanced at Bartlett with appeal in her splendid eyes.

"Well, as I said, her diary is at times incoherent." Crawford seemed anxious to allay her fears. "Still quoting from her diary, there is a close correlation between the dates when she wrote that she had decided not to make you the beneficiary and the visits of Mr. Dunn. And others." He plainly rejoiced in the "Others", thinking he had scored heavily.

"I said she was mad; you said she had a remarkable imagination," Katherine said coolly. "Take your choice, Detective. You might also take your leave, unless you come to the point straight away. It's late."

"As you wish, Milady. I'll go straight to the night Lord Carra died." He would quote from Henrietta's diary, he said as he pulled two sheets of paper from his breast pocket and laid them on his knees. "You had two guests for dinner that night, Mr. Dunn and Lord Whiting, both of them bachelors, as it happened." He glanced at Bartlett, who did not react. "Your voices got louder and louder, some sort of angry argument. Lord Carra seemed to be accusing you of being too familiar with one or both of the other men. He shouted something about Mr. Dunn and his damned dogs. You departed the dining room and ran up the stairs to your bedroom and slammed the door." He looked at her and raised his eyebrows. "Lady Carra? Any comment?"

"That's all quite true, Detective." Katherine seemed almost indifferent to his recital. "Henry had drunk far too much, again, and he was very angry. I left the table hoping that would calm him down."

Crawford resumed his story. "There was more shouting from the dining room, and after a long time you went back down the stairs. Your stepmother wrote that this time she opened her door to watch you. Lord Whiting and Mr. Dunn left the dining room and met you in the entrance hall. Mr. Dunn called out something over his shoulder in the direction of the dining room, but your husband didn't come out."

"He called to Henry that they would let themselves out. Lord Whiting said he thought Henry was too tight to hear him."

Crawford looked down at his papers. "One of the guests left, she thought it was Lord Whiting, and the other stayed talking to you."

"That was Mr. Dunn. He asked me to call a servant to help Henry to his bedroom."

"And did you call a servant?"

"No. It would have infuriated Henry and embarrassed the servant. Mr. Dunn and I left him in the dining room."

"Lady Carra heard nothing for a few minutes and then heard a loud cry – she thought it was from your husband. Then nothing more was heard by her."

"Mr. Dunn did not leave, or at least he did leave but then returned almost immediately. He and Lord Whiting went back to the dining room to wheel Henry to his bedroom on the other side. Henry objected loudly, I suppose. I went upstairs and to bed."

"You 'suppose', Lady Carra? Did you ask them about it later?"

"Yes. They said Henry had objected to being wheeled about. I can't say I blamed him."

"You didn't go to help him?"

"No, I was tired and angry at him. He could help himself."

"Were you very angry at him?"

"Yes, of course. He'd insulted me and my friends."

Crawford folded the papers and returned them to his pocket. "Lady Carra's diary contains no more regarding her stepson's death that is not in the public record. So if you'll allow me a few more minutes, Milady, I'll now refer to the inquest report, which is notably brief."

"How much longer, Detective?" Bartlett asked.

"A few minutes, no more." Crawford faced Katherine again. "Let me see. Lord Carra was found the next morning by the gardener in the small pond or pool in the center of his rose garden. He was submerged face down and was not breathing and was not alive at the time. The pond was four feet deep where he was found. His bath chair was on its side at the edge of the pond, about five yards from his body. The medical examiner found no injuries or bruises on his body. There was no evidence of suicide or foul play and so the coroner ruled that it was death by misadventure."

He took another look at his notes, cleared his throat and went on. "The police investigation was at best rudimentary, as is now admitted by all concerned. Only one local constable had the wit to attempt to determine how Lord Carra got himself to the pond. Do you remember that, Ma'am?"

"Yes. He wheeled himself on the flagstone path. He always used it to reach his garden."

"That path was covered with a thin layer of gravel, and there were no wheel marks on the gravel when the police arrived at your house. That week was completely dry, so the marks were not washed away by any rain. It's all here in the police report."

"Well, then I imagine he went over the lawn. If it was so dry, there would have been no wheel marks on the lawn, either."

"That lawn has a steep upslope at the bottom, up to the pond, you'll remember. The present owner, Lord Whiting, allowed us to carry out some experiments last week. None of us could wheel ourselves up that gradient alone."

"Perhaps my husband was stronger than you, from his years in his chair. Or perhaps the grass is longer now, or the ground is softer."

"Perhaps. We suspect that Lord Carra had to be helped up to that pond. He was a large man and, strong as he may have been, we doubt he could wheel himself up that slope by himself. We think it more likely that somebody pushed him up it, or, more likely still, carried him up it to the pond. And that it was two men, not one, seeing how large he was." Crawford wore a self-satisfied grin.

Katherine sounded annoyed. "Why are you telling us all this, Detective? Your suspicions are of no interest to either of us."

"Because they suggest that Lord Carra's death was not actually a death by misadventure, Ma'am."

"That it was murder, you mean," said Bartlett evenly. "And that Lady Carra may have been involved." He took Katherine's hand. "Lady Carra, tell Mr. Crawford that you'll answer no more questions, that if he has any evidence that implicates you he must produce it and that if he wants to question you again he must write to your solicitor."

"Murder or assisted suicide, Major. That's a possibility as well." Crawford put away his notes and stood up, still ignoring Bartlett's last sentence. "Thank you for your time, Lady Carra, and for the tea. It has been most kind of you to assist me in my investigation of both these matters."

Katherine had recovered most of her poise. "I'm pleased to help, Detective, but you understand that I endorse what Major Bartlett just said. You must do that if you hope for any more cooperation from me." She rang for Milly.

"I will advise my superiors at Staunton Street of the Major's remarks. Allow me to conclude by saying that I and my colleagues here and in Cork will continue our investigations, by interviewing other parties who may be in a position to shed new light on them." Milly appeared in the doorway, almost tapping her foot. "Good night, Ma'am, Major." He followed Milly out of the room.

"A long-winded young man," Bartlett observed at last, trying to ease the tension. "He's trying to make bricks out of straw, if you ask me. Has no evidence for almost anything he said."

"You're surprisingly casual, Charles," said Katherine, "considering that what evidence he has is against me and that he thinks he'll find more. Evidence of a very serious crime, need I add?" She was absorbing the implications of Crawford's visit.

"You're right. Sorry." Bartlett sighed and sat back down. "Does his lordship leave any of his good whisky around, do you suppose?"

"Good Heavens, Charles? Already?" She laughed lightly and moved to a marquetry chest and extracted a dusty bottle and two glasses. "Haven't you been warned? I've already killed one drunk."

"I'll drink this with care, then, and I'll stay well away from your garden. Thanks."

"I'll join you," she sighed, "just to keep you company." She downed a small measure and put down the glass. "Well! What do you think? What should I do now?"

"Get yourself a lawyer, fast. Crawford won't quit now; he smells blood." He would ask Pettigrew, the ministry's lawyer, to advise her or to recommend another man.

"Thank you. A specialist in criminal law, please." Another silence. "You know, I've never been in a situation remotely like this, suspected of a serious crime, and I don't know how to react. I'm just numb."

"That's natural. You'll have to rely on your lawyer, do what he says." Why couldn't he, Bartlett, give her any sensible advice? "When he hears the so-called evidence, he'll make you see that they have no case, that it's all a bluff."

They talked for another hour or so. As he took his leave he realized that he had learned much from the events of that day, much that he felt he should have already known from their previous conversation. It had been a harder life than he'd suspected. Had it made her harder than he knew?

Chapter 57

"Holyhead, Major? What on earth takes you there?" Adams' curiosity was genuine. He and Bartlett were on much better terms these days, but he could not help dreading that any journey out of London by Bartlett would bring down on his ministry's head a catastrophe of some sort. This dread was reinforced when Bartlett said he was going up there, dangerously near the Laird rams, to join forces with Jones, the loosest of cannons.

"Commander Jones needs a messenger boy, sir, in case those rams start to move."

Well, that was all right, Adams said to himself. "Very well, but if they do move, you will cable me at once, please, so I can protest to Lord Russell."

"Of course I will, sir." In a pig's eye. Adams wanted only to stop the rams. Bartlett wanted to capture or sink them.

*   *   *

From the Liverpool station, ten minutes' drive took Bartlett to the end of Wirral Dock, where Hull 294 was tied up in front of 295. He told the driver to wait and he strolled down the dock towards the two ships.

They looked much longer, taller and deadlier than Bartlett had imagined. The grey hulls rode high in the water, but even so he could see the lines of 294's forward turret, with an empty eye where her guns would go, and the sinister shape of the underwater ram projecting from her bow. Bartlett had not believed that a ram could be so dangerous in combat, but now he did. Our frigates will need to stay well away from those things, he thought. He shivered as they walked the length of the two ships.

Beside the stern of 295 he saw rows of large wooden crates. The markings on the first row all said Armstrong & Co. Ltd. The second row – shells. Palliser shells, by God, he said to himself. Look at the colors painted on the tops of the crates – black, white and red. They're Pallisers, all right. Two shells per crate.

But where were the gun barrels? None of the crates was big enough. He looked around for guards but saw none. That section of the dock was empty of workmen. He couldn't think why Bulloch left the crates out in the open. Surely they were in violation of the neutrality laws?

Bartlett had seen enough. And he was lucky. The first train to Chester made a quick connection with the new Holyhead line, and he rattled westward across North Wales in first class comfort. A cold lunch and a glass of warm ale in the dining car and he walked out the entrance of the Admiralty Pier Station before dark. There to learn that the Yardarm Inn, where Jones was lurking, lay in the old harbor section, ten minutes' drive away over the crowded cobbled streets

The damp salt air was replaced by the reek of stale beer that assailed him as he made his way to the public bar, where the tattooed owner assured him that his room awaited him on the second floor and Jones awaited him in the dining room. "Real pleased he was to get your telegram this morning, real pleased." Bartlett shook his head. Jones seemed to have a strange need for these malodorous inns.

One look at his closet-sized bedroom convinced him to move out in the morning, but that evening he owed to Jones. He shrugged, dropped his case and worked his way down the stairs.

"This place isn't too bad, is it?" Jones, wearing his anonymous grey suit, saluted him from a bare wooden table in the dining room. "The bar goes quiet before midnight and the wagons don't crash around in the street outside till about five, so we'll survive. We don't want to be too conspicuous, anyway," staring hard at Bartlett's uniform.

Bartlett reserved comment, ordered a brandy punch from the pubescent waitress and told Jones of his visit to the Birkenhead docks.

"Cannon and shells? Bulloch must have gone crazy. That'll – no, think, Jones, think, you idiot." He quoted what Burnett had revealed, that Bulloch had sold the rams to the French.

"He sold them to the French? The French, by God!"

"You see what this means, don't you?" Jones leaned forward as he whispered.

"It means we can't touch them. That we'll have to tell our ship captains to head right back to Carolina." Bartlett sipped his punch. "Unless of course they want to start a war with France, and lose their ships, by tangling with the two ironclads."

"No, no," Jones growled. "Look: we'll tell *no one* that they're French owned; not Adams, not the captains." Jones was excited now. "We'll deploy our ships so they'll be waiting for the rams when they come down the Mersey – unarmed – to the sea. Our men will believe they're rebel ships and will attack them. And sink them."

"*If* they're unarmed." Bartlett was doubtful. "We have to be sure that they *are* unarmed." He thought a bit. "And they will be armed unless they have to leave in a hurry -"

"Right. And they'll leave in a hurry only if Bulloch believes that the English will try to detain them. So – " Jones stopped, then started, "so the English will have to try to detain them. That's obvious enough."

"We could cable Adams about the cannon and the shells I saw, and he'll run to protest to Lord Russell." Bartlett paused. "No, that's no good. Russell would just demand to see a sworn affidavit and consult his tame law officers."

"Any other ideas, chief?"

"Just one." Bartlett spelled it out. "We can rely entirely on this man."

"It's worth a try. Will you draft the cable? I'll get another beer while you do."

A few minutes later, as Jones stared meditatively into space, Bartlett pushed a paper across the sticky table to him.

"TO PATRICK BURNETT ESQ", Jones read. "Do you have his cable address?"

"Yes, upstairs in my case."

> "HAVE TO ASK YOU MOST REPEAT MOST IMPORTANT FAVOR STOP URGENT THAT APPROPRIATE OFFICIALS MADE AWARE THAT VESSELS IN YOUR DRAWINGS WILL SOON BE EQUIPPED WITH MATERIAL ALREADY AT DOCKSIDE STOP THIS WILL BE CLEAR VIOLATION OF RELEVANT LAWS STOP AM HOPING THAT AUTHORITIES WILL IMMEDIATELY TAKE INDICATED ACTION STOP PLEASE REPLY TO JONES AT YARDARM INN OLD HARBOR HOLYHEAD STOP MANY THANKS AND BEST OF LUCK
> YOUR NEPHEWS FRIEND"

Jones handed the paper back. "Will he understand a word of this?"

"He will." Bartlett toyed with his glass. "But even if this works, and the rams leave unarmed, they'll still be flying French flags. How do we persuade our captains to attack them?"

"Easy. Flying a false flag, usually a flag of a neutral country, is common practice when ships face a battle at sea," Jones said with confidence. "These captains will know all about that."

"If you say so. I'll send this cable when the frigates arrive, which had better be soon."

"Oh, they're here, arrived at noon today. Dear me. Didn't I mention it? Not frigates, though. The *Arapaho*, the *Delaware* and the *Seminole*, three well-armed steam sloops of war, all ostensibly looking for the *Alabama*. *Delaware*'s at the coaling station now, the other two are anchored in the old harbor and will coal first thing tomorrow."

"You do like your surprises, don't you?" Bartlett had to laugh. "When do we see their captains?"

"Right now. Those three men coming into the room. They'll join us for dinner. Mind your manners, please, and eat nicely."

*   *   *

John Sherman

Patrick Burnett had no trouble understanding Bartlett's telegram when he read it at nine the next morning. He called for Harrison and sent him to find Captain O'Hara and bring him back to the house.

O'Hara entered Burnett's study an hour later, listened for ten minutes and was out the door, headed for Birkenhead in Burnett's carriage. "I'll swing by the rams first, sir," he'd said as he left Burnett, "and then go to the Customs office. I know just the man to talk to there."

*   *   *

Bartlett and Jones were on the quay, chatting with Captain Whetcraft of the *Delaware*, when the serving girl from the Yardarm ran up to Jones with a telegram in her fist. "For you, sir," she cried and ran back to the tavern.

It was from Burnett:

> "YOUR FRIENDLY CAPTAIN REPORTED DOCKSIDE MATERIAL TO SENIOR AUTHORITIES THIS MORNING STOP THEY PROMISED IMMEDIATE CABLE REPORT TO LONDON STOP WILL ADVISE ANY DEVELOPMENT STOP NOTE NONE OF DOCKSIDE MATERIAL LOADED SO FAR STOP YOURS IN LIBERTY
> PATRICK"

The three sloops of war had finished coaling. The wind had held on their voyage from Bermuda and they'd made most of the run under sail, so they only required about one hundred tons each to top up their bunkers.

"Right, Captain Whetcraft," said Jones crisply. "We'll leave as soon as your ships are ready. Major Bartlett and I will wait at the Yardarm for your cutter." Jones's manner was impressively commanding, Bartlett thought. There had been some respectful discussion at dinner about the chain of command for the operation, but Jones's orders stated that he was in overall charge. This actually suited the three sailors. They sensed that some tricky decisions were coming that would be made only on political grounds, and they had no wish to have to make them.

Jones's order also stated that Whetcraft was the senior of the three captains. Bartlett and Jones would therefore sail in the *Delaware* with him.

Whetcraft, short, white-haired and fighting a uniform that had grown too tight for him, saluted and left them. "How old do you think he is, Charles?" Jones asked. "Fifty ? Fifty-five?"

"Fifty-five, anyway. Just think, you have another twenty years at your same rank ahead of you."

A Friendly Little War

"Well, at least I'm seeing the world."

The elegant secretary pushed his head around the door to Lord Russell's room at the Foreign Office. This was his third year in his post and he was still unable to gauge his superior's mood. He brought what he feared was bad news, but one never knew.

"Yes, what is it, Carruthers? Come in. man, don't hang about the door like a, a - whatever. Come in."

"It's a dispatch from the Treasury, sir, a copy of a telegraphic report from the Chief Inspector of Customs at Merseyside." He held up a paper. "I can't think why they sent it on to you."

"They sent it on to me," Russell said with emphasis as he read it, "because the Chancellor is aware that the Prime Minister has made me responsible for dealing with those wretched ships in Liverpool. As you should also be aware, by now. You've made enough notes on the subject, I should think." He dropped the paper on his desk and pursed his lips.

At length he looked up at the hovering aide. "That law officer, the one dealing with this question of neutrality law – is he back at work?"

"No, sir, he's at home now."

"So there's no time left to involve him. Therefore, this is no longer a matter of law. Any action I can take will be an act of state, an exercise of prerogative, outside the process of law. Do you understand?"

"Yes, sir."

"Good. Then go find one of our tame lawyers and tell him for me to draft an Order in Council instructing the Chief Inspector of Merseyside to detain these two vessels immediately. They will be detained under armed guard until we can determine who their true ultimate owners are."

"Yes, sir."

"Then draft a telegram from me to the Chief Inspector stating that the Order has been issued and he should be ready to act tomorrow morning."

Carruthers was frantically making notes. He looked up when he finished.

"Then, send in a messenger. I'll write a note to the Chancellor asking him to stand by to sign the Order with me. Off you go, now."

Ten minutes later, the note on its way, Russell sat back and contemplated what he was about to do. First, he was stepping outside the established law, but the cabinet had the authority to do that.

Next, he would risk infuriating the Emperor – but he had heard Palmerston on that subject. Besides, the cannon and projectiles lying on the dock would prove that the alleged French owners intended to "arm or equip" the ships for combat, almost a clear breach of the neutrality law.

Then, he would also risk infuriating Jefferson Davis, but he could live with that. Davis had nowhere else to turn for help.

Finally, and most important, he would obtain for the Royal Navy two of the four most powerful warships in the world, ships that, armed with the new armor-piercing projectiles, would make scrap iron of the vaunted Federal ironclads and smash the Federal blockade.

The question of recognizing the Confederacy was boiling up again. Perhaps, after seizing the South's two best ships – for he had few doubts as to the rams' eventual destination – England was obliged in fairness to recognize it. In that event, the two rams would destroy the Federal navy in the war that was sure to follow.

Not a bad day's work, he thought contentedly. He sat back and waited for the papers he had ordered to appear on his desk.

The Foreign Office lawyers, all but the most senior of their number, worked in a large drafty chamber on the top floor. Carruthers approached the desk of the man he knew best, one Holloway, who listened intently, making notes, and then said, "Nothing easier. I know the form, done it dozens of times. Hulls 294 and 295 you say? Right. You'll have it in, oh, half an hour."

It was twenty minutes, in fact, and Holloway accepted Carruthers's breathless thanks with modesty. Then he headed for the main Westminster post office and its telegraph room. Captain Bulloch would pay him double for this one.

*   *   *

At least double, Bulloch was thinking an hour later. That man's the best investment I've ever made. He folded the telegram and put it in his coat pocket.

He had hoped that, if he did not load any of the brightly marked crates that contained the cannon accessories and the Palliser shells, the Customs would hold off detaining his ships in the confident expectation that he would in the end put at least one crate aboard and they'd have him dead to rights That would buy him the time to finish fitting out and provisioning the ships for the short dash to Bordeaux. But it was not to be.

Both vessels had enough water aboard and enough coal in their bunkers – brought over the gangplank at night in small loads – to get them to Bordeaux even if they had to steam all the way. All they lacked were officers and crew.

The dozen officers were lodged in his hotel. Bulloch called them together, told them that Plan Bordeaux was on and they would sail at seven the next morning. They left to dig their crews out of the cheap waterside inns that held them. Thirty men per ship were enough to reach Bordeaux, where the rest of their complement waited to join them.

Bulloch went back to his room. He had selected both captains and had complete confidence in them. His role was over. He could not take the slightest risk - if there was any trouble with the authorities - to be seen to be connected with 294 and 295.

He would watch in the morning from his window as they steamed past him, on the first leg of their way to devastate the Yankee blockading fleet.

Chapter 58

The River Mersey flows north into Liverpool Bay, entering it at the apex of the right angle formed by the bay. One coast of the bay runs north towards Scotland, the other runs west along The Wirral. Both coastlines are made up of stretches of barren sand dunes, and the shallow bay between them is a complex mix of shifting sand bars and narrow, winding channels. Many of the bars are visible at low tide, but those that remain under water are the greatest threats to navigation.

Dawn comes late at those latitudes in the late autumn, and the morning mist had just begun to clear and reveal a fine day, with smooth sea and a light westerly wind, when Bartlett and Jones joined Captain Whetcraft on the quarterdeck of the *Delaware*. The three screw sloops lay at anchor off Formby Point, at the edge of the Crosby Channel, the principal route north through the Bay from Liverpool. They were five miles north of the Mersey's mouth and half a mile from the eastern shoreline of the channel.

The three ships waited, steam up, sails furled, gun ports down, the guns pivoted to starboard and the whole battery loaded. The decks were newly holystoned, the guns polished and the brightwork cleaned. The crew had been inspected at quarters and dismissed, although every man expected the drum to beat to general quarters at any time.

"High water's not until noon," Whetcraft was saying, "and those ironclads will draw about thirteen feet unloaded. But there's already plenty of water in this channel and, if Bulloch knows that the English are after them, I believe they'll make a run for the Bay any time now. I would."

"There's no cover for us here, Captain," Jones observed. "Should we anchor farther down the channel?"

"If they identify us too soon and realize we're waiting for them, they can turn sharp west here, down the Rock Channel." He ran a finger across a chart. "Then we'd have to chase 'em around and across all these tidal banks and sand bars and they might get clean away. I think we'd best stick with our plan."

"Fine," said Jones.

A bowman shouted, "Two steamers, dead ahead!" The officer of the deck snapped his glass to his eye and confirmed it. "They're heading straight for us, Captain, at about five knots. I don't recognize their flags."

Through his glass Jones made out the French tricolor, the high grey sides and the two circular turrets. "It's them, Captain, the two ironclads flying French colors. Three miles due south."

Whetcraft raised his trumpet to order general quarters and the ship was cleared for action. *Arapaho* and *Seminole*, lying astern of the *Delaware*, were signaled to clear for action. Then all three raised anchor and steamed slowly south, line astern, on the starboard side of the Crosby Channel, leaving the lightship to port.

"We've probably given away our intentions by moving off together," Jones confided to Bartlett, "but I didn't see any alternative."

"Oh, it was a master stroke, Commodore," Bartlett joked. "Fooled them completely."

"Commander Jones!" Whetcraft called from the port side of the quarterdeck, telescope in his hand. "Those are French ships, flying French flags. They're not rebel ships."

"Look hard, Captain. You've seen the drawings. Look at those lines, look at the turrets. Those are the ironclads, there's no doubt of it."

"But the flags!"

"Damn the flags, man! Those are the rebel rams, I tell you, and I'll not let some Frenchman with phoney flags stop us from taking them."

"You'll take the responsibility?"

"Glad to. That's why I'm here."

"Major Bartlett, you're my witness."

"Yes, sir." Bartlett gave Jones a broad wink. "Your career's in my hands, Robert."

The rams put on more speed, as if they realized their peril and hoped to race past the Federal ships and out to the open sea. In response, the *Delaware* slowed to three knots. The two formations were now barely a mile apart. Whetcraft gave the preliminary orders.

Then he barked "Port your helm, hard!" and the quartermaster spun his wheel. Bartlett clung to a shroud as the ship heeled over and looked back to see the other two ships copy the maneuver.

The plan, worked out between the captains the night before, was to wheel the sloops in a tight half circle that would bring them around parallel to the northerly track of the rams and on their seaward side, so that they could not try to escape to the west over the shoals. With their batteries all pivoted to starboard, the sloops would then attack the rams' weak points - their rudders and screws – at close range with their eleven-inch pivot guns, mounted fore and aft. Their four 32-pound broadside cannon would rake the rigging and decks to prevent the skeleton crews from handling their ships well.

"And remember, gentlemen," Whetcraft had finished, "our objective is to capture these ships, not to sink them. We sure as hell don't want the English to salvage them. We want them alive and well and back in Boston Harbor."

The plan almost worked. But, when the *Delaware* had completed two thirds of the half circle, both the enemy ships had turned to port and were steaming straight at her, their long iron rams reaching for her waterline. They had waited until the Federals made their first move and then executed their planned counter. Whetcraft ordered the quartermaster to continue his turn to port until the *Delaware* was headed northwest with the rams two hundred yards behind her and gaining.

CRAASH! The *Delaware's* stern pivot gun opened with solid shot at the bows of her nearest pursuer. CRAASH! The bow gun of the *Seminole* fired at the pursuer's stern, to no effect. The *Arapaho*, third in line, steamed up behind the second ironclad and fired several times at her rudder, again to no effect. All five ships were now heading north or northwest.

"Shoal water dead ahead, sir, half a mile," the officer of the deck reported. Whetcraft expected this and ordered a starboard helm to stay in the channel. The pursuing ram, under rapid but ineffective fire from the *Delaware's* stern gun, anticipated the turn and turned to cut her off.

The *Delaware* could not turn quickly enough. The ram, under a full head of steam, came up on her at an angle of forty-five degrees, aiming for her midships and ignoring the stream of eleven-inch shot that bounced off her forward quarter and turret.

"You know, their armor plate's less than five inches," Jones called to Bartlett over the roar of the gun, "but look how it deflects our shot. Makes me feel quite safe behind the eight inches on my *Nantucket*."

As both ships continued their circle to starboard, the ram's angle of attack narrowed until it was on almost the same course as the *Delaware*. Whetcraft watched his onrushing opponent gain on him until, with fifty yards separating the two, he ordered two more turns of the wheel.

The ram could not respond in time. It slid by the *Delaware's* stern to port, missing her rudder by a miracle but carrying away her taffrail and half her stern timbers with a grinding crash that shook her to her keel. The ram's captain then made his first mistake. He sheered off to port, as if to escape to the west, counting on his speed to carry him out of effective range.

But the gun captain on the stern pivot gun was cool-headed. He had stopped firing useless rounds into the ram's bow when she was about to collide with his ship, and after the collision he opened up with percussion shells at about fifty yards. The first two missed the rudder, but the third and fourth exploded on target and locked the rudder into a slight port helm. A wild cheer went up from his gun crew and was taken up by the whole division when they saw the extent of the damage.

"We have the bastard now," Whetcraft growled under his telescope. "He – what in hell?" he lowered his glass and looked for Jones. "Commander! Can you make out her name?"

Jones raised his telescope. Across the ram's stern in gold was painted *EL TOUSSON*.

"Port your helm," Whetcraft told the quartermaster. "Follow her." Then he asked Jones, "French flag? Arabian name? What is she?"

"Does it matter, Captain? She almost sank us." Jones drew a big breath. "But, on my honor, she's a Confederate warship, one that is now trying to escape you."

The officer of the deck came up to them with his chart. "Sir, I think she's trying to head far enough north to stay in this channel, which turns northwest a mile ahead. But on her present course she won't make it. And if that port helm doesn't change she'll soon be heading due west towards this shoal here, the Burbo Bank."

"Can she get across the bank?" the Captain demanded.

"At low speed and with a lot of luck, maybe. In another two or three hours, with more water, probably."

"We'll keep after her until she runs aground or we can cripple her." Whetcraft gave the necessary orders and turned back to Jones, who had been watching the other three ships in the battle.

"*Arapaho's* aground south of us," he reported. "*Seminole* and the second ironclad are chasing their tails to the north."

"Damn. Why wasn't I told?" Whetcraft fixed his glass on *Arapaho*, then looked at the chart. "That's deep water over there and she's parallel to the shoreline. She must have just run up on a bar. Three hours to high water. Officer of the deck! Ask Captain Hills his condition, if you will, and report."

Seminole and the second ram were fighting on a circular track, each ship steaming clockwise around a common center and trying to attack its enemy's stern. Their circles were taking them slowly northwards.

"Captain Lane on *Seminole* is in no danger," Whetcraft said as if to himself. "If that ram he's fighting breaks westward out the channel I can intercept her. What's our own Arabian ram up to, Commander?"

Jones grinned. "She's aground ahead, half a mile."

EL TOUSSON was plainly hard aground, her bow tilted up and her screw churning the sea white as she tried to reverse off the bar.

"Engines one-third," called Whetcraft, "let's stay afloat." The ship crept to within four hundred yards of the stricken ram. The officer of the deck meanwhile reported that *Arapaho* was taking some water forward and would wait until the incoming tide floated her off.

"Well, Commander, what do you recommend?" Whetcraft asked Jones. "Try to disable EL TOUSSON from here, as I can't risk getting any closer; try to pull *Arapaho* off; or help *Seminole* take that other ironclad? What would they say at Annapolis, eh?"

"They would say: leave the *Arapaho* for now; fire a dozen shells at our Arabian friend there to try to disable her completely; and then go help *Seminole* capture the other ironclad. Right now, that ship has the best chance of escaping from you."

"Right. That makes sense. Officer of the deck!"

The forward pivot gun had by this time been shifted to port, and Bartlett went forward to watch it in action. The first explosive shell was loaded with great care, the gunner applied his eye to the sights and stepped back and the monster roared fire. The shell could be seen flying all the way to the ram's quarter, where it exploded harmlessly. The gunner adjusted his sights, the cannon was depressed slightly and roared again. And again a harmless burst along the armored waterline.

The gun captain worked his shots aft along the waterline and the fourth round found the top blade of *EL TOUSSON'S* screw. The gun crew cheered, threw their caps in the air and shouted, "That's it, boys! Give her another one!" The cry was taken up by the rest of the division, who had been watching as intently as Bartlett.

When the smoke drifted away on the light breeze it was plain that *EL TOUSSON* would be going no farther that day. Her propeller blade bent forward at almost ninety degrees and the rudder was twisted hard to port. Whetcraft sent the officer of the deck to congratulate the gun crew and told the quartermaster to make for the *Seminole* and her opponent

"Well done, Captain!" applauded Jones. "Damn good shooting, that was."

"Yes, it was," beamed Whetcraft. "We give those boys a lot of live firing practice. Uses up tons of powder but pays off in the end."

The *Delaware* changed to a more northerly course, where it could intercept the second ram if it broke off its circular chase of the *Seminole* and raced for the channel to the open sea. The ironclad was gaining relentlessly on its prey and ignoring the shot and shell being poured at it by both of *Seminole's* heavy guns.

Whetcraft exchanged signals with Captain Lane. The ram was at the northern end of its clockwise track and heading east, so *Delaware* moved to cut it off from the south when it was nearest the eastern shore of the channel. *Seminole* was to attack it from the north at the same point.

This time the plan worked. The ram turned sharply to starboard and attempted to escape to the west between the two converging sloops. It hoped to break free before they got close enough to find its rudder or screw with their pivot guns, but it was too late. The sloops had just enough speed to keep up with it and hammer its sides with solid shot, searching for the weak spots. *Seminole* also raked its deck with canister and grapeshot from her broadside cannon

"Where's her crew?" Bartlett shouted. "Dead?"

"No, they're all in the engine room," Jones called. "No sails, no guns, so no deck crew. Only the captain, the quartermaster and three others. There, on the quarterdeck."

"Very brave men," said Bartlett as a sheet of grape swept across the ironclad's lower rigging.

Suddenly the ram slowed sharply and swung to starboard, aiming to hole the *Seminole's* waterline. Jones lowered his glass and shouted again. "Another Arab, Charles! The - *EL - MONASSIR*, by Allah! Wonder what that means."

The *Delaware* followed the ram northward. Whetcraft ordered the bow pivot gun to switch to five-second shell and aim for its deck. Then he signaled *Seminole* to head for the eastern shore of the channel to tempt the ram to follow her.

Five rounds went off to no visible purpose. Then the sixth, by a freak of fortune, clipped the mizzenmast and was deflected slowly off to the smokestack. Its thin iron was just strong enough to stop the shell after it pierced one side and to drop it straight down.

Bartlett, watching, pointed to the stack and turned incredulously to Jones. At that instant, a blast of flame and smoke rose from the stack and the ram veered sharply to starboard. Then a jet of steam and more smoke erupted from the stack and it slowed to one or two knots.

"Engine room!" the officer of the deck cried. "We've hit her Goddamn engine room!"

"A bloody miracle," Jones muttered. "One engine's out for sure, maybe both."

But the ram recovered its balance and steamed at a steady four knots towards the sandy shore, now less than half a mile to the east.

Whetcraft came over to Jones. "He's going to run her up on the bank, Commander. We can try to stop her or let him do it. Your advice? Quick, man."

"I would let him do it, Captain. It'll be easier to pull her off the bank than raise her if we sink her. And her crew will escape, so we won't have to deal with them."

"Right." Whetcraft nodded and turned to order the signal to *Seminole*.

"Oh, and Captain – I'd leave *Seminole* to deal with this ram and then to help *Arapaho* off. We're needed to the west, with the first ram." Jones was so pleased by the ready acceptance of his advice that he began to feel like a master tactician. Command in battle was not that difficult, after all. At least, not when the enemy can't fire at you.

Ten minutes later, as the *Delaware* steamed towards the *EL TOUSSON*, his mind was changed for him. The deck jumped under his feet and the force of the blast staggered him. He knew what he would see before he saw it.

EL MONASSIR was sinking rapidly, two hundred yards from shore. Her back was almost broken amidships, her masts dragged in the sea and a swelling plume of thick smoke rose from what had been her coal bunkers. Through the smoke he spied two boats with crews pulling hard for the shore. Then came another blast and another eruption of smoke and fire. Cut in half, her stern and bows sagged beneath the calm waters.

Bartlett, his face dead white, looked up from a chart. "That stretch is seven or eight fathoms deep at high tide, Robert. We've lost it. Too bad."

Whetcraft came up, less shaken. He peered hard at Jones and raised both eyebrows. Jones stared back and nodded twice, slowly. Yes, he meant; he would take responsibility for the loss.

Now he *had* to capture *EL TOUSSON*.

He asked Whetcraft to maneuver the *Delaware* as close to the enemy as he could without grounding and to launch four of the ship's boats on the side facing the ram. "I estimate the boats will hold about sixty men armed with rifles, Captain?" Whetcraft agreed. Jones told him what he intended to do.

Whetcraft objected. "In another hour or two we can come up alongside her and board her. You say her crew is only thirty men? They won't be any problem – we have five hundred men in total on our three ships – and we can haul her straight out to sea."

Jones had considered doing just that. "That's all true, Captain, but we're in British territorial waters here, and I expect an angry Limey frigate or two to join us soon. And if the rebels decide to blow her up like the other one, I don't want to be alongside her."

Whetcraft pulled his beard. "All right. We'll try it. If it doesn't work, we can do it my way."

The *Delaware's* screw slowed and stopped when she was two hundred yards east of the silent, motionless ironclad. She dropped anchor and swung parallel to her prey. Jones scanned the ram's deck and made out a group of three officers near its stern, watching several crewmen working beneath them on its rudder. He hailed them though a borrowed speaking trumpet.

He first identified himself and the *Delaware* and then asked who was in command. The reply came at once: "Captain Jason Summerall of the Navy of the Confederate States of America, at your service. What can I do for you on this fine day?"

"A joker," Bartlett observed, "just what we need."

"You can strike your colors, sir," Jones bellowed, "and bring your men across to this ship. They will be treated well."

"And let you have this ship, Yankee? Never! We'll just stay here until the Royal Navy sends a ship to tow us back to port. We're still in their territorial waters."

"I hope your judgment is better than your charts, Captain. You are in international waters." He announced that he did not propose to wait for the Royal Navy, and that in five minutes he would send a boat across with a towline to attach to *EL TOUSSON's* rudder.

"That boat will be escorted by three other boats, with sixty men in all, heavily armed. They have orders to kill any of your crew who resist them. And we will sweep your decks with grapeshot until the line is secured. Do you understand me, sir?"

Whetcraft was giving his orders to the boat crews, each man now holding a rifle and ammunition. They made up almost half the ship's company.

Captain Summerall had conferred with his officers. "Now, you understand me, Yankee! You will not take this ship. That's final."

Was he bluffing? Should they wait until more men could be sent from *Arapaho* and *Seminole*, both now racing up from the south? Jones, his heart pounding, asked Whetcraft and Bartlett for their opinions. No, was their answer to both questions.

"Right," Jones said. He asked Whetcraft to order away the boats. "They'll go in single file behind the boat with the towline, and if they see any man, even one, leave the ram they return to this ship at once."

Whetcraft moved away but Jones stopped him. "Hold on, Captain. I'd better command this expedition. Charles! You're coming, of course?"

Two minutes later they were pulling slowly across a gentle swell, dragging the heavy towline behind. A reluctant Bartlett, seated in the stern beside Jones, was uneasy. The sea was not his chosen environment, and he recalled that every time he stepped in a boat with Jones danger followed as night the day. But he had to go along on this mad excursion, he couldn't back down. At least the sea was calm.

The other three boats trailed in line behind them at a cautious distance. Jones had ordered the junior officer in each one to turn back immediately on his command or if he saw crew leaving the ironclad. From the looks on their faces, he was confident they would do just that.

As they crawled forward, the *Seminole* and the *Arapaho*, now free of the sandy bottom, crossed in front of the ironclad's bows and took up station in front of it and on the side opposite the *Delaware*. The ram was now boxed in and shielded from any Royal Navy ship that might try to intervene. And its crew had nowhere to go.

With twenty yards left to the ironclad's grotesquely bent rudder, the towline was brought forward. They heard a gunshot on board, followed by another, and backed water and listened. A third gunshot, this time from the cabin in the stern almost above them. Then a boat dropped into the water alongside the ship, and another. Two men jumped from the rail and grabbed a boat's stern.

Jones waited no longer. "Give way, men! Hard, now! Pull!" he cried and "Starboard helm!" to the boatswain. The following boats needed no more instructions. Their oars flashed in the sun as they made all speed back to the *Delaware*.

Bartlett looked back and tugged at Jones's sleeve. Two boats from the ironclad were following their squadron, pulling as if the devil himself were in pursuit. "It's no bluff," he said and Jones nodded.

By the time the ram's two boats were alongside the *Delaware*, Jones's expeditionary force were all back aboard her and leveling their rifles at them. As he leaned over the rail to address them, he was knocked back on his heels by a series of muffled explosions along the ironclad's waterline, five in all. The ironclad listed sharply to starboard and began to fill. An uneasy cheer rose from the two boats and their captain, a handsome blonde figure, shook hands with his two young officers.

No one spoke; both crews watched as the ram listed a few more degrees and came to rest on its sand bank.

"Captain Summerall!" Jones called down. "Well done, sir. Your ship won't sink. The British will have her off as soon as we leave. Then her French owners can buy her back for salvage. And you can buy her back from the French. Is that your plan?" He ignored the gasp from Whetcraft.

Summerall grinned but said only, "Will you take us aboard, sir?"

"I will not, sir," said Jones in a relaxed tone. Whetcraft and Bartlett joined him at the rail. "You have not struck your colors or surrendered your crew, so by rights we can kill you where you sit."

Summerall shrugged, stood up and offered his sword to Jones. "Consider this my surrender, if you please, and consider that my colors are struck."

"I do not. Captain Whetcraft and I," he elbowed Whetcraft's ribs, "will consider your colors are struck only when your ship is beyond salvage. So you will now take one boat, go back to your ship and destroy her properly."

"And if I refuse your unlawful request?"

"We are still in combat. I will shoot one of your crew. And then another, until you do as I - request." Jones drew and cocked his pistol.

"You would not -"

Jones's bullet caught one of the young officers, standing on Summerall's right side, in the right forearm. He screamed and dropped to the deck, holding his arm and glaring at his captain.

Jones loaded and cocked his pistol. Summerall stared up at him, mouth open.

Chapter 59

Deeply pleased with themselves, Bartlett and Jones boarded the early train in Holyhead, sat back and made ready for the long trip to London. They had dined well and slept even better. Not at the Yardarm Inn this time, but at the Royal Hotel, which was fitted in every way, it claimed, for 'the highest grade of people in Society'. "And if we aren't them," Jones had asked, "who is?"

Bartlett linked his hands behind his head and hoped for a nap. "Well, we saved the world again, Robert, although we shouldn't be the ones to say so." A pause. "I haven't asked you yet - would you have gone on shooting sailors if Summerall hadn't, ah, cooperated?"

"Don't know. Probably."

"Then I probably would have stopped you. But I wonder - "

"Ah, there's no point in wondering about 'if'. It's over." After a while he added, "Still, I can't help wishing, you know, that I'd taken a more *active* role in the engagement. I felt a bit, um, extraneous out there from time to time, I'll admit."

"Whetcraft did well. Under your guidance, of course."

"He did. But maybe I should have yanked the wheel from his hands, metaphorically, and taken over."

Bartlett hoped he was joking. "If you're ever tempted to do that, you'll give me a few minutes' warning, won't you?"

"To jump ship, you mean?"

"I swim like a fish."

*   *   *

The next day, Adams' mood was as close to euphoria as his flinty nature allowed. "Well done, well *done!*" he repeated more than once as he ushered them into his office, beaming broadly. And well he might. The erratic Bartlett and the devious Jones had blown away his greatest headache, a headache that was leading England and the United States once again to the edge of war. So much for my diplomacy, he thought with a tight smile; often it's better to let the military sort these things out. It was a pity that the rebel ships were sunk and not captured, but even so it was a major victory. Russell would be furious.

He didn't worry that the sea battle was fought in England's territorial waters, or that the rebel ironclads were flying the tricolor. He could evade the coming diplomatic shrapnel from the safety, politically speaking, of the Union's triumph.

What he didn't know was that Hulls 294 and 295 were legally the property of French citizens, and that Bartlett and Jones had triggered Russell's order to detain the ships, the order that led them in the end to their sandy graves. Nor were they at all inclined to tell him. "The less he knows, the better for him and for us," Bartlett had urged, "He can shout back at Lord Russell with a clean conscience."

Adams made them relate all the details of the tactics Jones used to win the victory, how they dodged the underwater rams, how they drove the ironclads aground to their destruction, everything he could think to ask. Something Jones said at the end led him to ask about the rebel prisoners.

"Ah, that may be an opportunity for you, sir," said Jones. "The *Delaware* will bring them down to Plymouth, where one of our merchant ships has an empty hold. Captain Whetcraft hopes to drop them off there and get back to his blockade fleet as fast as he can. *Arapaho* and *Seminole* have already left for Savannah."

"Why not take them back to a prison camp?" Adams asked.

"Two reasons. That would delay his return to blockade duty. And we thought you might want to use those men to show the world that the rams were in fact rebel ships, whatever flag they flew."

"Excellent, excellent." Adams was in a repetitive mode that day. "I can use the newspapers for that purpose. It's time they did something for our cause."

"Good idea, sir," Bartlett approved. "Let two or three of them interview the prisoners, hear their cracker accents, ask them questions in French." He laughed. "That'll prove they're all Southerners."

"And then I can release them. Let them make their own way home, eh? Perhaps Captain Bulloch can pay their passage." A malicious grin crossed Adams's rocky New England features. He must tell his wife about all this.

He let them go after they promised to have a full report for him by the week-end. "Include everything, please. I want this ministry to get the credit it deserves – we deserve – for this stunning success. Meantime, I shall prepare myself for my inevitable, and most satisfying, confrontation with the Foreign Minister."

"I just had a thought, Charles," Jones grinned as they left. "The French might want to get their hands on Summerall and his crew, to charge them with theft of their ship."

"The theft of an ironclad, eh? A landmark in jurisprudence and we were there." He clapped Jones on the back. "Well, I have an errand. Come by my rooms before seven, in full dress." They were dining with Katherine and Lord Carra that night.

*　　　　　　*　　　　　　*

A Friendly Little War

Jones and Bartlett formed up on the Carra doorstep right on seven o'clock. It was still light enough to pick out the three modest medals on Jones's dress blue coat. Bartlett felt vaguely unmilitary in his new evening clothes.

Milly led them to the drawing room, where Bartlett introduced Jones to Katherine and her uncle. Katherine's hair was up, and she wore the dress of emerald green silk that she had worn to *Trovatore* the previous year. The effect was at least as stunning. Jones gaped openly and then shot a glance at Bartlett with more than a casual approval in it, and envy.

Carra poured with a flourish from a magnum of champagne and announced that they would drink to the Yankees' historic victory over the French off the Liverpool coast.

"Not quite Trafalgar, not quite Nelson, but it'll do very well," he declared. He raised his glass and called, "Confusion to the Emperor!" They followed and drank deep. "That'll teach the Frenchies a lesson they may have forgotten, eh? The papers are full of it, and so they should be. Not often we get a chance to show them who still rules the waves."

"Uncle, it wasn't the English, it was the Americans who won," Katherine corrected him.

"I know that, for heaven's sake, but we're all Anglo-Saxons, aren't we? That's what counts."

"And I'm afraid they weren't French ships, sir. They were Confederate – "

"Cunning devils, those Frogs. Flew the wrong colors from the mast, did they? But your lads smoked them all right." He took another long drink and waved the glass about. "Katherine tells me you fellows were there. Must have been quite a sight."

Jones spoke for the first time. "We were there, sir. In fact we were on the *Delaware*."

"Commander Jones here was really in command of the – " Bartlett started to say when Jones cut him off.

"I was advising the ship's captain on the fighting qualities of the enemy. I'm a naval architect, you see."

"Fascinating," said Carra as he poured the second round and squinted at the bottle. "Major, we have some time before we dine. Come over here to this table and show me how your ships maneuvered the French onto the sands." He gathered up a few ornaments. "Now, this corner will be the entrance to the Mersey, right here, and..."

Jones and Katherine watched Bartlett move the ornaments across the table top. She studied him at close range. "I confess, Commander, that I'm disappointed in you. I imagined you with red eyes, horns and a tail."

"As a rabid cow, or as the devil?"

"As the devil, of course. From what Major Bartlett has told me of your exploits, you led him straight into trouble."

"Guilty as charged, Ma'am, but he doesn't object, or does he?"

"No. Not to me, anyway. Oh dear, I must see to something in the kitchen," she said, moving off.

She was back in a minute, blushes all gone. "Do forgive me, but I always have to remind Mrs. Mostyn that Lord Carra prefers a roast that is not a charred lump. It goes against all her atavistic instincts."

Jones was learning how circumspect Bartlett was in his relations with this woman whom he plainly loved. It was reassuring.

They moved to watch Bartlett put the final rounds into the lacquer box that stood in for the unfortunate Frenchy. "A pity his lordship wasn't calling the shots at Liverpool Bay," said Jones. "We'd have finished off the Frenchies much sooner."

Dinner was a merry affair. Both men were still exuberant over their victory and both tried their best to impress Katherine, at least partly to impress the other man. Katherine was intrigued. Not since she rode out in Ireland with Jeremy Dunn and Oliver Whiting had two escorts competed for her attention at the same time and so genially.

The hansom cab came for Jones at eleven o'clock and he left them on the doorstep with profuse compliments for Katherine. To Bartlett he called, "*Hasta mañana, chico!*" as he rode away.

"'Until tomorrow, little one'?" Katherine lifted an eyebrow.

"He likes to show off his Spanish. In this context it means friend, or something like it."

"What an agreeable man he is, not at all the ogre I expected. And attractive, too."

He turned back to her. "Attractive? Jones ? My word!" he stammered. "What next?"

"You don't agree?" Her curiosity was genuine.

"It's not for me to say. But I can say that he performed brilliantly in that engagement. He was in command, and those rams could have easily escaped us."

"And you? What did you do, Charles?" she teased.

"Oh, stirring stuff: closed my eyes and stayed out of the way."

"I'm sure Jones would disagree." She took his arm to go back inside. "He's seems quite fond of you, you know."

"Perhaps he is."

"Why do you sound surprised? We all are – fond of you, that is."

*   *   *

A Friendly Little War

The two old men sat together in their corner of the Cleveland Club's paneled smoking room. They had dined lightly and now waited until it was time to go to the Lords. The other members ignored them out of respect for their positions, and their talk was overheard only by the flushed, haughty faces of their predecessors watching them from the walls.

"Well, John," said the Prime Minister, "this business off the Mersey seems an unholy mess. As I'd asked, you made sure those two ironclads didn't leave; they barely made it to the sea. But I never meant for the Northerns to sink them. We wanted them for ourselves, did we not?"

"We did. I issued the necessary order and instructed Merseyside Customs to detain them, but the rams left before their men could move." Lord Russell was most uncomfortable, and Palmerston's sarcasm was most unwelcome. "It was no coincidence. Somebody must have alerted Captain Bulloch to my order. A spy in Liverpool, I expect."

"Or in your Foreign Office, more likely." Palmerston signaled to the waiter. "Ironic, is it not? Your haste to detain the ships caused us to lose them, after I'd made you responsible for them. You should have put a guard on them before issuing the order."

"Perhaps. Perhaps." Russell paused until the waiter left. "But the real irony is Bulloch's. If he had allowed Lairds to announce that the French had bought the rams from him, he could legally have armed them – the cannon were lying at his dockside - and they would have easily sunk the Federal ships. We should not have detained them because France is not a combatant."

"This is all too ironic and complicated for my tired old brain, I fear." Palmerston sipped his brandy and looked at his watch. "We have little time left." He lowered his voice. "Having lost the rams, the main point now is what do we do to the Yankees? They entered our territorial waters and sank two friendly ships. Surely we must punish them?" His old lust for action against the Americans had flared up.

"Yes. The dilemma is how. I will see Adams tomorrow."

"That man you sent to see the Pasha. Has he reported?"

"Not yet. We must assume the rams were technically French-owned, so we will support any French claim for reparations. With respect to the territorial – "

"John, do forgive me. Time we were leaving." Palmerston stubbed out his cigar and rose to his feet. "Do as you think best with Mr. Adams and send me a note. Just be sure to make it painful for them."

As they waited for their coats Palmerston looked down at Russell and said, "More irony, John. You realize, don't you, that if those rams had not been sunk by the Yanks, they would have left port. And that we would now be at war with the United States."

Russell grunted his assent. "I know."

*   *   *

Katherine's last words a few nights before had carried Bartlett's imagination and his hopes to a new level, one he explored with New England caution. Did he dare hope for more? Could there be a future for them? She had never even hinted at anything like that. And – could he believe her? Had she said what she did merely to keep him tamely around her?

He decided to press ahead, to see her again soon, to take her out to – to what?

"No box this time, Charles?" she laughed as she followed him through the crush at the Royal Lyceum Theatre. "We have to sit down here in the stalls with the lower orders?" She tried to sound disdainful and failed. Theaters always excited her, wherever she sat, and her acquaintance with the box seats was limited and recent.

"Afraid so. Bannerman couldn't join us tonight, so we're condemned to sit with the rabble. Try to bear it, won't you?"

In the first act, the *Traviata* was a disappointment. The production was threadbare, the acting lamentable. Worst of all, the heralded young soprano from Verona froze early and only began to thaw after she finished the two famous arias in the act, both of which the critics kindly described as "unfortunate."

Things improved in the second act and they were cheerful as they made their way to the foyer where more champagne awaited them. Bartlett had to notice the admiring looks that Katherine, attracted in the crowded scene. Once the champagne was safely poured, he relaxed and savored the moment. She was wearing a dress he had not seen before which was probably new. Even he, who did not follow the latest fashions could see the envious looks being cast her way by the other ladies in the audience. She must have spent some of her new found wealth, he reflected. The dress was the color of port and had a much wider skirt than most of the others he saw around him so he supposed it was the last word in fashion. He decided to say nothing as anything he did say would probably be the wrong thing. He was however beginning to feel a bit of a rake, with this beautiful woman at his side who was not only looking quite lovely but who considerately gave every appearance of listening to his comments on the opera.

The final curtain dropped, Katherine gamely wiped her eyes with a bit of lace and they filed out to the street. Bartlett had booked a table at deLancey's, where they had once dined with Bannerman as host. He had told himself that he was not trying to appear the equal of the elegant banker, and that it was the only restaurant he knew near the theater, but he hadn't convinced himself. No matter, he thought, the food will be good and Katherine liked it last time.

As an apprentice man of the world, Bartlett was relieved to note that the service in deLancey's was as attentive as when Bannerman had played host. His own air of effortless authority needed more work, he conceded, and he took too long over the wine list, but otherwise he was content with his performance.

The supper was excellent and could be eaten with one good arm – a clear soup, a featherlight omelette and a *coup de marrons* that begged to be eaten. The sommelier ignored Bartlett's selections and served the wines he would have drunk himself, trusting his instinct that the host would not protest.

It was past eleven when Bartlett called for the carriage and they clattered off over the cobbles. They rode in amiable silence for a time, Bartlett humming the tenor's first act aria under his breath. Then Katherine spoke. "Charles, it's been a delightful evening and I hate to spoil it, but I must tell you. That creature Crawford called on me again." She shivered. "He said that he's heard from his 'mates' in Dublin and he has some new questions for me. But he really wanted to see me, I think, so he could frighten me again. I had to let him in."

"I hope you didn't answer more questions."

"Of course I did. Why shouldn't I?" She sounded annoyed.

"I thought you'd agreed not to until you retain a solicitor."

"Oh."

"Well, don't worry. Our man Pettigrew will suggest one for you."

She snapped under the strain she had hidden so far and the fatuity of this last remark. "'Don't worry'? Do you think that helps?" she cried. "Who knows what kind of crazy charge they may bring against me. I may be facing prison, facing the end of my life, and all you can say is 'Don't worry'?"

Never had he felt so inadequate. Minutes later he squeezed her hand and helped her to her door. She looked straight past him and went inside.

But that's not fair, he thought, suddenly angry. Damn it, after all I've... She's not being fair to me. He raised his hand to her doorknocker, but then he let it drop.

*   *   *

As the days went by, Adams became more nervous. He wrote to the editors of popular newspapers to persuade them to tone down the stridency of their reports on the Liverpool Bay 'crisis'. In this he failed utterly. They knew what sold their papers, and it wasn't soothing words from the American minister.

Russell was no help. It suited him to prolong the confrontation. It gave him the chance to emerge as the cultured, tolerant patrician in the dispute with the barbarians from across the sea. He waited for Adams to make the first move.

Chapter 60

Napoleon III never went to his clubs. They were crowded, fiercely political and totally masculine. The people he wanted to see came to him.

And they came to his Empress, Eugenie, who by now was almost a fixture at his private conferences in the Tuileries. But Morny was accustomed to her presence and often welcomed it, because she helped her husband order his scattered thoughts. Tonight they discussed the outrage in the waters off Liverpool.

"This is too much," the Emperor fumed, "intolerable." He despised his own reliance on his half brother but, on tricky problems of foreign affairs, Morny still gave sounder advice than anyone else. "These barbarians must be taught a sharp lesson, one they'll not forget. What do you suggest, my dear? Auguste?"

Eugenie was ready to poison every well north of the Mason-Dixon Line, but Morny got his oar in first. "Any measure we consider must be tempered by one inescapable fact. And that is that we have a mere six thousand men, one third of them sick, festering in Mexico and an easy target for the Northern army."

"He's right, Louis, because - we - have - not - yet - sent - the - reinforcements - we - need - there. Remember them?" Eugenie was beside herself at Napoleon's failure to embark the promised twenty-five thousand men needed to keep her beloved Mexico out of the grasp of the Yankee hordes.

Napoleon had given up trying to comprehend the repeated delays in putting twenty-five thousand obedient men on approximately the right number of ships and pointing them to the southwest. The only possible conclusion was that his new general, Forey, was waiting for cooler weather on the Mexican coast.

But he couldn't admit any of this. Although he was as angry with Eugenie as with the Americans, he held his temper. "I have to agree. Our men there are hostages, in effect, and for the present we cannot contemplate any military action. We shall protest strongly, of course, here and in Washington. What else?"

"Reparations," Eugenie said.

"Bravay paid one hundred thousand pounds for each ship, Louis," said Morny. "We must demand twice that and settle for no less. Seward will think he is getting off cheaply."

"What else?"

"Even before Captain Bulloch sold the rams to Bravay, he had ceased his attempts to build more ships in England. In fact, he ordered four corvettes from Bravay."

"You have told us this, Auguste," said Eugenie, an edge to her voice.

"Yes. France must now give him every possible incentive to build all his ships here. Besides the obvious reasons, such as more jobs, more foreign exchange and so forth, it will be the fastest and most effective way to strike at the Federal military." Morny's aim was to keep the American war going. He did not want France, weakened by Napoleon's unfailing indecisiveness, to confront an angry, re-unified America.

"Ironclad ships to help the Southerns to break the blockade, restore our cotton supplies, more work for our people." The Emperor approved with delight. "We shall do it; give them bank credits; move the best designers and workmen to work on their ships; ah..."

"Revoke our neutrality law," from Eugenie.

"Yes," Morny agreed, "but perhaps not yet. Just now Seward would see it as an act of war."

"There's no need to revoke it," Napoleon said. "We've never let the law stand in the way of our foreign policy objectives. The people don't know and don't care about foreign affairs." There was a note of pride in his voice. He persisted in his belief that the people trusted him to protect them against the ravening foreigners.

"But the Americans do, so all the support we offer to Bulloch must be offered with maximum secrecy," Morny cautioned. "The Northerns must not learn that we help him in any way or we shall have Seward threatening our forces in Mexico. Their Monroe Doctrine has not been repealed."

"Of course," said Eugenie, "maximum secrecy. Auguste, will you take charge of this program?" She had not bothered to ask her husband's opinion on this offer.

"I shall be happy to inform Commissioner Slidell of the new, ah, informal shipbuilding arrangements, but that must be the limit of my role, I fear."

"Why, for Heaven's sake?" snapped the Emperor. One never knew with Auguste, he thought, there was always something hidden in his motives.

"My health. I must absent myself from Paris for much of the time." Morny coughed delicately.

"Haven't we been through this before?" Napoleon asked pettishly.

"Yes," said Eugenie, "but this time he means it."

"I do. Sophie insists." Morny shrugged with easy tolerance. "So I shall ask Mr. Slidell for a list of the ways in which we can assist the Confederate shipbuilding effort here. Once I approve it, Louis, I shall forward it for your consideration and your instructions."

They chatted for another fifteen minutes. The imperial intestines were quiescent for once so Napoleon, forgetting his earlier anger at Eugenie, was in a temperate mood. The thought of giving the Americans one in the eye always soothed his digestion.

*   *   *

Lord Russell had looked forward all morning to confronting Adams. For months he had been on the defensive as the Confederates evaded the neutrality law. Then he had felt guilty for a day when he flouted the same law and ordered Customs to detain the Laird ironclads.

Today it was his turn. He had two legitimate complaints against the North, and he intended to reciprocate all the personal criticisms and sneers from Adams he had borne in recent months. With interest.

"You cannot possibly deny, sir, that those three ships were ships of your navy. That they attacked and sank ships of a neutral power. That the action took place in the territorial waters of Great Britain." He allowed himself the luxury of pointing his finger at Adams's truculent nose.

Adams was ready. "I accept your first and third points. As to the second, those were ships, not of a neutral power, sir, but of the Confederate navy." He held his hand up to forestall Russell's objection. "Those two ships were designed, contracted for and paid for by Confederate agents here in England. That *you* cannot deny."

"I do not deny it, but – "

The hand went up again. "And *manned* by Confederates, officers and crew. Have you sent anyone to interview our prisoners in Plymouth? No? Well, the press have, as you must know if you read your own newspapers, and they have no doubt that every man among them is a rebel. Their service papers are all rebel papers, and you cannot disguise an Alabama accent."

"All that you say is true, Minister, but those two ships were the property of the Bravay Company from Bordeaux, which bought them from Captain Bulloch weeks ago. And paid for them."

That jolted Adams. The French tricolors flown by the rams were not just a ruse, then. "You have the proof of this transaction?" Russell nodded, a slow smile on his lips. "Well, if this, um, Bravay bought them, it was a sham," he bluffed, "they bought them with the intention of selling them right back to the rebels. You can be sure of that."

"You may be right," conceded Russell with grace, "which is why I ordered Customs to detain them. So we could determine their real eventual ownership."

"But they got away from Customs?"

"Obviously."

"You did not put a guard on them before you issued the order? That, Foreign Secretary, was careless."

"So I've been told."

"And Lairds, or more likely Bulloch, was warned. That's no surprise." Adams savored the moment. "As I've mentioned many times, sir, England is stiff with Southern spies. It was probably one right here in your Foreign Office."

"So I've been told." The meeting was not going as Russell wanted and expected. He had to get back on the attack. "We shall determine their true ownership in due course, and you may be sure that I will advise you accordingly. But, whoever owned them, your ships attacked them in our waters. What have you to say to *that?*"

"Nothing much. The officers commanding confirm the facts." Adams sensed that he had been too aggressive, so he was anxious to let Russell score a few points, as long as they were harmless. The newspapers were screaming for retribution for this intolerable assault in the home waters, and Russell had to produce some Yankee concession to appease their editors and readers.

Russell blustered and threatened and Adams gave him his head. In the end, Adams undertook to recommend to Seward that he offer a full apology to England through Lord Lyons in Washington. That should let this affair rumble along for a month and then die a peaceful death, he thought, provided Palmerston tells his tame editors to let it die.

The honors about even, they parted in a spirit of professional amity, each content with the points he had scored and confident that serious trouble had been sidestepped.

Chapter 61

His work at the ministry seemed even duller than usual to Bartlett. He quickly read the dispatches that had accumulated on his desk and accepted or declined the routine invitations to the routine receptions that began to accelerate into the winter season. At these affairs, he would be forced to deny his participation in the sinking of the two rams, worse luck, and hope that his denials would be taken for what they were. It's my one chance at fame, he thought ruefully.

Robert Jones was in, out, and around the ministry. He spent much of his time with Morse, their heads close together in the consul's corner of the room. Bartlett guessed that Adams, who'd learned the value of espionage in the destruction of the rams, had relented and opened the ministry's pocketbook to his unacknowledged spymasters.

But one afternoon Jones came up to Bartlett, stuck out his hand and announced that he was off. "I'm back to New York from Southampton tomorrow," he said with a grin. "I figure you and Morse can stand on your own two feet now, so it's back to the *Nantucket* for me. If my executive officer hasn't parked her on a reef by now."

"Well, Robert, *bon voyage* and *hasta la vista,* etcetera. It's been a pleasure, I suppose." Bartlett's attempt at humor struck false notes in his own ear. "A winter in the southern sunshine for you, is it?"

"Yes, as I told you - fishing, flogging, sinking rebel skiffs. War is pure hell in the modern navy."

"All the best, then."

"Thanks." A painful handshake, a merry wave and Jones was almost out the main door. He stopped, paused and came back. "Charles, when I was in Washington on my way over here, your uncle Stoddard and Henry Wise mentioned a different kind of assignment, something that would need at least two men. I, ah, don't know any more yet, but if it does come up – "

"The answer is definitely maybe. You asked me once before, you know."

"I know. Just checking." Another handshake and this time he left.

Bartlett was left to think about their friendship, for that was what it had become. He had a simple test: If he found himself in terrible trouble, whom would he ask for help? The list was always disturbingly short, but that day he had to admit that the only name on it was Robert Jones.

*   *   *

Bartlett had no word from Katherine. Curious, and annoyed at her, he called at her house one dark evening as he returned from work.

"She's not here, Major." Lord Carra hoisted himself from his chair by the fire to shake hands. "Left for Ireland two, three days ago. Expect her back soon, though." Bartlett muttered his thanks and turned to go but Carra stopped him. "Stay a minute. You'll have a whisky with me, won't you?"

It would be rude to refuse him, so Bartlett accepted. Carra eagerly followed the headlines and wanted his guest's opinion on the likelihood of war. "It boils up every six months or so," he said, "we and you Yanks scream at each other for weeks, it looks as if the shooting is about to start and then it all goes quiet again. How do you account for that, eh?"

Bartlett told him his own theory. The belligerence of the United States, he said, was in direct proportion to its military success. For England, the reverse was true. The Battle of Liverpool Bay was an anomaly. Both countries claimed success: one military, the other moral. So each felt free to challenge the other. "But that's where it'll stop, I'm sure. The day is long past when England can win a war against us." He cited the size of the Union army, the new strength of its navy and the weakness of Canada.

Carra was impressed by Bartlett's command of the figures. "But then that's your job, isn't it? To frighten our military people."

"We call it liaising with them," Bartlett smiled.

The talk turned to prize fighting, and not by accident. It turned out that his host's dormant interest in the prize ring had been revived by the arrival of a splendid specimen from Mississippi. "Or so he says. Chap I know bought him from a promoter in Cardiff. Says he's an escaped slave. Shipped out on a cotton freighter before your war and been here ever since."

"Have you seen him fight?"

"Once. He beat a good Irishman the other night, a big fellow." Carra looked around guiltily and lit a black cigar. "I only smoke in here when Katherine's away. Anyway, the thing is this chap's offered me an interest in this black – pay a third of his costs for a quarter of the profits. The standard split. The idea is to promote him as an American hero. The punters will support him whether they're for the North or the South, you see."

"An interesting approach. Very topical," Bartlett observed.

"But I want to make sure that he is what he says he is. I don't want to invest in an American hero who turns out to be a West Indian, like that last useless nigger I had. Make me look foolish, it would." He peered sharply at Bartlett. "Could you take a look at him, Major? Talk to him? Tell me if he was in fact an American slave?"

That took Bartlett aback. He'd had no idea where Carra was leading the conversation. But – why not? "I'd be glad to, sir. I'm no expert, but I should be able to tell you that much. Whenever you want." What on earth would he say to the man? Ask him to describe the slave's life on a Mississippi cotton plantation?

"That's good of you. First I'll just have a word with young Bannerman about it."

"Malcolm Bannerman?"

"Yes. He helps me with my, ah, investments. Very sound. Not too keen on the prize ring, though." He stared into the middle distance and shook his head. "Damn shame Katherine hasn't married him."

"What a shame." Bartlett muttered.

*   *   *

Washington had turned cool after a hot spell, so the President wore a shabby pullover with his carpet slippers. It was a good week for him: Seward had reported that the Mexican legislature had approved his loan scheme. It was just a matter of time before the choicest bits of Mexico fell in his lap.

Now, even better, they were seated around the black table in his main office to celebrate what the press called the Battle of the Irish Sea.

Seward raised his near-empty glass: "To the greatest naval victory in our history, gentlemen, and to the brave men of *Delaware*, *Arapaho* and *Seminole*."

"Well, we've already had that one, Governor, but I guess we can't have it too often." Lincoln sipped his bourbon from a full glass. "I've said much the same to Welles and asked him to pass my congratulations and thanks down the line."

"In our history," insisted Seward. "Course, it's too bad we couldn't *capture* those two ironclads, instead of sinking them, but what the hell."

"What the hell," echoed Stoddard. This was becoming awkward for him.

"Also, the English insist that they were French ships." Seward wagged an unsteady finger, "but Adams reports that they've shown him no proof. And that, even if they were, the French would've sold them right back to the rebels."

Lincoln sat up straight. "The French? I haven't heard about that. Good God Almighty. Is the Emperor screaming?"

"Not yet. Stanley in Paris is getting reports that the Duc de Morny arranged some sort of transaction with the rebels, the French and the Egyptians, but he thinks that's all too fanciful to be true."

"Morny again, eh." The President was intrigued. "The fellow's everywhere. Next you'll tell me that – what's his name? The naval officer who got friendly with him? Next you'll tell me he was mixed up in this."

Stoddard coughed. "Commander Jones. He was mixed up, sir, he and Major Bartlett." He described how the two had led the three Federal warships to their prey and Jones had commanded them in the battle.

"They're quite a pair," Lincoln nodded. "Time they got a medal, isn't it, General?"

"Yes, sir. But with no fanfare. We may use them again and I don't want them to be well known, not even in this country."

"Fair enough. I'll leave it with you." Lincoln paused for thought. "Now, Governor, what do we do about the French? They're bound to kick up some sand over this."

"We wait to see what the Emperor says," Seward replied. "Then our response is low-key, accommodating. If they demand reparations, we pay them with a smile, while maintaining that those were really rebel ships." Now he paused for thought. "The same with the English."

"The English, always the English. Why?" Lincoln's tone was harsh. If there was an English dimension to the battle, it was sure to be tiresome.

"Their territorial waters, Mr. President. It's in my letter."

"Yes, now I remember," Lincoln said. "Well, we apologize nicely, don't you agree? You can blame the heat of battle, hot pursuit, inaccurate charts and so forth. But no reparations for them. Not one damn dime."

*   *   *

In his hotel room, James Bulloch took his last look out over Liverpool Bay as the sun set. The bitter taste in his mouth would not go away. So close. A day earlier and the rams would have been safely in Bordeaux by now, waiting for their cannon, poised to hurl themselves on the Yankee blockade fleet.

He had done all any man could do and it was not to be, not here in England, anyway. In France. The telegram from Slidell was encouraging and specific. Bulloch was to go to Paris as soon as possible to meet again with the man with the bell, who was giving certain assurances. Looking at his future, he foresaw that he was through with Liverpool and that the French would prefer him not to be visible in France. To London, then, with trips to France as necessary. Not a bad prospect.

He began to pack. The London train left at eight in the morning.

Chapter 62

Days passed with no sign of Katherine. Bartlett began to brood. He resented that he missed her so keenly. And she hadn't even thanked him when he gave her the name of the lawyer recommended for her by Pettigrew, saying that she was minded to retain the Messrs. Cunningham in Cork. "Patrick already knows about it, you see, and if they accuse me of doing away with Henry it will be in Ireland." Odd how she could appear so matter of fact about a possible murder charge, he'd thought at the time.

He had little else to think about, his arm still hurt and his resentment spread as it grew and as the whisky dropped nightly in his decanter. Made of Irish crystal, he recalled wryly.

He recognized that he was straining the facts to justify his resentment, but he resented her. Then he resented his resentment. That's enough, he thought, enough. I sound like a spoiled child.

At times he felt himself growing weary of his relationship with Katherine: too many emotional low points and not enough high points. There were plenty of other attractive women in London, he told himself, he'd met many of them at the official functions he was obliged to attend. Most of them were somebody's wife, but many weren't, and did it make any difference to him?

Besides, what did he really know of Katherine? Or of Henry? Or of the possible murder charge? Very little, indeed. A cloudy memory began to take shape at the edge of his thoughts and impressions. What was it? And then he knew. Her voice saying:

"Worst of all, Henry wouldn't believe that I wasn't attracted to other men. It was horrible. Unbearable. It reached the point where I had to - do something. So I - and my friend - oh, never mind. I must forget about that. I must."

His mind then turned involuntarily to that night when they had sat up drinking together after the evening at the opera. The evening when he had first felt that he might be falling in love with her and she had appeared to find him attractive. He had been so happy, if confused, by their sudden intimacy that he had failed to notice how very intoxicated he had become after not much alcohol. Why had he only just managed to get back to his rooms before passing out – to sleep until late the next morning? Why had she departed for the north early the following morning, having not mentioned that she was going?

He began to view her erratic behavior in a different light. Perhaps it wasn't just her womanly prerogative to change her mind? He had obediently forgiven her every time, but he couldn't help but suspect that she was playing him like an Irish fiddle. Why couldn't he remember anything from that night when Owen had escaped? His thoughts then strayed to her relationship with Bannerman. Had she already decided to marry him when she had been with him, Bartlett, in France? At what point had she broken off their engagement? Who was this Cunningham individual? This last thought brought him back to the present and Gilsenan's charge that she had murdered her husband. And this then led him to link thoughts of him, her husband and laudanum.

His imagination had run away from him again. These nights alone at home are bad for me, he thought. I must go out more. I must get to know other women.

*   *   *

Saturday morning came, brilliant blue with a high sky and a brisk wind. His mood was foul and his head was woolly from good whisky and cheap cigars. Fresh air, he thought, must get some fresh air. Too much thinking is bad for the system. He would walk to the park a few blocks away and just breathe for a spell.

Katherine bustled out of her doorway, a determined tilt to her chin and a book under her arm. One sight of her and his grievances instantly melted away – as if the clouds had suddenly parted. He waited for her to see him. "Good morning," he called, "not another row with the dreaded lord, I hope?"

At first he didn't remember, and then she laughed aloud. "And a good morning to you, Charles. What a memory you have. It was right here, wasn't it?"

"You carried a book and wore a frightening look on your face. Carra had said something terrible to you."

"He threatened to throw me out of the house because... Oh, I don't recall..." Another laugh, then a quick change of subject. "Where are you headed now?"

"To the park, Milady, for the air. And you?"

"To the same park, sir, to read this naughty novel. Shall we go together?"

"I'd be honored." She took his arm and they sauntered up the street.

"I haven't seen you for two weeks. Have you been away?" A harmless enough opening, he thought.

So did she. "Yes, to Ireland, to look after my farms. My estate, I should say, now that I'm a lady of property."

"Helping with the lambing, were you?" he teased. "Spreading a bit of muck here and there?" The vision of Katherine as a farm hand was delectable.

"Goodness, no." She laughed and assumed a grand manner. "My serfs do all that. I just tell my lawyer what to do – which is whatever he has recommended I do – and sit back fanning myself. And signing a few papers now and then. Agriculture is such fun."

He laughed with her. "Fun it may be, but it can be risky, as half of Ireland found out. Have you thought of selling up and putting the money in, say, gilts instead? A nice steady income, no worries, sleep at night and so forth."

"No. Why should I do that?"

"In New England we have a saying: Never let the sea get between you and your money."

"Do you? How provincial of you, poor lamb." Again the grand manner. "I'm quite content to let my lawyer look after my investment, thank you."

"Your lawyer again? Ah, the ever-present Mr. Cunningham, he of the Gilsenan letters."

"The same." She dropped the patrician air. "He's said he will continue to do what he did for Henrietta, manage the properties. Also, he will represent me if that dreadful Mr. Crawford or Henrietta's son make any more trouble for me."

They reached the park and selected a stone bench in the pale sunshine and far from the children chasing each other in a distant corner. Katherine took off her hat but put it back on and shivered. "Ooh, it's colder than I thought," she said. Bartlett found himself daring to hope that there might be a return to the intimacy of their time in France. They seemed to have grown so far apart since that time but now she appeared happy to be sitting beside him on the park bench and he was just considering the possibility of taking her hand when she shattered his mood of contentment with a long sigh, "Mr. Cunningham got a short note from Gilsenan saying he'd turned over Henrietta's diary to the Dublin police, who told him the London police would call on me." She sounded uninterested.

"Old news. Nothing since then?"

"Nothing at all." She peered hard at him. "Why do you ask?"

"Isn't it obvious? I care about you and this affair may be dangerous."

"Dangerous? Why? I've done nothing wrong. These extraordinary accusations that Mr. Gilsenan makes, there is no evidence for them, you said so yourself."

Good Lord, he thought, her mood's completely different from the other night when she berated me for saying: 'Don't worry.' What can have happened in Ireland? "Yes, but…"

"But what?" Now she sounded annoyed.

Bartlett was also annoyed at painting himself into a corner. "Well, there's always the chance that someone will say something to the police that looks bad." Escape was in sight, he thought. "Like Henrietta's diary. Or that someone once heard you say something threatening about

Henry," he blundered on. Part of his recent resentment rose to the surface. "After all, you told me your life with him was unbearable."

"I did? When?"

"Weeks ago. And you said that a friend had - You see, that's just the kind of thing someone might have overheard."

"Someone like you." Her anger was audibly rising.

"Perhaps. And come to the wrong conclusion."

"Like you?"

"Yes. *No*. I'm using that as an example, not as evidence, for Heaven's sake."

"Someone like you, Charles, with a suspicious mind." She lowered her voice.

That's totally unfair, Bartlett thought although he couldn't help remembering his thoughts of the previous night, somewhat guiltily.

"Good-bye." She picked up the book, trimmed her hat and took a step away.

"My word, Katherine, what's got into you? Stay a minute. Let's straighten this out."

"All right. That's easily done." She squared up to him, the matchless green eyes boring into his. "Tell me, on your honor: Do you think that I may, in any way, be complicit in Henry's death? On your honor." She meant it, no doubt about that.

He would not lie to save himself. "In any way? Yes, I think there is the remotest chance that – "

"Good day, Major."

"Katherine! Hear me out." He grabbed her wrists. "Look. I'm losing my patience." He breathed deeply twice. "I must – *must*, you understand – know the truth about Henry. You have to tell me. Otherwise, I – I – "

She stared at him, her hand at her mouth, blinked once and was gone. And there was no point in going after her.

*   *   *

Days of thick, brooding despair followed for Bartlett. Why was it that every time he and Katherine edged closer to each other they sprang apart in suspicion and bitterness? No simple disagreements for us, he thought, it's always war to the knife.

Her vivid emotional swings were wearying, to say the least, and were eroding his love for her. And even more threatening loomed the possibility that she was somehow involved in the death of her husband.

My God, he thought, now I'm assuming that it *was* murder, with no proof that it was. Does she think I assume that? Probably. Well, at least

I've told her I need to know the truth of it. I have to clear this up, one way or another. I don't see a future for us unless I can.

But maybe I never can.

Imagine then his surprise and delight to read the note left on his doorstep a few days later:

> "Dear Charles
>
> Can you forgive me – again? I am horrified when I think of how I spoke to you in the park. It was inexcusable. I felt betrayed by your suspicions and in despair because I could not imagine how I could make them go away.
>
> And I can understand your suspicions, I must give you that. Henry's treatment of me, Henrietta's diary, Gilsenan and other things look bad. I can see that now, but at the time what you said seemed monstrously unjust.
>
> What can I do? Your suspicions must be made to go away, as you rightly insist, so you must go to Ireland with me. Only there can you see the truth. And dare I say that you owe me that much?
>
> I leave for Cork on the overnight boat from Swansea next Sunday. I have business with Patrick Cunningham at ten o'clock on Monday at his room in Number Nine, The Broadway. Then I have been asked to Carra, where I lived with Henry, for two nights.
>
> Please meet me at Mr. Cunningham's office and then accompany me to Carra. I would like you to meet the two neighbors and friends who were present on the night of Henry's death and hear what they have to say. It may be our last chance to put an end to your doubts. It will certainly be our best.
>
> Fondly,
> Katherine"

Of course he would go. He had enough leave accumulated, and Adams would not object to his absence for a few days.

But how to reply, how to combine a dignified acceptance with enthusiasm? A dozen drafts later he settled on:

> "My dear Katherine,
> I am delighted by your note and will meet you in Cork as you suggest.
> You do not say how long we will be in Ireland, but for me the longer the better.
> Fondly,
> Charles"

He wasn't happy with that. It was weak and awkward, but he couldn't tell her again that he must know the truth. It would have to do.

Chapter 63

In Cunningham's waiting room Bartlett and Katherine sat in huge leather armchairs that faced each other across a fire. Bartlett had booked a hotel nearby and so managed to arrive ten minutes early to show the proper degree of willingness, but Katherine was there before him. She greeted him with a disturbing mixture of relief and apprehension.

"Will your conference take long?" he enquired politely.

"With Mr. Cunningham? No, I have to sign some papers, that's all."

"That's odd. Why do you come to Cork when he could post them to London for you to sign?"

"I enjoy the trip, the countryside, especially the Irish countryside, and the sea." She gave a fleeting smile. "Besides, just to get out of London does me good."

A great brown bear of a man lumbered through a door, kissed Katherine's hand and looked at Bartlett with a question mark on his face. Katherine introduced them and explained that Major Bartlett was a tenant and a friend who was taking some leave in the south of Ireland.

"Ah, yes, you told me he might accompany you," Cunningham said. "Well, Major, if you'll make yourself comfortable in here, Lady Carra and I will attend to our farming chores and make ready for our next visitor." They went inside and closed the door.

Bartlett had re-read the morning paper and was studying the passers-by through the window when a dark-haired, pleasant-faced young man entered, nodded and sat down with his own paper. Then Cunningham's head emerged from his door. He looked at the new arrival, said, "Good morning. Give us ten minutes more." and beckoned to Bartlett to come in.

Katherine sat white-faced on a chair next to Cunningham's desk and looked anxiously at Bartlett when he took the chair offered to him. "He's here, Lady Carra, right on time. That man, Major Bartlett, is Harry Gilsenan. He wrote that he had substantial new information in what he calls the case of Henry Carra. When I read Lady Carra's telegram, I invited him here today, ostensibly for me to hear this information and to discuss the proposal he made on his first visit, when I threw him out on the street."

"So he expects a friendlier reception from you this time," said Bartlett. "That might be dangerous."

"So it might." Cunningham didn't look at all concerned. "I've discovered more about Gilsenan. He has a worrying amount of influence with the Dublin police force, far more than one would expect of a moderately successful criminal lawyer. Especially one whose client list is heavy with men accused of membership in the Republican Brotherhood, and worse. The police loathe all Fenians."

"Where do you get your information, Mr. Cunningham?"

"Hah. It is well known that barristers are the world's worst gossips, especially Irish barristers and especially those who appear in criminal trials."

"Go on, Mr. Cunningham," said Katherine, "I want to hear all of it."

"All right. Well, it is whispered that Gilsenan buys his influence with the police. That he gives them evidence that men they do not suspect of anything are in fact Fenians. This he does in exchange for the police dropping charges against his clients. The prevailing rate of exchange, I'm told, is two Fenians for one client."

Bartlett said, "A dangerous game – for him."

"Indeed. So dangerous that he may be thinking of retirement, provided he can find enough money to live on." Cunningham bowed in Katherine's direction. "And here - "

"And here I am," she said bitterly, "with all the money he would ever need."

"Correct. And considering what I've just told you about him, I urge you not to show him any disdain, however much he deserves it." He looked from one to the other. "Right. Let's have him in."

Gilsenan greeted Katherine with excessive courtesy, Cunningham with caution and Bartlett with indifference. He showed no surprise at finding his intended victim and an American officer present and, after a brief hesitation, accepted the lawyer's invitation to tell them what was on his mind.

"You're quite right, Counselor, it'll save time if her ladyship hears me direct." He produced a page of notes and looked around the room. "Well, as you know by now, Counselor, some of the boys on the Dublin force are particular pals of mine, and they've persuaded Cork to work with me while I investigate the case of Henry Carra." He hoped to sound like a barrister addressing a jury.

Claiming to represent relations of Henrietta and backed by the local police, he had interviewed more than a dozen county families who had known Henry Carra. He found that these people assumed that Henry had been "done away with" and that among Katherine Carra's many admirers the guilty party was sure to be found.

"Ridiculous," Katherine said. "Who are these people?"

"I'll not reveal their names yet, Ma'am, but you'll see them at the trial, if it comes to that."

"I thought as much," she said.

"Oh, they talk about it openly, as if everybody knows it and nobody cares. They all liked you and felt sorry for you, thought your husband had it coming to him."

Bartlett intervened. "And will any of these citizens testify that they actually saw anything that might support their wild assumption?"

"No, but they all know someone who can." Gilsenan recognized this as a mistake before he finished so he hurried on. He had also read all the files on Henry's death. "There aren't many of them," he said, "considering who he was." The papers proved that the police inquiry was a joke, the coroner's inquest was a farce, and his verdict a scandal. "Death by misadventure? Death by accident? Lord Carra, a double cripple, accidentally fell in from his chair and adventitiously swam fifteen feet to the middle of the pool and drowned? Pull the other one, please."

But one file was pure gold, Gilsenan went on, and no one but he saw its value. When Carra was sold at auction that summer, the ponds and fountains in the garden were drained to save the cost of maintaining them. In the fatal pond a young under-gardener found a bottle, "a most interesting bottle", and turned it in to a policeman. As described in the file, it was small, made of pinkish rock crystal with a design etched on one side and a tight-fitting cork stopper. And it held a few drops of laudanum.

"It was found near the middle of the same pool," said Gilsenan with pleasure plain on his face. "The officer filed his report and put the bottle in store, where it still is, I suppose. Forgotten. But not by me."

"So?" said Bartlett dismissively. "So what?"

Gilsenan flushed. This was the sort of treatment he'd expected from these people. "So - I traced her ladyship's maid, Annie Westropp, to Kinsale. In the end she – she was very expensive – admitted that the bottle belonged to you, Ma'am. You used it nearly every night, she said."

"It sounds like mine," said Katherine mildly. "I wondered where it had gone." At first, Bartlett was incensed that Katherine had said anything in response to this heresay, but he was surprised by how casually Katherine had accepted this, so he said nothing.

"It had gone to kill your husband, that's where it had gone. He was drugged and then drowned."

This was too much - it was Bartlett's turn to snort. "You have no evidence for that. The bottle could have been dropped in the pool any time after that by anyone from the house."

"Quite right," from Cunningham "or Lord Carra drugged himself and crawled into the pool. He had drunk too much that evening, so a drop or two of laudanum would knock him out rapidly." For the first time, suicide was offered as the cause of Henry's death.

"That theory won't wash, Counselor," Gilsenan laughed. "He couldn't have wheeled himself up to the pool. No one could. Detective Crawford's explained that to her ladyship already. It might just about have been possible for someone to have pushed him up there but there is no way he could have done so by himself. I contend that Messrs Dunn and Whiting colluded with you to drug Lord Carra at dinner and then you all dragged him to the pond and drowned him in cold blood."

"He could have crawled up to it and pushed his wheelchair ahead of him." Katherine retorted

"Excuse me, Ma'am, but I doubt that theory, I doubt it very much. He'd have to be incredibly strong to do that." Gilsenan laughed again. "Besides, why bother with the chair?"

"To implicate my friends. Or me." Katherine said this with no inflection whatever. She's amazingly cool, Bartlett thought, almost *too* cool.

Cunningham flexed his enormous hands.

"So I maintain that he was murdered." Said Gilsenan as he looked at those hands, hoping they would not be laid on him again. "And so would a jury say. They would say that what's most obvious and most simple is what happened that night: he was drugged with her ladyship's laudanum, dragged up to the pool and held under water till he was dead."

"For which you have no evidence," Cunningham stated.

"Besides the bottle? And my mother's diary? And the police report that there were wheel tracks on the lawn? I don't need any more. Not for present purposes." Gilsenan smiled smugly.

"And those present purposes are?" Cunningham pressed him.

"To make an offer, a fair offer." Gilsenan leaned forward. "I'll drop my investigation into the murder of her husband if Lady Carra makes over to me the farms my dear mother left her." He stared at each of them for a second. "And I'll give her the diary. What could be more clear, or more fair than that?"

"Or more criminal," Cunningham replied. "That is blackmail."

"That's only a word. Call it what you will, Counselor. I call it an exchange." Gilsenan turned to Bartlett. "As they say in your great country, Major: Them's my terms, take 'em or leave 'em."

Bartlett rose halfway out of his chair. "You..."

"Sit down, Major. I've been thrown out of here by a man twice your size." A harsh laugh. "Well, Counselor? You're thinking: Should I report him? And you see at once that would be too stupid. If the police investigate your charge of blackmail, they'll have to re-open the case of Henry Carra. And that's the last thing your valued client wants. Am I right?"

Cunningham ignored this. He invited Gilsenan to wait next door while he conferred with his client. The lawyer sloped out with a sneer on his face.

"Well," Cunningham said, "that was pretty much what I expected to hear, except the business about the bottle. And we now know where we stand. He's quite clear, the sniveling viper."

"Is he bluffing?" Bartlett asked.

"I don't think so. He's a hard case. Remember what I told you of his reputation. We have to assume that he means what he says." He tried to reassure Katherine. "I'll look into his story about the bottle. Apart from that and those alleged interviews with the county gentry, there were no surprises."

"Also very little evidence against Lady Carra," said Bartlett loyally. To her reproachful look, he added, "Even if Lord Carra was murdered, he has absolutely no evidence that you were personally involved. Either Whiting or Dunn could easily have away with Lord Carra. The diary only recalls one guest leaving. Perhaps..."

Bartlett couldn't finish his sentence before Katherine had interrupted him: "What do you recommend I do, Patrick?" The use of his first name jolted Bartlett.

"What you must *not* do, obviously, is accept his so-called offer." Cunningham was emphatic. "And there are two things that you can do. First, try to recall if there's anything else he might stumble on that could be used against you – a letter, something you said to your alleged legion of admirers or to your staff." It was difficult for Cunningham to dig into Katherine's private life. "Second, think hard about any of that same legion who might have been involved in Lord Carra's death."

"You mean who might have murdered him?" Bartlett asked the question to spare Katherine.

The answer was oblique. "From what I know, which is limited, an accident is most unlikely, indeed improbable, and suicide most doubtful. Which leaves murder as the least unlikely."

"Dear God," sighed Katherine. "All right. I will do that." She lifted her eyes to Bartlett who saw in them a strange look, almost a hunted look as if she knew she was going to have to take some action she would regret.

"Fine." Cunningham stood up. "Please excuse me while I tell Mr. Gilsenan what we have decided. It won't take long."

There was silence between them as they waited. Cunningham was soon back and noticed it. "Well," he said. "That's that. We'll hear from him again before long, I'm sure."

"He won't go to the police, will he?" Bartlett asked.

"No, indeed, that's the last thing he'll do. But I mean that literally. He'll do it in the end if he sees no other option."

"Dear God," Katherine said again. "What a horrible man."

"And you won't go to the police with his blackmail?" Bartlett persisted.

"No. In that he was correct – forgive me, Lady Carra, it's your decision, of course."

"I agree with you."

As she left, Katherine held Cunningham's hand and said, "I'll do what you said I should do. I may even have some news for you before I leave Ireland."

"About the laudanum, Charles," Katherine said after their hired carriage began the long trip to Carra. "The maid was right. I did use it almost every night. I needed it to sleep."

"I can see why, and it doesn't bother me." He smiled benignly. "Many of my best friends are doomed drug fiends."

"Boor. I've not taken a drop since Henry died. I want you to know that."

Bartlett couldn't help but think back to the brandy night. Had Katherine laced his drink with laudanum to ensure that he was incapacitated when she went off to tell Owen that he could get on that boat? This was worse than he could possibly imagine. He had forgiven her for putting his career at risk to save her brother. He had even forgiven the possibility that she had seduced him in cold heart. But to risk his life with a narcotic would be much harder to forgive.

*　　　　　*　　　　　*

Carra was much as Bartlett had pictured it: The standard sweeping gravel drive, a three-story central section with two lower wings and the large formal garden at the back, running down to a stream. Built by an over-ambitious corn merchant in the 1780's who soon was forced to sell, it passed through the hands of another family before Samuel, the first Carra peer, bought and repaired it fifty years earlier. The architecture was undistinguished but, with two dozen rooms, it was grand enough for the average Irish noble family. Or it had been, until Henry Carra went for a dip.

Oliver, the fourth Viscount Whiting, snapped it up from the banks that had found themselves the reluctant owners of the property. When Bartlett and Katherine arrived late in the afternoon, the west wing was shrouded in scaffolding and twenty workmen were busy separating Whiting from the income he had accumulated from other property deals in the county.

Whiting himself did not appear until half an hour before dinner, which allowed his two visitors time to recover from their journey, bathe and change their clothes. He waited for them in the library and, after making sure that their rooms were comfortable and they lacked for nothing, pressed a sherry into Katherine's willing hand and a whisky into Bartlett's.

A Friendly Little War

Whiting was short, dark-haired, clean-shaven, bespectacled and unmarried. The word that characterized him was neat. His hair, ears, feet and manners were all neat. Everything except the most penetrating blue-eyed gaze that Bartlett had encountered, a gaze that seemed to be fixed on Katherine. In less than an hour Bartlett perceived that his host adored her.

"How excited I was when your telegram arrived, Katherine," he said. "I'd lost all hope of seeing you again and here you are, four days later. It's a miracle." He apologized for the scaffolding, reassured her that the workmen would not start before ten in the morning and turned to Bartlett. "You're my first American visitor, Major. How kind of you to accompany Katherine on her return." He might almost have meant it.

"Isn't it?" Katherine said. "Major Bartlett wanted to take some leave and see a bit of Ireland, and I needed someone to frighten off the highwaymen. And here we are, in my old home." She looked around the room and at the ceiling. "You've done wonders with it already, Oliver. The windows, the paneling. And the ceilings were quite tired when we – I left."

Dinner was a quiet, pleasant affair. Katherine and Whiting had silently agreed not to reminisce because it would have excluded Bartlett, so instead they talked of London. Like many provincial noblemen, Whiting badly missed London, or missed his conception of London, and wanted to know everything. His guests did their best to satisfy him with descriptions of the city's theater, of its opera and of its fashion. Bartlett attended enough official receptions and other affairs to hold his end up with tales, many of them real, of the higher military and political orders.

They retired early. Whiting saw them to their rooms at the opposite ends of the east wing and reminded them that his carriage would be ready at ten to take them to Kilveen.

Bartlett contented himself with a courtly wave as she shut her door. He thought he heard a giggle. His nightclothes were all laid out and a welcome fire threw sparks in the fireplace.

As sleep evaded him, his thoughts once again returned to the idea that Katherine might have given him laudanum back in London. He hated himself for having these thoughts, but Katherine was such an enigma that he couldn't help but think there were dark secrets in her past. Why was it that - whenever he was alone – he could be so suspicious of her, but that every suspicion evaporated as soon as he saw her face? She was beautiful, that was sure; he was in love with her, that was certain; but he did not consider himself to be the kind of person who was ruled by his heart. His belief in her was more than just emotions – he was sure he saw innocence in her face. No amount of evidence could outweigh his gut instinct. At least, that's what he thought for now.

Chapter 64

"As I expect every tourist to Ireland must have said, it sure is green, even in winter," Bartlett commented as he and Katherine left another village and reached the surrounding fields. "It's all that rain, I imagine."

"This is a lovely part of Ireland, Charles, and all of it 'sure is green'." She was much more relaxed than the day before, he thought. Could it be because she thought his suspicions of her, or some of them, had dissipated? If so, she was wrong. That bottle of laudanum had kept him awake half the night. He might be sitting next to a murderer.

"Where are your farms, Katherine?" he asked.

"Two of them are the other side of Kilveen, on the west, and the third is about ten miles south. We won't go there today – we haven't the time – but I mean to visit one of them after you go back to London."

They were all doing well, she went on. The catastrophe of the Great Famine and its successors had faded and Ireland's farms were recovering. It was still a dreadful economic system, where the individual plots of land were divided with each generation, but the larger farms, like hers, could prosper if they were well managed.

"I'm lucky in my tenants," she said, "or the Cunninghams were clever in choosing them. They're young and have modern ideas. They make me feel quite maternal when I visit them."

They contrived to avoid any mention of Henry, Gilsenan, laudanum, or gardens. Bartlett was itching to see the pool where Henry drowned but could not bring himself to ask about it. I'll look at it when we get back to Carra, he thought.

At length they pulled off the rutted main road and turned up a straight drive lined with elm trees. At the end rose a substantial house. "Kilveen," Katherine said simply.

The house was empty but Katherine had a key. Oliver Whiting had bought the estate along with Carra and done it up to attract a rich tenant, so far with no success. The fishing was unreliable and the hunting was worse each year, so no Englishmen were interested, and the farms were tied up in long leases at low rents, one of Henry Carra's last mistakes, so the few Irish families with any money stayed well away.

Their carriage stopped at the main entrance and they got down stiffly. The square, three-story house was built of reddish brick with black shutters and a steep slate roof. The entrance was reached through a small porch and in the rear a series of stone steps descended to a garden that was overgrown. Katherine gave a tiny cry of dismay when she saw it. "This is where I learned to be such a hopeless gardener," she said.

"Nothing I planted ever grew, so I hoped that once I left here it would flourish. But look at it."

She recalled that Malcolm Bannerman once talked of buying Kilveen, but that was at the time when she had come close to marrying him. Poor Malcolm; he had deserved better from her.

Inside, the house was spotless. The pine floors were polished, the furniture was under dustsheets and the windows were immaculate. The smells of soap, polish and beeswax were too strong. Katherine wrinkled her nose. "Shall we have the picnic outside, Charles? It's not too cold, is it?"

Bartlett agreed and after a quick tour of the grounds and the steadings, Katherine spread a linen cloth beside a bench and they tucked into the chicken, ham, salad and Rhine wine.

"This is delightful, Katherine," said Bartlett, wiping his lips. "And you? Happy memories? It must have been heaven here for a child."

"Oh, very happy ones," she smiled wistfully. "As you say, paradise for a child. Our summers we spent here and our winters in Cork, which was not so attractive for a young girl but exciting. Then it all changed so quickly when Father and Owen had to emigrate to Canada. And then not long after, Father died in Canada."

"I didn't know you were so young when your father died." Bartlett poured wine for both of them.

"Yes, I was but I remember him well. Before he left he gave me this chain" – she took it off and showed it – "And I wear it every day."

And every night, he almost said. This thought reminded him of their nights together in France and he found himself thinking I love this woman and if I find that she did murder her husband I don't know what I shall do. Return to Washington and the army, I suppose, if they will have me. But I will never stop loving her.

She looked so delectable stretched out on the grass that he couldn't stop himself from moving closer and kissing her lightly on the lips. She didn't appear to object and even put her hands on his shoulders as if she wanted to return his kiss. They looked at each other for a long moment and all Bartlett's suspicions flew out of his mind as they kissed lingeringly.

The sun was warm and they must both have dozed off because the next thing Bartlett was aware of was the air getting chilly and he sat up to find the sun had disappeared behind the house. Katherine was looking so relaxed and content that he was loathe to disturb her but they had quite a journey back to Carra so he kissed her gently again until she was properly awake and told her they should be leaving.

They set off in the carriage around three, in time to reach Carra before nightfall. Katherine looked back through a window at Kilveen until they reached the main road. As they bounced along he resumed the conversation that had been so delightfully interrupted by saying: "So after your father died and you went to live in Cork your life was far from a bed of roses for, how long? Six or eight years?"

"That's right. It was fine for the first few years, or as all right as it could be without my brother and father, but then there was a long bad patch. With Henry and the rest of it. But then out of the west came the Messrs. Cunningham bearing my three farms." She laughed.

"Dear, dear. That remark casts an unfavorable light on your character," he joked. "Almost money mad, one might unkindly think."

"My farms do not make me money mad, wretch; they make me independent."

"Financially, perhaps; but emotionally?"

"Is there a difference?" she teased him and took his hand. "Oh, Charles, I can laugh so easily with you. You make me feel that I'm amusing, even though I fear I usually appear so grim."

Whiting's housekeeper had pulled out the stops for dinner that night. Ancient silver, even older china and vases of fresh flowers adorned the table as they filed in from their champagne in the drawing room. Katherine gasped with pleasure. "The flowers, Oliver! Where does she get them?"

"Grows them herself, has a glasshouse in the stables. Don't know how she does it." Whiting sat at one end with Katherine on his right, Bartlett on his left and Jeremy Dunn at the other end.

Dunn called himself a farmer, technically the correct term for a man who owned five thousand acres of arable, unmortgaged land and a house to match. Large and dark, he was the same age as his great friend Oliver Whiting – late thirties – and a bachelor. He was also the joint master of the local hunt and the man who had taught the young Katherine Carra a proper seat on a horse. For years he had told anyone who would listen how deeply in love he was with her. Even Henry Carra heard about it.

The dinner was lively. Bartlett and Whiting began to discuss the Battle of Bull Run; Dunn and Katherine began to discuss Katherine. Whiting was struck by Bartlett's mastery of the Confederate tactics in the battle so Katherine said, "You mustn't be too modest, Charles, for Heaven's sake. He was there, Oliver, fighting with an Irish regiment. Do tell him about it, Charles."

"Ah, indeed? Then you can tell me, Major..." and Whiting was off again.

Dunn meanwhile leveled all his heavy charm at Katherine. He had pressed her many times in the past to leave Henry and marry him, making much of his financial solidity, his social standing and his everlasting love for her, all of them vastly superior to Henry's offerings. "He's never loved you, Katherine," he would argue. "He's never loved anything but his farms and his bottle. He married you because we all wanted to."

Bartlett watched her with fascination from across the table. He had never seen her so attentive to another man, not even to Malcolm Bannerman at the opera or at Rochester Place. Nor had he seen her so heart-stoppingly lovely. She had done something to her hair with a rope of pearls and she wore a décolleté dress of blue-green satin. The satin and the pearls glowed in the candlelight as she moved.

The recollection of the reason for his presence here and the company he was in hit him hard in the stomach. Following their delightful afternoon in the carriage and at Kilveen he felt relaxed and more confident than ever before that Katherine returned his feelings. But there was still a very large cloud hanging over any future they might have together.

The conversation became general and more animated. The pudding and cheese came and went, the wine came and stayed. Whiting toasted Katherine in extravagant terms, Dunn outdid him and Bartlett toasted their host. At the point when ladies conventionally withdrew to gossip in the drawing room, Katherine told Oliver she had something to say.

She would, she said, presume on her friendship with Oliver and Jeremy to ask of them an enormous favor. Charles Bartlett, out of kindness, had done her and her brother an exceptionally good turn. He had saved them both from a dangerous situation and they would for a long time be in his debt.

"Now," she said sadly, "partly because of that act of kindness, Charles is himself in an awkward position. Please forgive me if I say only that it is complicated, and that it involves Henry's death. I suggested as much in my telegram to you, Oliver." Her host nodded, intent on her tale. She went on. "Charles can help me, and himself, out of this situation if he learns *exactly* what happened here the night Henry died."

The strain was affecting her composure and she paused. Oliver gently asked, "So you want Jeremy and me to tell him what we know? Which is everything, I believe." He looked for confirmation to Dunn, who was staring intently at Katherine.

"Are you sure of this, Katherine?" he demanded. "Really sure?"

"Entirely sure, dear Jeremy. I wouldn't ask you if I had any doubts."

"Everything?" Whiting repeated.

"Everything, please."

Dunn and Whiting looked at each other. Dunn nodded and Whiting said, "All right."

"Thank you. I hope you can forgive the melodrama." They all rose as Katherine stood up, looked them each in the eye and left the room.

Silence. The butler presented the port. Dunn coughed and moved up the table to take Katherine's chair. Bartlett looked relaxed but his brain was whirling. Could he believe anything these two said? How could he question them?

Whiting filled his own glass, pushed the port to Bartlett and said, "More port, gentlemen? This will require time and strength. I'll begin, shall I, Jeremy, and you can fill in the gaps."

The fatal dinner was in April 1860, he recalled, a cold, clear night in early spring. Katherine liked to have guests for dinner because with other people present Henry was apt to drink less and abuse her less brutally. Whiting and Dunn were frequent guests because their schedules were more flexible than their married friends'.

"And she liked our company," Dunn interjected. "We stood up to that drunken boor more than the others did."

Whiting agreed. That night Henry was in an especially vicious mood. He insulted Katherine, accused her of seeing other men and of despising him.

"These were his normal run of accusations, Major," said Dunn, "and at times we could more or less laugh them off, jolly him along. Not that night, though."

"We did try to calm him down, hold back his drink, and nothing helped. He got more drunk and more insulting by the minute."

"I was his particular target. He always suspected that Katherine was attracted to me because we often rode together." Dunn was looking hard at Bartlett, as if he was trying to get across a message.

"I don't understand why you tolerated this treatment, and so often," Bartlett said.

The question surprised Whiting. "For Katherine's sake, man. To protect her, of course."

"Finally," Dunn went on, "he called Katherine a poxy whore, shouted that she and I were - and that he would never let her run off with me. He screamed at her like a woman. Never seen or heard anything like it. She ran out of the room and upstairs. That jolted him for a bit. Then he began again, on her, on me, on Oliver."

Whiting took up the tale. "We tried to get him to go to bed, and he wouldn't have it. Just kept the brandy going. We wanted to leave, but we couldn't go away with him still sitting there. We couldn't call a servant to take care of him, it would have been too embarrassing for everyone."

"Then Katherine came down to the hall," Dunn said. "She had a bottle in her hand, said it was full of laudanum and would put the bastard to sleep – my word, not hers. He could sleep all night in his chair. And Oliver and I could go home at last."

Dunn continued. "We decided to put it in his brandy, he'd never notice the taste of the stuff. Katherine said to give him a big dose as he was a big man. How much, I asked. A quarter of the bottle, she said. So I did. His eyes were closed and he never saw a thing."

It was Whiting's turn. "We thought he was asleep, so I started for the main door to go out, but Henry shouted something so I went back to the dining room."

"Excuse me, Lord Whiting," Bartlett cut in, "you didn't leave then?" Henrietta's diary said that one of the two guests, probably Whiting, left the house at that point.

"No... I remember it clearly - I went back in. Katherine stayed in the hall. Henry was wide awake and screaming filth about Katherine. I picked up the bottle and looked at Katherine. She made a motion as if to give him the rest of the stuff, empty the bottle. I did. And that did the trick. In two or three minutes he was out cold as a haddock. Katherine went back upstairs."

He stopped and glanced at a nervous-looking Dunn in silence. Dunn said, "You're the host, Oliver. It's up to you."

"No, I think you should tell him, Jeremy."

Dunn took a deep breath and appeared to gather his thoughts. "I suggested we leave him where he was. Then we looked at each other and without another word being spoken we made the decision and wheeled Henry into his bedroom, right next to the dining room. There are French windows in his room and through them we saw the fountain and pool in the moonlight. We didn't think or hesitate. We each grabbed a handle of the chair, pushed it out those windows, across the lawn, up the slope and into the pool. We never stopped or said a word. We pushed him off the chair face down and we held his head under water until we were sure he was dead."

Silence again. These two have just confessed to murder, thought Bartlett, because Katherine asked them to confess. They have nothing to fear from me because they'd simply deny ever telling me anything, and who would believe me? What's more, they must know my feelings for Katherine. They must know I would never do anything that would implicate her. But they appear to show no remorse, no repentance, no shame at all.

"Was he alive when you put him in the pool?"

"Couldn't tell. He didn't move at all," from Dunn.

"Were there any, ah, bubbles in the water?"

"Too dark to see."

"That slope up to the pool is steep. I had a look this afternoon. Why didn't you use the stone path instead?"

"From his bedroom it's much farther. And we weren't thinking, just reacting to this monster we suddenly had in our power and wanted to eliminate."

"I see. What happened to the bottle?"

Dunn said, "I don't know. I left it in the dining room at first but later, before returning home I realized that it would look bad there the next morning and as we didn't like to disturb Katherine we took it to the pond and threw it in. Never thought about it again."

"It was found months later in the pool and handed over to the police," Bartlett said. "Odd that you didn't dispose of it."

"Not odd, Major," Dunn disagreed, "we weren't thinking, as Oliver said, just reacting. Although I can see now it was a mistake. Let me say that, even if we had been thinking, doing away with Henry Carra was justified. He was a horrible man who treated his wife inhumanly and had become a very real danger to her safety. A man from whom she had no other escape. He would never have given her a divorce, never."

"I don't think Katherine meant us to justify what we did, Jeremy, merely relate it. But," Whiting stopped to reflect, "there's no harm if we do. And we can justify it from the other direction, so to speak. We can insist that we actually did Henry a favor. Surprised, Major? Look, he was a man who had lost his feet, his land, his money, his wife, his self-respect and his hope, all in five or six years. And he must have known he had no chance in the world of regaining any of them." He seemed to be directing this line of thinking to Dunn, more than Bartlett.

"You're saying he had little left to live for," Bartlett said.

"I'm saying he had nothing to live for, and he knew it."

Bartlett had to ask them. "Gentlemen, my last questions are personal ones, I'm afraid, but necessary if I'm to understand what happened here." He coughed slightly. "Am I right to think that you both are fond of Katherine? Please excuse..."

"Hah!" Dunn laughed. "'Fond'? We're both in love with her."

"We'd be strange if we weren't," added Whiting, "seeing as half the county are. The male half."

That took Bartlett aback. "Is that so? Well, may I ask if she ever encouraged you in any way to, um, help her with Henry?"

Dunn enjoyed Bartlett's discomfort. "You mean did she ever ask who would rid her of her turbulent husband? No. But there were signs..."

"Be careful, Jeremy, you see where our guest is leading us."

"Of course, Oliver, but Katherine did say to tell him everything and this is part of everything. Besides, if we don't tell him he'll guess the worst."

"Perhaps you're right," Whiting admitted. "There were certain signs, hints, whatever you call them, from her. You may not know how subtle she can be in these matters, Major, it's like catching a cobweb in the wind."

"It was no secret," Dunn said, "that if Henry died she would be left an indigent widow and in need of a husband. And I... we both believed, somehow, that if Henry was helped on his way her sense of gratitude might incline her choice towards – whoever helped him. There was no other way we could have helped her financially. We hadn't counted on Henry's uncle taking her in, damn his eyes."

"Or on Henrietta Carra's will."

Bartlett had heard enough and, he was sure, all they would tell him, certainly about Katherine's role in the play. She must have told them something before dinner to get them to cooperate like that. What could she have said to them? More hints, signals, cobwebs? There were too many questions for his tired brain.

He thanked them both for their frankness, thanked his host for his dinner and went slowly upstairs to his room. He could hear them still at the table when he closed his door. Much as he wanted to go to Katherine he knew this was not the right time or the right place.

*   *   *

Katherine left early the next morning. Whiting arranged for one of his carriages to take her to Brody's Farm, the nearest of her three properties. There she was to meet Patrick Cunningham to review with her tenant his plan to enlarge his barns. The lawyer would take her back to his father's house in Cork, where she would spend the night, or possibly two nights, before returning to Swansea on the morning ferry from Queenstown.

Whiting handed her up. She held on to his hand and said in a low voice, "Thank you so much, Oliver, you and Jeremy. You're both so kind. Ah – did it go well?"

"We did exactly as you asked, my dear. As always."

"And was he dreadfully shocked?"

"Not shocked, but shaken, that was plain. Perhaps we laid it on too thickly."

"No, that's fine. Now I'll see how he truly... how he reacts."

Bartlett had wanted to go with her. He worried that she traveled alone and he had no particular reason to be back in London that week, and she had refused him with a laugh. "I shall be fine, Charles, so don't fret. I managed the journey to and from Paris on my own, you mustn't forget."

He guessed that she would prefer to leave without seeing him, so he watched from his window as she bid Whiting good-bye. He saw her give her host a shy smile and kiss him on one cheek. Then he waited until her carriage swung down the drive before he went to breakfast. There he found Dunn behind a vast plate of kedgeree. They exchanged cordial grunts, Bartlett loaded a plate, reflecting on his changed tastes since that first morning with Mrs. Mostyn's finnan haddie at Rochester Place.

He picked up the morning paper and sat down. He couldn't tell if the silence was companionable and he didn't much care. Dunn had business with his bank in Cork later in the day and had offered to carry him to the ferry dock, an offer Bartlett had accepted. Conversation could wait until then.

They set off about noon, electing not to wait until after lunch and bidding their host enthusiastic farewells. Oliver Whiting gripped Bartlett's hand hard, looked intently in his eyes and nodded his neat head almost imperceptibly. Bartlett took that as some form of approval.

Dunn proved to be an engaging companion. He had been a soldier, a captain with a heavy cavalry regiment in the Crimea. "Nothing to do with Henry Carra, though. Never saw him there." Bartlett gave him an edited version of his one battle experience at Bull Run, and Dunn related two of the funnier fiascos of the British campaign near Inkerman. "It seems as though we're both experts in the ancient military art of the cock-up, Bartlett. I didn't mind too much because I'd no idea of staying in. You're a career man, are you?"

For the first time, Bartlett wasn't sure of the answer.

As they weaved their way towards the center of Cork, Dunn said, "Look here, your ferry won't leave for four hours. I can't give you lunch, but I'll put you out at Noel's Hotel. Use my name and they'll give you a good meal and look after your case if you want to wander around for a bit. It's a pretty town, Cork."

*   *   *

Bartlett boarded the *Swansea Flyer* thirty minutes before she sailed, dropped his case in his outside cabin and headed for the lounge. He needed a drink, and he needed to think.

He slumped down in the brocade armchair with a whisky in one hand and his head in the other. What was the point? He'd thought about her all night, he hadn't slept more than an hour or two and where had it got him?

Was she a murderer? Did she knock him, Bartlett, out with Laudanum that evening in London? Had she assisted Dunn and Whiting in the death of her husband? It was clear she had aided them, if only by giving them the bottle and suggesting, when half the bottle didn't do the trick, that they give him the other half – a dose which she must have known would likely prove fatal. If Whiting and Dunn's story was to be believed. Could he believe it? Had she done more than tip them the nod? But did he believe any of it? What if he didn't? Then she, Katherine, must have killed him. His doubts were endless, circular, hopeless.

I've lost more damn sleep over that wretched woman, he thought. First, I tortured myself over whether she seduced and drugged me. Then

462

whether I should lie to the police to prove she didn't harbor Owen when they were after him. Now it's this new torment - her part in a murder.

As all these thoughts chased themselves around his exhausted mind he knew that he would still love her – guilty or not. And he told himself that what Whiting and Dunn had said about the hopelessness of Carra's life was such that he would have wanted to die. This last thought was not of any great comfort to him as it was no excuse for causing his death. Her possible complicity mattered only because he wanted to marry her and spend the rest of his life with her but was still uncertain if he could do so if she was guilty? He didn't know. First he had to make up his mind if she was. Well, then, look at the facts, he told himself, break them down.

But what facts? Her innocence or guilt rested on two unknowns. One: Whether she encouraged those two men to kill her husband? Two: Whether she gave them the laudanum to put him to sleep or to kill him?

One: I listened to those two last night and my guess is that they exaggerated her so-called 'encouragement'. I'll bet she only *hoped* they'd do it but she didn't encourage them, hence all the talk of cobwebs. How to be sure?

Two: She must have known that a whole bottle of laudanum, however small it was, would put him out, if not down. However, they didn't say she did any more than gesture to them, so there was no proof that she wanted...

"Good evening, Charles. May I join you?" And there she was. He gaped at her. "Please? I can't stay in here unless I'm with a gentleman escort, as the waiter put it. He was most insistent on that point."

He jumped to his feet and pulled out a chair for her. Then he closed his mouth and signaled the waiter. Then he stared at her, speechless.

"Do say something, Charles. Perhaps that you're pleased to see me. Are you?"

"Very pleased, indeed." He was ordering tea for her but she intervened and asked for whisky.

She explained that her farm visit took less time than she had expected so she changed her plans and booked a cabin on that night's sailing. "Hoping to find you and that you would give me dinner on board."

"And the Messrs. Cunningham?"

"Oh, they didn't mind, and we'd finished our business."

There was a great ringing of bells and hooting of horns. The *Swansea Flyer* left the quay and was nudged gently out into the harbor. They watched the lights of the river go by and compared the merits and otherwise of their respective cabins. Katherine was disappointed to be given an inside cabin but conceded that it was after all the last one to be sold and refused his offer to exchange with him.

Her mood changed. "Whenever I leave this harbor I think of my father, sailing so hopefully to Canada all those years ago. From this same dock, I think." A long sigh. "How different my life would be if he hadn't died." A short laugh.

Bartlett decided that the direct approach was the only one. He thanked her for asking Whiting and Dunn to tell him everything about Henry's death. "And if you'd asked them to drown themselves, I expect they'd have done so," he said. "They're besotted with you. They told me they are."

"They have been good friends to me since I was married, always kind to me when things were difficult." She sipped her drink and lifted her eyes to his. "Tell me what they said about that night, please."

So he did, reciting the facts as he had been told them, including her encouragement of the two men to use the whole bottle of laudanum when half had not done the trick. "The first time I've had dinner with two killers," he joked, "and such pleasant company."

"Only two?"

The moment had come, and he dodged it. He'd thought of something else: "On one thing I'm not clear, Katherine. Whiting said that he objected to calling a servant to help your husband, but you told the detective that it was you who objected."

She looked blank. "One of us did. He or I? I don't remember. Does it matter?"

"Yes, you see..." But suddenly, blindingly, he saw the truth. She was guiltless. Completely blameless. Something – her blank look, or her emerald eyes, or her scent, or her nearness to him – something overpowering convinced him beyond all measure that she was innocent of Henry's murder although as these thoughts flashed through his mind he also knew that he had no proof nor ever would have. He was still fairly sure that the story told him by Dunn and Whiting was not the truth or not the whole truth but now it didn't matter to him.

Of course! He cried to himself. Forget the so-called facts. They're nothing but words, anyway. Trust your instincts, your senses, your knowledge of this woman who is gazing at you with innocent eyes.

His moral, rationalistic upbringing and beliefs had betrayed him. They had led him to look the wrong way, to look at what was unimportant. He had suddenly grown up; he knew that what mattered was his confidence in his own judgment and his love for her. He saw that now. His way was open.

"Charles?"

"What?" he said. "No, it doesn't matter." He took her hand. "It doesn't matter at all." His suspicions and confusion had vanished, like the dark shadows on a wall, when the door opens and the sunlight hits them.

A Friendly Little War

"Here we are again," he said as he blew out the candle in her cabin and turned to her.

She stroked his face. "Yes, it's been so long."

"Let me see if I can remember how."

"Ahhh. You haven't forgotten, after all."

They passed the night in boundless, joyful carnality.

Later:

"Charles? Are you awake? I'm awake."

"I've noticed. Stop squirming, it's too, um, exciting."

"*I've* noticed. I can't sleep. I have a guilty conscience. It's Malcolm. I told him I won't marry him."

"That's nice, my love. Now - what?" He went hot and cold . "Is he the most appropriate topic just now? Why not just tell him to push off ?"

"I *did*. I won't marry for ages, I want to see the whole world, I'm free, I'm rich."

"I know. How convenient. I have to marry a rich girl – some day."

"Why marry one when you can..?" she whispered something.

"My, but you're a hard woman!"

"Not entirely. See?"

Still later:

"Charles, do you love me?"

"Huhh? What? Yes, I worship you."

"I'd hoped for a less ecclesiastical response."

"To worship is to love. I imagined that all properly reared young ladies knew that. But all you seem to know is this."

"M'm-h'm. Now, *this* time..."

Finally:

"Charles?"

"Don't you ever sleep?"

"How do you feel about children?"

"Whose? I don't have any."

"If you were married?"

"They just come along, don't they?"

"You're very amorous tonight."

"No, too sleepy to be amorous."

"Oh? I'll have to see about that."

*   *   *

The other policeman had waded out into the River Liffey until the water reached his knees. He had snagged the coat with his boathook where he was standing in an eddy, and the powerful current threatened to push the corpse loose and carry it out to sea in the dark. There was no boat in sight at that time of night, so he had one chance only to bring the wretched thing to shore.

"Got him, I think." He pressed down with the boathook and pulled it back evenly. "Grab the end of this, will you, and help me bring him in."

Together they pulled the body onto the rocky shingle. They were at the downstream edge of Dublin, where there were no lights. They turned the fully clothed figure on its back and lit a lantern. His pockets were empty. An ordinary face, marked only by a welt along his cheekbone and a shallow depression in the bone of his forehead.

"No accident, this one," said the first policeman. "Look at his head. He was beat up before they threw him in." He held the lantern closer. "Look familiar to you?"

"Never saw him before."

"I have, but I can't think where it was." He snapped his fingers. "Wait. In court, it was, a couple of months back. He was – no, I've lost it."

"The defendant? A witness? A lawyer? Not the judge, that's for sure."

"A lawyer. Yeh, that's it, the defense lawyer for one of them Brotherhood thugs. I was on guard duty. Name of - Concannon? No. Gilsenan, that's him. A slick son of a bitch, he was, sure enough."

"I've heard of him. A young fellow. Wonder who did that to him."

"I heard he got on the wrong side of the Fenians, turned one of 'em over or something. This is probably them getting even."

"Yeh. Now how do we get him back to the station?"

*   *   *

Bartlett slept so heavily that the steward returned to his cabin twice to make sure he was out of bed to stay. After packing, he and Katherine ate breakfast at separate tables to keep up some sort of pretence.

Between sips of coffee Bartlett studied her face. Was she feeling as free, as exuberant as he was? She gave no sign of it, but then she hadn't suffered the kinds of poisonous doubts that he had had to overcome. Her demeanor was calm and a bit reflective, thinking he hoped of the pleasures of the night before and the prospect of a long journey with him. He blocked that image, though. Pull yourself together, man he said to himself. Try a little realism.

It was a grim, rainy Welsh day when they went ashore and found the Swansea terminus. The train to Paddington was promising to leave on time and their compartment was empty and fairly clean, so they settled in, Bartlett with his newspapers and Katherine with her naughty novel.

"We haven't missed much, it seems," he commented, scanning his paper. "Only... what's that? Someone's calling your name." He pulled down the window and leaned out. They both heard a boyish cry of "Lady Carra! Lady Carra!" coming closer.

"Here, boy!" he called and a pink-cheeked youth in a Swansea Flyer uniform panted up to their window and thrust a telegram envelope at Bartlett. He gave the youth a few coins and passed the envelope to Katherine. She saw her name on it, looked up doubtfully at Bartlett and began to read.

She gasped, read the paper again and handed it to him, her face as white as chalk.

> FOLLOWING TELEGRAM RECEIVED HERE
> LAST NIGHT STOP
> QUOTE DEAR LADY CARRA DUBLIN
> NEWSPAPERS REPORT TODAY THAT BODY
> FOUND IN LIFFEY IS THAT OF HARRY
> GILSENAN COMMA BARRISTER OF THAT CITY
> STOP
> POLICE DO NOT RULE OUT FOUL PLAY STOP
> WILL REPORT FURTHER BY POST AS MORE
> DETAILS ARE RELEASED STOP
> PATRICK CUNNINGHAM UNQUOTE
> GODSPEED DEVOTEDLY OLIVER

Bartlett dropped the paper. "Katherine!" he cried. "It's over! You're safe now!"

"Can it be true?" she whispered.

"Yes, of course. Cunningham wouldn't cable you unless he was certain of it."

But she was silently weeping into her handkerchief. "Come now," he said. "Tears of joy?" She shook her head. "Of relief?" She nodded, her head in her hands. She began to shiver and then to shake. Bartlett moved to sit beside her and put his arm over her shoulders. "What a curious woman you are," he said, "you cry at good news. You never react as I expect."

She wiped her eyes and inhaled deeply. "It's all part of my capricious charm, you see. I..." A last breathless sob. "What wonderful news. That horrible, horrible man."

"He was, indeed. But he's dead."

"Yes," she tried to smile, "and I suppose we should feel guilty that we're glad he is."

"Nonsense. We can rejoice in this death without a single twinge of conscience. Your world's a better place now."

"My world may be, but I'm still not safe, you know. That equally horrible Detective Crawford will try to prove I'm guilty."

"Perhaps, but think...how can he even begin to make a case against you? All he has is Henrietta's diary and an empty bottle of laudanum. He needs witnesses and he won't have any, will he? Who? Dunn and Whiting?"

"Of course not. They'll say they left Henry unconscious on his bed. That's agreed."

Katherine now excused herself and went out to repair the damage to her face, leaving Bartlett to reflect on their new prospects, which he hoped would be joint prospects.

He was confident that Katherine was indeed safe now. The laudanum bottle remained a teasing mystery. And he found himself thinking, fleetingly, of his previous suspicions regarding her behavior on the night Owen escaped. But no, he would put those suspicions out of his head forever because even if she had drugged him she had done so out of desperation at her brother's impending arrest. The question was: who threw it in the pool? He wondered how Whiting and Dunn had 'agreed' to answer that question if Crawford put it to them, for Whiting had told Bartlett that he didn't know what had happened to the bottle.

And he didn't like the word 'agreed'. Why did the two men have to agree on their story, when what they would tell the police was so obvious to them? Maybe they'd needed to agree it with someone else. With Katherine? Was it possible? No. But if not her, who else?

He felt a chill spread in his gut. Try as he might, he couldn't divert his line of thought; make it go in a different direction. So it moved to another loose end: Henrietta's diary, which said that Whiting had left the house before Henry passed out, although Whiting insisted that he had returned and stayed to the watery end. Had he? Maybe he wanted to convince Bartlett that he and Dunn were the two people it took to push Henry to his death.

The implications of that horrifying thought dragged into his consciousness the memory he was trying frantically to keep out: the memory of Katherine saying that her life with Henry had become intolerable and that she and 'my friend' – not 'my friends' – did... something she must forget about.

Do not go back there, Bartlett told himself, for God's sake. You've been there and you are past all that, past those corrosive doubts and suspicions. Do not go back or you are lost. Get a grip, trust your instincts and trust your love. You must.

Katherine entered the compartment a few minutes later, looking refreshed but worried. Bartlett was staring out the window at the sodden Welsh hills. She sat beside him, took his hand, and said "I know there are still many unanswered questions chasing around your mind, Charles, and I have decided to tell you the whole truth about Henry's death. As you will hear, the secret was not mine to share until last night when I obtained Jeremy and Oliver's permission to share it with you.

"The truth is that Jeremy Dunn alone was responsible for Henry's death. Oliver did indeed leave the house as stated in Henrietta's diary but he did not return that night as he told you. I went upstairs to my room leaving Jeremy, Henry and the bottle of laudanum. They had already given him half the bottle and it had had no apparent effect. I did not encourage Jeremy to give him the other half but nor did I remove the bottle when I retired.

"What happened next was that Jeremy, who was about to go home, realized that Henry, although by then showing signs of the drug taking effect, was trying to tell him something. He finally understood that Henry wanted him to give him the bottle, which at this point was still sitting on the dining room table out of Henry's reach. Jeremy understood at once what Henry wished and decided, perhaps thinking of me, to place the bottle within his reach. Jeremy then watched Henry empty the bottle.

"So you see, up to this point the death could have been viewed as assisted suicide. Unfortunately, however, the laudanum and alcohol consumed that night were not sufficient to stop Henry's heart from beating. He was still breathing an hour later. It was at this point that it became at least manslaughter, if not murder, as Jeremy made the decision to end Henry Carra's life. He managed to carry him up the path to the pond and then pushed the wheel chair up the lawn. If the police investigation had been more thorough they would have noticed that the marks on the lawn were not consistent with the weight of an occupied wheel chair. The rest of what happened is now as you were told last night except that it was only Jeremy who was there."

"But..." stammered Bartlett, who had not even suspected this explanation: "I still don't understand why you told me so many conflicting stories which you could see were making my suspicions grow when you might at least have told me that you were not implicated."

"No – I couldn't tell you. Not without denouncing Jeremy as a murderer. Early the next morning Oliver and Jeremy returned to Carra and told me what had actually happened the night before. They came before Henry's body had been found so we were able to dispose of the bottle in the pond – a foolish mistake, I suppose, but we didn't have much time before one of the gardeners would find the body and were not thinking very clearly. Of this I am guilty. It was I who disposed of the bottle in the pond.

"I still do not understand why you couldn't have told me sooner."

"Because we had agreed that we would all take the blame. Frankly we had all considered the possibility of ending his life and I certainly knew my life would be a thousand times easier without him. So although I had nothing to do with his actual death, I am guilty of having wished for it on countless occasions. Jeremy, Oliver and I decided, that morning, that if we ever had to tell the story of Henry Carra's death it would be that we all colluded in the death but that they had actually put him in the pond. When you started getting suspicious, I became convinced that you were going to discover Jeremy's guilt. If that had happened, I had a feeling that you would deliver Jeremy into the hands of the law, or – worse – Gilsenan. I know you would have done it to save me, but it would not have saved me. I really do feel as responsible as anyone for Henry's loss. My only hope was that you could be convinced that I was complicit in the incident and therefore back off to protect me."

"We had seldom seen each other in the intervening years, and so we had not had an opportunity to agree the finer points of our alibis. Also we had not reckoned with Henrietta's diary, Gilsenan's blackmail or Detective Cunningham's re-opening of the case.

"Oh, Katherine," Bartlett took both her hands in his, "I am so glad you have told me this. There appeared to be so many loose ends which I was trying to tie up in my head, without success - now I understand why. You should know that I had already decided that you were completely innocent before you told me the truth, but I am very glad to have my decision confirmed by you." He looked out the window again and saw that it was raining harder now but it didn't seem to matter.

Epilogue

Bartlett returned to work at the Ministry where he found his life as boring as it had been before Jones had entered his life and led him into all the adventures they had shared in the past two years.

The weeks went by and his relationship with Katherine strengthened as they spent more time together. He had finally succeeded in laying his suspicions almost entirely to rest. No more had been heard from the Irish or London police and he doubted if it ever would be.

Then one day, two bits of news were received. The first by him in the form of a telegram from his Uncle Miles requesting his return to Washington as soon as practicable for another assignment. The second by Katherine, who waylaid him as he returned to Rochester Place and invited herself to tea with him.

"Owen has written to tell me that he has been wounded and is therefore out of the fighting so he has returned to Boston to work for his paper," said Katherine when they were ensconced with cups of tea and Mrs. Mostyn's scones, which were slightly less leaden than usual.

"He suggests that I join him there – to get me away from Lord Carra's servitude as he puts it – and to keep house for him at least until he is fully recovered from his wound. I am most tempted by this suggestion I must say and, as you know, I have been experiencing a desire to travel since inheriting those farms and having a decent income from them."

"But, Katherine, you do realize there is still a war going on over there?" said Bartlett.

"Yes – but I don't believe Boston is much affected by the fighting?"

"That is true, but what about me and our relationship? You know I love you, do you not?"

"Well, actually, you've never said so," she smiled slightly as she said this, remembering Bannerman's proposal those months ago.

"Well I do and I want you to marry me, but I know I don't have much to offer you. No fixed abode and little money. But in spite of that I think we would be happy together. Do you agree? I pray you do, Katherine my dearest."

"Oh Charles, that is the first time you have called me your dearest and it makes me so happy. However, before I answer your question, I must lay to rest what I pray is your only remaining suspicion of me – no, don't protest – I know you are still uncertain whether I put laudanum in your drink the night before you were due to sail for France, enabling Owen to escape on the ship in your place. There must be no secrets between us from now on so I must tell you that I did add a small dose of the drug to your drink that night and I did flirt with you with the intention of allaying your suspicions. I had to get Owen away or he would have hanged - this was the last chance for him.

"As to your question, yes, I do love you - very much and I too think we could be happy together, but it would have to be far away from Rochester Place and Lord Carra. Would you be willing to live with me in Ireland? Patrick says that one of my tenants would like to vacate his farm so perhaps I can sell it and buy back Kilveen. I know Oliver would be happy to get rid of it. We could live there together very happily, I believe. Do you agree?"

"Well, Katherine, it is not an easy decision. I too had some news today to say that my presence is requested back in Washington as soon as I can tidy up my affairs here in London. As far as the Ministry is concerned this will take only a day or two. However my personal life is, as you know, more complicated. I want to spend the rest of it with you and would ask you to marry me immediately except... oh what the hell! Will you marry me, my darling Katherine?"

There was a long pause as she looked at him with her glorious green eyes, which filled with tears. "I think the answer has to be yes, because I don't think I could live without you, but it is clear that you will not or can not come and live with me in Ireland."

"Not yet, I cannot, but would you consider coming to America with me? I know there is a war on and that it is being fought not too far from Washington. If you feel uncomfortable being there perhaps you could spend some time with Owen in Boston until things improve? At least we'd be on the same continent."

"Do you know, dearest Charles, that logistics seem unimportant, we will manage – somehow – as long as we are together. Ireland can wait. Owen must manage without me. I'll come with you to Washington as soon as I have told Lord Carra and straightened out my affairs in Ireland. As you know, I have a considerable income now, and will have some capital if I sell the farm. You have your army pay and perhaps your Uncle Miles might help us to find a house?"

"I'm sure he would," said Bartlett, completely dazed by her response, stunned that he had actually proposed marriage to her and she had accepted. "Come here and kiss me and then we must go over to Lord Carra and persuade him to open a bottle of champagne. Although that may be the hardest obstacle we have to overcome."

The End

Lightning Source UK Ltd.
Milton Keynes UK
21 May 2010

154453UK00002BA/5/P